A Mother
and Two
Daughters

This Book Belongs to.
    Ann-Marie Anderson.
    Please return it..

Also by Gail Godwin
and published in Great Britain

The Perfectionists
The Odd Woman
Dream Children
Violet Clay

A MOTHER AND TWO DAUGHTERS

GAIL GODWIN

HEINEMANN: LONDON

William Heinemann Ltd
10 Upper Grosvenor Street, London W1X 9PA

LONDON MELBOURNE TORONTO
JOHANNESBURG AUCKLAND

First published in Great Britain 1982
Copyright © 1982 by Gail Godwin
434 29750 X

Printed in Great Britain by
Mansell (Bookbinders) Ltd
Witham, Essex.

TO PAT

PART 1

PART I

Our epoch is over,
a cycle of evolution is finished,
our activity has lost its meaning,
we are ghosts, we are seed . . .
—D. H. Lawrence,
"Dies Irae"

1.
THE OLD GUARD

ere we all are again, thought Nell Strickland, entering the party on the arm of her husband. The prepossessing old room, flickering with stout holiday candles and spiced with pine boughs, looked exactly the same. Time had shriveled some of the guests, expanded others, snuffed out a few altogether, but here was the room, a predominance of deep reds and browns, with not even a piece of furniture rearranged since 1938 when Nell, a new bride, already expecting a baby but not showing yet, had first crossed its threshold on Leonard's arm.

Theodora Blount, their hostess and the undisputed leader of their social set, sailed toward them, her late mother's diamond brooch pinned low on the bosom of her dress. The brooch had looked much bigger when the tiny old lady had worn it, presiding happily from her wing chair over Theodora's former parties. "Here comes my eggnog man," proclaimed Theodora in her rich, assertive alto. To the room at large, she added, "I would never dream of mixing the eggnog without Leonard's supervision." Theodora granted a flushed, high-boned slab of cheek for Nell's kiss. "My, you feel so frosty," she remarked, looking at Nell sharply in order to gauge her mood. Theodora did not reign quite so complacently under Nell's observant and occasionally satiric eye, though she knew the wife of her childhood friend had the good manners not to provoke her openly. "May I borrow him for a while?" Theodora asked Nell. "Azalea already has the cream and the eggs separated into bowls."

Leonard Strickland gallantly offered his hostess his arm, and, with an affectionate backward glance at Nell, who he knew could take care of herself, departed with Theodora to the kitchen.

Maiden Queens handpick their vassals from the ranks of other women's husbands, thought Nell, stopping before an old pier glass to smooth her hair; it is their compensation.

Once upon a time, a young blood named Latrobe Bell had gotten a girl "in trouble"—a girl nobody knew, from Spooks Branch Road—while his fiancée, the heiress Theodora Blount, was having her *Wanderjahr*. Theodora had retaliated by returning from Europe and crowning herself Queen for Life of Mountain City. Stopping off first in New York and working for a candy factory, so she could say for the rest of her life, "I know what it's like to be a girl on her own in a big city."

Years before that, she had crowned herself May Queen of the Spenser School, now defunct, which used to be at the top of this street. There were five girls in the class, four of whom loyally voted for one another. Theodora voted for herself and was the only girl with two votes. Rachel Stigley, who had been one of the other girls in the class, had told Nell that story. Also the story of how Theodora stayed in the Junior League an extra ten years because nobody had the nerve to suggest she had turned forty. Rachel Stigley was dead now.

Ex-Congressman Bell and his wife, Lucy, had not yet arrived, but they would be here for certain. When Latrobe Bell was serving his one term in Congress, Lucy (that girl from Spooks Branch Road nobody had ever heard of till she stole Theodora's consort-elect) left Washington a week early, missing all the good parties there, in order to represent her husband at Theodora's annual Christmas party. Lucy Bell, who after her marriage had promptly metamorphosed into the soul of propriety, "worshiped" Theodora, as she put it.

Theodora was godmother to the Bells' younger son, who now made missiles down in Huntsville, Alabama. She was also godmother to Nell and Leonard's older daughter, Cate. But eight years ago, Cate and Theodora had had a terrible falling out. In the late spring of 1970, Cate had been at home licking her wounds over having been fired from the staff of a private girls' school in New York, after leading her class of twelve-year-olds to block rush-hour traffic at the Lincoln Tunnel to protest the invasion of Cambodia. Theodora had summoned Cate to her house for lunch. The following day, Theodora had telephoned Leonard and informed him ominously that "my responsibilities to that girl are at an end." Theodora told Leonard that his daughter had said unforgivable things that breached the bond between godchild and Sponsor; but she would elucidate no further. So Nell had asked Cate point-blank what had been unforgivable. Cate had stuck out her chin in that way she had, and drawled in her ironic voice, "Well, after she told me how I was confusing the mess of the world with the far greater mess of my own life, and how I would end up either in jail or the insane asylum, I merely pointed out that over sixty years of having to be right had atrophied the part of her mind that could respond to the truth."

It was most likely the "over sixty years" that *really* did it, thought Nell. Theodora was paranoid about her age. She didn't even like Leonard to tell people he had reached retirement age because she had already told too many people about how, when Leonard was a little boy, "I'd pick up his hind legs and he'd walk around the carpet on his little hands, and I'd tell him, 'Leonard, you are my wheelbarrow.' "

On this very carpet where Nell stood now. A ceremonious old Persian with too much red. Nell could imagine the busy red designs swirling close to a terrified child's eyes. ("I dreaded those visits when she turned me upside down. Thea was a large girl, even then; and, as now, there was no saying no to her" had been Leonard's version.)

What gives people power? Maybe simply their willingness to take it, thought Nell, her intelligent eyes narrowing in her handsome face as they roved among the early guests in search of the least possible bore. Not Dexter Everby, he'll start pumping me about how much acreage Leonard's cousin Osgood's got out there on Big Sandy Mountain. And *not* Grace Hill, the society editor and hypochondriac. Why did I ever tell her I was once a nurse? And the Harley "brothers" look so self-contained, sipping their tonic water beneath the hanging poinsettia. (Who had coined the convenient euphemism of calling them brothers? Nell wondered. Theodora, probably. Mr. Harley taught Greek and Latin at a nearby private school for boys; the younger and more feminine Mr. Harley, whose real name no one remembered anymore, had once been an up-and-coming tenor, it was said.) Too bad Theodora's best friend, Sicca, did not come to evening parties. Sicca was always amusing, even when drunk. That left the young Lewises, who had only two current topics of conversation: their latest jogging mileage and the efficiency of their new wood-burning stove. But at least they were relatively new in town and she did not know every dusty bone on every skeleton in their family closets.

Although she had come to Mountain City at age fourteen to board at a girls' school while her mother was treated at the famous TB sanatorium nearby, and though she had remained here ever since, going on to nursing school after her mother died, and then marrying a Mountain City man, Nell still thought of herself as a comparative newcomer. Even when she thought, "Here we all are again," she excluded the innermost kernel of herself, that unsocialized observer who had masqueraded adequately since puberty as a "Southern Lady." She did not feel thoroughly Southern, though she had never lived farther north than Delaware. But, unlike her older daughter, Cate, Nell had always felt obliged to suppress what her own elegant father would have called her "ungainly aspects." Nell could not quite forgive Cate for not making more of an effort to blend gracefully into the landscape and keep her unruly instincts to herself.

Theodora intercepted Nell as she was about to bestow herself on the young Lewises. The Maiden Queen had a small, pale, delicate young creature in tow. She wore black velvet slacks and a white smock with ruffles up to her chin. If she had not been pregnant, she might have passed for Theodora's page boy.

"You haven't met my little houseguest," said Theodora,

beaming down on the diminutive girl. "Wickie Lee, this is Mrs. Strickland, the wife of that nice man you met in the kitchen."

"The one you drug around when he was a kid?" The girl's twangy mountain voice made the statement, which she had probably meant to be "conversational," sound awkward, rather presumptuous. But Theodora only laughed dotingly.

"How do you do, Wickie Lee." Nell, who knew about Theodora's new protégée, offered the girl her hand. Since Wickie Lee's mysterious advent a month ago, Theodora had availed herself liberally of Leonard's advice—though she did not always follow it. The small, blue-white hand of Wickie Lee wavered tentatively toward Nell, who was then surprised by its grip.

In early November, the girl had shown up at New Hope House, the home Theodora's church ran for unwed mothers. All she would volunteer was that she was expecting, that she intended to keep her baby, and that she had heard about the home from someone who had previously been helped there. But she refused to give the name of this reference. She would not even give her own surname. "I'm sorry, but I got to be careful," she explained quietly. Judging from her accent, she was either from the depressed valley region of Ruffin County or the adjoining and more violent Sharpe County, where there was much inbreeding and strangers still got shot at. But her refusal to comply with forms put the church ladies in a quandary. They tried to avoid unnecessary friction with the nosy federal agencies even though their parochial hearts smarted against outside interference: why, they had been taking care of their own perfectly well without it! But . . . what if the girl were a runaway? (She wouldn't even tell her age.) Or wanted for some crime? The church ladies were doing their best to coax Wickie Lee down to the Welfare Department, which she was resisting anxiously, when, enter Theodora on her charger. She took one look at Wickie Lee and satisfied herself that the girl was no criminal. Moreover, she fell in love—as she told Leonard over the phone—with that proud little face ("that long-ago face" was Theodora's actual description). "There's pure blood in that child's face, you can tell it a mile off. A lot of families up in those coves can trace themselves all the way back to the first English settlers. They haven't intermingled with outsiders and you can tell it because their faces don't have that *homogeneous* American quality. My father's people first settled in Sharpe County, you know, and tougher, more stubborn individuals you won't find anywhere. Welfare is *anathema* to them. I don't blame her one bit for resisting all this bureaucracy. She came to us through a friend, some previous girl we'd helped: we can take care of our own kind down here. I'll tell you one thing: distressed women were having babies and being helped by their own kind long before federal agencies had ever been dreamed of. The girl said she'd be perfectly willing to do a little housework. Azalea's knees are acting up, and everybody knows it's excellent exercise for expectant mothers to scrub floors. But officially she's my little houseguest. It's not against the law to have a houseguest, I don't suppose."

Leonard had said things would be a whole lot easier if the girl would just tell her age.

"Why should she?" Theodora had barked back. "I don't tell mine. Besides, her condition proves she's not a child anymore."

Theodora was going to pay all the doctor and hospital bills herself.

"Wickie Lee made the hot fruit salad," Theodora told Nell. "Azalea told her what we always put in, but Wickie Lee did the work. Wickie honey, take Mrs. Strickland up to your room, why don't you. I want her to see those droll little dolls you've been making." To Nell, "Wickie Lee's dolls were the hottest item at the Republican Women's Christmas Bazaar." To Wickie, "How many did we sell, hon?"

"Nineteen," said the girl placidly.

"Isn't that something? And all she had were some walnut shells from our marathon nutcracking session and the choice of scraps from Mother's old workbasket. Wickie, take Nell on up and show her. I'll bet you've made nineteen more just since that bazaar."

Nell followed the girl up the old curved staircase, whose banister had been worn down to bare wood in places by decades of trailing hands. She was frankly curious to see how the "houseguest" had settled in.

Theodora had installed Wickie Lee in her old girlhood room, which faced the rear garden and looked directly down on the old carriage house, in the upstairs laboratory of which Theodora's grandfather had first mixed his famous "Energy Tonic," which was still on the market. Theodora claimed she had taken a dose every day of her life, and everybody knew from the write-ups that the state's world-renowned Evangelist had big batches of the tonic made up for him at a local pharmacy to take on his world tours to keep up his energy. Later the carriage house had served as stable for Theodora's succession of horses, the last of which had been a mean old stallion named General, whom she had pulled over backward on herself in a test of wills. She broke her hip, but he broke his leg and had to be shot. In the last few years there had been some talk of converting the upstairs laboratory into an apartment for Azalea, who could hardly make it to the bus stop anymore. But Theodora said Azalea was happier living among her own people. Though her own people had robbed Azalea twice within one year.

Wickie Lee's dolls populated most of the console table in front of the window and spilled over onto the high four-poster bed. "My, you have quite a little family up here," said Nell, picking up one of the dolls, an old woman with a kerchief and apron made from some lovely scraps of old sprigged muslin. Even the kerchief, minuscule as it was, had a tiny, perfect hem. "What an elegant little whipstitch!" exclaimed Nell, truly impressed. "Where did you learn to sew like this?"

But the girl, on guard, eyed her suspiciously. "I just picked it up," she murmured. You won't get anything more out of me, said the sullen gaze. She's proud and scared to death, thought Nell; I wonder what the real story *is*; but now I've ruffled her feathers. What a delicate, tragic little face; it does have a "long-ago" quality.

"Well, they're very sweet," said Nell, examining a few more. There were dolls of all ages: old men and women, younger adults, even children of assorted ages and one little swaddled infant with a tiny nut face. You could tell the old men by their beards and the young women by their rounded figures and the absence of headscarves. Nell laughed aloud when she saw that one of the young women was pregnant. "You really do have a knack," she complimented the girl. "No wonder you were the hit of the bazaar."

"Yes, ma'am," replied the girl.

"You must be sewing constantly."

Wickie Lee rolled her eyes. "What else is there to do?"

"Well . . ." Nell cast about for more conversation, but it was clearly going to be a one-way effort. "Shall we go down again?"

"I'll stay up here for a while," said the girl, already hoisting herself onto the high bed. "I tasted some of that hot salad and it made my stomach burn. I think I'll rest awhile. Could you shut the door as you go out?"

The Bells had just arrived. Latrobe, who sustained a ghostly replica of his boyish, high-blooded spirits via alcohol, was preceded into the room by the plucky Lucy, who was smiling and blinking rapidly like one of those small cars with flashers that escort an oversized vehicle which might prove dangerous on its own. Right now, Latrobe was not dangerous, being in an early stage of rosy geniality. It would take "politics" to incite him. Later in the evening someone—not necessarily someone with the best intentions—would ask Latrobe his opinion on some current configuration of world events and, in doing so, press the button which would activate the concomitant rage, resentment, or fear inside the ex-congressman, and off he'd blast into an orbit of diatribe. This was what politics was about, for many men. Then there were the other men, like Leonard. Leonard regarded the passing parade of world crises from the austere vantage point of some ancient philosopher, or historian, shaking his head in gentle, Olympian dismay over the mismanaged future. People like Latrobe usually went to Congress; people like Leonard usually didn't. Which, Nell supposed, was some sort of comment on the world in which she lived.

Leonard, in his shirt sleeves, was just carrying in the cut-glass punch bowl of fresh eggnog, to the accompaniment of loud cheers from those guests who had been stanching their thirst at Theodora's parsimonious and eccentric bar. (The same dusty bottles of crème de menthe and Grand Marnier stood like wall-flowers, year after year, while everybody tried to dance with the brand-new fifths of bourbon and scotch.)

Nell did not like the feverish, wrung-out look of her husband; he did not look well, at all. But on her way to him she was blocked by Lucy Bell and was first obliged to field her ecstatic questions. Yes, Lydia, her younger daughter, was coming for Christmas; yes, she was bringing those darling boys. The darling husband, too; yes, Max was very capable, wasn't he? No, Cate would be staying at her college. No, the college in New Hampshire had closed; Cate was now at *another* college, in Iowa. Thank you, it was the dress she had worn to Theodora's last Christmas party, but she was glad Lucy still liked it.

Leonard had disappeared back into the kitchen, but Lucy was not yet done with Nell. "Have you met the . . . 'little house-guest' yet?" asked Lucy. Her voice had its customary upbeat lilt, her smile stretched the Cupid's bow she had painted on her mouth for years, but her eyes, fringed by heavily mascaraed lashes, communicated daggers. Nell said she had met Wickie Lee. "I do hope we can all persuade Thea to be *careful*," Lucy went on, but in a very low voice. "A person in her position, at her time of life, is more vulnerable to"—Lucy searched for the non-pejorative word which could nevertheless convey the deadly sting—"*ingratiating* people."

Sounding brusquer than she had meant to, Nell remarked that Theodora had always done pretty much as she liked, hadn't she, and excused herself to go after Leonard.

"Now I know what you girls go through," said Leonard, mopping his perspiring face with his handkerchief. "Azalea's bursitis was bad, so I offered to beat the egg whites and heavy cream myself. Whew, that old handbeater is ancient. Wonder why Thea doesn't get herself an electric one like you have?"

Nell looked with fury at the mess in Theodora's kitchen. It looked as if a bomb had hit it. Always clean up as you go, Nell had taught both her daughters; and had been gratified when Lydia reported that the first thing they taught you at the Cordon Bleu was, Clean up as you go. "Why didn't you call me?" exclaimed Nell, resenting Theodora's imposition on her husband. Leonard was not a young man anymore. He was no longer anyone's wheelbarrow—or eggbeater, either.

"Now, honey." Leonard touched her arm. It was a gesture she knew well. Early in their marriage, Nell had gotten shrill about something and Leonard had touched her arm in this way. "I just can't . . . abide a scene," he had said apologetically. He was not much changed from that younger man. The cheeks had indented more above the lantern jaw; the shoulders, always slightly stooped, were simply more frail. But he still had all his hair, and his large eyes, magnified since childhood behind thick glasses, still retained their unworldly innocence. "Let's go in and enjoy the party," he said, putting his jacket back on over a damp shirt.

"Hey, Latrobe, you're the expert on foreign affairs. What you think's gonna happen over there in Iran?"

Azalea's ham biscuits were all gone, the crumbled edifice of fruitcake lay in shards upon its Spode platter, the guests were into Leonard's reserve batch of eggnog, and all that remained were a few brandy balls with their powdered sugar fingered beyond appeal and a great deal of Wickie Lee's hot fruit salad (no wonder the girl's stomach had burned; she had put in way too much curry powder). Dexter Everby, who sold real estate, had decided the time had come to set Latrobe in orbit.

"What do I think? I'll tell you what I think." You could see Latrobe—who had baby-sat for one congressional term till the son of the favorite son came of age—trying to rouse himself to perform the role of statesman. "I think we got a plan up our sleeve. It may go into operation any minute."

"What kind of plan, Latrobe?" Young Lewis, his faithful junior partner.

Latrobe's alcoholic gaze swung ceilingward, as if to consult a blueprint. "It may be a little military action," he slurred mysteriously. "It may be a strategically placed little bomb; it may be a strategically placed *threat*. But lemme tell you one thing: those fist-shaking fanatics are gonna be mighty sorry when it's over."

"Well, if you ask me," said Theodora in her husky alto, "we'd better hurry up and start making them sorry. Don't you think so, Latrobe?"

Latrobe looked intently at his former fiancée. Then he laughed rather unpleasantly. "You could make anybody sorry, Thea. Why don't they elect you President?"

Those who dared to look could have seen a rare sight: Theodora at a loss.

"Well, I think it's just plain ungrateful," exclaimed Lucy Bell, flashers on alert. She looked from one to another, smiling and blinking until she had rerouted all their attention. "I mean, the Shah led them out of the Dark Ages."

"Some people prefer to be left in the dark," said someone.

"Well, they can mill around in their dark all they want," put in young Lewis, "but when the lights start going out over *here*, it's time to do something. If we didn't have our wood stove, I don't know where we'd be. The price of *oil*—"

"Those wog sheikhs are meeting right now, in some backwoods Hilton, to raise it again," someone said.

Lucy Bell tugged at Leonard Strickland's coat sleeve. "Don't you feel we owe it to the Shah, who's been our friend, to help him out?" she appealed.

It was December 16, 1978, a date Nell would remember for the rest of her life. But not because of the Shah's problems or because some sheikhs waving Russian rifles danced on the Hilton tennis court in Abu Dhabi to celebrate their power.

"Loyalty to friends is certainly important," said Leonard in the slow, courteous singsong that had driven many an opponent (and a few clients) crazy in court. "But so is the self-determination of a people trying to shape their own destiny. What we have here, it seems to me, is a question of moral priorities."

"The Russians wouldn't be stopped by a few moral priorities," said Dexter Everby.

"No," said Leonard, "because their government runs on the principle of dehumanization. Ours runs on the principle of human decency. That's where the real conflict is today."

"Human decency's not a very effective weapon," said Dexter, "when your enemy's got missiles with nuclear warheads."

"That's what my boy makes, down in Huntsville," said Latrobe Bell, coming alert again.

"We've got those warheads, too," said Leonard gently, "but the crucial challenge is for us to show, by our restraint, that the world has outgrown the need to use them."

Somebody groaned.

The older Harley "brother" quoted something in Latin. When nobody asked him to translate, the younger "Harley," whose real last name everyone had forgotten, said, "What was that in English, Al?" In his way, he was as good a spouse as Lucy Bell.

"Lucretius. 'May pure reason rather than experience persuade us that the universe can collapse, borne down with a frightful sounding crash.'"

"Amen!" cried the young Mrs. Lewis.

Nell raised her eyebrows at Leonard in their time-honored signal: In five minutes we leave.

Grace Hill was edging her way over. What is the disease of the week? wondered Nell. But it would not kill her to listen for five minutes; Nell felt sorry for the hypochondriacal society editor who had been widowed so long most people thought she was an old maid.

Grace had noted, since yesterday, a *tingling* down the backs of her thighs. Did Nell think it might be sciatica?

"It might." The kindest thing you could do for hypochondriacs was encourage them in their small diseases; it kept their minds off the big ones. "Do you have a good heating pad?"

Grace did, and happily promised to use it as soon as she got home. She looked around, then lowered her voice. "Have you by any chance heard about poor Taggart McCord?"

"No! Where is Taggart now, anyway?" Taggart McCord was

the town's wildwoman. Of impeccable upbringing, she had somehow gone off the rails soon after her (good) marriage. She had left her husband, joined the WAVES, and after the War had done just about everything else: played piano in a nightclub, jumped out of airplanes, worked with poisonous snakes in a circus. Whenever she got low in spirits or in funds, she would come back home to visit her mother, and even people passing their house in cars could hear wild Taggart McCord thrashing the piano on the sun porch as if she were taking out all her discontents on it. Taggart would be in her fifties now.

"Honey,"—Grace's mouth was working in a strange way—"Taggart was found dead in a trailer in Opa-Locka, Florida. We just got word down at the paper."

"Oh no! Not *Taggart*." Nell was truly shocked. Taggart was not the kind of woman you could like, but . . . it was an affront to life to imagine her dead, somehow. "But what was she doing in a trailer?"

"Living in it," said Grace. "She was teaching at some aviation school nearby. They're trying to keep her poor mother from finding out it was suicide. She's out at the Episcopal Retirement Home, but still quite lucid. Please don't say I told you, I—"

"Grace, shame on you!" Theodora loomed suddenly. "I should have known you couldn't be trusted."

Grace blushed. "It'll be in the paper tomorrow, anyway, Theodora."

"Not all of it." To Nell, "They didn't find her for several weeks. She'd had a run-in with the aviation school and they assumed she'd quit and gone home. I didn't want poor Taggart to be the ghoulish centerpiece of my party. It would have ruined everybody's mood. They're going to keep the suicide part out of the paper. It's nobody's business. After all, she was a McCord."

"But suicide seems so unlike Taggart," said Nell. "Now if she'd jumped out of a plane and her parachute failed to open . . ."

"I'll tell you something," said Theodora ominously. "I always had a feeling it would be something like this. I'm all for tough, independent womanhood, you know me, but there's a limit to the traces anybody can kick over, I don't care how privileged or intelligent she is." She gave Nell a meaningful look. "Nobody can live on the edge of possibility forever, especially not women. Lord knows it's not fair, but a middle-aged woman with no *base* attracts more pity and censure than her male counterpart."

Cate's unspoken name hovered between them.

"Well, don't worry about my telling anyone," said Nell. "We've got to be getting on home."

"Nell dear, do you think you and Leonard could do me a big favor and drop Azalea on your way home?"

It was hardly on their way, being in the opposite direction. "I suppose we could," said Nell, and it was in this sort of response that she revealed she was not truly one of them. One of them would have replied, eyes flashing social daggers, "Why, it would be a pleasure!"

"You're so sweet," said Theodora. "I'll go tell Azalea to get her things together."

Neither would have felt it right to "discuss the party" with Azalea in the backseat, so, after a few commonplaces (there had also been some difficulty about adjusting Azalea's seat belt, which Leonard insisted on for everybody), driver and passengers separated into private reveries as the sturdy Oldsmobile wound confidently through the Christmas-lit residential streets toward the dark inner city where Azalea lived. Nell was thinking about Taggart McCord, impatient to discuss her with Leonard. Who could tell what Azalea (her last name was Clark, if anybody was interested) was thinking, that inscrutable figure who hindered their normal intercourse but who came from the generation of those servants who knew better than to start a conversation with those in the front seat.

Leonard was trying to recall, now that it was too late, how Montaigne would have answered Dexter Everby. About learning to do for conscience' sake what we now do for glory. That perspicacious part about how one could easily imagine Socrates in Alexander's place but not vice versa. How did that passage go:

"To storm a breach, conduct an embassy, govern a people, those are brilliant actions. To scold, laugh, blank, blank, blank"—he intended to consult his Montaigne as soon as they got home—"and deal gently and justly with one's family and oneself, blank, blank, blank: that is something rarer, more difficult, and less noticed in the world."

The car entered the badly lit, narrow streets behind the courthouse. Nell automatically reached over and locked her door, and then felt embarrassed because of their passenger. As the vehicle shifted into its lowest gear when it began the steep climb up the unpaved road, with no streetlights, toward Azalea's house, which perched on an ungraded bank at the dead end, Azalea began to moan softly in the backseat.

"What's the matter, Azalea?" asked Leonard.

"Oh Lord, Mr. Strickland, I scared to go in that house by myself. They was waitin' for me once." The robbers. "I come in in the dark and they liked to knock me down runnin' out."

"Well, in that case, Azalea, I'll go in with you and we'll have a look around. All right?"

"I don't want to be no trouble."

"No trouble. Nell, can you find the flashlight in the glove compartment?"

Nell complied. But once Leonard and Azalea were out of the car, their figures toiling up the steep, undrivable driveway, the erratic circle of light dancing along beside them like a capricious child, she indulged in a mental diatribe against the exploitative Theodora.

Azalea had had a husband once. As a young man, Leonard had discussed with him one afternoon whether drinking a glass of ice water fast could kill you if you'd been working in the sun. Though Azalea had no children of her own, she had raised two of Clark's from a former marriage. The girl worked in Chicago, had a family of her own, and never visited Azalea. The boy, Jason, had been repeatedly in trouble, and Leonard had gone to bat for him more than once; but then there had been an armed robbery and a man had died. Jason, now paroled, worked in big construction in the state capital. He never visited his stepmother, either, but, from time to time, mailed her expensive presents wrapped by himself in brown paper and twine and never insured. He had sent her several Swiss watches, a transistor radio, a cameo brooch framed in seed pearls and diamonds, and a set of antique fruit knives from Tiffany's. Azalea carried her gifts proudly across town on the bus to show Theodora. "Let's try not to think too much about where they come from," Theodora had told Leonard with a husky laugh.

Azalea's house had a new roof of smart green tiles, though Leonard could not see them in the dark. He had spent several days calling around town for the best price; Theodora, who preferred Azalea to stay under a roof in her own part of town, had magnanimously paid. Just as she had paid all of Azalea's medical bills till she became eligible for Medicare. Theodora would give Azalea the last egg in her refrigerator and even her old Persian lamb coat, the soft whorls of which brushed against Leonard's wrist as he supported the old woman up this last terrible stretch of hill.

Once inside the house, they searched the three small rooms and inspected the glassed-in back porch, which smelled of apples rotting slowly in a bushel basket. At Azalea's request, Leonard poked into the recesses of a closet. He recognized many old dresses of Theodora's and sniffed, faintly, her brand of perfume. Theodora would give her beloved Azalea everything in the world but the minimum wage.

"There we are, Azalea. Not one bogeyman."

"I sure appreciate it, Mr. Strickland." She walked him to the door. "You and your family have a nice Christmas, hear?"

"Thank you. We'll sure do our best."

He waited outside till he heard her fasten all her locks and bolts. His thumb was already poised against the flashlight switch when something—a kind of light-headedness amounting almost to exhilaration—arrested him. Feeling guilty about keeping Nell waiting, he nevertheless allowed himself to go on standing up here in the clear, cold air. As his eyes grew accustomed to the dark, he looked up and made out first one, then another, of the familiar constellations: the same stars looked upon by Socrates.

There was his own name-star, Leo. Funny that Ptolemy should have seen the shape of a lion; it had always looked to Leonard more like a question mark seen through a mirror. A dog barked inquiringly from a cluster of shanties below: Is there another dog like me out there? Stillness enwrapped Leonard as he waited with the dog for a reply. None came. A low, chill wind started up suddenly in the tall grass at his feet and played a dry, metallic tune on something, probably a rusty tin can. He felt the cold through his socks, but still he did not turn on the light and start down. A configuration of things (the Montaigne, the terribly steep hill, the smell of apples on Azalea's porch) had stirred his memory. And then it came to him, that other hill he had climbed, in a long-ago passion for Beauty and Justice. He was twenty-three. Beauty was a girl named Mercedes, who taught Spanish in the high school. Justice was what the two of them wanted to go off to Spain to fight for. It was September 1936, and he had just passed the bar. The smell of apples in Osgood's orchard gave him courage as he climbed the jagged, straight-up road to his hermit cousin's house. He was going to ask Osgood to justify him in his decision to go to Spain. "If you cross that ocean," Leonard's father warned, "I'll fill your place in the firm. There's plenty of injustice here to take care of." As a young man, Osgood had left these hills against his own father's advice, to fight in World War I. And been disfigured.

Leonard had stayed with Osgood for three days. He had asked to see his cousin's medals, but Osgood had shown him something else. Leonard went back down the hill and entered his father's law practice. Mercedes vowed angrily to go for both of them the following summer, but by that time the militia they had hoped to join had been dissolved, and Mercedes had married and moved away.

"To storm a breach, conduct an embassy, govern a people . . ." He'd check that passage as soon as they got home. Leonard switched on the light and started back down the hill. I have been constructive, he thought, in my limited sphere. It was as if he were answering to somebody, but to whom?

*   *

"I think I'll take the expressway home," Leonard said, strapping himself into his seat belt.

"Are you sure you're feeling all right?" asked Nell. He hated the expressway for the same reason he preferred to take trains to New York and Florida and ships to Europe. He liked to keep track, he said, the whole way.

"Yes, but I want to look something up."

As soon as they were on the expressway, she told him about Taggart McCord.

"Oh no. Not Taggart."

"That's what I said, but it's apparently so. She'd had a run-in with her employers and I guess she just felt down on her luck."

"I would have expected Taggart, of all people, to give Death a hell of a go-round before ever giving in."

"Theodora said she always thought Taggart would end up like this."

"Well, you know Theodora. She tends to be a bit melodramatic."

Nell wondered whether to go on. She decided she would. "Theodora actually seemed to be making a sort of ominous comparison. Between Taggart and Cate. She said middle-aged women couldn't live on their possibilities anymore."

"Well, Cate's not a middle-aged woman."

"Leonard, she'll be forty this coming June."

This seemed to come as a surprise to Leonard. But after a moment he said, "Forty today isn't like forty when we were that age. Or Taggart, either. Life is changing so rapidly. The expectancies are stretching."

"Some would say they are shrinking. I just wish Cate would hurry up and find . . . happiness." She had been about to say "find herself," but the overused phrase stuck in her throat.

"Maybe she's looking for something else."

After a bit, Nell said, "It will be nice, having Lydia and the boys for the holidays."

"And Max. I like Max."

"Lydia warned me that he might be able to come only for Christmas Day."

Lydia had warned Nell of more than that, but had sworn her mother to secrecy. Lydia said she did not want to spoil Daddy's Christmas.

"Oh. Too bad. But understandable, with the economy in such a mess."

But Lydia would not go off the rails. It was not in her.

"Listen, Nell," said Leonard in a constricted voice. "Did you eat any of that hot fruit salad?"

"Precisely one mouthful. And if Theodora wouldn't persist in using damask napkins, I would have spit that out. Wickie Lee made it. I don't think she knew what curry is. What a strange little creature she is. Such a peculiar mixture of defiance and complacency. I wonder where she *came* from. I wonder—"

"I'm going to pull off the road," said Leonard, slowing the car. "I have the most terrible indigestion. It seems to be spreading all over. . . ."

He angled the car toward the emergency lane. Nell looked over, saw he had passed out, guessed what was happening, and prepared to unhook her seat belt to do CPR. But instead of stopping, the car continued to roll, at about thirty miles per hour. Trapped in her seat belt, she could not reach the brake with her foot. The next few seconds had the familiarity of a nightmare. She started to scream as the car skimmed softly from the pavement, like an airplane taking off, bounced rather gracefully down a steep, grassy embankment, and began to turn over. Nell's body was shaken violently from side to side, her head cracked against something, her chest felt as if it were being bisected. She passed into a darkness.

She was being released from her straps and eased onto something flat and then strapped down again. She opened her eyes and heard voices excited with their own importance and saw a skyful of stars. Her confused brain registered a distinct memory of having released Leonard from his bindings and laid him back on the front seat and breathed into his mouth. He had raised himself up and kissed her and patted her elbow. "You always were so competent, Nell," he had said. There were only two things wrong with the memory. The first was that they were in their old Packard with the long front seat; the second was that, even as she worked to save him, a group of Girl Scouts to whom she demonstrated resuscitation techniques each year was watching her. "The brain begins to die after four to six minutes without oxygen," one of them chanted.

The pitch and cadence of Leonard's voice, praising her competence, were still in her ears when she came to in the emergency room and found a young nurse with a fat face taking her pulse.

"My husband?" A pain shot through her chest.

The nurse's eyes went uncommunicative. "Just rest, honey." Was she actually chewing gum?

Nell took her arm away from the nurse. "I was a nurse in this hospital before you were born." Each word cut like a vise into her diaphragm. "I know what 'just rest' means, but I never called people 'honey.' Get rid of that gum."

She woke again in another room. A doctor they knew was there. Leonard had once helped his son. A trooper had stopped the boy for speeding and found marijuana in his pockets; the boy could not have gone to law school with a felony on his record. "What time is it?" she asked, trying to sit up.

"Easy, Nell. You've got all the time you need." His eyes told her everything.

"Did he ever regain consciousness?" she asked.

"Never did. The rescue boys tried everything. Do you remember what happened?" He watched her carefully.

"I remember the car turning over . . . we were upside down . . . it was awful. And then it seemed to me I was saving him, but I guess that was a delusion." A tear slid from her eye. "I was giving him CPR and then he sat up and thanked me."

"Was he having a coronary before you all went off the road?"

"Yes. Yes, now I remember." She was glad she could remember. But then she thought, What good would it do him? And she remembered how, as a young nurse, she used to have to wrap the dead in this hospital. Close eyes. Insert dentures, if any. Prop up chin. Put on diaper. Cross and tie wrists and ankles and label big toe. Wrap in shroud. They probably used paper ones now. Cate had received her Ph.D. in a paper gown. The morgue was not listed as such on the elevator. Once Nell had opened a drawer to put in a body and found two legs, left by the interns. Did she give them a piece of her mind. That was when this was still a training hospital.

"That's good," said the doctor. "You're probably not concussed. It's a wonder. You've got a bruise on your head the size of a pancake."

"The girls," said Nell. "I have to phone the girls."

"Phone's right here. Let me dial for you. Remember their numbers?"

Nell reached into the recesses of her mind and pulled out Lydia's number. Cate moved around so much, she had given up trying to memorize hers. As the doctor was dialing, Nell remembered that Lydia was not living at that number anymore. But it was all right. Max would take care of everything. Max was so good at that.

There was a fine obituary in the Sunday paper. Leonard had died early enough before deadline for there still to be time for someone to look through the files and write a piece that did him justice. There was even Leonard's quote, the most memorable of his career, which won the bus station's lawsuit after its new building sank: "If we cannot trust our foundations, what *can* we trust?" Someone had also taken the trouble to track down a decent photograph, recent but flattering. That someone was the night city editor, an old beau of Lydia's. That final summer, when she had played him like a fish, raised his hopes that she was going to catch him . . . until he looked behind and saw that he was merely bait for the bigger fish. But the night city editor had a romantic soul. Though comfortably married, he prided himself on having suffered so thoroughly in unrequited love. Perhaps he would go to Strickland's funeral, just to see if she still had the power to hurt him. As long as you could sustain a youthful ache for thwarted passion, that meant you were not yet middle-aged. Didn't it?

Below Leonard's generous obituary was a brief item about the death of Taggart Staunton, née McCord, formerly of this city. At her home in Opa-Locka, Florida. Mrs. Staunton had attended the former Spenser School on Edgerton Road, graduated Magna Cum Laude in Music from Converse College, and served with the Women Appointed for Volunteer Emergency Service in World War II. She was survived by her mother, Mrs. T. G. McCord.

In the Monday-afternoon paper was the yearly write-up of the Christmas party given by Miss Theodora Blount of Edgerton Road. Centerpiece of hemlock, holly berries, and Advent candles. The guests included ... Refreshments served were ... Grace Hill, her sciatica aggravated by the office typing chair, bravely endured an emergency rewrite. It would be dishonoring the dead, would it not, to mention his "incomparable eggnog," so, after much agonizing over how to fill his space (for Society must go on), Grace wrote: "Miss Wickie Lee, houseguest of Miss Blount, contributed the piquant hot fruit salad."

2.
THE SISTERS

Lydia Mansfield, née Strickland, was an exceptionally organized woman. Fifty minutes after Max arrived at her new apartment with the sad news, she was on the Interstate, heading west, the backseat of her Volvo crammed with family Christmas presents which she had bought and wrapped weeks ago, and a giant picnic cooler stuffed to the lid with frozen cuts of meat and casseroles. Her dark suit, sealed in its dry-cleaning bag, swayed gently from a backseat hook. The child in her ached to sob, but it was more important for everyone concerned that the woman behind the steering wheel drive. Her shapely, lacquered nails fished in the compartment between the bucket seats, where Leo, her fifteen-year-old, kept his tapes; she jammed the first available one into the deck. The toe of her boot depressed the accelerator to the floor until she saw the speedometer hit seventy. Eastern-sounding chimes, then an electronic chord filled the car. With a glance in the rearview mirror, she settled back to speed. If a trooper sneaked up on her, she would admit she was in the wrong, explain the reason for her hurry, and then burst into tears, if necessary. She deliberately focused her mind on the mundane details of the living in order to postpone, till a more appropriate time, her grief for the dead.

She had remembered to pack Dickie's sheet music on top of his pajamas. Dickie's new kitten, Gregory, was staying with the young woman in the next apartment; Leo's old dog, Fritz, had seniority. Dickie would stay in the old house with his father and brother till she got everything under control. Then Max would fly them up to Mother's in his Piper Archer and they'd have the sad Christmas together.

Sounds of wind followed the electronic chord. Not the kind of music she had played as a teenager. Yet as the sounds accumulated into a sort of theme, she grew to like its soothing, inhuman texture. Nothing sentimental, just good accompaniment for a stranger in a moving capsule on the dark highway of life, speeding along beneath the galaxies. Thank the Lord, Mother was alive and in one piece. Both of them would have been too much. She and Max had wept like children; she had let him nuzzle her hair as they held each other. A certain part of marriage was for life, you might as well face it. Some part of Daddy lives on in me, like a filament of power, she thought. And it will live on in Leo and Dickie, and in their children. She would probably give Max the wool shirt from Bean's she had ordered for Daddy.

She had tried at least six times, while packing, to reach Cate. The phone rang and rang. Was it too much to expect her to be home at a time like this? Max had promised to dial every fifteen minutes for the rest of the night till he got her. But what if she were away for the weekend? Or had gone somewhere for Christmas? She might even be out of the country. You never knew what to expect with Cate.

Cate was attending a student production of *Dracula* at Melanchthon College, a small, Lutheran-affiliated institution on the Iowa shore of the Mississippi. Afterward she was invited to the cast party out at the rented farmhouse of the Drama teacher, who was elated by the success of his play. Though coming down with a cold, Cate, who believed one of the best ways to keep from atrophying was to move continually forward to meet the advance of the unpredictable, went. Infected by the holiday spirit and the group's exultation, she danced with faculty colleagues and students, both men and women, and even by herself some. When she got home, it was almost three a.m. and the phone was ringing.

She made the early-morning flight to Chicago, but because of heavy Christmas bookings could not make connections to North Carolina. She settled for an Atlanta flight and completed the trip in the window seat of a Greyhound bus. In a weird state of mind from sleeplessness, Coricidin, and the miniature bottles of scotch she had purchased from the stewardess (which probably hadn't been such a good idea), she put her head against the cool glass and wept, in an unashamed and rather meditative way, until her fascination was aroused by a couple on the opposite side of the bus.

Lydia went to the bus station to meet her sister. She parked in the loading zone next to where Cate's bus would pull in. A young dispatcher came over and told her she couldn't park there.

"You must be new around here," said Lydia. "My father saved this place from sinking out of sight in 1952. Besides"—she flashed her smile at him—"the Atlanta bus is due any minute, isn't it?"

He said it was and sauntered off, won by her lovely arrogance. He was unimpressed by 1952: he hadn't even been born then.

Each time Lydia saw Cate, she was surprised that her older sister showed so few signs of degeneration. Cate swung off the bus looking like a cross-country adventuress in her tight jeans, dark-blue down jacket, and cowboy boots. Her dark blond hair was slipping down from its topknot and her nose was red, but she swaggered toward Lydia with that pelvis-first walk of hers, her chin lifted at its habitual forty-five-degree angle. She carried a brown leather suitcase, the twin of which Lydia had: they had bought them for eleven guineas each at Simpson's in Piccadilly, when Max was with First National City Bank in London and Cate's first husband, Pringle, was stationed at nearby Ruislip. Cate's suitcase had more nicks and scratches, but in her person she had managed still to outdistance retribution. How?

The sisters hugged. Cate said, "Hold that bus, driver, for the little Strickland girls." Referring to the old days when, out of gratitude to Daddy for winning their suit against the careless architects, the station gave orders for the three-thirty Lake Hills bus to wait for the Strickland girls' school bus.

This made them both start to cry, but when they saw the young dispatcher watching them with interest, they drew themselves up like offended princesses.

"You look gorgeous and svelte as always," said Cate. "How do you do it? I know your love of food is second only to mine."

"I've been swimming for my life," said Lydia. "Let me take that bag. You remember the day we bought these together?"

"God, I sure do. Three days before Kennedy was shot."

"And two weeks before Leo was born," Lydia reminded her. "You insisted on carrying both of them out to the taxi because I was so big, remember?" She laid the suitcase in the backseat.

"How is Mother?" Cate asked when they were both inside the car.

"Well, she broke a rib and she's got some nasty bruises on her right side. And, naturally, she's in grief. But, thank the Lord, she's in one piece. The car turned completely over. That reminds me, you ought to put your seat belt on." She fastened hers, with a decisive click, over her tweed jacket.

"No, thanks, I'd rather not. I'm always more afraid of not being able to get out."

"Suit yourself," said Lydia, who had decided it was too early to start fighting. "All I can say is, I'm glad Mother didn't feel that way." She angled the Volvo left, down the ramp to the new expressway.

"Oh! Aren't we going the old way?" asked Cate

"This is much quicker. I thought we'd go out to the house first. You can have a drink and freshen up from that horrible bus ride before you see Mother. Then I thought we'd go by Mr. Morgan's, where Daddy is. The funeral's on Tuesday. Oh, and I talked to the Gulf station that towed the Oldsmobile in. They can fix it, but Mother may prefer to trade it in for another car."

"My, you've certainly been efficient," remarked Cate ironically. She drew out a sodden handkerchief and blew her nose. It was probably morbid, but she had wanted to drive past the old landmarks and send each of them a message that Daddy had died. Places had their rights, too. As they zipped past the old town that shimmered like a memory of itself below the soulless expressway, she squinted hard to pick out the places she wanted, trying to carry out the ritual, anyway. At least they would be going to the hospital. That was a major landmark, even though the old building had been covered completely by renovations and expansions. One spring day in 1938, Daddy had come out of his father's law office, across the street from the hospital, and had seen a furious blond nurse rush out onto the balcony of the fire escape. ("You should have seen her face. It went through the most remarkable series of changes. Now there's a girl of temperament, I thought. And then I thought, If I can make her look my way, I can make her smile. And when she *did* smile, I knew I would marry her.") How the little girls had loved that story. "You helped matters along, you know," their mother always interjected. "You cleared your throat. And I smiled because I felt silly. The day was so beautiful and you looked so calm and collected down there. I can't to this day remember why I was so angry."

"You've got a terrible cold," said Lydia. "That awful bus ride didn't help it any, I'm sure."

"No, but there was a strange couple across the aisle. They helped pass the time."

"Oh, *how* strange?" Cate did have a knack for observing interesting things.

"Well, they got on with me in Atlanta. They were clearly a *couple* of some sort, but she made him sit in the seat behind her, though there were plenty of double seats. She was young, extremely well dressed, and pretty, in a lowbrow sort of way. He was about the same age, but terribly fat. He wore shapeless, baggy clothes that looked old and cheap. All during the trip, she sat there with her nose in the air, gazing straight ahead, or sometimes she would read one of her magazines. Or glance through it, is more like it. Except when, get this, he would pull out a big brown paper bag, and reach over the seat and hand her a half a sandwich with the crusts cut off, or a segment of tangerine, or another half a sandwich. He got to choose the order in which she ate, and she would accept each morsel in her regal fashion. And, about twice during the trip before I dozed, I saw her come across something she must have found interesting in her magazine, and then she would fold it over carefully, hold it up above her head, point with her fingernail—she had beautifully manicured nails—to the spot she wanted him to see. And he would take it from her, study it intently, and hand it back. And she would look satisfied and continue leafing through it."

"Lord, how strange!" cried Lydia, fascinated with the story.

"Isn't it? But then I dozed, as I say, and when I woke up they were gone. Now, either they got off in Greenville or I hallucinated the whole thing."

"Describe her clothes," said Lydia. She wanted the couple to be real.

"She had a very nice brown herringbone tweed overcoat. It might even have been a Burberry. And a dark-gray, either mohair or cashmere, turtleneck sweater, and matching skirt. And some gold chains around her neck. And a gold watch. Only the boots were the slightest bit cheap. The stitching wasn't good."

"Well, if you could see all that, it wasn't any hallucination."

"That's no criterion. My hallucinations are always full of details."

"You sound like you have them all the time," remarked Lydia edgily. Cate's "mystical" side, or her pretension to one, had frequently spoiled things between them.

But Cate had caught Lydia's tone, and as she was determined they would not fight when their father had not been gone twenty-four hours, she amended offhandedly, "When I'm tired, I sometimes . . . don't you ever, after a really exhausting day, close your eyes and see all these people doing things? You don't control the images, they just come."

"I wonder if they were husband and wife," mused Lydia. She wanted to love and admire her sister.

"Maybe. Or brother and sister. I got the feeling that he was the one who made the lunch and bought her clothes, though I couldn't say why."

"Yes!" cried Lydia. "I got the same feeling when you were describing them. I wonder why."

"Maybe they were symbolic of something," said Cate.

"Well, you're the expert on symbols. My life is complicated enough without them. But you know what? She probably made him sit behind her because he was so fat and they couldn't be comfortable otherwise."

"That's a realistic explanation," murmured Cate, turning to look out the window.

After a few minutes, Lydia said, "I'd better tell you, we're going right by the spot. There. See those first track marks going off into the grass? Daddy thought he had indigestion and pulled off the road. His caution saved Mother's life. They weren't going so fast, then, when it went off the embankment. The heavier set of track marks is where the wrecker towed it out of the field afterward." Her own voice sounded unfamiliar to her as she narrated these details to her big sister. She had slowed the car a little.

Cate looked. Then bowed her head and began to sob defenselessly.

Lydia felt guilty. Though Cate had made *her* cry often enough through the years. But she wanted to make amends.

"Listen," she said, speeding up again, "I have something to tell you. Max and I have separated."

Cate's sobs subsided to a snuffle. She reached in her pocket and brought out the soggy handkerchief, decided it was too far gone to use, and jammed it disgustedly back into the pocket, which was also damp. She sniffed deeply and wiped the residue delicately with the outside of her sleeve. "I must say, that surprises me."

"Well, yes," grumbled Lydia. "I surprised myself, I guess."

"But I thought you two got along."

"We did. We do. There is nobody in this world I respect more than Max. Except Daddy. I know a lot of people will think I'm crazy, but I can't help it. Daddy never knew, by the way. I made Mother promise not to tell him I'd moved out till after

Christmas. I didn't want to spoil his Christmas." Now she began to sniffle.

"Poor old Max," said Cate. "When I talked to him last night . . . or God, was it only this morning . . . he sounded sort of poignant. But I just thought it was because of Daddy. *You* moved out?"

"It was the fairest thing. After all, I was the troublemaker." Lydia sounded rather pleased with herself. "Dickie's with me in an apartment, and Leo's staying on at the house because it's nearer his school. We're all being very civilized."

"What kind of trouble were you making?" asked Cate.

"None—yet," said Lydia, flushing to the line of her dark curls, which she kept cut short as a boy's because they suited her pixie face and because there was no chance, ever, of anyone's mistaking her for a boy. "It's just that I didn't feel free to make any. I guess this all sounds vague, doesn't it?"

"Not if you read between the lines, it doesn't," said Cate matter-of-factly. "You married when you were practically a child. He finished raising you, and now it's perfectly natural, you want to fly out of the nest and see the world for yourself."

But she had gone too far; Lydia resented this neat interpretation of her decision, over which she had agonized for months. "It's a bit more complicated than *that*," she said. "I mean, I didn't just read a sentence in a novel and walk out, like you did when you left Pringle in Keflavík."

"It was also the novel I read *after* that novel," Cate felt she should admit. But when Lydia didn't pursue it, she asked, "So what will you do now?"

"Well, eventually I intend to earn my own living. Right now Max is supporting the boys, of course, and I'm paying all my own expenses out of my dividends from those good stocks Max bought for me when we were in London. I think that's okay, because, after all, they are mine. They're in my name. But I consider this just training. I want to learn to *do* something I can make my living at. So I'm going back to college in January at UNC–Greensboro and get my degree."

"Don't get it in English. There are no jobs."

"Oh Lord, I wasn't going to. I was thinking of something much more practical."

Now it was Cate's turn to feel slighted.

"Meanwhile, it's good for me to learn how to economize," Lydia went on. "For instance, the other day I saw this most marvelous purse. The leather was so soft and it was woven in strips, like wickerwork; it was the exact shade of gray to go with my tweed jacket. But the price tag was a hundred and fifty dollars and I said no."

"Jesus Christ, that's disgusting," said Cate. "It would have been disgusting for a Rockefeller to have bought that purse."

"I don't see that. If I'd been a Rockefeller, it would have been between me and the man who was offering his time and craftsmanship in the form of this purse."

"Lydia, I can't believe you are that naive. The poor exploited bastard in Taiwan who wove your precious purse probably got thirty cents out of that hundred and fifty dollars." Despite all her good intentions, Cate had started to harangue.

"It's not 'my' purse," Lydia had the satisfaction of replying in a calm voice. "And I really think we ought to try to get along, today, at least, simply out of respect to Daddy."

When it came time, in his first period of prosperity after the War, for Leonard Strickland to move his family into a larger house, he and Nell finally narrowed the choices down to two: Commodore Hawkins's "old colonial" of weathered gray shingles, which had just come on the market in the elite section of town known as St. Dunstan's Forest, or a house built to their own specifications in the desirable, but not so exclusive, section of Lake Hills. Leonard, who was partial to the architecture of the past, and romantically drawn to anything or anybody remotely connected with the sea, favored the old yachtsman's house, even though it sat rather low in a dark grove of spruces and despite the fact that St. Dunstan's Forest's unwritten policy of excluding Jews went against his egalitarian grain. But, to counter this, "The Forest," as it was called, would be so safe for his little girls; its private police force had rendered the section a preserve for privileged children. Nell liked the fresh air and the hilly lots of Lake Hills; she despised the shadows and the dampness and the snobbery of "The Forest" and said she didn't need any policemen to help her take care of her own children. Recently she had noticed several "modern" houses going up on lots around town. They rambled rather than perched and had large picture windows which let in great quantities of light. She had her heart set on a certain high lot, with a view of the lake and only a few roofs of lower houses (she was a snob in the antisocial sense) and the mountain ranges beyond.

Without ever raising their voices, they compromised. Leonard got his new "old colonial," and Nell got her fresh air and view. The townspeople nicknamed the house "The Gray Puritan" because it loomed so stiffly atop its open, casual slope: a boy had told Cate about this in high school. But when the family had first moved in, at the end of a summer, everybody was pleased with the house: Leonard with its exterior and the fact that he had also managed to please Nell; the girls because they didn't have to share a room anymore; and Nell with her multiwindowed kitchen that faced the mountains and drank in the afternoon light.

It was only when autumn came, and the trees lost their leaves and the winds began to blow, that the flaw of the house manifested itself. The house shrieked. The contractor and the architect were summoned. There was nothing to be done. When the wind blew in a certain direction, the house wailed like a banshee. They would have to live with it: the condition was inherent in the incompatibility of the structure and its high lot. Sometimes the wailing would make Mother wail back at it, on winter afternoons, when Daddy was still downtown. Mother never wailed when he was home. He could not abide shrillness in people. Even the house seemed to respect his wishes. The wailing was at its worst from four to six, but subsided to a soft, plaintive moan after that. It could sound almost elegiac when Daddy was home.

Yet the house and its lot did seem to have settled down together, thought Cate, surprised at how good the place looked as Lydia turned into the driveway. As in an old marriage, its disharmonious elements had, through long proximity, adjusted themselves into a semblance of mellowed accord. The evergreens planted by Leonard Strickland to muffle the wail were at last tall enough to allow "The Gray Puritan" to sit back more restfully on his winter-tarnished turf and form a benevolent, weathered backdrop for the beauty of two well-grown willows, one planted on either side of the flagstone walk, shaking their naked spun-gold branches to the tune of the wind.

Door key already in hand, Lydia moved ahead of Cate across the close-clipped lawn. Cate inhaled deep breaths of air while she waited for Lydia to open the house. They went in. There was an awful stillness, and the afternoon light was at the stage which makes everything look dusty. Cate's heart began to pound in the dreaded rhythms of her old claustrophobia. Lydia, seeing that her sister looked suddenly quite ill, said gently, "I'll fix us drinks while you go upstairs and wash up. Is bourbon all right?"

"Fine. Though I probably shouldn't. With the Coricidin I might collapse."

"Well, if you do, I'll be right behind you to pick you up," said Lydia, her large, long-lashed eyes brimming with emotion at her own goodwill toward this sister who, it seemed, moved each year a bit closer to the precarious edge. The edge of what, Lydia could not quite say, but she often caught herself having a fantasy of how she would *minister* to Cate, or even help put the pieces of her back together, like Humpty Dumpty, if she happened to fall.

"Ah, Lydia," said Cate, rewarding her baby sister with a kiss for her motherly overture, "you and I might make it, after all."

"I hope so," said Lydia, a little embarrassed now by the waves of affection she had set in motion. "Wait a minute"—she handed Cate a section of folded newspaper, which she herself had placed earlier today on the hall table for precisely this moment—"you might want to read this while you're freshening up. It's Daddy's write-up."

Dear Lydia, why do just one thing when you can be doing two? thought Cate, going upstairs with her suitcase and the newspaper. But she was moved by Lydia's offer to "pick her up." There had been times, lately, when she had yearned to collapse into the protective embrace of someone else's responsibility. But it was too early for that, in one sense; and too late for it, in another.

The furniture and pictures were the same in her old room, but what little of her own spirit she had managed to infuse there during her intense adolescence and budding womanhood had drained out again. "And this is *your* room," said Mother and Daddy, leading her proudly over its threshold, while the twelve-year-old Cate struggled to overcome her dismay and say something grateful. For the room was too full of things; there was hardly space to walk around, and certainly no place to dance. Mistaking her silence for awe, Mother had said, "With those twin beds, you can have your friends spend the night now." And Daddy had said, "Because you are the eldest, we decided you had the right to the mountain view." He went over to the window, bumping into a bed on the way. "Look there: if they'd framed it for you, it couldn't be more centered—Pisgah and the Rat." There had been a reproduction of a Renoir still life, framed by them and hanging above the beds. Full-blown roses in a vase crowded the canvas. Later, in high school, she had replaced it with a poster: Paul Klee's *Saint at a Window*, which, with its mystery and simplicity, left her room to breathe. Curling and browning at the edges now. Why had she never thought to frame it?

She tossed the suitcase and the newspaper on a bed and went to the window. Pisgah and its lower, rodent-shaped twin peaks still had sunlight on them; the ranges below were swathed already in the deep melancholy blue of evening. Those mountains had formed the basis for many aspirations; she must have looked out at them at least a thousand times and imagined what it would be like when she had got beyond them, to the world to be conquered on the other side.

Now she had flown over the mountains many times; she had seen and learned many things; but what had she conquered?

She sat down on the bed and read Daddy's obituary. "... survived by his wife, Nell, and two daughters, Mrs. Max

Mansfield, of Winston-Salem, and Mrs. Cate Galitsky, of Davenport, Iowa." Why had they put Lydia first?

She sat there pondering the strangeness of her own identification, as it appeared on the page. If she did not know herself, or remember her sexy, roguish second husband, Jake . . . if she were just anybody-who-did-not-know-the-Stricklands reading this page, she would imagine "Mrs. Galitsky" as some old immigrant widow, living out her days among tea cozies and antimacassars in a safe Midwestern town.

Then her eye drifted on down the page and she saw the item on Taggart McCord. Surely she was too young to be dying "at her home" in Opa-Locka, Forida. Funny, Cate had not known her married name had been Staunton till now. Taggart McCord "Mrs. Staunton"? that sounded about as surprising as herself as "Mrs. Galitsky." (The kind of friends they had, during their marriage, had simply called her "Cate," or, sometimes, "Jake's woman.") She had never known till now, either, what WAVES was an acronym for, and the full name of the women's branch of the Navy struck her as demeaning and condescending. Women *Appointed* for *Volunteer Emergency* Service. Emergency, meaning otherwise nobody would think of using you. And besides, there was a contradiction: you couldn't volunteer for something you had been appointed to, or be appointed when you'd already volunteered.

Once, when they were still living in the old part of town, Cate and Lydia had been treated at the drugstore soda fountain by Taggart. She was already sitting on a high stool at the counter, drinking something she called "Dope." Cate and Lydia were a little scared when she called out to them in her deep, mocking voice to come and sit beside her; they had heard she was "wild."

But she looked so glamorous in her bare-toed sandals and peasant skirt, her bright auburn hair flying out from underneath a bandana, and everybody knew she was the daughter of the irreproachable Mrs. McCord. The little girls climbed up on the stools that Taggart patted. She wore gold hoops in her ears like a Gypsy.

"Come on," she said. "It's my treat."

"We each have a nickel from Mother, for our cone," said Lydia, a prim second-grader.

"Oh well," said Taggart. "I was thinking of more of a splurge." She must have seen Cate's greedy look, because she casually tossed each of them a menu. "I really wish you would splurge on me," she said. "I'm loaded."

The man behind the soda fountain snickered through his nose.

"If you're really serious," Cate said after a minute, "I'd like this." She pointed to a forbidden treat on the menu, too shy to say it aloud.

"What?" cried Lydia, who had been pretending she could read the menu just as well as Cate. "I want it, too."

"Two Pig's Dinners," said Taggart to the man behind the counter.

The little girls sat bleary-eyed, their waistbands about to pop, playing with the remains of their glorified banana splits. Taggart narrowed her eyes at the big Baptist Church across the street. "You know, Chip, that is the most erotic piece of architecture in town, and those poor Pharisees don't even know it."

"Chip" looked toward the girls and shook his head.

"Well, I don't care." She toed the rail of the counter with her sandaled foot. "I'd like to write a book exposing this place. I could do it, too. The things I know. But my talents lie in other directions."

She and "Chip" began to laugh hilariously.

When Lydia got home, she threw up her Pig's Dinner. Cate asked Mother what "erotic" meant. "That woman is just crazy," Mother said. "I hope you have learned your lesson, Lydia." "That woman" would have been slightly older than Cate's students at Melanchthon College. Nell never did tell her what the word meant. She looked it up in her father's dictionary. "Pertaining to or prompted by love." Even by the age of ten, Cate often got the feeling that there was a great conspiracy at home, at school, and even in books, to withhold from her the very information she needed to make sense of the world.

*   *

"So, how are things out there at that college?" Lydia asked. The sisters were curled up at either end of the couch in the living room, sipping their drinks. Lydia had also prepared an appetizing cheese board, with a sprig of grapes at each corner. She took pride in such things.

"Well, it's not Harvard," said Cate. "It's not Chapel Hill, either. The kids are somewhat bland. It's not their fault. Most of them have lived on farms all their lives. And it is a Lutheran school. But some of them are quite beautiful." She was thinking in particular of a boy she had danced with at the cast party. Even if he had used her mostly as a post to dance around. He was the son of the local pesticide magnate and had played the part of Count Dracula in the college production. "Iowans are really the pure, true Americans, in a way."

"I don't see how an Iowan is any more American than I am," said Lydia.

"There's nothing *coming between* an Iowan and his America. Whereas, with us . . . well, you know being Southern is a whole way of life; and New Englanders still have one foot aboard the *Mayflower*; and New Yorkers are their own country; and California is the end of the world. But there's still that air of pure, pioneering America in the Midwest. Though, instead of being proud of it, they are so defensive because they have no pretensions."

"Mmm," said Lydia. Cate certainly had a way of wrapping things up. "What is your place like? Your apartment."

"It has no pretensions, either," Cate said, laughing. "It has a bedroom and a kitchen and no living room. If you stick your neck out the bedroom window far enough, you can see the Mississippi River."

"Do you have 'a man in your life'?" Lydia put it in self-mocking quotes, but that was because she was so interested.

"I had. A sort of one. I've dropped him." She gave a dry snort. "Though he doesn't know it yet."

"Oh? Why?"

"He had it coming. He's the 'Resident Poet.' Married to a docile little woman who takes his shit. He writes poems about how life wouldn't be the same without Alice, then goes around screwing himself silly. We got along, though; he had wit. Until he attacked me in a Ways and Means Committee meeting. The President was threatening that the college might have to close because of skyrocketing fuel costs, lower enrollment, etcetera. I suggested we all take a cut in salary in order to keep the place open at least till the end of the school year. He flew into a rage, my little poet in residence. Got all huffy and puffy and said that those people who 'had only themselves to please' had no idea of the responsibility of heads of 'nuclear families.' The meeting was only a few days ago, but next time he comes mewling around my balcony, I'll stick my head out and tell him to go away, I'm in the middle of pleasing myself."

"I hope you won't get lonely," said Lydia after a moment. She could see the poet's side, but didn't want to spoil this rapport.

The early-winter sunset was filling the room with shadows. So much family history had happened here. Cate had petitioned to be allowed to drop out of the convent school and go to public high school. In this room, Lydia, hardly able to contain her triumph, had made hasty wedding plans so she could accompany Max to his new job in London. Every six months, Nell Strickland would declare the room off limits the night before it was her turn to hostess the Book or Bridge Club. In the southwest corner, next to the huge Magnavox console, their father would sit on Saturday afternoons, upright and motionless as a Pharaoh, tuning out the worries of family and work as he gave himself up to his operas via earphones.

"Well, if I do get lonely," Cate said, slurping the last of her drink through the ice cubes, "I'll take a demon lover. Or maybe I'll try women. As a matter of fact, there's a woman I was going to spend Christmas with. She just kicked her husband out; he sounds like a bastard. She's established a very attractive solitude for herself, with her antiques and her translating. She even looks a little like Virginia Woolf."

Lydia, rather alarmed, slid her eyes to Cate's face. The chin was tilted up to its forty-five-degree angle and Cate was watching Lydia, from under hooded eyes, with a little smile.

Lydia swallowed. "You don't really think your school will close, do you?" she asked.

"It may. It may not. Those kinds of threats keep people in line. Just like, when we're always hearing bad things on the newscasts, we shrivel into ourselves and say, 'Oh, Walter, don't let them take our cozy homes away from us, at least.' That way, they keep us from going out and having a look around for ourselves and seeing what the news *really* is and demanding what we want."

Who is "they"? thought Lydia. Was Cate just the tiniest bit mad? If so, what had done it? Being married to a man who flew U-2s on secret missions? Being married to another man who lived off her salary and took drugs? Was it being alone too much, or knowing too much, or . . . had that little spark of madness always been there, glowing at the heart of her personality, waiting for the right event to fan it into flame?

"But if it does close," Cate went on, grimly cheerful, "I'll find something else. Maybe I won't teach for a while, but I'll find something else to do. There's always *something.*"

Lydia looked at her watch. "I guess we ought to go on over to the hospital and check on Mother," she said.

When the sisters walked into their mother's hospital room, there sat Theodora Blount, already dressed in the deepest mourning. From the look on Nell's face, they had got there none too soon. Theodora had been carrying on as if she were the new widow.

"I really don't know," she blubbered hoarsely, "what I'm going to do without him. It won't even be the same world. He was the last real gentleman. I have no wish to live in a world without his influence." When she saw Cate follow Lydia into the room, she buried her face in her handkerchief, to give herself time.

"Why, here's Cate," said Nell, in the tone of a proud but beleaguered country which has just received a fresh shipment of weapons. "Cate darling, come and kiss me, but be careful, I can hardly move."

Cate kissed her mother gently. "Hello, Aunt Thea," she said, without a trace of repentance.

"Well," snuffled Cate's godmother, fumbling on the floor for her purse, "I know you want to be alone with your family. I'll go on home." She carefully avoided even the word "daughters," because that would be acknowledging Cate.

Lydia, in a gesture of solidarity with Cate, merely nodded sadly at Aunt Thea in greeting. She was afraid if she spoke, Aunt Thea might make a big thing of saying hello just to *her*.

"Try not to grieve so," said Nell, the real widow, from her hospital bed. "He would want us all to go on." Her voice was a little slurred from tranquilizers.

Why, she's shrunk, thought Cate, as Theodora drew herself up to her full height. Theodora saw the sudden softening of Cate's look and interpreted it as a desire on Cate's part for reconciliation.

As the old lady approached Cate, she inclined slightly toward her errant goddaughter. Her sharp old eyes, reddened with the sorrow that could have reopened her heart to Leonard's child, *willed* Cate to make the first move. Cate knew that all she had to do was spread her arms a little, or murmur "Aunt Thea?" in a voice devoid of irony, and an exchange beneficial to both would be reinstated. But though her brain flashed its message of generosity and pity, her reflexes, dulled by fatigue, bourbon, and antihistamines, clung to their well-established pattern of stubbornness, and Cate herself saw the moment become lost.

"Azalea offered to come to me today"—Theodora addressed Nell in a higher-pitched voice than usual—"even though it was her day off. But Wickie Lee said she'd make us some sandwiches, bless her heart. As if I could eat anything. Well, Nell, I'm going to pray for you. We're all going to feel his loss heartily." Draping her head with a black lace mantilla, she turned her back on Cate. "How are those two fine boys?" she demanded of Lydia, her eyes shining with fury, as she passed through the door.

"Poor Theodora," said Nell drowsily. Though she felt fuzzy from the tranquilizers, the scene between Cate and Theodora had not been lost on Nell, and even though she had been lying here all morning blaming Theodora for precipitating Leonard's death, she had to admit she was a little repelled by Cate's obstinacy.

"Who on earth is Wickie Lee?" asked Lydia.

"Theodora's new protégée. A little mountain girl who showed up at New Hope House and wouldn't tell anything about herself. She's expecting a baby and living at Theodora's."

"Poor old Azalea," said Cate. "I guess it never crossed Aunt Thea's mind that Azalea might *want* to come over and fix supper. Azalea loved Daddy, too. Lydia, why don't we go get Azalea and ask her to come fix *our* supper?"

"No, please," protested Nell with such force that her rib hurt her. "That would only complicate matters."

"I don't see how—" began Cate.

"I've already prepared a casserole," put in Lydia quickly. "And we'd have to take her home again afterward."

Nell began to cry softly. Lydia's words had brought back last night's image of Leonard and Azalea toiling up the hill, accompanied by the bouncy circle of light.

Lydia said to Cate, "I'll leave you two. You all haven't seen each other yet." She went out of the room discreetly.

Cate summoned the reserve energy she had not been able to muster for Theodora (though Theodora's inconsiderateness about Azalea made her feel absolved) and sat down by her mother in the chair Theodora had vacated.

"Mother, I'm so glad you're all right." She smoothed away a lock of graying blond hair from the ugly bruise on her mother's temple. My light hair will go gray like this, thought Cate.

"I don't know what we'll do without him," murmured Nell, "he held things together."

"Mother, tell me about last night. I think if I could just picture what his last hours were like, I'd be able to accept it better."

"We're all going to have to accept it whether we like it or not." Nell felt suddenly tired. Wasn't that just like Cate? Wanting her to dredge up everything when she hadn't even had time to go over things herself. No, that wasn't fair: Cate had loved her father. And Leonard had loved Cate. "We'll talk about it all later," she told Cate. "You don't look very well, darling. You ought to take that cold home to bed. There'll be plenty of time to talk later."

"All right, Mother," said Cate sorrowfully. She kissed Nell and got up to go.

As soon as she had gone, Nell felt guilty. Then she felt angry at Cate for making her feel guilty. Oh, why was it that Cate had only to enter a room and life became immediately more turbulent and complicated.

The next stop for the sisters was Morgan's funeral home: not pleasant to either of them. They drove home avoiding any mention of the effigy of their father that lay in Mr. Morgan's viewing parlor. Though Cate was troubled. Something was missing from that effigy. What was it?

"You saw about Taggart McCord," said Lydia. "It was under Daddy."

"Yes. Remember those Pig's Dinners? I wonder what she died of."

"It didn't say. That usually means cancer. I've never been able to eat ice cream and bananas together after that day."

While they were eating one of Lydia's good casseroles, the phone kept ringing. Condolences from ex-Congressman and Mrs. Bell. "That woman sounds like a wound-up doll," said Cate. "Your turn next."

Lydia took so long on the next call that Cate put her plate back in the oven, which was still warm. "Lord," cried Lydia. "You remember Hugo Miller who hung on like a tick when Max was courting me? He's the night editor or something down at the paper. He wanted to 'go over' Daddy's funeral announcement that I dictated perfectly well to Mr. Hays this afternoon. I think he just wanted an excuse to talk to me. Too bad you didn't answer." The phone was ringing again. "Oh no! I can't believe this."

"It's my turn," said Cate. "Would you mind sticking my plate in the oven when you take yours out?"

"I'll wait for you," Lydia called after her, glowing with

goodwill. To think of poor Hugo carrying his torch all these many years.

Cate came back chuckling. "Why, God bless you, child, you waited."

"Who was *that* on the phone?"

"Mr. Morgan. A 'suspicious-looking' old man with an 'unfortunate facial disfigurement' just showed up, wanting to see Daddy."

"Oh *hell*," said Lydia. "What did you tell him?"

"I said that was our cousin Osgood and to put him on the phone. He saw it in the morning paper and hitchhiked into town in the afternoon. I invited him over to spend the night at the house, is that okay?"

"Oh, for Christ's sake, Cate!" Lydia sputtered. Then saw from her sister's face that she, Lydia, had been had, for the millionth time.

"Don't worry. Actually, I *did* invite him. But you know how hermits are. He's going to hitchhike back tonight. God, he has to be at least eighty, if he fought in the First World War."

"Can you imagine," said Lydia, shuddering, "stopping your car for him in the dark and then seeing a man with no nose get in?"

"Oh, don't start *that*, Lydia. You'd think he had a hole there or something. He still has more nose than a lot of people walking around feeling perfectly pleased with themselves."

"I guess he'll come back to town for the funeral."

"Why shouldn't he? He and Daddy had a special understanding."

"So there he'll be, in his bib overalls, in the family pew."

"You know, Lydia," said Cate conversationally, "some of the biggest hicks in the world have their closets full of three-piece pinstriped suits." Then she went on quickly, because, after all, they had almost made it through one whole day without a fight, "This casserole is superb. I can identify the hamburger meat, the summer squash, and the potatoes, but *what* is this interesting fourth ingredient? It's not water chestnuts, is it?"

"I hate water chestnuts. They're overrated. Do you really want to know what it is?"

Good, she had fallen for it.

"It's those hard little cucumbers you use for pickling. The ordinary ones won't do. They go all soft and tasteless if they're cooked."

After they had loaded the dishwasher, the sisters pecked each other's cheeks and said good night. Lydia made them both toddies, and she remained downstairs with a currently popular book about the life crises of modern womanhood, while Cate, feeling light-headed and knocked out beyond caring, took her hot drink and cold upstairs to bed.

One of their biggest fights had been over Uncle Osgood. Cate had been twelve, Lydia nine. It was their first year in this house. Their school was visiting the annual Mountain Crafts Fair at the civic auditorium, where Osgood always had a booth. He carved animals. EVERYTHING THAT WALKS, CRAWLS, OR FLIES— WITH THE EXCEPTION OF HOMO SAPIENS, read his hand-lettered sign, which grew dirtier each year. Mother said he had probably seen such awful things in World War I that he had given up on humans. He lived a hermit's life on his disability pension; he had an apple orchard, but gave most of the apples to anyone who would come and pick them; he raised fancy brands of chickens, sold their eggs, but kept the chickens as pets—or models: his chickens were beautifully carved, as were all his animals, in that patient, highly detailed way that was dying out. The eccentric old man carved all his animals on the same scale, however: a chicken stood shoulder to shoulder with a bear; the shells of a turtle or a ladybug were the same circumference. It disoriented some buyers. But Osgood's booth was very popular at the Fair. His deformity made him interesting and the folklorists stalked him. But he could smell a hidden tape recorder clear across a room, even out of his abbreviated nose. And if he didn't like a person, he refused to be drawn into talk so that they could hear (or record) his "quaint mountain accent." "Hit's no telling," he would say politely, or, "Reckon I cain't help you none." And that was that. The folklorists would have to try their luck at the booths of the few other old-timers left: genuine mountaineers, descendants of the first English and Scotch-Irish settlers who had hewn their way into the most isolated pockets of these hills and holed up for generations, preferring to eke out a bare subsistence for the reward of living as they damned pleased. Some children of these cussed independents rebelled and came down into the cities as soon as they could get away. Leonard Strickland's grandfather had been one of these; Theodora Blount's grandfather had been another. But others, whether from inherited disdain of organized life or from apathy of spirit, clung to the old, dwindling homesteads, to the old ways and the old speech, and refused to admit the most distrusted of all outsiders: the future. Osgood Strickland's father had been of their number. Osgood himself had gone out of these mountains only once in his life. And lost most of his nose.

By chance, Cate and a seventh-grade friend had been passing near Osgood's booth at the Fair, when Lydia hurried by with some of her fourth-grade friends. "Lydia, what happened to his nose?" asked a little girl. "I have no idea," replied Lydia with a toss of her braids. "But you're related to him, aren't you?" persisted the other. "That old hillbilly? I most certainly am not!" Lydia had retorted.

Cate had been furious with her little sister. She had marched right up to Osgood's booth with her friend and waited till he was free of customers. Then, in a rather prissy voice, she introduced her friend to Uncle Osgood so she would be completely in the clear when she tattled on Lydia to Daddy. When Cate's friend drew back and would not shake the old man's hand, Cate was mortified. But he cocked his head to one side and snorted out of his exposed nostrils divided by a ragged stump of cartilage. This was the way he laughed. "Do you ever let *little things* bother you?" he asked Cate, his thin shoulders still shaking with mirth. "I'm afraid I do," Cate replied, thinking he was referring to her friend's rudeness, and walking right into his trap. "Then don't sleep in the same room with a mosquito," he told her, doubling over with his joke. He had given each girl one of his carved animals, which he took a long time selecting himself, sending them canny glances as he made his decision. Cate got a cat. Cate's friend got a mouse. Both, of course, were the same size. At least the girl had been able to say thank you. Stupid Sue Ridley.

That night, Cate had lurked in the downstairs hall, outside Daddy's study, listening to the result of her handiwork.

"Lydia," Daddy was saying, "when you deny your relatives, even when they are unfortunate or eccentric, you deny part of yourself. I want you to understand that."

"He is not part of me!" came Lydia's scared but adamant protest.

"His father and my grandfather were brothers. If you're related to me, you're related to him. He's your own flesh and blood," Daddy reasoned.

"He's not my flesh! He's not my blood! That no-nosed old hillbilly!"

There was a very distinct *whap*. Followed by a shocked silence. Then Lydia's outraged wail. Cate, gloating outside in the hall, began to tremble. Daddy so seldom hit.

Then there were sounds of snuffling and comforting. Daddy's reasoning voice, thick with some emotion Cate could not identify, said, "Promise me for my sake to try not to feel that way. Osgood's a brave man. Why, if it weren't for Osgood, all our lives might have turned out very differently."

Lydia, always a formidable grudge-holder, had not spoken to Cate for one week.

Not surprisingly, Lydia had remained entrenched in her revulsion against Uncle Osgood, while Cate, having "claimed" him, felt obliged to adopt him as a sort of personal talisman. She made a myth out of him, the proud, sly-humored hermit-craftsman, mutilated in his stubborn stand for freedom, who at seventy . . . eighty . . . ninety (she had been adding a decade to his age for years) often climbed one of his apple trees and hid his face in its white blossoms. When she brought her colorful second husband home from New Mexico to meet her family, the only person Jake got excited about was Uncle Osgood. (That was actually the one and only time she had seen him in a tree.) But Jake had eulogized that spring day until the day he walked out of her life. "We hiked up this impossible hill and when we get to the top there are *miles* of apple trees in blossom, and the old guy obviously heard us talking because all of a sudden these legs in overalls swing down from a branch, and then this slim old body, and then this funny face with a sweet smile and a snout like an animal. And he takes us into his house and gives us a Dr Pepper and introduces us to his pet chickens—he's a vegetarian, just eats their eggs—and shows us his carvings. And I ask him why he doesn't carve people, and you know what he answers? 'I don't *feel* fur carving them.' Isn't that fantastic? I loved that old guy!"

And throughout the rest of their colorful marriage Jake had used the expression as his own. "I don't *feel* fur getting a job," he'd say. "I don't *feel* fur kicking the habit." And, finally, "I don't feel fur YOU!" Just before he stopped speaking to her altogether and would curtain himself off from her in their Greenwich Village apartment and play imaginative messages of hate and obscenity on the tape recorder when she came home from teaching at her swanky girls' school.

The little rabbit Osgood gave them for a wedding present, made out of poplar wood and poised to sprint, had long ago been smashed. During a violent fight, Cate had thrown it at Jake's head. He had ducked and its head was crushed against the mantelpiece.

Well, at least I gave Lydia nothing to file away against me tonight, thought Cate, shivering under the blankets in her girlhood room. The mattress of the twin bed was too soft and her legs ached. She was pretty sure she had a fever. The thought did not displease her. I kept the peace and didn't raise any of her formidable resentments, Cate thought. But the thing she had exerted self-control to avoid during waking hours awaited its own time. She slipped into an uncomfortable sleep and dreamed Lydia was seating people at the funeral according to some special plan of her own, handing them elaborate menus as she showed them to their pews. There was much excitement in the crowded church because this was to be an unusual funeral, during which the dead man would stand in the pulpit, sum up the meaning of his life, and give advice to the living about how to face the future. Cate was glad she was of the immediate family, because she wanted to be right up front. She had a feeling Daddy was going to answer the questions she had been asking all her life. But Lydia led Cate to a bench in the very back of the church, where several old men, in overalls, the kind you saw chewing tobacco outside the court-house, sat. "I'm supposed to be up front," Cate told Lydia. "No," said Lydia officiously. "You're back here." Lydia was wearing her white coming-out gown from the Rhododendron Ball. "I will not sit back here." "Shh!" someone hissed. "It's starting!" Lydia slung a menu at Cate and flounced off to the front of the church. Out of respect for her father, Cate sat down by the old men. She heard her father begin to speak in his patient, singsong voice. She could not see even the top of his head. She thought he spoke her name several times, but was unable to make out a single sen-tence.

She woke up in tears, sweating profusely. "This is really too much, I don't deserve this," she heard herself say. Not sure if her voice was an echo from the dream or if she had spoken aloud. She sat up in the dark, trying to free herself of the dream. I mustn't be too sick to go to the funeral, she thought, panicking; that would be awful, it would be fulfilling the dream. Then, with a crushing disappointment, she realized that the real funeral would provide no forum for her father's posthumous wisdom. Unfair! That's what a funeral should be for. The world was sick and in a fever; her ideals were still perfectly good. She was thirsty, but unable to move out of bed to get a glass of water. I was not a total disappointment to him, she thought. I atoned for my divorce from Pringle by getting a Ph.D. And I believe Daddy understood about my marrying Jake. He sent a case of Piper Heidsieck to Albuquerque, even though he and Mother couldn't make it to the wedding. He kept a bound copy of my dissertation on his office shelf downtown ("Designs for a New World in the Poetry of D. H. Lawrence"), and when he introduced me to strangers, he'd say, "She's a *doctor*, you know." And even these last few years, whenever I talked to him on the phone, and on my rare visits home, I got the feeling he hadn't given up on me. It was as if he were almost *anticipating* how I might surprise him next.

Her eyes adjusted to the dark, and from where she sat, propped up on two pillows, she could make out the silver slice of lake, through the window; it hung like a flying saucer atop the points of the evergreens on the slope below the house.

Then she felt her heart constrict and knew someone was in the room with her. It took all her courage to turn her head slowly toward the door. The flat silver disc of lake still lay, like a thin cloud, across her retina.

But through this cloud she saw her father standing in the doorway of the room, his figure silhouetted by the light from the hall. His face was in shadow, but somehow the cloud upon her eyes provided its own illumination. She could see his eyes roving under the dark brows, searching for something. What? She felt his distress knocking in her own heartbeats. He needed something, wanted something. Was it something to do with her? She swung her feet out of bed and started toward him. But then there was a sort of turbulence, followed by darkness, and she lay flat on the bed, not even propped on the two pillows as she had thought she had been; not sitting up. And she couldn't see the lake from this angle of the room. And the door to her room was closed.

Shaking, she reached—really, this time—for the switch on the bedside lamp. (The old fear: there's a ghost in the room, but if you can just reach the switch in time . . .) The light was on. The ghost was gone. She wanted more than anything for him to have been there.

"Jesus Christ! I knew it! I knew there was something missing!"

Lydia, curled up downstairs with a book she was growing to despise more by the paragraph, heard Cate speaking to someone. But surely that was not possible. She would have heard the phone ring. Curious, she closed the book and put out the downstairs lights. It was time to turn in, anyway. She would look in on Cate. She had remembered something she wanted to ask her,

while turning the pages of this inane book which put women, individual women like herself, into simplistic categories chosen by
the author.

She found Cate sitting up in one of the twin beds, clutching
the sheet and blanket to her chin. Her eyes were wide and staring
and her face shiny with sweat.

"Lord, you're *sick*," announced Lydia.

"I think I may have some fever," agreed Cate. "Could you
bring me a glass of water?"

Lydia returned with the water and a spoonful of some whit-
ish stuff.

"What the hell is that?"

"Liquid aspirin. I'm sorry, that's all I could find. Mother
kept it for the boys, you know. It's a little old, but it'll help bring
your fever down. Tomorrow you stay in bed and I play nurse."
She sounded pleased by the prospect.

"Thank you, baby. Oh God!" Cate looked wildly around the
room, then focused hard on Lydia and started to say something.
Then decided not to.

"Cate," said Lydia, "I was wondering, downstairs. Did the
fat man eat any of that lunch himself?"

Cate looked as if her little sister had gone mad.

"The one on the bus," said Lydia, "who fed the pretty
woman her lunch."

"Oh. Yes, he must have. No, come to think of it, I didn't actually see him eat anything. Are you still worrying about them?
Maybe he was on a diet"—she laughed—"so in future she'd let
him sit up front with her. But listen, Lydia,"—her eyes roved
about hyperactively, impatiently—"we've got to call up that Gulf
station first thing in the morning."

"Why?" asked Lydia, totally confused.

"To see if Daddy's glasses are still in the car."

3.
FAMILY BUSINESS

Like most American males of his generation and circumstances, Leonard Strickland had begun at a relatively youthful age to make provisions for his own death.

During his lifetime he had made five wills. In the first, written in his sixth month of marriage, and Nell's third month of pregnancy, he left all to Nell. And, in the event of her death, all to their child, with Leonard's father as trustee. "All" at the time consisted of a life insurance policy and the faith that Mr. Strickland senior would leave *his* all, when the time came, to the orphaned child. In the event that both Leonard and Nell died without issue, Leonard's all would go to his father. Nell's father was also alive at the time, but she said he could take care of himself, and he could. After Nell's mother died, the elegant doctor had lost no time in marrying a rich widow.

In the second will, he left all to Nell. In the event of the death of both, all to the trustee, the trusted Mr. Teague at the bank (for Leonard's father had died), for the care of the children. Theodora Blount was designated as guardian for Cate and Lydia. In the event of Theodora's death, Lydia's godfather, a cousin of Nell's who owned a furniture factory in Delaware, was to take the children. "All" now included an augmented life insurance policy and the net worth of Strickland Senior's estate, which came to much less than expected after Leonard had paid his father's numerous creditors and taken care of his gambling debts.

(There was also a sizable legacy to a certain woman in town; Leonard preferred to pay this, rather than contest the amount.) "All," in Leonard's new will, now included his and Nell's new home as well as Strickland Senior's beach cottage at Ocracoke, on the Outer Banks. Leonard made a trip alone to the island to clear out most of his father's effects (delivering a box of cosmetics, colorful undergarments, and a brand-new Jantzen swimsuit with the price tag still on it to a certain house in town when he returned). Leonard made Nell joint owner of the house in Lake Hills and the cottage at Ocracoke to save her taxes in the event of his death.

Then, before he knew it, the girls were grown. Cate married Lieutenant Pringle Patchett, USAF. Lydia married Max P. Mansfield and went to live in London. Leonard had felt downright dilatory when Lydia wrote announcing the impending arrival of a grandchild. He had drawn up over a thousand wills for others by now, and executed half as many, and he knew the perils and loopholes of incomplete provisions. The more family members, the more permutations of mortality to be anticipated. He knew some horror stories resulting from the testator's inability to foresee all the ways people have of predeceasing one another. He agonized long over Will Number Three. He believed in the family as the bulwark of a moral and stable world, and therefore his ability to provide, in foresight and fairness, for its continuation through all contingencies would be, truly, his last testament.

He belabored his choice between making a *per stirpes* or *per capita* distribution to the grandchildren. He discussed it with Nell. "For heaven's sake, Leonard, Lydia hasn't even had *one* baby yet," said she, finally exasperated. "But the *per stirpes* sounds fine. What could be fairer than Lydia's children dividing up her share and Cate's children dividing up hers?"

"If you knew how I've seen the *per stirpes* abused. What if Lydia has one child and Cate has six? Or vice versa? One child could get a whopping sum and his poor little cousins have to divide everything up six ways."

"Then put in the *per capita*," said Nell. "Though, frankly,

Cate may not have any children. You know how she's always maintained she hates them, even when she was one herself."

"Pringle will change her mind on that."

Will Number Four was made when Lydia (pregnant again), Max, and little Leo came back from London. Max had shown such a talent for investment that Dick Broadbelt, who had founded the prosperous family-owned and -operated state bank, Broadbelt Commercial Trust, just after the Depression, was making Max his investment officer. Leonard concluded that if Broadbelt was making Max "one of the family" in this way, he would be wise to follow suit. Max had already made some excellent investments for his father-in-law. In Will Number Four, Leonard therefore appointed Max trustee of Nell's residuary assets with the stipulation only that Max follow the Prudent Man Rule, which Max had been doing, anyway, quite profitably, with Leonard's portfolio. The Marital Deduction Trust devolved on Nell, as executrix, to be assisted when necessary by the attorney for the estate. And the feelings of the old trustee, Mr. Teague of the local bank, were not hurt, because, at just this time, Mr. Teague suffered a stroke.

Leonard's fifth will, which turned out to be his last, could have been satisfied by a codicil to his fourth, but, in his experience, codicils led to ambiguity; and, moreover, they could sometimes wound, when compared to the original clauses. And he did not want to wound Cate, but to protect her and any children she might have by Mr. Galitsky, whom Leonard had just met.

Upon the death of Nell, Cate's share would go into a trust. She would be able to draw five hundred dollars a month from this trust. Upon Cate's death, the trust would be continued for the benefit of her children. Should she die without issue, it would revert to her sister's estate.

At only one other time had Leonard been tempted to redraft his will. That was in 1970, after he had been obliged to fly up to New York to bail Cate out, following her arrest for obstructing traffic during the rush hour at the Lincoln Tunnel, and for biting an officer. (The little girls whom she had been leading, in a protest against the invasion of Cambodia, were hurried away in two

station wagons by shocked school officials.) Cate was her confident, ironic self by the time her father arrived at the precinct station; she had been using the time to make some last-minute
notes on her dissertation. She gave Leonard an amusing playback
of the entire incident—the little girls in their uniforms making a
chain across the mouth of the tunnel for outgoing traffic; the
things drivers had shouted at them; the flashing lights of the
police cars. Then she did a devastating imitation of the head-
mistress, her jowls trembling violently, calling, "It goes without
saying, you're fired!" from the departing station wagon. But she
played down her own violent biting of the policeman, explaining
with a shrug, "I didn't like the way he *took possession* of my arm. It
was rude and it hurt. I decided to make *his* hurt, a little."

"Why don't you come on home and rest for a while?" Leonard had said to his daughter.

And she had spent a few months back home, completing her
dissertation, which Leonard had had his secretary type. And she
had gotten herself disinherited by Theodora. And had flown
away again, to New Mexico, to defend her dissertation.

It was during that summer of 1970 that Leonard had been
tempted to make an outright bequest to Cate upon his own
death. Would it not be fair? With Lydia so well fixed with Max
(who was already on his third will), and with Mr. Galitsky gone
(he had decamped from Cate's life earlier in the year), it did seem
hard on Cate, now in her thirties, twice divorced and with no ali-
mony, cut off by Theodora. But, after giving the matter much
consideration, he decided against it. As things had always stood,
Nell was to be sole beneficiary during her lifetime. Would not a
separate bequest for Cate cause friction between the sisters, cast
doubt on Nell's capacity to deal fairly with both daughters, undermine the very solidarity he had exerted so much tact and patience to preserve in that household of three very strong, and
very different women? And might not Cate, the only woman in
the family who had been supporting herself, interpret his special
provision as a lack of faith in her? His gift might rob her of the
thing she valued most in herself (and he in her): her stubborn insistence on following her own star, even if it meant getting ar-

rested. (Leonard always cringed and smiled, at the same time, whenever he pictured Cate biting the policeman.)

In some ways, Cate had done as he would have liked to do, had he been less prudent, more furious and full of fire. Perhaps it was wrong in him, but he did look forward, with anxious eagerness, to whatever his older daughter might decide to do next. Not that he wished her any danger; or rather, not any danger that his prudence and foresight couldn't get her out of.

He left in the old five-hundred-dollar-a-month stipulation. Her Ph.D. was her bequest to herself: her passport to a good job, with three months off every summer. And Cate was still a handsome woman; she would very probably marry a third time. If not another Galitsky, whom she had supported, then another sort of man, who, with the best of intentions, might wish to use her capital for his own projects. And Cate was still in her childbearing years; there were those innocent unborn grandchildren to protect, as well. Cate's capacity to hold down a good job (give or take a few splurging protests for noble causes), plus a six-thousand-dollar-a-year income, payable at five hundred a month, and quite possibly a wage-earning third husband as well, was infinitely better than a sudden lump sum of two hundred thousand dollars or so, should Nell die suddenly, and becoming prey to a husband's unsound schemes. Or worse: Cate's possibly giving in to a sudden fit of outraged charity, donating it all to some Just and Noble Cause. If Leonard had been willing to squander his life at twenty-three on the Spanish Cause (till Osgood brought him to his senses in a powerful and generous way), why shouldn't Leonard's daughter, who was even more of a firebrand in her thirties than Leonard had been in his young manhood, squander two hundred thousand dollars on some scheme for a utopia? Since the age of fifteen, when she had insisted on going to the public high school "so I can meet some people other than the members of the select bourgeoisie," she had made no bones about her socialist tendencies. She believed the wealth should be spread around, and was just proud enough that if, having announced this belief of hers for the thousandth time, someone said, "Okay, comrade, let's start with your two hundred thousand," she would feel compelled to write a check then and there.

And so, much as he admired his Cate, Leonard's very reasons for admiring her made him wish to protect her from herself. That he was, in effect, punishing her for her independence and her egalitarian tendencies did not, perhaps, occur to him. Or perhaps it did. But Leonard, for whatever subterranean motives unclear even to himself, for whatever divisions in his personality, could not bring himself to relinquish his paternal hold on his interesting, troubling elder daughter even after his death.

It was Christmas night, nine days after Leonard's death. The visits of condolence had slackened off, but, to be on the safe side, Nell and Lydia were in the kitchen making a fresh supply of cookies. The day-after-Christmas lull would undoubtedly inspire the family's slighter acquaintances with a sudden moral urge to get in their cars, especially if the day turned out nice, to go to pay their respects to the new widow. While mother and daughter made up batches of dough, talking in low, confidential voices between the screeches of the old Waring mixer, Cate—still nursing her cold and a growing depression—watched a Dracula documentary with her nephews on the big color TV in the living room.

Max, who had flown his plane back and forth twice now, once for the funeral and to bring the boys, and then again for Christmas, sat in his late father-in-law's study and watched the evening news on a black-and-white portable. The black-and-white suited him fine: a child of the newsreel era, he was more inclined to trust news if it was not in colors—and unreal colors, usually, at that. The atrocious sensation of the Guyana Massacre was beginning to die down (those piles of face-down corpses hugging one another in their cheap, colorful cottons would have been granted more of the dignity suitable to the dead on a small black-and-white set such as this) and the networks were relying once more on the revolution in Iran for their "crisis." Max, sitting forward on the couch, which would later be turned into his bed, since he was no longer permitted to go upstairs and climb into one of those too-short twin beds in his wife's girlhood room, watched with a sort of angered fascination a close-up of some bearded Iranian youths shouting into the cameras and brandishing their fists as if on cue. He, the self-made, fatherless boy, saw into their hearts all too clearly, and he resented them deeply, much more deeply than he had once resented rich people, in those days when he had only his enterprise and his compulsive capacity for work and his "good name" (his mother had been born a Powell, which went a long way in this state).

Of course it was more fun to be out on the streets raising hell, being glorified for it by the cameras of the world, than to be trapped in some stuffy old bazaar selling rugs for your uncle, or sweating away ignominiously down at the oil fields, or sitting through a dull class over at the university, fees paid by your father. The "Revolution," that pet word of his sister-in-law, was, Max suspected, for many young people down through the ages just a timely carte blanche to abandon the slow and diligent task of making something of themselves and to go out in the open air with their friends and make trouble.

Max's father had been killed on a country road in 1937 while demonstrating a new Studebaker to a prospective customer. An old tractor had come out on the road and Jack Mansfield was going too fast to stop. He passed it and crashed head-on into an oncoming truck. Everybody dead except the old fool on the tractor, who testified that the Studebaker had flown out of nowhere, coming at him at ninety miles an hour. Earlier, Mansfield had been seen at the local bar. The Studebaker people had got out of paying compensation to the widow and six-year-old son of the reckless man.

It would serve those militants right if they did succeed in bringing that fanatic old dervish back from France. (Max made a mental note to liquidate certain shaky stocks in the bank's portfolio and pick up some more Norfolk & Western. Now was the time: if the crunch did come—and the latest antics of those OPEC bastards certainly portended it—then Eastern coal would have to supply Eastern energy.)

Max felt sad, in a comfortable way, making himself at home

in Leonard Strickland's retreat. The room was so full of the man. His law books on the shelves. The Hatteras seascapes, more professionally framed than they had been painted, on the knotty-pine walls. Strickland had been a nut about the Outer Banks, and these were his holiday efforts to pay homage to the same sand dunes and sea oats and lighthouse through several decades of his life. They were honest primitives, most of them painted on the back porch of the family cottage on the island of Ocracoke.

Just think, being able to sit down with a box of paints and dabble away the livelong day. And he read his books, too, you could tell; the ones on his personal shelf above the desk. Markers all over the Montaigne and Cicero's letters to Atticus. The Emerson. But why three copies of Orwell's *Homage to Catalonia*? Valuable editions, perhaps. Strickland could have been a much wealthier man. But he was reluctant to take cases he didn't approve of, and he hated to fly.

One of these days, maybe after things quieted down and *he* retired, Max planned to read the classics.

Max had "asked for the hand" of Lydia in this study. With a father like Leonard Strickland, it was the sort of thing you did. Even when you hadn't meant to propose when you went down to Chapel Hill to catch the Duke–Carolina game and "say good-bye" to your pretty first-year nursing student before you took up the gay bachelor life in London. Nope, couldn't use that word anymore. The whole society turned completely on its ear the last ten years. Look at marriage: in the same state now as the dollar since it was cut loose from gold. And now here he was on the same sofa where he had sat when Strickland had welcomed him into the family; only now he was the "estranged husband," forbidden the happy discomforts of "going visiting" between the too-short twin beds in the frilly girlhood room overhead. The irony was, he loved Lydia now more than he had when he proposed for her in this room in 1960. Then he had been captured (literally) by her adoration of him. When she beat those wet lashes at him when he came to say good-bye at Chapel Hill, a sweet cruelty came over him: she was at his mercy, she would be devastated if he left her now. He gathered his soft, weeping bundle close to his chest and in his mind's eye he watched the "other" Maxwell Powell Mansfield fade off into the might-have-been realm: that bachelor with the rolled umbrella who was going to have a playboy's flat in Chelsea and make a pile on the Exchange and break the hearts of a few London debs before coolly proposing to Lady Jane, or the Honorable Arabella somebody-somebody. And yet his soft little kitten had grown into this woman who knew her mind. He had shaped her, or helped to, and now he had the pleasure of realizing that the woman who was tailor-made for him (the fact that he had cut the cloth only made her more dear) was on her way out the door.

Lydia's charm was that she was strong as steel without forfeiting one ounce of her femininity. This last week, for instance. Nell in grief, tranquilized and taped up. Cate up in *her* bed most of the time, sneezing and dozing. Who down in the kitchen, or pouring sherry and cutting fruitcake for the condoling hordes? (That Mrs. Bell had taken Max aside, asked him if he could "do anything" about the pregnant hillbilly Theodora had taken in. What could he do and why should he? *This* family stood to gain nothing, thanks to Cate's foolish tantrum. What did he care whether Buddy Bell, the godson who made missiles, came into a damned windfall through no effort of his own?)

And Lydia at the funeral. Old Theodora honking hoarsely behind her black lace. Cate coming out of church in that hippie-looking dress, too long for her coat, with her arm around Azalea as if *they* had been sisters. (Azalea, to give her credit, had cried silently and looked discomfited by Cate's determined embrace.) Nell, stunned by drugs and blotchy-faced, could not help looking less than her handsome best. It was Lydia who did most justice to the dignity of the occasion in her neat dark suit, her face ghastly white but firm. During the service, she had stood straight as a soldier, a son on either side of her, and Max, next to Leo, had looked over at her and had seen her bite the soft pad on her upper lip until he expected the blood to come spurting out. A funeral was a public ceremony. Like it or not, people came to look at the family, too. Was Lydia's grief any less genuine—and Max of all people knew how she had worshiped her father—because she had spared a crowded church full of people the sight of a red, rubbery face and the harsh, broken cries of her woe? (He had heard her in her room above this study sobbing her heart out the night of the funeral, and it was all he could do to keep from taking the stairs three at a time and going to comfort her.)

It was to her they owed the appropriate, muted Christmas, as well. There had been a tree under which to place the presents which had already been bought and which the boys would have been unhappy without. And it had been just the right thing when, before they opened their presents this morning, she had said, "I know this family has never been a bunch of showy prayers, but just this once I think it would be nice if one of the boys said a little prayer for Granddaddy. Leo, you're the oldest, you're his namesake. Come on, you can just make it up." Leo, a critical, formal boy who would rather die than appear ridiculous, shot his mother a pleading look. But she wouldn't let him off, she stared him down until he lowered his long lashes and muttered a brief, conservative reminder to God to watch over his grandfather. Then Dickie, to everyone's surprise, blurted, "I want to say one, too. Granddaddy, we know you're with us, somewhere in this room, and we all love you and miss you very much." This made Nell cry. Dickie was the artistic one; he felt things. Lydia was an excellent manager; she stated her expectations and stared the boys down until they fulfilled them. Usually. Why, Max wondered, did she not tell Dickie, "I would like for you to lose twenty pounds"? But, generally speaking, she was a wonderful mother.

Then they'd opened their presents. Dickie got his Mozart records; Leo, his dark-green velour pullover; both boys, their Calvin Klein jeans. Nell, her perfume from Lydia (Cate had not brought gifts); and Cate, some stationery from Lydia, who had gone out to buy it at the last minute. And he got the wool shirt from Bean's which Lydia told him had been meant for Daddy, and—thanks to Dickie, who had been his gift consultant—Max had given Lydia something she had wanted but had denied herself. But why had she flushed up when she opened it and Cate commented wryly, "Your purse!"

Old Osgood had sent Cate a beautiful little carved turtle. Dexter Everby, the real-estate man, had brought it by the house. She and Osgood had had a lengthy tête-à-tête on the sidewalk after the funeral. What a pair!

Cronkite was not on tonight, it was a holiday. SALT II planned for mid-January, and two weeks later the Chinese were coming. IBM going democratic with its stocks. Inflation rate of 7.5 projected for the new year. Friends and enemies changed; management philosophies bowed to the times. The younger anchormen signed themselves off with shy smiles, or a bit of harmless word play, or an ironic lift of the eyebrows, before dutifully identifying themselves with the network. But nobody except Cronkite, squaring his papers with an authoritative snap, got to say, "And that's the way it is." The phrase would probably retire with him. Good night, Cronkite, wherever you are; good night, Strickland. (There on Leonard's desk lay the December issue of the *North Carolina Review of Supreme Court Cases*, still in its wrapper, along with some other mail that had arrived too late.) Be glad you lived out your days when you could say, "That's the way it is," and halfway believe it yourself, thought Max, pressing the OFF button on his late father-in-law's little Japanese set.

"Why am I so fascinated by vampires, Aunt Cate? I'm scared and fascinated at the same time." Cuddly Dickie wriggled happily against Cate; they were sharing a box of peanut brittle. "Do you ever feel that way?"

"I know what you mean," said Cate, who always talked to him in the same voice she used with adults. "I was thinking about that myself. I must say I'm not all that enchanted by this Vlad the Impaler, who they say was the 'real' Dracula. Sadism doesn't fascinate me one bit."

"I know," agreed Dickie. "Do you really think anybody could torture and kill twenty thousand people?"

"Sure they could. The Shah of Iran probably has that many under his belt by now."

"But why? Why would anybody want to do that?" Dickie's voice, which had not yet changed, rose to a squeal.

"Dickie," complained Leo, who had appropriated his grand-father's sacred chair by the Magnavox, "if you don't want to watch this program, why don't you go talk somewhere else?" He was too well brought up to include his aunt Cate in his repri-mand, even though he had heard his parents say she was a little crazy.

"It's not a program," said Dickie, "it's just a documentary." He fished in the box and took another piece of peanut brittle.

"Well, I'm trying to watch it." Leo in his new dark-green velour made an elegant figure in the high-backed wing chair. He had his mother's slender, long-waisted frame and her dark, curly hair. Ever since he had been a small child, his face had had a fin-ished, adult quality which made his peers attribute superior wis-dom to him and which delighted the kinds of adults who recoil at more exuberant, loose-limbed children. "So like a *little man*," was the cliché most often used by them about Leo. But Cate found her older nephew's self-possession oppressive and somehow desiccated, as though the life in him had dried up before he ever had a chance to live it. Though small children in general set her nerves on edge—you could never express a complete thought when they were around—she believed in principle that children should be experimental, healthy insurrectionists. From what she could remember of her own childhood, she had sat on the fence, playing the adults' game in order to get on with her own thoughts, but smoldering within. She looked over at Leo to see if she could detect signs of smoldering; but all she saw was an aloof young man, rather rigid in posture, gazing hypnotically at this documentary which could have been put together with more imagination.

But Dickie's question interested her and she sat there, munching on more peanut brittle, though she was beginning to feel a little sick from it, trying to figure out why the vampire mystique had taken hold of the American imagination. There were two Dracula productions currently running on Broadway; she had just watched one at the college where she taught; and here, on Christmas night, no less, a major network had set its imprimatur on the current fad.

It was more than just the fascination with horror. Did it go all the way back to the eternal pull between Eros and Thanatos? That beautiful boy in the college production, in his cape that must have been at least nine yards around: now why had she felt such . . . such *satisfaction* when he enwrapped the female lead in that big black cape and slowly bent his pasted-in fangs to her arched neck? There had been humor in the moment, too, she couldn't deny that. What did these pretty children know of Thanatos, or even Eros, for that matter? But audience and actors colluded with one another in the prearranged *frisson:* good-natured shrieks echoed from all parts of the darkened school auditorium; the local Dracula sank his teeth and the prostrate maiden felt the will to resist ebb out of her. Sex, of course; good old-fashioned sex. But also the wish to be transformed. A nice, modern, instant, prepackaged transformation. A quick, clean bite by some outside force and it would all be done for you, you could stop trying.

"Thus he continues," a pompous voice-over intoned against a background of the "real" Dracula's ruined castle in Rumania, "wanting to live, wanting to die. Not truly alive, not really dead. All of these legends attest to the fact that man fears death, but"—ominous pause—"he fears some things even *more.*"

"What?" cried Dickie. "Isn't he going to tell us what?"

"Shut *up!*" came Leo's imperious growl.

"It's over now, Leo," protested Dickie. To Cate he whined, "He didn't even tell us what!"

"It's not over," said Leo. "I want to see the credits."

"Aunt Cate, what do you fear more than death?" asked Dickie.

"The loss of my will to resist," Cate replied immediately. And realized that this spontaneous utterance was the truth.

"To resist *what?*"

Leo stood up. The credits were over. "Do you all want this thing left on, or what."

"Turn it off," said Cate, "if you would."

"Boy, Dickie, you can sure spoil a program," said Leo, leaving the room with his erect-shouldered, zombielike walk. Since he had been in this house, three girls had called him long-distance, two from his hometown and one from her parents' vacation home in Key West.

"To resist what?" repeated Dickie, relieved to have his repressive brother gone.

"Oh," said Cate, taking what she had determined would be her very last piece of peanut brittle, even if she had given Dickie the money to buy it (she had shelled out ten dollars to each nephew in the spirit of Christmas, though it left her woefully short of cash), "compromise. Cowardice. The sucking pull of the Status Quo . . ." Trying to declaim and chew at the same time, she bit down wrong on the candy and a sharp, tingly pain shot through her whole system. She knew what she was going to find before she reached into her mouth to extract it: a substantial portion of her lower right molar with the big filling in it. "Oh shit," she said, her eyes smarting with tears of pain and frustration. Even her own body, it seemed, had joined the popular crusade to make her lose faith in herself.

Max, having apprised himself of the gains and losses of the world on the anniversary of the Lord's birthday, took a tour of the house to stretch his legs. Nell, with her back to him, sponged the kitchen counters. A lovely smell that reminded him of his own mother's house emanated from the oven. Toll House cookies, his favorites. Lydia, a paperback book clasped in an armpit, was just leaving the kitchen, slathering a creamy-looking lotion all over her hands and wrists.

"Oh hi, what have you been up to?" she asked. Not waiting for an answer, she lowered her voice. "Listen, I want to thank you for that purse again. You shouldn't have, but it's just beautiful. It's a piece of real craftsmanship and it was nice of you to go to the trouble."

"Dickie said he'd been with you when you all saw it in the store." Although he had (sort of) been going in search of her, she had come up on him before he was ready. He stood in the softly lit alcove wrapping his foot around his other ankle like a high-school boy trying to stall the girl he aspired to. "What's that you're reading?"

"Oh, just a stupid book." But she looked guilty. "So far it hasn't told me one thing I didn't already know. I'm giving it one last chance in the bathtub. I never really read in the bathtub, though. You leaving tomorrow?"

"There are some things I've got to see to. I ought to get away by nine."

"I'll drive you out to the airfield."

"If you'd rather sleep, I can easily get a taxi."

"No, I want to."

A tiny acrobat of hope somersaulted in his chest. "I'd like it very much, then."

"I'll make popovers for breakfast," she said. "Dickie likes them. Then we'll drive you out there."

"Dickie could do with a few less popovers," he said bitterly.

"It's baby fat. Thirteen's the worst for that. Anyway, we're going to go on a diet when we get back to the apartment. Well, I'm going on up and take my bath."

Up Lydia clopped, in her Dr. Scholl's exercise sandals, because she wanted her bath more than him. Up the same stairs the girl had floated down, eighteen years ago, having bathed and dressed just for him.

She never did say what the book was.

Max drifted toward the sound of his son's and his sister-in-law's voices in the living room. He was not averse to a couple of rounds of sparring with Cate.

"Aunt Cate lost a piece of her tooth in the peanut brittle," Dickie told his father.

Max stood on the thick carpet in his black socks, taking in the scene. The aunt with her witchy hair hanging down, an Indian shirt open one button too low. His younger son, already pouching out of his new Calvin Klein jeans. The half-empty box of peanut brittle open between them. Nephew and aunt were examining the pulpy, yellow-white artifact of Cate's tooth with scientific interest.

"Well, I don't wonder. The dentists are probably the major stockholders in the peanut-brittle business. I would have thought you all had enough turkey and pie."

"It was just something to munch on while we watched the documentary," said Dickie.

"Well, it looks like you're already munching yourself right out of those jeans," said Max, unable to keep his disgust from showing.

Dickie looked as if he'd been struck. Cate saw it and tipped up her chin to her brother-in-law. "None of our waistlines are what they used to be," she drawled, focusing her catlike eyes on Max's paunch.

"How was the documentary?" Max sucked in his stomach, regretting he had come in here at all.

"Not terribly original," said Cate, willing to be friends now that she had punished him. "It didn't really explain why we're all so fascinated by the Dracula myth."

"The real Dracula was pretty sadistic, Dad. He maimed and killed at least twenty thousand people. But Aunt Cate says the Shah of Iran has done that many himself."

"I don't think that's been proved," said Max. "It was a mutually profitable relationship we had with the Shah, and we may wish we had stood by him a little better, before this thing is over."

" 'Woe to you who are at ease in Zion,' " said Cate, with a strange little grin at her brother-in-law.

"What's that?" asked Dickie. "The Bible?"

"Just a little family prayer to end this bountiful Christmas Day," said Cate. "We had one this morning, or rather two—I thought yours was perfect, Dickie—and now I'm making my small contribution." She continued to smile, with her hooded cat eyes, at Max.

"Well, I've got a few things to do," he said, turning abruptly on his heel. "I'll leave you children to your peanut brittle. But don't stuff yourself too much, Dickie, because your mother is making popovers before you all drive me to the airfield."

"Oh boy, popovers!" shouted Dickie, his brief anguish forgotten.

Nell found Max back in the study. He was inserting new pages into his flight manual and looking slightly forlorn. She handed him two hot Toll House cookies on a paper towel.

"Nell, you're a fine woman." He bit into a cookie: the warm chocolaty part reminded him of his childhood. He felt bad about fussing at Dickie.

She sat down on the couch beside him, giving a little wince. The seat belt which had saved her life had broken a rib. "I've been thinking in the kitchen," she said in a wry voice, "in a few more years I'll die and then you'll all have to traipse up here again and the girls will have to bake the cookies for people to eat over my dead body."

"Come on, Nell. You're going to be around for a long time yet. You're a healthy, attractive woman, and fortunately he left you well off. You can lead a very comfortable life. And that's what he would have wanted."

"But what am I supposed to do with my 'life'?" she said sarcastically. "I'm sixty-three years old. It would have been simpler and neater for everybody if I'd died in that accident, too."

"Nell, you're just not yourself right now and it's understandable. Ordinarily, you are one of the toughest, most sensible people I know."

"Well, I don't feel tough," she replied. She looked around the room, resting her eyes on Leonard's things. Max saw her lower lip quaver. "If I seemed tough to you, it was because he was there to back me up."

Max didn't believe this; he had always thought Nell was the strong one in that marriage. He said, "I suppose they've both seen the will by now."

"Oh yes. I gave each girl a copy. That's what he wanted. And if I had been the first to go, he had my will all ready to give each a copy the day after the funeral. Who got what jewelry, and the china and silverware. Honestly, Max, there's something a little ridiculous in all this. People leaving themselves behind in so many pounds of metal and piles of dishes and acres of dirt. It's almost an insult, really, to the dead *and* the living."

Had Cate been influencing Nell? Max wondered. "What did Cate say about the will?" he asked.

"Well, of course she knew—they both knew—that I was to be life beneficiary. At first, Cate said she didn't need to read it, whatever Daddy had done was just fine with her. I said, 'But he wanted you two to read the will and know *just how* everything had been set up.' She said in that case she'd read it. So I sat there and she read it through—we were in my bedroom. She said, 'Hmm,' once; I'm pretty sure it was at the part about her annuity. I was a little worried that she would feel slighted by that. But when she handed it back to me, she said, 'Thank you, Mother, I'm sure you're going to live a long time, as we want you to, and that's all that matters. By the time it gets to Lydia and me, the world will have altered so radically that we won't need it.' "

"God knows what she meant by *that*," said Max, irritated. "Doomsday, probably. Or socialism. She was quoting some prophet of doom in the living room a few minutes ago."

"I wonder what *will* happen in the future," mused Nell. "Not that I'll be around to see it."

"Of course you will. It's happening all around you now, and it's neither as simplistic nor as bad as a lot of people make it. In my opinion, the world is growing closer, not farther apart. I mean, you've still got eruptions now and then, like over in Iran, but in the long run, progress works itself out. It's got an in-built self-correction mechanism. No, what you're going to be seeing more of is better management of things, more consolidation. The people who are always complaining about the evils of bigness don't understand that it's the bigness that's going to save us. Like I was telling Leo the other night: just take a little tour around the house and pick up objects and look at where they're made. That'll give you some idea of how interdependent we all are already. Why, I could show you some printouts from the bank, listings of depositors and borrowers, that would make you wonder what country you were in. A state bank in North Carolina, too. Nossir, the world is not a bunch of isolated nation-states anymore. We're all in this together. We're going to think twice before we send one of Buddy Bell's missiles screaming into a country that's in debt to us for several billion dollars."

"Let's hope so," said Nell. "And let's hope they won't send anything screaming over here, to get out of paying their debt."

"That won't happen. The little countries don't have the technology. And the ones we used to be most afraid of are coming closer to our way of life every day. Look at Russia, it's getting more capitalistic than we are. And the Chinese are coming over here to be wined and dined and shown through our industrial plants next month."

"You make things sound very optimistic," said Nell. But she cocked her head to one side, as though weighing his opinions against reservations of her own.

"In my opinion, it's the people who're afraid there's no place for them in the future who go around preaching gloom and doom," Max said. "I believe in investing in the future. I have to."

"*Leonard* was often hopeful," mused Nell, "but in a different way from you. He could always cite you an instance in history where whatever you were worried about had happened before but had come out all right." She laughed softly. "But it didn't always come out all right for the people concerned." She stood up and gave another little wince. "Well, I'm going to bed. These tranquilizers make me so sleepy."

"Is that rib giving you much pain?"

"Yes, but, you know, I'll be sorry when it goes away. Every time I feel it, I think, As long as I carry this pain, I carry the last time I was with him." She glanced around her late husband's room wistfully and then went over to one of the little paintings, the view of the Sound from the cottage at Ocracoke. "I remember so well the day he did that. He started it early one morning and got more frustrated as the day went on. The light kept changing on him. He couldn't make it stand still and pose for him. He refused lunch. I had to bring him a sandwich and he hardly touched it. Max, how on earth am I going to take care of that cottage? It's clear at the other end of this long state, on its isolated little island. We used to take two days driving there. Do you think I ought to sell it? But it would hurt me so, for his sake. He was always talking about how Lydia's boys would take *their* children there one day. And Cate's children, their children . . . if she had any."

"Hasn't that option about expired now?" said Max.

But the critical edge in his voice aroused Nell's maternal loyalty. "Cate's not yet forty," she reminded him. "Modern women are hanging on to their options to the last minute, nowadays. Not that I believe Cate *will* have any, but—"

"Tell you what, Nell. Why don't you let me fly over from time to time and check on the cottage for you? The island has that nice little airfield, I remember. I could hop in my Piper after work and be down there in an hour, maybe get in a bit of fishing in the early morning or just relax. I need to take it easy and the only way I can ever do it is to get clear away from the bank. I'd enjoy doing it for you."

"Max, that's very thoughtful of you, but I couldn't take advantage of you—"

Max put up a palm, as if stopping traffic. "Nell, I don't want to hear another word about it."

"The water has to be turned on," mused Nell, as if thinking aloud. "There's a valve under the sink; sometimes it's hard to turn. And the damper of the fireplace is tricky; you have to reach up into the chimney and open it with your hand. And the oven is slow. I never was able to bake a perfect cake."

"I guess I can manage the valve and the flue," said Max. "And I won't be baking any cakes."

A smoothness had come into Nell's cheeks as they talked. She was looking more and more like her handsome, confident self again. There was something in her expression that reminded him of Lydia when he offered to do something that had lain, flashing little signals at him, in her mind for some time.

"It would be such a load off my mind, of course," admitted Nell tentatively. "Though, really, Max, why should you? I mean, what are we to you now, when Lydia . . . though I still have hopes that she'll come to her senses."

"Whatever Lydia feels she has to do," Max assured Nell, "won't change how I feel toward her. And besides the fact that I've always admired you, and that Leonard thought well enough of my capabilities to put your investments in my hands, well, dammit, I'm the father of your grandsons, and you're the grandmother of my sons, and"—he decided to go the whole way— "you're the mother of the woman I'll always love."

"Oh, dear Max," said Nell, giving him a look of compassion.

Cate had read recently that a famous New York hairdresser said not to brush your hair anymore; far from adding luster, brushing merely pulled out good hair and damaged the ends. But she sat in front of her teenage dressing table, brushing hers, anyway. Rules for what was good for you and what wasn't changed so fast these days that you had to use some discretion on your own. Let the hairbrushing suffice as a form of meditation, then; *that* was supposed to be good for you.

On the kidney-shaped glass top of the dressing table were Osgood's little turtle and the large chunk of her tooth. As she brushed, in her old rhythm of a hundred strokes a night, she poked these two objects around with a finger. From time to time she looked up, quickly, into the mirror, trying to catch sight of the old hag who awaited her somewhere on the other side of forty; and then she wondered if she were deluding herself, out of sheer familiarity with her own face, that she still looked good.

She opened her mouth, revealing the new hole; there, now she looked less good. Was there enough remaining tooth for the dentist to make a cap, or would he have to pull it out and attach a false one to those on either side? Many people would just have the tooth pulled and forget about it. Pringle had once told her that there were enlisted men who *wanted* all their teeth pulled while the government still had to pay for a nice set of dentures.

There was nothing like a lost tooth, or even a piece of one, to remind you that Old Father Time was chip-chipping away at the cherished edifice of self. She wondered if Taggart McCord had died with all her teeth intact. Or were there some bridges or gaping holes, each signaling a further erosion of confidence in herself?

Cate had been shocked when Mother said Taggart had committed suicide. She had felt slightly betrayed, as though Taggart had let the team down. And then she had worried that she considered *herself* on Taggart's team. She didn't, really. It was just that she was afraid others did.

Yet how am I different from Taggart? she wondered. I believe that my life, so far, has shown courage; but then, the things she did showed courage, too. You have to have a certain amount of courage to spring yourself from the kind of milieu into which we were born.

In a way, she showed more courage. She left her husband and joined the WAVES and even learned to fly her own plane. I merely married a man who flew planes, convincing myself I loved him because he was my ticket out of here. I have supported myself for almost ten years; but so did she, except for those times between jobs when she came home and dipped into her mother's coffers. But, if Melanchthon College closes, I might have to do just that until I find another job.

Cate put down her hairbursh. And then there was Daddy's will. She couldn't help it, it had hurt her feelings. No matter how many times she reminded herself that the will was dated the same year she brought Jake Galitsky home and he did not try to hide the fact that she was supporting them, the terms of that will—her father's last message to her—undermined her. It cast doubt on the kind of life she led. Why should he show less faith in her because she lived for seeing things and feeling them honestly than he did in Lydia?

Of course, he had died assuming that Lydia was still safely ensconced under the protecting wing of Max. But that was undermining Lydia, in a way, wasn't it?

Was it possible that Daddy's ideals of freedom and equality were bigger than his passions when it came to acting on those ideals?

But if that were true, she was not ready to accept it yet. She would almost rather think of herself as not being good enough to satisfy his ideals.

She picked up the little turtle and cradled it in her palm. Well, at least Daddy had been buried with his glasses on, thanks to her vision, or whatever it was. He had worn them ever since she had known him. They were a part of him. If there was an afterlife in which the dead continued to perfect themselves—and some very fine minds believed there was—Daddy might need them to see with.

"Didn't you bring that purty black-haired boy of yours?" old Osgood had asked her after the funeral. And she had found herself telling him the story—well, part of the story—about the meteoric rise and fall of her marriage to Jake Galitsky. The old man nodded sagely, as if he had no reason to expect to hear any other story. Cate wondered if the old man had ever had a woman before he got his nose shot off in the War. "Do you still have yore little rabbit that I give you all that day?" he wanted to know. And she told him how sorry she was, but no; that she had thrown it at Jake during a fight, and Jake had ducked, and the rabbit had been smashed. Osgood gave his dry snort, thin shoulders shaking, that passed for a laugh. He was wearing an old tweed overcoat that looked as if it had come from the Salvation Army store and a white shirt with a frayed collar and a thin brown machine-knitted tie. He leaned on a hickory cane, and Cate had been amazed by the youthfulness of his hands. Though raw from the cold day, they were supple and had no discoloration on the backs or arthritis in the fingers: did the carving keep them young?

"Well," he said, after thinking for a minute, "that little rabbit was only poplar wood. It was too soft."

And then Dexter Everby had come up to them. "How much acreage you sitting on out there, Osgood?" Osgood's family, Daddy had said, had once owned the entire mountain ridge; but they had sold off timberland indiscriminately to greedy outsiders, whenever they were short of money.

Osgood took his time answering. "Oh, reckon enough to

stick my head out the door and holler without anybody gettin' upset."

"How are you getting home?" Dexter wanted to know.

Osgood held up his thumb.

"No need of that, fella. Be glad to drive you."

"Mighty nice of you," murmured the old man, with a look at Cate that said, Might as well suffer a fool. "You come up and see me again, young lady," he had called, going off with Dexter, who had come by the house in Lake Hills several hours later to deliver the turtle, wrapped in brown paper, with a piece of cardboard stuck in the flap.

To Cate. Merry Christmas. From Osgood.

Cate stuck her thumbnail in the turtle's shell. Hard wood, this time. But why a turtle? Did that mean he thought she was slowing down, that her rabbit days were over? Or that he still believed in her ability to win the race, even after everyone else had given up on her? Or maybe he didn't mean anything at all. Maybe he was just a simple old man whom people invested with meaning because of his circumstances.

Cate caught herself frowning in the mirror. So that's how she looked when she thought. Jake had always been taking pictures of her. He said a great photographer could catch the elusive personality behind the face that other photographers thought was the whole person. That was when he had decided to be a great photographer. He had snapped her as she laughed, preached, clowned, slept, vamped it up. Once he had berated her until she burst into tears and then snapped her while she sobbed. "It's interesting," he had said later, showing her the print, "you always keep your chin up even when you're crying."

She and Jake had made love on the floor of this room. First removing the mattresses from the twin beds and making themselves a soundproof nest on the floor so Mother and Daddy would not hear their frolics. They had lain in the dark giggling as Cate had told Jake how Mother had said, "And now you can have your little friends over to spend the night."

Maybe Jake wasn't the soul of responsibility every father dreams of his daughter marrying, thought Cate, but Daddy should have had more faith in me. I'm not an aimless or irresponsible person. I simply want to see things for what they are, and I believe in following my instincts—as far as civilization will allow me to. Why is it that these things get me in trouble, and even cause people to regard me as dangerous? In reply, the wind blew, causing the house to shriek, but not nearly as loudly as it had before Daddy's evergreens attained their height.

Once, when Cate was four years old, she had been spending the day at Theodora's. They were in the front yard, which faced Edgerton Road. Theodora was pruning her rosebush, when a brown bus labored slowly up the road. It was full of people, mostly women and children. They looked different from the people Cate knew and she was fascinated. She waved at the people on the bus, but only one child waved back. The others just looked out the window at her in a sad, mute way.

"Who are those people, Aunt Thea?"

"Well, darling, those are Japanese people. They're going to be staying up at the Edgerton Park Inn."

"But only rich people stay there. And they were in that dirty old bus."

"Well, they're going to get to stay there now," said Theodora. "They are going to be guests of our government. Isn't that nice?"

That was the first instance Cate could remember in her life when she had heard "the tone." It meant someone was not really answering your question. She had heard "the tone" thousands of times since, and, as she grew older, it roused the demon in her more and more, and she took pleasure in smoking people out of their hideouts of sweet words. It had become one of her missions.

"But we're at war with Japan," the four-year-old Cate had persisted. "Why should we be nice to them?"

"These people whom you saw on the bus haven't done anything, honey. They just happen to be living in this country."

"You mean they have homes here? Then why can't they just stay home?"

"Because they just can't," said Theodora, a little impatiently.

"And they're going to have luxurious rooms and all they want to eat at the Inn."

"Then why do they look so sad?"

Theodora closed her pruning shears and put the safety latch on. "What a lot of big questions for a little girl! I think it's time we go into the house and have us a glass of lemonade, don't you?"

Cate was bought off that day, but Theodora had nursed a viper at her lemonade pitcher. It had been Cate's persistent question ever since that day: What right did one set of people have to push another set of people around? What right did the Theodoras of the world have to dictate how others less secure than she lived their lives? The question had led Cate to the Lincoln Tunnel at the head of a group of privileged little girls, and it would probably be leading her a few more places before it was over.

So, my life has moved in a significant pattern, she thought. I've deceived myself periodically, but who hasn't? The point is, or should be, that the mistakes are constructive. I shouldn't have married Pringle without loving him, but, to be fair to myself, I didn't know what love was. I had read about it in books, but the pull of tradition was stronger on me then, and I confused it with what others thought was desirable. Pringle was a good catch, and I did achieve a sort of erotic high as I ordered my monogrammed sheets and towels. I really believed that the act of marrying him would create the love. And I did feel exuberantly snug and loving, those years when I followed him around the NATO bases. In a way, I sort of worshiped him: his radiant calm when he dressed in his uniform and tied his white silk scarf before he went off in one of those sleek phantom planes nobody was supposed to talk about. He was radiant and cool as an angel.

But when things got bad for me, I had the intelligence to see it. And fate has always been good about providing me with convenient messages, little metaphors woven right into the texture of my life. I looked out of the apartment we had in Keflavík and I saw those stunted trees sitting in the soil of dead volcanoes; I watched the sun set at two p.m. on a winter's day. I watched

Pringle and his fellow pilots playing Death at the Officers' Club in the evening, shooting champagne corks out of three-dollar bottles of Piper Heidsieck and bragging about the games they played in the sky with the Russian pilots. And one day I was sitting alone in the apartment in the noon twilight, reading Durrell's *Justine*. I had just been fantasizing a scene in which I was packing up all our things and returning to the States as a widow because Pringle had fallen out of the sky playing airplane games with Russians.

When suddenly I looked down at my book and read the sentence: "Justine was a happily married woman, but she dreamed of widowhood."

That message was almost *too* clear.

And then take the "coincidence" of my finding that Lawrence novel. Browsing in the American Forces Library under "Travel/Southern U.S.A." (because thinking about packing up and going home had made me homesick), I found *St. Mawr* mistakenly shelved in the adjoining "Travel/Southwest U.S.A." And it was the story of that headstrong American girl who flees her English husband and returns to America and buys an abandoned old ranch in the mountains outside Taos that made me decide to go home. And when I got home and was applying to graduate schools around the country, it was remembering the scenery descriptions in that novel that made me apply to the University of New Mexico. And when I got out there on my scholarship, of course the first thing I felt bound to do was drive right up to that ranch in Taos.

And when I got to the top of the mountain and parked in front of the caretaker's cottage, whose beautiful bare feet were sticking out from under the white Jaguar he was repairing? Not the caretaker, but the caretaker's friend, that Jake of all trades— who, I later learned, was the local expert at stashing dope in places on a car where troopers never thought to look. And when it came time for me to pick my dissertation topic, who was more fitting than the author of all this: whose heroine despaired of finding Dionysus in the flesh and settled for him in nature, but who had led me to mine?

And even if Jake wasn't Dionysus forever, or even the embodiment of the New American Dream, as I first thought, nobody can say that's not a pattern. So now I just have to wait for the next part of the pattern to develop, and go toward it zestfully, but with a modicum of discrimination. One does learn discrimination as one goes.

Perhaps if Taggart McCord had waited, she would have seen the next part of her pattern. Or God, maybe she *did* see it, and decided she'd rather die than live it. Maybe there are people whose patterns are meant to provide warning to others.

Please. Don't let that be my pattern.

In the kitchen, which was below Cate's room, someone prowled stealthily about, not bothering to turn the light on.

Under the sink, in the metal pail lined with white plastic, a paperback book, *Life Crises of the Modern American Woman*, had joined the orange rinds, toast crusts, avocado peelings, turkey bones, and other wet garbage of this Christmas Day. If some unsqueamish person, who didn't mind finger contact with a few oily lettuce leaves or coffee grounds, had been curious enough to fish the book out again and take it into the light, that person would have found a page turned down in the middle of a chapter toward the middle of the book, the chapter being entitled "Your Now-or-Never Years." Whether the reader had marked this page earlier and continued on further for some pages before she grew disgusted, or whether she had grown weary at the marked page and, as an afterthought, decided it deserved the wet garbage rather than the honor of another try, the unsqueamish detective would have had to hazard a guess.

The prowler, munching on a Toll House cookie, reached unerringly into the recesses of an overhead cabinet and brought out the fifth of Old Crow. It would be nice to have a couple of cubes of ice, but the *plinks* in the glass might alert Max, who might not yet be asleep in the study next door, and then there would be an awkward confrontation in the hall. ("Couldn't you sleep, either?" "No, but not for the same reason you couldn't.")

Why was it when someone loved you more than you wished him to, you found yourself trying to hurt him all the time?

Because he put pressure on you, that's why. The pressure made you squirm and then it made you feel bad and then you retaliated.

If the situation had been reversed, if he had come to *her* one day and said, "Look, I want us always to be best friends, but I want to go off and live by myself for a while," she would have let him have one moment's satisfaction of seeing her regret, but after that she would have resumed her composure. Even if her heart had been broken into a dozen pieces, she would have resumed, for him and the world to see, her composure. Not one pleading look would she have sent him if they had happened to meet. He would not have had a chance to feel guilty or to pity her. He would have begun to wonder if she had ever really cared for him. And, eventually, she would probably have got him back.

She took another cookie and tiptoed barefoot with her drink and the cookie through the downstairs hallway where, earlier, she had met Max. A low-watt bulb burned all night in the lamp on the hall table, and she admired herself glide by, in her brandy-colored silk negligee with the beige lace décolletage, in the oval mirror that hung above this table. When they had first moved into the house, she could see only the top of her curly head in this glass, but now she was completely centered in it. She had to admit she was better-looking now than at any previous time in her life. These were her peak years. If she didn't get fat or let her skin dry out, she could enjoy a few more of them. . . .

(*"If you are in your mid-thirties and put your mind in mothballs during those busy years when you were nurturing your children, now is the time when you may find yourself sneaking trips to the attic to take it out again and try it on for size. Have you become too small for your old ambitions? Too flabby for your former capacity for rigorous thought? And what about those secret dreams of adventure and romance? If there is a dusty old mirror, you clean it with the corner of your apron and look in. Why, you're still there. You look pretty good! It's now or never, you think."*)

I will find my own way, thought Lydia, climbing the stairs; I will not be regimented into one of your fatuous popular-psychology categories.

Cate's door was closed. Also Mother's and . . . just Mother's, now. The boys were in sleeping bags in Mother's sewing room because they couldn't have Cate's room. Lydia paused outside this door, which was ajar, until she heard the separate rhythms of their breathing. Leo's was deep and quiet. Dickie, who had trouble with his sinuses, wheezed a little.

In her own room, she lay in the dark, sipping her drink till she began to feel warm and drowsy. Her tongue explored the crevices of her mouth, routing out any latent cookie crumbs; she was too cozy to get up to brush her teeth. Recently, at the Health Club where she swam, a slim, dark man had started swimming in the lane next to hers. Her stomach did a little flip as she summoned up the memory of this man's body beating softly next to hers in the chlorinated water. Through her goggles she could watch his long feet fluttering in the wake of bubbles from his mouth. One day, he might be waiting for her on the edge of the pool. They had not spoken yet, but she had watched him noticing her.

Lydia put her glass on the bedside table and wriggled down further into the covers. She considered venturing, via imagination, into an affair with the stranger, but her concentration was diverted from this activity. It would not be showing respect for her father. And poor Max lay directly beneath her, one floor below. And also—perhaps the most decisive factor—it would be just the sort of activity that clever Yankee bitch who had written the book would be *expecting* a thirty-six-year-old woman, recently separated from the only man she had ever slept with, to be indulging in, alone in her maiden bed.

PART II

Ku—WORK ON WHAT HAS BEEN SPOILED (DECAY)

The Chinese character ku *represents a bowl in whose contents worms are breeding. This means decay. It has come about because the gentle indifference of the lower trigram has come together with the rigid inertia of the upper, and the result is stagnation. Since this implies guilt, the conditions embody a demand for removal of the cause. Hence the meaning of the hexagram is not simply "what has been spoiled" but "work on what has been spoiled."*

—The I Ching

PART II

—The I Ching

4.
DRACULA'S FATHER

C ate stayed on with her mother through the first week of the new year. The family dentist, a cheerful man with social pretensions, whose wife flew to New York every spring and fall to buy her clothes, had been able to make a crown for the broken tooth, and Cate felt rather bad about flaring up at him. When she had gone back to have the gold tooth formally installed, he had started sticking a little square of X-ray film into the other side of her mouth, where nothing had gone wrong.

"What's that for?" she asked.

"Oh, I thought we ought to take ourselves a new set of pictures." He pronounced it "pitchers," probably because he talked to so many children in the chair; since Cate was last here, he had taken to wearing sporty plaid smocks and a heavy gold chain around his neck.

I'll be damned if I'm going to get cancer so his wife can buy an extra blouse at Bergdorf's, thought Cate, and had harangued more than necessary about an article she had read about dentists who took unnecessary X rays. She had hurt his feelings and he had got back at her by hinting darkly at the sorts of diseases that lurk below and between healthy-appearing teeth. "You're flying back to that college of yours in the Midwest, aren't you? Well, you'll get the same dose of radiation that this film series would have had."

She couldn't stop herself from replying, "Well, that's all the more reason I shouldn't have these."

When Cate told Nell the story, Nell said, "You ought to have told him you just had a set taken by another dentist in Iowa."

"Then why didn't I go back to that dentist to get my gold tooth?"

Nell gave her daughter a look that caused Cate to despair of ever being understood. Then Nell said, more humorously, "Poor Dr. Musgrove, I've heard his wife runs around on him. And Lucy Bell told me she was over at their house once and Mrs. Musgrove has a whole closet just for her shoes."

When Cate got back to Melanchthon, there was a message from the President in her office mailbox. "Please see me."

She went upstairs to his office.

The President was a rawboned man whose shirt collars were too big for him. His round eyes had a way of gazing past you rather than at you. He was an ordained Lutheran minister and conducted college business as if it were a sort of unavoidable distraction from a colloquy with God. Cate was a little afraid of him because she disliked him so much and was worried that it would show.

"Dr. Galitsky, how would you like to teach a Drama course?"

"But Mr. Terry teaches the Drama courses," Cate said.

"Mr. Terry had to leave us." The President raised his round, abstracted eyes toward Cate's general direction.

"But how come? I mean, he was so devoted. He was so pleased with the success of his *Dracula* production. Everybody was."

"He had to leave us," said the President. "We're compressing all his classes into one. It's the best we could do at such short notice."

"How strange," said Cate, thinking of how settled Mr. Terry had seemed in his farmhouse, where, after the cast party, she had danced herself into a frenzy on the night of her father's death.

Not knowing. Had Mr. Terry known that night that he was going to be leaving Melanchthon? She could swear he hadn't. The way he had fitted out the house with all those lamps and curtains and cushions and hangings: the aura of the place was just not that of someone who already had his bags packed. "He seemed so happy with things here," she said.

"We live in a changing world," said the President, edging something out from under his thumbnail with his other thumbnail. "I was very impressed with your spirit of cooperation at our last Ways and Means meeting. So many people today are just out for themselves. Your community spirit is inspiring."

"Well, I meant it," Cate felt compelled to say, even though the last thing she needed at the moment was a voluntary salary cut. The gold tooth and the air fare home had set her back.

"I'm sure you did. But we couldn't take advantage of your fellow-feeling like that. None of our salaries buy as much as they used to. But if you could help us out with two hours of your time per week, I'd be very grateful. It would keep our young Thespians from being disappointed."

"I'd be willing to try," Cate said, begrudging the loss of two precious hours of her already hectic week. But if she had offered publicly to give up her money to help the school stay open, she couldn't very well deny it two hours a week of her time. "But I ought to warn you, the last time I did anything remotely theatrical was when I played one of the Wise Men in our eighth-grade Christmas pageant."

The President rewarded her with a smile that looked slightly painful to him. "I'm sure you'll be fine. You'll tide us over. Mr. Terry had them read scenes from plays, or he devised exercises for them to do in class. Just use your imagination. Of course, there is usually a play at the end of the semester. But I wouldn't want to take advantage of your good spirit. Let's see how things go. If you *did* decide to do a play, I would appreciate it if you picked one with more large parts than the *Dracula*. Some people felt the *Dracula* was too much of a showcase for Jody Jernigan. Not that we don't all like Jody, but some students felt their talents were wasted, just lying propped up in those coffins."

"I'll see how it goes," said Cate warily.

"Good. And next year, we'll of course get someone full-time."

"Do you think there might *be* a next year, then?" Cate felt she had earned the right to ask this.

"I have more hopes of it than I did before Christmas," the President replied, staring past her left shoulder with his round, abstracted gaze.

Well, well, thought Cate, driving home, I wonder who pledged some money. Or maybe some rich old alumnus died and left some.

It was not till several hours later that she began to fume. She'd been ripped off. That son of a bitch with his missionary gaze had ripped her off. After subtracting for the Easter holidays, that left sixteen class weeks. Two hours a week made thirty-two hours of her time, and she knew she'd be expected to direct the students' play, as well. It would end up being more like a hundred hours. Gratis. Because she had no choice. And this sort of thing was happening to teachers like herself all over the country because the administrators knew they could get away with it. There weren't enough jobs to go around anymore.

But then she turned herself around. She preferred to feel noble rather than helpless. It wouldn't kill her to give two hours a week, or to put on a play. She might learn something; it might lead to a new experience. And though Karl Marx had become very much abused, she did honestly subscribe to his famous maxim: "From each according to his ability," etcetera. And I got off with my tooth, she reasoned. Maybe this is the payment being exacted for it. If so, I'm happy to pay. As long as I am granted my vitality and élan, I am perfectly willing to give my tithe.

But the sudden abdication of the enthusiastic Mr. Terry, with his intense little run-walk, and the way he had exulted on the night of his production, continued to puzzle her.

*　　*

Cate started off by having the Drama class read *The Glass Menagerie*. It had a theme sympathetic to the young (how parents spoiled the lives of their children), and four people at a time got big parts, so Cate could see who could act.

The best actress was a quiet, plain girl named Nan Tyler. A graduating senior, she was taking the class for the third semester. That meant she was really serious, because after two semesters the course ceased to count toward the liberal arts requirement. Nan had played the female lead in *Dracula*, but at first Cate didn't connect the vivacious actress she had seen in that production with this thin child with wispy hair and an unmemorable face. But when it came Nan's turn to read Laura Wingfield, Cate saw that here was the real thing. The other class members were neither awed nor resentful when Nan acted. They accepted her quality as they would have accepted the sharpness of a good knife or the pure notes of a songbird. Nan planned to go to New York to try her luck when she graduated, and Cate felt that if fate was at all kind the girl would make it.

The best actor—by default of there being no better one in this group—was Jody Jernigan. Jody had played the elegant Count Dracula in Mr. Terry's swan-song production. Whereas Nan Tyler was nothing till she became whomever she was portraying, Jody simply portrayed himself, whatever role he was playing. As Tom Wingfield, he was a graceful, dreamy brother, sealed away from the rest of his family in a little package of self-love. Which was okay; just as it had been okay to be a graceful, dreamy vampire, whose very way of stalking in his purple-lined velvet cape proclaimed he lived his days on another plane. As long as he hid behind the right parts and kept his exceptional beauty, he wouldn't make a fool of himself.

Jody reminded Cate of those willowy youths in Burne-Jones's paintings, gazing narcissistically at themselves in brooks, or floating several inches above the ground beside maidens who were their mirror images. Jody was sort of the class pet. The girls seemed to admire his grace and beauty; they complimented him on his outfits and fingered the cashmere sweaters and silk shirts and suede pants he wore to class, but there was nothing sexual in the exchange. The boys in the class tolerated him affably, condescending to him a little—especially the jocks who were taking the course because it met only once a week and had no written homework. One or two of them called him "Count" since the production, and exchanged amused glances with one another when Jody pranced into the classroom like a young horse, flaring his nostrils and shaking his mane.

But Jody was set apart, with a certain respect, by them; and not for his good looks but because he was the son of Roger Jernigan, a local figure of some notoriety. Everybody knew who Jernigan was; you couldn't drive or walk in any direction through this town or its outskirts without coming across at least one sign or billboard advertising Sunny Enterprises. The latest one Cate had seen had been done by a famous illustrator whose "honest primitive" style, combined with a shimmery mystical overlay, made him a favorite with big corporations. Cutting down thousands of trees couldn't be so bad when you saw pictures of all the helpful activities mankind engaged in as a result; monstrous communications monopolies became rather touching when represented by sweet little businessmen floating about a blue sky like so many balloons; and now here was Sunny Enterprises, maker of insecticides and herbicides, advertising itself via a simple rural morning scene: fields and farmhouses under a bluer-than-blue sky, and in each neat square of field, symmetrical rows of tall and perfect corn. In the upper part of the pure, unpolluted sky danced a string of plump yellow letters that bulged as if they had been filled with helium: SUNNY ENTERPRISES. You looked at the sign and felt a guarantee of your share of America's blessings—health, freedom, fertility—whether you knew what products were being advertised or not.

Roger Jernigan was the founder and president of Sunny Enterprises, which had its mammoth chemical plant on a lonely country road southwest of the city. There was also a lucrative crop-dusting subsidiary with branches throughout the state. Jernigan had started his business just after World War II, when DDT came on the market, but he had made his breakthrough (and first fortune) with a chemical which had proved the most effective against the European corn borer, a devastating pest which had been introduced into this country in 1917 and had spread westward across the continent, laying waste not only to corn but to soybeans, sorghum, potatoes, and even gladioli. Jernigan's first product had since been taken off the market when an ingredient turned out to be hazardous in residue; but he and his chemists had developed another product to replace it. The local newspapers chronicled his ongoing battle with the Environmental Protection Agency, but, so far, he had managed to keep one step ahead of them. Sunny Enterprises was named after his first-born son, Sunny, who, according to rumor, was some kind of playboy or wastrel. Both sons lived with their father and a house-keeper in a castle on the bluffs, some forty miles upriver, where a number of such extravagant old edifices dotted the shoreline. These "castles" had been built by German settlers who had made good in the New World but could not relinquish their nostalgia for the architecture of the Old; so they disdained their timber-rich surroundings and hewed out chunks of stone for the dwellings they modeled as closely as possible after those they remembered hulking above the Rhine. Jernigan had apparently taken a fancy to one of these, remodeled it at great cost, and it was to and from there that young Jody commuted, in an enormous old Lincoln Continental, safe as a tank.

Cate got the lowdown on the Jernigans from her friend Ann, who had kicked her husband out and had such an attractive solitude with her antiques and her translating. Ann had had Jody in her French class. "He came bleating to me that he hadn't been able to finish his take-home exam because he had to drive to the airport to pick up a girl for his brother. Apparently this Sunny has girls flown in. I asked why Sunny couldn't go get her himself. He said, 'My brother's not allowed to drive.' All very mysterious. Jody cultivates the mystery a little, I think."

"Perhaps he did something dangerous, this Sunny, and got his license taken away," said Cate, taking up the mystery.

Ann shrugged her elegant shoulders. She did look a little like Virginia Woolf, but Cate had just been goading Lydia when she said they might have an affair. If Cate had been going to pick her first female lover, it would have been someone with greater energy and curiosity about life. Ann's life was neat and shapely, but there was a complacency about her that bordered on the decadent: she was too comfortable inside her old house with her old French editions arranged around her in fusty bindings.

"*Tant pis,*" said Ann. "You get these American Gothic types out here. Maybe Jody's brother is a satyr and has hooves instead of legs. I'll take their papers home to grade, but I won't take their lives. That's where I draw the line."

At first, Jody had a chip on his shoulder toward Cate. Despite the fact they had danced together at Mr. Terry's party, he kept his distance from her now. He seemed either to resent her teaching this class or else to be testing her. When not called on to read, he sulked in the back of the room, tossing his head quite a bit, daydreaming, and flaring his nostrils. But Cate knew from experience that you never wooed recalcitrants. You ignored them till they came around—or called too much attention to themselves.

One day when she was working with a rather hopeless student, Jody made himself particularly distracting. He fidgeted and tossed and flared; then he started in on the most violent of his mane shakings to date. His thick black hair had been cut for maximal fullness, and these vigorous head shakings were his way of combating any creeping lankness.

Other students began to notice. Then to look toward her to see what she would do. That's enough, thought Cate.

She looked pointedly at the back of the classroom. "Are you all *right?*" she asked, feigning concern.

Jody was so immersed in fluffing his feathers that he did not realize she was addressing him. He gave his thick hair a few more energetic fluffs and shakes. Then, slowly, still unaware that all eyes were upon him, he lifted his hands to his hair and lovingly examined the restored coiffure with his long, tapered fingers. As he finished doing so, he raised his eyes and met Cate's solicitous stare. A slow flush crept up the white column of his neck and mounted to his hairline.

"I'll bet you have a bug in your ear," said Cate. "Am I right?"

"A . . . bug?" repeated the boy, his thin skin flaming.

"Well, an insect, if you like," said Cate. "We sometimes call them bugs in the South. The best thing to do when a bug crawls in your ear is to shine a flashlight into it. That way, the bug follows the light and crawls out all by himself. You may be excused from class to find a flashlight. It'll be much more effective than trying to shake it out, as you were doing." She gave a wickedly exact imitation of Jody's mane shaking, even down to the way he dreamily shut his eyes and flared his nostrils. The class snickered. Cate felt her hair slipping down out of its topknot, but it was worth it.

Jody got himself together admirably and said he'd just as soon stay in the room, if she didn't mind.

"I don't mind at all," she said sweetly, and finished working with the untalented student while a subdued and interested class watched her with increased respect. Then she assigned them an exercise for next time. "I want you to come prepared to reveal the character of a certain person by acting out another person's reaction to that character."

After class, Jody followed Cate down the hall, shrugging into his gray silk paratrooper's jacket with the silver fox collar. "Does it have to be another *person* who reacts to the character?" he wanted to know.

"What else could it be?" asked Cate, striding along in her brisk pelvis-first walk. She looked forward to a long bubble bath, with a glass of wine and some incense.

"Could it be a sort of animal? Who would communicate in words?"

Cate didn't see why not. She was curious to see what he would do. But she appeared to consider his request while she buttoned up her coat and he pulled from his pockets two gray suede gauntlets. He awaited her answer with humble attention.

"Oh, okay," she said. He actually seems to like me since I embarrassed him in class, she thought. Maybe it's a novelty for him, somebody coming down hard. "Just be sure you make the character of the person come through."

"Oh, he will!" promised Jody, wriggling his fingers into the beautiful gloves. "Can I give you a lift somewhere?"

"No, thanks, I've got my own transportation." She stepped first into a mean blast of prairie cold while he held the door. They parted amicably. He trotted off to Student Parking to fetch his Lincoln Continental and drive upriver to the castle; she bowed her head against the awful wind and headed for her little red Volkswagen, which awaited her in the faculty lot.

When Cate had arrived here, a year and a half ago, because it was the only job she had been able to find after her college in New Hampshire closed, she had taken a careful look around and cataloged the various possibilities for coping with the place. She admitted she suffered from the Easterner's bias about the Midwest, and had even felt a mild panic as she drove her car across the bridge over the Mississippi. She felt she was going into exile. The college put her up at their alumni house while she looked for permanent living quarters; she met her colleagues and found out what living arrangements they had made. The most fashionable ones, for untenured people, seemed to fall into two categories: you could hide out from the reality or you could parody it. If you chose the former, you might purchase one of the many available old Victorian houses that sat back, like compromised spinsters, on once-desirable streets now lined with the stumps of diseased elms. Then, like Ann, you could refinish the old oak floors so the house would fetch a higher price when you sold it, and you could hang the warm greens and browns of Cézanne's southern landscapes and draw your bamboo shades against the real one outside your window. Or, if you chose the latter alternative (as the Resident Poet and his nuclear family had done), you could rent a farmhouse outside town and stomp around in mail-order hunting jackets and gumboots and baby-sit with your landlord's livestock while he and the missus took their comfy mobile home down to Florida on your rent money.

Cate drove around and walked around for several days, then made up her mind. Everybody thought it was terribly original and daring of her when she settled on the little flat above the TV repair shop on a street marked for urban renewal near the river. It had one large room, sunny in the morning, a kitchen large enough to eat in, and a bathroom with a tub. To show their pleasure in such a respectable tenant, the TV repairman and his wife had painted and scoured, and even installed a little color set where she could watch it from the bed she bought at Goodwill. When the few remaining shops that had not relocated closed down at five-thirty every evening, Cate had the street all to herself. She felt akin to that contemplative order of nuns who do their serious praying during the hours when most people sleep, in the belief that someone must hold up the world during the dangerous hours. Here she was, presiding over a street already doomed to the wrecker's ball; she was the link between the end of the old and the beginning of the new. She had good locks installed on her doors, of course, but couldn't really bring herself to be scared. She had lived alone in New York after Jake left; once a black man had exposed himself to her on a train. She had been scared then, but she had heard her own voice remark good-naturedly, with just a touch of humor, "Now I don't think we need to do *that*." The man had got up and gone to another car.

Nothing was going to happen here. Perhaps that's why she needed to live right on the edge. If she raised the sash of her window and leaned out, she could see the Mississippi River and the eastern shore on the far side. She felt a little like a drunk who is secure as long as he can sleep with one foot on the floor.

Once, when the Resident Poet, lying next to her in the bed from Goodwill, had asked her, "Just *why* did you pick this place?" she had answered that, of all the places she had looked at, the spirits here seemed friendliest. It fascinated him when she talked like this. Another way of putting it would have been to say that, in this location, she felt she could keep faith with whatever the spirit of the place had to reveal to her and keep her sanity at the same time, but that would have frightened him. Well, as it had turned out, she had frightened him, anyway. He had not phoned her since their altercation in the Ways and Means Committee when she had suggested everyone take a salary cut for the common good. He had been nervous or evasive when they passed in the halls. So it looked as if she was not to have the pleasure of dropping him first. Living on an abandoned street because the spirits were cheerful and interesting was "daring" of her; but her socialist leanings were something else.

She was sorry to lose his companionship, even though she knew she could live without him. When he wasn't frightened, he could be a kindred soul with his barbed wit and his sharp eye for the social dynamics of people in institutions.

Jody's "animal" turned out to be a European corn borer, that small larva upon whose annihilation Roger Jernigan's fortune had been erected. But in Jody's presentation, the little larva was the sympathetic character. The villain, the "character being revealed" was *its* enemy: Jody's father. The corn borer's plaint was in the form of a Country and Western song which Jody accompanied on a handsome guitar.

> *I'm just a pore little corn bore*
> *Tryin' to do my thing*

sang Jody in a nasal baritone, sitting gracefully on a low stool with his legs crossed. He wore a peach-colored silk shirt and a dark-brown cashmere V-neck, a fringed leather cowboy jacket, tight brown leather pants, and dark-brown boots.

> *But Mister Poison in the Sky*
> *Has it in for me:*
> *Here come his yeller angels*
> *With their foul, stinking breaths*
> *Blowin' all over this lovely day,*
> *Tryin' to do me in—*
> *And the universe, as well!*

Jody choked and sputtered. He clutched his throat. He raised his guitar above his head, as if fending off the low-flying "angels," reproducing their engine sounds by a low rumble in his throat. By this time the class had caught on and they adored it. It was not quite what Cate had had in mind when she assigned the exercise, but she was amused, too. Nan Tyler's presentation had been disappointing; she was obviously better at filling the roles others created. Nan had portrayed a prisoner being tortured by a jailer in such a way that the jailer's sadism was revealed. Most of the kids had chosen to portray some passive victim being acted upon by an authoritative figure—was this how Today's Youth perceived their chances? No wonder they were all howling with laughter and applauding each time the singing corn borer hurled another insult at Daddy. At least he was fighting back.

> *Mister Poison! You . . . [gasp]*
> *Almost got me that time!*
> *O-ooo!*
> *Gotta breathe now, like grandpappy taught me—*
> *We'll see who outlives who!*

When Jody reached into a Woolworth bag and brought out a real gas mask and sang the final verse behind it, he had his audience in his hand.

> *While you sat on your hill,*
> *And counted your money*
> *And said what we could and couldn't do,*
> *All us Lepidoptera down below*
> *Were outevolving you.*

Jody sang softly, but clearly, behind the gas mask (a real one, probably snitched from one of his father's crop dusters).

"We were outevolving you," sang the class, to Jody's refrain. Even Cate joined in, though she felt sympathy for the powerful absent father being mocked by the young and untried. There sat the son and heir in his expensive clothes, paid for by the father, strumming on a costly guitar, paid for by the father, leading the whole class in song against the values of the father. I'm probably soft on fathers, she thought, since I've just lost mine.

But after class she congratulated Jody. "It was the best prepared and the most entertaining exercise of the class."

He was delighted with her praise. "Actually," he said, indicating his peach-and-brown outfit, "these are the colors of the corn borer, but you couldn't be expected to know that."

Several days later, Cate was in her office grading some papers from her Composition class. It was already dark outside the window, but she stayed on, partly because she dreaded the trudge to Faculty Parking and sitting there shivering till her car warmed up, and partly because these papers were so disappointing that she didn't want to take them home with her. In her writing courses, she went to great trouble to think of themes that might wake up drowsy minds or ignite a rare spark of genius, and the first theme she had set for this new bunch of students was: Describe the thing that has excited your interest most, this past week. It had become clear to her, after having marked about six papers, that this class was even duller and more conventional than the one last semester. The most exciting thing that had challenged the interest of the writer of the current paper was that he and some friends had driven over to Iowa State for a basketball game. She forced herself to read on, feeling that her talents as a teacher were wasted and that she did not really exist in the mainstream of life anymore. Last night she had made the mistake of watching the news on her landlords' little color TV, and there was a depressing interview with Sara Jane ——, she had already forgotten her last name. The woman who had taken a shot at President Ford, several years back, and been sent to jail. Well, for several hours, Sara Jane and another woman had escaped from jail and wandered under the stars and into a town past a lighted restaurant before they were recaptured, and, in the interview, Sara Jane was telling how good it had been to be outside, in the real world, even for that short time. What had got to Cate was that the woman was so articulate; and she looked into the camera with a calm, sad intelligence that Cate would have liked to see more of in the faces of the world's so-called leaders. And yet this woman was crazy, or, at least, had done something pretty crazy. Cate had tried to imagine Sara Jane's life: her parents, her education, her lovers. What combination of events had compelled her to go out and get a gun and track down a harmless President she didn't even mean to kill? What was the statement she was trying to make? And Cate recalled her godmother's parting threat, nine years ago: "You are going to end up either in prison or the insane asylum, if you don't watch out."

Cate sat on in her office, aware of footsteps passing in the hall. Other teachers locking up their offices, going home. She had left her door ajar—you never knew who might wander in. Perhaps she was kidding herself that she could do without the Resident Poet the rest of this cold, lonely winter. She was trying to envision what awful thing she might be capable of that would land her in jail (not just the precinct arrest, like the one in New York, but the behind-bars kind, for years and years), when some footsteps came to an abrupt halt outside her door and a man's voice announced:

"*Doc*-tor Galitsky." He was reading it off the sign on her door.

She looked up and saw a stocky, thick-necked man, wearing a down jacket like hers and a knitted cap pulled down to his bushy, reddish eyebrows.

"Yes?" answered Cate. It crossed her mind that this might, at last, be the handyman she had been asking for since November. Her office thermostat was stuck at eighty, and this seemed wasteful, considering the college's financial straits. But as he sauntered through the door and she got a closer look, she realized her mistake. His eyes were too shrewd and too keen and the musculature of his ruddy face had a willful, energetic set that did not go with taking orders from someone else.

"Saw your sign and thought I'd say hello." He looked her "up and down," as the saying goes, and seemed pleasantly surprised at what he saw. "I've been hearing your praises from the President and from my son. I'm Jody Jernigan's father. Or 'Mister Poison' if you prefer." He grinned, showing a mouthful of sturdy teeth with little spaces between them.

"Oh!" Cate swiveled around in her chair and offered him her hand, which he crunched enthusiastically. "So you heard about that. Won't you sit down?" She indicated the "conference" chair alongside her desk.

"Heard about it, I helped him compose it." He pulled off the knitted cap and sat down in the chair. He wore work pants and lace-up boots. "His brother and I were his first audience. You know that line he had about the 'angels' blowing their foul breaths over the lovely day? He was going to have them spewing chemicals, but I said, 'Son, you've set up an interesting situation, now take advantage of it. An angel would breathe. You've got to follow through with your—' I guess you have a technical name for what I'm trying to say." His reddish-blond hair, thinning on top and graying at the sides, seemed to have a life of its own. It had been doing a little electric swaying-dance ever since he had pulled off the woolen cap.

"I think you mean personification," said Cate, smiling. "Well, it was a big hit, your son's song, everybody loved it." In all her years of teaching, she still got thrown, again and again, when matching up students with parents. She would never have guessed that this stocky, rather homely man was the father of beautiful, willowy Jody.

"Glad to hear it. Glad things have worked out." He made an effort to tame his electric hair with both palms. Then he looked around her office, took in everything, and finished his inspection by giving her another old-fashioned once-over. His snapping green eyes, set deep in the ruddy, crinkly skin, seemed delighted or amused, or perhaps a little of both. "His song's perfectly true, you know. The little devils are evolving. They're becoming immune to the stuff."

"Are they really? But what will you do? Isn't that bad for business?"

"It's been bad before. It'd be bad again, if I let it, but I won't let it. You keep one step ahead of progress or it plows you under. I'm not ready to become fertilizer yet. I was over at the experiment station in Urbana yesterday. They're doing some interesting work with pheromone traps—that's where you use his own sex drive to lure him into these scented traps. Dispose of him that way. But I've still got a few new chemical formulas up my sleeve. We're testing 'em now. I don't mind a little evolution now and then. Keeps me interested." His eyes grazed her once more, as if checking whether *she* was still interesting. And Cate, who until now hadn't found him attractive, found herself wondering if he considered her attractive.

"It keeps me interested, too—evolution," she said. "I just hope I can keep up with it."

He laughed. "You seem to be doing all right. Well . . ." He got up. "I left my motor running outside. I just stopped by to drop some papers off to your President."

Cate tipped up her chin a few extra notches. "It was a pleasure to meet you," she said cordially. "Thanks for stopping by."

He was pulling on his cap again. "Aren't you putting in overtime around here?" he asked, tucking some loose strands under the cap.

"Well, I took over Mr. Terry's Drama class, you know. He—"

"I know all about that turd Terry," he said impatiently. "No, I meant, weren't you staying around here awful late?"

"I was just postponing the inevitable."

"What's that?" He looked down at her, his green eyes alight with curiosity.

"Going out into the cold and warming up my car."

"Well, hell, why didn't you say so? My Jeep's right outside the door. Come on, I'll drive you. You can sit in the Jeep while your car warms up."

"No, that's silly," said Cate, wishing she hadn't mentioned it. "I'll be fine. I want to stay here and do a few more papers."

"Come on. Get your coat on." He had spotted her jacket hanging on its peg behind the door and was already taking it down.

"Please," said Cate, beginning to get annoyed. "Go on. Your motor's running."

"It's not going to run anywhere without me." He danced her jacket at her and stood his ground. His look said: Now don't waste a busy man's time.

"Oh, all right. Thank you." She stood up. No sense making a scene. She turned her back to slip her arms into the jacket he held for her. In her boots she was taller than he was; as she rocked back on the heels to accommodate the difference, she lost her balance slightly. He ended up catching her under her arms just after the sleeves whisked over them.

"Steady," he said, his breath close to her ear.

"I'm fine," she heard herself reply, rather prissily. She drew herself up to her full height before turning to face him. Which had it been, chemistry or just plain exhaustion, that had made her want to sink, sink, sink back against him? She fastened her jacket with brisk, angry snaps, aware that he stood watching her with that grin on his face.

When she was locking her office, he said, "I have an idea."

"What?"

"Let me buy you dinner. That way, you can postpone the inevitable even longer."

"You mean tonight?" She looked down at her jeans. "I'm not really dressed . . ."

"Neither am I. But I know a place that'll be honored to have us." The green eyes under the bushy brows sparkled at her. Was there an added degree of familiarity in them since he had caught her off balance? She was not sure she wanted to put herself in that position with him again, lonely Iowa winter or not. Yet she was curious about him; it would be fun to have dinner. "I know what," she suggested. "Why don't you drive me to my car and then I could meet you at the restaurant. That way, you won't have to bring me back to the school afterward."

"I've got nothing against the school." He pressed down the heavy metal bar of the exit door and held it open for her. "We'll go in my Jeep," he said, as she passed first into the blast of arctic wind.

"Well . . ." She bridled at his bossiness, but, on the other hand, it was a relief to have someone else take charge, for a change.

A giant yellow four-wheel-drive Jeep, its headlights burning and its motor idling, crouched on massive snow tires across the two vertical parking spaces reserved for the handicapped.

He helped her in gallantly, then went around to his side and revved the motor once or twice. The Jeep was very warm.

"Just let me call home," he said, "and check on things."

He spoke into a two-way radio. "Rollingstone? Anybody home?"

A burst of static blared from the dashboard. A woman's voice said, "Hilda here."

"What's new?" asked Jernigan gruffly.

"That pilot's lawyer called again. . . ."

"I said new. Where are the boys?"

"Sunny's down in the gym. Jody's in his room. You want to speak to him?"

"No, just tell him all he has to do now is graduate. I'll be eating in town. Don't anybody wait up."

"All right."

"Thanks, Hilda. Ten-four." He switched off the radio and U-turned the jeep toward the exit road.

"Is Rolling Stone the name of your castle?" The little interlude on the two-way radio had intrigued her. She had so many things she wanted to know. Why was Terry a turd, for instance?

"How'd you know I had a castle?"

"People talk," she said. "You must know that. Especially around here, where your son's in school."

"What do they say? I know they call me the pesticide baron, the liberals on the faculty. What else?"

"Not much. Just that you live in a big old castle on the river. Is it named after the rock group? Or the gathers-no-moss variety?"

He laughed. "Neither. Certainly not the rock group. It's named for the famous paper city of Rollingstone. You know, that famous scam in the last century."

"No, I don't know."

"You Easterners amaze me. You never seem to know about anything that happened west of the Mississippi, and you don't feel guilty about your ignorance. Actually, this happened on the east shore of the Mississippi, so you've got no excuse. *Doc*-tor Galitsky." He nudged her elbow with playful familiarity.

"I do feel guilty, especially since I don't even know what a paper city is. But please call me Cate. Spelled with a *C*."

"Cate. That's a nice name. You don't look at all like a Galitsky, you know."

"What would 'a Galitsky' look like?" asked Cate dryly.

"Not like you look, that's all." He managed neither to fall into her trap nor to back down.

"It was the name of my second husband."

"Was? Is he dead?"

"No. We're divorced."

"You divorced both times?"

"Yes."

"Struck out twice myself. Why'd you keep Galitsky's name? I thought women all wanted their maiden names back these days. What *is* your maiden name?"

"Strickland. I suppose I kept Galitsky because that's the name on my doctorate. But what's the difference? A father's name or a husband's name. 'Maiden name' is a misnomer, isn't it? But you were going to tell me about Rolling Stone." He was getting ahead of her in the questions.

"It's one word. Rollingstone. Well, it was a city that never existed, except on paper. Around about 1850, people from the East Coast began showing up out here with these beautiful maps of a city called Rollingstone, where they'd bought parcels of land from this fellow back east. They took the steamboat upriver and asked the captain to let them off at Rollingstone. When he told them there was no such place, they got out their maps. They showed him the layout of the town, with its town hall and its church and its library—it even had a library—and where they'd bought their land. And even when the boat got to the place where Rollingstone was supposed to be, up near the Wisconsin border, and they saw with their own eyes that there was nothing there except a few old Indian fortifications, many of them *still* got off the boat. They just couldn't believe they'd been had like that. Some of them died, trying to last out the winter there.

"But the damnedest thing: when I was knocking out the walls in the basement to build the boys a gym, we found stacks of those old maps."

"You mean the maps of Rollingstone?"

"Yep. A friend of mine works in the state archives and they had one up there and it matched with these exactly. Now, what do you conclude from that? We concluded that the scoundrel may have been the man who built my castle. They never did catch the person connected with that scheme, you know. Fascinating story, isn't it? A genuine bit of old Americana."

"I'll say," agreed Cate, picturing all those stranded people unable to believe they'd been fools. "Tell me about your other son. Is he as beautiful as Jody?"

"Sunny's a nice-looking boy. He's a blond, like you. My sons have different mothers, but they were both lucky enough to take after their mothers in looks. Though Sunny's got my build. Sometimes I think Jody's a little too beautiful for his own good. But so was his mother."

"Sunny's the older, isn't he?"

"Sunny is thirty-three," said Jernigan. But a defensive note had come into his voice. "I'm taking you to a restaurant called The Power Plant. You know it?"

"I've heard of it, but I haven't been there."

"What have you heard?"

"That you can get a good steak and the decor is nice. The building was once the town's old power plant."

"That sounds about right," said Jernigan.

When they got to The Power Plant, Cate noticed that most of the diners were dressed. The place was practically full. People ate shockingly early out here. She was drawing herself up to look her most arrogant, to offset her jeans, when a young headwaiter hurried toward them, all smiles and respect. "Mr. Jernigan! Why didn't you let us know?"

"I didn't know myself till this lady agreed to have dinner with me," said Jernigan, removing his cap. Once more the hairs swayed electrically above his rosy face. "You can fit us in somewhere, can't you?"

The headwaiter led them to a nice table by the window, which looked out on the spotlit frozen waterfall that had once turned the dynamos for the old power plant. Someone had done a clever job of remodeling, leaving in the high ceiling and painting the air ducts that snaked overhead in bright primary colors. You looked up and got a sort of Mondrianlike ceiling mural, in three dimensions. Cate just had time to read the name on the handwritten RESERVED sign on their table before the headwaiter whisked it away.

"Mr. and Mrs. Axel Ollin bite the dust," she commented to Jernigan, who had also seen it, when they were seated. "How do you rate that?"

"Well, the fact is," he said, almost with embarrassment, "I'm part owner of the place." He tried to calm his hair with the palms of his hands. "A friend of mine asked me if I wanted to buy in. He sells heavy farm equipment and needed a place where he could bring his farmers for a good solid meal; and it's fairly near my plant, so I could bring people for lunch and dinner. The EPA boys who come to snoop around my plant love this place. Especially the salad bar. In the summer, all the produce is locally grown. That turns them on no end. Tell me the truth, what do you think of the decor, the ceiling and all?"

"Very striking. It was a wonderful idea, leaving those old pipes exposed."

"You think so, eh?" His eyes danced. "That was Jody's idea. He has a flair for that sort of thing. He had a pretty free hand in decorating our castle when we moved in. Really enjoyed himself. He ordered the furniture and I wrote the checks. But I put my foot down when it came to my room. He would have had me sunk into the upholstery and surrounded by mirrors, like some

Hugh Hefner. I like a big, hard bed and a couple of windows I can open without getting lost in the curtains, and I can do without the mirrors. But he made old Hilda happy. Hilda's a cousin, from my mother's side of the family. She's been with us since Jody was a little boy. Jody fitted out her apartment like she was a German princess. She *is* of German descent—my mother was a Schmidt—but"—he laughed—"poor old Hilda isn't exactly a princess. But she's a godsend to me. She's one of those old maids who should have married and had fifteen children. So she consoles herself by spoiling mine rotten. You want a cocktail first?"

"Are you going to have one?"

"I'm not much of a drinking man, but don't let that stop you."

"Maybe we'll just order a bottle of wine with dinner," said Cate.

"You sure?"

"Sure. I prefer wine. But only if you drink some. I'm not going to drink the whole bottle myself."

"I'll help you out. But why don't you order us something good. I'm sort of a country bumpkin when it comes to wines."

There was that hayseed grin again. But counterbalanced by the acute green eyes in their crinkly settings. Cate could just imagine him over a business lunch, letting the man across the table drink himself silly because he felt he had nothing to lose with the "country bumpkin," who would remain good-humored and confident and sober—and end up getting exactly what he wanted. As much as she would have enjoyed getting cozily sozzled with a nice bottle (or two) of wine, she was determined to keep her wits and find out everything she wanted to know about Jernigan. He interested her as a type; she had known very few "tycoons"—well, none, really; there had been none hanging around the various NATO bases when she was with Pringle; there had certainly been none in Jake's world—though she had met one or two dope dealers who drove Rolls-Royces and flew back and forth to South America a lot; Max was not even a tycoon, he was simply a servant to one; he had sold his talent for predicting what money was going to do under given circumstances to Mr. Broadbelt, who was a tycoon. (Wouldn't it be fun if Lydia could see her now, having dinner with a tycoon; no, seeing wouldn't be enough, because Lydia would take one look at Roger Jernigan's Pendleton shirt and work pants and heavy boots and dismiss him; she would have to be told.)

Cate was curious as to how, in the real world, a man like Jernigan had established his base of power, and how far he could make it extend, and by what methods. Why did she assume automatically that those methods would not be honorable? Where had this bias come from? As far back as she could recall, she had nourished a contempt and a mild, righteous fury for what she called "robber barons." A "liberal" term, Jernigan would say; yet her father had not been a liberal and she had heard him use it. Her father had been honest and scrupulous in his business, but then, in the world's terms, her father had not been a success. Prosperous, yes; admirable, yes; the kind of man people refer to as "a rock." But he had not been brilliant or daring, and had not pitted himself against any jagged elements or been in the vanguard, or even the middle ranks, of any important causes or discoveries. He had stood for fairness and for preserving the foundations others had built—the status quo, in other words.

And, having known him, she wondered if any man could become a success and remain compassionate and civilized and honorable in the bargain. Her father hadn't really thought so, she was pretty sure. But why was she sure? Had he, in his steady, quiet way, while egging her on to be outstanding, instilled this scorn of success into her?

A robber baron was, in the original sense, a nobleman of feudal times who robbed people traveling through his kingdom. In modern times, it would be someone who used his wealth or power to take advantage of others. The "scoundrel" who had gotten away with the Rollingstone hoax wasn't even a robber baron. He was a mere embezzler. He would have had to get away with it openly, and prosper in the eyes of his community, to attain the class of robber baron.

Was Jernigan a robber baron, in the real sense of the word? She realized that she wanted to find out enough about him to convince herself that he was not honorable. Then she could dismiss him; he would no longer be a threat, or a reproach. *If I knew I could not be powerful without being dishonest, I think I would be able to accept myself better*, she thought.

And it shocked her to realize this about herself. All this time, she had been bending over the wine list, not really reading it, and, just as she was beginning to register what wines were there (there was a good Mondavi red—she remembered it from the summer she and Jake had waited tables at the El Tovar Lodge at the Grand Canyon), she had a further insight that made her shudder. It was about Sara Jane Moore (that name had suddenly, ominously resurfaced), the articulate middle-aged woman with the sad-wise eyes who had shot at President Ford. Could it be that Sara Jane Moore, looking into the glass one day and seeing her chances dwindle for the success she felt she deserved—whatever form that might have taken—had been struck temporarily insane with fury at Success? And to know that less deserving people than herself had found power, claimed power—that one had had it thrust upon him simply because another man was dashing madly for the exit—must have been galling. She may not have *seen* Gerald Ford, even, when she aimed that gun. She may have been shooting at that fickle, undiscriminating aura, called Success, which hovered briefly above his head, and that's probably why she missed. Missed all the way around, poor thing; because if she had succeeded in killing him, she would have made it into the history books, at least.

Cate told Jernigan they should order the Mondavi. When they got back from the salad bar with their heaped plates, she asked, "What are those Environmental Protection people hoping to find when they 'snoop' at your plant?"

"Horrors. Everybody's on the lookout for horrors now. It's big business, looking for horrors. It might even be the number-one industry in America." He grinned and stabbed a circle of cucumber with his fork.

"What kinds of horrors in particular?"

"In my case? Well, my current horror is that certain little residues might escape from my smokestacks. Then not only would I have the EPA down my neck, but a whole town's liable to sue. Lawsuits are another big industry these days. I have a pilot, sprayed *part*-time for me *one* summer, *eight* years ago. His baby's been born with a defective heart, and he's suing me. Claims it was exposure to a weed killer I made, which he's read has now been taken off the market."

"Do you think it might have been?"

"Nothing conclusive has been proved yet. But I would be the first to feel sorry if it turned out to be. The point is, there's no guarantee that every new wonder science discovers is going to be good for us. A penicillin mold is; a hydrocarbon might not be. It's trial and error and the goodwill of all men. Or should be. I've certainly never made anything thinking, Let's hope this wipes out all the robins or deforms some children. But what gets me is the current fashion for accusations based on after-the-fact knowledge. I have to spend half my time and a great deal of money just foreseeing *potential* horrors. I've spent one night out of every three this past month down at the plant preparing for lab audits by the government and so I can be there early in the morning to watch the crew who're installing my scrubbers, these chemical filters that go in the stacks. They collect the horrors before they escape into the wide blue yonder.

"But somebody's got to produce those scrubbers. And I've got to buy 'em from him. Safeguards are another booming industry in this country today. Horror hunting, lawsuits, and safeguards. The ironic thing is, when I started my business, *it* was considered a safeguard industry. We were the saviors; now we're the villains." He popped the cucumber into his mouth and crunched thoughtfully. "What gets me is how short people's memories are. I remember when everybody thought DDT was the answer to all our prayers. Right after the War. You're probably too young to remember that."

"I'll be forty this year," said Cate, who refused to be coy about her age.

"Really? You don't look it. I know I'm supposed to say that, but it's the truth. You have any children?"

"No," said Cate.

"Why not? I know I'm *not* supposed to ask that, but I'm interested."

"Well," began Cate, annoyed with herself for feeling defensive, "my first husband and I didn't want any for a while, and after *a while* was over, we were divorced. I remember having a couple of weak moments with my second husband, when I wouldn't have minded, but luckily nothing came of it. Maybe I'm not fertile, I don't know." She laughed rather harshly. "My father, who died this past December, left provisions in his will for my children, so I don't guess he could close the door on the possibility. Of course that will was made a few years ago."

"And how about you? Can you close the door?" asked Jernigan.

"Yes. I think I can." But after all these years, she still expected the sky to come crashing down on her in punishment every time she said she didn't want children. "I think I have come to terms with being the exception. But what about you? Aren't you somewhat of an exception yourself? From what I gather, you've raised your sons alone."

"Not quite. Sunny's mother was around till he was almost ten. But she wasn't strong. I mean emotionally. We had some problems with Sunny, and her way out was to have periodic breakdowns. She spent a lot of time in and out of clinics. Now, Jody's mother was something else. She was a very beautiful woman, a Brazilian. I think she married me for security and to get to America. I was the one who talked her into having a child. Scared to death it would ruin her figure. Well, it didn't, but she was never crazy about Jody. There are women like that; don't like their own kids. I had to learn that from Manuela. I learned a lot from Manuela. One thing for sure, she cured me of beautiful women."

Thanks a lot, thought Cate. "Where are they now, the mothers?"

"Both remarried. Selma, Sunny's mother, operates a fishing-boat concession with her husband down in Florida. Says she's happier than she's ever been. Manuela runs a modeling agency in LA and is married to a rich Oriental. She claims to have fulfilled herself and is dying to get her hands on Jody so she can turn him into a model. She likes him better now since he's turned out to be beautiful." He bestowed his innocent, spacy-toothed grin on Cate. "What do you think it is about me, drives women away? Maybe"—he laughed—"I exude some kind of womanicide."

"No you don't," said Cate, quick to the rescue of the under-dog. "You're a very sturdy, virile man. Those qualities are prac-tically extinct. And you have confidence and energy and you *ask questions*. You're curious about people. If you knew how rarely anybody asks me half as many questions as I ask them. Curiosity is attractive. And also,"—the wine had come and half a glass had made her generous—"also, you exude a sort of personal energy, a power. And power of that kind is very attractive." Embar-rassed, she ducked her head and sipped more wine.

"You think so?" His face glowed with undisguised pleasure. "Well. Have some more wine." He refilled her glass.

"Oh no. Not until you catch up."

He picked up his glass and downed every drop. "Okay?"

"Okay." She laughed. "I like things to be even."

He refilled his glass. "I'd like to propose a toast. To pleasant surprises."

"I'll drink to that."

During dinner, he said, "After my scrubbers are installed, I promised to take Sunny skiing in Colorado. When I get back, may I phone you?"

"Certainly." She was attracted by his combination of straightforwardness and shrewdness; she was intrigued by his touching bondage to his sons, and curious about their lives; and she had to admit she had not heard "the tone" when he was de-fending his business. He was not her "type"; he had neither the imperviousness of a Pringle nor the Dionysian charms of a Jake (had Jake cured *her* of beautiful *men*?). She couldn't enjoy the witty, intellectual-catty repartee with him that she and the Resi-dent Poet had excelled in. But there was a comforting and refreshing solidity about this man who, like herself, moved through the days trying to stay one confident step ahead of all the forces that might do them in. Maybe, at this juncture of her life, it was enough to have the company of a fellow mutant. "I could make dinner for you," she said, "if you don't mind eating it in a kitchen upstairs over a TV repair shop on a condemned street."

"Which condemned street? Where do you live, anyway?"

When she told him, he laughed and laughed.

"What's so funny?"

"Just the coincidence, is all. You know, that area has been purchased by a group of local developers. They're going to build a complex down there. A theater, a couple of restaurants, shops, some terraced apartments."

"Yes, I heard something about it. From my landlords. Oh God. Wait a minute. Don't tell me you're one of them. One of the developers?"

He nodded.

"Well, well, this is getting a bit feudal. But at least I'll know who to blame when I get evicted. How much longer have I got, anyway? My landlords weren't even sure themselves."

"You've got as long as you need," he said.

"What do you mean by that?"

"Oh ..." His face tensed and then became purposely bland—he had been tempted to tell her something, then thought better of it. "I mean that I'd never evict you. We'll leave your building standing, like a little landmark. We'll open a restaurant downstairs and call it Cate's Kitchen."

"Well, I may need a job cooking there, if the college closes. Do you think the college will close?"

Ah-ha. The guilty look. He did know something.

"Not in the *immediate* future," he said.

She was reminded of another question she had wanted to ask. "Why did you call Mr. Terry a turd? Do you know why he left Melanchthon in such a rush?"

His face went through a few more tensings. Then he looked

at her as if assessing her trustworthiness and, after a further pause, said, "Yes, I know why he left. I asked that he leave. He tried to seduce my son Jody."

Cate sipped her wine slowly. "I'm surprised I didn't think of that. But how did you find out?"

"I know my son. I've observed him at close range for almost twenty-one years. I saw some signals and I asked him right out. He told me. Jody's flighty, but he's not secretive. He loves to be admired, and he loves to talk about it, when asked."

"Did he actually say, 'Mr. Terry tried to seduce me'?"

"Oh no. He said Mr. Terry had asked him to go to Europe with him this summer, to some drama festival. I pursued it from there. Then I paid Mr. Terry a visit at his overdecorated house and pursued it some more. Then I paid a visit to the President."

"Just like that, eh?" said Cate, indignant on behalf of the ousted Mr. Terry. What chance did he have in the territory of the feudal lord? "Didn't Mr. Terry stand up for his rights?"

"What rights? Have you read your contract lately? There's a morals clause. If *you* had tried to seduce Jody, there would've been grounds for dismissal. As it was, Terry got off with his reputation and severance pay. The President told him if he'd go without a fuss, there's be no mention of the trouble on recommendations."

"Well," said Cate, "I'd better watch my p's and q's, hadn't I? As a matter of fact, I danced with Jody once. At the *Dracula* cast party. I may even have batted my eyelashes at him once or twice, just to keep in practice."

"You don't need any practice," said Jernigan. He picked up her hand and covered it with both of his. "You're a very attractive woman. I was very surprised when I walked in your office. I'd expected an angry-looking lady with ... with little black ringlets and rimless glasses, I guess. And don't go getting huffy on me about Terry. I'm not a man who goes around shoving his weight just for the fun of it. I believe in taking care of what's mine and what I've contracted to take responsibility for. If every person would do that, the world would be in one hell of a lot better shape."

" 'To deal gently and justly with one's family and oneself is a worthwhile glory for any man,' " said Cate.

"That's nice," said Jernigan softly, not releasing her hand. "Who said that?"

"My father. Paraphrasing Montaigne."

"Your father sounds nice. He must have been proud of you."

"I didn't always please him. And the blasphemous thought grows on me that he didn't always please me."

"Fathers don't have an easy time. Mothers, either, I guess. If Jody were yours, you wouldn't want him to grow up queer. You would want him to meet a girl and marry for love and have your grandchildren."

"But what about Sunny? Isn't he likely to present you with the first grandchild?" She remembered what Ann had said about Sunny's having girls flown in.

She knew at once she had said the wrong thing. He withdrew his hands and smoothed his hair away from his temples, even though it was quite calm now. When he did speak, it was kindly, as if he desired most of all to protect her from her own tactlessness.

"Sunny's an end in himself," he said. "I got used to that idea a long time ago. If we get to know each other better, maybe I'll tell you all my troubles. Maybe you'll even meet him sometime. But I'd rather not go into it now."

"Certainly." Oh, Jesus God, what was wrong with Sunny? Now she had to withdraw her grudge against him for pushing Terry around, in order to feel sorry for him. He was obviously a beleaguered man. Left by both wives, one son threatening to go gay (and she was pretty sure Jody was headed in that direction) and the other son . . . 'an end in himself,' whatever dire thing that might mean. Some hereditary disease? But he had girls flown in and went skiing in Colorado.

The thing was, dammit, she was attracted to Jernigan for the very qualities she had enumerated when she was trying to build his confidence. (What made her think he needed it built?) Speaking his attractions aloud, seeing them register on his lively, strong-ugly face, had made her prey to them.

When their dessert and coffee came, Jernigan gave the keys to their waiter and asked him if he would mind going out to the parking lot and starting the Jeep. He gave the boy his own jacket.

"But what for? We're not ready to leave yet," said Cate.

"I want it to be warm," said Roger Jernigan. "I want to postpone the inevitable for you a little longer." He put his hand back over hers.

For the umpteenth time in her life, Cate decided to go halfway to meet the advance of the unpredictable. Rather defiantly, she put her free hand over his.

But he had one left, and he put that on top.

They sat there, grinning at each other over the pile of hands, until the waiter returned with Jernigan's jacket.

Within the hour they were lovers.

5

LYDIA AND EROS

During her married life Lydia had been a great sleeper. She was the one who had a hard time waking up in the morning and the first to doze off at night. "I always thought it was the woman who was supposed to lie awake afterward and stare at the ceiling," teased Max, who was the one in their family who kept vigil with the ceiling. After Leo was born, in London, Max had hired a part-time nanny so Lydia could have her afternoons free. But she often used the time to steal a delicious nap while Nanny pushed Leo to Kensington Gardens in his pram. And all during the years when the boys were small, Lydia would promise herself naps, the way other people promised themselves drinks or candy bars, after she finished her day's duties. It was only several years ago, when she overheard a conversation between Dickie and a school friend in the kitchen one afternoon, that she was forced to review her pet habit. "Is your mother an invalid or something?" asked the friend. "Oh, no," said Dickie airily, "she just likes to sleep a lot." Hearing her child say it so matter-of-factly put an unflattering focus on her sleeping. But I get everything done, she told herself; it's just that I'm so organized, I have time left over for a nap. Other women gabble over bridge lunches, or rush off to their Modern Dance class, or sneak out for a quickie with their lover. I've never run with the pack and I don't believe in adultery, so I go to my room and empty my head of the confusion for a while. I'm available to everybody the whole time if there's an emergency, and my nap restores me to optimum efficiency again.

But it provoked her, this new, unwelcome image of herself as "a woman who slept a lot"—not to mention "an invalid"!— and the result was she could no longer take her pure, childish pleasure in her naps. Her profound bouts with sleep *were* a kind of umbilical cord connecting her to her childhood, she saw that now: when she lay down her head on the pillow, she sometimes even thought little phrases to herself, like, "There, there," or "Don't worry your little head," or, "Everything will be all right." The mother in her put the child to sleep. But, thanks to Dickie's friend, whom she never could bring herself to like after that, her sleeping did not seem so innocent or wholesome anymore. She began to ask herself what kind of life would make one want to stay awake.

It seemed hard to believe, to the Lydia who now got up before dawn to commute to UNC–Greensboro, that that other woman who had rushed home in the sunlight hours to draw her curtains and relinquish herself to oblivion had been herself. It made her slightly queasy to think about it, the way a person who has regained health looks back on a long illness. But Lydia had never wasted much time going back over her mistakes, and if the sleep was a mistake, well, it was over now. These days, she hardly got in her eight hours and didn't begrudge the deficit. It was as though she lived her new life in a climate twice as bracing as the old; and when you had more oxygen, you didn't want to sleep.

She was enrolled as a first-semester freshman and taking a full course load. There was a lot to catch up on. But in a sense, Lydia did not regret her late start. Her mind was more focused now than it had been at eighteen. She could concentrate better. At eighteen, she had gone around in a daze, unable to give anything her undivided attention for long, for fear of missing out on something else. Urges and ambitions contravened one another: she had wanted to dazzle everyone with her abilities as a great nurse; she had wanted the good-looking dental student to ask her to the dance; she had wanted Max to propose to her and take her off to London. (And if she'd had it to do over again, Lydia decided, cruising toward college on the I-40, playing that tape of Leo's which she had grown fond of, she would do it in the same order. She had married the man she had aspired to—then; she had had the children she wanted and she had had them young, which was best; and now she wanted to improve her mind and do a few other things. It really did seem to her that she had a chance of getting it all in.)

Her courses were: Introduction to Modern Economics, Survey of Renaissance Literature, General Psychology I, and—she had originally planned to play it safe with only three courses till she got into the habit of school, but who could resist the lure of such a title—History of Female Consciousness.

School had changed. The last time Lydia had been in a classroom, you opened your notebook, wrote down what the teacher told you to think, memorized it the night before the test, and wrote it back to him in an exam book. The closer your version matched with his, the better your grade would be. Lydia had not minded this method, because she had an excellent memory.

Now they seemed to want you to think. To play mental games with yourself, even. On the first day of the Economics class, the teacher had passed out cards and told everybody to make a list of his or her economic beliefs. "I believe in our own system of capitalism," Lydia had penned, in her neat, slanted, convent-school script. "I believe in competition, free enterprise, and rewarded initiative." She had handed in her card feeling pleased with herself. At the next class meeting, the teacher handed the cards back. On the bottom of each card, he told the students, he had assigned individual readings designed to challenge their beliefs. Lydia had gone straight to the library with her list of readings. She read selections in a book about Karl Marx. She read an offprint, written by her teacher, about how multinationals controlled governments from behind the scenes. In a book called *The Twilight of Capitalism* she came upon an utterly new version of why we were in an energy crisis: it was because in 1943—the year after she was born—President Roosevelt had backed down and let the oil companies run the Saudi Arabian concession rather than insisting that the Petroleum Reserves Corporation he had established for the purpose run it. So it was not because of OPEC but because of a generation of government policy that subsidized the priorities of the oil companies *out of the taxpayers' pockets* that the energy crisis had resulted. Good Lord. Did Max know this? She decided to ask him next time they met; then decided not to. He might refute this interesting argument with one blow and she'd be right back where she started with her little note card of beliefs. Not that she didn't believe in those things still. But she liked feeling this invigorating tension in her mind, as if a wrestling match were going on in there. These new facts didn't threaten her, because she didn't feel guilty about them or in any way responsible for them. How could she? She had been only one year old at the time. But being in possession of the facts made her feel more in control. The more facts she learned about the world, the more stock she felt she owned in it. When anyone mentioned Karl Marx to Lydia after she had read those two chapters about him, she felt a pleasant proprietary tug inside, as if he belonged partly to her now. And the same with Aristotle and Descartes and Spinoza, those first psychologists she was reading about in General Psych I: she felt possessive about them, too, as if her learning about them had suddenly brought them into existence.

The Professor of Renaissance Lit was a courtly older gentleman who had actually cried while reading "Lycidas" aloud to the class. Something about the way he held his shoulders, and the soft-consonated, singsong cadence of his voice, reminded her of Daddy, and when he had come to the lines, "Weep no more, woeful shepherds, weep no more, / For Lycidas your sorrow is not dead, / Sunk though he be beneath the watery floor," Lydia took out her cambric handkerchief and sincerely sobbed along with the old man. He thought she had been moved by his reading and, from then on, his eyes sought her out whenever he read aloud.

But it was History of Female Consciousness that Lydia looked forward to most. Though she had been drawn originally to the title of the course, and the promises of themes contained, she was now equally, if not more, fascinated by its teacher. Lydia had never met a black person like Renee Peverell-Watson.

Renee was a striking woman, about the color of President Sadat of Egypt. She *looked* rather Egyptian, with her Nefertiti hairstyle. She was possessed of a precise East Coast drawing-room drawl which she could shut off like a valve, when she chose, and replace with the kind of speech people like Azalea used. It made Lydia nervous when Renee did this; it was as if she, Lydia, had deliberately begun to talk like Uncle Osgood, saying "hit" instead of "it," and "I come" instead of "I came." But there was something wickedly arrogant about it, when Renee did it, as if she were showing her listeners that, though she was equally at home in both worlds, she was actually above both. She was a few years younger than Lydia and had her Ph.D. in Sociology from Harvard. Though she had had offers from all over the country, she had come back to North Carolina because, first, she said, she was a North Carolinian, and secondly, she preferred the climate. Renee's great-great-grandmother on her mother's side had been a house servant on the famous Peverell Plantation up in Halifax County. "What you must bear in mind," Renee told the class in her haughty lecturing voice with a touch of irony that reminded Lydia of Cate, "is that being a 'house nigger' was once as envi-able an aspiration for a black person as 'wife and mother' used to be for a female person." A few women in the class tittered ner-vously. Lydia had winced when Renee used the word "nigger."

For over a century, all Renee's relatives on her mother's side had kept Peverell in their name. Renee told the class how she had enjoyed driving over to Chapel Hill to the library's Southern Collection and spending the day reading the Reverend Peverell's meticulous plantation diaries. "My backstairs ancestor kept scrupulous records," she told them in her silky contralto. "I think his diary was his conscience. In many ways he was an en-lightened man. He made his own slaves overseers for the farm work, which was *very* enlightened. And when he went on trips he would write instructions to them. They couldn't read, of course, so a neighboring farmer would come over and read the letters to them; and they would dictate their replies to this farmer." She held out one of her long bronze-colored arms and inspected a handsome coral bracelet with gold links that dangled from her bony wrist. "I really think, given his time and circumstances, that the Reverend Peverell behaved pretty well."

During her drives to and from college, Lydia would play her older son's weird electronic tape that set cosmic vibrations strumming in her, and fantasize how she and Renee would become friends after she had proved her mind to her teacher. Lydia even constructed a satisfying little scenario in which she introduced Cate to Renee, and how Renee's ironic wit and vocabulary would impress Cate.

As Lydia drove, she also fantasized about the object of her amphibious dalliance at the Health Club, where she swam on Tuesdays and Thursdays, when she did not commute to Greensboro. Things were progressing at a decorously sensual pace with the slim, dark man in the next lane. And at last the day came when Lydia exchanged her commuting fantasies for mental recapitulations of physical realities that brought the blood rushing to her head while she drove to the space-age music of "The Alan Parsons Project."

Lydia and her stranger had progressed from mutual scrutiny of each other's bodies via their goggles to chitchat about laps and strokes while resting at the shallow end; he had an unusual accent she could not place. After that, he would frequently brush against her thigh or arm as they plied their watery parallels to the deep end. There had been obstacles to their progress: although they arrived at roughly the same time, there were not always adjacent lanes free. Lydia wanted to kill the interlopers. There was a woman who wore a towel around her head while swimming, because she had dyed hair, and Lydia had kicked her legs hard to splash this woman who, on several occasions, had dared to come between her and the dark, slim stranger. And then there was that awful priest who took up two lanes with his flailing backstroke, smiling as he ruined everybody else's swim, and nobody would say anything to him because they had seen him go into the Club wearing his collar; Lydia, practically apoplectic, had watched the priest head straight for the free lane next to her, just ahead of the stranger, who was, of course, too polite to rush ahead of the priest and claim the lane. Lydia wondered if her beautiful man were a Catholic.

And yet it was on one of the days when the priest had come between them that the stranger had at last made his move.

He was waiting in the Club's parking lot, ostensibly rubbing at some imperfection on the hood of a silver BMW. He squinted toward her over the top of his tinted glasses as she emerged from the swinging doors into the sunshine. Why, he almost glowered at her. He's saving his pride in case he's presumed too much, thought Lydia: after all, he can't know for sure how my stomach does a flip-flop every time he brushes against me in the water, nor can he know how I can cause the flip-flops in myself for the rest of the day just by *remembering* our bodies touching.

She had never, before today, met him coming in or going out, and so this was the first time she had ever seen him fully dressed. The sight of his light, open-necked sport shirt framing a discreet V of dark chest hairs, and his slacks cut low and pocket-less on his eel-slim hips, seemed even more exotic than his almost-naked body. She had already grown used to his sleek, muscled arms and honey-colored skin and the forest of little dark curls that descended from his shoulders all the way down to the line of the brief swim trunks; she had even grown used to the fascinating codpiecelike bulge perched just beneath the Lastex.

Well, here we go, thought Lydia, frowning in his direction, her senses toppling over one another in the soft prespring air. Squaring her swimbag over her left shoulder, and clutching her handsome new gray purse of woven leather strips, she marched in her prim, resolute style toward the man whose name she didn't even know.

With Max, it had been just the reverse. She had known his name for years, before she ever saw him; and she had decided to marry him before ever imagining him undressed.

The first time Lydia saw Max, even though they had grown

up in the same town, was at the Rhododendron Court banquet, the year she was being presented. He had been crowned King of the Rhododendron Festival twelve years before, when Lydia was only six and hadn't even begun to worry whether she would get asked to participate in the town's highest social event of the year; and then he had gone away to do all those things young men from good families with no money have to do in order to prove themselves. And now here he was, back home for a visit, and Proven, providentially still a bachelor, escorting his young cousin Snooky Powell, a classmate of Lydia's who was also being presented.

Max was wearing the red cutaway jacket, the black tie and trousers, that all the Brigade Guards wore. The festival had been modeled, back in 1928, on somebody's idea of how such things would be done in England, and, before World War II, the Guards' uniforms had been exact replicas of those worn by Buckingham Palace Guards. Cate said the new red jackets looked like bellhop uniforms, but then Cate loved to mock formal occasions—she had told Lydia she had been forced by Mother and Daddy to come out at the Rhododendron Ball because they said if she refused she would ruin Lydia's chances for being asked.

Lydia had taken it as a nudge from Providence when she found herself (and her escort, poor Hugo Miller) seated across from Max and Snooky at the banquet; she had blessed whoever had arranged the place cards. (It turned out to have been the serviceable Lucy Bell, who had no marriageable daughters.)

"You're Leonard Strickland's baby girl, aren't you?" Max had asked Lydia, in a big-brotherly way, over the shrimp cocktail. "I used to see you and your sister holding hands on the way to the drugstore on Ashe Street. Where is your sister now?"

"Oh, Cate's already married," Lydia was pleased to be able to report. And felt grateful to Cate for rushing through four years of college in three, to fly off with Pringle, so that she, Lydia, could now report it. She lowered her gaze to her shrimp. "And I'm still a big baby in some ways, I guess."

She daintily speared a shrimp and took it between her teeth, nibbling it solemnly with her mouth closed, the way she had seen movie stars eat on screen. When she looked up again, she saw that her last remark had amused him, as she had intended it to.

As the waiters removed the silver bowls with melting ice and began to put down the main course, she had cataloged his assets. He had that nice thin beaky Powell nose. He had the right combination of worldly ease and unaffected affability. He was tall. And several girls had actually proposed to him; Snooky had told her that. Of course, they had been older—older than Cate, even. On the shelf already. Oh, thank you Cate, for once doing something right, thought Lydia, turning to say something nice to poor Hugo so Max could see he had competition; that looks good for our family, Cate being married already at twenty-one. A Strickland woman gathers no dust, she doesn't even know what a shelf looks like.

"Where are you off to college?" Max asked, during the Rock Cornish game hens and wild rice with baby peas.

"Chapel Hill," replied Lydia.

"Is that right? But girls can't go there till they're juniors, can they?"

"They can if they're in nursing school."

"You're going to be a nurse, huh?"

"Don't you think I'd make a good one?" Lydia postponed attacking the hen, which she really wanted, and chose a small forkful of rice instead. She looked at him while she ate it.

"I'm sure you'll be good at whatever you set your mind to," said Max gallantly, but, for the first time, he sent her an unbrotherly look.

That's more like it, thought Lydia; and now, for the rest of the dinner, I must be completely sisterly. Don't want to frighten him off. And when the dancing starts, I'm going to find Daddy and ask him to cut in on me several times. We'll dance together and I'll look at him the way girls do who have no intention of growing up yet. That will make Mr. Mansfield feel even safer. Snooky says he's going to London in November. June, July, August, September, October . . .

When Max cut in on Daddy at the ball, he engaged her

without missing a single dance step. "And what made you want to be a nurse?" he asked, spinning her around as if he had danced with a million girls. He was over a head taller than she: perfect.

And while Lydia explained to him, not *too* earnestly, but in fetching little phrases uttered at appropriate times during their dance, all her good reasons for wanting to be a nurse (her mother had been a nurse before she married . . . it was a good career for a woman . . . it was so useful . . . it was something you could do for the rest of your life . . . Mother had always been so wonderful when anyone in the family was sick . . .), her imagination raced on ahead, making battle plans for the summer months, when she would still be on her own territory, where she knew her shops and her mirrors and her best props: poor Hugo numbering among the most valuable of these.

And she actually heard the voices of various friends—and the even sweeter voices of enemies—exclaiming, "Well, you'll never guess who got Max Mansfield in *three months!*"

"Ah, I can see you *are* serious," said Max gently, with just a touch of rue, when the charming sylph he was dancing with broke suddenly into a rapturous smile.

"Oh, I am," agreed Lydia, looking up at him and seeing he found her twice as enchanting now that Nursing stood between them, like a jealous beau.

It had taken her a little longer than the three months, during which she had had very little time to dwell on what his naked chest might be like, or any of the rest, which was very vague, anyway, to Lydia in those days.

The slim, dark man stopped rubbing so desperately at the hood of his BMW as Lydia approached. Oh come on, smile now, thought Lydia, a little annoyed as he blinked at her behind his green-tinted glasses but still withheld any facial acknowledgment of the ritual in which they were engaged. Hell, we've already gone farther than this in the pool.

"That's a Three-twenty, isn't it?" inquired Lydia, to put him at his ease, even though it made her look a bit stupid: 320 was right there in little silver numbers on the back of the car, and she was approaching from the back. "I was tempted to buy a Three-twenty myself, last year," she went on, as if she had come over purposely to talk about cars, "but then I finally decided on my Volvo. I wanted a sunroof and the BMW man said I'd have to wait six weeks for a sunroof."

"Yeah, I kind of wish I'd gotten a sunroof myself," he said, looking woefully at her, as if she were in the same class as the sunroof he hadn't gotten. He went on rubbing at the spot, rather ineffectually, with the ball of his thumb.

"You've got a spot there!" announced Lydia, deciding the time had come for her to take charge. She sauntered around to the front of the car. She was slightly surprised when she saw his shoes. They were kind of pointy and in a peculiar shade of orangy-brown.

"I think it must be resin," he said. "I park under a pine tree at my office. But isn't it too early for resin?"

"Here, let me have a look," said Lydia. She slung her swim-bag to the pavement and put down her gray purse on the hood of the car. As she bent over the spot, she was aware that he was using this opportunity to reassess her with *her* clothes on. She admired her own youthful hand as it moved in and out of the jacket sleeve of soft gray tweed as she worked on the hard, sticky spot with a thumbnail lacquered in a new shade of dusky rose. "It's resin, all right," she informed him brightly as she scratched away. Silence. If he hasn't made a move by the time I finish with this spot, she thought, that flailing priest and the woman in the towel can divide him up between themselves. Lord! Things haven't changed one bit since I got out of high school. From all I've been hearing about the sexual revolution, I got the idea that people just moved through the preliminaries with a fluid grace. We were doing better than *this* in the water.

She finished her task, straightened, and held up her finger-nail, with the little brown glob of resin under the tip, for his inspection. "Spring comes earlier down here," she said challeng-ingly. "You're not from here, are you?"

"I grew up in New York," he said. "But I've moved down

here to set up my practice." And he more than redeemed himself by taking her hand firmly in his and removing the glob from under the nail.

Practice, thought Lydia, her nerve endings going all tingly from the contact. That must mean doctor. It couldn't mean lawyer unless he'd passed the state bar.

Then the glob was stuck under his fingernail. But this made them both laugh, which broke the tension. He had nice, small, white teeth and healthy-looking gums. He took the glob over to the nearest tree and wiped it off on the trunk. "Go back where you belong," he said, and she liked this touch of whimsical mastery.

"Have you had lunch?" he asked, coming back.

They had been in the water since eleven. To have had lunch, she would have had to eat it around ten o'clock.

"No, not yet!" she sang brightly.

"We could go somewhere. Or I have some cold cuts and beer back at my apartment. It's not far from here."

"But don't you have to get back to your . . . practice?" Now that she was getting what she desired, some perversity made her want to delay.

"Thursday's my half-day off." He smiled.

Doctor, she decided. Most of the local doctors take Thursdays off for golf. She liked the way his smile combined a gentle shyness with male pride. Oh, he knew he was attractive, all right. "Then let's go to your place," she suggested, "if you're sure you've got *enough* cold cuts." She had not yet appeared in public with any man since her separation from Max, and wanted to make sure she knew what she was getting into before she did.

"We can always get more," he said. "Will you come with me, or follow in your car?"

"I'll follow in mine," said Lydia.

But as she was marching off to her Volvo, he laughed and said, "Hey, come back a minute."

Lydia retraced her steps.

"Isn't there anything you want to know about me?" he asked.

She gave him a puzzled smile. "Well, sure. But, I mean, like what?"

"My name, for a start. If we got separated in traffic, you wouldn't know how to look me up. And if you changed your mind and decided to give me the slip, I wouldn't know how to find you again."

Good heavens, thought Lydia, I don't believe he has the slightest intention of behaving like a cad. His sincerity was touching, but it put her on guard for trouble later. "My name's Lydia," she said, wondering whether or not to make up a last name. "Lydia Mansfield," she decided on. Truth was simpler.

"Mine's Stanley Edelman," he said. They shook hands.

I wonder if he's Jewish, thought Lydia, as she walked to her car again. Well, that's all right. Cate *married* a Jew. She once said that Jews and Southerners had a lot more in common than Southerners and Yankees, because they both liked to show their emotions and knew how to live well.

Stanley lived in an apartment complex very similar to Lydia's. In fact, they might have been designed by the same architect, with their two-toned mansard roofs and the little overhung porch that went with each unit. Stanley's complex was called "Maple Villas"; Lydia's, "The Colony." This provided them with an ice-breaking topic during that otherwise awkward moment when they climbed the outside stairs to his second-floor unit (Lydia's unit was on the first floor).

"I wonder where they get these pretentious names," she said, "but at least yours is better than mine. The colony of *what*? Ants live in colonies; so do artists and bacteria. I'd like to know what the owners of my apartment complex think we're a colony *of*. 'Singles,' probably. Which is also a very condescending assumption."

"Well, aren't you a single?" asked Stanley, unlocking his front door.

"Oh, yes. Well, at least since December I have been."

"That's good," said Stanley. "I'm a single, too." And he gave her his sweet smile, though tinged with nervousness, as he motioned her in.

He had left his curtains drawn, and the sunlight shining through their light-green synthetic material made the room appear the same greenish hue as the bottom of the Health Club pool. As he moved to open them, Lydia quickly took in the rest of the furnishings: some modular pieces, in an okay color of light brown, which could function either as one long sofa or a short sofa and two chairs (he had them arranged the latter way), a chrome-and-glass coffee table whose surface was bare except for a strangely shaped, large ashtray of pinkish marble that didn't look as if it had ever been used. There was also a goose-necked chrome floor lamp and, of course, the awful "neutral beige" wall-to-wall carpeting which she had in her apartment. He couldn't be blamed for the carpeting.

From the looks of things, he hadn't completely moved in yet. Two large picture frames backed in brown paper and sealed professionally with masking tape were propped against the wall in the kitchen, which was directly through the archway from this room. The kitchen was also carpeted, in a sturdy nonshag beige, just as hers was. She would have liked to take a peek and see what sort of pictures he planned to hang on his walls.

"Let me show you the rest of the place. . . ." He interrupted her just as she had begun exclaiming in an overly hearty voice about how the layout of his apartment was exactly the same as hers, only mirror-wise. They were both ill at ease.

But for the second time he saved things with a touch. He simply took her purse and laid it down on the lonely-looking glass table, and then he put a hand on each of her shoulders and stood smiling at her as if to reassure her. But his large brown eyes with their long, girlish lashes feasted on her face with a kind of awe.

"I still can't believe you're really here," he murmured.

So he had been fantasizing, too.

"You could . . . you could kiss me," Lydia stammered, "and find out for sure."

It was the strangest thing, but she believed she actually felt his swoon as well as her own, as his eyelashes fluttered once and he bowed his face into hers. He began to kiss her mouth as though trying to absorb her essence into himself. She held herself to him on tiptoes, her wrists crossed behind his bent neck, a handful of his soft hair secure under each of her palms, until her legs trembled and her knees began to buckle. She felt the hard knot of his desire against her. For a moment she thought she was going to pass out.

"Let's go lie down," he whispered.

He took her by the hand and led her away, but she had enough presence of mind to retrieve her purse as they went. They turned right into a hallway. In her apartment, it would have been to the left. So that meant the first door on the right was probably the bathroom.

"I'll just slip in here a minute," she said. It was.

He understood. "I'll be next door. If you get lost, I'll come and look for you." He gave her a little pat on the shoulder, as if for courage.

What a nice man. Somehow she had not expected that.

She was surprised to see that her face in the mirror still retained its precise shape, for she felt all blurry and melted down. He had good thick towels on his racks. A soft terry-cloth bathrobe hung from the hook on the back of the door.

On the wall facing the toilet, at eye level when you sat down, was a framed steel engraving of a foot with its bones, tendons, and muscles exposed. All the parts were labeled. "Astragalus," recited Lydia softly, as she leaned forward to make sure everything was secure inside, "os calcis." Parts of the body sounded so much nicer in Latin.

She draped her clothes in a neat pile over the rim of the tub, hiding her bra and panties under her blouse, as she always did when she undressed at the gynecologist's. She had decided she wouldn't be able to carry it off, stripping in front of him; for an old married woman of eighteen years (half her life!), she was still quite maidenly.

She slipped into his terry-cloth robe, which smelled of some nice manly spice, and hoped he would have had the tact to remove some of his clothes.

Once again he had been thoughtful. He was already in bed, the sheet pulled up to his chin. Something about the *dependency* of him as he lay there, and the long, fringy eyelashes lowered in modest cunning, reminded her of her pretty Leo as he looked when she came to kiss him goodnight. Leo knew he was beautiful, too. And then suddenly it struck Lydia that this man had a mother who probably worshiped him. For the first time, she saw him as somebody's child. All these new juxtapositions made her stomach lurch. She crawled in beside him with a long shuddery sigh, hardly noticing her surroundings, except for the fact that he had closed the blinds; or maybe he had never opened them when he got up that morning.

Before marriage, Lydia had thought of the sex act (that is, when she thought of it; she preferred dwelling on the more graceful and gratifying preliminaries) as something the man "took" and the woman "gave." "He took her quickly," the books would say; or, "She gave herself to him." If anything in these verbal images aroused Lydia, it was the idea of making a present of her virginity to the man to whom she would then "belong." He would then be grateful to her forever and protect her in return, and, according to the books, if she had chosen sensibly, she would "learn to love him." It also aroused Lydia to think about this well-chosen man setting about his long, arduous task of making her love him, using all his patience and skills to instruct her toward a passionate, wifely response.

Thus schooled by premarital reading and by her social education, Lydia took care to "choose well." That was where her task was; the rest lay with the man. And with Max, everything seemed to go according to plan. He had at least a twelve-year head start on her; he was a man of the world, to whom desperate women had actually proposed. It was clear, on their wedding night in Mr. Broadbelt's Blowing Rock cottage (the refrigerator stocked with champagne), that Max knew what he was doing. But she had never expected him not to. He would do that well, as he did everything else well: dancing, making conversation, choosing the right clothes, making the right investments. He conducted himself like a sportsman in bed, making sure he followed through the proper moves and elicited from her the proper responses. Well, *that's* not so bad, Lydia had thought, the first morning she had waked up as Mrs. Mansfield. And it continued to be not so bad during the excitement of the first year in London and into the second, and then she had found pregnancy to be truly erotic . . . somehow the best of all. And afterward she couldn't wait to get pregnant again. There had been a miscarriage between Leo and Dickie. And then there was the move back to the States, with Dickie on the way and Max with his important new position. Then came the years when everybody was tired all the time, Max with his responsibilities at the Bank, she with two small children, but all during that period they had been scrupulous in their conjugal duties: they had *both* behaved like sporting people. Though sometimes, accelerating right on schedule toward her weekly quota of spasms, she wanted to cry out impatiently, "Oh, what's the *point* of going on and on like this? What does it *accomplish*?" And she had looked forward more and more to the moment when she could fall asleep afterward with a clear conscience: both she and her partner having done what was expected of them.

When she had begun to test out, in a quiet corner of her mind, the idea of leaving Max and living by herself, it was not any images of more impassioned, steamy lovers that were summoned up, but images of quiet, free spaciousness: spacious hours in which to structure activities that would express her; a spacious bed, with cool sheets, with nobody in it but herself. The Health Club had come after the official separation; she had noticed, one shocking day, that she could no longer eat everything she wanted without putting on weight, and had rushed to sign up for the only form of exercise she could tolerate. "You can swim lying down," she liked to say, "and you don't have to do it with anybody else."

The stranger in the next lane had been an afterthought. She had become aware of him one day because she saw him notice *her.* That was the way it had begun. He had taken her in his thoughts first, she was sure of it, and by doing so had aroused something in her she didn't even know she had to give.

He wanted her now in a way she had not been wanted before. She knew it. How did she know it? Because he was not going to tolerate the little barrier she always left up, at these times. Max had tolerated it; he had approved of it, she believed. He had one himself, so they could engage sportingly, with matching handicaps. Really, she and Max had done very well all these years when you considered that it was their barriers that did all the entwining, in the fleshly dance-step of love. But this man was not being decorous or sportsmanlike; he was going down willingly into those dark, swirling currents of pure feeling where you could lose yourself. He wanted her to let go completely and be swept away in his waves of ardor. His need for her was so great that he wasn't going to let her reserve one tiny molecule of dry self from the torrent. They'd go down together or not at all.

Oh *Lord!*

"I'm so sorry," whispered Lydia, her mouth all wet against Stanley's ear.

"For what?"

"I screamed, didn't I?"

"It's okay." He smiled exhaustedly. His hair was plastered in wet little curls, all down the front of his body. "Everyone's gone at this hour."

"*I'm* gone," moaned Lydia, pulling as much of him back to her as she could get her limbs around; off she roared again, into the surging currents. She heard his awed voice, somewhere far off, saying, "Darling . . . oh my darling," as if he were trying to keep them both from being frightened, by offering his little life preserver of repeated esteem. It was touching, but she didn't want it, didn't need it: it didn't even belong here, in this place where they were.

She'd had to drive around town for more than an hour after that first time with Stanley. She had needed time alone, to re-

sume her boundaries and get herself in shape for the boys; Leo
was coming for supper that night. In her time-proven stratagem,
she amassed mundane facts as a barricade against the waves of
feeling that still pounded against her composure. As she drove,
she kept catching herself grinning sheepishly, in a way that
would never do in front of her sons.

Her lover's middle name was Albert. After his mother's
brother, Alberto. His mother was second-generation Italian, and
yes, she did worship her son. That had been one reason he'd
wanted to move so far away: as long as he stayed in New York,
she expected him to have dinner with her every Sunday. He was
thirty-one (Lydia's first "younger man") and he was a podiatrist.
Better than a dentist, thought Lydia, though not as good as an
M.D., of course. The two frames turned to the wall had housed
well-known Dufy seascapes; he had bought them in a hurry to
have something for the walls, he said. At least they hadn't been
paintings on velvet. Everything was just beginning for him. He'd
get better pictures later and tone down his taste in shoes. The
Edelman *was* Jewish, and Cate had certainly been right about
their expressing their emotions. Lord! But here came the pounding waves against the barricade. Lydia pulled into a Burger King
and ordered a Whopper over the intercom; neither of them had
been in the mood to eat much afterward. But she had appraised
his refrigerator while she stood there in his robe and nibbled a
slice of Genoa salami. Here there was still room for improvement
in the art of living well, and she had ticked off in her head some
of the delicacies she would bring for their next Thursday's picnic. He had laughed when she told him she couldn't quite place
his accent. It was "Judeo-Italian Brooklyn," he said.

Lydia had been quite herself again by the time she took a
second shower at home and served her sons plates of spaghetti
and meatballs—except she didn't have her usual appetite, because of the Whopper. Leo had told her she was more interesting
to be around since she had started back to school. "You're more
animated," he said. It was the longest compliment she had ever
gotten out of Leo, that tactiturn perfectionist.

*   *

It was time for Lydia to go to discuss term-paper topics with Renee, as she insisted her students call her. "Ms.," when pronounced aloud, sounded like a bumblebee, Renee said, and "Doctor" was parochial.

Renee's office door was open. She was sitting at her desk, reading an aerogram with an English stamp and smoking a little brown cigar. Framed by shelves full of glossy books and wearing a twill pantsuit with a low-necked cerise silk blouse, she was the advertiser's dream-image of the woman who has "made it."

"Oh, hi," said Renee. "Come on in." She folded the aerogram and slipped it into her purse.

"Lydia Mansfield," Lydia reminded her, as the class was a large one. Women's Studies were very popular.

"I know that," said Renee, blowing out a plume of cigar smoke. "Born in Ruffin County. Attended half a semester at Chapel Hill, School of Nursing. Live in Winston-Salem. Two sons, thirteen and fifteen. Separated." She motioned Lydia to the chair beside the desk. "Sit down."

"How do you know all that?" Flattered, Lydia sat down.

"All what? Those statistics? I always check out my students' admission forms. I like to know where they come from and where they're going. I'm a sociologist, you know."

"Well, I haven't gone very far, so far," said Lydia in the easy tone of sociable self-disparagement on which she had been weaned.

"Everybody has her own starting point," replied Renee, with equal ease. "Will you have a cigar, or does smoke bother you? They're very tasty. I don't inhale." She opened a slim yellow tin box that said DUNHILL MONTECRUZ and offered it to Lydia.

"Thank you. I believe I will. I've never smoked a cigar before. But these are so nice and thin."

Renee rummaged in her desk drawer and found a book of matches. She handed them to Lydia. "I don't keep a lighter; I'm not that much of a hardened smoker."

"Oh, Antoine's," said Lydia, glancing at the matchbook. She had a bit of a chore lighting her cigar, but made a joke out of it. "What do you think of the French food in New Orleans? *Really.*"

"What do I think of it? I'll tell you. I think the same as you do, judging from your 'really.' They think French means swimming in sauce down there. One night my boyfriend, Calvin, wrote a note in French and asked the waiter to give it to the manager next morning. The waiter thought it was a complimentary note, but what the note *said* was, 'If you are ever in Greensboro, North Carolina, come to my house and I will show you how to prepare *pompano en papillote* properly.' But the manager of that so-called French restaurant probably couldn't read French, either."

"My husband could hardly eat his oysters Rockefeller when we were down there," said Lydia. "I had one and I could swear they'd put those Pepperidge Farm bread crumbs on top. That was before we got separated, of course."

"Of course," said Renee.

The two women puffed on their cigars, exchanging looks of mutual approval.

"Well, about my term paper," said Lydia, her eyes scanning Renee's books. On the shelf directly beside Lydia's chair were several impressive-looking volumes bound in green. *Social Class in Black America* was printed in gold at the tops of the spines. And, farther down, in smaller gold letters, *Peverell-Watson.* "Good Lord, is that whole thing your thesis?"

"Duplicates," said Renee. "I figured after all that slaving, I could treat myself to a few Xerox copies."

"I'd love to read it. That is, if you ever lend copies out," said Lydia. "It sounds so"—she was not sure what adjective she should use—". . . fascinating."

"It's fascinating, all right." Renee laughed in her smooth contralto. "The Harvard Press thinks so, too, apparently. They've asked me to expand certain parts and then they want to publish it."

"Publish it! Aren't you excited?" Oh God, thought Lydia, she's younger than me—not to mention other things—and she's already accomplished so much.

"I guess I am. I would have been more so if Oxford or Yale had wanted it. There's always that sneaking suspicion that Harvard wants it because I'm one of theirs."

"One of—? Oh! You mean you got your degree there. Right." Lydia was a litle flustered. This was a relatively new social situation for her.

"Now about your term paper," said Renee. "You got any ideas on what you want to write about?"

"Well, I was thinking about doing something on Eros," said Lydia. The word sounded a little silly when she said it out loud; yet, earlier today, rehearsing what she would say in this conference, she had thought the topic sounded splendid.

"Eros," repeated Renee, as if testing the word. "The *Love* God," she added, faintly sarcastic. "Well, there's certainly plenty of material. . . ."

"I don't know, maybe there's too much material," said Lydia. "Maybe I ought to look for another topic." She felt confused and unsure of herself.

"No, wait a minute. Hold on," said Renee, puffing her cigar. She narrowed her eyes at her bookshelves. "Eros, Eros . . . it's just that I haven't thought about old Eros lately." She gave a low, harsh laugh. "I guess I've been too *busy* to think about him. What particular aspect of Eros were you interested in exploring?"

The sheepish grin Lydia had to struggle so much to suppress these days plucked at the corners of her mouth as Renee regarded her steadily. Renee's eyes were hazel, with peculiar yellow flecks in them. They turned up at the outside corners, above her accentuated cheekbones. Lydia saw that she encouraged the Oriental look by the use of eyeliner.

"Oh, I don't know," said Lydia gruffly, choosing to grimace rather than give in to the silly grin. "I'd just like to get to the bottom of Eros, once and for all."

Renee's eyes widened in amusement. She put down her thin cigar in a little metal ashtray. Her mouth twitched under her well-formed nose. (There must have been more than just a Peverell in those genes, thought Lydia.) "Well, if you *do* get to the bottom,"she drawled in the ironic singsong that reminded Lydia of Cate, "kindly send me a note up, will you?" And then she switched. "I'd like to get the lowdown on that ol' jitterbug myself."

The switch had come so fast that it caught Lydia off guard. She flushed, then giggled. The giggle got caught in an intake of breath and she snorted. Then Renee began chuckling, too. She must enjoy doing this sort of thing—especially on her home ground, where everybody knew exactly when the switch came.

"The aspect of Eros that *I've* always found interesting"— now Renee was back in Harvard Square—"is the Socratic idea that Eros is a striving for what one lacks. The concept of Eros as unmanageable sexual desire has been a little overdone, I think. Especially in our times."

"A striving for what one lacks?" said Lydia, sitting forward in her chair. Renee had set her mind off. She put down her cigar in Renee's ashtray.

"Well, *yes*. Listen, what time do you have? I can't wear a watch. My ions screw up the time."

Lydia consulted her expensive quartz timepiece, a gift from Max on her last birthday. "Oh dear, almost noon. I've taken up too much time, haven't I?"

"Not at all. But I have to go home and let my dog out. He kind of runs my life. My house is in walking distance. Would you like to come home with me and have a light lunch? I have to reduce so I can get into my bikini. Calvin and I are going to Bermuda for the spring break. You and I could continue our conversation over a ladies' lunch."

Lydia had her Survey of Renaissance Lit at one. Today they were going to do Donne's Holy Sonnets, and, while preparing them last night, she had also prepared at which lines she was going to reward the old Professor with looks of solemnity or appreciation: he was sure to read the sonnets aloud. He would be terribly disappointed if she didn't show up.

But you had to make choices in this life. "I'd love to come home with you," Lydia told Renee.

Renee lived on a genteel old street several blocks from the college. "I usually ride my bike," she told Lydia, "but this particular pair of pants gets caught in my spokes." She had the striding gait of the long-legged, and Lydia had to stretch her own legs to keep pace. Though the street had seen better days, judging from the size and age of most of the houses, there was still an air of pride about Renee's block; people tended their lawns and trimmed their forsythia and planted new azalea bushes. "This is me," said Renee in her sarcastic contralto, but Lydia could sense her new friend was proud of the two-story frame house whose hedge-lined walk they had just entered. There was a grand old Japanese maple about to bud in the small front yard. Someone had carefully mulched it with heaps of pine needles. The house was freshly painted in a greeny-gray shade, with black trim and shutters; the color scheme made it look more sophisticated than its neighbors on either side. They mounted the steps to the screened-in front porch. There was Renee's three-speed Raleigh tilted on its kickstand. Even as Renee took out her key to unlock the door, Lydia could hear wild scratching noises and excited whimpering from within.

"Cool it, Judge!" called Renee. "Just cool it, will you?" To Lydia, she said, "Watch your stockings. He's not mean, he just gets overexcited."

She unlocked the door and pushed it open cautiously. A sleek silver-blue beast took a flying leap at Renee; his front paws landed against her chest; they stood practically chin to chin as he slathered her face. He must have weighed close to a hundred pounds. "Down, Judge, down!" ordered Renee. "Oh, you great big baby! Want me to smack you one?"

At the word "smack" he went down at once on four legs and contented himself with shimmying his rear end in ecstasy. He had initiated an experimental lunge at Lydia, who was offering her closed fist as her father had taught her, when Renee clapped her hands together threateningly and sent the dog streaking the length of the house, dislocating several small rugs in passing; he skidded to a stop at the back door and turned to look back appealingly at Renee.

"You going *out!*" said Renee with tender menace. She followed the dog to the back door and unbolted it and released the tormented bundle of energy into the outdoors.

Lydia, at a glance, took in Renee's downstairs rooms. She would not have thought it possible to get so much light and space into a house that looked so conventional from the outside. Walls must have been knocked down to free the old-fashioned separations of living room, dining room, and kitchen. There was lots of bare floor, but the nice small rugs kept it from being *too* bare; there were green plants, some as large as small trees; there was a grand piano, with its lid propped up and a Chopin mazurka open on the rack. Later Lydia would look more closely at the pictures on the wall, but instinctively she knew they would be exactly right, exactly what Renee knew was right for the walls of a house in which she lived.

"Well now," said Renee, "sorry about that. Come on back here and we'll see what we can find us for our ladies' lunch." She had already opened an olive-green refrigerator and was removing things, stacking them along one arm.

"He's a beautiful dog," said Lydia. "A neighbor down the street from us had a weimaraner when I was growing up, but he was more of a brown color. Have you had him long?"

"Well, prepare yourself for a fairy tale," said Renee. She was opening a tuna-fish can. "No, maybe it's more like a ghost story. That dog just walked up on my front porch one rainy night and rang the bell. I'd just moved in. I thought maybe it was a neighbor wanting to borrow a cup of sugar, or maybe"—she gave a husky, sarcastic laugh—"maybe it was the Welcome Wagon or somebody, working late. But no, I open my door and there stands this dog, looking like he doesn't understand why I haven't invited him in already. He was all wet . . . and thin and shivering . . . I can tell you, he didn't look so good that night. I couldn't for the life of me understand how anybody could have let a fine dog like him get in such bad shape. So I let him in and got a bath towel and dried him off. I had to follow him around, upstairs and downstairs, because he was running around all over the place, sniffing and carrying on. He seemed to know the place, even where the closets were. I fed him some chicken livers I was saving for a pâté and decided to let him stay the night. I couldn't put him out in all that rain. So when I went upstairs to get undressed, he followed right along, as if he knew the whole routine. And he goes to the closet in the bedroom and starts whining till I open it up. Then he pops inside and throws himself down in a heap and looks up at me as if to say, 'Now I'm all settled, thank you very much.' Do you like tuna fish?"

"Oh sure," said Lydia. "And it's very good for slimming."

"Well, I'm not planning to starve you. I make it with garbanzo beans and a little touch of wine vinegar and some mayonnaise and alfalfa sprouts. Speaking of wine, would you like some? I've got some"—she opened the refrigerator and peered in—"Piesporter. It's opened. Calvin tries different wines, and then if he likes them, he buys a whole case."

"Maybe a little," said Lydia, "but I've got to drive to Winston-Salem, so not too much."

"How about if I mix it with a little soda water? We can have spritzers."

"Great! I don't know why I didn't think of that. But what about your dog? I mean, did he really ring the *bell?*"

"He sure did. My story's not over yet, I just had to catch up on my hostess duties." She took down two fragile-stemmed wineglasses and filled them half with the wine and half with club soda. Lydia watched the glasses frost over from the cold liquids. She felt very content and interested in life: she could not believe she had wasted so many precious years in a stupor. "Cheers," said Renee, smiling. She looked content to have Lydia here. She went back to mixing the tuna-fish concoction. "Anyway, the next day, his 'owners' showed up and I learned the whole story. He had belonged to the judge who owned this house before. But then the old judge had a stroke and was in a coma for a while, and the judge's secretary was given power of attorney, to handle his affairs. He was a bachelor and had no family. The secretary couldn't keep the dog because she had five cats, but she wanted to make sure somebody responsible got the dog, because she knew how much the judge loved him. *He* had taught him to ring the bell, by the way. So she asked these people—the man had done some outdoor work for the judge; they had a place out in the country—if they would keep the dog till it became clear whether the judge was going to get better, in which case he'd want his dog again. They agreed, these people, because they liked the old judge and I guess they also thought it would be prestigious, having a dog like that for a while. But then the judge died and the dog got to be too much for them. He ate too much; he kept breaking his chain and running off. I don't blame him, they kept him outside in a doghouse! The minute they showed up here, I could see they weren't the kind of people who could appreciate a dog like that. But I let them take him away. I hadn't really thought it out yet. But when he ran away *again* and rang my bell, I just opened up that door and said, "Come on in, Judge." I'd decided that's what I would call him, the moment I opened that door the second time. His first name had been Blue Boy and those stupid people in the country had shortened it to Blue, and I guessed his old name was ruined for him. And then I went to the phone and called those people and offered to keep the dog. They were a little uppity about it. When they'd come to the house and seen who had bought it, well . . . I can tell you, all sorts of sociological nuances started whirring around in the air. But I was determined to have that dog. So I told them I needed a big dog for *protection*, and, after all, it was *his* house, in a way. That seemed to mollify them. That and a check for a hundred dollars." She curled her lip contemptuously.

"So now, as you can see, he runs me. He doesn't even sleep in his closet anymore. He sleeps right on the bed with me." She laughed. "That made problems with poor Calvin. When Calvin and I want to indulge in any hanky-panky, I have to go over to his place. The Judge won't even let Calvin *sit down* on that bed upstairs."

"Are you—are you in love with Calvin?" Lydia asked, wondering whether or not Calvin was black. Talk about sociological nuances: Lydia's head was reeling with them. It was all thoroughly fascinating. Maybe she should go into Sociology.

"No," said Renee. "It would be convenient if we were, but I'm not in love with Calvin and he's not in love with me. We get along well, though. You might say we're two upwardly mobile pilgrims keeping each other company on the trip." She was arranging the tuna mixture on a bed of endive leaves, with black olives and pimientos. "Calvin's a TV producer over at the local channel." She took some lovely Japanese plates from a cabinet and got some silver salad forks and bread knives from a felt-lined wooden chest in the same cabinet. The table was already laid with a checkered cloth.

There was a peremptory thud against the back door.

"You don't mind if The Judge joins us, do you? He's real sociable. Likes to have his Gainesburger alongside, on the floor."

"Good heavens, no," said Lydia. "It's his house, after all." Both women laughed and exchanged looks. Each knew she had found a friend capable of appreciating her.

The Judge came in, dispensing welcomes and animation in abundance. Lydia went into the small downstairs bathroom to wash her hands; she took a closer look at the walls as she came out: Renee had hung antique maps, matted in soft greens, with thin silver frames. There was an old map of North Carolina.

Renee sliced some black bread, arranged a stick of butter in a cut-glass dish; she selected two Gainesburgers from a box as if they had been patties of steak tartare. These were laid in a plastic dish and placed with great ceremony at The Judge's feet.

"You know about bread, don't you?" Renee handed Lydia a soft damask napkin. She sat down and spread her own napkin on her lap. "Even when you're dieting, it's important to have at least one slice of bread a day and a glass of milk. I learned that at Weight Watchers. It keeps your face from wrinkling."

"That's good to know," said Lydia, reaching for the bread. "And, of course, a little butter helps, too."

"Of course!" Renee laughed, passing Lydia the little cut-glass dish.

The Judge, who had dispatched his lunch in two gulps, sat beside Renee, his silver muzzle on her knee, soulfully eyeing her tuna fish.

"And what about you?" Renee asked Lydia. She separated some alfalfa sprouts from the tuna fish and offered a bit of tuna on her fingers to The Judge. "Is there an Eros in your life?"

Renee had caught Lydia unawares, and before she could stop it, the sheepish grin had spread across her face. "What makes you ask that?" she asked. But she was already smiling her admission.

"I'm psychic," said Renee. "No, I'm not psychic. I'm a good observer of people's faces while they talk. It's become one of my specialties. When you said, 'I'd just like to get to the bottom of Eros, once and for all,' I could see you were right in the middle of him."

"Well, you were right," said Lydia, buttering her bread generously, since she was only going to have one piece. "I'm in the middle, all right. Honestly, sometimes I think this sort of thing is like . . . well, having a virus. Some kind of fever comes over me whenever I go to his place. I can't let him come to mine, as I live with my younger son, and even if Dickie were in school when he came, I'd be afraid he could sense something afterward."

"Y'all don't go out openly, then?" asked Renee.

"Oh no! I mean, there's nothing wrong with him . . . with, er, Stanley—that's his name. But I just want to see how things go before I start dating in public again. It's like making a statement, you know, when you start dating a particular person after you've separated. And I have to consider Max, too—that's my husband . . . ex-husband . . . ex-husband-to-be, I mean. Max is a sort of leader in the community and, though I don't want him anymore, I owe it to him and the children not to embarrass him. So I have to be careful."

"I see," said Renee. Who looked as if she did see.

"But like I said," Lydia went on, "this *fever* comes over me when I'm around him. I just behave like . . . I don't know what. It's as if I abandon the self I've always known. And, to tell the truth, I don't know where this sort of thing *fits* in my life, or whether I can make it fit, or whether I even want it to fit. That's why I'd like to get to the bottom of whatever this thing is. Then I can look at it rationally and say, Yes I want this in my life, I can make a place for it, or, No, that's enough of that. I'm probably not making sense."

"Oh yes, you're making sense," said Renee, watching Lydia with those yellow-flecked, know-it-all eyes. "You sound like the essence of sense."

"Well, I don't know," said Lydia. She lowered her eyes away from Renee's gaze. She felt she had betrayed Stanley a little, but, in doing so, she also felt free; she felt more herself again, and that was a relief.

After their dieter's lunch (which left Lydia still hungry) Renee showed her the upstairs; and it was the revelations of upstairs that Lydia thought about as she drove home in the fading sunlight that afternoon. She went over her friend's house in her mind, still seeing the rooms and the old maps and the big vase of forsythia, with their buds forced open, upstairs in Renee's bedroom, which she shared with The Judge. It was just what she would have expected of Renee, to have flowers in the bedroom for herself. And Renee's bed: a high, old four-poster, with a patchwork quilt. "Mamma was born in that bed," she said. "It was her housewarming present to me when I bought this house. She went to school here, you know. She met my father in this town, so it's all very significant."

"You mean they went to college here?"

"No, they went to Palmer." Renee had waited for a sign of recognition from Lydia, but when none came, she explained, "It's closed now. But it was a sort of coed Foxcroft for the black elite. Only"—she had laughed—"its founder, Miss Charlotte Hawkins Brown, would have seen herself in Hell before she used the word 'black.' My mother and father met at Palmer and they married right after graduation and went back to Atlanta, where my father's father started an insurance company. Here they all are, my family, right on the wall. I've made myself a sort of family album on this dormer wall. I can lie in bed and contemplate my origins at night. But you have to sit down on the bed to see it properly."

And she and Lydia had sat down on the bed where Renee's mother was born and Renee had given Lydia a tour of the Peverell-Watson family. "That's my great-great-grandmother in the daguerreotype. The Reverend Peverell bought her in 1810 in Newport News. She was with a consignment from the West Indies and she was the first female to be sold. It's all documented in the Reverend's diaries, over at Chapel Hill. She was five feet ten inches tall and wore real gold earrings in her pierced ears and was 'comely for a wench of color,' to quote him. That likeness was taken when she was close to sixty, we figure; and her face is in too much shadow. It's a pity the photographic processes couldn't have been invented a bit sooner, so we could have seen her when she was young. That old guy in the wheelchair she's standing behind is the Reverend Peverell. After his wife died, she moved into the big house and took care of him. And that young man standing beside the chair, with his hat in his hand, is my great-grandfather. We think this 'family portrait' was a present from old Peverell to my great-great-grandmother; that he sent for the photographer one day and had a whole bunch taken and gave them all to her. Mamma's got some others, slightly different poses, and my first cousin has some. But there sure isn't a one of these in the Peverell family papers over at Chapel Hill.

"And that's Mamma with her mamma. And that's Mamma and Daddy on their wedding day. And that's their class picture from Palmer. And I won't bore you with these relatives, though they're amusing in their way. And that's my older brother, Warren, who's a lawyer in Atlanta. . . ."

"And who is this beautiful girl?" Lydia had seized on a recent-looking photograph of a statuesque young beauty, very like Renee, only darker, wearing a school uniform of some kind. "Is this your younger sister?"

"No, that's Camilla, my daughter." Renee's voice, though cool, had the slightest catch of pride in it. "She's at school in England. Mamma raised her, so I could get on with my education and all. In fact, a kind of sad thing happened when poor little Camilla was about three. I was home from Wellesley and Camilla came and jumped into my lap—she was so glad to see me—and put her little face against mine and called me her sister. And Mamma, who is one for the truth at all costs, said, 'No, honey, Renee's not your sister, she's your mother.' And that poor little child started crying her heart out. 'No, Mamma, you are my mamma, you are!' she was crying. Meaning my mamma. I guess the mix-up came about because Mamma had always referred to me as 'Renee' when I was away, rather than 'your mother.' But I was so sorry for Camilla that day that I would have gladly become her sister if I could, just to make her feel better. It all turned out okay, though. She's a product of Mamma's raising; it shows all over her. And that's an advantage. Mamma is a lady if there ever was one; me, I have my lapses. Camilla's at the top of her class over in England. And she likes me a lot. She writes me things in her letters that she won't tell Mamma. So maybe I got the best of both worlds, after all."

As Lydia commuted home on the I-40, she could hear the rich shifts in Renee's voice as it switched from irony to frank amusement, lapsed into the easier home-rhythms during intimate narrative, then paused on a note of wistful reflection. As Lydia had been leaving Renee's, she had asked her if she played her piano a lot. "Not as much as I *should*," drawled Renee, stroking the curve of the instrument in passing, "after all my training. I usually play now only when I'm sad. Which is only on the average of about twice a month, now."

Renee's life intrigued Lydia; her progress pricked sharply at Lydia's competitive spirit. Lydia ticked off what Renee had against what she herself had; and what she had had that Renee hadn't. She looked forward to learning all she could from her new friend. But though she acknowledged Renee's superiority over her in many of the areas the world values, Lydia felt, at bottom, a sweet, secret security in being who she was that all the striving, achieving Renees in the world could not topple. Lydia knew she could and would learn a great deal from Renee, but without the humiliation of Renee's ever being a threat.

That evening, while Dickie practiced his clarinet, Lydia phoned her mother. Nell provided her with the perfect opening to talk about Renee. Nell told Lydia she had been to lunch over at Theodora's. "Honestly, it was ridiculous," said Nell. "There the three of us sat around the dining table, me and Theodora and Wickie Lee. And Azalea sat in the kitchen having *her* lunch. Theodora spent most of the time hollering back and forth with

Azalea, and Wickie Lee and I sat in silence, picking at our shrimp salad. The shrimps were *tiny* and also they were the slightest bit off. I've been expecting to get ill all evening, but so far I haven't."

"Mother, this is so interesting. Let me tell you about my lunch today." And Lydia related the salient details. She told Nell about The Judge, and about that Palmer school (Nell had never heard of it, either), and about Renee's great-great-grand-mother's alliance with the Reverend Peverell, and of Renee's illegitimate daughter at the top of her class in Battle Abbey, England.

She was frankly disappointed at her mother's reaction. Nell listened with interest and a couple of "oh, *really*'s, but she did not pursue any further details. She wanted to get back to Theodora and Wickie Lee.

"Theodora seems completely taken in by her. I mean, the girl is a mystery, and that's always interesting, but she doesn't contribute very much. She's getting too big even to do house-work—Theodora won't let her—and when she did do it, Azalea had to come along behind her and do it over. All she does is sew on those dolls. And watch the afternoon soap operas. Theodora says at least she sews while she watches them. Theodora has a theory about the dolls. She thinks Wickie Lee is homesick and is making herself dolls of everybody from wherever she came from. Now she's started making their faces out of stuffed nylon stockings; then she sews in the wrinkles and the expressions. Theodora has brought her a closetful of clothes, and she fusses over her about her food and makes Azalea prepare special little meals; Theodora even reads to her out of the childbirth books the doctor recommended, because Wickie Lee says her eyes are too tired from making dolls. What I can't get over is Theodora's total . . . capitulation. It's as if she sees a different girl than the rest of us see. Theodora seems completely *charmed*."

"Dickie was saying about Gregory, his kitten, the other day, how there's something charming about how Gregory is just him-self and pleases himself and isn't even grateful. Maybe Theodora is charmed by Wickie Lee's ingratitude."

"Oh no, it's not that she isn't grateful," said Nell, ignoring

Lydia's theory. "I think she probably is, in her way. She just hasn't been brought up to show it right. Is that Dickie practicing on his clarinet? I hear the sweetest little tune."

Mother and daughter chatted on for a few minutes. Nell told Lydia that at Max's suggestion she was having a burglar-alarm system installed. "Max has been very thoughtful," said Nell. "He calls at least once a week, to see how I am."

"Have you heard from Cate?" asked Lydia.

"Yes, even she's been attentive. Not as attentive as Max. Or you, of course. But for Cate, very attentive. She sounds in very good spirits. Very sure of herself; you know how she can sound when everything's going her way."

"That's good," said Lydia, trying to sound sincere. "I'm glad about that. She seemed down, at Christmas. I mean, we were all down, because of Daddy, but she seemed to be . . . I don't know . . . sort of giving up on things."

But Nell wanted to get back to Theodora and Wickie Lee. "What's going to happen when that baby is born? Will they just stay on there? Will Theodora *adopt* Wickie Lee and her baby? That would be something, wouldn't it?"

After Lydia hung up, she sat with her legs curled under her on the sofa and, to the background music of Dickie's clarinet— the piece he was practicing now was really lovely; it was sweet and spritely and yet sad at the same time—she imagined Stanley, her Eros, prowling the rooms of his apartment, trying to imagine which room of her mirror-image apartment she was in. She knew Stanley thought of her; perhaps even now he was demolishing her last barrier in his imagination. Her womb did a funny little flip, right there in her living room, with Dickie's music ascending in a succession of pure, hopeful notes from the closed door of his bedroom. She and Dickie had both been trying to diet, and Lord! was she hungry.

She was popping corn when her son came out to join her in the kitchen.

"I'm afraid I've had a little relapse," she told him.

"May I have one with you?" asked Dickie. He came up and

slipped his arm around her waist and laid his head on her shoulder. She remembered how his head had smelled when he was a baby; it still retained a trace of that clean, newborn smell.

"Of course you can. It's better that we have a little butter in our systems; that way we won't wrinkle so soon. What was that lovely thing you were playing? Even Mother commented on it, when she and I were chatting just now. Was it Mozart?"

"Oh Mother, I love you for that. It was *me*. It was something I wrote."

"You wrote that? What you just finished playing in your room?"

Dickie nodded. He was shining with pleasure. "But I'm really behind, in some ways," he said. "Mozart wrote his first symphony when he was eight."

"Every person has his own starting point," she said, quoting Renee. "Or hers."

As she and her younger son sat across the table, sharing the bowl of popcorn, an ecstatic shudder of well-being rippled all through Lydia's body. She suddenly had a prescient feeling that she had crossed her own starting point and that she had a very interesting future ahead of her. She had not worked out all the details yet, but she felt it as certainly as she had felt she was going to marry Max, that first time she had danced with him at the Rhododendron Ball.

6.
THE BOOK CLUB

With her bare fingers, Nell poked through the wet leaves and other winter debris on the border of the garden, on the lower slope behind the house. There. She had known she was going to find it as she had lain in bed earlier this morning watching the first light turn the top branches of the trees pink.

The cool little sword-shaped leaves stood guard around the newly opened flower. It was a purple crocus with darker etchings in its petals. At its center glowed the golden-yellow pistil. The first crocus of the year: from a bulb Leonard had lowered into the earth with his own hands, more than twenty years ago.

Nell's vision misted over and she bowed her head. She felt the wet ground come up through the knees of her old gardening slacks. If only we were not mortal, she thought; if only we were not personal, there would be so much less pain. But how do I know that? This flower is not mortal, it is not personal. But if I wrenched off its taut, prim petals, if I snatched the bulb from its hole and left it lying to bake in the sun, to die, it would feel its own kind of pain and betrayal. Would I prefer to be this crocus and take my chances on suffering its kind of pain? Even if I could live longer than the human being who planted me, even if I could be spared the human pains of memory, or anxiety about the future?

No.

Once, about fifteen years ago, she and Leonard had been working down here in the garden. It was the closest activity they had in common, and they had had some of their truest conversations between the relaxed silences during which each raked and dug and planted and plucked. Nell had never been able to stand wearing gloves; they interfered with the tactile pleasure of gardening. That day, she had looked down at her right hand, engaged in smoothing earth around some flats of impatiens she had just planted, and she noticed for the first time a dark brown splotch on the back of the hand. Her first age spot. Disgust had filled her, followed by a sort of helplessness: here came age, and its loathsome debilities. She remembered an unkind remark she had heard her father make, years ago, about some beautiful woman who couldn't hide her age anymore because of her hands. Nell put the hand down by her side and tried to work with the other one. But the day had clouded over for her and soon she gave up and sat back on her heels, breathing deeply to counter the unpleasant truth that seemed to have lodged physically in her chest.

Leonard noticed that she had stopped gardening. "Tired already?" he had asked, looking over. He wore his silly-looking old straw hat with the pointed crown, and his glasses were steamed up from his sweating. There was dirt in the creases of his cheeks, on either side of his mouth. He's getting older, too, Nell had thought. But suddenly she felt better.

She raised herself up from her heels and surveyed the garden. "You know, I think an entire row of delphiniums would look good there, at the very back," she said. "Just imagine: that rich line of blue backing the pink and white phlox. It would be extravagant, of course, because it would take at least two dozen plants to fill in the space, but I think I've reached the point where I'd rather look at flowers than look at myself in the mirror."

Leonard's eyebrows had gone up, over the tops of his glasses. "But why deny us the one pleasure for the other?" he had asked, truly surprised. "Surely we can afford both."

She could tell he really meant it; he was not just being gallant. He actually thought her body was still worthy of raiment and care and expense, to give them pleasure. He had said "us" so naturally.

And afterward when they had been dressing—they had been going out somewhere for dinner; where?—she had looked at herself in the mirror and her "moment of truth" down in the garden appeared slightly mad. Highly out of proportion to the facts. We all get older, and "when you considered the alternative," as Churchill had once said . . . She had seen the reflection of a healthy, handsome, prosperous-looking woman, dressed to go out to dinner with a husband of compatible age and looks. She had even looked down at the offending hand: why, the spot was hardly more than a freckle in this light!

He protected me from so much, thought Nell now, kneeling alone in the dirt. From my harshest judgments of myself as well as of others. I don't know where I got that supercritical streak from. From my father, I guess. He couldn't stand ugliness or ineptness in people. He didn't really like sick people very much; I wonder what made him become a doctor. Maybe that's why Mother went on and died, out at that sanatorium, just when she was supposed to be getting better; perhaps she felt that her long illness had spoiled things between them and she didn't want to go home and face it. It's funny how character traits reappear in different family members: I'm critical, as my father was, only he never criticized himself the way I do myself; and Leo not only looks like Dad, but has that same perfectionist streak; and, probably, that's where Cate's faultfinding propensity comes from, only she focuses it out on the world when she might do better to focus a little closer to home.

Nell heard the telephone ringing in the house. It wasn't the time either girl usually called, and it was too early for Max to call. It was most likely one of the Sympathy Brigade, that cluster of friends who seemed determined not to leave her alone for more than a few days at a time. What were they afraid of? That she might learn to find resources in herself?

Leonard protected me from them, too, she thought, getting

up off her knees and starting for the house out of habit, to quell the ringing phone. When they knew Leonard was home, they thought twice about telephoning. Except for Theodora, of course, who always wanted to speak to Leonard.

She ended up running toward the house and was breathless when she picked up the receiver. Of course, the person at the other end had just hung up.

Miffed (with herself for running to answer, as much as with the caller who had interrupted her garden reverie), Nell made herself a cup of tea and got out all her Sabatier cutting knives and started shining their dull blades the way Lydia had learned in that Cordon Bleu course: by rubbing Ajax into them with a wet wine cork. The Sympathy Brigade, as she had dubbed them privately, operated from mixed motives. She supposed they felt sorry that she had lost her mate (or they told themselves they felt sorry), but there was at bottom a kind of *gloating*—yes, that was it—an exultancy they could hardly suppress, that she was now . . . one of them. Even as their lips eulogized the many qualities of Leonard and deplored her loss of such a companion, there was an excited flush in their faces, an unhealthy glitter in their eyes, that celebrated, as much as they tried to conceal it (possibly even from themselves), the leveling process. She had seen the glitter in the eyes of Theodora, who had never had a husband; of Grace Hill, whose husband had been dead for decades; yes, even in the eyes of Lucy Bell, whose husband was technically still alive but, for the large part, pickled in alcohol. *Ah, darling Nell*, the bright eyes glittered (though the mouths puckered or turned down with sorrow at the corners), *this is what we all come to, in the end.*

Here we all are, together, the long-lived females of the race, the proverbial "survivors," thought Nell, brandishing a newly gleaming blade in the morning light; condoling and consoling and casseroling one another as we shrivel into old dried husks of ourselves, like those nut-faced dolls of Wickie Lee.

And she would have worked herself into a rage of remorse, laced generously with the sarcasm that seemed to be dominating her moods more and more these days, had her attention not been arrested by a large, sleek crow alighting in the garden below.

Nell, whose ophthalmologist had told her at her last checkup that she had the distance vision of a jet pilot, watched the crow through the kitchen window. What lovely, single-minded arrogance it emanated as it strutted up and down amid the same debris she had been picking through. It was gathering materials for its nest. Nell watched it send a couple of wet leaves flying: Not good enough, the crow seemed to be saying, with a toss of its head. Then it found what it wanted, a nice pile of dried grass. It filled its beak with the grass, greedily, till it began to stagger from the weight. Its beak, hung with the yellow grasses on either side, made it look as if it had whiskers. Nell craned forward across the kitchen counter to watch the crow take off. Was it going to get off the ground with its load? It faltered in the first seconds of flight, but gained momentum without having to relinquish one strand of the grass. Good for you, thought Nell, feeling the achievement of the crow as it flapped off toward one of the tallest of Leonard's white pines, the ones he had planted when they had first moved in, to muffle the house's "shriek." The crow disappeared into a thicket of high branches. Nell felt pleased that she knew where the crow was making its nest.

The phone rang again. Nell answered it on the second ring.

"Nell honey," announced Theodora's magisterial growl, "I rang a few minutes ago, but you were probably out in your garden, weren't you? Isn't it a lovely morning?" (She pronounced it "maw'nin," the way people did in the eastern part of the state, and the affectation irritated Nell.)

"Yes, I was down in the garden," said Nell. "I ran up to the house as fast as I could, but you'd just hung up."

"Oh, pity," said Theodora, not really apologizing. "Listen, Nell. I'm calling about the Book Club. What do you want to do about the April meeting? You're signed up for it, but it's completely up to you. If you don't feel up to it yet, I'm sure one of the other girls will be happy to change with you. On the other hand, it might do you good to get back in the swing of things."

Theodora's tone made it clear she thought Nell ought to hold the April meeting at her house. Had they really been calling one another "girls" all this time? The idea was ludicrous.

"You'll have to fill me in on what people have been doing," said Nell, who had not attended the monthly meetings since Leonard's death. They had not expected her to come to the first two, and she had begged off the March, saying she was not back into reading yet.

"Well, you know the book list," said Theodora. "Last Saturday we did Mr. Michener's *Chesapeake*. Wonderful book! I want you to read it. So rewarding. Grace Hill made a cake in the shape of the state of Maryland, where the novel is set. So imaginative of Grace. She even tried to put in all those little inlets, which made the cake kind of crumbly on the one side. Grace works so hard at these things."

Meaning: she works *too* hard. Poor Grace had got into the Club late in life, and only after she had become society editor at the newpaper.

"Let's see, my book is that one about . . . I don't have my list right handy," said Nell. She'd just as soon have the April meeting and get it over with.

"That was just the thing I wanted to discuss with you, honey. What we have *scheduled* is that novel about the Rabbi's wife. Little Jean Lewis wanted it on the list, and as it was her first year in the Club, we all said yes. But Lucy Bell just finished it and brought it over to me, and I've been dipping around in it, and I find it a little tacky. Lucy did, too. But luckily, we have a perfect out. It's so well timed it's practically Godsent. The educational channel is doing *The Scarlet Letter* in installments, and it finishes just before our April meeting. It would be so rewarding, don't you know, to compare the programs with the book."

"Won't Jean Lewis be hurt if we scratch her book at the last minute?" asked Nell, just for the sake of arguing, really. She didn't care which book they did. *The Scarlet Letter* would be easier on her: she could watch the progams and skim the book, which she vaguely remembered.

"Jean's a sweet girl," said Theodora. "She'll want to fit in with the Club's wishes. Lucy's going to talk to her. After all, young Lewis *is* Latrobe's junior partner. I think we'll all get so much more out of *The Scarlet Letter*. Don't you?"

"It's fine with me," said Nell. She imagined the effect she would create if she were to cut large *A*'s out of red felt and ask each member to pin one on her breast, as a "favor," as she came through Nell's front door. ("Nell's always had an odd sense of humor," she could hear Theodora saying behind her back afterward. "She spent her formative years in Delaware, which is a rather peculiar state, neither Northern nor Southern; in a way, we could say the same about Nell.")

"I'm so glad," said Theodora. "And I'm so glad you'll be hostessing. Please let me know if I or Azalea can help. That goes for Wickie Lee, too, of course. Perhaps she could make favors or place cards. That child's a wizard with her hands."

"I'll let you know," said Nell. "We still have time." She had never been one who agonized for months ahead of time about her menu and centerpiece and cake.

"Not a *great* deal," warned Theodora. "The first Saturday in April is less than a month away. But I won't keep you any longer now."

"Well, I'll be in touch, Theodora," replied Nell (who knew what she would have said had she been truly one of *them*: "Why honey, you're not keeping me at all. This is delightful. Aren't we all going to have *fun* with *The Scarlet Letter!*"). But she could not rise to it, even in parody. She had never been able to do it, even for Leonard's sake, and now that he was no longer here to protect her from her worst self, she supposed she would turn really brusque.

That night Nell dreamed it was the day of the Book Club. Each member took a turn standing at Nell's fireplace, with her back to the room, while the others pinned a donkey's tail on her. Nobody was blindfolded, and there was no gaiety about the game in progress. Everybody was deadly serious, as if it were some kind of religious service. As it became Theodora's turn to face the fireplace and stick her rump out, Nell realized that she herself was not participating in the ceremony; she was standing off to one side, next to a man who was whispering obscene remarks about the other members. "Look at that old cow," he whispered, pinching Nell's arm. "Wrinkled old hag-face . . . old sow's tits."

Although she knew she was *allied* with him in some diabolic way, Nell was upset by his behavior. She had just turned to him, planning to remonstrate with him that these were, after all, her friends, the only ones she had, and since she was their contemporary his ugly descriptions must also apply to her. But at that moment, Theodora, who had just had her tail pinned on by the other members, let out an awful noise. As a nurse, Nell recognized its full and terrible significance: it was not just the sound of someone breaking wind; it was the sound a newly dead body makes when its bowels give way. "We've got to do something!" cried Nell to the man. She saw now that he was dressed in doctors' whites, so he should understand. But, to her horror, he just shrugged and beamed at her. We're not concerned with all this, his complicitous smile said.

Nell awoke alone in the dark, in the bed she had shared with Leonard for forty years; out of habit, she still kept to her side. Her heart was pounding from the frightful dream. She knew it would be a smart thing to turn on the bedside lamp, look at the time, anchor herself in the real world; to put on her robe and go downstairs and make a cup of tea. But she felt weak and sickened by the dream. "Who was that man, I know him!" she moaned, pulling the covers up higher and moving toward the middle of the bed, toward Leonard's old side, for comfort. But his side of the bed was quite cold. She retreated to her own part again.

She dozed off once more and had one of those dreams that simulate a wakened state. In this dream, she did get up and tie her woolen robe around her and go downstairs. The light was on in the living room. Leonard was sitting in his chair by the Magnavox, where he used to listen to his Saturday operas over earphones so as not to disturb the rest of the family.

"Leonard," said Nell. "Oh, Leonard, I've had such a bad dream."

She went over and climbed into his lap, as if she were a little girl, and put her head against his. She felt his hand come up and smooth her hair in his old familiar gesture.

This time, she awoke crying. She forced herself to get up, like a sensible woman, turn on the light and get out of bed. The clock said three-ten a.m. She put on her robe, blew her nose on a Kleenex she found in the pocket, and went downstairs to make a cup of tea.

Her kitchen comforted her. Before the house was built, she had told the architect how she wanted this room designed. "I want to be able to look at the mountains while I'm chopping vegetables, cleaning pots, or sautéing onions," she had said. "Then you're going to need lots of windows," he had answered; she had liked him for knowing enough about her activities so that he would understand she would need that much space. As she watched the coils turn red under the kettle, she poked the soil of her Swedish ivy plant and watered it; she warmed her small teapot and spooned in a teaspoon and a half of Russian Caravan blend. These rituals of exercised choice and taste laid a groundwork of calm while she mulled over her dream.

Basically, she had a pragmatist's approach to dreams. "Dreams take the events of the day before," she had often told her daughters when they had had peculiar dreams or nightmares, "and mix all the events up in a bowl indiscriminately, and the result is that you often get a pretty inedible pie." But Nell's Book Club dream seemed significant for the very reason it had the power to upset her even after she woke up.

The donkey's-tail part was easy. That was her wickedness about giving them each a red felt *A* to pin on themselves. And the division in herself in the dream, she understood that, too. She made fun of them, though she was one of them: there had been that division in her for years. And she had, the day before, been thinking about age, its ugliness and helplessness. The man in the dream was a bit of her father, the doctor who didn't like sick people; but she had known the man, she remembered that face. It was the face of a small, fastidious man, with blond, curly hair and a neat mustache above thin, very rosy lips that were habitually curled in sarcasm.

The teakettle became turbulent, and Nell allowed her mind

to go blank as she concentrated on listening for the exact moment when the heavy, pressurized rumble shut off and became a release of singing steam.

She made her tea and carried her cup into the dark living room, where she switched on the lamp that had been switched on already in her second dream. She sat down in Leonard's wing chair and lay her cheek against the back. She remembered the day they had bought this chair and what it had cost. And she remembered how, when it came time to have it reupholstered, she'd had such difficulty matching the material: Leonard hadn't wanted to change; he'd gotten used to that blue linen, he said. . . .

Dr. Grady Moultrie.

A mortified smirk spread over Nell's face, which, moments before, had been slack and heavy with sorrow. She took quick, scalding sips of tea, marveling at the treachery of the subconscious. What a tireless vigil it must keep, waiting for the vulnerable moment in which to pounce.

She would have preferred not to remember Grady Moultrie after all these years of blissful amnesia, while sitting in Leonard's favorite chair for the first time since he had died.

Grady Moultrie had been the young resident surgeon at the hospital, when Nell was a nurse. She had never known why he had singled her out for his favors. She had been a handsome girl, in her healthy, high-colored style, but never delicately pretty; and one would have thought the small, fine-boned doctor with his aesthetic squeamishness and his elite proportions would have been drawn to a matching partner. There were several pretty nurses who possessed in abundance those flirtatious graces that Nell, at twenty-three, had despaired of mastering. But the more they practiced their charms on the fastidious little doctor, the more he seemed to despise them. It was Nell he sat by, in the staff cafeteria; it was Nell he consulted about the places to go, the sights to see, in the town—he came from a small textile community just across the South Carolina line, and did not disguise the fact that he had been raised in a mill village. Nell felt at ease with him because he was the first man her age she'd met who didn't expect her to affect the female wiles she didn't possess naturally; also, neither of them was "from" the area, and they could judge it more dispassionately than the majority of their colleagues, who had grown up here. And Nell and "Dr. Moultrie," as she was required to call him at the hospital, did a lot of judging. They judged their colleagues, their patients, the townspeople, the shops and stores, even the shapes of the mountains that surrounded the town. As the two of them huddled over their coffee cups during breaks, they might have been a royal couple in exile, disguised for the time being as doctor and nurse, consoling each other for their comedown in the world. Nell startled herself by her talent for verbal abuse. Before Grady Moultrie, she had *thought* in critical patterns, using these patterns to figure things out for herself (and, in some cases, to anesthetize some pain inflicted by society), but now she heard herself expressing aloud the most scathing configurations of insults in a voice that sounded strange. It came out of her, this dangerously calm, lower-pitched voice, from depths only the little doctor had managed to tap. The strangest thing was, Nell didn't feel all *that* strongly, either way, about the people and institutions she so brilliantly reviled in the presence of her new friend; it was a form of flirtation in which they indulged, she somehow knew that.

Then they began to go out. Nurses were not supposed to date the resident physicians, that was the official rule; but it simply meant people sneaked, which gave the forbidden dates a certain piquancy. Nell and Grady Moultrie would "meet accidentally" in a darkened movie theater; soon they were driving to roadside diners a few miles out of town; and then they began "parking," in the doctor's little convertible roadster, in a secluded lookout spot on Beaucatcher Mountain (over the name of which they had quite a few laughs).

During these parking sessions, Grady would tickle Nell into a fine frenzy with the points of his lips, or sometimes with the tip of his tongue. He did things to her with his hands that she had never allowed anyone to do before; and he went places with his mouth and tongue that nobody had ever tried to go before. He seemed to derive pleasure from her abandon, though he panted and moaned very little; and once, on a clear, bright night, when they'd had the convertible top down, she had caught a look on his face that had frightened her: a sardonic look, almost contemptuous.

And yet, he wanted to marry her. He had not proposed in so many words, but he had taken her to the little mill town to meet his mother and sister, two imposing women who seemed to take it for granted that Nell would marry him. The sister was divorced and had a good job as a legal secretary, and the two women lived outside the mill village now, in a respectable frame house with lots of gingerbread trim. They went in for collecting old china, and Nell remembered an endless afternoon inspecting paper-thin teacups while Grady was over at the church rehearsing a song he had promised to sing at a friend's wedding. At the end of that visit, he had given her a head-and-shoulders photo of himself, in an elaborate silver frame. "This is one of Mother's," he said, "but she would like you to have it. On the condition that, if you don't stay in the family, you return it."

Nell had not replied. She knew she was in a kind of sexual thralldom to him, but surely she would not marry him. Or would she? Her father, already remarried to a rich widow, would have no objections to such a match. Wasn't that what all nurses were supposed to desire: to marry the doctor?

Soon after this, in one of their necking sessions, Nell reached for the zipper of his pants. She couldn't stand all this pressure a moment longer. But, to her great surprise, he stopped her hand with the shocked virginal modesty her sex was supposed to manifest at such times. "Uh-uh," he said, "mustn't touch." He pushed her hand away and continued to go where he liked with *his* hands. She was angry and humiliated. What was going on here? When he said "musn't touch," did he mean until they were married? Or never? She didn't even consider asking him. She was afraid he might turn his famous sarcasm on her.

Nevertheless, some healthy instinct came to Nell's aid. She knew that if she allowed things to go on this way, they might get married; and it would be a very peculiar marriage. She didn't believe the doctor really liked her. Perhaps he didn't like women. It made her uncomfortable to imagine what it would be like waking up beside that look of his every morning; she would have to be so careful, always on her guard. So she returned his picture to him, saying she was confused and needed time to think things over. How calmly he had taken the news! For once, he wasn't sarcastic; on the contrary, he was almost gentle. Ah, what a good show he had put on. She had thought she was free. And then had come that awful confrontation in the hospital elevator, when she was wheeling old Mr. Steckeroth down to the morgue.

Nell had become attached to Mr. Steckeroth when he came out of intensive care. She was drawn to patients who fought to stay alive, who battled their way back to health and did not flourish on pity. And here was this old German, a gardener for the city parks, struck speechless and partially paralyzed by a stroke, but determined to walk out of the hospital again and tend to his flowers. As Nell massaged and exercised his arm and leg, they established a kind of dialogue. She asked him questions and he responded with nods or shakes of his head. He walked the fingers of his good hand across the counterpane, pointed to the door of his room, and then began making gardening motions and smiling and nodding, and Nell understood perfectly. She looked forward to going to the old man's room every morning, and, when his stricken hand grasped her hand firmly, after several weeks of exercise, she knew how God must have felt when he brought Adam out of inanimate clay. She could now elicit half-coherent sounds from him as his speech center struggled out of the primordial confusion into which the aneurysm had thrown it. "You know, Mr. Steckeroth," Nell told him one day, "I really think you're going to make it." She walked her fingers over the counterpane. The old man shook with soundless laughter and tears came into his eyes. I'm proud to be a nurse, thought Nell that day; even if I don't ever get married, being a nurse will be enough.

And then one morning she came into his room and saw that he had relapsed. He lay there listless and scarcely breathing. His eyes met hers with a look of sorrowful apology. He had decided that, after all, he couldn't make it. And he didn't. Before noon he was dead, and Nell went in to perform the last tasks: the propping and tying, the labeling and diapering. She wept as she worked, and Dr. Moultrie came into the room and watched, a thoughtful little smile on his face. Nell stiffened and kept her back to him as much as possible; there was something disrespectful about the way he stood there, as if he were amused by death, or by her feelings, or both.

"I'll give you a hand in the regions below," he said casually, following Nell and the trolley to the freight elevator. Nell said she could manage by herself, but she couldn't very well stop him from getting into the elevator with her. If a doctor wished to accompany a body to the morgue, what nurse could forbid him?

The doors to the old freight elevator clanged shut and they started down. Then Grady Moultrie pressed the STOP button. They were between floors. He pulled up Nell's uniform and began stroking her thighs, his tongue darting in and out of her mouth like a snake. He put one finger in her. But then he put two, and, when she began to writhe and moan, he roughly inserted a third, which was very painful. And then he reduced her to a quivering blob of sensation: she half climbed up him and begged him to stop. When he was finished, there was blood on his three fingers. He wiped them on the sheet which covered Mr. Steckeroth's body. Then he pressed the START button and the elevator continued its slow, jerky progress downward. He did not even get off with her at the morgue. She wheeled out the trolley and when she looked back the doors were slowly closing, like curtains, on his sardonic smile.

After she had tucked the old gardener away in his cold drawer to await the undertaker (and disposed of the sheet —somehow, that had been the worst part: Grady's wiping his fingers on the sheet), Nell went back to her own floor. She went to the bathroom. She hurt, and there was more blood on her panties. She took them off and flushed them down the toilet. Then, because she was still trembling, she went out on the balcony of the fire escape to pull herself together. She was afraid she might scream, or attack Grady Moultrie if he came into sight, or do something that would disqualify her from her profession. She looked down at the ground, two floors below, and imagined how another kind of girl might well be tempted to throw herself off: the kind of girl who would feel Grady had disqualified her for marriage to a decent man. But, whether because she was a nurse or because she had lost her mother before that good lady could instill into her the exaggerated respect for that tiny membrane one must preserve at all costs for one's husband, Nell could not waste much time grieving for her actual physical loss in the elevator. She had been willing to seduce Grady on the mountaintop, but it infuriated her that he had *cheated* her out of her maidenhood; he had not taken her as a man should.

Then her anger deepened into a more philosophical one: what a sick world this was, in which the people who longed to live died and the healthy ones went around belittling life and casting scorn on things. There was poor Mr. Steckeroth cooling down there in his drawer, never to plant another flower; while people like Grady Moultrie used their hands and voices to cheapen and shame life.

And there she had sat with him, day after day, indulging in their sick little game of belittling things around them.

Ah, if only there were a war on! Look what Florence Nightingale had been able to do with the Crimean War.

And Nell clenched the iron railings of the balcony and threw all her energy into imagining some grand way she could renounce life and get back her self-respect in the doing. Her face must have gone through some interesting changes, those changes she was to hear described again and again as Leonard later built up the story. Or what Cate would call "a family myth."

As Nell wrestled with her demons on the hospital fire escape, a man below cleared his throat.

She looked down and saw a tall, gangly man standing in the parking lot of the law office across the street. When he saw he had gained her attention, he smiled. It was a modest, shy smile. He was about her age and had a long, kindly face, still raw with its own youth. He wore horn-rimmed glasses, and a cowlick of lank brown hair had flopped out of his side parting. He looked like a man who had never had a scornful thought in his life.

Embarrassed that she had been watched, going through all her emotions, Nell smiled back at the man. She gave a little lift of her shoulders, not quite a shrug, as if to say, Aren't I silly, when I'm still alive and young and it's a nice spring day. She noticed a sweet circle of grape hyacinths planted around the sign across the street that read STRICKLAND & STRICKLAND, *Attys. at Law.*

("I'd come out of the office to get a breath of air, and that's when I saw a furious blond nurse rush out on the balcony of the fire escape of the hospital across the street. You should have seen her face. It went through the most remarkable series of changes. Now there's a girl of temperament, I thought. And then I thought, If I can make her look my way, I can make her smile. And when she *did* smile, I knew I would marry her.")

Had he known? At the time? Or had he convinced himself he had known, during one of the many tellings of this family myth to their little girls? Leonard loved a romance.

And, at this point in the family romance, it became Nell's cue to say, "You helped matters along, you know. You cleared your throat. And I smiled because I felt silly. The day was so beautiful and you looked so calm and collected down there."

And then the lie: *"I can't to this day remember why I was so angry."*

The Father's wistful romantic narrative. Balanced so admirably by the Mother's wry common sense. Not an unhealthy combination of forces for a pair of little girls. Morgues and bloody fingers and perverse deflowerings had no place in such a story. Not even Leonard knew the truth about that day. Nell's conscience had pained her in the first months of their marriage when Leonard, wanting to share everything with his wife, made a clean breast of his previous love for Mercedes somebody, the high-school Spanish teacher he wanted to go off to Spain with, to fight in the Civil War. Now it's my turn, Nell had thought, the burden of her concealment expanding in her chest until it actually interfered with her breathing. But she couldn't speak. I'll wait a few days, she had decided; I'll wait for the right time.

How she had wished then that she had a mother to call up on the telephone. ("Mother, which is right? To be scrupulously honest, no matter how I might shock or disillusion him? Or to live with my hateful little memory and protect his innocence and optimism?") Though Nell could too well imagine what her own mother would have answered: "Don't give him anything he can hold against you!" No, what she had yearned for, during that crisis of conscience, was an Ideal Mother, an all-wise female whose advice would be based on far-reaching principles of benevolence. But in the absence of the Ideal—which was usually not to be found when you most needed it—you had to rely on your instincts and common sense.

Nell had decided that Grady Moultrie would haunt their marriage more if she were to give Leonard certain visual pictures than if she kept them to herself. She had done nothing more disreputable than allow the doctor to bring out a certain side of her nature which was dark and a little frightening. But wasn't it better to know she had such a side? She was sarcastic and she was highly sexed. But maybe she could turn the sarcasm to uses of intelligence, and the sex . . . well, here she was, already pregnant in her third month of marriage: she was pretty sure she could find enough to keep her body busy. Lovemaking with Leonard didn't have the frenetic, sinister sensations of being swept away and slightly demeaned in the process that her sessions with Grady had elicited; but her husband soothed and satisfied her in quite another way. It was like deep breathing compared to panting. Leonard's careful, trusting *assumption* of her body touched her in remoter places than Grady's aloof experimental probes.

So, Nell had told herself, I *did* save my deepest wifely responses for my husband, and that's an end to that. And each time he told their love story to the girls, she held her head up and came in on her cue: *"I can't to this day remember why I was so angry."*

And the goddess of memory had been benevolent. One day, she *had* forgotten. She had lived in Leonard's story until it became more true than her own suppressed version. The lonely, self-defensive, sharp-tongued nurse with her young appetites all a-jangle seemed more like a younger sister who aroused Nell's dutiful attachment, but also her impatience. That young woman had not passed out of existence, but she had become encased in a smoother, wiser, rounder version of herself—made possible by Leonard's belief in her as a woman of temperament, but also a good and capable woman.

"But what will I be without him?" wondered Nell, huddled in his chair, clasping the cold teacup to herself. The sky was growing light. She could see the first touches of dawn on the mountain ranges which the rear of the house had been built to face. She reached up and switched off the lamp and got up and went to the window, still holding her cup to her breast as if it were a talisman of some kind. Down below, in the garden, the crow was already at work, rejecting leaves, gathering more of the straw, which it seemed to like best. Nell felt as if they were old friends now. "I will not turn into a mean, sarcastic old woman," she informed the crow through the glass panes.

Neither could she immolate herself at the shrine of her sainted husband. She was not the type, any more than she had been the type of girl who could have thrown herself off a balcony in 1938 because she had lost her technical virginity to a cad. Besides, Leonard hadn't been a saint. He had known quite well how to use his gentle unworldliness to evade confrontations; he exempted himself from family squabbles with a maddening sublimity: there he'd be, sitting under his earphones, rapt with opera, or in his study reading a dead Roman lawyer's letters to a friend, while the rest of them tiptoed around, hissing and smoldering at one another. He had driven her crazy many a time while he decided upon a parking place. And even though she had learned to curb her "shrillness," as he called it (in others; he would never have said, "Nell, you are shrill"), she had lost her savor for arguing with him early in the marriage: she would lose track of her best points while waiting for him to finish a sentence.

Some men dominated by force; Leonard had dominated by leisure. He had slowed them to his stately pace. Though they would have expressed it, "We must protect Daddy from this," the truth was that, by instilling in them this desire to "protect" him, he restrained them.

So here I am, thought Nell, big old solitary sixty-three-year-old me. I might live twenty more years. Or even thirty. Who is going to restrain me now? Restrain me from what excesses and eccentricities? There's Theodora trying to amuse herself with a stray hillbilly girl; and Grace Hill with her imaginary ailments (though, at least, she has a *job*); and Sicca Dowling drinks, her face is a shambles; and Gertrude Jones makes a pilgrimage to Europe every year and affects a lively interest in all things architectural. And poor Taggart McCord, who was more than ten years my junior, kills herself in a trailer.

The crow took off toward the white pine with another load of straw. "That's right," said Nell. She approved and envied the bird's absolute and unreflecting oneness with its task.

The Mountain City Book Club had been founded in 1886 by Edna and Dora Hildebrand—known to their friends as "Eddie" and "Dos." At the time, they were youngish spinsters who kept house for their father, Adolf Hildebrand, who owned a jewelry store which specialized in watch repairs and the restringing of pearls. Eddie Hildebrand, the "bluestocking" sister, appointed herself founder and president of the Book Club. Dos, who preferred working in the vegetable garden and tending her goats, was made cofounder and vice-president. (After her death, she was remembered chiefly in the town because, late in life, she had married a man named Prince Albert.)

The Club's first secretary was Bernice Taylor Blount ("Biddie" to her friends), who lived in the beautiful new house across the street and wrote a perfect private school hand. A vivacious young married woman who was extremely proud of her singing voice and her eighteen-inch waist, Biddie would have laughed in the face of any interloper from the Future who might have had the audacity to suggest that she would one day be remembered in this town primarily for being the grandmother of Theodora Blount. Biddie would have been insulted; she had other plans for herself. Had she not captured the rough-edged but enterprising Sam Blount, who had known just when to sell his patrimony up in Sharpe County and come down out of the hills into this pretty town which the new railroad was transforming into a booming tourist center? (Sam's patrimony being eight miles of valley, from ridge to ridge, including the virgin timber; and that being only a postage stamp compared to the holdings of his ancestor, Blount of Beaufort, who, after the Colonial Act of 1778, had bought up 320,640 acres of Sharpe County, which were later sold off for as little as a nickel an acre as the family began to "go down.") "You've got the class, Biddie honey, and I've got the cash," Sam liked to say in his heavy mountain twang. "We ought to rub on right tolerable together." And, though Biddie was weaning Sam of such language as well as his rough edges, she believed they would. After Sam got all his businesses going well (he owned a livery stable which rented horses and equipages to tourists; he had part ownership in a funeral home; he had just opened the town's first detective agency), Biddie pictured them taking a tour of Europe, where—through a combination of his means and her social talents—they would be invited to English country houses and Paris salons, where she would be begged by the guests to sing. Meanwhile, one must take what culture one could find in one's own area, and Biddie took seriously her membership in the City's first Book Club.

All the minutes and scrapbooks of the Club had been preserved since its first meeting. In 1976, the members wanted to do something historical to honor the Nation's Bicentennial (and the Book Club's ninetieth year) and it was decided that each member would "research" one of the Club's founding members and do a report on her. The names were drawn out of a bowl, and Nell had drawn the name of Biddie Blount. Theodora provided Nell with an amplitude of photographs and biographical details. Nell spent several hours poring over the Club's old scrapbooks and the leatherbound minutes, which were lodged— according to the bylaws—at the current president's home.

Biddie had had four babies, three of whom had died. One was stillborn; the twins had been carried off by diphtheria; only Teddy, the firstborn, who was to become Theodora's father, had survived. Nell studied the visible metamorphoses of Biddie, documented by the photographs. Her face had been too round, even when in its prime, for those high-necked blouses, but she *had* had a tiny waist. And she must have had a voice of some kind, because there was a note from Dr. William James of Cambridge to prove it. In 1904, when the great American philosopher had made a railroad stopover to visit the town's Normal College, the Mountain City Book Club had captured him for tea in the interim before his train north. In his bread-and-butter note from Cambridge (addressed to "Mrs. Samuel Blunt," who was then Club president) Dr. James professed himself charmed by "Mrs. Blunt's" Verdi aria and secure in the knowledge that Literature and Culture in the state would "grow and flourish under the capable guardianship of such groups as yours."

"Granny was just sick that he'd left out the *o* in her name," Theodora told Nell. "She worried for years over it, and then one day she picked up a pen and put it in herself. She said the family name was more precious to her than the authenticity of the letter. All sorts of people have tried to get this letter, you know. The library wants it for their Historical Collection; and some man who was doing a biography of Dr. James pestered Mother practically to death—he wanted her to send the letter to him, out in Ohio somewhere, so he could look at it. Mother wrote him that if he wanted to look at it, he was welcome to come to the house and look at it. They finally compromised by her copying out the message of the letter and sending it to him; but, you know, it never did get in the book. I call that careless and ungrateful."

"I'm surprised this letter isn't in the Club scrapbook for 1900–1910," Nell had said.

"Oh, honey, Eddie Hildebrand made such an ugly fuss about that. But, after all, the letter *was* addressed to Granny. It came to her house. It mentioned *her* name alone, in the body of the message. And besides, it was too valuable to be pasted away in an old scrapbook which got dragged around to every new president's house. And if it hadn't been for Granny, Dr. James would never have come to the Club. She worked so hard to make the club into a real cultural asset to the community. Before she took over, it was . . . well, kind of parochial." Theodora laughed huskily. "In fact, Granny used to say that if it had been she who had founded the Club, she would never have let the Hildebrand girls in. They weren't really—" Theodora tilted the flat of her hand from side to side, as if weighing invisible social evidence. "I mean, their father was this nice little German who repaired watches. And Dos, running around with her billy goats, wasn't ever a lady."

Poor Biddie Blount, whose singing voice outlasted her eighteen-inch waist, never sang in a Paris salon or an English country house. She never even crossed the ocean. First came the babies; and by the time little Teddy became old enough to travel, Sam Blount had lost most of his savings in speculation and sequestered himself in his "laboratory" above the carriage house, where, with the help of a local pharmacist, he worked on formulas for an "Energy Tonic." He still owned a share of the funeral home, and his friends joked with him that he couldn't lose either way: "You can always bury 'em if the Tonic doesn't work." But the Tonic did work. Sam put it on the market, and within three years he had made a new fortune. The Energy Tonic tasted good, and it made you feel peppier almost as soon as you swallowed it; it was packaged attractively, and druggists loved it because they could display it in their windows in winter and it wouldn't freeze. By 1919, when little Teddy took over the business, the family nostrum (as the Blounts called the Tonic) had entered a new period of prosperity. The Volstead Act had been passed, and tourists unable to make contact with a local bootlegger found that the Energy Tonic served them almost as well; you could even take it with some foods—it was good with cheese dishes, for instance. Teddy went into partnership with another druggist in town, and they expanded their "line" to include skin preparations, the most popular of which was a bleaching cream made of lard, oil of almond, and hydroquinone; this preparation had spectacular success with the colored population.

And so, in 1930, when most people were suffering from the Depression, young Theodora Blount was able to sail first class to England, egged on by fat, deaf Granny (though Biddie was only sixty-four at this time), who shouted from her chair at Theodora, "If you don't see Europe before you marry, you'll regret it the rest of your life! Make your young man wait!"

Theodora had seen Europe. The young man had made a tactical error with Lucy somebody, the girl from Spooks Branch Road, which had rendered him unable to wait. But, at least, Theodora's father had been able to save most of her inheritance for her. When the Food and Drug Administration was established in 1931, Teddy smelled trouble. He converted his profits from the Energy Tonic into good railroad stocks and municipal bonds rather than plowing them back into the business. The skin preparations remained on the market just as they were, but the Tonic underwent a subtle adjustment. It looked the same, it tasted *almost* the same, but it became less desirable to its most ardent purchasers; but, even to Teddy's surprise, there remained a local demand for the Tonic. These faithfuls, many of whom were good teetotaling Baptists, continued to proclaim the healthful merits of the nostrum even after Prohibition was repealed.

When Nell had read her "report" on Biddie Blount to the Book Club, she knew her voice sounded strained with fake enthusiasm. As she droned on about Biddie's inestimable influence on the history of the Club, her reputation as the town's social leader and arbiter of style, she never lost awareness that Biddie's granddaughter (now of grandmotherly age herself) monitored her, making sure Nell kept to the accepted version of the family story. Nell had toed the line, boring them all, probably; meanwhile, a subterranean commentary eddied around in the backwaters of her mind.

That night at supper, she had told Leonard, "You know, Theodora's family is so representative of so many things. The way people come out of the backwoods and rise to power by lording it over the people they have tricked into taking them seriously. And all these sacrifices that are forgotten later, or erected into monumental *pretensions*! My goodness, when you really get down to it, 'the aristocracy' simply means whoever got there first."

"That's been true all throughout history," mused Leonard.

"Though, getting there first does imply a superior energy; and *staying* there demands a certain concerted effort. But sweetheart, if the Club has begun to bore you, don't think you have to stay in for my sake. . . ."

"Oh no, I find it interesting," Nell had replied honestly. She laughed in her dry way. "I find *them* interesting."

" 'Them,' after all these years?" remarked Leonard the lawyer. "I find *that* interesting."

But Nell was wound up with her topic and couldn't stop. "Do you know what, Leonard?" She had started laughing. "Whenever Biddie Blount gave a luncheon, she insisted that the paper say: 'Covers were laid for twelve—or fifteen or whatever—guests at the home of Mrs. Samuel Blount.' Can you beat that? 'Covers were laid for'! Oh Lord, Leonard! How can anybody take society seriously? We're all a bunch of hicks from the backwoods, it's really only a matter of when we came out of the underbrush and put on our skirts and trousers and began 'laying covers' for one another!" Her stomach began to cramp with spasms of her hard, dry laughter.

When she had wound down a little, Leonard examined the tines of his fork. "That's true, in a sense," he murmured, the softness of his voice such a contrast to her sharp hilarity. "But, you know, I think that Club meant a great deal to my mother. She used to read the books so carefully and make little notes on a card so she would have something pertinent to say. And when she was hostess, she used to plan her table months ahead. She put so much thought into her favors. I remember one time she sewed little stuffed bookworms for each member. Daddy used to tease her. But that was the tradition, you might say; the men teased the women for dressing up and going to all that trouble just for one another. But I believe the Book Club kept Mother's mind alive. Having something to prepare for like that—it took her mind off other things. Daddy didn't always make her life easy, you know."

"Oh dear, I'm so callous!" Nell had wailed, as remorseful as she had been sarcastic before. "Please forgive me, Leonard. I've gone and hurt your feelings."

"You have?" He looked through his thick glasses, which had kept him out of World War II, with what seemed genuine innocence. "Well, I'm not aware of it, then. Nell, this roast beef is done just right."

Thus he tempered her bursts of sarcasm and self-castigation; he dampened any sparks between them before they could gather enough glow to become dangerous. Sometimes Nell had felt herself *poking* at a promising-looking ember: How much fire could we make, if we really went at it? she had wondered, though not in so many words. Somewhere, far below words, she had known that she could have gone the furthest in any confrontation. On the level of violence or animal passion, she felt sure she could have won. But he never let her put it to the test.

Just as well, maybe, thought Nell, the widow; though, as a wife, she had sometimes longed for a flame, even if someone got burned a little.

One evening, around the middle of March, when the spring winds were doing their best to bring out the house's banshee song, and as Nell lay in bed trying to get through the "Custom House" preface of *The Scarlet Letter*, the bedside phone rang and it was Cate. She seemed particularly chatty and Nell sensed from an uncharacteristic rambling in her daughter that Cate had really called to ask something very specific, and wanted to camouflage it. She chatted on about her classes. She said she had been going out with a "local magnate," the father of one of her students in the Drama class. She said she had been sitting at her kitchen table doing her income tax. "I just got out my Teacher's Insurance Annuity papers, to check something," Cate drawled on, "and I suddenly came across my retirement date. Two thousand and two. I got the strangest feeling. It seems so far away and yet it isn't. It's only twenty-three more years. Listen, Mother, this is a silly question but I've been wondering—probably because of that retirement date: when does one . . . I mean, when am I likely to expect the first signs of menopause?"

Good heavens, thought Nell. Can she be, already? My child?

"Well, it's variable," Nell said in her most practical and

professional tone. "Some women start as early as their late thirties, some diehards go on into their fifites and even conceive. You've heard of 'menopause babies.' But it's generally conceded that the earlier the onset of the menses the longer they'll keep functioning. And you started very early for your age. You were ten. Lydia was a little later, she was almost twelve. So I don't think you have to worry for a while yet."

She waited for Cate to contradict her.

But Cate said, "No, I guess not. But just tell me, while we're on the subject, what the first signs are. So I'll be prepared for the great ordeal." She said this last ironically.

"Well, your periods taper off," said Nell. "Or you'll have a heavy one followed by a very light one . . . or maybe miss one altogether."

"I see," said Cate. Her voice was very low, though she was trying to maintain the irony.

"Have you . . . missed one?" Nell decided to venture.

"Goodness no, Mother!" snapped Cate. "Can't we just talk theoretically? I just like to know what's going on in my body." She amended herself. "I mean, what's *going* to go on."

"Well," said Nell, slightly provoked, "that's a rough idea of what's going to go on. But there are so many excellent books on the subject nowadays. So many modern books." She could not resist a little backlash. "After all, things may have changed since I was a young woman. They may have revised the system completely."

To her surprise, Cate laughed appreciatively. "That's always to be considered," she replied amiably.

Then Nell felt she had been mean. She asked all about Cate's new beau. "Is he attractive?"

"He has a certain vital masculine charm. But he's shorter than I am and his face is red and rather homely," replied honest Cate.

"Is he very rich, then?" asked Nell.

"Pretty rich," said Cate.

"Is he . . . I mean, *interested* in you?" That had not been exactly what Nell meant to say, though it was what she thought.

Cate laughed. "Strange as it may sound, Mother, some men still find me attractive."

"I didn't mean *that*. . . ." Nell thought. "I meant, well, is he *free* to be interested in you. That's what I meant."

"He's not married. Both wives left him."

"Oh, really? Do you know why?"

"More or less. The first marriage sort of eroded; and there was some trouble with the first son. The second marriage was just a mistake. Or rather, she liked his money, he liked her beauty; but he raised that son, too."

"Goodness. That would be a handful for you. Or no, how old are the boys?"

"The boys are raised now, Mother. One is thirty-three and one is going to graduate this spring. And why should it be a handful for *me*? I didn't say anything about marrying him, did I?"

"No. But if you *liked* him, and if he could take good care of you, and you enjoyed being together . . ." Nell halted; *why* must Cate always fight her tooth and nail, even in a phone conversation? "What I mean is, it's not such a piece of cake spending your old age alone."

"I'm hardly old yet, Mother. Neither are you, for that matter. Old today is not what old was yesterday."

"Funny," said Nell. "Do you know, your father used almost the same expression the night he . . . well, just before we went off the road. We were talking about . . . about you girls, as a matter of fact. And I said, 'Cate will be forty this coming June,' and he said forty for a person today wasn't like forty when we were that age. He said the expectancies were stretching."

"What did he mean by that?" Cate asked. "Did he mean it about me?"

"I *think* so," acknowledged Nell. Though she had not thought it desirable to tell Cate why they had been discussing her that last time: that she, Nell, had been quoting Theodora's ominous statement that middle-aged women couldn't live on their possibilities anymore. "And I think he also meant *generally*, as well. For the whole human race. He usually did mean generally, as well."

Cate laughed. "I know exactly what you mean. Dear Daddy. But look, how are you getting along? Okay? That's really the main reason I called. Not to discuss menopause."

"Oh, I'm fine. I have the Book Club here in a few weeks. So I'm up here in bed trying to read *The Scarlet Letter*. It's so strange. I was sure I had read it before, but it's obvious I haven't. There's this whole first section I'm sure I never saw before in my life. To be frank, I'm not completely in the mood for this book, but I suppose I'll persevere. And it's going to be on television, so I can always watch that."

"The main thing to remember about *The Scarlet Letter*," said Cate, with a resumption of her jaunty confidence, "is that it asks the very crucial question 'Can the individual spirit survive the society in which it has to live?'"

"Well, I'll try to remember that," said Nell, smiling at her daughter in spite of herself.

They said their good-byes and Nell tried to go back, unsuccessfully, to the dusty Custom House. She finally switched off the light and lay on her pillows, hands folded between her breasts, trying, as she had done many times before, to figure out her older daughter's motives.

The first Saturday in April, the day of Nell's Book Club, turned out to be clear and sunny, with the temperature in the mid-sixties by nine o'clock. Early April in the mountains could be tricky, so much so that women who could afford it often had two outfits ready for social events occurring around this time. Nell laid the lightest of her two dresses—a gray linen with tiny gray pearl buttons down the front—out on her bed, and went down, still in her robe, to put the finishing touches on her luncheon preparations. Though each hostess operated under the illusion of freedom, she was bound by a great number of strictures and traditions regarding menu, decoration, and order of events. Some customs were contradictory to other customs (you were supposed to serve a selection of "nonfattening" salads, for instance; but you were also expected to keep an endless supply of hot rolls circulating around the table); and some customs had always seemed to Nell to be downright uncouth, for a group that laid so much stress on the refinements of culture. Guests arrived at eleven-forty-five; you were supposed to have them seated at the table by noon; there were no cocktails first, no alcohol ever; coffee, hot coffee, was supposed to flow from the same endless source as the hot rolls, and be served straight through, from soup to nuts; and—this was the tradition that got Nell—the hostess was not supposed to sit down at her own table. The hostess was expected to circulate around and around the table, pouring the coffee and passing the hot rolls and—during hurried refuelings of coffeepot or refillings of roll basket in the kitchen—stuff what she could get of her own food in her mouth, like a servant between trips.

Where on earth had such a custom come from? wondered Nell, as she applied hot towels to the rings of her aspics and fruit molds and waited anxiously for the reassuring *clump* of the preparations sinking onto the platters below. Was it some old-fashioned mountain notion of high courtesy to guests? That must be it, because even the women who had maids followed the protocol. The maids were allowed to serve the plates in the kitchen, but the hostess did the circulating in the dining room. Once, when Theodora was hostessing, Nell had choked and gone into the kitchen to get a glass of water, and there sat Azalea at the kitchen table, a nice selection of the day's goodies arranged on her plate, a steaming cup of coffee on one side, while Theodora stood at the sink, trying to chomp a mouthful of roll and chat with Azalea at the same time, while waiting for the next pot of coffee to perk.

At ten o'clock, the florist delivered Nell's centerpiece. That was another custom: even if you had won every Garden Club award in town, you were expected to order the flowers for your centerpiece, which came prearranged from the florist's. She set down the rather conventional-looking arrangement in the place reserved for it: nice, serviceable flowers, cut low, so the women could talk over them. Then, as a reward to herself for obeying so many rules, she went to take another look at her cake, which had turned out splendidly.

The ladies wouldn't have to pin red *A*'s on their breasts, but they were going to get one served to them at the table. Nell was especially pleased with the red glazed frosting. She had experimented with raspberry juice and vegetable dye till she got exactly the shade she wanted. And the elaborate yellow tracery effected with a paper funnel: well, she wished Hester Prynne could have seen it. (Nell had not quite finished the book, but she had dutifully watched every installment of the work on TV.)

At eleven-thirty-nine, the first car drew up. Nell looked through the curtains and saw Sicca Dowling get out of her little sports car with the bashed fender. Chiffon scarf trailing like streamers behind her, she wandered halfway up the flagstone walk, then obviously recalled something she had left in the car. She retraced her steps, her ankles wavering in the high-heeled sandals. She poked her head into the passenger side of the car, removed something from the glove compartment, and (after a quick look around her) swigged from a silver flask. She put the flask back and sauntered up the walk a second time, looking jauntier. Sicca's one son had been killed in a helicopter accident in Vietnam; she had had a nervous breakdown; her husband had run off for a while with a young girl he had met on the golf course. But now he was home again and they drank together. Sicca carried her sorrows by making a joke of everything, including herself. But there was no malice in her. Nell had seen her fall flat on her face and pick herself up and make a joke about it. She had been Theodora's maid of honor–elect, before Latrobe Bell had made himself ineligible for that wedding. Nell liked Sicca and was always sorry when she was too indisposed to come to a meeting; even though she occasionally fell or knocked over a valuable glass or told one of her questionable jokes.

As Nell came out of her house to meet Sicca, Theodora and Wickie Lee pulled up in Theodora's impeccably preserved 1954 Buick Special.

Sicca floated up to Nell and kissed her. "Nell, you look truly wonderful. We've all missed you very much." Her breath was fragrant with vodka. She still had her slender figure even though her poor face was a ruin.

Theodora, bearing a basket covered with a snowy cloth, and Wickie Lee, carrying a small box in which Nell presumed were the place cards Theodora had volunteered for her to make, approached with the ceremony of guests who know they are indispensable. Wickie Lee, whose baby was due this month, had a new dress that flowed with old-fashioned majesty, and a quaint upswept hairstyle. Nell had a poignant image of Theodora dressing and grooming the little protégée like a life-sized doll about to give birth to another life-sized baby doll. But she had to admit, Wickie Lee's sojourn with Theodora had bestowed a luster: the girl looked rested and healthy and less suspicious of everyone; she carried herself better. And there was a dignity about the pale, finely made "long-ago" face that peered impassively upon the three older women overdoing their greetings to one another.

"I declare, it's so good to have you back with us," said Theodora, kissing Nell. Theodora's eyes were actually wet. "But look here what Azalea sent you. Two dozen of her special cornbread sticks. They'll need to be heated up. Sicca, where did you find that suit? It's exactly what I wanted, but who can ever find anything out at that new mall?"

"Dowling ran me down to Atlanta and gave me carte blanche at Rich's," said Sicca. "There's a lot to be said for the dividends of repentance."

The two old friends hooted with laughter and drifted toward Nell's house arm in arm. Two more cars pulled up: Lucy Bell and Jean Lewis in Lucy's new Toyota; and Gertrude Jones, who lived in the country, in her wartime Jeep.

"I've brought the place cards," Wickie Lee told Nell, offering her a Yardley's Old English Lavender soap box at just the moment Nell was preparing to greet the new arrivals. "They're in here. Want to look at them?"

"I certainly do. Let me just—" Nell heard the phone ringing inside the house.

"I'll get it," shouted Theodora, who had reached the house with Sicca. "You go on and greet your guests!"

"Nell, you look wonderful!" cried the fresh chorus of women. Lucy Bell had a new suit that looked dangerously like Sicca's new suit from Rich's; Jean Lewis, glowing in the superiority of her youth, carried a library copy of *The Scarlet Letter* crammed with page markers torn from yellow legal paper; Gertrude Jones was still in her trusty old tweeds and had mud on her shoes.

"Oh, aren't they sweet!" cried Lucy Bell; for Wickie Lee had the top of the box off and was showing the place cards to anyone who would look. "What a darling idea! A little pearl stuck on a sprig of evergreen."

"That's really symbolic. You caught the spirit of the book," said Jean Lewis, who wasn't much older than Wickie Lee. (Nell wondered what Jean told her husband about the meetings when she got home. Did she say, "I do it for your sake, darling; otherwise those old biddies would drive me mad"?)

"Very simple and tasteful," said Gertrude Jones, also admiring the cards. "Oh look, here's mine. You used one of those lettering pens, didn't you? I always think simplicity is best in the long run. Look how Norman architecture has held up."

"Thank you," said Wickie Lee with equanimity. "They aren't real pearls. We bought them at Woolworth's."

"It's any day now, isn't it, precious?" Lucy Bell asked Wickie Lee, who stood perfectly still until Lucy had finished hugging her. "You must be so excited. I remember how excited I was, even after all these years. I hope you've been doing your exercises like a good girl. And Theodora says you all saw a movie—"

"We walked out," said Wickie Lee, putting the lid back on her place cards. "As soon as it got messy, we left. I don't need a nasty movie like that to help me have my baby."

"It was Grace!" called Theodora from the house. "She said

not to wait lunch. She stepped in a pothole on the way to her car and thinks she sprained a ligament; she's at the hospital waiting for an X ray. She'll be here when she can!"

"Won't you all come in?" said Nell, to get the show on the road. "Come on, Wickie Lee, I'll show you where the cards go. They are very nice." She had to stop herself from putting her arm around Wickie's shoulders as they walked beside each other to the house; the stoic diminutiveness of the child, rounded with incipient motherhood, touched Nell today. But she saw that Wickie Lee didn't like being handled, and she respected that.

Lunch was madness. Nell expected this. She moved like a gracious robot, refilling coffee cups and passing rolls and Azalea's corn-bread sticks, which went fast. Sicca Dowling told a funny story about old Mrs. Wyatt, who went downtown to buy a maternity bra at age eighty, because her doctor told her it would be more comfortable with her pacemaker. Several of the members exchanged glances as Wickie Lee carefully cut off the tips of her cold asparagus, pushed them to one side of her plate, and ate only the stems. Gertrude Jones stepped outside on the screened-in porch to smoke. She exhaled through the screen and the smoke drifted onto the top blossoms of Nell's Japanese cherry, in bloom in the garden below. After Rachel Stigley had died of cancer of the sinuses, all the Book Club members but Gertrude had stopped smoking. At twelve-fifteen, Grace Hill hobbled in triumphantly with a taped-up foot and regaled the others with stories of the unbelievable inefficiencies of the emergency room. Nell served the cake, and, after the ohs and ahs died, Nell saw Lucy Bell, the current secretary, jot down a few words in her notebook: a description of the cake, to be read in the minutes at the next meeting. Sicca, who had taken a fancy to Wickie Lee, who sat beside her, asked her if she'd heard about the Pole, the Jew, and the Negro who went to heaven. Wickie Lee said she hadn't. "Well," began Sicca, "Saint Peter told them they'd each have to spell a word before they could get in—"

Nell took the coffeepot back to the kitchen. She had another one ready on the back burner. "—the Pole said, 'C-A-T,' and Saint Peter said, 'Okay, you can go on in—' "

Nell dipped a piece of asparagus into the leftover home-made mayonnaise and ate it head first; she wished she could start loading the dishwasher. "—the Jew said, 'R-A-T,' and Saint Peter said, 'Okay, you can go on in—' "

Nell had stashed two of Azalea's corn-bread sticks under a dishtowel. She bolted one and then the other and washed down the remaining sweet, greasy crumbs with a glass of water from the tap. "—'and now,' said Saint Peter to the Negro, 'it's your turn. Can you spell "chrysanthemum"?' "

Nell came back with the fresh pot of coffee just as the laughter was abating.

"In my day," said Theodora, "there was another version of that joke. He had to spell 'parthenogenesis.' "

"That's strange," said young Jean Lewis, who tended to be earnest. "Because, actually, 'parthenogenesis' is easier to spell. You can sound it out. It seems to me the words should be getting easier. Even in the jokes."

"I heard this version from my little shoe-repair man," said Sicca. "He was so pleased with the way he told it that his laughter was just infectious."

"Well," said Wickie Lee, who did not look as if she had laughed, "I can't spell *either* word."

There was a short, baffled silence. Then Nell said, "Ladies, shall we move into the living room?"

There followed an interval of about seven minutes, during which the members repaired to one of the three bathrooms; several dozen gallons of tank water went rushing through the pipes; then, one by one, the members reassembled, with noses repowdered and hairdos set in order.

Wickie Lee, who had been given first chance at the bathroom due to her condition, had claimed Leonard's high-backed wing chair; she seemed scarcely larger than a doll in it.

Theodora, reelected for a third term as president, brought the meeting to order.

Lucy Bell read the minutes from the March meeting. There was an eloquent description of Gracé Hill's cake, shaped like the state of Maryland, with no mention of the fallen inlets Theodora had told Nell about over the phone.

Theodora asked if there was any new business; there wasn't. "Well, I have one little item I'd like us to think about," she said. "Girls, we are diminishing. This past year, we lost Rachel Stigley. Montgomery Starnes has gone to live with her daughter in Texas, and I think we have to face the sad fact that though Portia Jane Woodcock has made remarkable progress after her stroke, she will never be an active member again. We have, in effect, three empty spaces, whick I think we ought to fill with . . . bright new faces. Young faces. After all, if this Club doesn't survive, who is going to research *us* when the Tricentennial comes around?"

Everybody, except Wickie Lee, who looked preoccupied, laughed.

"I therefore move that we establish a committee for new membership and that Jean Lewis, *our* youngest face, be put in charge."

The members clapped. They voted unanimously for Theodora's motion. Jean Lewis blushed and said earnestly she'd do her best to have a slate of potential new members by the next meeting.

Theodora should have been a politician, thought Nell; she knows just when to give, after she's taken away. Now Jean Lewis's feathers are calmed about her Rabbi's-wife book's being scratched at the last minute.

"If there is no further business, I move that we proceed to the discussion of Mr. Hawthorne's fascinating novel, which many people agree is the first American masterpiece." Theodora paused, as if she could not quite bring herself to relinquish her hold on the group. "And it's going to be especially rewarding to compare the novel with the series we've just finished watching on TV. Who would like to begin?"

Jean Lewis was busily leafing through her library copy, consulting tiny notes written on the yellow strips of paper. Everyone waited. "What I found particularly rewarding," she began in an earnest voice that made it inconceivable that she should be parodying Theodora's pet word, "was my own opportunity to compare the two *books*. I mean the book we had first planned to read, *Rachel the Rabbi's Wife*, with *The Scarlet Letter*. What struck me particularly was that both these books are about the same thing: a strong-minded, independent young woman living inside a repressive, patriarchal society."

"That girl's eyes on TV were such an uncanny blue," Lucy Bell was heard murmuring to Sicca Dowling. "Was she wearing contacts, do you think?"

"Maybe she was high on something," said Sicca, a little too loudly. She had stepped out to her car again when the other members had been freshening up.

Several members laughed, and Wickie Lee, frowning, wriggled in her chair as if she were uncomfortable. Jean Lewis half shut her eyes and hardened her jaw.

Nell the Hostess said, "That's a very good point, Jean. Or, to put it another way: Can the individual spirit survive the society in which it has to live?" There now, Jean looked mollified and Nell could report to Cate that she had quoted her.

"Perhaps I'm out of turn," said Grace Hill, who often prefaced her opinions with this phrase, "but I thought it was more of a love story. An *unhappy* one, of course, in that Puritan setting, but—"

"I didn't watch the programs," said Sicca. "I'm always conked out before those prime-time shows. But I did read the book, years and years ago, when I still had all my brain cells, and it seemed to me it was about people who enjoyed wallowing in their exquisite guilt."

"Oh nonsense, Sicca," boomed Theodora. "We read that book together, when we were at the Spenser School. You cried like a baby. You wanted it something awful for Hester and Dimmesdale to run away on that ship."

"There you go again, Thea, creating memories out of whole cloth because you know you're safe. You know my memory's awful. Well, even if I did want them to get off, they didn't. He died and she spent the rest of her life wallowing in exquisite guilt. . . ." Because they were such old friends, Sicca and Theodora felt perfectly comfortable fussing in public. It was almost as if they felt others were privileged to be allowed to hear.

"Excuse me," cried young Jean Lewis. "I simply must take issue with you, Sicca. Hester Prynne did not spend the rest of her life wallowing in guilt. She came back to that community of her own free will and helped a lot of women with their problems. She was the brightest, most positive force that community had!"

"Speaking of bright, didn't you all feel the television made everything *too* bright?" inquired Gertrude Jones. "I mean visually. The atmosphere was more like a Gypsy camp. There were too many colors. They did violence to Hawthorne's stern little Puritan setting."

"Wickie honey, I wish you'd tell us some of your thoughts," said Theodora. To the group, she explained, "Wickie Lee was extremely moved by that last episode. We neither of us wanted it to be over, did we, Wickie? Afterward we got out the book and I read the conclusion aloud and we both cried."

"Maybe you're confusing that with your 'memory' of me crying at Spenser," said Sicca dryly.

"I for one would love to hear Wickie's thoughts," said Grace Hill effusively. "Why, I mean, especially in your—er—" Realizing she had gone too far, Grace wildly backtracked but found all her exits closed. She bravely pursued, "I mean to say, there are such interesting parallels. Both of you young girls—er, alone—and—"

Theodora cut her off. "Let's let Wickie Lee speak for herself," she said sweetly, with a dark look at Grace.

Wickie Lee had been shifting more than ever in her chair since she had received notification she was expected to speak. Nell's heart went out to her now as she eased herself forward in Leonard's big chair and fidgeted with her hands a little. As she spoke, she kept her eyes down on her extended belly.

"Well, I loved her," she said in her small, flat voice. "I loved him—Dimmesdale—too. He had such a sad, beautiful face. I felt so sorry for them." She wriggled in her chair and frowned. "But I felt sorrier for him. He lost everything. But she had—"

The girl's face contorted. Oh Lord, thought Nell, she's going to cry. How cruel of us to put her on display like this. What can I say to help her out?

But at that moment, Wickie Lee gave an exclamation of distress and lurched awkwardly out of the chair. A puddle of water was forming on the rug at her feet.

"She's broken her waters!" cried Lucy Bell.

"She couldn't have!" said Theodora. "The doctor said the fifteenth of April. This is only the seventh."

Lucy gave a wild laugh, the likes of which Nell had never heard from her. "Theodora, there's some things even the doctor doesn't have control of. When baby's ready, baby *comes*."

Though it lasted scarcely longer than a second, Nell would never forget that frozen scenario in her living room: Wickie Lee, eyes round with fright, or surprise, clasping her belly with both hands and looking down at the rug; the women, some sitting, some who had risen in excitement or confusion; and—across it all, *above* it all, somehow—Theodora Blount and Lucy Bell, their gazes locked in the mutual animosity they had managed to hide from their friends for decades: Theodora could never forgive Lucy, that nobody from Spooks Branch Road, for robbing her of her rightful partner and any children they might have had; and Lucy hated Theodora for patronizing her and lording it over her, even though she, Lucy, had "won."

"Oh!" gasped Wickie Lee, with an intake of breath. The scenario came unfrozen then.

"How long have you been having contractions?" asked Nell, going to the girl.

"Well, I felt—oh!—these twinges starting at lunch, but"— the girl turned so pale she was almost blue—"this is a right smart one."

"Call the ambulance, somebody!" ordered Theodora. "Grace, go call the ambulance."

"Hold on a minute, Grace," said Nell. "We don't have time

for the ambulance to get here. Grace, you call the hospital and tell them we're coming, and ask them to locate the doctor. Wickie Lee, sit down in that chair and start counting aloud and tell me as soon as the next one starts. I'll just get some towels and we're off. Whose car are we taking?"

"But I'll ruin the chair," said Wickie Lee.

"It was my husband's chair and he would have insisted you sit right down."

"Towels!" cried Theodora. "You mean she might have it in the *car*? Shouldn't we call at least . . . a taxi? I know I'm too upset to drive."

"My waters didn't break till hours after the contractions started," Lucy Bell was telling someone, sotto voce.

"Sicca, do me a favor," said Nell. "Pour everybody a drink. You know where our liquor cabinet is. Grace, go on and make that call. Theodora, when I bring my car out of the garage, you and Wickie Lee be ready."

". . . sixteen . . . seventeen . . . eighteen . . . nineteen . . ." counted Wickie Lee.

"You know best," said Theodora humbly. "I'll do whatever you say."

They were settled in the car before Wickie Lee had another contraction, and well onto the expressway before the third. "Don't worry, Wickie, we're going to make it," said Nell. "First babies usually do give a little leeway, even when they're eager to get here, like yours is."

The girl started to laugh, then gasped.

"Remember to pant, darling," said Theodora, who sat in the backseat, holding Wickie Lee's hand. And the older woman stuck out her tongue like a dog and set the example.

Grace had done her job well. An orderly with a wheelchair awaited them, and a nurse informed them that the doctor had answered his beeper; he had called in from the St. Dunstan's Forest golf course and was on his way.

"You all go on ahead," said Theodora at the admissions desk. "I'll take care of these dreary forms." She seemed anxious to get rid of Nell.

But as Nell followed Wickie Lee and the orderly to the elevator, she overheard Theodora dictating to the woman who was typing the form: "Wickie Lee Blount. No, B-L-O-U-N-T. That's right. She's my little niece and we'd like her to have a private room. . . ."

Wickie Lee, in the throes of another contraction, had overheard, too. She rolled her eyes up at Nell. "It was her idea," she said, as if she felt called on to explain Theodora's whims.

Two hours later, Nell drove Theodora back to the house to pick up her car. Wickie Lee had, with very little fuss, given birth to a seven-and-a-half-pound baby girl. Theodora was crowing with pride. She told Nell how Wickie Lee had scorned the movie the doctor made them go to. "Wickie said to me, 'I don't want to watch this naked woman with her socks on any longer. You're not supposed to see it from the outside. You're supposed to feel it from the inside.' And just look how she came through! And the baby almost as big as she is!"

"Will they be staying on with you?" Nell asked. They would soon be passing the spot where she and Leonard had gone off the road on December 16; she was driving the same car—all they'd had to do was hammer out the roof and realign the wheels. Her broken rib had mended and she had resumed her social life. Existence went on.

"As long as they like," said Theodora, with feeling.

Back at the house, Nell found that the women had washed and put away all the dishes. There was a note to Nell from Lucy Bell that she had shampooed the rug but that she was afraid there was nothing to be done about the water mark on the linen upholstery of the wing chair. Sicca, who had told Theodora she'd stay to "congratulate" her, was stretched out on the sofa, with a snifter of brandy on the table beside her. Nell made fresh coffee and the three of them sat around, discussing childbirth. Theodora could join in with the rest; she said she felt as though she'd been through it herself. It began to get dark and Theodora said she had to get back to the hospital "to check on my chicks." Nell walked Sicca to her car in the soft spring evening. "You're sure you're able to drive, Sicca?" "Honey, I'm a walking coffeepot. I haven't been this sober at this time of day for years."

That evening Nell decided to call Cate, who would be able to appreciate the many amusing and significant ramifications of such a day. But, though Cate seemed pleased that her mother had taken the initiative in phoning, she did not respond with the satirical verve that such an account would ordinarily evoke from her. She sounded depressed and—for the first time that Nell could recall—bitter. She listened to Nell's recounting of the highlights of the day, laughed without much enthusiasm at the expected places, and said at last, when Nell was speculating on the future of Wickie Lee and the baby under Theodora's roof: "Wickie Lee is the Third World, and I hope Theodora gets the full benefit of her."

Then Cate asked her mother if she had been following the nuclear reactor disaster at Three Mile Island.

"I've been keeping *up*, of course," said Nell. "But it was my impression they have things more or less under control. Isn't that your impression?"

"My impression is that we're never told the truth about these things," said Cate. "I'm not sure I'd even want to bring up a child in this day and age. And some goddam huge piece of spacecraft's due to fall out of the sky on us this summer." Nell did not care for the gloomy satisfaction in Cate's tone.

"Where are you going for Easter?" she asked brightly.

"To Chicago on Easter Monday, for a couple of days."

"Oh! Are you going to do something with that nice man you've been dating?"

"No, I'm going to do something all by myself," said Cate.

"Oh?" inquired Nell. In the space she left for Cate to elucidate, she could hear another conversation out there in the airwaves. It sounded like businessmen. Finally Nell said, "I used your quote in our meeting today."

"My quote?"

"About *The Scarlet Letter* being about the individual spirit trying to survive in society."

"Oh yes." Cate laughed harshly. "The individual spirit."

"Well," said Nell, beginning to tire of Cate's intransigence. "It's been a long day. You call me when you feel like it."

"I will, Mother." A little surge of contriteness. "I really do appreciate your calling to tell me all your news."

"Have fun in Chicago," said Nell.

She heard Cate's intake of breath and thought she wanted to say something more. But "Good night, Mother" was all that came.

Nell went into the living room to turn off the lamps. Yes, there would be a faint water mark on Leonard's chair. He would not mind it. She extinguished the lights and stood in the quiet room, which bore no other trace of the day's hectic activities. She thought with tenderness of Wickie Lee in her private room getting used to the fact that she had a small creature utterly dependent on her. At this moment, Nell felt closer to Wickie Lee than to Cate. As she went up to bed, she said aloud, almost angrily, "Wickie Lee is not 'the Third World.' She is a mother."

7.

ROLLINGSTONE

When Cate, as a young wife of twenty-three, flew from the States to Ruislip Air Force Base to join Pringle, she was subjected to the most thorough physical exam in her life. For the better part of a day, she was conveyed down an assembly line of Air Force doctors. They made her run up and down a little portable staircase and then listened to her heart; they shut her in a booth with earphones and told her to press a button the minute she heard a high-pitched sound; they asked her to sit at a desk and give an oral account of her life so far (she had the good sense to be brief and euphemistic); they X-rayed her chest, shone lights into her eyes and ears, hit her kneecaps with a little silver hammer. Last on the agenda was the gynecological examination: an inscrutable older doctor had palpated each of her breasts with grim thoroughness, as if they had been mined with tiny explosive devices; then he switched on a goose-necked lamp and disappeared like an old-fashioned photographer under the sheet that covered her raised legs. She felt him locate each ovary and, one hand in- side her and one hand outside, squeeze them until she could feel their shape.

After she was dressed, he sat her down in his office and, using a small female doll with its insides exposed, explained the reproductive process. Cate thought it best to listen attentively. When he was finished he told her that her "equipment" was in excellent condition and inquired if she would be starting a family while stationed at Ruislip. Cate told him she and Pringle did not want to have children just yet. When the doctor ascertained Cate used a diaphragm, he seemed to approve (whether because he thought it safest or because he thought it proper for her to take the responsibility, she wasn't sure); and then he gave her some extra advice concerning her chosen method of contraception. Though nothing was foolproof, he said, there were ways to be *additionally* careful. One was to insert a dollop of contraceptive jelly at the tip of the uterus and around the rim of the diaphragm, in addition to the tablespoon *in* the diaphragm; two was, never have intercourse a second time without a second application of jelly into the vagina; and three was—he could not stress this enough for "active married women"—hold your diaphragm up to the light, good strong daylight, at least once a month, and examine it for thin spots. ("Some women allow their diaphragms to get thin as Belgian lace and then wonder why they've conceived.")

Seventeen years later, Cate was doing just this: holding her diaphragm up to the early-morning sun streaming through her window. This was her sixth or seventh diaphragm. Over the years, the compacts in which they came got progressively cheaper-looking, just like the covers of American passports. There was probably some interesting moral significance to be derived from this comparison, but on the early April day in question, Cate felt too demoralized to do much symbolic devising.

The little rubber cup passed the Belgian-lace test; there were no thin spots. So, either she had been careless about inserting it or else the manufacturers of the jelly had decided to cut costs and put less spermatocide in; you read about such corporate duplicities every day now. But whether from her own carelessness or from corporate neglect, the result was the same: Cate was eight weeks pregnant.

When she had missed a period at the end of February, she had passed quickly over the suspicion of pregnancy. She had never been pregnant before in her life; why should she be now?

Early menopausal symptoms seemed more likely. And after that talk with Mother, when Nell had said one of the first signs was you missed a period, she began to look at the positive side of menopause. No more birth control; no more standing in front of a classroom and having a sudden liquid feeling that reminded you, too late, you should have brought Tampax today; no more paranoia and bad temper just before your period. As for all the terrible side effects that were supposed to go with menopause, Cate was sure you had those because you were told you were supposed to. She planned not to have any of them. If, by any chance, she were to have a hot flash, she would open a window. If she wept, she'd weep. But she would not feel her life was over, she would feel—on the contrary—she was entering the stage where she would be free to be herself and nothing but herself. She would not have to be anybody's mother or grandmother. She would not have to be Anyman's idea of "a real woman." After she had passed through menopause, if a particular man were drawn to her, she would know it was for her own self and not what her body could produce for him.

During March, Cate had prepared so well for menopause that she had been startled on several occasions to come across her reflection in a window or mirror. Who was this blond young woman in jeans striding fiercely along, her chin stuck out against the wind? Where was that wise, mellowed person of middle years who had outlived the treacheries of her body and was loved and admired for herself? She was almost disappointed to have lost touch with this reassuring future self.

Who knew? All those years when she was spending her hard-earned money on birth control, she might have been infertile; she might have had something wrong with her "equipment" that even the ovary-squeezing Air Force doctor had failed to detect.

When she missed her second period, she got scared. She loitered in a drugstore, near the shelf where they kept do-it-yourself pregnancy-test kits. When the duggist's back was turned she picked up one of the kits and read the instructions. If it was positive, she would have to see a doctor, anyway; if it was negative . . . how could she be sure? It might be a false negative. She went home and consulted the yellow pages and made an appointment with a gynecologist named Dr. Eric Happe, because the name seemed a good omen. But after he had examined her and told her the news, it became clear that his ideas and hers of what her happiness should be did not coincide. Trying to maintain a professional neutrality, he nevertheless managed to let her know he was a Catholic, the father of six children. He advised her to consult a family-planning service; he was sorry, he could be of no further help to her. "I wouldn't wait too long," he said. "His brain waves can already be measured, you know."

"That sadistic son of a bitch. What an irresponsible thing to say! *Cochon!*" snarled Ann, Cate's only woman friend in the state of Iowa. Her nostrils dilated and she almost achieved a flush, which was an extreme for cool, orderly Ann.

"It was the one thing he thought could get to me," said Cate. "He probably took one look at me and decided, 'Academic type. I'll go for the brain. She wouldn't be moved by the mention of tiny little hands.' "

"I'm glad you had the sense to stop by here. I can put you out of your misery at once. You don't even have to let your fingers walk through the yellow pages. I know an excellent clinic in Chicago. Very near the Palmer House. I've been there twice. Would you believe I fouled up twice within one year? Though one of those times wasn't completely my fault. My ex-husband sabotaged me. His sick little idea of keeping the marriage together."

"Is it very expensive?" asked Cate.

"Reasonable. Two-fifty. In New York, you can get one at the Eastern Women's Center for a hundred. Or at least you could four years ago. But New York's too far to go. Your air fares would eat up the saving. My advice is, we book you at my Chicago clinic for the Easter break. You stay at the Palmer House and pamper yourself—"

"But the Easter break is two weeks away, Ann. I'm eight weeks gone."

"I've heard of people having them up to eighteen weeks. Or so much as twenty-four, only that's pretty stupid. But you'll be ten weeks and ten weeks is nothing. I had my first when I was sixteen weeks. That was back in the Dark Ages when you had to locate a butcher and pay him a thousand dollars in cash, though. I was really scared. I let it go so long because I was hoping it would go away by itself."

"I know," said Cate. "I was even hoping it was menopause. That way, I would still be going along with nature's way."

"Don't get qualmish about this," warned Ann. "You wouldn't get qualmish about a D and C, would you? Well, this isn't even a D and C. Up to twelve weeks, they can do it with suction. It's nothing."

"I wish he hadn't said that about its brain," said Cate. "I mean, if he has brain waves, that means he's *thinking*, doesn't it? What kinds of thoughts?"

Ann delivered an impressive set of French expletives. "In my opinion, that doctor did something much more immoral when he said that to you than he would have done by removing the little growth inside you that's about the size of a grape. The power of brainwashing! You called it a "he," did you know that? Who was the father? Or sperm donor, I should say. It's best to keep this impersonal. No, forget I asked that." She waved her graceful hand, as if brushing away a fly. "It's none of my business."

"It's Roger Jernigan," Cate told her, without hesitation. Any signs of curiosity in Ann should be encouraged. "And, if the doctor counted right, it was a dead hit. The first time we ever went to bed together." Cate started laughing; she was a little out of control. "That would be his style. All enthusiastic force. Pushing right ahead." She veered into whimsy: "Maybe he learned it from those little bugs he can't spray to death anymore. They've evolved, you know. They're immune to his chemicals. Maybe his brainy little sperm sent brain messages to the brainy little bugs and the bugs told them how to resist my Ortho-Jel."

"Let's have a drop of Remy Martin," suggested Ann, who, though insular and incurious, did have an active compassion for the few people she liked. "Then I'll call the Chicago clinic. I'm sure they'll remember me. And we'll book you in at the Palmer House."

"I can't afford the Palmer House." Cate had stopped laughing and had begun to shake.

"You have a credit card, don't you? We'll charge it to that and then when the bill gets here, I'll lend you the money. It's not that much. Believe me, Cate, what you have to insure against is any suggestion of the sordid at a time like this. You are going to a clean, first-class clinic—it has *Vogue* and *The New Yorker* on its waiting-room tables; you'll have a medical examination; then you'll go back to your hotel and order yourself a bottle of wine from room service, or go down and have dinner at Trader Vic's; the next morning, you go back to the clinic, lie down on a table, just like for an ordinary annual checkup; they may give you a local; then the uterus is dilated and they hook up a little tube, and—*whoosh*—just like turning on the vacuum cleaner."

"Oh God," said Cate, burying her face in her hands.

Cate replaced the diaphragm in its plastic compact of streaky blue. She wondered when she would be needing it again. Maybe not for a long time. The appetite for lovemaking had gone out of her. It appalled her that her few times of pleasure and fellow comfort with Jernigan should have landed her in such murky moral waters. Today was Saturday, one of the first decent spring days here so far. Easter vacation did not begin till next Thursday. Her abortion was not until Easter Tuesday. Ten days to go, counting today. She was having second thoughts about the leisurely way she had decided to go about this: "booking in" coolly, as if she were going to have her hair restyled and didn't mind waiting, as long as she could get into a really good place, where they had *Vogue* and *The New Yorker* on their waiting-room tables. Of course, the reason behind the wait was that she would have a whole week to recover: classes would not resume till the following Monday. And ten weeks was "nothing" now. Ann had assured her of this; the woman on the phone who had taken down details of her medical history had assured her of it. This was the Modern Age. Medical technology, enlightened legislation, frequent airline flights, and the amenities of a good nearby hotel made it possible for the professional woman to sandwich her first-trimester abortion between classes and have a whole week off to pamper herself against infection and deal with any remorse.

But between now and Easter Tuesday was a special kind of Hell. Cate felt she was keeping a secret from her own body. Here it was, going happily along, thinking it was preparing for the future of the baby. There was no way she could send it a signal saying, You are wasting your efforts. And that was another thing. Her body seemed to have taken so well to its new state. Between her first and second missed periods, one reason she was so sure she wasn't pregnant was that she manifested none of those symptoms she had heard women complain about. Lydia had been unable to keep anything on her stomach for the first three months with Leo; and with Dickie, she had begun with a deadly lassitude and having to go to the bathroom every fifteen minutes. Cate had experienced nothing but a sense of well-being and a tenderness in her breasts, which she always got before her periods, anyway. She felt a certain arrogance in her own good health, that she was capable of such a model pregnancy.

But on this Saturday, when she had to mark time for ten more days, she determined that her best plan for the good of everyone (herself, her fooled body, and the "it" slightly larger than a grape, with brain waves) would be to immerse herself in nonreflective activity. She gathered up every item of clothing that could be put through the Laundromat machine; she packed herself a lunch; and off she drove into the Iowa spring morning, her chin tipped up an extra notch, singing along with the song on her car radio.

There was therapy as well as a housewifely sense of accomplishment in folding and stacking dozens of warm, clean-smelling personal garments: jeans and blouses worn soft and faded from long use; her sprigged flannel nightgowns; her colorful collection of bikini panties. Today she even liked her old Fieldcrest towels, with the white CPS monogram on the royal blue. The fact that these towels from her first trousseau had held up so well gave her a solid sense of being able to survive her own past. And even to carry it with her into her future—the parts of it that were useful.

She had lunch in the sun at her favorite city park. The tips of the deciduous trees were red with bud, but it would be another few weeks before their leaves unfurled. She missed the South most at this time of year; its earlier spring. There were a few children playing close to their parents. Cate narrowed her eyes at them and waited to feel something that would make her rush to the nearest pay phone and cancel her appointment at the private Chicago clinic. But none of the children appealed to her. They were just not her type of people. Thank goodness. She could lift her face up to the sun and take another bite of chicken sandwich and count her blessings. There still were some. She was healthy, she was smart, she was free; she was not even old. How many people in the world today could tote up four such blessings?

She thought about Roger Jernigan. He was a busy man, but ever since that first night he'd kept her informed about his movements. "I'll be in Vail for six days, with Sunny." "I'm off to LA for some meetings; guess I'll take you-know-who to lunch. She's invited Jody to spend Easter with her." "I'm driving up to Ames to check out a few things at Ag Research. I went to college there, you know. I don't guess you'd care to drive with me. Oh hell, that's right. That's your Drama day. Well, Jody will have the benefit of you, at least."

Right now he was in Washington, meeting with his old enemies at the Environmental Protection Agency. ("Progress has created stranger bedfellows. But one thing's for damned sure. The world will go on eating. So I guess we'll have to work out something between us.")

He was attracted to her. He enjoyed her mind. He liked lying beside her in bed and testing her reaction to various subjects. The more independently and assertively she expressed herself, the better he seemed to like it. Some of her ideas were strange and unworkable, he told her, but they made him see that there were more worlds than his. He liked that: there were more worlds. He told her she was "classy." He once asked her, just as he was covering her body with his own, "What are you doing with an old country hick like me?" But the playful, confident green eyes sent a message that contradicted his professed humility.

Though his physical type did not attract her, she responded to his physical presence. She could not be aesthetically objective about him when he looked at her or touched her. His sheer personal energy commanded her response. And it impressed her that a man so busy in his own world (which many men would have thought was the only world) took her so seriously. It made her like herself and him better. And each time he had come to her apartment on this street he already owned, he had shown a touching respect. He took everything in, wanted to know where things were kept, asked questions about how she lived. She understood he was trying to imagine her in her own world and that her different way of life, her independence, both baffled and charmed him. "That's pretty. I like that," he would say, picking up a trilobite fossil she used as a paperweight. "Did you find that yourself? Where?" "That's a nice picture"—of her Georgia O'Keeffe print, *The Lawrence Tree*—"I could be comfortable with that, myself." "Did your mother make you this pillow? You made it? You embroidered all those little flowers?" "What do they charge you for this place? Hmm. Not too bad. They could have at least given you a bigger TV. You watch it much? Where do you sit when you grade papers? Are you reading all of those books on that table?" "Do you cook for yourself when you're alone?" "Has anybody in your family been to visit you here?"

He kept a bed for himself at the plant and slept over when he had early appointments, rather than drive the forty miles up and back from the castle. "The castle," he called it, in the same tone as you would say "the cottage." Architecturally it was a castle, that was all there was to it. He had spent several nights with her in February, while his scrubbers were being installed, but he always left early, before dawn. "I don't want to bump into your landlord." "I don't care if you do," said Cate (who did, a little). "Besides, you're his landlord now, in a sense." "All the more reason," muttered Jernigan, wrinkling his nose disapprovingly at the sock he was putting on for the second day.

There was no getting around it. Roger Jernigan was a nice man. But did she love him? He had come into her life when her self-esteem was ailing and her defenses were low, and he had made her feel safe and appreciated. She was pretty sure he wasn't in love with her, either. He liked to take her out to dinner; he liked to talk to her; he liked to go to bed with her in her quaint lair with its brave starkness and its feminine touches. He was, perhaps, a little flattered that "a woman of intellect" should find him interesting. But he had never invited her to his home—or castle, rather. After their first dinner, he had never again suggested that she might meet the mysterious Sunny sometime. Probably he was the sort of man who draws a firm boundary between the territory of his mistress and the territory of his family life.

Stupid word, "mistress." It didn't apply, really.

But, whatever she was to him, she had made up her mind to keep the pregnancy to herself. He was never going to know about it. She thought she knew him well enough to know it would make him feel sad; he'd already had enough problems with children. He was not to know. And then she would have to be chaste for a while after the abortion; Ann had explained that. So that would probably be the end of things between them: he would think she no longer wanted to go to bed with him. That was a pity. Though her present circumstances had dampened desire, she *had* enjoyed sheltering beneath his solid warmth. "I want to postpone the inevitable for you a little longer," he had said, that first night. He had meant the cold. Well, they had got each other through the winter. Now there was another inevitable to be faced, and he could not help her postpone that. All his money and warmth could not protect her from having to make the lonely decision she had come to.

She put the crumpled trash from her solitary picnic back into the brown bag, like a good citizen, and left the park. It was still quite early in the day, but the sun was not as warm as it looked. God only knew how she was going to get through the rest of the weekend. But she knew she would see it through somehow, even if she had to resort to sleeping it through. Two things comforted her. Though, as Jernigan would say, they made strange bedfellows. She was as proud of her stoic decision to keep her condition from the man who had helped cause it as she was of her wholesome, symptomless pregnancy.

She managed to sleep away the rest of the afternoon. She watched the evening news. Dire ramifications continued to multiply from the accident at Three Mile Island. Now everybody knew what the inside of a nuclear reactor looked like, and how it could go wrong. But it had taken a near catastrophe—or maybe it would turn out to have been a slow-blooming catastrophe—to make people pay attention.

Maybe it was already too late for everybody. In their greed and shortsightedness, maybe they had set too many things going that were now curling inevitably like boomerangs and heading back, even at this very hour—like those pieces of Skylab due to fall this summer—to do them in.

How could a world know when it still had one more chance, and when it had reached the point of no return?

How could an individual know?

She decided to get drunk, and opened a bottle of wine. But, after a few sips, abandoned the idea. Drinking wine had lost its savor for her lately. Now why was that? Nature's way of protecting? What was already booked for extinction.

She considered calling Ann for reassurance. But she knew what Ann would advise. ("Avoid sordidness. Avoid qualmishness. Above all, avoid philosophy. One of our most fundamental rights as women is the right to choose whether or not to have children. That's all the philosophy you need. And stop torturing yourself by picturing a little Einstein in there sending out brain waves. I'd like to send that Dr. Happe a poison-pen letter. He's never had to decide whether or not to have a child.")

And when the phone rang, Cate almost didn't answer because she thought it might be Ann. She had reached the point where she preferred her own individual suffering-through of her experience to listening to sterile assurances from someone who obviously had not suffered in the same way. In the end, curiosity won, and Cate picked up the receiver and it was Nell.

But as the call went on, it seemed more and more like a bad joke. Daddy had died less than four months ago, krypton gases were wafting invisibly across America, and here was Mother, light-headed to the point of being a little silly over the social politics of the Mountain City Book Club. And here she was, Nell's daughter, about to have an abortion, and all Mother could do was speculate on the future of Wickie Lee's seven-and-a-half-pound baby girl which had taken less than three hours to deliver. Of course Cate knew she was not being fair: her mother didn't even know she was pregnant. But she didn't feel like being fair. She felt like bursting into blubbery, childish tears and dumping the whole problem in Nell's lap: "Oh, Mother! What shall I do *now?*"

And when Nell said, "Have fun in Chicago," Cate felt as if the top of her head were going to blow off. She could hardly speak. She heard herself imitating some other daughter's voice as she said, "Good night, Mother." That her mother did not seem to know the difference only reinforced what Cate had suspected all along: Nell would have liked her to be a different daughter.

Cate hung up and waited to go mad. It would have been a relief. Complete abdication. Let others take over. She remembered how she had lost her balance and fallen back into Roger Jernigan's arms. The temptation she had felt to keep on falling. To give up on keeping her stubborn, weary balance and just sink.

What good was she doing anyone by trying to be herself? What good was she doing *herself?*

But, because she was herself, she couldn't stop believing in her future, even at a moment like this. She would probably be believing in her future even as they were lowering her into the grave. Her dry, feverish eyes scanned the room, searching for something that could ratify her existence and shine some light on her future. She sprang off the bed with a cry of relief when she spotted her trusty *I Ching* languishing among other neglected books on her brick-and-board shelves. How could she have overlooked its mysterious potential for instruction for so long? She carried it back to bed as if it were a cherished companion. It was full of strips of paper, note cards, a few envelopes, on which past hexagrams had been recorded. Goodness, here was one of Jake's: *Kuei Mei,* The Marrying Maiden. There was a date on it, March 21, 1967. Oh yes, she remembered what that one had been about. Jake had thrown the coins, shortly after they were married, wanting to know whether he should go into a foreign-car venture with a friend (Jake always asked very literal questions of the old Chinese oracle), and they'd had a fight when he got Six at the Top, which was crammed full of images of violence and failure, which Cate had then tried to convince him were symbolic, not literal. But unfortunately, the language had worked against her. The last sentence of Six at the Top read: "This impious and irreverent attitude bodes no good for a marriage."

Cate got three pennies from her purse, returned to bed, and smoothed the sheet flat. When Jake had asked his literal questions, he had done so with the luxury of genuine old Chinese coins, bought in an antiques shop in San Francisco. Though Cate had only Western coins, she phrased her question in the spirit of the ancient Chinese philosophers. She felt she would receive a better answer that way. They had used the book to discover the truth of a given moment, and thus to decide how to behave in accordance with all the ingredients which made up that moment. So she did not ask anything so literal as "What should I do about Chicago?" She closed her eyes, shook the coins passionately, and asked, "What is my present situation?"

The pennies fell, with muffled clumps, upon the sheet. When she had thrown them six times, she had *Ku* for an answer, Work on What Has Been Spoiled (Decay). Her heart sank as she began to read. *Ku* was the Chinese character for a bowl in whose contents worms were breeding. But then she read on and her spirits lifted a little. The *I Ching* never left you without some hope. Her conditions were bad, but not yet spoiled. She must *work on what had been spoiled.* Oh God, were the ancients backing her up on her Chicago decision? No, she must remember not to be literal. All the *I Ching* could tell you was the truth of the moment. She read further and it told her she did not have fate to blame for her present state of corruption, but rather the abuse of human freedom.

She was looking up her Nine in the Third Place when the phone rang. Nine in the Third Place meant "setting right what has been spoiled by the Father." There would be a little remorse, no great blame. Well, thank you, oracle, for small favors.

It was Jernigan calling from the airport. "I'm back early. We didn't accomplish a damn thing. I've been thinking of your quiet little haven all the way back. I don't suppose I could drop over? Or were you already in bed?"

"I'm in bed with a book. But I'm dressed. As you know, the bed is the only comfortable place in this haven." She heard her jaunty, ironic voice with a bit of mistrust. Why was she encouraging him to believe she was her confident old self as usual? She felt she ought not to want to see him. On the other hand, he was the only person she could think of who actually seemed to admire her for what she was.

"I have to get a bite to eat. Or shall I bring something for both of us?"

"You know what? I'd love a pizza." Suddenly she wanted a pizza more than anything in the world. Chicago and bowls full of writhing worms seemed manageable, if only she could have a pizza. "With pepperoni and sausage and anchovies and green peppers, if that's not too greedy."

Roger Jernigan laughed. "You don't know how nice it sounds after all the pussyfooting I've been through in Washington to hear someone say what they really want. Will that be all? No mushrooms?"

"Oh yes, have them put mushrooms on, too."

"Good. I like mushrooms. Well, expect me in about thirty, forty-five minutes."

She ran herself a bath and pondered over which incense to burn while she soaked. As incense was one of her weaknesses, she could choose among "Lumière," "Song of Bengal," "Purity

Jasmine," "Radha's Devotion," and "Krishna Musk." Philosophy dictated "Lumière," but humor egged her on to "Purity Jasmine."

She lit a stick of "Purity Jasmine" and lowered herself, with a gratified sigh, into the tub. Enough bowls of worms for one day. Now to eat pizza and enjoy being Jernigan's fragrant, intelligent priestess of higher sensibility after his frustrations in bureaucratic Washington. Not a flicker in her face would give away her secret. She looked forward to this exercise in self-effacement.

She put on one of her freshly laundered pairs of jeans and found she couldn't zip them all the way up. Already? She sucked in her stomach and turned sideways to examine herself in the mirror on the back of the door. A bloated look, but no actual curve yet. She put the old jeans back on and wore a white satin shirt outside, like a tunic. She heard his Jeep prowling softly down her deserted little street; there was no time left to pin up her hair.

She opened her door and watched him come trudging up the creaky stairs in dark, shiny shoes. He looked very official in his man-of-the-world clothes. He carried a large, flat cardboard box that emanated irresistible smells. His face was in shadow, but she could tell he was smiling. She realized she envied him. She would have liked to be Jernigan, climbing toward herself, having only the kinds of problems that can be left outside.

"Lady ordered a large pizza with everything on it," he mumbled, trying to sound like a delivery boy. His jaw was etched with five-o'clock shadow and he wore a severe dark pin-stripe suit. He had hunched his shoulders obsequiously to go with his delivery-boy act, but even through his weariness you saw the habit of command. He was no more capable of passing for a delivery boy than he was for the handyman she had briefly mistaken him for when he had first entered her office in his work clothes.

He presented her with the pizza box and gave her a spousely peck. "Peace and sanity, at last," he said. "Your hair looks nice, down like that. I've never seen it down. Of its own accord, I mean." His eyes flashed slyly, reminding her of their intimacies. He handed her the box.

"I've never seen that suit before," she said. There would be the problem of going to bed. He would expect it. But, having given him up in her mind, wouldn't it be unfair to them both to go to bed again? Yet she couldn't tell him she had given him up. Or why.

"It's my East Coast business suit," he said, going into her sanctuary. "If I stay out of strong light, you can't even see my red neck in this suit. But now that you've seen me looking respectable . . ."

He took off his coat and tie and hung them on a wall hook just inside the door. He stood with his hands on his hips, a stocky, solid man in dark trousers and a blue oxford cloth shirt, and surveyed her walls and ceiling with the air of some harassed person who has just entered a cathedral. "Damn. Let's you and me trade places for a month. I'll stay up here and read your books and you be me and go out there and make the decisions I have to make. I'll accept whatever you decide. Just come back at the end of the month and say, 'Roger, I decided to scrap the new Tru-Gro Formula because with these new registration laws it'll cost too much to test. I decided to go ahead with the viral formula instead, even though we won't see any profits from it till the mid-eighties, by which time you might be dead. And, speaking of your son and heir, I decided to allow Jody to pierce his ears.' What do you say? Will you trade places for a month?"

Cate stood looking at him. She was still holding the box, which was very warm on the bottom. She was full of conflicting feelings: resentment that he saw her life as so effortlessly lofty; envy that *his* major decisions concerning profit and loss lay outside himself; affection for the way he at least tried to imagine her life, and for the way he allowed himself to be yoked to the aberrant whims of his younger son. She had also felt an unexpected shock and grief when he had joked of his own death. What did that mean? She decided she would rather not explore it, just now.

"You might not enjoy making some of my decisions," she said. She had meant it to come out with a light irony, but instead it sounded bitter and accusing. This was not at all the gracious level on which she had planned to meet him tonight. Where was her self-control? "I'll just stick this in the oven for a few minutes so it'll be good and hot," she added, in an upbeat "everything's-under-control" voice that suddenly recalled to her how Mother, whose moods ran the gamut from wry humorist to ferocious disciplinarian when she was home alone with the girls, would turn into a smooth hostess the moment Daddy came through the door.

She went into the kitchen and switched on the oven and slid the pizza onto a baking sheet. She got out silverware and cloth napkins and, though she knew he was standing quietly in the doorway watching her, his arms folded across his chest, she affected more concern for a soap spot on one of the wineglasses. She held it up to the light and polished away the spot with a dishcloth. She kept Jernigan at a distance in her thoughts as a safeguard against the capitulation she had felt coming on in the other room. To make herself hard, she remembered her mother's telephone call. How funny that her own "hostess" voice a few moments ago had been an exact duplication of Mother's, even though she, Cate, hadn't been sincere. Maybe, all those years ago, Mother hadn't been sincere, either. They had both been acting out the old scene of getting their man from the outside world to the kitchen, sparing him the household battleground in between. But it had confused her and Lydia, as little girls, when their mother suddenly became smaller and smoother when Daddy came home. Cate's way of steadying herself against the sudden chemical change in the family mixture had been to assume the more ferocious properties of the vanished mother, while Lydia, the baby, had retreated into the quiet, neat shell of herself. Which, Cate saw now, not only kept Lydia from being noticed (i.e., punished) but made Lydia resemble a small copy of the "tamed" mother.

But what good was such knowledge, years too late? That old family configuration was dissolved now. Probably when Cate was ninety-six, she would wake up one morning and all the ambivalent dynamics between herself and the important people in her life would snap into place, like a completed picture puzzle. And she could sit there all by herself and gaze down at the understood patterns and revel in the fruitless wisdom of hind-sight.

"Why wouldn't I?" asked Roger Jernigan, leaning against the doorframe with his arms folded across his chest. "Why wouldn't I like making your decisions?"

"I just don't think you would, that's all." This time she kept out the bitter tone and even managed a nonchalant shrug.

"Try me," he persisted, grinning. "I might be very good at your decisions, just as you might be very good at mine. Beginner's luck, intuition, that kind of thing. Or maybe your decisions are so esoteric you don't have faith in my capacity." He raised his bushy eyebrows, still grinning. He was enjoying this game they had started—*he* had started—as a conversational gambit to ease the transition between their separate existences and the moment when they could lapse into a shared meal, or a shared bed. It was obvious to her that he had missed her bitter undertone and that he was oblivious to how far away from him she had roamed just now. Jake would never have missed these things, even though he had often used them against her; the Resident Poet would have picked them up from her face, read them in the air. Did Jernigan lack the finely tuned radar that could pick up the subtle shift of mood, the small nuance that registered—infinitesimally—a large lie? Despite his curiosity and willingness to imagine her life, was there a thickness in him that would make it easy for her to avoid his scrutiny on what he called "esoteric" levels?

It disappointed her to think so. Yet it made things easier for her if she could discover a fault in him that must keep them apart. Such a fault reinforced her Chicago decision. And having provided herself with this "proof" of his inadequacy, she felt strangely tender toward him, as if she must protect him from the knowledge of his stunning flaw.

"They're not esoteric at all," she said good-humoredly. "They're very practical. They're so practical they're boring." If he persisted, she could always rattle off some *other* decisions that hung in the immediate future: the kinds of decisions that, though annoying, she knew she could make with the upper half of her mind.

"Well? Try me," he persisted.

"Oh, I ask myself whether I should try to find another apartment, since this one's going to be torn down, assuming I'll have a job here next fall. The President has been evasive. He offers hope but no contracts. Several of us have been to see him. Or I ask myself whether I shouldn't be getting rid of everything but what I can pack into my car, come the end of May, so I can drive right off after I've turned in my grades. And if so, should I drive east or west? And whose hospitality can I impose on while I try to find an opening at another college that's just about to go under." She had achieved her old mocking irony and grew more cheerful as she spoke, doing a graceful knee bend to remove the pizza from the oven and transfer it to a large, round ceramic platter. She poured his glass full of wine, hers half-full so he wouldn't notice she'd gone off it, and waved him graciously to his place at the table. "So you see?"—she helped him to the first slice of pizza—"my decisions offer neither the excitement of big business nor the novelty of Jody's earrings. Does he want to pierce both ears, by the way, or just one? There's a difference, you know."

"He said both. At least, I think he did. But he'll do what he wants. When he goes to California to visit his mother next week, she'll no doubt encourage him. I'm sure he asked me only for form's sake. Or to get a rise out of me. He knows I can't fill the holes back in." He surveyed his cutlery thoughtfully, remembered to spread his napkin in his lap, and began cutting up his slice of pizza with a knife and fork. "What do you mean about there being a difference?"

"Well, there's a complex system, it seems. Depending on whether you wear two earrings, or one, and in which ear, it's supposed to signal your sexual preference. Or preferences."

Jernigan groaned. "I guess I'll just wait and be surprised." When he saw that she was eating her pizza from her hand, he put down his knife and fork. "Think I'll join you with the fingers."

"It's the only way, isn't it?"

They both ate silently, a little greedily. She poured him more wine as soon as his glass was empty.

"You're not drinking your wine," he noted.

"Oh yes I am." She picked up her glass and took a showy sip. "There. I'm drinking my wine." The bitterness was back, she could feel it emanating in thick, dark waves from herself. She looked forward to his leaving.

At last he scrubbed his mouth with the napkin and pushed his plate away from him. "I wouldn't plan on a job at Melanchthon next fall," he said, not looking at her. "That's confidential. It's not to go out of this room. But you and I are friends and I think you should know."

"Well, thank you. That takes care of two decisions. No job at the college, no need to get another place to live. Is the college closing, then?"

He nodded. "But remember, it's confidential."

"All right, but I'm annoyed. Why couldn't the President tell us that? My God, it's April. People need time to write letters for jobs."

"Just be grateful you weren't laid off in December."

"Grateful to *whom?*"

He picked up his napkin, started to fold it, then crumpled it into a ball and threw it down on the table. "Well, dammit, to me. Jody's last semester at Melanchthon College is going to cost me approximately three hundred thousand dollars."

"I suspected you were . . . *helping out,*" said Cate dryly. "But I still don't see why we couldn't know, those of us who have to find jobs for next year, that the college would be closing. The President lied to us. He let us think that there might be a chance."

"That's partly my fault. I told him I'd help out next year if he could find others to carry part of the load. He hasn't found 'em. He's had five months. Damned if I know what he does with his time. Seems to have his head up in the clouds with Jesus. Well, maybe Jesus will come through. But I'm not running a one-man charity show any longer. I want Jody to have his diploma, and I want his class to graduate and have the fun of it. Not feel like they're going down on a sinking ship. I want the college to act like a college right up to the last minute my son graduates from it. If that's selfish or 'devious,' I'm sorry. Like I told you once before, I try to take care of what's mine."

"In other words, you haven't told the President you won't be helping out next year."

"No, I haven't. I'll tell him the day after Jody gets his diploma. If he knows now, he'll start cutting corners. He'll probably cancel the speaker, or something. If I'm running this show till the end of May, I'm running it my way."

"I see," said Cate. She gave him a thin, sarcastic smile. "I'd best keep my mouth shut since you're paying my salary, sir."

Oh good, she had wounded him. He looked up at her, surprised. "I thought we understood each other, Catie. Seems to me we had a similar argument over Mr. Terry and after I explained matters you saw my side. I guess I was wrong."

"We can never understand each other," said Cate bitterly. "And when did you start calling me 'Catie'? Nobody in my life has ever called me 'Catie.' It's not your right. I don't belong to you, even if you are paying my salary."

The bitterness overflowed from her eyes. So much for her exercise in graciousness and self-control. She picked up her wineglass and drained it. She felt the wine hit her stomach and bounce back. Bolting from the chair, she made it to the bathroom just in time.

She spewed forth what seemed gallons of undigested tomatoes and cheese and dough and peppers and sausage and mushrooms. So much for the girl who wanted everything and could tell you what she wanted. So much for satisfying one's greedy appetites. Payment was always demanded. You always had to pay in the end. Weak from vomiting, she struggled from her kneeling position and flushed the toilet. She washed her face and swished toothpaste around in her mouth. She listened and heard nothing. Please God, she prayed, let him be gone. I certainly gave him every reason to leave without saying good-bye.

He was sitting on the edge of her bed when she came out of the bathroom. His shoulders slumped and his face looked old. When he was not feeling confident and in charge, the jaw was rounded and slack. She saw how, if life had gone differently for him and he had not believed in himself, he *could* have looked like someone's handyman. She felt pity and repugnance. Better for him to have gone than for her to see him like this.

"What's this all about, Cate?" he asked. His voice was cold and weary. "You've been acting strange ever since I came in the door. If you didn't want to see me, why didn't you say so on the phone? But you sounded so friendly and then when I got here you acted like we were enemies. Yes, you did. Even before I told you about the college. I may be a simple man, but I'm not that simple. Something's missing in you. You're different. Will you be good enough to tell me what's going on?"

"I was sick," she said, to defend herself against this hard, impersonal tone. He frightened her when the curiosity went out of his eyes and they looked upon her with this weary gaze. He just wanted their business summed up between them so he could cut his losses and go home. "I was sick in the bathroom."

"I know that. I have ears. But why? Is it because you're sick of me?" But here he could not stop the old playfulness from creeping back into his expression. It undid her.

"No, it's because I've become allergic to wine," she said, slowly. She measured her words to the cadence of a stately death march. "I've become allergic to wine because, contrary to what you said about there being something missing in me, something's been added. I *am* different. I'm pregnant."

He got up from the bed. He looked her over, narrowing his eyes as though he were trying to penetrate her womb with X-ray vision. "I know I'm not supposed to ask this, but is it—"

"Yes," said Cate. "I'm old-fashioned. I only have one lover at a time."

"But how in hell—I mean, don't you always use all that paraphernalia?"

"I can't figure it out, either. It shouldn't have happened." She repeated the whimsical joke she had told to Ann, about the sperm becoming immune to the jelly; then wished she hadn't: it sounded lewd. It certainly spoiled the stately death-march mood.

He gave a sharp, joyless laugh. "Nothing's impossible. I gave up thinking I could control nature a long time ago. You can surprise it, or divert it, once in a while, but it always has some surprises of its own."

"Yes," said Cate. They were standing several feet apart, their arms dangling at their sides, like combatants who have lost the zest for any further engagements.

"What should we do?"

"What I'm *going* to do is go to a clinic next week. In Chicago. Over the spring holidays. It's a simple procedure, I'm told. I'm sure I'll be in excellent shape to finish up the semester without cutting any corners." She couldn't resist one little dig.

"That's what you want, then?" Did he sound the slightest bit relieved? She could tell if she could look at his eyes, but somehow she couldn't quite meet them.

"Yes," she said.

"I'm really sorry. I wouldn't have had this happen for the world."

"Well, it did. Besides, it's one half my fault. Takes two, you know."

"The Chicago thing, how much is it going to cost you?" For one horrible moment she was afraid he was going to reach into his back pocket and fish out his wallet. But he was only steadying his back with his hand. Now she did look at his face. He looked deathly tired. He had expected to come up into her sanctuary of truth and light and be washed clean of his manly cares. The human condition suddenly appeared very hopeless to her, and she simply wanted to end this exchange with dignity.

"I'd rather you didn't worry about that. They're very reasonable." She laughed sharply. "They've got to be, to fit into the working girl's budget. I'm not saying it won't set me back some, but I want to pay. Like I said, I'm an old-fashioned girl in some ways. It will soothe my conscience to have to pay. So please don't say any more about it."

"I feel responsible. What about my conscience? How am I going to soothe *it*?"

"You mean you've been a free man all these years and you've never had this happen before?"

"As far as I know, it's only happened twice. And they're

both at home asleep now." There was just a touch of moral smugness, the way he said this. It set Cate off.

"Well, maybe you ought to be heading home to tuck them in. Take care of what's yours. And leave me here to—to take care of what's mine."

Their eyes met, then, in shocked awareness of what she had said. She was appalled at her crudeness. She could feel the tears just about to come down.

For a minute he looked as if he were going to stride over and take her in his arms and offer enough tenderness to absolve them both. But either she had imagined it because she wished it, or else he had decided he didn't have enough to offer.

"Maybe I ought to be heading on up the river," he said, glancing at his watch. "They don't expect me until tomorrow but I can certainly understand you've had enough trouble from me." He went over to retrieve his coat and tie from her wall hook.

"It hasn't all been trouble." She wanted to stretch out her arms in front of the door, to prevent him from leaving her alone with her thoughts. Thus she appeared all the more rigid as she stood there, half turned away from him, watching his departure movements out of one eye. "We kept each other warm during the coldest part of the winter."

"There's that," he said sarcastically as he put on his coat. He whisked his tie from the hook, gave it an angry look, then balled it up and jammed it in his coat pocket.

"Try to remember the good times," she said inanely as he was unlatching the Yale lock to let himself out.

"I'll phone you in a couple of days," he said. "We'll hurt each other if we go on tonight."

"Thank you for bringing the pizza." She was crying now and hoped he could hear it in her voice, though she was too proud to move. It was not too late. He could still stride across the room and comfort her.

"You're welcome. I'm sorry you didn't enjoy it more. Good night, Cate."

Then he was out of her vision. She heard the door relatch itself softly. Heard his footsteps beating a brisk retreat from her

Sanctuary. She fell across the bed and slammed a pillow over her head, but it didn't prevent her hearing his Jeep's engine catch and rumble away down the silent, condemned little street.

She lay there, in her jeans and satin shirt, too dispirited to get up and undress. There was a pounding in her temples. She remained motionless, sprawled horizontally across the bed, trying to imagine a way out. There was no way out. She must find a way to relieve some of the pressure of being unable to get out of her mind and her body.

Then she remembered something she had used during the last months with Jake, when he was going crazy and trying to make her crazy, too. It was a little mental exercise that had appeared of its own accord, one night, as she lay alone in bed in their Greenwich Village apartment and awaited Jake's next assault on her sanity. By then, he had built himself a platform in the living room and piled it high with blankets and pillows and hung ragged tapestries and Indian bedspreads all around so she could not "spy on him" in his "home." When she came back from teaching at the Upper East Side girls' school, he would be behind the hangings, on his platform. He had stopped speaking directly to her by then, but as soon as she came through the door, she would hear him switch on the tape recorder behind the hangings, and his recorded voice would begin its daily mad harangue, listing her faults, calling her insulting names, and accusing her and her petty bourgeois notions of impeding his progress to godhood.

She would fix supper and leave a plate for him on the kitchen counter. She would take her supper into the bedroom and shut the door and grade papers or work on her dissertation—to the accompaniment of the tapes. When one finished, he would put on another. There seemed to be an endless supply; he must have spent most of the day recording them. All that work and energy dedicated to madness; and, though he had done his best to burn out his mind with drugs, some of his accusations were so perceptive, so inventive. He knew her; he knew what would shock and hurt. At some point during the evening, she would hear him creep to the kitchen, like a cautious animal, to seize his supper. She knew he was taking drugs. The only thing she couldn't figure out was where he got them and how he paid for them.

Her sanity was very important to her at this time, and her self-concern must have been what had brought on the little exercise. If she could hold on, long enough to write her dissertation and get them out of here—Jake had fared better with more open space around him, though she had taken this job because he had wanted to "try New York"—she could bring him through this period. She didn't mind being the strong one with the most to give. She had married him, and she wanted to honor the difficult part of the vows. One failed marriage was regrettable, but two might mean the failure had something to do with her. At this time, she could not quite bring herself to imagine a second divorce. She preferred to cling to the dwindling hope that she might yet save Jake; they could move to Vermont or New Hampshire, where she could teach at one of the many small colleges there, and he could farm or do carpentry, which was more face-saving than waiting for her in a city apartment. He felt he had been jilted by his own times. He had quit school and prepared for a revolution that didn't seem to be coming, and now he was falling apart because he saw that the future intended to pass him right by, even though he had offered it his youth and brightness. He was metamorphosing back into a raging infant, but he could still use his adult intelligence to think up new ways to test her loyalty and devotion. The longer he lived off her salary, the more violent became his efforts to force her to admit the contemptuousness of money. Contradictions abounded. He wanted to lean on her as an infant leans on Mommy, but also to show her why she was too "bourgeois" to be a god like him.

One morning, while she was in the bathroom, she heard his tape-recorded voice inviting her to come immediately to an "art show" on his platform. Like the optimistic fool she was, she went. He had sneaked out of the apartment. On the walls behind the platform were smeared childlike drawings. In shit.

But even that hadn't been the end. She had washed down

the walls with ammonia. As he had known she would. Didn't Mommy have to clean up Baby's mess? It was when she came home early, one afternoon in November of 1969, and discovered him sitting around perfectly sanely, in a perfectly friendly way, with his customers. There were little packages out on the coffee table and a pile of money. Jake was the local dealer. She kicked him out then. She was "bourgeois" enough to see the necessity of doing that.

But before the packages on the table, she had gone to her bedroom every night and taken a grim pride in her ability to keep this household going. After she had done her work, she would turn off the light and try to empty her mind. A favorite trick of his was to wait until she had fallen asleep, and then to put on a fresh tape. She was never quite prepared for what she might wake up hearing about herself. One night she had lain there in the unsafe dark, wondering whether he was asleep or awake and, if the latter, when the next tape would start, and she had begun to split. She had felt her sanity threatened for the first time.

Then the little exercise had thought itself into her head. It was as if she stood in the center of a circle, which was her mind, and she was provided with a broom, and every time a bad thought tried to cross the borders of the circle, she must sweep it out with her broom. As long as she could keep alert and hold on to the little broom, she could keep the thoughts out. She could see them: dark, amorphous blobs, rather like the shapes she had washed off the wall behind Jake's platform. Sweep, sweep, went her busy broom, and the shapes fell back.

She knew that if she could keep the circle clean long enough for her energies to regenerate themselves, she would survive. The circle needed time in which to heal itself.

She got so good at the exercise that she could keep sweeping the circle clean even if one of the tapes did start. The words had no power over her. She got so she could sweep herself into sleep and wake up able to go on. Even during sleep, she left the guardian part of herself turning around and around in that circle, ready to attack the first dark encroacher with the broom.

*   *

So, after Jernigan left, Cate lay rigid and quiet, with her eyes tightly shut, and stood in the center of the circle with her broom. Nothing must be allowed in. Not the future (whatever and wherever that would be), not Chicago, not the outline of Jernigan's face, cocky and commanding or weary and sagging, as if she had managed to defeat him ... no. Out, thought. Sweep the circle clean. Not the dirty plates waiting on the table in the kitchen, attracting roaches and mice. Not even that. She turned and swept, swept and kept turning, until at some point her circular vigilance went on automatic and she was rewarded with a sort of sleep.

Later, a dream crept in, but it was a mild dream, neither healing nor awful. It could have been much worse. She dreamed that she was packing her car and doing a neat job of it. Books, clothes, cooking pots, a large exotic potted plant, the likes of which she had never seen, were all fitted snugly into their allotted spaces. The leaves of the plant waved intelligently, as if they were expressing the plant's thoughts, and she was thinking how well she had managed all this and how nice the plant would be for company on her journey. Then a large black woman appeared beside her car. She was like Theodora's Azalea, but she was also, somehow, Cate's friend and maid. She was carrying a bundle in her arms, something Cate had forgotten to pack. It was a baby. For a minute, Cate was annoyed. Where was she going to put it? But then she saw a place for it, next to the intelligent plant. She took the baby from the black woman, who promptly disappeared. Then Cate looked down and saw that, though the bundle was wrapped like a baby, it contained a stuffed teddy bear she had owned as a child.

She awoke, her clothes tight and twisted around her body. A motor switched off on the street below. Then there were brisk steps on the stairs and someone knocked at the door. Through the window shades, she could see it was already light.

It was Jernigan, freshly shaved, wearing his familiar work pants and plaid shirt.

"What time is it?" was all she could think of to say.

"A little past seven. I spent the night at the plant."

"You mean you didn't go home?"

"No. I worked for a while. I went over the field manager's reports. Then I took a shower and tried to sleep." He looked at her rumpled clothes. "You don't look like you've slept much, either."

"I slept some," said honest Cate.

"Let's go out and get some breakfast. I know a diner that's open on Sunday. I think we should talk." His voice was low and serious, his countenance grim. She noticed patches of crinkly skin, where all the color had drained out, beneath his eyes.

"I need to change my shirt," she said.

He looked her over again and nodded. "Yes, I guess you do."

She took as long as possible in the bathroom, brushing and flossing her teeth, washing her face, putting some makeup on. She brushed out her tangled hair and pinned it up. She had her pride. There had been no need for him to *agree* with her that she needed freshening up. She removed the crumpled shirt and scrubbed each armpit with soapy, hot water. Then she put on the shirt she had discarded before her bath the evening before.

Neither of them spoke much as he drove. The streets of the town were quiet at this hour, but as the Jeep passed a church, Cate saw two men unloading stacks of palm fronds from a florist's truck. It was Palm Sunday. She noted this fact to Jernigan, just to break the silence.

"So it is," he said. "I haven't been to church in years. Hilda goes faithfully every Sunday. When Jody was little, he sometimes went with her. But he doesn't go anymore, either." He sighed. "It was nice, believing in God. I remember the feeling, as a kid."

"I had a distinct feeling of relief when I stopped believing," said Cate. "I was tired of God spying on me all the time. It was a relief to know I was in charge of my life, not God."

He gave her a funny look. "When did you stop believing?"

"Oh, I didn't come to a dead stop till I was in college. But I'd begun to suspect when I was in this convent school my sister and I went to as children. I was always getting into arguments with the nuns, and there was always a certain point where they'd paint themselves into a corner. One time this nun—actually, she was one of the most intelligent—and I really got into it, and there was a moment when I saw her face go pale with dread. I'd made her doubt for a moment. I felt bad about that; after all, she had given her life to her belief. But it was in college that I became sure that it was entirely up to me: I was entirely responsible. No wonder Kierkegaard felt such dread. All that freedom and its responsibility! I felt pretty scared myself till I combined my new belief—or rather nonbelief—with socialism. That made things cheerier. I'd do my part and if everybody else would do theirs, we'd all be architects of the world's soul. Which, in a strange way, brings you right back to God. Each person has to be a tiny part of God. Or what we used to think of as God." Now they were out on the highway, driving past fields that had been freshly turned by the plow. Cate felt better. She soared a little on the wings of her intelligent testimony: her life did make sense, and she could put it into words. "When did you stop believing?" she asked cheerfully.

"When I was in the Army, I think. I was in Italy. It was in 'forty-three and the Allies were bombing villages left and right. I was with a small detail of men who had to go ahead into a village. We had to see if the enemy had got there. The place was deserted. Even after the bombs, you could tell it had never been much. And then one of the men in our detail went berserk. There was this chicken. It came out of a house. He picked it up and just started tearing it to pieces. I don't mean just wringing its neck. I grew up on a farm. I know how you kill a chicken humanely. But he was tearing it into bloody shreds. About that time I saw an old woman in black. She was looking at us through the window of where her house had been. There was just this one wall left. And everything switched around in me, and I saw that, to her, we were the enemy. We had bombed her house. Now we were tramping through her village, and one of us was tearing her chicken into little pieces, with it still screaming. *We* were the enemy; not the enemy we had come to save her from. I was nineteen then. Up until then I never questioned that we were the

good guys and God was on our side. Don't get me wrong. I think
we were the good guys in that war. But after that, my simple faith
was gone. I still believed in some kind of force, but I wasn't so
sure whose side he was on. And, like you, I felt more alone after
that. More like it was up to me. But I never went in for socialism.
That's not my kind of thing."

"You just believe in taking care of what's yours." Cate was
irritated with him again. How could he be so intelligent one minute, then short-circuit himself right back into deliberate, provin-
cial ignorance the next?

"That's right," he said softly. And gave her a look that set
her vibrating with ambivalence: she wanted to lean against him,
lapse wearily into his care; she also wanted to press down on the
handle of the door and leap from the Jeep. She clenched her
hands in her lap and stuck up her chin and narrowed her eyes
at the dark, fertile fields that stretched away on either side of
them.

After they had eaten breakfast, he said, "Let's go over this
thing one more time. You go to Chicago when?"

"Easter Monday. First I let them look me over, then I spend
the night at a hotel, then next morning I go back for the . . . procedure. I spend another night at the hotel, then I fly back. I'll
have almost a week to take it easy. Then back to my duties at
sinking Melanchthon. I'm luckier than most. Most women have
to go back the very next day."

He gave an impatient wave of his hand. "Most women don't
concern me. How far along are you?"

"Ninth week. That's nothing much, I'm told. By friends who
have been there before."

"And you've really never been pregnant before?"

She shook her head.

"Amazing. Not to, all this time, and then *now*, despite pre-
cautions. Damned amazing." But there was a tinge of male pride
in his voice. He covered it up at once, adding humbly, "I'm truly
sorry to have messed you up like this. It was on my mind most of

the night. You're a damned fine woman, Catie—excuse me, I mean *Cate*. Sorry about that, too."

"That was churlish of me last night. It's just that I'm touchy about my name. I never liked 'Catherine,' which was my father's mother's name. I never even knew her well—she was trodden under completely by the time I was six—but even the way other people pronounced her name, '*Catherine*,' had a gloomy, *pitying* sound to it. I was determined not to be a '*Catherine* '"—and Cate rolled her eyes back as she intoned her Christian name. "I've fought hard to make people call me Cate. It's the only version of the name that fits me. Not Catherine the martyred wife, or cute little Cathy, or anybody's Kitty or Catie. Now, my younger sister had it easier. First of all, she wasn't named for anybody. Mother and Daddy picked Lydia's name out of a dictionary. It means 'soft and gentle.' I guess they realized by then they were going to have enough trouble with me. Also you can't chop 'Lydia' into any silly nickname. Lydia is Lydia."

"And Cate is Cate," he said. He actually looked pleased by her little diatribe. "Listen, Cate, I want you to do something for me. To ease my conscience."

She lifted her eyebrows.

"I'm putting Jody on the noon flight to Chicago on Friday. From there he goes to LA, to spend the Easter holidays with his mother. I've given Hilda the Easter weekend off so she can go to her family in Waterloo. Sunny and I were going to batch it out at the castle. But now I'd like you to join us. Come up and spend that weekend at Rollingstone. I've seen how you live. I want you to see my life. Wouldn't that interest you? To see how Mister Poison lives on his hill?"

"I don't know. . . ." She frowned. She hadn't been prepared for this. Still, the offer was appealing. It appealed especially to her curiosity. And it *would* be a fitting conclusion to their affair. She owed it to herself in a way: seeing him in his habitat might provide her with some useful perspective on this difficult interlude in her life. She ought to learn from her mistakes.

"I could pick you up at your place on Friday," he went on,

"after I take Jody to the airport and see him off. Then, I can either take you back to your place or straight to the airport for your Monday flight. At least allow me to spend the countdown hours with you, since you won't let me contribute anything else."

Cate thought for a minute. Somehow, she didn't like the idea of being trapped in his habitat without her car. "I'll tell you what," she said. "I'll drive to your castle. I'll come up on Friday afternoon, and then I'll leave early Monday morning. But I'll need a map. Is that okay?"

"It will have to be, won't it?" he replied, studying her with thoughtful amusement for a moment. "All right, I'd better take what I can get." He unclipped a ball-point pen from his shirt pocket, took a paper napkin from the dispenser, and, with an obvious relish for the map-drawing process, traced in hard, sure strokes the road that led up the Mississippi River to Rollingstone.

Cate was no stranger to castles. When she and Pringle were at Ruislip, they had spent many weekends traipsing through English castles. When they were stationed in Iceland, they once flew to Copenhagen, rented a car, and drove up the coast to Elsinore, where she had broken one of her heels while creeping through the dungeons of Hamlet's castle. In her hometown there were two bona fide castles. They were both on the mountain that overlooked the town. One was a sinister gray-stone fortress, surrounded by a tall spiked fence, inside which, it was rumored, German spies posing as the owner's houseguests operated a signal station in World War II. Now it was owned by an ex-ballet dancer who had turned it into an exclusive restaurant which catered to private parties only. The other castle was a friendly yellow-brick one, which sat right out in the sunshine; but it had the requisite number of battlements and turrets and even a moat. During Cate's teens, after its businessman owner and builder had died, this empty castle had been *the* place for parking; she and her dates had driven over the rattly moat bridge and pulled in beside the next car in the wide gravel lot and smooched away in the romantic atmosphere overlooking the twinkling lights of town. That castle was now a business college.

So, as she drove upriver on Good Friday, Jernigan's paper-napkin map on the seat beside her (though, so far, she had had only to follow the river road), she did not expect to be surprised too much by the actual lineaments of her lover's home. She had a pretty good idea of what it would be like, give or take a turret or a moat or a battlement. The thing about American castles, poor things, was that they were, by nature, a little hoaxy. They were the harmless decorative descendants of an institution that had been constructed from grim realities: the people who had sheltered inside the real castles had done so because there were people outside willing to cut their throats in order to steal their hard-won positions and possessions. The people inside knew this all too well because, not long before, they had been outside, sharpening their knives to cut the throats of others and win *their* hard-won goods. As Mother had often remarked: "What were aristocrats but simply the barbarians who got there first?" Mother had her points.

Cate drove through the old lumbering town of Clinton. She had been up this far before, having once come here to climb the bluffs to a city park which provided a wonderful view of the Mississippi. Here the river was about two miles wide. The bluffs were becoming steeper and lighter in color: enormous sheer drops of limestone, as perpendicular in places as if they had been masonry. To think that once there had been a time when the water was on a level with the tops of these walls! The idea was strangely restful. It depersonalized her finite agonizings, to be able to remind herself that her perishable body would be outlived by many more centuries by these mute, grand bluffs. That is, unless some idiot, acting on orders, pushed the button. But, either way, she was secure in the promise of her own eventual personal extinction.

And having canceled herself out with the help of the majestic bluffs, Cate found she was looking forward intensely to whatever she would find at Roger Jernigan's castle.

She was upon it almost before she was prepared. "Just after the toll bridge," he had said, "turn left at the old stone warehouse. Then you go up, up, up, almost to the top of the hill, and turn left again into the private drive. That's us." He had sketched two short left turns on the paper napkin, but she had expected the approach to be lengthier in reality. Within minutes of turning off the river road and urging her car in low gear up an incline she wouldn't care to confront in snow or ice, she was completing the curve of gravel driveway that ended abruptly in a retaining wall into which a two-car garage had been built. An arched stairway through the wall led to the next level above. Cate, from her car, could glimpse a sweep of lawn, still recovering from winter, and, above that, the castle.

Its proportions were a little disappointing—it was about the same size as a three-story house—but its architecture *was* that of a castle. It had four square towers, two at the front and two at the back, and the whole top of the building was notched with battlements. Except for some large modern windows, obviously recent renovations, and a connecting balcony joining the two tower rooms on the second floor, the structure looked like a child's drawing of a castle.

Jernigan, in Levi's and a red sweater, appeared above the retaining wall. "Well, you got here," he observed gruffly. "Look what nice weather you've brought, too. Uncommonly nice, for this time of year." But he looked ill at ease and wary. Had he, in the interim, regretted inviting her?

"The weather is lovely," agreed Cate, slamming the door of her VW, "but I can only take credit for bringing myself." She hadn't meant it to sound so threatening; she guessed she was nervous, too. Being on someone else's turf did make a difference.

"Well, I hope you at least brought an overnight bag. Didn't you?" He sounded worried. Maybe he thought she had changed *her* mind about spending the weekend, and would drive off again after supper.

"So I did." She opened the door again and ducked into the

backseat and swung out her faithful brown English suitcase, the twin of which Lydia had.

He was down through the wall's staircase in a second. "Here, give me that," he ordered. His alarm was rather comic. It made her remember for the first time in at least an hour that she was pregnant.

He was obviously thinking of it, too, because his eyes swept over her body in a searching, tender way. "Welcome to Rolling-stone," he said. "Was my map okay?"

"I didn't get lost a single time." She followed him up the tunneled stone stairway. "It's a lovely drive. I had some beautiful views of the bluffs." Her cheerful, "social" voice bounced back at her from the limestone walls.

They surfaced on the lawn, which sloped left, toward a magnificent view of the river, spanned by the bridge she had driven past just a few minutes ago. About thirty feet from them stood a rocklike blond man, tending a barbecue pit. He was dressed identically to Jernigan, in Levi's and the same red sweater. His back was to them.

"Come meet Sunny," said Jernigan. "Then I'll show you where your room is."

Somehow she had assumed she would be sharing his room.

The blond man heard his father's voice. He turned to watch them approach. He was not beautiful, like Jody, but he had pleasant, clean-cut features. His eyes were green, like Jernigan's, but they were rounder and not as shrewd. It was hard to believe he was thirty-three. His countenance had the smooth, unfinished surface of a boy's. Except for a certain dryness in the cheeks, and a deep double-slash of frown lines between the eyes, his face had no other signs of aging. His body was hard and knotty, like a weight lifter's. He watched Cate come toward him with the unembarrassed stare of a child.

"This is Sunny, my elder son," said Jernigan. "Sunny, this is Cate, Jody's teacher."

"Hello, Cate!" responded Sunny with a great deal of enthusiasm, as if he had been primed.

"I'm so glad to meet you. At last." Cate stuck out her hand, but Sunny ignored it.

"Remember the night Jody rehearsed his song about the corn borer?" said Jernigan. "Well, that was for his class with Cate, at the college." He spoke to the other man with a patience Cate had never heard him use before.

"Yes, I remember," said Sunny. He turned back to the barbecue pit. "Roger, the coals are ready. They're white on both sides."

"That's great, son. I'm going to take Cate up to her room now. Maybe she'd like to wash or unpack. Then you and I can cook the steaks."

"She's going to sleep in Jody's room," said Sunny, looking from his father to Cate.

"That's right," replied Jernigan. To Cate, he said, "It has the best view, and the most rugs and mirrors. Jody made it up for you himself before he left this morning."

"I want to go, too," said Sunny, bouncing up and down on the balls of his sneakers. "Can I go, too?"

"Sure you can," said Jernigan. "Here, take her bag and run on up to Hilda's rooms. You wait for us there."

Looking as if he had been granted a great favor, Sunny took the brown suitcase from his father and sprinted off across the lawn to the castle. His run was a little erratic, as though he were constantly being distracted from his path.

"He's excited today," said Jernigan, taking Cate's arm. "I don't often have people up here. But I've told him who you are. I've prepared him for your visit. He's used to routine. He thrives on it. As long as he knows what's going to happen and what's expected of him, he's fine. He's very helpful, too. He helps Hilda with heavy cleaning; he does all the yardwork. He was wonderful when Jody was small. Tied his shoes, dressed him; then taught him to do it for himself. He was always carrying Jody around on his back, till you thought of them as some double-headed animal. His mind . . . it has its own special way of arranging things. One minute he'll seem oblivious to what's happening around him. The next, why, he's telling you details of things you've forgotten, things that happened years ago. Five years from now, you wait, he'll be able to remind you of things about this day that you'd hardly noticed yourself."

Cate felt very sad, both because she now understood the secret of Sunny and because, not only did she not know where she was going to be in five years, but she doubted she would ever meet such a solid, comforting man again.

"He's a very likable person," she felt she should say. "He has so much—so much *energy*."

"He has that, all right," said Jernigan with a sigh. "He has to take medication or he'd go off like a rocket. Yes, he's a likable, affectionate boy. And nice to look at, in his way. I mean, he's not—it could have been worse. Although I didn't think so when we first found out. We didn't know anything was wrong till he was three. We thought he was just a slow developer. But then this little boy just about his age moved into the house next door, and we got to worrying about the difference between Sunny and him. We took him for tests. We got the news. My wife went to pieces. She felt it was her fault because one specialist said it might have been caused by a too-rapid exit from the birth passage. The oxygen get cuts off, see. Poor Selma had a bad time. For a while there, she was more of a problem than Sunny. But you gradually accept these things." He laughed harshly. "What else can you do? Then the rationalizing games set in. In some ways that's the worst part. 'Maybe it won't be too bad. Maybe he'll grow out of it.' And the doctors don't know everything, either. They encourage you to 'wait and see.' Especially when it's a borderline case, like Sunny. If you've got the means to do it, you go around buying the theories of different specialists and then picking the one you like the best. I was fortunate enough to be on my feet pretty well by the time he needed schools. He could have the best. He was away at a boarding school for a while, a good place. Organized like a little community. The big ones take care of the little ones and the . . . less damaged take care of the more damaged. But Sunny's happiest at home. I made the decision to bring Sunny home when Jody was two, and I never regretted it. Jody loves his brother more than he loves anybody in the world. And Sunny takes such a pride in Jody. He tells Jody he's his bodyguard, and hangs on Jody's every word, and is always surprising him with gifts. Sunny's made Jody a better person. He's made me a better person."

Jernigan stopped and turned to Cate. "He'll always have the mind of a child. But I'll tell you something. I couldn't have said this thirty years ago, but I can say it now. If I had the choice of Sunny never existing, or him existing exactly as he is now, I would choose to have him. Can you understand that?"

"Yes, I can," said Cate.

"Good." He put his arm lightly around her and they continued toward the castle. "That's enough about that. I want you to enjoy your weekend. Make yourself at home. By the way, I ought to warn you, Jody prepared a little surprise for you."

"Why should you warn me?"

"Because. He meant for it to scare you. In an amusing way, of course, but"—he glanced significantly at her stomach—"you shouldn't be scared too much."

"I don't scare easily," retorted Cate good-humoredly, adding before she had time to think better of it, "Besides, so what? It would save me a trip to Chicago."

Jernigan flinched. "Anyway," he said, more coldly, "you'll see it when you open the door to his room."

"I'm surprised you told him I was coming," she said, feeling his rebuff. All right, so the remark had been crude, she wished she hadn't made it, but what right had he to be offended. Did he take it as a slight against "what was his," even when they both knew she was going to dispose of it on Tuesday?

"He would have heard it from Sunny. I try and make the most of my opportunities for candor with Jody. In hopes that he'll be equally candid with me."

They found Sunny pacing restlessly up and down in Hilda's "Parlor," which was awful. It reminded Cate of some of the most stifling "formal" rooms in the Hapsburg Palace, through which she and Pringle had dutifully dragged themselves, both half-dead from a bout with food poisoning but not wanting to miss the highlights of Vienna. Now her throat began to close on her, and her heart started pounding; it was the beginning of her old claustrophobia, which attacked whenever she knew she was going to have to stay in a place that made her feel trapped. Could she get through *one* night here? Things were already off to a less than ideal start, thanks to her careless remark. But if she were to leave, wouldn't Jernigan take it to mean she was fleeing Sunny, that she found him depressing, poor Sunny who was at the moment proudly reciting an inventory of Hilda's dreadful furnishings? Jernigan had been right: Sunny's memory for details was prodigious. He remembered which pieces had been bought at which auctions, and he seemed particularly urgent about having her know which things they had brought with them from their other home, the one they'd lived in before Roger—as Sunny always called his father—bought the castle. It was both sad and thought-provoking that his brain, though damaged, retained these specialized circuits through which past images and information—unadulterated by any of the abstractions and conceptions that the healthy mind delighted in—could flow so accurately. Sunny could not think the thought she had just had, for instance.

And so she took herself in hand and breathed deeply and said, "Oh *yes*," when Sunny asked if she'd like to "peek" into Hilda's bedroom; she exclaimed suitably over the canopied monster of a bed, complete with faded rose satin hangings. With tassels.

"It makes Hilda happy" was Jernigan's quiet comment. He had been watching Cate. As he led the way upstairs, he called back to Sunny, "We want to keep Hilda happy, don't we, son? We'd be in a sad fix without her, wouldn't we?"

"We'd be in a sad fix!" Sunny called back, laughing hilariously.

Cate had forgotten Jernigan's warning about Jody's "surprise," and let out a shriek when she entered his room, where she was to sleep.

Suspended from the ceiling was Jody's voluminous Dracula

cloak from the college production. Handpainted cardboard hands with long, deformed green nails had been pinned to the front of the cloak. The hands held a sign lettered in Gothic script:

WELCOME, DR. GALITSKY
(HEH, HEH)
TO: DRACULA'S BEDROOM

Her shriek set Sunny off again. His delighted laughter infected Jernigan, who lost his thoughtful scowl for the first time since the lawn. Then Sunny had to recite the history of the cape. When Hilda had bought the eight yards of black velvet and the seven and a half yards of purple satin, and how, while sewing the cape, she had bunched the satin in the sewing machine and cried for a whole hour. "Here, you want to see where she bunched up the satin?" He started pawing through the yards of cape.

"Come on, son," said Jernigan. "Let's let Cate get settled. You and I have things to do downstairs." To Cate he said, "Will you be warm enough if we eat outside? He likes it. It will be the first opportunity we've had this spring. But if you think you'll be cold, just say the word."

"Of course I won't be cold. Besides, I brought my heavy sweater. It'll be much more fun to eat outside."

"Good. You'll be okay here? Not too much fluff and foolishness for you?" He glanced around with wry forbearance at his younger son's room.

"I revel in fluff and foolishness. On occasion."

Their eyes met. Good humor had been reinstated between them.

"You take as long as you like," he said, brushing her arm lightly with his fingers. "We'll be getting things set up downstairs."

Alone, Cate unpacked her few things. There was no reason for her to feel pity for Jernigan. As he had said himself, it could have been much worse. It was a luxury to allow herself to pity Jernigan. His situation was rich and picturesque enough to make it a comfortable area for pity. "See how the mighty are fallen"— but with a castle and a sweeping view of the river; the happy, at- tractive face of the victim; and steaks on the grill. If Jernigan had been a poor man—if he had been, say, the real handyman she had first mistaken him for at the college—and had dragged into her office one day his retarded son, a son maybe not so nice to look at as Sunny, she would have felt the real pity, the kind that is so painful that you want to dissociate yourself from it.

Jody's bedroom was rife with fluff and foolishness. But it was luxurious to the senses, with its sinfully thick white rugs, and amusing in a campy sort of way. She went to the window to make sure it could be opened. It could. Down below, the two men in their look-alike outfits were carrying out a table. It looked like the dining-room table. She stood back, out of sight, and listened to them discussing the best place to put the table. "Do you think Cate would like to look through my telescope?" she heard Sunny ask his father. His voice, high-pitched for a man's, floated up to her through the brisk, late-afternoon air. Beyond and below them, the river curved. She felt a bit like a medieval princess, looking out of her tower room at the pleasing, distant vistas of Illinois, which from here appeared a soft, indis- tinct blue. Then she reminded herself that she was not a medie- val princess, nor did she want to be, and, come Monday, she would be crossing that river to do a very modern thing in Illinois.

Jody's bathroom was carpeted in thick purple. As Cate washed her face, redid her hair, and performed other necessary functions, she found it rather disconcerting to be unable to lose sight of herself for a minute. While sitting on the purple toilet seat and shyly averting her eyes from her seated reflection on the opposite wall, she counted forty-three mirrors, ranging from the big one she was trying to avoid to little ones the size of a magni- fying glass. Some were framed ornately, others were cut in the shapes of hearts. She chose to think that Jody meant them partly as a parody of his own beauty. Dear Jody. Accepting the burden of the Drama class, she had rationalized that, at least, it might lead to a new experience, and so it had.

*   *

They dined in sweaters, in a patch of late sun, off a mahogany table that would have seated ten; its thick legs sank progressively into the turf as they cut their steaks. There was a rich potato salad (a little too rich), homemade bread, and a chocolate sponge cake for dessert—all prepared in advance by the faithful Hilda before she departed for Waterloo. Cate was obliged to undo the button on her jeans discreetly before the end of the meal.

Whenever a barge or a boat of any kind passed on the river, Sunny sprang from his chair and followed its progress through a costly-looking telescope which had been set up on a tripod. He called for Cate and his father to come and look, too, and the first few times they went.

"He never tires of the river traffic," said Jernigan. "And we've lived here almost six years now. You aren't getting chilled, are you?"

"I'm fine." She smiled at him. "I'm very fine. I feel very secure and relaxed."

He reached for her hand and stroked it between his two. "Good. That's the general idea."

Suddenly she felt sorrowful that this lovely security would end on Monday.

"Cate?"

"What?" God, she really liked this man.

"Could you stand watching a movie?" He stroked each of her fingers, as if he wanted to learn each one of them. "He always has a Friday-night movie. It's a sort of tradition."

"I'd love a movie, then. What's playing?"

"*The Magnificent Seven*. It's one of his favorites. Come on, now. Are you sure? A cowboy movie? I won't feel hurt if you'd rather read in your room. I could join you later."

"No, I want to watch *The Magnificent Seven*. I remember liking it. Can we hold hands in the dark?"

He laced his fingers through hers and held their two hands aloft, as if they were the referee and the winner of a boxing match. "We can hold hands in front of the whole damn world," he said, grinning. Then he stood up and released her hand. "Son,

I'm going down to set up the projector," he called to Sunny at the telescope. "You and Cate can clear things, but don't you two try to move that table. It's too heavy for Cate."

Sunny showed Cate where to put things in Hilda's kitchen, which was as admirable a room as Hilda's living quarters had been impossible. Cate couldn't help thinking that Lydia would adore this kitchen. There was a restaurant-sized gas range, an enormous butcher-block chopping table, a rack of gleaming knives plentiful enough to supply a gang war. Metal and porcelain surfaces shone; storage shelves groaned with portly reserves. Every inch of space was immaculately ordered. Cate felt the absent housekeeper peering jealously over her shoulder as she spooned the leftover potato salad back into the see-through container labeled SALAD FOR STEAK. All of the containers in the refrigerator were labeled with explicit directions: HEAT FOR 30 MIN. AT 350. PREHEAT OVEN! or SALAD FOR COLD CHICKEN. It was obvious that Hilda did not expect them to get along very well without her. Had Jernigan told her that he was having a woman spending Easter weekend here? Would Hilda return and frown when she detected an alien touch in the way Saran Wrap was crinkled over the remains of the sponge cake?

During the movie, there were two phone calls for Jernigan. He took the first call leisurely, from his comfortable armchair beside Cate's. "Yeah, my son and a friend and myself are down in the gym watching a movie." He went on to speak in an easy, friendly tone about the resistance of some rootworm, about "target-site insensitivity" and "benefit/cost ratios." When he hung up he was in a mellow mood and retrieved her hand and laid it on the arm of his chair and began playing with it some more. She was aroused and so was he. But Sunny had to have his movie, even though he was not exactly glued to the screen. At frequent intervals, he would spring restlessly from his chair and go over to the Universal equipment and do some chest lifts, or raise himself by the arms and hang in midair while he watched the movie for a while. When the second phone call came, Jernigan mumbled cautious monosyllables into the receiver. Then he said, "Let me take this on another phone." He asked Cate to hang up when she heard him pick up on the other end and left the room with an exasperated sigh. "Okay, Kevin, I'll explain my position one more time," she heard him say when he came on the line. She hung up.

Sunny had to have a sedative every night in order to "defuse," as his father put it. Jernigan went upstairs to Sunny's quarters on the third floor while Cate undressed slowly in Dracula's bedroom. When Jernigan had returned to the movie after the call from "Kevin," he had slipped her a note on a piece of memopad paper which had the logo of a smiling sun and *Sunny Enterprises / "We make your garden grow" / herbicides, insecticides, crop spraying* at the top.

Cate, wearing her nightgown, sat down on Jody's bed and curled her toes in the thick white rug and reread the note in Jernigan's brusque scrawl.

Gentleman residing in North tower room desires tryst with Lady in South tower room. If agreeable, please answer to three clandestine knocks on Lady's door leading to balcony.

She had not expected him to have such a delightful sense of romantic occasion. She had not expected the awakening of this vigorous lust in herself, either. She sat there, among the *fin de siècle* ruffles and clutter of Jody's harem lamps and silk flowers and ostrich and peacock feathers, and the Beardsley poster of the Chevalier Tannhäuser (who looked a lot like Jody, with his cape and floating hair), and tried to figure it out. Why this lust now? Why here? Was her body trying to trick her into some kind of trap? Or were these surroundings arousing the atavistic female in her who wanted to receive the Dracula bite from her man so she could lie down forever within the protection of his castle walls?

"Oh shut up, Cate," she said, "quit philosophizing. Give yourself up to temporary lust and theater. See this weekend for what it is; his doing his ceremonious best to salve his guilt by making you feel appreciated, before sending you off alone to do what you have to do on Tuesday."

And so, when the "three clandestine knocks" came at the door leading to her balcony, she opened to him, prepared to continue the playful fantasy he had set up in his note.

But she found herself being crushed to the breast of a groaning man wearing clean striped-cotton pajamas.

"I've waited all evening," he murmured angrily, his voice muffled in the curve of her neck. "Dammit, we deserve some happiness, too."

She let herself be pressed, enfolded. He ground himself against her as though he were trying to escape into her. His urgency was contagious. She wanted it, too. She was tired of being conscious and witty and responsible. She wanted to get down to basics, to take and be taken. Nevertheless, she was surprised when she heard something like a growl escape from herself.

"Let's go to my room," he said hoarsely. "Jody's feathers give me hay fever."

He led her outside, across the balcony connecting the two rooms. A big moon lit up the curling river and the grounds below. The nippy air made her skin tingle under her gown. Oh hell, she thought, why couldn't this be the thirteenth century? Then it would all be decided for me.

And in the dark of his room, tinctured with moonlight, she found it all too easy to abandon her modernity, to give herself up to basics. She was his female and he was her male. They knotted themselves together, struggling and clinging for a total closeness, a self-obliterating closeness. They were connected utterly in intention, and by something more. Already inside her was the tiny life they had created together. What else was necessary? What on earth was the rest of the fuss about? Why not go back to this, stay inside this, get rid of that nervous, worrying self?

And if, at that moment, someone had pushed forward a document ("Do you hereby sign away all your troublesome, thought-provoking rights to your unclear and insecure future? Do you, by placing your signature on the dotted line, pledge yourself to care for, and be cared for by, this male creature who is reducing you to your essential female creatureness?"), she would have signed.

And her sense of honor would have made her stick to it, even when she was restored to her habitual rational, worrying, worrisome, sometimes female and sometimes androgynous self. She would have signed. And stuck to it. Well, probably.

She would question herself afterward: if he had asked her, there in the moonlit room, after they had tried and almost (but not quite) obliterated their modern selves; if he had struggled hard, back into the land of words, just enough to ask her . . . what he would ask her on the next afternoon—might she not have said yes, and sealed her fate as a happy woman?

But instead they fell asleep, still connected, having renounced everything outside. She was safely walled away from her past, and from Chicago, and from whatever came after Chicago. He, buried close to the life he had helped to engender inside her, was out of reach, for the time being, of the guilts and responsibilities he had set in motion, many of which were time bombs, due to go off in their own separate hours of the future.

The next day, which continued unseasonably mild, the three of them drove up to Bellevue, to a state park on a rocky promontory high above the river. At Sunny's instigation, they sang Jody's "Pore Little Corn Bore" song, delighting Sunny each time he had to supply someone with a line. He knew the song perfectly.

They consumed Hilda's sumptuous (labeled) picnic, having to weight things down with rocks to keep the wind from blowing them away. After lunch, Sunny went off to explore the trails he knew from other picnics here, and the "adults" relaxed against a warm, friendly rock, absorbing the sunshine and the view of the river.

"Does Sunny ever have . . . girl friends?" Cate asked.

"In what sense do you mean?" Jernigan sounded defensive.

"Does he ever have girls come to visit him?" She was remembering the gossip from her friend Ann, who said Jody had told her he couldn't do his exam because he had to pick up some girl for his brother at the airport.

"Funny you should ask that. He did have a friend, from his old boarding school. She came out here sometimes. Melanie would be thirty-four now. I wonder what she's doing these days." He closed his eyes and tilted his face up toward the sun. "It didn't work out like everybody hoped, but, hell, you can't mate people like animals. The young people sensed we were trying to corral them and they weren't having any. You know, they call people like Sunny and Melanie 'subnormal,' but there are times when I think they've developed finer senses, when it comes to feeling, than we have."

"What happened?"

"Well, I met her parents, on a visiting weekend at the school. This was when they were just children, Sunny and Melanie. Melanie was the adopted child of this couple. They couldn't have any of their own. Some people have rotten luck, don't they? But when they found out late about Melanie—it happened like it did with us, they didn't know until she was several years old— they determined to do everything they could for her. Like me, they were able to afford the best school, the ninety-nine thousand consultations with 'specialists.' We were all so pleased about it, when we saw how well our two kids got along. So we encouraged them to keep in touch after they left the school. I used to help Sunny write his letters to Melanie, and her mother, I'm sure, wrote Melanie's letters to Sunny." He took Cate's hand, stroking it absently but possessively as he talked. "Sunny visited Melanie, and Melanie came out here to see Sunny. This went on for fifteen years. They played like two children—it was touching to see it, even though they weren't physically children anymore. Then, last fall, Melanie's father called me with a proposition. He and his wife were getting on in years and he was afraid if something happened to them Melanie would have no one to love her and look after her as they had. His wife had gone over to Sweden to check out some community they have there. The Swedes are damn smart. People like Sunny and Melanie can marry and live in this community. But that was in Sweden. Melanie's father wanted to set up something *here* for our kids. What he proposed was that he would settle an old-fashioned 'dowry' on his daughter and entrust it to me. Then Melanie and Sunny could marry and live here. Hilda could teach Melanie how to do the things she's always done for Sunny, and I'd have myself a sweet, docile daughter to care for me in my old age. Well, I wasn't too keen on *that* angle, but I decided to consult Sunny on the marriage part. And Melanie's father consulted her. Then she flew out for the 'betrothal visit,' I guess you could call it, and it was awful. They'd lost their freedom around each other. They were nervous and embarrassed. Melanie had shrieking spells and we had to put her on the plane home. And that was the end of that."

"Oh *God*," said Cate. And she confided to him what she had thought; that Sunny was some kind of wastrel playboy who had women flown in for his pleasure.

He laughed bitterly. "I'm aware people have strange ideas. I don't discourage them. For one thing, it's none of their damn business. For another, Jody is extremely protective of Sunny. He'd rather people think there's something mysterious and leave it at that."

"But did Sunny and Melanie—no, I shouldn't ask that."

"I know what you're going to ask. I honestly don't know, myself. I didn't spy on them. All the more power to them if they did, but I think they mostly just cuddled a lot. Sunny isn't all that interested in sex. He likes to work out, and he can ski fairly well, but he isn't highly sexed. That's often the case, you know. But it wouldn't have hurt anything if they had; Melanie'd been sterilized. Some town boys tried to get at her once, and that was enough for her father."

"Oh God. Why is there so much sorrow in the world?" She crouched against him and closed her eyes as if to blot it out.

He put his arms around her. He kissed her forehead, her nose, each of her cheeks.

"It's not all sorrow. Is this, right now, sorrow? Was last night sorrow? When we were together?"

"No." She kissed him back, kiss for kiss, forehead, nose, and cheeks. "It was a lovely postponement, that's what."

"Listen, Cate. Look at me. Don't you know why I asked you here this weekend?"

She looked at him and of course she knew. Once again, she felt schizoid in his presence: she wanted to run away as fast as she could, and she wanted to curl up in his pocket.

"You do, don't you?" He prodded her relentlessly with his sharp green eyes.

Cate hung her head, like a maiden.

"Now, listen. Don't interrupt till I've finished. I'm fifty-five years old. I'm in pretty good shape. You've seen that I have a responsibility to Sunny. But, so far, I've been able to meet my responsibilities. Unless all the Furies turn on me at once, I'll be able to go on meeting them. Even if I get hit with a rash of lawsuits. This Kevin, the pilot who called last night, is trying to get me to settle out of court. They've had another baby that's normal and he just wants to go somewhere and start over and for me to contribute fifteen thousand to his new future and pay his lawyer. I told him I couldn't, I had to tell him that. So, what I think you ought to do is call this Chicago clinic first thing Monday morning and cancel that appointment. I'd like you to go on and have that child. And I'd like to marry you."

"Oh, Roger, I appreciate it. I really do."

"Wait a minute. Don't you believe I'm serious? This isn't some kind of courtesy offer. I thought this whole thing out. More seriously than I thought out my other marriages, in fact. I'll admit, I didn't plan to marry again. I had everything nicely separated. My work at the plant, which I love, by the way, if it weren't for all these crippling restrictions. I will not apologize for being in toxicology. It's a science, not a crime. And I had the boys and Hilda up here. I had women, occasionally; I like the company of women. When you told me your news last Saturday, I wasn't prepared, at first, but then I drove out to the plant and thought about it. The more I thought about it, the more attractive it seemed. We're neither of us teenagers anymore. But we're not *old*, by a long shot. We could have quite a good time together. I know you'd be good for me. You know things I don't know. And I know things you don't know. I flatter myself I'd be good for you."

"You would. I know that, but—"

"But what? You wouldn't have to be stuck up at the castle, if that's what you're worried about. I know you like your independence. We could have a nurse for the baby. Hell, what's my money for? And there'd be Hilda. And Sunny is wonderful with children, he's already proved that with Jody. You could travel with me. I'd like that. I have to go places all the time. Especially now that this business is changing so much. In June, I have a big Integrated Pest Management conference in Switzerland. Ever been to Switzerland? We could make it sort of a honeymoon."

"I just wasn't prepared for this, Roger." Cate was growing alarmed. He spoke as if, having thought it all out, it was as good as done.

"So? I'm preparing you now. Only, we better get started pretty soon, because of . . . circumstances." He glanced down at her stomach.

"I'll be forty in June. The chances of a woman my age having a child that's not—"

"Already checked into that. You can have a test done in another month. Even if you were twenty, I'd want you to have it done. After what I've been through with Sunny. If there's something the matter with the baby, we'll make you another appointment. But not at some damned impersonal clinic."

"And then you'd be stuck with just me," she joked.

"Can't think of anybody I'd rather be stuck with. That's the truth, Catie . . . Cate. You liked last night, didn't you? You even enjoyed Sunny. That's something I had to be sure of."

"Oh, Sunny's *fine*—"

"But?" He sounded the slightest bit annoyed. He had offered her everything he had. What more did she want?

What more *did* she want? She looked away from him, across the curving river, at the trees and farmlands and houses on the Illinois side. That was the trouble. She couldn't think of what more she did want, she could only know what she didn't want. But how could you tell a man like Roger Jernigan that, though you knew your life was not perfect, your hopes for the future lay in keeping a space ready for what you did want, even though you didn't know what it would be until it came. She knew how that would sound to a man like him.

"It would be an escape," she tried to explain. "A lovely escape, but—I don't want to escape my history." She heard her words as he must hear them: they sounded ponderous, a little pretentious.

"I don't see how marrying me would interfere with your history," he reasoned humorously. "That's in the past, isn't it?"

"I mean my future history, as well," she amended lamely. "The whole pattern of my life, as it defines me. What I am, what I'm meant to be. The thing is, I know it would be good with you, but—" She saw Sunny's head cresting the promontory; he was returning to them from his climbing expedition. How could she convey to this man how much his offer had touched her, *tempted* her, honored her, yet also make him see why, outside of a storybook, it would be doomed to failure? "I would feel as if I had retired from the struggle without having finished facing it."

Two more heads appeared. Sunny had picked up two companions, adolescent boys.

"Hell, I'm not offering you immunity from struggle. I don't have that myself. I assure you, we'll have our share of struggle. Unless you mean some esoteric kind of thing I'm too stupid to understand." He had seen Sunny and the boys, too. He stood up abruptly, brushing off the seat of his pants. "Well, give it some thought, at least. You've got till Monday morning. Will you do that for me?"

She owed him that. "I'll do it, of course, but—"

Brusquely, he waved off anything else she was about to say and went to meet Sunny and his new friends. There followed an awkward scene, unpleasant for everybody. It had happened many times before, judging from Jernigan's carefully friendly attitude toward the two young boys: Sunny had often befriended people much younger than himself who had at first been flattered; then, after being with Sunny for a while, they would begin to sense that this big, cheerful, muscular man who was pretending to be their equal was not only not their equal but their inferior. The new friends would become increasingly patronizing and then bored and impatient to get away.

Sunny's present friends must have reached this point when Sunny had dragged them back to meet his father. Jernigan asked them where they lived and, when he found out they lived in the town, asked what their fathers did. One father was in the Coast Guard; the other father "lived somewhere else." Jernigan asked the boys what the cost of an ice cream was, these days. They told him, and, within seconds, each disappeared down the path between the rocks with thirty-five cents.

On the drive back, Sunny wanted to know, once more, exactly when Jody would be back. Then he asked his father if he could join the Coast Guard. Jernigan said, "No, son, we need you too much at the castle." Sunny nodded, as if he expected this answer. Then Sunny wanted them to sing all the verses of the Corn Bore song again.

> I'm just a pore little corn bore
> Tryin' to do my thing
> But Mister Poison in the Sky
> Has it in for me . . .

they sang, Sunny happily from the backseat, Jernigan pensively at the wheel of the Jeep, Cate with determined enthusiasm while staring out the window and trying to imagine her life as Mrs. Roger Jernigan. She pictured herself sleeping late and then, dressed in an expensive maternity wrap (which Jody would have picked out for her), descending into the kitchen to ask Hilda (tactfully) not to put quite so much sour cream in the potato salad; she saw herself get out her embroidery again and work on a tapestry she had once planned to make when she and Pringle were in Iceland that long, dark winter: it was going to be a crewel tapestry representing all biological life, starting with simple, colorful fishes at the bottom and working up to a row of blithe, graceful Blakean figures which would represent what men and women could be. She saw herself in June, visibly pregnant, her amniotic fluids having been pronounced healthy by the doctor Jernigan had picked, accompanying her husband via Swissair to an Integrated Pest Management Conference.

> *While you sat on your hill*
> *And counted your money*
> *And said what we could and couldn't do,*
> *All us lepidoptera down below*
> *Were outevolving you.*

That night, for the first time, Jernigan was impotent with her. They lay in the dark talking about his lawsuit problem. "The trouble is, with this fad for suing, if I were to pay Kevin off, every man who had ever worked for me, every pilot who had ever sprayed for me, the next time anything in his life went wrong—his wife miscarried, he developed a wart or a rash—it would be my fault. I have nothing against Kevin, but nothing has been proved. I frankly don't know myself whether the chemicals in my spray made that hole in his first child's heart. I'd be more than willing to help Kevin out with a loan, if only he hadn't gone and sued. Do you think I should pay him his fifteen thousand? I suppose you do."

He seemed a little disappointed when Cate said no, that if it hadn't been proved, then he would be asking for more lawsuits, probably.

They lay in silence for a while. Cate imagined how, as his wife, she would have to take on the burden of his conscience. The burden of her own was a full-time job. They would lie here (or in some other room which would be hers, which she could decorate in any way she liked—with plenty of advice from Jody, no doubt), and, on the nights when they did not make love, they would lie next to each other, companionably discussing the slippery moral crevices in the terrain of toxicology.

*   *

On the night of Easter Sunday, she lay in his arms and cried herself into hysterics. He soothed her and fathered her. At last he gave up and tried humor. "It's asking a lot, isn't it, Cate, to want me to console you for leaving me." She stopped crying soon after that, and they made love, not passionately, but with determined goodwill on the part of each. He even left his reading lamp on. His room was the most undecorated in the castle. She lay beside him, afterward, approving of its starkness, while he stroked her head. She closed her eyes gratefully and, after a while, he must have assumed she was asleep, for he put on his reading glasses and leafed through the current issue of the *Journal of Economic Entomology*. Several times she peeked up at him; it was like watching him going on with his life after she had gone.

The next morning they breakfasted together, while Sunny worked out on the floor below. They ate in silence, listening to the thuds and clanks of the various body-building instruments as Sunny made his daily rounds on the Universal.

Her plane to Chicago would leave shortly before noon.

"You don't want to take the river road back," he said. "Here, you like maps. I'll make you a map of the quickest way to the airport. What you want to do is get on Sixty-four at the bridge, then go south on Sixty-one at a town called Maquoketa. Too bad you won't have time to see their archaeological museum. It's probably closed on Easter Monday, anyway. The Indians around there used to bury their dead in trees, and there's a piece of elm with an arm bone in it. Sixty-one will take you right down to Eighty, which is what you want for the airport."

"Thank you for the weekend," she said, taking the map and putting it in her purse. "I'll always remember it."

"I expect I will, too. You know you can always call me if you need me, don't you?"

"I know." They both knew she would not be calling.

"Well, Jody will be disappointed."

"You mean you told him?"

"Just that I was thinking about asking you to marry me. Not

the other. That was between us, until you gave the go-ahead. He thought it was a great idea. He likes you."

"I'm sorry if I raised false hopes."

"No harm done. It appealed to his imagination. And he probably thought it would make it easier for me when he left. He's got to go soon. He's got to make his own way."

"Yes. . . ." She wanted to go. This was getting painful for both of them.

"So what will you do, come June?" He watched her with interest, but not so much personal, she thought, as scientific: what would a stubborn, esoteric creature like herself do next?

"I'll look for another job, I guess. I'll look for . . . whatever comes next."

"Well, that's sure to come. I hope you like it, whatever it is." He put a hand on each of her shoulders, looked her in the eye, kissed her firmly on the lips. "Good-bye, Cate."

"Good-bye, Roger." She grimaced, to keep back the tears.

"Come on," he said. "Smile, for Sunny's sake. Let's go down and tell him good-bye. If he asks when you're coming back, would you mind saying something like, you hope you'll see him again sometime? He wouldn't understand if you said never. It upsets him when people come into his life and then go out."

"It upsets me, too."

"Well, it's your choice, baby."

On the inland route Jernigan had marked for her to the airport, Cate counted three billboards advertising his company. Three times she passed the simple scene of early morning in rural America, under a bluer-than-blue sky, where every ear of corn grew straight and perfect as its neighbor and in every little farmhouse you could imagine a family eager to finish breakfast and go out and reap the blessings of the day. And hovering above this idyllic guarantee: the string of plump, dancing yellow letters: SUNNY ENTERPRISES. (The company had been founded and named by Jernigan only a few months before they had decided to consult the first of the "ninety-nine thousand" specialists about the disturbingly slow progress of the firstborn son.)

Cate wondered if he had planned it this way. That she would have to make her getaway past these billboards which reminded her, like silently chiding sentinels, that she was now leaving the kingdom he had asked her to share. Not that his kingdom was as simple as that promised by his billboards; even he would admit that such simplicity had never existed. Even in "pure, free" early America there had been tragedies in the farmhouses and blights on the corn. (More, in fact. One must give science, progress, their due.) As he had said, he couldn't exempt her from the struggle. The world he had asked her to share had its portion of uncertainties and sorrows; she had seen them for herself. But there would also be comfort and security, usefulness . . . and passion: she had felt those things, too.

What between-worlds kind of freak was she, then, who could say no to such an offer? What kingdom did she keep expecting to discover just over the next hill?

She was beginning to wonder whether whatever drove her had her best interests at heart, or whether, indeed, *it* had any heart at all.

8.
THE OUTWARD IMAGE

Once, during a teenage argument, Cate had scornfully accused Lydia of "only caring what other people think." For a moment, Lydia had been stung. Was that the way she looked to others: one of those insecure girls who "only cared what people think"? But Lydia clung for dear life to her self-esteem. She had learned that the best defense against her sharp-tongued sister was a counteroffense, the more arrogant the better. Lydia had thought for only long enough to get her phrases straight and then retorted, "Well, of *course* I care what people think. Everybody does. And the people who say they don't are only saying it because they *want other people to think* they don't. They're the worst of all. At least I'm honest with myself."

Her retort had gone over with surprising success; she had seen Cate go abstract with that self-examining look she sometimes got. Cate was thinking, Am I one of those people who say they don't because they want other people to think they don't? Am I less honest than Lydia? Lydia could read Cate's thoughts. You learned a few tricks by living under the same roof with your tormentor.

And having admitted that her self-esteem was bound up with the image others had of her, Lydia became fondly protective of this "trait," and set about enhancing it with her individuality. For, all her life, Lydia had had the tendency to think well of herself and possessed the related faculty of turning criticism to her own advantage. If "caring what others thought" was her "trait," then it couldn't be all that bad. Especially if she was honest in claiming it.

And so, "Oh yes, I'm a conventional person," Lydia would always assert, after the argument with Cate, in the same assured tone someone else might say, "Oh yes, I'm an artist."

"I guess you could say I live by the forms," Lydia would say. "Frankly, it saves me so much more time for other things."

"There are things life expects of you," Lydia told her boys as soon as they were old enough to be her captive audience, "and there are things you have a right to expect of life. You just have to learn which is which. And get yourself organized."

And, on the whole, Lydia's system had served her well. She organized life into neat compartments and tended to each compartment at the proper time and place. She grew accustomed to hearing herself praised for this. "Lydia's so good about channeling her energies," Mother often said. "It's a miracle," said her friends, "how you always manage to get everything done." (Even during her "afternoon-nap years," she was always scrupulously careful to tend to the other compartments before hitting the pillow; why, the nap itself could be said to be a compartment. There was a time and a place for it, and while she was doing it she did it well.)

And, until the late spring of her thirty-sixth year, Lydia's system had never broken down. It had never even been seriously threatened.

In high school, Lydia had been a good student during the week and a good date on the weekend. That was the main reason she had chosen to remain at the convent school, rather than dissipate her energies as Cate had after transferring to the public high school, where you knew boys were watching you even as you tried to study.

Her first semester at Chapel Hill had been a little tricky; too many expectations warred with too many temptations. It had been exhausting and confusing trying to fit everything into its proper place and time. But Max had arrived just in time with his offer, which seemed to combine perfectly what life wanted from her with what she could get from it.

And during her marriage, her compartment system had served her well. Her compartments organized *her*. If she had labeled them in her neat handwriting, they would have read something like: MOTHER. COOK. HOSTESS. INTERESTED WIFE ("What exactly *is* a bond, Max?"). WELL-DRESSED LADY SHOPPER. AMIABLE BED PARTNER. If, frequently, when going from one compartment to the next, she sighed, or muttered in her thoughts, "Now. *That's* over," well . . . that didn't mean she hadn't done it properly, whatever she was glad was now over.

And when she had felt she could no longer be Max's wife with the proper enthusiasm, she had moved out. There: that compartment closed now. Make a few new labels: MOTHER. (And she was scrupulous about having Leo come at least once a week for supper at her apartment so he wouldn't feel she had abandoned him.) STUDENT. RESPECTED FRIEND OF MAX. SECRET LOVER OF STANLEY. STILL A LADY.

But, just when she had been congratulating herself for managing everything so beautifully, serving everyone's needs including her own, her system had let her down. Or rather, circumstances (beyond her control?—well, that was debatable, she guessed) had posed a serious threat to her system. First, the contents of one compartment had leaked into another, causing her some surprise and embarrassment. And then, just when she was figuring out how to mend the walls and clean up the spillage, another compartment—the most sacred to Lydia—had come under scrutiny and attack from outsiders.

With the threatened system went the foundering of her image—what others thought of her, or what she thought they thought. And her self-esteem was currently at a shaky point until she could get things organized again.

At the moment, she was sitting on the sofa in her apartment, the noisy air conditioner ruffling the pages of the yellow legal pad poised on her lap. She was nobly forcing herself to draft her term paper for Renee even as she worried about the rest of her life. "There is a time and a place for everything," she told her boys, and she had already reserved the evenings of this week to write the term paper ("Eros: Friend or Foe?") before everything had fallen on her head.

Max had taken Dickie and Leo to see *Close Encounters of the Third Kind,* and she wanted to have a rough draft sketched out before Dickie got back. Would Max come in? It was still a little embarrassing to see him after *that* unfortunate encounter. Lord, what did he think of her? That fool Stanley. How could someone so feeling as a lover be such a fool? Or did feelings lead to such foolishness?

Max probably would come in. They had both agreed it would be best to stress "the family" at every opportunity, for Leo's sake. Leo was not in school at the moment. Ever since "the Cookie Cunningham thing," as she and Max now referred to it, Leo had refused to go to school. His pride had been severely hurt. *His* system had betrayed him. But if he didn't go back soon, he was going to lose credit for a whole semester's work—and all because of that spoiled little operator, Cookie. Max and Lydia had each had a session with the school psychologist, a Dr. Karen Small, but nothing had been resolved. Max had found Dr. Small humorless and slightly pitiful (she had a great many moles on her face and arms) but had jollied her along the way he did bank customers whose powers of investment exceeded their personal or intellectual charms. And Max was always especially amiable and polite to people he considered his inferiors. But Lydia had taken an instant dislike to Dr. Small, with her button-bright eyes so eager to peer into intimacies, and her deplorable jargon. She had turned Lydia right off by explaining she wanted to "triangularize Leo's situation." By this she meant that she wanted to hear from Leo and Max and Lydia. But why not say so? And Lydia could not resist replying, "But why not 'quadrangularize' the situation? We have four in our family. I have a younger son, Dickie." "I know all about Dickie," the button-eyed Dr. Small had told Lydia complacently, without a trace of humor. "Leo and I have already discussed Dickie. You took Dickie with you, to live across town, isn't that right? And left Leo with his father when you and Mr. Mansfield separated?"

Lydia had detected a definite slant in the way this woman perceived their "situation." She saw herself through Button Eyes' eyes: the fickle mother departing in a *whish* of graceful garments, her suitcase in one hand, the plump hand of the favored child in the other; away they went in the callous mother's car, leaving behind that nice, polite father (who had been so amiable to Dr. Small) and the dark, brooding older son, who would then be bound to resort to "an attention-getting device."

Was Dickie her favored child? Did *people think* she favored Dickie over Leo? But that was just not true. It wasn't true.

And Lydia felt herself go cold with the slap of this unearned accusation, although just a few minutes ago she had been sweltering despite the ineffectual air conditioner that came with this apartment. She got up and turned it off; it was so noisy, besides. At least Max and Leo had central air conditioning at the house. They had the color TV and all the good furniture and the familiar amenities. They could spread themselves out. Really, though the Button Eyes of the world might not think so, Lydia had bent over backward to be fair about this thing. She had left Max the house because he needed a house like that more than she did. (Lydia had wanted to live in an apartment all her life; she had the idea it would be glamorous. Whereas Max had grown up in a sort of combination apartment/boardinghouse, where his widowed mother had to share her kitchen with another woman. Living in his own house was extremely important to Max.)

Well, she could not expect every nonentity in the world to appreciate the careful arrangements she had made for everybody when she had decided she could no longer live with Max, but, really, it was downright *hurtful* for them to think she had abandoned Leo for Dickie. That was just not so. Leo had *wanted* to stay on at the house. It was within walking distance of his school. He and his two best friends had formed a little club; they called themselves, for some reason, "The Ghouls," and they liked to meet at Leo's house and shoot basketball goals or play pool, and their mothers would pick them up there. She had known Leo would be all right. He had his routines; he kept his room neat without any coaxing; he was so self-contained. Even as a baby, he had been able to entertain himself. Whereas Dickie . . . well, bless his heart, Dickie was a mess. If you didn't keep after Dickie every minute, he would abandon his schoolwork and just climb on top of the piles of dirty clothes and other mess and play his clarinet, or listen to music with his eyes closed and eat too many Clark bars. Dickie needed more attention.

But when Lydia had explained this, grudgingly, to Dr. Karen Small—grudgingly because who the hell was this young woman, younger than herself, who had no children of her own, who wasn't even married and wasn't likely to be—when Lydia had explained how Leo had always been the "good child," that people, even when he was a little boy, had called him a "little man," Dr. Small had fastened her flat little bright eyes on Lydia, as if she were reading some subtext—in jargon, no doubt—and, when Lydia had finished explaining the differences between her sons, had asked blandly, without a touch of tact or grace, "Did it ever strike you, Mrs. Mansfield, that Leo felt you were *punishing* him for being good?"

Lydia had not been able to speak for a moment. Waves of dislike all but blotted out her consciousness. To have to be subjected to this . . . this creep. Where was she from, anyway? She had no accent from anywhere. Perhaps they ironed out your accent at . . . wherever Miss Small had gone to do her graduate work in psychology . . . and programmed in this jargon. (Lydia had squinted at the prominently framed degree behind her adversary's desk . . . Rutgers University. Where in the hell was Rutgers?)

"That is the silliest thing I have ever heard," Lydia had finally blurted, when she had regained her voice.

"The silliest thing I ever heard!" she now said aloud, angrily, in the apartment that was already growing stuffy again. She decided to sweat rather than turn on the noise again. She must get on with her paper. "Eros: Friend or Foe?" Or *fool*? No, she must not think of Stanley now. Of the two problems, Leo was more important, and she shouldn't even think of *him* now. He was safe at the movies with his father and brother, and this was the time she had set aside to do her paper. There is a time and a place—

But: to punish a child for being good! Lydia suddenly recalled a motto that had particularly enchanted her in seventh
grade. She had been president of her class and had convinced her
fellow students they should vote it in as the class motto. But Sister Delaney had protested; the nun had almost wept. "You *can't*
have that as your motto, girls. It isn't suitable." "But it's true,"
Lydia had said. "It's the *truth*, Sister." "I know dear, but . . . it's
not a nice truth. It's not hopeful. It's cynical." Finally the nun had
won them over. They voted to have "Hitch your wagon to a star"
as the class motto, instead of "The wheel that squeaks the loudest is the one that gets the grease."

And yet that motto had gone straight to Lydia's seventh-
grade heart. It *was* true. The people who made the fuss and got
into the most trouble did end up getting more attention. How
often had she heard Mother and Daddy say, "Lydia's all right,
we don't have to worry about Lydia, but—*what are we going to do
about Cate?*" One half-minute discussion of Lydia, followed by
hours of discussion of Cate, who, though supposedly causing them grief, also caused their voices to rise with a curious,
taut fascination. What, oh what, was Cate going to do next?
Whereas you knew what Lydia was going to do; you could depend on it.

Enough of that, thought thirty-six-year-old Lydia. This is
not the time to go into all *that* or I'll never get to Eros.

"We were brought up believing it is possible to find everything in one man," Lydia wrote in her neat, flowing hand across
the yellow page. "My generation grew into womanhood certain
that if we were nice-looking and chaste and pleasing in manner
and dress, that Mr. Right would come and marry us and satisfy
all our desires. He would take over our father's functions in caring for us, he would be an intellectual equal (or superior), and he
would be the perfect lover."

She read over what she had written. It flowed nicely, but
was it a little too glib? Did it fall too much into the currently popular ruts of blame? ("Look what a mess we're in because *they* told
us all those lies.") But how else should she start it? She looked at

her watch and realized she had wasted almost an hour getting started. She began to panic, as she used to, long ago, whenever she had to write a book report for school. One night she had worked herself into hysterics because she couldn't get the first sentence of her book report. Daddy had taken her downstairs to his study and sat her down on his leather sofa with a soft, sharp pencil and one of his brand-new legal pads. "Now all you have to do is write me down one true thing about that book," Daddy said. "I haven't read it, so anything you can tell me about it will be of interest. Don't think of what your teacher expects you to write, or what you think you should write. Just write down one true thing about that book."

Ever since that night, Lydia had always used legal pads and soft lead pencils, sharpened to stabbing points, when she had to write something.

Was what she had written true? Well, yes and no. She was not exactly "brought up believing" those things, but, all the same, she had expected them. And, during her first few years of marriage, if anyone had asked her, "Did you manage to marry that All-in-One Package of Manhood?" she would have answered, "Of course."

She read her paragraph over once again, hoping to spring from the momentum of its final words to her next idea.

". . . and he would be the perfect lover."

For her birthday last November, Max had flown them to New Orleans in his Piper Archer. This was a trip they had wanted to take for years. New Orleans, to Lydia, had always suggested an interestingly decadent amalgamation of races, foods, and pleasures. It was where Rhett Butler had taken Scarlett on their honeymoon. It was where you would go with a man who could protect you, and the two of you would order course after course of rich French food, drink some absinthe in a dark, seductively sleazy little bar, and then wander along, safely anonymous in a crowd of revelers, until some Negro playing a saxophone called you out of your tight, civilized self and you and your partner carried the rhythms of the jungle successfully back to your hotel room.

For three consecutive days, Lydia and Max had eaten one rich meal after another, dragging their stupefied digestions back to their hotel in order to lie down and rest them for the assault of the next meal. After the evening meal, they wandered dutifully up and down Bourbon Street, where a music that sounded very little like Count Basie and a smell that they both recognized as marijuana assailed their middle-aged senses. Absinthe had been outlawed long ago; they each had a Pernod in the Absinthe Bar, but it was not the same. In fact, it made Lydia rather sick, on top of the oversauced French meal. When, by ten-thirty at night, they turned to each other to put the Good Housekeeping Seal of Approval on their married vacation, not the faintest throb of the jungle drum beat in their veins. But each had been painstakingly solicitous of the other's self-esteem. Their tired, bloated bodies struggled together to preserve the illusion of a belated honeymoon. Besides, Clark Gable was dead and, several years ago, when Vivien Leigh got off the plane in Atlanta to attend the revival of *Gone with the Wind*, some reporter had come up and asked her, "What part did *you* play?"

On the morning they left, Lydia went into a shop on the Rue Royale and bought two boxes of expensive Christmas cards, "Christmas in the Old French Quarter": fine line drawings of how things used to look in the Vieux Carré, done by a local artist. On the trip home, she sat beside Max at the controls and addressed the cards. She was glad she had remembered to bring along her address book. She hardly glanced at the clouds and patterns of light they were flying through. They assured each other several times what a good time they had had, though New Orleans had changed, obviously, from what it used to be. But didn't everything? *Max and Lydia Mansfield*, she signed the cards.

She waited till the end of November to mail the cards, because having your cards arrive in November would be as bad as wearing your white shoes after the first of September.

She had moved out the first week in December, the day after Leo's birthday.

But you couldn't put *that* in a term paper. Even though, in an indirect way, it was very important background for Eros.

Lydia selected another sharpened pencil from her pile. "Eros," she wrote, indenting for a new paragraph, "is what we mean by physical passion, or romantic love." Then she remembered what Renee had said in their first conference and added: "But Eros can also be thought of as *a striving for what one lacks*, even though he is more often equated in our times with unmanageable sexual desire." This would please Renee. Teachers liked to have their own words quoted back to them.

Lydia's upper lip had begun to perspire. She consulted the notes she had made at the library. In the absence of inspiration, she chose simply to elaborate on a note card. "The Greeks personified these longings (or strivings) into a god. Sometimes they gave him wings. (Meaning Eros can't last?) In Boeotia, an ancient Greek state where the people were still uncouth, Eros was worshiped as a large phallus. In antique art and on very old tombs, he is often portrayed aiming a bow and arrow or sadistically burning the wings off a butterfly with a torch. Eros is almost always displayed as a young boy."

Here intruded an image of her own boy, Leo, on top of Cookie Cunningham. It was a speculative image, but it filled Lydia with jealous pain. Leo's hips . . . that perfectly sculpted little butt she had wiped and powdered . . . and once, in London, in an ecstasy of mother love, had planted kisses all over before stopping herself: she didn't want to turn him into a queer or something. It made her sick, the thought of Leo and Cookie Cunningham. Not that she didn't want her son to be normal, but somehow Lydia prayed that his initiation into sex had not been with that manipulative girl. Cookie was one more "wheel that squeaked the loudest and got the grease."

Lydia bristled with anger. But this was not the time for anger. It was the time for Eros.

"From no source that I know of," she wrote, beginning a

new page, "have we been led to expect permanence from Eros, or peace, or self-respect." Was that going too far? Well, leave it in for now. Lydia had a fetish: every time she changed something, even one word, she had to go back and do the page over. "Eros is no respecter of family ties or social class. He doesn't care a hoot for propriety. He may come dressed in a variety of garbs, not always in the best of taste, or he may speak in an accent foreign or unusual to the ear. Yet once we are pierced by his arrow, we become consumed with a desire that often seems isolated from the rest of our lives."

Just writing the words "consumed with desire" had a physical effect on Lydia. Despite all the trouble Stanely had caused, she was still under his physical spell.

But what was she to do with him?

After Lydia had been to Stanley's place a few times, he had begun making elaborate plans for all the things he would like to do with her. He wanted to take her to dinner at that new Plantation Inn where you could dance afterward; he wanted to drive her west for a weekend in the mountains ("Your mother lives in the mountains, doesn't she?"); he was thinking about taking horseback-riding lessons at a stable in town: perhaps they could ride together, pack picnic lunches behind their saddles and eat in sun-dappled woods, their two horses tethered to a tree.

As he came up with each idea for expanding into the world as a couple, Lydia had run the corresponding picture through her head. She saw at least a dozen couples she had known in her life with Max that they would be sure to run into if they went to any fashionable new restaurant in town. She saw herself and Stanley, each self-conscious for a different reason, walking toward the front door of her mother's house in Lake Hills, where Nell, wearing that unsettling smile she could get on her face when one part of her found something amusing but the other part told her she must behave, would be waiting to serve them tea, or drinks. ("Well," Nell would say, when they were all arranged in the living room. "What a nice surprise. This is wonderful weather for a trip to the mountains. I'm so glad you let me know you were up

here. I hope you'll stay to supper. Stanley, Lydia tells me you're
from New York. What do you think of our ways down here? No,
really. Tell me, what do you really think of us, so far?") Oh,
Mother would carry it off; she would probably enjoy the unex-
pectedness of it. But what would she be thinking of her daughter? ("Well, well, not what I would have expected Lydia to
choose, but why not? He *is* sweet. Those long eyelashes. And
such an attractive physique. I suppose they are passionate
lovers. . . .") Lydia burned with embarrassment when she
reached this part. Why? It was true. They *were* passionate lovers.
Mother would probably not even mind. It was Lydia who could
not bear the thought of Nell's thinking of her in this way.

As for the horseback-riding picnic, it was out of the question: the two of them bouncing and sweating atop two dusty
rented hacks who would stop and eat grass until you kicked
them. They would sneeze, and swish their tails, and probably
worse, during the picnic. Stanley was imagining something out
of an English rural-wallpaper scene. Lydia felt she had to protect
him from his own romanticism.

He was really a touching man, surprisingly sensitive and full
of all sorts of softnesses and feelings that did not seem to conflict
with his masculinity. He was always surprising her with sweet
gestures, or vulnerable statements that were almost frightening
in their nakedness or originality. Once while they were lying together, he shocked her by saying he wished he could have a
baby. On guard, Lydia had instinctively pulled the sheet up to
her chin and said that, though she adored her sons, she didn't
think she wanted to have any more babies. "No, I didn't mean
that," he said dreamily. "I just meant I wished *I* could have one.
Just one little baby that would come out of me and be all mine."
What a strange thing to say! Lydia had felt repelled. No, she had
felt that she *ought to feel* repelled. But after she had gone home
and thought about it, it had grown on her. What a strangely
attractive, almost erotic idea: her beautiful, slim, deferential
Stanley as a male mother. The strange vision helped Lydia, temporarily, to a fresh reimagining of the world: gentle male mothers with their long brown arms and legs cuddling infants; male

mothers with healthy penises dangling freely beneath loincloths, but subjugating their male force to the care of a small creature. But, lacking practice in transferring vision into symbol, Lydia fell back into literal territory with a thud and Stanley's vision seemed preposterous, even slightly obscene. From where was the baby going to come out of him? Would he still be able to have a penis? What about breasts? She remembered a story in the newspaper about some man, left alone with a starving baby; the man's nipples had begun to leak milk.

And in a way, this thing she and Stanley had between them was like that vision. As long as it remained softly focused, slightly blurred, with plenty of seclusion and shade, it could survive. But expose it to too much light of day, to the scrutiny of the wrong people, and it might disintegrate. It might "self-destruct" on the spot, like those secret instructions on the tape at the beginning of the old *Mission: Impossible* shows which all four of them—she, Max, Leo, and Dickie—had loved to watch.

Lydia therefore told Stanley a lie, to protect this nice, private thing they had between them for as long as possible. She told Stanley that, though Max, her estranged husband, was in most ways a gentleman, he was extremely jealous; also, he had powerful connections in this city, and if she aroused this jealousy before the divorce came through, he might prevent her from having custody of the children. "We're getting one of those divorces where nobody's at fault," she told Stanley. (This part was the truth.) "The two of you live separately for one year, and then it's done. Without any ugly accusations. So it will be December before I'll feel comfortable about going out."

This seemed to convince Stanley. "But you can at least come and see my office," he said. So she let him take her to his office on his day off and show her all the equipment of which he was so proud (bought with money borrowed from Broadbelt Commercial Trust): the examining tables and reclining chairs with great big trays for your feet, the X-ray machine, and some very nice etchings (similar to that one in his bathroom back at the apartment) of the bones and muscles of the feet. "A friend of mine in New York who's an artist picked those up for me in Rome," said

Stanley. "They're by a fifteenth-century Italian artist. You know, the artists used to have to go out at night and rob graves in order to learn the bones of the body." Lydia was almost in love with Stanley as he took her through the rooms where he worked, explaining everything proudly in his soft voice with its emphases so different from the ones she was used to. She saw him in his hometown, New York, surrounded by his own network of friends, who would bring him things from Rome. It had taken courage for him to come down here and start all over again, friendless. And later that afternoon, when they were lying naked and damp from their loving exertions, she confided in Stanley how, recently, since starting back to school—and since meeting him—she felt she had crossed her own starting point and that she had a very interesting future ahead of her. "I don't know what it is yet," she told him, "only I know it's going to make me more alive than ever. I will be living a life in which I do something that's important. It will be something I can do well and care about doing." And he nodded and squeezed her hand. "That's exactly how I feel about what I do," he said. And then he confided to Lydia another of his startling visions. "You see, I feel I have to convince as many people as possible to get their feet in shape." (At this point, Lydia had to suppress a snicker; Stanley saw it and looked slightly hurt.) "No, listen," he went on, "it's important. People have got to take better care of their feet. You don't know how it hurts me, every time a patient shows me a pair of ruined feet. It's not just that it's an ugly sight, it's that . . . well, they've signed their own death warrant. They can hardly walk. And I don't mean just old people, either. Young people come in with their arches fallen and their toes all bunched together and their metatarsals already deformed. My heart sinks. I do what I can, but I want to tell them, 'Don't you know we're going to have to run?' I can't tell them that, they'd think I was crazy, but I really do think that we've all got to get in shape the next few years. I think we're going to have to run for our lives. And the ones who hobble along or get out of breath just aren't going to make it."

"Run *where*?" Lydia asked. "From *what*?"

"I can't tell you that. I'm not a prophet. All I have is this feeling. I'm not the only one. Why are all these people suddenly getting in shape? They sense something. I'm not saying *what* they sense. I'm not sure exactly what it is *I* sense. All I know is, I want to be ready. And I want to help other people be ready."

"But are you thinking of *war*," Lydia pressed him, "or *what?*"

"I can't tell you. It's like an animal instinct. I've just got this feeling that we all may have to move pretty fast and be in the best shape we can. I try to run every morning except on the days I swim. Here, let me see your feet a minute."

"No," protested Lydia, shoving them beneath the sheet. "I don't want you to see my corn."

But he bent down and found her feet, anyway. "The corn's okay. It'll go away when you start wearing sandals this summer. But you shouldn't have worn the shoes that did this." He rubbed his thumb professionally across the bunion on Lydia's right big toe. "Your arches are still terrific, though. That's a good girl."

His benevolent "doctoring" approach had aroused Lydia again. She bent down after him and they were soon locked together with their heads where their feet had been. Lydia found herself entertaining fervid visions of a catastrophe that would wipe out all her need for secrecy with Stanley. If the world suddenly turned into a place where the best people were the leanest runners with the most durable lungs and the sweetest intentions, she could do no better than Stanley. She had held on to Stanley, blotting out the world where you always had to be dressed in the image you wanted others to see, and imagined their two slim naked brown bodies (she would have lost some weight and got a suntan) running, running, swift as animals, on healthy, high-arched feet, toward a safe, quiet haven where they could begin to build a gentle civilization which could throb with a few rhythms of the jungle.

A week or so later, Stanley had said, "We're going to the movies this week. The next time Dickie spends the evening with a friend, you and I will go and see *The China Syndrome* at the movie house near my place. You're going to have to trust old Stanley more. You've gotten too uptight about this divorce." He had looked so certain and so mysteriously pleased with himself that Lydia had been convinced. What harm could there be, after all, in going to a nearby movie house and sitting in the dark with her lover? Going out with a person after you had been married for a long time was, as she had told Renee, like making a statement, but this would be a harmless statement. It was not as if she were posting banns with Stanley in church.

And so they had gone to an early-evening showing of *The China Syndrome* at the first opportunity Lydia could find to nudge Dickie into spending the evening with a friend. And she had to nudge, because, at the moment, Dickie was feeling very comfortable with just the two of them playing house, trying to be good about their diet, each going away after supper to do homework, and meeting at ten for a "reward" snack.

Though Lydia had her reservations about Jane Fonda (one more wheel that squeaked the loudest . . . about things that had nothing to do with the profession of acting), she had enjoyed the movie. Having Stanley sit next to her in a public place, his arm draped casually around the back of her chair, was as erotic-in-reverse as seeing him for the first time in his clothes after they had made each other's acquaintance practically naked in the pool. And the movie, about a near-miss nuclear catastrophe, was made all the more riveting by the fact that real life—up in Harrisburg, Pennsylvania—had copied the scenario only a month ago. Perhaps that world of the leanest runners was coming closer.

Lydia came blinking out of the dark theater with Stanley. She was still under the spell of the movie and poor Jack Lemmon's death. Then she heard Stanley speaking in a friendly way to someone in the line of people waiting for the nine-o'clock showing. The someone was Max.

"Hello, how are you?" Max was saying in his amiable voice. To Lydia, he said simply "Hel-*lo*," but in a way that spoke volumes. With Max was a svelte, athletic-looking girl, wearing tight jeans and a T-shirt that showed off her thin, muscular arms. She looked vaguely familiar; she was wearing running shoes.

"Hello," she said, flashing a mouthful of teeth that no longer wore heavy silver braces. "I guess we haven't seen each other since I was about thirteen."

It was Lizzie Broadbelt. Lydia had known she was back from the London School of Economics, and from an ill-fated romance with some Arab she had met in England. But in Lydia's mind, Lizzie had remained the fat-faced child with a mouth full of silver (and usually some bits of food) who had whined around her grandfather's chair during those awful, stiff dinners at the Broadbelts'. Max had told Lydia that he was "showing Lizzie the ropes" of the Trust and Investment departments, and Lydia had heard the information absentmindedly. She wasn't prepared for this streamlined, smiling, poised female who looked so eager to be friends.

"Hello, Lizzie," said Lydia in a daze. Everybody but Lydia herself seemed to be smiling, relaxed, and at ease. She felt the victim of some kind of conspiracy. "How are you liking things at the Bank?"

"Well, it's a job," said Lizzie. She looked up at Max, who laughed, as he was supposed to.

Lydia's head was buzzing with confusion; but she remembered her manners. "I'd like you to meet Stanley Edelman," she said to Max and Lizzie. "Stanley this is—"

"Oh, we've already met," said Stanley, sounding very pleased with himself.

"Dr. Edelman is a valued customer," said Max, nodding cordially to Stanley.

"We've met, too," Lizzie told Stanley. "I was in with Max, having my lesson, when you came up."

The four of them stood smiling at one another until Lydia thought her face would break. Then, thank the Lord, the line in which Max and Lizzie were standing started to move.

"You all enjoy the movie," said Lydia, "if enjoy is the right word." Then she looked pointedly at the handsome quartz which Max had given her for her last birthday. "Goodness, I'd better get a move on if I'm going to collect Dickie by nine-thirty from the Roberts' house." There. That ought to make that clear. To Max she said, "Is Leo okay?"

The enduring priorities had been flung down, like respectable gauntlets, across this embarrassing scene.

"I left him talking on the phone to a girl," replied Max. "When I get back, he'll probably still be talking."

Everyone laughed, as they were supposed to, and the two couples moved in opposite directions. "Let's have lunch sometime," Lizzie Broadbelt called after Lydia. "We can compare our experiences in London!" At Stanley, Lizzie flashed her orthodontic gems in an open salute to his dark, athletic attractiveness. They were, Lydia realized, near enough in physical type to be brother and sister.

She walked, in a hot bubble of rage and confusion, beside Stanley to the parking lot where both their cars, wheels turned toward each other as if they'd been having a date of their own, waited side by side. She could hardly think, she felt so dislocated and humiliated. She was trying to sort out what she had won or lost from the unexpected encounter, when Stanley crowed happily, "There now, didn't I tell you to trust your old Stanley? The ice has been broken and nobody's mad at anybody."

"Do you mean to tell me," said Lydia, stopping in her tracks, "that you . . . set this whole thing up?"

"You mean tonight? Just now? Oh no, *that* was pure luck. But I guess you could say I laid the groundwork. I went in to see him last week. I just wanted to meet him and have a look at him myself. It was the simplest thing in the world to arrange. I had some business there, anyway, and I just inquired casually whether Mr. Mansfield happened to be free, and he was, and they sent me right up. He was going over some charts or something with *her*—she's the boss's granddaughter, isn't she?—but she went out while he and I talked."

"Talked . . . about *what*?"

"Oh, I had that all planned. I told him I was considering making some investments and wanted to know what he would recommend."

"And what did . . . he recommend?" asked Lydia, her chest so constricted she could hardly breathe.

"Well, he asked me approximately how much I wanted to

invest. Then—he was so modest—he said that he had to spend so much of his time thinking in terms of the whole Bank instead of any individual investor that one of the younger officers might be more up on what I needed. But he said I couldn't go wrong by starting with a couple of CDs. Those are—"

"I know," said Lydia, in a choked voice. "I know what CDs are." Poor Stanley had been condescended to royally and he only thought Max was being "modest." She didn't know whom to feel sorrier for: Stanley or herself. Now that Max had seen them and put two and two together, he must think they were both fools: Stanley for going on such an ill-considered errand to the upstairs offices of the Bank; herself for going with a man who would do such a thing. And Lizzie Broadbelt, what must she be thinking? She must be sitting there in the movies next to Max having herself a private chortle over the comedown of the irreproachable Mrs. Mansfield, who used to shoot her such cold looks when she was an ugly little girl hovering behind granddaddy's chair. Or were Max and Lizzie already *discussing* the unexpected meeting that had just taken place (which Stanley called "luck"!) and all its ramifications? For the first time it occurred to Lydia that Max and Lizzie were sleeping together. Well, that was to be expected; Max was a normal man; the two of them were thrown together every day. But . . . surely Max wasn't *serious* about her. The sleeping together was one thing, but if he could go so quickly from loving her to loving Lydia Broadbelt, well, didn't that undermine the eighteen years' worth of devotion Max had professed to feel for her?

"Would you mind telling me," Lydia asked Stanley in the parking lot, "what you hoped to gain by going to . . . his office?" She had almost said "my husband's office."

"I told you," said Stanley, who was just beginning to see that Lydia was not as pleased as he had expected her to be that "the ice had been broken." "I wanted to meet him face-to-face. I wanted to judge for myself. I have good instincts about people. I wanted to see for myself how much we had to fear from him—"

"To fear?" In the confusion of all these revelations, Lydia had, for the moment, forgotten about her lie: the little story she had made up about their having to be careful because of Max's jealousy.

"Yes. But I knew the minute we started talking that he was a reasonable man. I trust my instincts, and my instincts tell me we have nothing to fear from Max." He spoke the name as if they'd known each other, he and "Max," since kindergarten. He pulled Lydia to him. "I thought you'd be more pleased. And tonight! Can you tell me how things could've worked out any better? Now it's all out in the open."

"Yes, it's all out in the open," repeated Lydia slowly, testing the thought as she spoke.

"You're with me," said Stanley, muzzling her neck, "and he knows it. And he's consoling himself with Miss Broadbelt, and we know it. So nobody's going to take your kids away from you. And now we don't have to sneak around like we have something to be ashamed of. I can take you out proudly." He parted his lips and played his warm breath upon the back of her neck. "And I'll be proud."

Lydia stood with her head bowed, allowing Stanley to plant his necklace of kisses. She was overwhelmed by the blurring of lines that had suddenly complicated her new life, the life she had intended to have control over. She didn't know where anything fitted, with all these new developments, and she was not going to know as long as Stanley kept melting her down with kisses. He turned *her* into a blur. "It's too much," she said, her voice breaking. He turned her around joyously and kissed her all the harder. He thought she was overwhelmed with relief.

"Come back to my place. Just for a little while."

"I can't! I have to pick up Dickie. I'm already late, as it is." She began to sob with frustration. All these demands on her, it was too much. Why couldn't life be simpler? All she asked was the space in which to be herself, and a simple, innocent passion with a man like Stanley, and the respect of other people. "There's too much going on," she accused him tearfully, "everyone asks too much of me. I have to go away and compose myself."

He was still in awe of her tears; they were relatively new to him. After they had arranged to meet as usual on Thursday, he reluctantly put her into her car. She drove off, still sobbing, and saw him in her rearview mirror. He was standing beside his BMW, in the space her Volvo had left. He made a romantic, forlorn figure, under the blue-white glow of the parking-lot lights: her devoted knight who had climbed the wainscoted staircase of the Broadbelt Bank to confront the dragon for her sake, and had found only a modest, condescending fellow who advised a couple of Certificates of Deposit. He doesn't want to get into his car and drive home to a place I'm not in, thought Lydia; he dreads getting into a bed where—

She started to bawl.

But by the time she had reached the Roberts' house she was in control again. Dickie came running out to the car, jumped in, and didn't notice a thing.

Well, here comes the showdown, she had thought when Max had phoned, several days later, in the morning. "I have to talk to you," he had said, in a businesslike voice. "Can we meet for an early lunch?" It just so happened it was Thursday, Stanley's day. It's his own fault, he brought it on himself, thought Lydia, and couldn't help feeling a perverse vindication as she hung up after making an appointment with Max, and dialed Stanley's number. He had wanted things out in the open, hadn't he? Well, he would have to sacrifice part of their lovely Thursday ritual (their "knowing swim," they now called it, swimming their laps side by side, just as they had done before they had ever exchanged a word, only now "knowing" what was to follow afterward). Stanley was disappointed she would not make it to the pool, but hoped she would come to him by early afternoon. "It's best to have it all out now," Stanley said, sounding pleased, if a little groggy, over the phone. She had waked him up; he slept late on his day off. Now he would turn over and dream of her while she dressed for her "having-it-all-out" lunch with Max. She felt she had been thrust, against her will, onto the set of a soap opera.

Max was waiting for her at their old table in the little restaurant near the bank. The headwaiter seemed ecstatic to see her again. To think! Once this had been the favorite part of her life: getting dressed to kill as "Mrs. Max Mansfield" and going downtown to have lunch at this restaurant. Only, in the old days, she had gone to the Bank to pick Max up; how she had reveled in marching past the tellers, eliciting from each a little greeting of homage before she turned right, past the glass cages of the credit and loan officers, and up the carpeted stairs into the somber, wainscoted regions—the regions where Stanley had so recently and intrepidly trod—where the brass titles on the doors grew more hallowed the farther down the hall you went. And Max's was the last door but one from the end; the end being Mr. Broadbelt, who had stopped coming in every day.

Max stood up from the table, kissed Lydia with respect, and assisted the headwaiter in seating her. "You're looking very well," he said.

Lydia felt herself blush guiltily. "So are you. You've lost weight, haven't you?"

"Thank you for noticing. I'm making an effort."

But it annoyed her when, after she had ordered a daiquiri—just as in the old days—he asked for Perrier on the rocks with a twist of lime. "No martini?" she asked.

"Not today. I've got to write my speech for an investment seminar and I need to keep my head clear. And, like I said, I'm trying to get rid of this potbelly." He slapped the front of his lightweight jacket, but rather complacently.

He *is* sleeping with her, thought Lydia; or getting ready to. It irritated her to remember all the times she had nagged him to slim down, to no avail. Yet he had professed to be devoted to her. "I will never love another woman the way I have loved you," he had said, just before she had walked out the door. But he would drink Perrier for Lizzie Broadbelt.

"How's Dickie?" asked Max. "Is *he* losing any weight?"

"We're all doing our best to improve ourselves," replied Lydia, lowering her gaze to the menu, which she already knew by heart: it had not changed in ten years. "I'm going to have my usual, the shrimp salad."

"I'll join you." Max ordered two shrimp salads and gave the

waiter the menus. In all their years together, Max had never ordered a salad for lunch. Things must be more serious than she'd
thought.

"And how is Leo?" she asked, sipping her daiquiri: stalling.

"That's what I want to talk about. It's why I needed to see
you."

"About *Leo*?" She was surprised, and her voice revealed it.
And she saw Max notice it, saw him register what it was *she* had
thought he wanted to talk about, and saw him look away, embarrassed that she would have expected this. You sometimes saw
more than was comfortable, when you had been married to a
person and reading his face for eighteen years. Max was embarrassed for *her*, that she would expect him to sink to soap-opera
tactics.

"This morning, right before I phoned you, I had a phone call
from Marshall Cunningham."

"The psychiatrist?"

"And the father of Cookie Cunningham, the girl Leo's been
dating. Hell, maybe I will have that drink." Max motioned the
waiter over. "One vodka martini, please."

"Oh Lord, don't tell me she's pregnant or something." Lydia
nevertheless felt her spirits rise when Max ordered the martini. It
anchored her back in the secure old times, when she knew where
she was with him.

"Nothing so simple." Max sighed. "Cookie tried to kill herself night before last. She swallowed almost a whole bottle of
some powerful tranquilizer Marshall kept around for patient
emergencies. She had written a suicide note. It seems it was because of Leo."

"Because of *Leo*?"

Max's drink came. He took a liberal sip. "Marshall said
they'd had a fight, and Leo refused to see her anymore, or to take
her to the Cotillion Club Dance."

"Oh *really*," bridled Lydia, already on Leo's side. "In my
day, we didn't swallow pills; we accepted another date for the
dance." She bit savagely into a stalk of celery from the little *cru-
dités* dish. It still had strings on it: this place was going down.

"Luckily," Max went on, lowering his voice, "Cookie's mother stopped by her room to say goodnight. The Cunninghams had been out for the evening. If they hadn't come home when they did, Cookie might be dead now."

"Oh for Pete's sake, I don't believe this." Lydia shook her head violently. Then stiffened when she saw the headwaiter covertly watching. He probably thought they were having a fight. "I mean, we're talking about death, when all Leo did was refuse to take her to a *dance*?"

"He'd already invited her to the dance, Marshall said, but then after this fight they had, Leo dropped her, refused to let her explain her side. Cunningham insinuated we had brought him up too rigidly, which I didn't like one bit. But the reason he called was this: Cookie refuses to return to school until Leo goes to see her."

"I don't see the point of that. Why should Marshall Cunningham want his daughter to see Leo if he's such a monster?"

"I told you. She refuses to go back to school until—"

"Oh pooh! Can't Marshall Cunningham make her go back? If Leo 'refused' to go to school, I'm sure we wouldn't put up with it. But of course, according to Marshall Cunningham, we're 'rigid.' " Lydia was so furious with the Cunninghams that she couldn't help adding, "I'll bet you anything that girl waited until she heard her parents drive up before swallowing those pills. And what kind of doctor is it who'll leave that kind of pill around for his children to swallow every time the least little thing doesn't go their way." Then, because she did not want to seem heartless, she amended, "I'm sorry for the girl, of course. She must have been unhappy, even to fake it."

Max drained his martini. She saw him debating with himself whether to have another, then pull himself together and go back to his Perrier. "There's a further complication. Leo won't go see Cookie. He absolutely refuses. I spoke to him just before he left for school. After Cunningham called. He was adamant. He says it's the principle of the thing, that he made his decision after their fight, and, as far as he was concerned, that was the end of it."

"Good Lord, what did they fight about?" Lydia's first reaction to this news was to be a little shocked at her son's hardness. But principles were principles. Hadn't she herself drummed that into him? She was not going to desert his defense so easily. And hadn't she herself been feeling hard toward Cookie? Lydia could not get the image out of her head of the contriving little "heroine," peeking out of the window as her parents drove up, then swallowing the pills.

"There wasn't time to go into it much. Leo said Cookie had 'made her decision and had to live with it,' whatever that means. Then he rushed off to school. He doesn't like to miss his first period. That's that Social Studies course all the kids are wild about. Clever of them to put it first thing in the morning. He didn't even finish drying his hair. That was another thing: it was kind of hard to talk, with him running that dryer."

"Maybe I can get it out of him. Though you know how closemouthed he can be. Even when he was little, he'd go into his own world and you couldn't get a peep out of him." Though Lydia had always admired this about Leo: his self-containment gave him a mysterious, finished quality. He had mastered a sort of cunning silence that made you think he knew more than perhaps he did.

"I was hoping you'd say that." Max sounded relieved. Their salad plates came. Lydia counted the shrimp. Nine. There used to be twelve. The place was really going down. "Do you think you could pick him up at school today, maybe? Catch him before he goes off somewhere with his friends? If you could spend the afternoon with him, he might talk to you. I could pick him up around eight this evening. Just between us, I have a feeling it might be simplest for everyone if he'd just go over there and see the girl. I know the Cunninghams aren't particularly our friends, but maybe that's why it would be kinder all the way around. I wouldn't want them to think that Leo's behavior indicates any rejection of their daughter on our behalf."

Typical Max. Always bending over backward to keep people he didn't even like from thinking he thought he was better than they were.

"I'll have to drive back across town to my place and leave a note for Dickie and put the keys in the flower box for him," said Lydia. She ate a shrimp and thought, Well, Stanley, this is just not our day. And she wouldn't be able to phone Stanley until he came back from *his* lunch—by which time he would be expecting her and would be doubly disappointed. And if Leo was going to stay for supper, she would have to buy more hamburger meat.

"You always know how to make him be sensible," Max said. "You've always been better at that than I have. You can make him see reason. Of course, I'd be against forcing him. We're not rigid. I must say, I didn't like that implication of Cunningham's."

"In the first place," said Lydia heatedly, "he has no right to set himself up as any arbiter of morality. Dammit, they were *his* pills. And I know for a fact that, even when I was living at our house, Cookie telephoned Leo half to death. She practically forced him into taking her out. I don't see that we owe these Cunninghams anything."

For the first time today, Max looked at Lydia in "the old way." "You're a tigress, aren't you," he said, "when it comes to defending your own. Just see how the land lies, will you? We owe *Leo* that."

He continued to look at her admiringly, however, and she felt she had regained a little of her lost pride from the movie incident the other night. Whatever became of them both, it was important for Lydia to retain a hold on Max's admiration.

Max then steered the conversation to other things. He said he wanted to update Lydia's portfolio. Get rid of some General Motors and buy more Texas Instrument. And the oil stocks would soar out of sight in the short term; and, in the longer term, railroads, coal, and microchips. "I want you to be in the best shape possible," he told her.

"You sound like you're planning to die" was her alarmed reply.

"No, no. I just want to get things set up for you before the divorce comes through. Not that I won't always be available for you, but it's good to do these things sooner rather than later."

It was the first time that Lydia could recall that he had said "before the divorce comes through." Previously, it had always been "if we go through with the divorce."

And over coffee, Lydia could not resist broaching "the subject." "How is Lizzie Broadbelt working out at the Bank?" After all, they'd discussed her before; only, Lydia, imagining the ugly child with food in her braces, had not paid much attention.

"She's going to be okay. Broadbelt wants to groom her for foreign operations—we're getting more and more into that; she'll be a great asset, she even speaks a little Arabic, which doesn't hurt anyone today. But she's still very young. She has a few wild ideas. Not that they're not good ideas, but you can't change the system overnight."

"What kind of ideas, for instance?" Lydia was suddenly extremely interested.

"Oh well, like an international currency." He laughed. "I told her, 'Lizzie, you'll have us all up the creek here if you try to implement all those fancy ideals you got at the LSE.'"

Lydia made a note to ask her Economics professor why, exactly, an international currency would have us up the creek. "I suppose she learned her Arabic from that Arab she had the affair with."

Max blinked, but looked less concerned than Lydia would have expected. "No doubt. Old Broadbelt told me it was just typical of Lizzie to fall in love with an Arab from the one country whose oil is running out. He would have been okay, though. His family owns one of the main banks in Bahrain. It was the family and cultural stuff that didn't work out. She went over there and met the family, Lizzie did. But she was a little too modern for them. Lizzie's a woman of the future, all right."

Lydia recalled how, when she and Max were courting, he had told her how proud he was that she was still a virgin. "I'm old-fashioned, I guess," he had said. "I want to be the one to teach you." And she also recalled how he really didn't mind that she didn't understand the intricacies of finance. He had often laughed dotingly over her worst mistakes, even going so far as to rumple her short curls and tell her "not to worry her pretty head."

"There's one other matter," Max said.

"Yes?" *Here it comes,* she thought, rather anticipating it.

"I've been feeling remiss. I promised your mother I'd fly to the Outer Banks sometime this spring and check on the cottage. And now the spring's almost over. I don't think I'm going to be able to make it. Not this month, for sure. I really had meant to go. Not only because I said I would, but because that cottage will belong to the boys one day. Your daddy would want it kept in shape for them, and *their* children. What I had wanted to do was see about turning it into a rental property—for very select tenants, of course, the kind that take a house for a whole summer. There are special tax deductions if you turn it into a rental property. But this kind of thing is best arranged in person, on the spot, rather than by phone. I was wondering if you might find a weekend or so to drive over. I could tell you what you'd have to do."

"Well, I have my school till the end of May," said Lydia. "I suppose I *could* go then. But the boys don't get out of their school till almost the middle of June. I suppose you'd want me to take them, too." In their eighteen-years-of-marriage code, Lydia was saying, *I can cope with anything you ask of me, because I'm organized; but I just want you to know that you're on the verge of imposing.*

"I can keep the boys with me," Max put in, receiving the code. He had probably hoped to get out of everything, but, when put on the spot, he was usually fair. "You go on out there whenever you can. Have yourself a little vacation."

Oh no, you don't, thought Lydia. Why, they were right back on the old marriage-go-round; staking claims on who got to be the biggest martyr. And he probably expects I'll go with Stanley, she thought; he thinks I'll take Stanley to Daddy's cottage and we'll have a passionate weekend while he sits home with the boys. When he probably meant to sit home with Lizzie while I took the boys. Lydia thought for a minute. "I know," she said. "I have the perfect solution. *Mother* and I will go. As soon as my school is finished, Mother and I can drive to the Outer Banks and take care of everything. We'll need to clean our stuff out if we're going to rent the cottage. And it will be good for Mother.

It will be a sort of sentimental journey. We'll have a chance to say good-bye one last time to Daddy in the place he really loved."

Lydia's eyes filled. She snapped open her purse, the intricately woven gray leather one that Max had given her for Christmas, and took out a clean handkerchief with her initials on it.

"Oh, honey," said Max, looking miserable. He put his hand over hers after she had finished blowing her nose and put the handkerchief back. She saw the headwaiter watching. He probably thinks we've decided not to get the divorce, thought Lydia.

Lydia straightened her shoulders. She decided to leave while she was ahead. "Well," she said, looking at the quartz watch, "I guess I'd better get a move on if I'm going to get everything done. I'll pick Leo up at school. Shall I see you at about eight? Try to make it by then, as I have lots of homework to do for my classes tomorrow."

"You're a wonderful woman," he said, rising when she did. He paid the bill and they separated outside the restaurant.

Not one word had been said about Stanley.

And, parked in front of Leo's school, waiting for the dismissal bell, Lydia had thought, Yes, that's the way "people like us" do things; we relegate them to the outer fringes by simply not mentioning them. As long as they are not mentioned, they do not exist in our world. And how can they be a threat if they don't exist? So, according to our luncheon topics, "our" world includes Leo and Dickie, it includes Mother, it includes the Broadbelts, it even includes Lizzie's Arab; and it includes the Cunninghams, who don't like us one bit more than we like them, but whose melodramatic daughter has changed the shape of my day. I'm sorry, but I don't for one minute believe that girl intended to kill herself. Or am I being hard? Am I lacking in feeling? But I am fiercely protective of what is mine . . . my nearest and dearest . . . a tigress, Max called me. That counts as feeling, doesn't it? What was it Renee said, when we were talking about Eros? That he could be a striving for what one lacked? Am I attracted to Stanley because he has the feelings that I lack? But if what I have for him isn't feeling, then what *are* feelings, I'd like to know. And it isn't just the sex. When I phoned him to say I couldn't come this afternoon, and he asked, "What did Max say, at the lunch?" I said, "It was *mostly* about our son Leo. Some girl took an overdose of pills because Leo didn't want to see her anymore." That wasn't a lie, we *did* talk mostly about Leo; but I couldn't stand to let him know he wasn't even mentioned—not even "How did you and Stanley like the movie the other night?" I felt so protective of him. My pride hurt for his pride; if that isn't feeling, I don't know what is. And then he said, "Your son obviously has the fatal charm of his mother." Meaning what? Would Stanley ever take pills if I said I wouldn't see him anymore? No, I don't think he would do that; I wouldn't want him to do that. But I could tell he was really disappointed that I couldn't come today. Strange: traditionally it's been the woman who waits at home for the man to "call in" and say whether he can get away from all the demands of his busy schedule for a stolen hour of secret love. Only our love isn't entirely secret anymore. The thing that gets me is that, if Max should marry Lizzie Broadbelt, who is twenty-three years younger than he is, people would think it was perfectly suitable. They would consider it a "good match" for both of them. Whereas, if I married Stanley, which I have no intention of doing—I'm not sure I ever want to get on *that* merry-go-round again—people would consider it a comedown for me. "Oh, she married a *younger man*," they would say, "someone from New York. Not that he's not very *attractive*. You can tell she's very physically attached. . . ." And Stanley is only five years younger than I am. Jake Galitsky was four years younger than Cate. But Cate couldn't care less about such things. Why do I? I *don't*. But it infuriates me for others to judge me. People like . . . the Cunninghams . . . whom I don't even like. Why is it I have spent so many hours in my life worrying about and working for the good opinion of people I don't even like? Because I don't want to give them the opportunity to misjudge me. If I conform outwardly to their approved image, then I can keep my distance from them and control what they think about me. But why should I care what they think of me?

Lydia had gone around and around this maze for a while and then relaxed her brain with a brighter image: the huge, unspecified (so she wouldn't have to imagine the ugliness and physical pain) disaster, from which she and Stanley and other swift, durable people with sweet intentions would be allowed to escape, running on healthy feet to a gentler, less critical world. In her mind, she blew up places like The Plantation Club and all country clubs; she had just reached the Broadbelt Bank and had her deadly weapon poised (What about Max? Should she give him a chance to escape? And Lizzie? She didn't really hate Lizzie; only why was it that, even when you didn't want someone for yourself anymore, you didn't want anyone else to have him, either? And the children? What was she going to do about Leo and Dickie in her catastrophe? Leo could run, but Dickie would have to lose some weight if he were to make it to the New World...). Lydia had just reached this complex set of decisions in her fantasy when Leo, tall and beautiful, flanked by his usual sidekicks, The Ghouls, came out of the modern school building.

He saw her at once—as if he had expected her to be waiting in front of his school—and indicated her presence to his friends; the three boys strolled toward the car with the practiced nonchalance of very young men.

He really is lovely, thought Lydia, her chest filling with pride. But there *is* a sort of heartless self-containment about him. Lord, what would I have done if I had been in love with someone like Leo when I was fifteen? Eaten my heart out, I suppose. I know I would have died before I ever picked up that phone and called him. And she felt sympathy for Cookie Cunningham. It pleased her that she felt the sympathy. That meant she wasn't heartless. But what was Leo feeling? Surely, behind that reserved exterior, he must be feeling something. Well, that's why she was here, to find out.

Leo leaned one elbow against her open window. "How come you're here?" he asked innocently. His two friends greeted her respectfully; they hovered, just within earshot, to see what would happen. Lydia knew from the atmosphere that they all knew why she was here; they had already discussed the whole thing, just as girls would have. Lydia supposed that if some boy had tried to kill himself over her when she was fifteen, that, yes, she would have gone right to school and found her sidekicks and related everything in a hushed, self-important voice: it was drama, after all.

"I was wondering if you'd care to spend the rest of the afternoon with me," she said to Leo so his friends could hear, too. "That is, unless you've got something better to do." She was flirting with her own son, a little. But she knew she could get away with it; she was one of the "young" mothers, whom the boys still thought of as an attractive woman, as well as "a mother." And she didn't want to humiliate Leo in front of his friends; he would not forgive her so soon for that. Leo could hold a grudge as long as she herself had been able to, at his age. (Once she had not spoken to Cate for a whole week, that time Cate tattled to Daddy about her "denying" Uncle Osgood at the Mountain Crafts Fair. She had marked off each day on her little calendar every night, and prayed to God to "harden her heart" like Pharaoh's till the end of the week; for Lydia had been sure God was on her side.)

"We were thinking about going over to the house and shooting some goals," said Leo, watching her; but he was intensely conscious of his friends in the background.

"*That's* always fun," said Lydia. She included his friends in an appreciative glance, as if to say, *With two such interesting friends, how could it help but be fun?* "But today I was hoping we could go off alone, just the two of us. I need to talk to you."

Leo shrugged. But she saw that she had carried it off.

"I guess I'd better come, then," said Leo. He ambled around to the passenger side. "See you guys later."

The friends stuck up a hand each in a casual wave. "See you later, Leo. So long, Mrs. Mansfield."

There, now; everyone felt respected.

Lydia drove them to Tanglewood, a vast park of over a thousand acres bequeathed to the city "for the recreation of all" by the late heirs of Richard Joshua Reynolds, who, in 1875, at the age of twenty-five, had opened a small factory to produce chewing tobacco. Lydia had begun bringing her children here when Dickie was still in his stroller. It was almost a ten-mile drive, but she loved its spaciousness. On lucky days, there would be whole stretches of park filled only with the sounds and presences of birds and small animals—and herself and Leo and Dickie. She had preferred being alone with her own children in a huge park to sitting on a bench with other mothers in a smaller park where the children were isolated into a screaming pack. At Tanglewood, Lydia had invented a game for herself and the boys. It was called "Philanthropy"—although, for a long time, Dickie called it "Philandropy." The game had come into existence when one of the boys had asked why two dead people, William and Kate Reynolds, had left this enormous park—which to two small boys seemed as big as the world—just to play in. "Well," said Lydia, thinking it out as she went, as she was often called on to do, "rich people—that is, *certain* rich people—reach a point where they have everything they want. And then they decide to use the money they have left over to make other people happy. That's called philanthropy. Of course, another reason they want to do it is because they may be getting old and they want to be remembered after they die."

And, from then on, on every trip to the park, the three of them would tell what they would "leave for others" after they had got all they wanted for themselves.

Lydia smiled now as she walked through the park with Leo, who would soon be taller than she. "Do you remember when Dickie wanted to bequeath a huge open-air zoo, where all the animals would be allowed to roam free? Then you said, 'But Dickie, if they are allowed to roam free, then *people* couldn't, and, what's more, the animals would eat each other up.'"

Leo laughed in that soundless way he had. "Yeah. And Dickie cried."

"Lord, yes, he did, didn't he?" And, all these years later, Lydia's stomach turned over with pity for that poor little boy who'd had his dream dashed by reality.

But this was Leo's day. "And you were once going to bequeath a baseball field. And once you and Dickie were going to bequeath allowances for every child so he could finish buying all the things his own allowance wouldn't quite cover."

They both laughed. This time Leo laughed aloud. "You said you were going to leave a big quiet house with bedrooms, where mothers could go and have naps while the children were right next door in another house, watching movies and things."

"Oh Lord, was I that transparent? How awful! What did you all *think* when I said that?"

"You were tired an awful lot," said Leo. Then he added politely, "Not that you were *always* tired."

"Having young children is such a strange time," said Lydia. "I went around in a daze sometimes. But, in a way, you have to be in a daze, or the sheer terror of your responsibility could overwhelm you. Can you understand that, at all?"

"I think I can," said Leo, whose voice expressed willingness to try, even though he did not quite understand.

"Of course, it's different now," Lydia went on. She knew what she was doing on this walk. Getting Leo to open up was a little like eating spareribs or lobster claws: you had to expend a lot of effort for the little you got. "Now you two are reaching the age where our interests are mutual. You, particularly. Soon you will be making the same decisions I have to make. What kind of work to do. What kind of life to lead. Whom you want to have as . . . friends. I feel we really have a lot we could talk about now. I'm no longer in a daze. Since I started back to school, I feel the world's opening up for me. I don't have the terror about you two anymore. As much. Of course, I still worry. Only, whereas I used to worry about you all falling off swings or sticking knives into the electric sockets, I now worry about . . . well, the same things I worry about for myself."

"Like what?"

"Well, those things I said. Finding the right work to do. And how to live your life so you'll like yourself and look forward more to getting up in the morning than going to bed at night. And choosing the people you want to . . . be with in your life. Here. let's sit down." They sat down on a wooden bench in the arboretum, which, at this time of spring, was dizzying with lovely scents. He knows it's coming, thought Lydia, and he'll resent it if I sneak up on him: the direct approach is best. "This is fun, being here with you. It's the first time we've ever been here alone, just you and me. This may sound awful, and I certainly don't want to underestimate her pain, but I have to be grateful to Cookie Cunningham for bringing you and me together like this. Only, from now on, let's take matters into our own hands and find time for each other without any outside agency. Do you think we can do that?"

Leo lowered his profile in a semi-nod which could be a yes, a maybe, or an undecided.

Lydia pulled a leaf from a shrub and began shredding it. "Do you think she really meant to kill herself, Leo?"

"Probably not."

"That's funny, I didn't think so, either. I don't know why, do you?"

"She called me up and told me she was going to do it," said Leo, looking straight ahead as if watching some movie in the azalea bushes across the path. "But I thought it was just a way to get me to come over. She said if I wasn't on her doorstep within fifteen minutes, she was going to take the pills. She already had the glass of water ready, she said."

"But you couldn't possibly have got there in fifteen minutes! It would be impossible without a car, and you can't drive yet. Or was your father home?"

"No, he was taking Lizzie to see *The China Syndrome*. Cookie told me I could call a taxi."

Lydia kept her face still so as not to show her surprise at some of this information. So Lizzie was already a household word. So much for Max's enduring devotion for "the only woman he'd ever love." Though maybe he was just saving his pride or looking for companionship. Lydia couldn't rule that out yet, till she had further evidence of how far things had gone.

Leo and Cookie's drama had been going on while the adult foursome were having *their* drama in front of the movie house. Hadn't Max said he had left Leo talking on the phone to a girl when he left ... and that they would probably still be talking when he got back? And they had all four laughed. Possibly at the same moment Cookie was swallowing her pills.

"In the first place, a taxi would never have made it to our house in fifteen minutes," said Lydia practically. Then she added skillfully, "Had you and Cookie had a fight, or what?"

After another forty-five minutes of Lydia's graceful prodding, Leo had provided a sparse scenario. He and Cookie *had* had a fight, several weeks ago. They were at a party, over at one of The Ghouls' houses, in Leo's neighborhood, when Cookie suddenly announced she had a headache and wanted to be driven back to her house by Rodney Bradshaw, the only person in their crowd who had turned sixteen and had his own car. Leo told Cookie to call her mother and have her mother come and get her (her mother had brought her), or he offered to take Cookie home in a taxi. But she said that would be trouble to everybody and she would just go on with Rodney. Leo told her if she went with Rodney, then she could just keep on going wherever she liked with Rodney, but not to expect to go anywhere with him again. Cookie, a headstrong girl, used to getting her own way, called Leo's bluff and departed—a little too happily for someone with a splitting headache—with Rodney in Rodney's car.

Only, Leo wasn't bluffing. That was the end, as far as he was concerned. That was the way he had been raised: you honored your ultimatums; otherwise, people wouldn't believe you the next time. But Cookie refused to believe Leo was through. All she had done, she said, was ride home with someone because she had a headache. (For whatever reason, Cookie and Rodney had extinguished their brief, incipient flame during the ride home; perhaps Cookie had felt too divided over Leo and her new attraction and Rodney had decided to quit while he was ahead; or maybe Cookie did have a headache, but, Leo said, a headache wasn't all there was to it, and he'd had enough. Cookie was the one who'd chased him, to start with.)

But Cookie had phoned and pestered and wailed. She had sent her girl friends to Leo as emissaries. They told him not to be "rigid"; "You don't want to be a male chauvinist, do you?" they told him. "That's not the point," Leo had said, and held fast. "Cookie was testing her freedom," the girl friends explained; "She has her freedom now" was Leo's reply.

"But you have to take me to the Cotillion Club Dance!" wailed Cookie. "That's been set up since February." Leo had said, "Get Rodney Bradshaw to take you." "But he's already got somebody. And—and—besides, I'd rather go with you." "Thanks, but no thanks," said Leo. "But people don't break dates for the Cotillion Club! It just isn't done." "Well, this person is doing it," replied the intransigent Leo.

The only thing left in Cookie's arsenal was to threaten suicide—"if you're not on this doorstep in fifteen minutes."

Leo had told her it was her life. Just as it was her freedom.

After Lydia had finished extracting this story from Leo, she picked another leaf from the shrub. This one she did not mutilate, but simply brushed softly, back and forth, across her cheek. "Listen," she said, "this is a hypothetical question, but what would you have done if Cookie *had* killed herself?"

"She wouldn't have! It was all an act! Everything's an act with her. She's all over a guy, but even that's an act. It's really herself she's in love with!" More emotion than he had shown all afternoon. Lydia began to understand.

"I said it was hypothetical. I mean, what would you have *felt* when you found out?"

"I would have felt I was to blame, I guess."

"*That* would have been awful to live with for the rest of your life," said Lydia, suddenly furious with the hypothetical Cookie who had killed herself and ruined Leo's life. "Well, I certainly am glad she didn't kill herself."

"So am I," said Leo. "But now I want to be done with it."

Lydia detected the anguish in her son's voice. She could

pretty well fill in the rest of the picture. There were a few things more she would have liked to know, such as: Had Cookie seduced him? How had she gone about it? (For Lydia was almost positive it would have been her initiative.) Another mother, emboldened by her progress, might have risked prying further. But Lydia's fastidiousness prevented her. She didn't discuss her sex life with others, and Leo was enough like herself to share the same reluctance about putting certain things into words: something had to be left private in this overly vocal world.

"Daddy says Dr. Cunningham wants you—or rather, Cookie wants you—to come and see her at home," said Lydia. "Daddy and I had lunch together today. The thing is, Cookie won't go back to school, she says, until you come and see her."

"What did Dad say I should do?"

"He didn't say you *should* do anything. He said it might be easier if you went on over there."

"What do you think?" And Leo turned and looked at her.

"What do I think? Lord, what do I think?" Lydia sat pensively, the leaf poised against her chin. Leo was right, in principle; but she had this feeling he was going to be ostracized if he didn't compromise, at least *outwardly*. His peers would make his life hell for being *too* principled, if they were already calling him "rigid." They would want him, for their own melodramatic satisfaction, to play out the rest of the scene. To go over to Cookie's house and stand solemnly in her ruffled bedroom and let her cry a little and enjoy to the maximum the trouble she had caused everybody.

But how could she advise her own child, so much like herself, to go against his own principles, just to placate the prurient, melodramatic crowd?

"Leo honey, I think it would be easier to go on over there. Could you do it in the spirit of noblesse oblige—remember how Granddaddy used to talk about noblesse oblige? She's obviously a mixed-up girl and has more to lose than you do. If you could get it over with in *that* spirit, I don't think you would be sacrificing your principles."

If I conform outwardly to their approved image, then I cheat them out

of their chance to misjudge me. This way I can get on with being myself:
her own silent credo as a schoolgirl.

"But it wouldn't be over!" protested Leo. "She'd think I was making up. She'd expect me to start over with her again. She would have won. I can't do it, I just can't."

Maybe he is stronger than I was, thought Lydia. I knew my limitations and I knew what barricades to build. But if he is stronger, why should I hold him back from testing his strength?

"Listen, Leo," she said, dropping the leaf, which, still intact, fluttered away in a little eddy of warm air, then boomeranged at the last second and landed on her foot. She reached down and picked it off. "I'll stick by you, whatever you decide to do. And I'm sure Daddy will, too. We've both got faith in your good sense."

"I appreciate that," said Leo gruffly.

They got up, at Lydia's instigation, from the bench and headed back toward the parking lot. Lydia feigned greater interest than she felt in the bark of certain trees, the blossoms on other bushes. She was careful to keep from looking at Leo because she knew he was struggling not to cry.

And that same evening, after Max had come by to pick up the resolute Leo and take him home, how proud Lydia had felt. She had coped with it all, on this trying day. She had stood by her son and reinforced Max's opinion of her as a "wonderful woman." She was so charged up with her own efficiency, she couldn't bear to sit still studying. She had called her mother instead, to inaugurate the June trip to the cottage. Nell had seemed amenable, if distracted. There was, it seemed, more trouble across town with Theodora and Wickie Lee. Wickie Lee had met some young woman in the hospital, named Rita, who was on welfare. Theodora had told Wickie Lee that Rita could not come to the house on Edgerton Road anymore because she was "common" and a bad influence. Now Wickie Lee was threatening to leave Theodora and move in with Rita and Rita's children, who lived off the state.

Oh, everybody's soap opera! thought Lydia. But that was

one more thing done: Mother had agreed it would be a good idea to make the cottage into a rental property. They would drive to the Outer Banks in early June, talking about old times and reinforcing their bond. *Just as Leo and I reinforced our bond today, Mother and I will reinforce ours in early June,* Lydia had thought.

And then an added realization had come: *Both Leo and I are the "good" children in the family.*

And when, shortly after that, the phone had rung (Lydia snatching it up on the first ring because Dickie was asleep) and Stanley's voice, low-pitched and with those different emphases, announced that he was in a phone booth less than fifty yards from her front door because he couldn't go the rest of the day without having seen her at all, when this was supposed to have been *their* day, she had thought, Well, *hell,* I deserve some reward for all I've done today. And out she had slipped, locking the door behind her, and had walked swiftly through the soft night toward a well-earned embrace from her importunate lover. As she had climbed into his car, which he had parked in the darkest shadows, so what they did would be their own business, and yet (thoughtfully) had parked within full view of her apartment, in case it caught fire or anything, Lydia had felt like an accomplished secret agent, equally at home in all the territories which she must oversee even as she lived in them: territories which, because of certain conflicting interests, must be kept separate from one another.

But her pride turned out to have been short-lived. Leo, abiding by principle, had stood firm in his refusal to go to see Cookie. And Cookie, more and more the tragic heroine each day he did not come, refused to go back to school.

For one week, the stalemate held: Cookie at home, Leo going about his business at school. But at the beginning of the second week, things shifted. Lines were drawn; pressure was put on. The pressure came from Leo's friends (though Lydia and Max thought they detected some behind-the-scenes machinations from the good Dr. Cunningham, who counted among his patients at least a fourth of the parents of Leo's classmates); the girls quit talking to Leo, or, when a group of them passed him in the halls, they would chant under their breaths, "MCP, MCP" (for Male Chauvinist Pig). And Leo's favorite teacher, Mrs. Epting, who taught the popular Social Studies, a sort of free-for-all forum in which the kids discussed marriage and the family, teenage sexuality, violence in today's world, and the loneliness of our senior citizens, had kept Leo after class and begged him to "have a heart." No man is an island, Mrs. Epting told Leo; we are all interworking parts of the human community. Up until then, Leo had thought Mrs. Epting, a curvaceous, well-married matron with slightly protruding teeth, was his friend. But when Leo explained his principles to his friend, Mrs. Epting said principles were one thing, but she was disappointed in his lack of humanity.

Next, The Ghouls abandoned Leo. Not in so many words, but there seemed suddenly to be a rash of dental and doctor appointments after schoool. The Ghouls' girl friends were Cookie's allies.

Leo, left alone with his principles, wandered the halls like a pariah for two more days. On the third day, when Max came into Leo's room to get him up, Leo, lying in his pajamas, with his arms around his half-blind old dog, Fritz, told Max he would not be going back to that school anymore. "But you'll lose credit for the semester," said Max, trying first for practicality, which usually worked on Leo.

"I can go to summer school," said Leo. "With no friends, there'll be nothing *else* to do. And maybe next fall you could send me to a private school. I think I would be able to concentrate better at a private school, anyway."

Leo stayed in his room, playing a song on his "I Robot" album over and over gain. On his second day at home, when Lydia cut all her classes at UNC-Greensboro to come over and be with him, he was still playing it. She put a spinach quiche in the oven—ah, how nice to have a see-through oven, at eye-level, again—and came into his room and sat on his neatly made bed and listened to the song with him. It was by that same Alan Parsons Project chap whose solitary space-age music she had played on cassette, the night Daddy had died and she had sped across

292 ~ GAIL GODWIN

the I-40 to be with Mother. Only this song was much more sentimental than the usual Alan Parsons. Lord, if she'd heard this
song on the night Daddy had died, she would have driven off the
road in grief. This song *abetted* grief. It was exactly the wrong
song for Leo to be listening to in his situation. Why, even the
words, starting off against a background of choir music, seemed
sinisterly tailor-made to Leo's predicament.

> *It's getting harder to face every day*
> *Don't let it show, don't let it show*
> *Though it's getting harder to take what they say*
> *Just let it go, just let it go*

Lydia was practically in tears by the third or fourth verse, as
she and Leo sat raptly absorbing the song. But by the last verse,
things had got better. The singer's martyrdom and pariahhood
had undergone a transformation; now, against a fast, defiant rock
beat, he belted out his singularity—he was enjoying it.

> *Even if you feel you've got nothing to hide*
> *Keep it inside of you*
> *Don't give in*
> *Don't tell them anything*
> *Don't let it*
> *Don't let it show*

At last the song faded triumphantly into pure instrumenta-
tion, and then it faded out altogether. Good-bye, human community; then, good-bye, world.
Which was just fine for a young Englishman who had recorded these albums and who was probably a millionaire by
now, but where did that leave Leo? Who really was suffering and
confused, with or without musical accompaniment. Who *needed*
his education.
After Leo had been out of school several more days and

Max, then Lydia, had had a conference with Dr. Karen Small, who had also come by the house to have a "one-to-one dialogue" with Leo, Cookie Cunningham saw fit to rise from her tragic bed and return to school. Everyone, even the teachers, thought she was "so brave."

Once again it had happened: the wheel that squeaked the loudest had gotten the grease. Lydia felt it was a defeat for them both: for Leo and his princples; for herself as a mother—after all, who had taught him his principles? But, more important—and this was what really made her angry (no wonder she was having trouble concentrating on her "Eros" paper)—she felt it was a defeat for the Individual trying to live by his lights. Once again, the sloppy, inconsiderate "feelers" had won out over the quiet, diligent "reasoners," who had their feelings, too, but kept them inside. Cookie Cunningham had initiated this whole fake soap opera, beginning with her "headache," because she wanted to sample another boy on Leo's time, and ending when she returned to school a heroine. To be rewarded. While Leo was punished. And it was happening all over society; the more mess you made of your life and the louder you were about making it, the more "funds" the government provided you with, so you could go out and make some more mess. And who had to pay for all these generous, "humanistic" funds to sustain the messer-uppers? The quieter, reasonable people who did what they were supposed to do and earned the money: the *workers* in Mrs. Epting's "interworking human community."

And to add insult to injury, this point of view that Lydia subcribed to was considered unfashionable and inhumane. She could just hear, for instance, Cate's diatribe in answer to her own protest. What the "liberals" had done was somehow to pervert the old noblesse oblige by making it into a drab duty, a *fashionable* duty. You couldn't make noblesse oblige into a duty or a law. That took the charity out of it. The true charity, not the sounding-brass kind. The whole point was to have the freedom to say: God, look at that poor deserving beggar, I'll help him because he's less fortunate than I, and because I'll like myself better if I help him. But when the undeserving messer-uppers pushed in your door with their hands out (or laughing behind their hands because they had learned how to work the system), where was the charity or dignity or equality or anything else?

Lydia seethed. God, I wish I had some power in this world, she thought. How can I get some power so I can make people listen to good sense?

Max brought Dickie home from *Close Encounters*. "I can't stay," he said. "Leo's waiting out in the car. He's pretty low and wants to go to bed. I thought the movie would cheer him up, but it didn't."

"It wasn't supposed to be a cheerful movie," said Dickie, who had gone at once to find Gregory and now had the young orange cat draped over his shoulder. The cat hung limp, purring and pumping the air with his two front paws. "It was a *thoughtful* movie about what might happen. You really should have stayed, Dad. It was something when those little creatures got off the spaceship."

Max looked as if he wouldn't mind clobbering Dickie. "I just couldn't concentrate on a movie," he told Lydia, smoothing the front of his Lacoste golf shirt with the flat of his hand. This was a new gesture, as if he were molding himself a waistline with his flat hand until the Perrier could do its work. "I had too much on my mind. So I went down to the office for a while."

"We all have so much to do," assented Lydia, looking around at all her discarded pages. "I had planned to draft this whole paper, but I had so much on *my* mind. . . ." She wondered if he had seen Lizzie.

Dickie, having shot his arrow, had retreated to the kitchen, where he was feeding Gregory for the fifth or sixth time that day. She heard him shake more Friskies into Gregory's bowl. "Poor old Greg, here's a few crunchies for you," Dickie crooned in his child's voice, "you must be *starved*."

Max, suspended in the doorway, said, "Private school wouldn't be such a bad thing for Leo, if he wants it. I took a look at his history book. I was shocked. It looked like a fat issue of *Look* magazine. A tenth-grade history book. Do you remember your tenth-grade history book? I remember mine: there were words in it; whole blocks of print without any pictures."

"If he wants to go next year and you're willing to pay for it, I don't have any objection," said Lydia. "I know I did a lot better at a private school. Of course they're all coed now. But I want him to go back and finish out the year here. Otherwise, it will seem as if they've driven him away. And he'll lose the semester."

"He said he's willing to go to summer school. Though I agree with you, he ought to go back and face them down. But that's easier said than done for a fifteen-year-old boy. A day is still a long time for him. We're talking about a whole month. And he might not be able to concentrate. So far, he hasn't been able to open a book at home. Where nobody's glaring him down."

"Oh damn," said Lydia.

"I agree," said Max. "It's hot in here. You look hot."

"Well, I *am* hot. This air conditioner belongs in the Smithsonian."

"That's another thing," said Max. "If Leo does go to summer school, I'd like it if you'd come back and take the house. I'd like you to be there for him. I could move in here, or somewhere like it."

"You couldn't last a week in a place like this. You like your luxuries and your space."

"Oh, come on now. I'm not that much of a tenderfoot. Well, think about it. I believe it might be the best arrangement."

"Okay, I'll think about it. Only I wish you'd get yourself a house."

"Well, I may, at that."

Lydia stood up, brushing aside a dozen or more crumpled balls of yellow paper. "I'll walk out to the car with you. If Leo's too tired to come in and say goodnight to me, I guess I'll go out and say goodnight to him." She felt oddly let down. It would have been nice to have a drink and talk. That was one of the things she missed most about being married: talking, over drinks and meals. Dissecting other people's lives; taking a certain comfort in their problems, which helped you gloss over your own.

After Max and Leo were gone and Dickie and Gregory had bedded down, Lydia dialed Renee's number in Greensboro. She had been tempted to check in with Stanley, but decided against it; it might get his hopes up by convincing him that she was growing dependent. That wouldn't be fair. She still didn't know what, in the long run, to do about Stanley.

Renee answered right away, in a soft, faraway voice.

"Oh damn, I've waked you," said Lydia.

"What are you talking about, girl? It's only nine-thirty. No, I was typing up a paper, to send off to *Southern Studies*."

"Oh, what on?" Lydia's heart was thumping. She was still a little nervous about calling Renee. The new had not yet worn off their friendship, and there was still a flirtation going on—as it does even between women—where each delicately tested the other's boundaries and tried to be her best and most interesting self. Lydia's first reaction, for instance, when Renee announced she was working on a paper, was: Oh, what a coincidence! I was just working on my paper for *you*! But that might have been seen by Renee as mixing business with friendship, if Lydia had blurted this out.

"Well, it's really no more than a footnote in my thesis. But this editor at the Southern Studies Institute found it interesting and asked me to expand it. Actually, it's about a tiny aspect of black snobbery."

"Black *snobbery*?"

"That's right. You see, blacks who are descended from slaves who worked on plantations in Virginia and the Carolinas think they're several cuts above those who worked farther down, in Georgia and Mississippi and those places."

"They do? Why?"

"Well"—Renee's tone became playfully mysterious, as it did in class when she was about to reveal something she knew people would find interesting—"it all goes back to when slaves arrived from Africa or the West Indies at major slave ports, such as Charleston or Newport News. The planters of Virginia and the Carolinas had first choice of the lot, so naturally they picked the strongest, the smartest, and the best-looking. Then the other Southern cities had to take what was left over."

"Oh Lord, Renee, is that true?"

"It's true in that way that never gets written down. I can remember my great-aunt saying once about a friend of hers: 'Maybelle sure does put on a lot of airs, for one who's only descended from *Georgia* niggers.' "

They both laughed, Lydia a little too loudly, out of nervousness. It still made her uneasy when Renee said "nigger."

"You know, I've been thinking a lot about . . . well, about snobbery," Lydia confided to Renee. "I feel embarrassed even admitting I've been *thinking* about it. Like you said, it's a thing that doesn't get written down, but everybody thinks about it. I know they do. Nobody wants anyone to look down on them, and everybody likes to have someone to look down on. I wish I knew why. Why do we *care* what other people think, when good common sense tells us they're just as worried about what we think— or somebody thinks? I wonder who the first snob was, anyway."

"I can't tell you why we care what other people think," said Renee, "but I sure can tell you who the first snob was, if that'll help any."

"You *can*?"

"Sure. He was a Scotch cobbler's apprentice. That's the origin of the term. The Scotch took the word from an Old Norse word that meant 'dolt,' because, as an apprentice, he was expected to make lots of mistakes."

"No! I don't believe this!" exclaimed Lydia happily.

"Well, it's true. You can look it up in a good dictionary. And then, later, the word 'snob' came to mean any person belonging to the lower classes. . . ."

"Oh, what a good joke on all the snobs today! Walking around feeling snobbish and not even *knowing*—"

"Yeah, it made me feel good, the day I discovered what a snob was," said Renee. "Then, somewhere along the way, the word got turned around to mean . . . just what you said: people who walked around feeling snobbish."

"Renee, you're wonderful."

"No, just educated," drawled the other, "or attempting to become educated." She graciously switched subjects. "How's Leo. Is he still staying home?"

Lydia filled Renee in on the latest, which was only a couple of days' worth since she had last talked to her friend. "I saw him tonight. Max had taken them to the movies. He really seemed depressed and wanted to go home and sleep. Leo's never been a sleeper, and here he was wanting to turn off at nine o'clock."

"It's very tiring, trying to prove a point," said Renee. "In high school, I once stayed in my room for three days to wear my parents down. The whole protocol of a protest can tire you out. First you discover you need things that aren't in your room; then there's the problem of meals—I mean, how hungry should you allow yourself to be when you're pretending to be beyond food? And the boredom gets to you, especially if you're young. I bet Leo's boring himself. That's what's tiring him out."

"But he isn't trying to wear *us* down. We're already on his side. He's protesting something else, I think. He's protesting the world, for not being fair."

"Well, he might as well get over that, because it's not always fair," said Renee.

"It's been two weeks," said Lydia. "It'll be two weeks tomorrow that he refused to go back. And I really do think he's capable of sticking it out. He's got my stubbornness. But he lacks my expediency. I wouldn't have let them cause me to lose a semester. I would probably have played their game and despised them quietly. Leo's more honest."

"Now, don't start running yourself down. That gets nobody anywhere. But you ought to get him out of that *room*. Why don't you bring him to school with you tomorrow?"

"You mean, take him to my classes?"

"Why not? It'll be a change. If he's bored, at least it'll be a fresh kind of boredom. The more outside influences, the better. If he'll come."

"Oh, I can get him to come. That's no problem. Renee,

you're just full of good ideas. But why were you trying to wear your parents down? Did you win?"

"I guess you could say it was a draw. I wanted to get engaged to this boy, Navarro. I was madly in love with him; he was the basketball hero. They didn't think he was good enough. Well, I finally came out of my room, after three days. Like you, I didn't want to miss my school. But Navarro and I continued to go out, and, just about the time I was realizing my parents were right about him, I conceived Camilla. I ended up missing *two* semesters of school, though, and it didn't ruin my life. That should make you less uptight about Leo."

"My God. What—what happened to Navarro?"

"Oh, he's around. In and out of the state penitentiary. Navarro has to have action. He was fine as long as he could work it out on the basketball court, but after he graduated from high school he needed more challenges. So he tried embezzlement, he tried armed robbery—so far, thank God, he hasn't killed anybody. I wouldn't want Camilla's father to be a murderer."

"Does Camilla ever see him?" How could anyone ever think life was boring, Lydia was thinking, when there were people like Renee to interpret it for you?

Renee sighed. "She's seen him. He has this way of coming around. That's one reason she's at school in England. She doesn't need him waiting outside her school or weeping crocodile tears through the bars of the playground. Not that he would hurt her. He just likes to make scenes. Look here, why don't you and Leo plan to have lunch with me if you can get him to come tomorrow. I'd like to meet him."

"I'm going to phone him right now," said Lydia. "If he's asleep, I'll tell Max to wake him up."

"If he can't come tomorrow, you come on and have lunch, anyway," said Renee.

"I'd love to. Either way, though, please let me bring the cold cuts. I can pack them right up tonight in my picnic cooler." Either way, with or without Leo, it would be fun with Renee. If Leo didn't come, they could talk some more about Navarro; and maybe some about Stanley; linking it all together via the subject of Eros: troublesome old Eros—"Friend or Foe," fool or felon. But as much as Lydia admired everything else about Renee, she had to protect herself against her friend's weird "salad" combinations. That tuna and vinegar and chick-pea thing, the first time; the mango and green-bean combination, the second time. After that, Lydia had protected herself—and Renee's pride— with a little white lie. Lydia said it made her feel bad, always having lunch at Renee's when she lived too far away to have her back. She'd feel better if they could have indoor picnics, provided by herself. Fair was fair.

Leo was not yet asleep when Lydia called. Despite his nonchalant monotone, it was clear he felt rescued from one more dull day with his principles.

No sooner had she hung up than the phone rang again. *My sweet Stanley. My reward for coping with all the trials in my life?*

It was Renee again. "Is he coming?"

"He's coming," said Lydia.

"Then here's an update on tomorrow's plans. I talked to Calvin. He says for us to come on over to the TV station around three and he'll show Leo around the studio, and then at four they're taping part of a Mary McGregor Turnbull show. You ever watch that? *Southern Kitchens?* The other guys at the station call it 'Southern Kitsch,' but Calvin has a soft spot for old Miss Mary. Has Leo ever watched a show being taped before? Calvin thought it might interest him."

"It would. It would interest me; I've never seen one, either. I watched *Southern Kitchens* a few times, but that was *years* ago. That Mary McGregor Turnbull must be *ancient*. I always like a good cooking program. But the strange thing was, on her show, they never showed the finished product, the times I watched."

Renee laughed. "Honey, that was because they almost never turned out right. They were going to take her show off the air, but Calvin rescued it. He put new life in that show, *and* he solved the problem you spoke of. The recipes *always* turn out now." She giggled. "You wait and see."

"I'm really looking forward to tomorrow," said Lydia. She was a little disappointed that Renee hadn't been Stanley, but you couldn't have everything in one day. "I could tell from Leo's voice, though he was playing it cool, that he's looking forward to getting outside that house."

"We'll broaden his horizons," promised Renee. "At least he won't spend another beautiful spring day playing that old record to death."

It was not, as it turned out, "another beautiful spring day," but as Lydia drove through the pouring rain, her windshield wipers on high speed, to fetch Leo, she was determined to make the day count. The rain slowed them down on their thirty-mile stretch of I-40, and they were late for General Psychology I. The instructor was lecturing on William James's belief in Voluntarism. There weren't two seats left together and Leo ducked self-effacingly into a backseat before Lydia could stop him. She had to take a seat up front and was unable to watch his reactions. That was a shame, because the instructor, an earnest young man—younger than Lydia—who often came to class with sleep flakes in the corners of his eyelashes, warmed to his topic today. "James, more than any other major American psychologist, apotheosized the human will," the instructor told them. His eyes kept returning to a certain spot in the back of the room, where, Lydia was sure, Leo was sitting. The class was a large one and maybe he was trying to figure out if Leo had been a student he had overlooked all semester. "James believed that many of our desires can be achieved, at least in part, as a result of desiring them. But he struggled all his life against his own depression and even made a doctrine out of it. 'Life *in extremis*' was one of his favorite terms. He described himself as one who welcomed a bit of tension—or, as he put it, 'a stinging pain in the breastbone.' "

"*Life in extremis*," Lydia wrote quickly in her notebook. "*Desires achieved as result of desiring.*" "*A stinging pain in the breastbone.*" So far, she had an A in this course.

The next hour was History of Female Consciousness. Not having been forewarned about Leo's aversion to being picked out in a crowd, Renee had introduced him to the class; whereupon, he immediately became the focus. This was partly because of the demographic makeup of the class (at least 90 percent women, a substantial portion of whom were older townswomen, some of them auditors, and old enough to be Leo's mother or grandmother); it was partly because of the topic under discussion: Moon priestesses and priests in ancient cultures. All the older women looked anxiously toward Leo, as if fearing for his soul, while the *hieros gamos* rites of sacred prostitution were being discussed; the minority of men in the class could be seen, in a body, swerving their eyes protectively in Leo's direction while the Phrygian rites for choosing new priests for Cybele were being discussed. Even Lydia shuddered at the thought of young men in an orgiastic frenzy cutting off their sex organs and then running through the streets and flinging these organs at houses. Whosever house got hit had to supply the new eunuch priest with women's clothes for him to wear in the temple. Lydia looked over at Leo, whose cheeks were pink with their usual high color, but whose expression was a study in neutrality. He'd make a good diplomat, thought Lydia, or gambler; at the same time she ached at the thought of his vulnerable male organs, which would, from now on, live their own life and make their special demands on him, causing him much longing and confusion.

"That was kind of heavy, Leo," said Renee, when the three of them—four, counting The Judge—were eating Lydia's cold cuts over at Renee's. "I hope it wasn't *too* heavy."

"Oh, it was interesting," said Leo, eating with one hand and caressing The Judge's silver-blue forehead with the other. "Everybody is so quiet in college."

"Quiet?" asked Lydia.

"Yes. Everybody listens to the teacher. Nobody interrupts anybody else when they're trying to talk."

Lydia and Renee exchanged a look. Lydia said, "That's because we want to find out what's going on. Especially us old-timers, who've wasted too much time already." Leo had pronounced a judgment on his school and didn't even know it.

Renee went away and came back with an envelope. "I've got

some new pictures of Camilla. They're quite good. Her room-mate from Persia took them with some fancy camera. My daughter, Camilla, is just your age, Leo; she's at school over in England."

"So Mom said."

They all looked at the photographs. In several, Camilla was jumping a horse, her thick pigtail flying out behind her derby. Her lips were set in a cool, confident smile, but her eyes were round with excitement and a touch of terror.

"She's so elegant, Renee," said Lydia. "Look at the way she sits on that horse."

"Yeah, but you know what? The poor child says her teeth chatter the whole hour before riding lesson. But she just plops on that hard hat and goes right on."

Leo looked carefully at each of the photographs but made no comment. He's taking in so much today, thought Lydia. I hope we're not overloading his circuits. Life *in extremis* with William James; young men flinging their severed organs at people's houses; and now this black girl dressed like Princess Anne, leaping her fences. Why, come to think of it, this is probably the first time in Leo's life he's met a black person like Renee, a person who is black but "one of us."

But he must have liked something about Renee's, because, when given the choice of going with his mother to her Survey of Renaissance Lit class or staying behind with The Judge, he chose the latter. Lydia rushed away in the rain to Professor Spruill's class. She was a little disappointed because she had been especially eager to introduce her pretty Leo to the old man: Professor Spruill would have approved so of Leo's grave beauty. But this was Leo's day, after all. She would skip Economics so they could go to the TV station and have their tour, but she really could not let the old Professor down. The class had thinned dangerously since they'd begun "The Faerie Queene"; everybody was skipping out on the dreary sessions, crammed full of all those late-Tudor imperial and ecclesiastical trappings. But as Professor Spruill had said, "The Faerie Queene" was the heroic farewell to an empire, and Lydia wanted to pay her respects—just as you would want to attend the funeral of some famous person who had influenced history. She would always be grateful that they had still been living in London when Churchill had died. Max had arranged for them to watch the funeral procession from an upstairs window of his solicitor's office in Piccadilly. She would never forget Field Marshal Montgomery, seventy-eight years old, doing a slow march (which Max said was extremely painful, even for young legs) behind Churchill's coffin, all the way from Westminster Abbey to St. Paul's Cathedral.

Calvin Edwards, Renee's friend Calvin, whom she had once described to Lydia as a fellow pilgrim on the upwardly mobile trip, awaited them in the lobby of the TV station. He was a large, round-faced black man—much blacker than Renee—with easy, expansive, almost floppy gestures; but his eyes were intently watchful, rather Machiavelian. It would have been hard to judge his age, but Lydia knew it was the same as her own. Calvin fluttered over them protectively, making them assure him nobody had gotten too wet in the rain; he caressed Renee verbally with his rich bass voice. ("How's it going, gal?") and told Lydia and Leo they "favored each other strikingly," making it quite clear it was a compliment to them both. He was dressed in well-pressed chino pants, a red-and-white-checked gingham shirt worn on the outside to conceal a potbelly, blue topsiders which gave him a stealthy, soft-footed walk, and a lightweight blue windbreaker with CAROLINA FOOTBALL printed across the back: clothes as loose and casual as his deportment. But the eyes took constant scans of their little group, assessing, judging, almost mind-reading, it seemed—for he had at once picked up a slight discomfort on Lydia's part (her hair had been blown during the walk from the car, under the umbrella, and she was feeling untidy) and he said, "Listen, folks, if anybody wants the Ladies or Gents, I suggest the ones right here, off the visitors' lobby; they've got more amenities than the ones upstairs."

"I think I *will* just—" said Lydia gratefully, and went off to set right her appearance; Leo, seeing her go, decided he needed the Gents. He was shy about making conversation with adults he had just met.

When they returned, Calvin and Renee were waiting in companionable silence, Renee with her usual air of cool insouciance, Calvin in his relaxed, loose-limbed manner. The two of them were together, that much was obvious, but Lydia found herself suspecting they had not had much more fun on their trip to New Orleans than she and Max had had.

Calvin spread his long arms and bundled them into the elevator. "We'll go by my office first and warm everybody up with a cup of my special tea. Surprising, isn't it, how rain like this can chill, even in May?" He broadened his *i*'s, Northern-style, and sounded his final *g*'s as if striking a gong, but he blocked his phrases in Southern rhythms. Meanwhile, back and forth, up and down, went the ever-watchful brown eyes, canvassing his little group. *As if*, thought Lydia, *he has to keep an eye on all our thoughts.*

As he led them down a fluorescent-lit hall, a man's voice called from a darkened room, "Hey, Calvin, you giving the twenty-five-cent tour or the fifty-cent tour?"

"These folks are so special I'm making up a new tour, Ernie, and it begins with you. You all come on in and meet Ernie." And Calvin ushered his brood into the dark room, where three men sat, relaxed, behind a long control panel. The one named Ernie was drinking Diet Pepsi from a can; the other two were smoking. On the picture monitors opposite them were a soap opera in progress, a bar of colors, a cake-mix ad, and some black-and-white footage of a tobacco auction: all silent. The rest of the screens were blank.

Calvin carefully introduced everybody to everybody else. His eyes moved faster, as there were three more people to scan. But, on the surface, everything was a joke. "Now officially, folks," said Calvin to his guests, "this is the control room where we build the local evening news. These gentlemen are setting things up—the films, tapes, charts, graphics, all those things that seem part of the news, but can be set up beforehand. But what these men are *really* doing is watching the soaps. Ernie here hasn't missed an episode of *General Hospital* in years. That's what's on the master monitor now. Only, Ernie's wife tells me, when they go on vacation every year, she lets him watch it with sound."

Everybody laughed. The man named Ernie tossed his Diet Pepsi into a wastebasket. "Takes one to know one, Calvin," he joked.

In his small, windowless office, which Calvin had nevertheless arranged to resemble a gracious parlor, he explained to them the importance of "goofing off" for TV people. "Those guys looked pretty relaxed, Leo, wouldn't you say?" (A quick look at Lydia, which read: See, I'm making your son the center of things; I know all about his problems.)

"Kind of," Leo admitted.

"Well," said Calvin, spooning five teaspoons of tea into a teapot with dragons on it, "you go back to that room in two hours, you'd see something else. You'd see a highly calibrated technical unit, working controls, speaking in code, every action timed to a minisecond. No time for jokes, no room for mistakes." To Lydia, he said, "This water ought to be boiling any minute now." The water in question was inside an authentic samovar, not one of those fake ones that have to be plugged into an outlet. Lydia saw that her admiration for its genuineness was not lost on Calvin. "That man I introduced you to, named Ernie," Calvin went on, ostensibly to Leo, "is one of our highest-paid men. They pay him because he doesn't make mistakes. Conversely, he's the biggest goof-off when he's not on the air. He's got to be, to break the tension. Ernie's one of the most talented news producers in the state; if he had to, he could build the evening news around the death of a June bug." Calvin refastened his little bag of tea and put it back on a small butler's table; the bag's label was turned so Lydia could read that Calvin ordered his tea from McNulty's in New York.

"What happens if you make a mistake?" Leo wanted to know.

"Well, after you make about two of them, you find yourself another job—like selling vacuum cleaners. Mistakes cost too much money in this business. You know that soap I was kidding Ernie about, *General Hospital*? Well, it costs sixty thousand dollars just to make one episode of a show like *General Hospital*." The water was boiling in the samovar. Calvin opened the brass tap, and scalding water steamed into the waiting pot. To Lydia, he said, "Renee tells me you lived in London for a while. Did you pick up the habit of using milk in your tea? If so, I'll get some for you from our communal refrigerator."

"No, thank you," said Lydia. "Perfectly plain for me."

"Leo?"

"Same here," said Leo, who hated tea but would drink it out of politeness to his host.

Lydia saw that on Calvin's wall, beside a small framed diploma from the RCA Institute, there was a Carolina Playmakers poster of a 1968 production of *Look Homeward, Angel*, directed by Calvin Edwards. "Oh, you went to Chapel Hill," she said.

"Got my M.A. there," said Calvin in his resonant, chesty bass. "Did my undergraduate work right here, over at Ag Tech. I'm a Greensboro boy." He checked his Accutron watch. "Tell you what, I'm going to go ahead and pour out this tea, even though it's only been three minutes. You won't tell the Queen on me, will you, Lydia?"

Calvin poured out tea into thin china cups and passed them to his guests.

"What kind of mistake would you have to make, for instance?" Leo wanted to know. "Before you had to go and sell vacuum cleaners."

"Oh," said Calvin, "well, there are the technical mistakes. But it's mostly the beginners that make those, and they're not in the position to do much harm. Then there are the big mistakes. The biggest mistake of all is to produce a show nobody wants to watch. The show you're going to see me tape part of in about half an hour was on its way to being one of those shows when I took it over."

"Calvin rescued the Mary McGregor Turnbull show," put in Renee, who had been keeping a low profile so her new friends could get to know her old friend.

"Let's say I saw its potential," corrected Calvin modestly, sipping his tea. "There is a need for a show like Miss Mary's, but my predecessor hadn't quite found the *focus*. He had more of a radio mentality. He was wasting what Miss Mary had to give and forcing her to give what she didn't have."

"This is marvelous tea," said Lydia. It was: a fruity, spicy tea. "What did she have and what didn't she have? By the way, I saw that show once, years ago, I was telling Renee; Mary McGregor Turnbull was doing syllabub, but you never got to see it after it hardened. That was before your time, I bet. Renee says you have a foolproof method now."

"I do. I have a caterer. He delivers whatever Miss Mary's been whipping up, in an identical container, and she takes it out of the oven, or refrigerator, or whatever. Sometimes Miss Mary's concoctions do come out okay, but we save shooting time by using the caterer. Would you believe, my predecessor used to *wait* for Miss Mary's recipes to *cook*? 'You boys take a break,' he'd tell the cameramen, 'and come back in fifty-five minutes when this banana pudding is done,' he'd say. Can you beat that? The guy had no video mentality whatsoever. Furthermore, here was Miss Mary, not only a fabulous raconteur and walking history book, able to get into any home in North Carolina, and he has her *read* Mrs. Reynolds Tobacco's recipe for peach cobbler, he has her *read* Mrs. Burlington Mills' recipe for salmon croquettes, when the name of the program—the name *he* picked—is all but hitting him in the eye with the potentialities. *Southern Kitchens*; and there he is, making Miss Mary squint at the studio TelePrompTer to *read off* Mrs. Reynolds Tobacco's or Mrs. Burlington Mills' favorite recipe when the viewers are dying to get into those houses the only way they can—through Miss Mary and our cameras—and find out whether Mrs. Burlington Mills uses a chopping board or a butcher-block table to chop her celery, and whether Mrs. Reynolds Tobacco's copper-bottom pans are shiny enough to hang from pegboard hooks, or whether she has to hide them under the sink."

"Everyone likes to see into other people's houses," agreed Lydia. "It's human nature."

"What happened to your predecessor?" Leo asked Calvin. "Is he selling vacuum cleaners?"

Calvin's resonant, chesty laugh vibrated through the small room. He gave Lydia a look which read: Isn't your boy something? A look Leo was meant to see. "If he isn't, he ought to be!" He checked his watch again. "What you all are going to be watching us tape this afternoon is the studio part of a show we've already taped most of down in Beaufort. There's a fantastic old man there, retired Coast Guard, lives in the same house his Huguenot ancestors built back in the seventeen-hundreds. Miss Mary and I went over with a crew to get his recipe for a crabmeat soufflé that's just out of this world."

"And have a look around his old house?" asked Lydia.

"You got it," said Calvin. "Those old houses in Beaufort are something to see. Do you know Beaufort?"

"We have a summer cottage right across Pamlico Sound," said Lydia. "On Ocracoke."

"Hey, isn't that where Blackbeard the Pirate lived?" asked Calvin.

"He died there, too," said Leo. "He was run to ground right in his own hideout. Teach's Hole. You can wade down to Teach's Hole from my granddaddy's cottage."

"It'll be your cottage one of these days," Lydia told him.

"You know," said Calvin, taking them all in with a look that announced confidential intent, "we're all North Carolinians here, so I can say this. I believe our state has the most interesting past and the most exciting future of any state in the Union. After I completed my courses up at the RCA Institute, they wanted to give me a job as assistant director over at NBC; but I thanked them very much and said I thought I'd get on back down here where the air is good and I know my way around. I like the *cultural* opportunities in New York, but those people up there are too tired and cynical; they get off too much on decadence and catastrophe. There's something self-righteous about the way they assure you they're right at the *center* of all the decay. Well, who wants to be right at the center of the decay? I'd rather be back in the Old North State, where there's still room enough to turn around in and we still have *hope.* No wonder a million new people a year are moving to the South, and a great proportion of them to North Carolina. And what with the new communications satellites we've got now, and the prospects very soon of cheap light-wave cable, nobody's going to have to live in New York to have themselves a network."

"Calvin wants himself a network," drawled Renee, with a fond, if rather platonic, look at her friend.

"Well? What's the point of dreaming if you don't dream big?" said Calvin. "My dream is a cultural network. There'd always be something worth watching, just as there's always something worth reading in a good library. I'd rely on subscribers and endowments." To Lydia, he said, "Don't you think, just within this area of the state, what with all our furniture factories and tobacco and chemical companies and textile industries, we could drum up enough support for one dial on the TV set where there would always be something worth watching? Don't you think we've got enough people right here in the Piedmont who know what's good?" He made it clear with his eyes that he thought Lydia was one of these people.

"I want to think so," Lydia told him. "It's certainly a dream worth pursuing."

"Thank you," said Calvin, with a gracious nod. "I need all the encouragement I can get. Now, folks, let's go on down to the studio and meet Miss Mary."

It was a small studio, but very modern, Calvin explained to them, pointing out the expensive, computerized color cameras, already set in place around a "kitchen" area. Calvin explained, ostensibly to Leo, to whom he directed all technical information in the old "man-to-man" style, how the floor of this studio had been specially leveled so that there would not be one jiggle or bump in a picture when a camera rolled across it.

There were three cameras, a complicated array of overhead lights, at least ten people running around looking very knowledgeable and indispensable, and, all by herself in a corner, a small blue-haired lady with a face like an angry mastiff's; she wore a cotton-print shirtwaist dress, circa 1959, and sat forward on a velvet Empire sofa—obviously a prop for some other show. She had a carton of eggs open on the marble-topped coffee table before her, and was in the process of breaking one egg after another, not very neatly, and trying to separate the whites from the yolks, not very successfully, into two glass bowls.

"Calvin," she called, in a gruff, peremptory voice, as soon as she saw the producer approaching with his friends, "how come you trapped me into doing a recipe that calls for nine eggs? You know my arthritis. And I never could break an egg right, anyway, even in my prime." She cocked her head to one side as she said "prime," and you could see the eyes of a girlish flirt still exercising their rights through the old and wrinkled lids. She took in Calvin's visitors but did not acknowledge them. "I brought this box of eggs from home," she told Calvin, "to practice on, before the show. I know how it throws you into a tizzy to go over your budget. And I don't intend to waste these eggs, either. I'll just eat scrambled eggs for the next week, that's all."

Lydia had met at least a score of old ladies like Miss Mary in her life. No matter how old or dotty or ravaged in the flesh they became, they kept faith with their own arrogance. It was an arrogance built on the rock-safe foundation of Who One Was and it kept them in love with themselves even after everybody else who knew who *that* was had died; it kept them in love with themselves till *they* died. But, unlike Cate, Lydia knew how to get along with the breed; Lydia had often thought what a pity it was that Theodora Blount had not been *her* godmother—she would have known how to handle Aunt Thea. She rather admired these old dragons, the way they took charge. And had this way of *knowing* they were right. It was better to be a dragon when you

were old than it was to be a meek, quaking sheep; that way you
still retained some power over others, just as Miss Mary retained
power over Calvin, who was now humoring her the way you
would a petulant movie star ("Now, Miss Mary, you know and I
know that nobody traps you into doing anything you don't *want*
to be trapped into doing. Have you taken your Arthritis Pain
Formula?")

And yet, thought Lydia, Calvin had "saved" this old
dragon's show. But she could understand why he would want to.
It would provide a certain gratification to a North Carolinian like
Calvin to save a fellow North Carolinian like Miss Mary. And for
an ambitious fellow like Calvin, Miss Mary could provide entrée
into the houses that would most likely contain the people who,
as Calvin had put it, "knew what was good."

"You've met my friend Renee Peverell-Watson," Calvin told
Miss Mary, "and now I'd like to present Lydia Mansfield and her
son, Leo Mansfield. Lydia is taking Renee's class over at the college, and Leo came along for the day."

Mary McGregor Turnbull nodded graciously toward Renee.
She turned slightly on her velvet sofa and gave Lydia and Leo the
once-over. Lydia went forward and offered her hand, and, as she
said, "How do you do, Miss Turnbull," she dipped a small
curtsy. She was careful not to squeeze the old hand, since it was
acting up with arthritis.

Miss Mary narrowed her eyes at Lydia. "Where are you
from?" she demanded.

"Well, I live in Winston-Salem now, but originally I'm from
Mountain City," said Lydia.

"We used to go up to Mountain City in summer, when I was
a girl," said the old lady, "We went for the climate. My father
was never really well after he came home from the War. The
Spanish-American War, I'm talking about. You have to specify
wars so carefully today, or nobody knows which one you're
talking about. I take it Mansfield is your married name, if that
good-looking boy is your son."

"Yes, ma'am," said Lydia. "My maiden name was Strickland."

"Strickland." The old lady narrowed her eyes in concentration. "There was a George Strickland, used to play poker with my older brother, Royall; he was a lawyer, I believe, and he smoked the most awful-smelling cigar."

"That sounds like my grandfather," said Lydia. "His name was George, he was a lawyer, and he smoked an awful cigar. So I'm told. He died right after I was born."

"Yes," mused Miss Mary. "My brother Royall is dead, too. Of course he was much older than I. Are you a good cook? I'm not. I lie awake nights marveling over the fact that here I am with a cooking show—I've had a cooking show for fifteen years—and I'm not even a tolerable cook. But I have quite a following, you know. I get letters. I have *fans*. Especially since Calvin took over. So I guess I must have something else."

"You have presence, Miss Mary," said Calvin. "You have charisma." His eyes had been working overtime, keeping track of all the personal dynamics going on, as well as the preparations in the studio. He looked at his watch. "You about ready to start, Miss Mary? Don't worry about the eggs. Tell you what. You do the best you can. One out of nine is bound to come out right. We'll just repeat that shot nine times."

"I don't know, Calvin," said the old lady. "We sure are cutting a lot of honesty corners. I still don't feel completely right about reaching into that oven and taking out what the man from the catering truck's just sneaked in one minute ago." She looked at Lydia. "Can *you* break an egg? Even in your *prime*?"

"It's one of the few things I learned how to do at this Cordon Bleu cooking class I took once," said Lydia. "They taught you to clean up as you went, how to make little ridges in a potato so it would roast better, and how to break an egg using only one hand. Those were the first things we learned. After that, it got more complicated. But I love to cook. I don't know how *good* I am, but—"

"Come here and sit beside me," said the old lady, patting a place on the hard Empire sofa, "and do show me how you break an egg with *one hand*."

Lydia sat down, tucked the corners of her skirt beneath her, picked up a brown egg from Miss Mary's carton, and cracked it in half with a single deft movement of her wrist. She held the two parts, still connected by a thin membrane, poised over the bowl Miss Mary had been using for her whites. "Do you want it separated, or what?" Although there was a shocking amount of yolk in Miss Mary's bowl of whites.

"How fascinating," said Miss Mary. "How truly fascinating." There was reverence in her tone. She looked up at Calvin and cocked her blue-tinted coiffure to one side. "Why can't you let this little girl from Mountain City stay down here in the studio with me and help me break my eggs on the show?" she wheedled.

There flashed across the producer's countenance an ill-concealed look of annoyance. He glanced, this time pointedly, at his watch. "Well, Miss Mary, it's a little *late* to be changing the format of the show—"

"Oh, pshaw," retorted Mary McGregor Turnbull, who had chosen not to notice Calvin's disapproval. "We've already done three fourths of the show down in Beaufort at Captain LaForgue's house. All that's left is for me to pretend to be making the Captain's soufflé. She can break the eggs and I can mix up that crabmeat stuff and we can talk, just like any two people in the kitchen. Any two civilized people can *talk*."

Lydia sat, still holding the egg. Everyone's eyes were upon her.

Calvin said, "I asked Lydia and her son Leo here as guests, Miss Mary."

"Well," said the old lady triumphantly. "She can be my guest down here in the studio and he can be your guest up in the control room."

Calvin groaned. But it was a token sort of groan. He said to Lydia, "Have you ever been in front of a TV camera before?"

"No," said Lydia, "but I'm willing to try. If I can be of help." Her heart began to thud, but nobody could feel that but herself.

"Good girl!" exclaimed Mary McGregor Turnbull. "We'll have us a fine time," she told Lydia, turning her back on Calvin, who was already motioning for the makeup girl. "There's nothing to it," the old lady told Lydia, sotto voce. "It's not at all intimidating, like the theater. I mean, there's nobody *out there*, in television. Not a live, breathing audience, like the theater. And if they're not live and breathing, why should anybody take any account of them? That's my theory. Now what did you say your married name was, again?"

Thus, Lydia found herself on television. A little microphone was clipped to the open collar of her cotton-knit polo dress; she felt the heat from the lights through a matte veil of makeup (but she had insisted upon applying her own lipstick and wiping most of it off); she somehow, thank the Lord, managed to break all nine eggs into elegant, still-connected halves and separate them, without mixing any yolks with whites. And she did it with one hand, at the same time chatting with Miss Mary about sundry topics: how she, Lydia, had decided to take the Cordon Bleu cooking classes in London because, as a new bride, she had been terribly lonely with Max away at the Bank all day, and she thought it would be better to learn some fancy recipes than to stay home feeling sorry for herself; how she had started back to school now, in her thirty-sixth year, "and, frankly, I'm not sorry I did things in the order I did them. I enjoyed being young when my children were growing up; it was more fun for us all that way; and I find I can concentrate better in college now than I could eighteen years ago." She told how she had brought her son to visit her college classes today, "so he'd get a taste of what's in store for him when he goes to college," but did not mention, or even allude to, the fact she was separated. That was nobody's business. Especially if—as Miss Mary said—there was nobody out there, anyway. Lydia tended to agree with Miss Mary's theory. When all you could see was blazing light and the lenses of some big cameras, how could you "take account" of anything but what you were doing, or of anybody but yourself and what you were saying? Lydia couldn't even see her friends, or her own son, up in the control room.

"You know," said Mary McGregor Turnbull to her guest, Mrs. Lydia Mansfield, "there's a mystery about Mountain City that has always intrigued me. Since it's your hometown, maybe you can tell me the answer."

The egg yolks had been poured into the crabmeat mixture, the whites had been whipped to stiff peaks with the electric mixer, and the two parts of the recipe had been folded and transferred into sixteen individual bakers, which Miss Mary, assisted by her guest, had placed upon a baking sheet and put into the preheated oven. Now they were "waiting" for their recipe—or rather, Captain LaForgue's recipe, which was his "company" recipe, proportioned especially for annual LaForgue clan gatherings at the old bachelor's house; the floor manager had motioned that Lydia and Miss Mary had one minute and a half left of their "waiting" period. Then there would be a cut, and the men from the catering truck, already waiting outside the door, with sixteen identical soufflés, would hustle the delicately risen props from the truck's ovens into the studio's. And the cameras would roll again as Miss Mary opened the oven and took out the soufflés she had not put in.

"What is the mystery?" asked Lydia. She thought it was a shame that their soufflés wouldn't ever have a chance to rise; what a waste.

"Well," said Miss Mary. "You're too young to remember the old Battery Park Hotel. It sat up on this enormous hill. It was called Battery Porter Hill; or sometimes Porter's Battery Hill. Then they tore down that old hotel and built a brick one in its place, but whatever happened to that hill underneath? We came back one summer and the whole hill was gone. I never could figure out how they got rid of that hill or why anybody would want to get rid of it."

"It just so happens I can solve your mystery," said Lydia. She could not keep from smiling. The old lady really didn't *know*? "They leveled that hill for two reasons: first, to give more space to the growing business center of town; and second, to use the dirt to fill a big ravine just at the edge of the business center, because it was dangerous and ugly. But, years later, the bus station built its new depot where this ravine used to be before it was filled up with dirt, and the pilings sank. My father was the lawyer who represented the bus station and won the case against the architects. My sister and I were allowed to skip school to go and hear his final argument in court. My father said, 'If we can't trust our foundations, what can we trust?' " Lydia felt her eyes go bright with pride and emotion; she had completely forgotten she was on TV, until Miss Mary clapped her hands and exclaimed, "Indeed! How very true! Well, Mrs. Mansfield, I'm sure our viewers will all agree you have been a very charming . . . and very *serendipitous* guest." Miss Mary winked right into the lens of the nearest camera. "And thank you for clearing up my little mystery. That vanished hill has worried me for years."

Why, the old fraud, thought Lydia, she is aware of an audience out there every minute. Unaccountably, Lydia began to shake just as the floor manager brought his hand down in the swift, clean gesture meaning it was all over.

"You were great," Leo told his mother as they drove home on the Interstate. It was rush hour, and the rain was still falling lightly: the most treacherous combination of driving conditions. Lydia had to keep braking and changing lanes. There was a little knot of tension at the base of her neck. She leaned back against the headrest, without removing her eyes from the road.

"I don't know about great," she said. "Just so I didn't make a fool of myself. What a day! My mind feels like that dark room we went into, with all those monitors showing different pictures, all going on at once. Was I really all right?"

"More than all right. Calvin said you looked like you'd been doing it all your life. He was worried, at first. But then, after things got going, he chose more shots of you than he did of her."

"He did? How do you know that?"

"I heard him tell the director. The monitors have numbers on them and he kept saying he wanted the numbers you were in. Oh, and he said you didn't have any bad angles. Renee thought you were terrific, too."

"Well, just so I didn't embarrass you," said Lydia. "There was one terrible moment—just after Miss Mary said she wanted me to be on the show—when I panicked. I had to decide which would be worse: to go on the show and make a fool of myself in front of you, or to beg off and have you think I was a coward. It didn't take long to make up my mind."

"You cared about what *I* thought?"

"Well, of course," Lydia said. It was true, she *had* thought first of what Leo would think; and then the others, too, but Leo was such a perfectionist. "Of course I cared. Don't you care what I think about you?"

After a moment, Leo said, "I guess I do."

They drove in silence for a while. Both of them were exhausted. Lydia wondered what Stanley was doing, right that second; wait till she told him she was on TV. Maybe they could watch the program together; Calvin had said all her angles were good.

Leo, looking out of the window on his side, said, "Then you think it's worse to be a coward than to make a fool of yourself?"

"Oh, absolutely. Say I *had* made a fool of myself"—and Lydia's stomach clutched (partly because they had all crammed themselves full of the crabmeat soufflés—the ones made by the caterers—before they fell) as she imagined all the ways she might have been laughable. "Even if I had, I would at least have known I had had the guts to try. But if I had refused to try, I would always be wondering what it would have been like. You know those people who go around moaning, 'Oh, if only I'd done such-and-such, my whole life would have been different.' Well, I don't want to be like that. If you get into the habit of retreating from challenges, you're just a sitting duck for regrets. When I get old, I don't want to be trapped in a room with a lot of old regrets."

She was thinking of what she was going to fix for Dickie's supper to make it up to him for having been off on all these adventures with Leo. If it had been Dickie with her today, they would now be having an animated, gossipy analysis of Calvin and Renee, the "new North Carolinian" that Calvin represented, and the interesting trade-offs apparent in Calvin's relationship with Miss Mary. But Leo did not go in for that kind of talk. She was also watching the slick road for their safety. And she was frankly basking in how well everything had gone: the classes, the way Leo had been treated by her friends, the way she had been "great," "terrific," on TV, "as if she'd been doing it all her life."

She really had no ulterior motive as she preached her small sermon on how it was better to risk contempt than to be a coward. With so many separate pictures of the day going all at once on the overcrowded monitor system in her brain, she had forgotten, for the moment, the reason for this mother–son outing: the Cookie Cunningham soap opera was not, for the moment, on any of Lydia's channels.

But when she thought of it later, after she had dropped Leo off at his father's, she said to herself, That *was* a rather appropriate conversation for us to have had; now, if only he'll apply it to his life and go back to school. But you couldn't control which, out of a day's events, would lodge themselves in your child's memory, to apply to his life and maybe alter the course of it. That was one of the most frightening aspects of being a parent: you never knew *what* a child was going to remember, or how he was going to remember it.

Leo spent the weekend working on his suntan and shooting a lot of vigorous, thoughtful baskets. On Monday, he ate breakfast with his father, spent the next hour blow-drying his hair, and arrived at school just after Mrs. Epting's loosely structured Social Studies hour was ended. He was polite to Cookie, asked after her health and said he was sorry she had suffered, but he never took her out again. He never went back to Mrs. Epting's class. He forced her to fail him, which seemed to give the teacher more pain that it gave him: that compassionate Mrs. Epting who was known to take pity and pass any student who showed up for class and "made an effort." Leo would make up the Social Studies in summer school, he told his parents. And even though The Ghouls were a trio once again, Leo was adamant about wanting to go away to school. A boys' school, if possible. He liked girls, he said, but he was tired of mixing everything up. Maybe he could go to school in England? After all, he had been born in England.

Lydia naturally gave herself some credit for Leo's return to school. And she gave some to Renee and Calvin, and told them so, which pleased them very much, though Renee said: "He just needed to get out and see there was more to the world, that's all. He was boring himself to death in that room."

In later years, Lydia was to construct a very inspiring success story, based on this day's events, about how, if you believed in yourself and did what you were supposed to be doing at the time and place you were supposed to be doing it, your destiny sometimes came right up and tapped you on your shoulder. She was referring to herself.

The people who admired Lydia, and found her an inspiration and a model, never tired of hearing the story, which contained the details of how it had all begun to happen for her. The people who did not admire Lydia, who felt she had neither earned nor deserved her "destiny," found the story tiresome.

But, as she became more influential, she grew less concerned about what these people thought, though she was never to conquer her concern entirely. Indeed, she came right out and admitted it, which (her admirers said) made her more lovable. "But if you do anything in this life," she would say, "anything *worth* doing, that is, you are bound to make some enemies."

PART III

The only thing to be done, now,
now that the waves of our undoing have begun
to strike on us is to contain ourselves.

To keep still, and let the wreckage of ourselves go . . .
—D. H. Lawrence, "Be Still!"

9.
GHOSTS

Nell drove out to Meadowland Mall—formerly Crabtree Meadows, where she had picnicked as a schoolgirl—to buy a bathing suit for the trip to the Outer Banks. Lydia would be driving up on Monday, and they would leave early Tuesday morning.

But there had been a last-minute change in plans: now Cate would be coming, too. Cate's college had gone bankrupt and Cate was bringing all her things to store in Nell's basement until she could find herself a new job. Nell expected Cate to arrive around midday tomorrow.

Cate had called a week ago to announce this, and to ask if she might live in the cottage at Ocracoke for the summer. She had sounded both demanding and on the defensive, as if she were daring her mother to deny her request. Nell did not deny it, because Cate had sounded almost desperate. Who would deny her daughter the use of a beach cottage if the daughter had no other place to live? Of course, that meant upsetting Lydia's plans about renting the cottage, but, as Lydia had been doing this (on Max's advice) to save Nell trouble, Nell really had not expected Lydia to blow up as she had.

"But I don't see what choice I had," Nell told Lydia, "other than to ask her to move in with me; and I don't think that would have suited either of us."

"No, but just because *she* never plans, she thinks she has a perfect right to mess up everybody else's plans. It's going to mess up your whole year's tax benefits if she lives there. If a family member lives for more than a certain percentage of the year in a vacation home, then the IRS won't let you claim it as a rental. It says so in the pamphlet Max gave me."

"She could hardly plan for her school to go bankrupt," said Nell. "They only told everybody for sure at the last minute."

"Oh *Mother*! She was talking about it last December when . . . when she was here. We sat right in the living room, before we went to see you at the hospital, and she said it might close, and if it did she might not get another teaching job for a while. She said she might try something else. Well, how do you know she won't decide to take up . . . *crabbing* or something? She might be living in Daddy's cottage for *years*."

Nell decided the time had come to inject some humanity into things. And also to set a few priorities straight. She was slightly repelled by Lydia's hard, "business" tone. "I think you and Max are worrying yourself too much about things you don't need to worry about," Nell said. "I'm richer than I've ever been in my life. I have more money than I need. I can certainly afford to give up some 'tax benefits.' Especially if it means giving my daughter a place to live. You have a place to live; I have a place to live. Would you want your sister not to have one? And besides, it's just until she gets herself sorted out, she said. She sounded as though she's had a hard spring. Besides, I don't believe she could stick it out on that island for more than a few months. She's too restless. Don't you remember how she was always so ecstatic to get to Ocracoke, and the first day or so she swore she was never going to leave, and then she'd be the first one to be ready to leave?"

In the silence that followed, Nell could all but hear the retorts that sprang to Lydia's mind, and which Lydia then rejected. That Lydia might think, but not voice, these things, restored Nell's faith in Lydia's basic goodness. In Nell's opinion, Lydia had grown more exacting and bossy since she had left Max, and since Leonard had died. (Was it some compensation for the loss of these men in her life: that she thought *she* had to be "the man" now?) But as long as Lydia's tact and loyalty and basic good judgment continued to overrule her tendencies toward authoritarianism, she would be okay. In many ways, Lydia's sentiments concerning Cate paralleled Nell's own, but it would have been a violation of some mutually held value for them to discuss these sentiments in too much detail. As a child, Lydia had exercised to the fullest her rights to criticize and complain against her sister; but when she became an adult she gracefully relinquished these rights. She established for herself a certain measure of superiority by refusing to name—beyond a point—the things in Cate that gave them all such pain and trouble. Lydia even defended Cate, on occasion.

"Well," Lydia had said finally, "I guess she's not the only one who had a hard spring. I mean, *you* had to . . . to *adjust*, and all . . . and if anybody had more complications in their life than I had, I'd sure like to know about it. But I tried to keep things under control, and to a large extent, I'm relieved to say, I succeeded. I had been looking forward to this trip, I really had."

"But we're still going, aren't we?"

"Well, *yes*, but . . . it won't be the same." There crept into Lydia's voice the whimper from her baby years. "I mean, you and I have never been anywhere just by ourselves. Do you realize that, Mother?"

Nell, surprised, thought back. Good God, was it true? Had there always been someone else around? But there *was* always someone else around when you were a family; surely Lydia, with her own family, knew that now. It was always a balancing act: so much attention to one, then, quickly! compensate the other by paying attention to him.

She said, "We'll find time to be alone, honey. Wait and see. And you and Cate should go off together some, too. I think you two could enjoy and benefit from each other if you had some real time together. Besides, I have selfish reasons. If you two aren't friends, then when I'm dead there'll be no two people to get together and talk about me. You and Cate know me better than anyone else alive."

This last had been meant to "lighten" the dialogue, but, to

Nell's chagrin, Lydia had burst into tears. Nell had had to spend the remainder of the telephone conversation bending over backward the other way: assuring Lydia, in earnest tones, that yes, she was in the best of health, she had only just last week had her annual checkup; that she had no intention of dying; that she fully intended—here the humor crept in again, she couldn't help it— to live into her nineties, till everyone was sick of her, and spend every drop of the money Daddy had left on herself.

"Good!" Lydia had cried passionately. "I hope you do!"

Such emotion, thought Nell, waiting in the line of cars bottlenecked this side of the tunnel that separated the old business district from the new shopping mall. Where had all that emotion come from, suddenly, in Lydia? Why this passionate, jealous outburst *now*, when Lydia's own children were almost grown?

For, when the girls were growing up, Nell remembered, she had felt . . . well, loved, yes, but with the distinct air, on the girls' part, of toleration. Now both daughters were homing in on her with their frenzied, passionate demands for her attention. What forms did they expect it to take? Was she to dispense wisdom? Advice? Consolation? Approval? Admiration? Was she to compensate them for not demanding these things from her sooner, all those years ago when she prowled around the house with nothing better to do than give these things, if asked, but knowing quite well, even then, that people never listen until they are ready? Then, she had had all the time in the world to be in demand, and would have welcomed it if either girl had invited her into the sanctuary of her room and demanded, "Mother! On the basis of your experience, how should I live my life? What, in your opinion, is the best way to get along in this world? Mother, what is the world really *like*?"

But each was shut away in her own room, perfectly confident that she was plotting the best of lives for herself, deaf to any advice or suggestion that might slow down or mitigate or impede the racy lines of her idealistic young plot.

Which was as it should be, thought Nell; which was in the nature of things. Now the traffic was inching through the tunnel.

Some fool, as usual, blew his horn to hear it echo, to disconcert those people who hated being trapped in tunnels. This tunnel was due to be blasted away, any day now; the city fathers had finally relented to progress, over the protest of the nature lovers and the people who owned property on the mountain that was to be blown away. There would, within a year or so, be wide, swift access from the old part of town into the modern new shopping malls springing up in what used to be meadowland, forests, even wilderness, in Nell's lifetime. In a year or so, everybody would be able to get in his car and drive the necessary ten or twenty or thirty miles (in Nell's case, it was thirty-two miles, round trip, from Lake Hills to the Meadowland Mall) without having to wait in a bottleneck at the tunnel.

That is, if there was any gas left. This spring, the Iranians had cut off their oil, and already people were saying, "We should have kept our perfectly good stores downtown, with the convenient bus system that only the blacks use now."

Misplaced, thought Nell, who, though no fearer of tunnels, was always glad to emerge into the light. So much in life is misplaced and mistimed, even when people mean well and have the highest aspirations.

But that was in the nature of things, too. People, city fathers, countries, had that in common with children: they could not hear until they were ready to listen.

So I'll buy myself a bathing suit and we'll all three go to the beach, thought Nell, and Lydia will want to be praised for getting Leo through his crisis and for doing so well in her courses and for being invited back by Mary McGregor Turnbull to help her with her program; and Cate will want her feathers soothed after yet another migration (though, this time, it really *isn't* her fault that her college closed). I must be careful not to praise Lydia too much, or soothe Cate too much, and . . . oh! speaking of feathers, I was so much looking forward to watching those baby crows learn to fly! Now I'm going to miss it, I'll be gone at just the wrong time.

One more misplacement, but how could she help it? You couldn't put a crow family before your own daughters, thought

Nell wryly, circling the rows of the shopping-mall lot for a space near her store; though she had begun to find a pleasure she had not thought possible in simple solitude. There was a sort of mellow ecstasy in just letting yourself go in the sun, contemplating the shifts of light in a day, or the wind in the trees, or the life of a bird family. When the struggle to "be yourself," and "hold your own"—and hold on to the people you thought you could not lose and still live without—was over, you could actually find pleasure in being nobody. Or you could *be* yourself, but without all that unnecessary pain of assertion, and simply sit and possess all the moments in your life that a certain sunlight or a particular wind reminded you of. So many moments had come back to Nell recently. Lost moments were capable of finding themselves in you if you let "yourself" go.

("There is a great deal to be said for just *being nobody*," Nell heard herself enlightening her grown daughters, against the soft lapping of the tides in Pamlico Sound. There the three of them would sit on the cottage porch, each with a frosted mint julep, rapt with mutual understanding at last.)

Then, getting out of the car, she had to laugh at herself. For, of course, they were nowhere *near* ready to let themselves go and be nobody. If she were to say such a thing, they would glow at her indulgently, each girl preoccupied with her own present needs, and simply not hear what Nell was saying.

And here am I, thought Nell, smiling, as she walked toward the ugly brown windowless mall spread like a baffling construction of the future across the landscape she still remembered crowded with crabapple trees in blossom when she and the girls from her boarding school had picnicked here; here am I, plotting how I can resume the running of their lives—as if they weren't old enough to do it for themselves. Some "nobody" *I* am!

She entered the mall, not really tempted as she passed the first offering at this entrance of the giant trading mart: a Baskin-Robbins ice-cream parlor. Then came a pet shop, a jewelry store, and a bookstore—one of those big chains. The pet shop was featuring a windowful of Siberian husky puppies, asleep in a desolate heap as far away as possible from a fresh pile of excrement; the jewelry store was crammed with shiny gold and silver "suggestions" for "Your Graduate"; and the bookstore, from the looks of its window, seemed to have only one book in stock, but lots of that one.

She was faintly depressed by the time she entered the vast, open emporium of Blum's—formerly the most exclusive store in town, but which had undergone some qualitative change simply by having been moved from its old quarters to this mall. Everything in the new Blum's was open, accessible—almost *too* accessible—and plentiful. But why, thought Nell, did that accessibility have to alter the actual feel and smell of the merchandise? Did we just *think* a dress was better when we had to ask for what we wanted and some helpful saleslady in black disappeared into a room and came back with that one dress? No, the quality used to be better, I'm sure of it.

But now she was beginning to sound just like Theodora, who loathed this mall where she was "forced to shop" since all the "good" stores had moved out here, and who went on a little too long about "the *people* you saw out there."

Poor Theodora. That was Nell's next stop: Memorial Hospital, where Theodora, now out of intensive care, was recuperating from her stroke. Nobody had quite pieced together what had happened. It was Lucy Bell's opinion that Wickie Lee had actually struck Theodora when Theodora had tracked the runaway Wickie Lee and her baby to the old apartment house on Depot Street where Rita and her babies were living on welfare. But Grace Hill, the only one who had actually gone to see Wickie after Theodora's stroke, testified on Wickie Lee's behalf: despite the fact that Theodora had barged in on them, had called Wickie Lee and her friend Rita "awful names," all Wickie Lee had done was, well . . . maybe told Theodora a few home truths. "It was about time *somebody* did," Wickie Lee had told Grace Hill (who afterward rushed back to the newspaper office and conveyed her findings, via telephone, to the other women, though speaking in a hushed, apologetic tone, as if she half expected the stricken Theodora to rise from her hospital bed, fly through the air, and boom over Grace's terrified shoulder, "Grace Hill, shame! Am I never going to be able to trust you behind my back?").

"She thinks she can own you," Wickie Lee had told Grace Hill. "She thinks, just because she helps you out, that you're her property. Well, nobody's anybody else's property. Least of all, I'm not. And my baby's not, either. I told her if she came up here again, when nobody invited her, I was going to take one of those sheriff's warrants out on her."

A sheriff's warrant against Theodora!

That had been on Sunday morning, a week ago tomorrow. And then, somehow, Theodora had ended up on Azalea's porch. Azalea, toiling up her hill after church, had seen Theodora's old Buick Special parked at the foot of Azalea's undrivable driveway. Azalea had known something was wrong right then, on account of Miss Blount never took that Buick up Azalea's hill, even in the worst weather when she brought Azalea (almost) home. Theodora said it would ruin the Buick's springs and undercarriage, otherwise she wouldn't think of making Azalea walk up the hill in bad weather.

So Azalea, already knowing something bad had happened, had panted up the last remaining stretch of driveway, which *no* car could drive . . . and found her protectress lying unconscious in a pool of vomit in the hot sun, her arm twisted under her, her face pulled oddly to one side.

Azalea had no phone. She dragged the unconscious Theodora into the shade (and out of her own vomit) and ran as fast as her old, swollen legs could carry her, down to the Buick, where she had already seen the keys dangling from the ignition, and— regardless of groaning springs and bashed undercarriage—got that car *fast* to the nearest source of help, other than the police, which Azalea would never go looking for on her own. She drove to the fire station, just behind the courthouse, and they called the rescue squad. Azalea rode with the rescue squad back to her place, to show them the way.

(Azalea, later waiting in the emergency room, started shaking so bad she had to be given a tranquilizer. She had never, it turned out, driven a car before in her life. "I jus' turned that key to the right, like I seen Miss Thea do, and put it in 'D,' and the Lord helped me do the rest, because somebody had to.")

Theodora was conscious now, but nobody knew yet whether or not she would be completely herself again. Latrobe Bell (to whom Theodora had given power of attorney after Leonard died; and whose son Buddy—now that Cate had forfeited her claim—was Theodora's heir) was talking about flying a specialist up from Duke. There was talk of an operable aneurysm lodged in an artery in Theodora's skull.

I am glad I have my own daughters, thought Nell; not that Latrobe won't be overscrupulous in all this—he'll know everybody will be watching—but I'm glad I've got that little extra padding of blood devotion, in case I fall over unconscious on somebody's porch.

She flipped cursorily through the rack of one-piece size thirty-sixes in the swimwear department before being descended upon by an eager saleslady. But no, this was the "new" Blum's, where no salesperson (as they were called now) seemed at all eager to descend. They kept their distance until you went in search of them. And then, the most frequent reply was "If it's not there on the rack, we don't have it."

Nell selected four suits of cut and color appropriate to her build and time of life, and headed for the dressing rooms. A young man stationed at a desk halted her at the entrance to the curtains: "Sorry, ma'am, I have to check you in. It's the procedure now."

"Check me in for *what*?" asked Nell. The young man wore skin-tight leather pants and a soft shirt, open down most of the front of his tanned chest. He was attractive, but not in the conventional masculine sense.

"Oh, you know." He made some graceful wavy motions with his hands. "People like you have to be inconvenienced because others have sticky fingers."

"Oh! You mean shoplifters," said Nell, enlightened.

"They've been robbing us *blind*," said the young man dramatically, rolling his eyes up to show the whites. "How many have you got there? Oh dear, I'm afraid they only allow three at one time." He fingered the suits, looked up at Nell, cocked his wavy head to one side. "I'll hold this one for you and solve the problem. You aren't going to want this old thing, anyway. It's years too old for you." He relieved Nell of the one suit she really hadn't been fond of. "Here, let me see those others. This is going to look stunning, I bet." He indicated a black, streamlined one, cut lower in the back than the others. "You have such a nice *straight* back."

Nell, inside her dressing room, tried the young man's choice on first. They did have an eye. She did have a nice back, smooth-skinned and straight. Some of her contemporaries already had a little hump. I'm not nineteen, thought Nell, observing her angles in the three-way mirror, but I'm not disgusting. She looked at herself through the eyes of that young man and saw a solid, taller-than-average woman with grayish-blond hair pulled back from a strong, high-colored face. She had never had to use makeup, other than a little lipstick for fashion's sake.

And to think, mused Nell, trying on her second-favorite suit, these very looks that have served me well used to give me such pain. For, when she was young, she had thought she looked like a cross between a peasant and a Valkyrie: she had yearned for small bones and delicacy and elusive feminine airs.

The other bathing suits seemed dowdy, after the sleek black one. It had turned this whole outing into an unexpected pleasure. Nell decided to buy two, so she would always have one dry. She looked forward to telling the young man, but when she returned to the desk, he had been replaced by an older woman.

She emerged into the bright sun of the parking lot with her two look-alike suits folded in tissue and nestled in a shiny green-and-white-striped carrier bag that had BLUM'S IS MY BAG printed in big black letters across both sides. In the old days, the Blum bags had been a simple green, with "Blum's" scrawled discreetly in one corner. One knew simply from the color of the green that the bag was from Blum's.

But I don't want to get into that "old-days" rut, thought Nell, remembering when this parking lot was grass underfoot and crowded with crabapple trees in blossom where her girls' school had come to picnic in the spring. There, or about there, where that small Mercedes was parked, she and her friends had spread their blanket and begun to unload their basket of school-packed sandwiches. She was happier today, a sixty-three-year-old widow standing on the hot asphalt under the noonday sun, than she had been as a fifteen-year-old girl. Then, she had been desolate most of the time. She was too big and clumsy and her sentences always sounded too . . . exact. She had no music in her gait or her voice, like some of the girls she admired.

No, thought Nell, the "old days" had their charms, but they had their sorrows, too. These are the new days, and my back is still straight. Why, come to think of it, I'm living in what those young girls shaded under that long-ago crabapple tree would call "the future." Hey, girls! I made it into the future!

Where are they all now? she wondered, setting off for the hospital to see Theodora. Prissy and Lynne-Anne and Merle and Sophie? A pity I didn't keep up with them. But I was so eager to get out of that school. I couldn't wait to say good-bye to them and disappear into this strange mountain town, where my mother had died, where not a soul knew me outside the school. I wanted to become a nurse and forget. Forget *what*? Why did those girls cause me such pain? They meant well, they wanted to be my friend more than I wanted to be theirs. I held back. It hurt too much. It hurt that Prissy had that wonderful father who worked for the Department of the Interior and was always coming and fetching her to take her away on camping trips, when my father didn't even want me to come home and live with him after Mother died here in the sanatorium. It hurt that Lynne-Anne was so beautiful *and* smart; and that Merle, dainty Merle, could attract any man from the eighty-year-old school gardener to someone's three-year-old brother; and that Sophie had such scads of money she could bring her own horse from El Paso, in his own private train car, and board him near the school. They thought I was standoffish. I remember once Merle cuddled up to me and accused, "Nell, why won't you really love us?" They were attracted to me because of my aloofness. But it *wasn't* aloofness, it was just plain jealousy. I was so jealous it hurt. And what good did my jealousy do anybody? Oh, silly, silly self, with all its wasteful *assertiveness*. What pain I would have saved myself if I could just have gone on and shared what they wanted to share with me. We all had our points. We were all aspects of . . . of that season's girl. It takes a variety of flowers to make a garden. But who can think of oneself as an *aspect*—or even as one flower in a garden—at the age of fifteen?

I wonder how many of them have made it into the future. Who still has a straight back, who still has her husband alive, what wisdom do they think they've gained? I hope they all *are* still alive. And well? Not, like poor Theodora, looking at the walls of some hospital room and wondering, Where am I?

She met Buddy Bell and his wife, just leaving the hospital elevator. Nell exchanged with Buddy the overenthusiastic greetings of people who have never really cared for each other, meanwhile racking her brain for the name of Buddy's wife: for Nell had nothing against the young woman (Sue? Sally? Jo-Anne? . . . years ago she had been in Nell's Girl Scout Troop . . . she was the same age as Lydia).

Buddy announced with a proprietary air that, though there had not been a great deal of change in his godmother's condition, Theodora was "holding her own." "Daddy's up there with her right now. He's on his lunch hour, you may just catch him. Nell, you remember Janet, don't you?"

"Of course I do," said Nell, shaking the young Mrs. Bell's hand. "Janet was in my Scout Troop."

"Way back in the Dark Ages," replied Janet, with the easy self-deprecation such girls relied on as a staple of social exchange. Only, poor Janet had not quite mastered the knack: Nell noted the fleeting dismay that darkened Janet's smooth forehead as soon as the words were out of her mouth—would Mrs. Strickland think the "Dark Ages" referred to *her*?

Nell helped her out. "You and my younger daughter, Lydia, were in at the same time."

"Oh Lydia!" breathed the grateful Janet, on sure footing again. "How *is* Lydia? I always admired her so much!"

"Oh, she's fine," said Nell, "she's gone back to school now that her boys are almost grown." Nell recalled something Lydia had once said about girls like Janet. "There are 'middle-of-the-list' girls," Lydia had declared, with the assurance of one who knew herself to be at the top of the list, "and, no matter what they do, or how hard they try, you just never think of them first."

"And what's old Cate up to, these days," interjected Buddy Bell, in a tone just a shade too familiar for Nell's liking. The tone invited her to collude with him in condemnation of "old Cate," who was always "up to" something . . . the kinds of things that caused her to lose out on the spoils of godchildship. When Buddy Bell was fourteen years of age, he and some rowdies had gone on a Halloween rampage, ringing people's doorbells and then throwing unwelcome things on these people's porches, while the boys waited in nearby bushes to observe with much hilarity how the homeowner dealt with burning brown-paper bags full of garbage . . . or excrement. Then, Buddy Bell, with the same instinct for "stepping up the experimental odds" that would later make him a valued member of missile-research teams, got the bright idea of leaving a lighted firecracker on a man's porch. What would the man do? The man answered the doorbell, took one look at the destructive sizzling thing, attempted to throw it clear of his porch, and lost all the fingers on his right hand. Oh, what woes and wails ensued from the Bell family! Lucy Bell was in tears or on the verge of them whenever she showed herself in public for weeks after. Latrobe, grave-faced as a preacher, spoke about the "misdirected energies of youth." A repentant Buddy was briefly exhibited, before being sent down to Atlanta to finish the school year from the house of his older brother, married and working for the IRS (the same brother whose conception had altered Theodora's life). An out-of-court settlement was negotiated by one of the "flashier" lawyers in town, and a year later Buddy Bell was back in town, on the high-school football team. It was all as before; only, there were four fingers fewer in the world.

Now Buddy stood before her, thick-necked, middle-aged,

and prosperous, the swagger of the preferred citizen implicit in the very hang of his low-belted plaid trousers, and condescended to Cate, as if she were the outlaw in their midst whom they all had to cover up for.

"Cate is coming home," said Nell brightly. "I expect her sometime tomorrow."

"Is *that* so?" The small blue eyes of the smiling Buddy narrowed to inscrutable pinpoints, but not before Nell had glimpsed the alarming vision she had set off in his head. "I know you'll be glad to see her," he managed to say with forced heartiness. "Is it for a nice *long* visit, for a change?"

"I hope so," said Nell, deterring the closing doors of the elevator, which had already left once without her. "She's welcome for a day ... or ... for a year. With Cate, you just have to wait and see what her plans are!"

She stepped into the elevator with a cheery wave, leaving Buddy to his unprofitable vision of a certain disastrous bedside reconciliation which could still occur.

Nell tapped softly at the door of Theodora's room. The private nurse on duty cracked open the door suspiciously, but her face brightened when she saw Nell. The nurse was Mrs. Talmadge, who had been with Rachel Stigley to the last. Nell and Mrs. Talmadge had taken turns reading *The Godfather* to Rachel, who was conscious right up to the end and said she wanted to know how the story came out before she died.

"How is she?" whispered Nell.

"She's awake," said Mrs. Talmadge. "You come in. Mr. Bell's been reading her get-well cards to her."

Latrobe sat with his back to the window, whose sill was crammed with flowers. Theodora lay propped at the crucial twenty-degree angle, to prevent recurrence of hemorrhage; she was being fed intravenously, and was attached to a catheter (Nell knew she would be furious if she were aware that the plastic bag full of her urine was visible, just this side of the bed). Her head was turned to face Latrobe, who was in the process of reading a card, though he looked up briefly to acknowledge Nell. It made a rather devoted scene: white-haired Latrobe intoning a well-wisher's message to his stricken friend lying still and rapt upon the bed.

If the young Theodora, while she was engaged to Latrobe, had been granted this particular glimpse of the future, thought Nell, *she would have had every reason to believe they were an old married couple, Latrobe as affectionate and dutiful as ever. She would have been pleased by this scene.*

". . . that one's from Reverend and Mrs. Cato Jones, out at Free Will Baptist," Latrobe was telling Theodora. "See, Thea, you got friends of every race, color, and creed. You know who Reverend Jones is? You remember Reverend Jones?"

". . . I . . . think . . . so," came a weak, shy voice. It was Theodora's rich alto timbre, but all the imperiousness was gone.

"What do you mean you think?" said Latrobe, shooting Nell and Mrs. Talmadge a look that said, Jollying her along is the best thing for her. "Of *course* you know who Azalea's preacher is. Reverend Cato Jones is Azalea's preacher."

"Oh. That's right." The voice expressed a willingness to please.

"Now look who's here to see you." And Latrobe stood up, to recognize Nell "officially." "Come on around here, honey, and have my chair," he said to Nell, magnanimously. Nell could see Theodora trying to turn her head.

"No, no, darling," cried Mrs. Talmadge, rushing forward to her patient. "Be careful with that head. When you get ready to turn, I'll help you out. Would you *like* to turn away from the window for a while? I can set Mrs. Strickland over here, if you like."

". . . away from the window . . ." came the pleading, child-like voice.

While Mrs. Talmadge performed the necessary steps to turn Theodora, Latrobe shuttled over to Nell. "She's much better," he murmured, in the same proprietary tone Buddy Bell had used downstairs. "Doc Watson says if she continues to improve like this, we can fly Damrosch, the neurosurgeon, up from Duke to take a look. They think there's a good chance of ligating that little bastard and keeping him from causing any more trouble. Then we can get to work on what we have. The physical therapist has already noticed good response in the left hand. But we're still in the touch-and-go period. We got to be mighty careful."

At last Nell sat down beside Theodora. She was alert but, Nell suspected, still very confused. Nell doubted whether Theodora had known who the Reverend Jones was—or even, for sure, who she, Nell, was—but she knew that *she had better pretend to know* as much as these kindly, looming faces demanded of her to know. Even in Theodora's confused state, she knew her survival depended on getting along with these people who had domination over her veins and the angle of her head and which way she could turn on her bed.

Nell took Theodora's left hand, which lay on the side nearest her. "How are you feeling, Theodora?" she asked, squeezing the hand gently.

The hand returned a faint pressure. "Just fair, thank you," said Theodora politely, as a child—a child brought up the old-fashioned way—might answer an adult. Even the words were old-fashioned, from another time.

"Who is this here, Thea?" Latrobe quizzed, hovering behind Nell. "Can you say who this is sitting next to you?"

"Oh please," said Nell, annoyed at Latrobe and distressed for Theodora, who ought to be allowed to emerge from her confusion at her own speed, reconnecting her memory circuits according to her own clues and not someone else's forced exam. It was quite possible that Theodora was four years old at the moment, or eleven years old, and that Nell and Latrobe and Mrs. Talmadge were three puzzling old strangers crinkling up their faces at her in parodies of concern. "It doesn't matter," said Nell to Latrobe, but seeking Theodora's eyes, "I'm just . . . nobody." Without her blue-rimmed harlequin glasses, Theodora's eyes were much larger and softer and without guile. The glasses had been wrong for her face. They had minimized her lustrous gray eyes and given her face a slightly sour, conniving look. How odd, thought Nell, that Theodora, who was so vain over her appearance and her age, would have worn glasses for decades that made her look harder and older than she was.

The hand faintly pressed Nell's again. "It's ... nobody," said Theodora, like a good student. But Nell could swear she saw a triumphant flash of humor in the large gray eyes, as if Theodora were saying to her, Well, I answered him, didn't I? and also understanding exactly what Nell meant when she said she was nobody.

One still knew so little about the brain: how it knit itself back together ... what stitches were dropped irrevocably ... after a stroke. One could describe "the stroke syndrome"; one could classify the stroke according to symptoms; one could now even locate the damaged or obstructed part (what Latrobe referred to as "that little bastard") and go in, under a microscope, and cut and tie and segregate the deteriorated area from the rest of the healthy brain. But every stroke was different, in that only one person in the world could know for certain what was going on inside, however much or little he or she "knew" according to outside standards.

Latrobe's dutiful laughter at Theodora's "nobody" answer receded in the room, and Nell sat on with Theodora quietly for some minutes more. Theodora's eyes remained on Nell's face; she seemed to be focusing as if trying to read a book whose contents didn't quite make sense. But Nell felt a calmness flow between them; she could not help but feel Theodora knew Nell wished to give her all the room she needed: that Theodora—whether a four-year-old or an eleven-year-old Theodora—trusted her.

What faces would my real trust flow toward if I were in her situation? wondered Nell.

But when she got up to go, Nell could not resist one small experiment to assess the current state of Theodora's mental processes. "Well, I've got to run on," Nell said, watching Theodora carefully. "I've got *Cate* coming tomorrow."

"Oh, is that right?" asked Latrobe, a little too enthusiastically.

Theodora's eyes slammed shut.

"I believe we're going to sleep a little," said Mrs. Talmadge, approaching the bed to make the obligatory smoothing and tucking motions.

Latrobe walked Nell to her car. "How does she seem to you?"

"I would say the prognosis is hopeful," said Nell. "I think she knows who she is, even though she may not know names yet. Of course, there's always the chance of a relapse or a reruption, and nobody can tell at this point what the extent of disability will be."

"Oh Lord, she isn't going to like being disabled," said Latrobe. He was still afraid of his former fiancée's displeasure. "You mean she'll never walk again, or what?"

"Latrobe, I wouldn't dare to predict. Not even Dr. Damrosch from Duke is going to predict. You really do have to take one day at a time, in things like this."

"Oh God," exhorted Latrobe, taking out a handkerchief and wiping the sweat from his face and neck. "It's such a damned responsibility. She left me in charge of everything, you know. I mean, well hell, Nell . . . you know our story. She could have been my wife." He laughed strangely. "In a way, it's like she *is*. You know, in those Arab countries they have a bunch of wives. There's always a senior one who kind of runs everything. By God, if Thea isn't like a kind of senior wife to me. She's godmother to Buddy, and, like I say, she's left me in charge of all her affairs, just like you'd leave a husband in charge. This may sound out of place, Nell, but I can tell *you*: I'm feeling this thing. I declare, I am. I think a heap of that girl lying up there. It just kills me that somebody as proud as Thea should be reduced to a dependent invalid. It's just a damn shame."

"Don't give up on her yet," said Nell. "She may rally and surprise us all." She turned her head away, toward a row of cars in the hospital parking lot. For Latrobe had started to cry. Nell saw a little orange Datsun with an M.D. license plate. On the bumper below the plate was a sticker which read I'D RATHER BE

ON THE GOLF COURSE. That's going a bit far, thought Nell, even in humor.

Latrobe recovered himself and blew his nose. "I declare I'd like to kill that little hillbilly hussy. I went over there, you know. To that apartment they have on Depot Street, she and that other rip-off queen, Rita. I told 'em a few facts I thought they ought to hear. I think I put the fear of God into Wickie, though that Rita . . . well, she's a mean 'un. She's mean as the Devil himself. She has spawned two welfare bastards you and I are paying for. That's the biggest racket going now, for a certain kind of young woman. Have yourself a passel of babies—the stipend goes up for each one—and then sit back and take a vacation for the rest of your life. What a racket!"

"Well, but they do have to take care of the babies," said Nell. "That's not exactly a vacation. Though I agree, the system does have a few too many loopholes. How *is* Wickie Lee? She must be a little distressed about Theodora. Those two did seem to have developed a certain understanding."

"I'll tell you the kind of understanding they developed. Theodora gave and Wickie took. That was the understanding *they* had. Then Wickie wanted to move her friend Rita in, but that's where Thea drew the line. That Rita is a mean, ugly thing. You ever seen her? No? She practically camped in Thea's living room till Wickie moved out. Distressed? I guess old Wickie is a bit distressed; she pretended to be real sorry and all. I guess she *is* sorry that gimme-time is over. Thea bought that girl an entire wardrobe and paid all the doctor and hospital bills and installed her in her own girlhood bedroom and gave her the benefit of her highly cultured mind. And look what gratitude she got. I expect, unless Thea recovers enough to tell us herself, we'll never know what happened last Sunday, whether she broke Thea's heart or made her so mad she busted a blood vessel in her brain, but I'll tell you one thing for damn sure: that hillbilly slut has got her last dime out of Theodora Blount. Oh, she pretended to be sorry and all that, when she found out how sick Thea was; if I'd of had my way, I would have told her Thea had gone on and passed away, but Grace Hill, who never could mind her own business, beat me over there. But I think I got it through both their heads, the hillbilly hussy and her mean, dark friend, that there would be no more free rides from Theodora Blount. They were welcome to steal what they could from the government—every other no-count is doing it—but they'd be wise to think twice before making any claims on Thea."

"But what kind of claims could they make?" asked Nell, puzzled.

"Lord God, Nell, what kind of *claims*? Look here, honey, I've been a lawyer forty-six years—I turned seventy last March, you know—and I can tell you people make claims when they've got a lot less to go on than Wickie Lee—or whatever the hell her real name is. Did you know that that bastard baby's birth certificate is made out in the name of 'Tiffany Blount'? Hell of a first name to stick on any child, bastard or not, but Thea couldn't talk her out of it. That's when they began to fall out, you know. But how Thea could have been so foolish as to let the girl use her own name is beyond me. That's Theodora's whimsy. Her arrogance. God knows I love her, but she always was too damned arrogant for her own good. You know what else she did? She put that girl up to claiming 'Arthur Dimmesdale' as the child's father! Now I'm no literary man, but I did watch that *Scarlet Letter* series with Lucy and I know who 'Arthur Dimmesdale' is. Thea probably thought that was cute as hell. She always did consider herself above the law. But that's because she's always had people like me—and your late husband—to shield her from her follies. But Jesus *Christ*, Nell—excuse me, but I'm wrought up—Theodora filled out the birth certificate *herself*. In her own verifiable handwriting. I went over to the courthouse and checked the photostat. Not only did Thea sign that girl into the hospital as her 'niece,' but she falsified a legal document in her own verifiable handwriting. So, you better believe I worked harder than usual to put the fear of God in that girl when I went over to Depot Street. To protect Thea."

"How did you do that?" They had reached Nell's car.

"Well, I let it be known that if we heard any more from her, that, as guardian of the law and a former Representative of the

U.S. Congress, I would set in motion certain ways to find out which particular little hollow of Dogpatch she had crawled out of—and make sure she got sent right back there."

"And what . . . did she say?" Nell liked Latrobe less than usual at the moment, though she was sure that he believed himself The Champion of Justice.

"She didn't open her mouth again. She just turned sort of blue. All of 'em from up in those coves are kind of blue, anyway. From malnutrition and inbreeding. I wouldn't be surprised if that baby of hers isn't a half sister or something. You remember that song that was so popular about thirty years ago? 'I'm My Own Grandpa'? No, I hit the mark all right. No more was uttered from Miss Wickie Lee. Her spokesman, the terrible Rita, took over. 'Mr. Bell,' she says, in that mean low voice like the Devil, 'we want to be rid of you even more than you want to be rid of us . . . if such a thing is possible.' She doesn't talk like people around here. She talks more like one of those agitators who come down here to 'test' situations and make trouble. But God, is she mean, and swarthy as sin. I wouldn't be surprised if she hadn't got some Indian in her, as well. Those Indians have started rising up again. Did you read about those ones up in Maine—or one of those New England states—that are going to get all their land back?"

Nell put out her hand. "Latrobe, I really must be going now."

She saw him make the effort to recall himself; he had been just about to blast off into orbit on one of his circular diatribes: round the Cape of Fear to the Sea of Blame to the great, wide Continent of Anger, and back to Fear. "I appreciate your stopping in to see Thea," he said. Then, in case that had sounded too presumptuous, he added, "I'm speaking for her, of course, since she can't speak for herself yet. She can *speak*, but I mean not—"

"Of course," said Nell, opening her car door. "I understand, Latrobe."

He looked reprieved. "So you're expecting Cate, huh? Is she coming home to roost for a while, or . . . just passing through?"

For some reason, Nell did not feel like torturing Latrobe as she had Buddy. She pitied Latrobe. Why was that? Because he was a seventy-year-old child who would go to his grave without ever knowing himself? Did Buddy know himself any better? Or maybe she had exhausted her torturing quota for the day. "No, she and Lydia and I are going to take a little trip to the Outer Banks, to Leonard's old cottage at Ocracoke. Then I think Cate plans to spend most of the summer in the cottage."

"Oh, is that right?" Latrobe's relief was highly visible. Were they that afraid of Cate? Or were they afraid more of Theodora's penchant for "arrogant whims," even in her barely conscious condition? "Y'all going to drive?"

"Yes."

"Whenever you see a gas station, better stop and fill up. They're saying up in Washington there's going to be a panic. I don't know if it'll hit here, but it's already hitting the Northern states. You girls be sure and keep your tank topped off, hear?"

"Thank you, Latrobe." Nell ducked into her car and smiled up at him as she switched on the ignition.

She took the old route home. Leonard had liked it best, and she did, too, especially since the accident. Every time she had to drive past the site of their accident when she took the expressway, she lived through the whole thing again, each time compounding it with all the ways it could have been worse.

I miss him so, but I'm glad he didn't linger in such a way that he was helpless . . . or just conscious enough to feel something was terribly wrong . . . or that he was being a burden, thought Nell.

You never knew. You never knew from what angle Death would approach. Those fruitless speculations everybody indulged in, from time to time: about how they wanted to go. Swift and clean in sleep. Or a massive coronary just after one had kissed all one's loved ones good-bye. Or a moment of understanding everything before the lights were put out. And everybody hopes to escape any of the awful embellishments. Leonard had been lucky there: it was pretty certain he did not live to feel the car turn over.

But you could not choose, even if you were as willful and prosperous as Theodora Blount; even Theodora could not fill out a little order form specifying preferred manner of death. Not even—Nell smiled—in her "own verifiable handwriting." How Theodora must have loved writing in "Arthur Dimmesdale." The girl, too. Nell bet they had both had a chuckle. She couldn't believe Wickie Lee was all bad, though she, Nell, had had her doubts about the girl, at first. But she had blossomed under Theodora's care and attention. Nell could understand any young person with an ounce of independence rebelling against Theodora sooner or later, but she couldn't believe Wickie Lee was no better than the stock character of "a rip-off queen." If that were true, it would be a bad prognosis for human progress. Nell wanted to believe Theodora's ministrations to her little stray had made a difference to the girl's outlook. Or was that being romantic?

She was driving through the part of town where they used to live, before they built the Lake Hills house. The McCord house, empty for several years now, had the shades drawn on the sun porch where Taggart, home on her prodigal-daughter visits, used to thrash the piano like an instrument of discontent. Mrs. T. G. McCord lingered on in the Episcopal Retirement Home; she had been told that Taggart had died instantly of a heart attack. There was a Dexter Everby Real Estate sign in the front yard. Which reminded Nell that, sometime this summer, she really ought to go out to Big Sandy to visit Leonard's old cousin. It was not right that Dexter Everby was always reporting to Nell that he had just "stopped in to see old Osgood. He asked how you all were getting along." Family was family. Leonard would want her to keep tabs on poor Osgood.

Although she had lived in Lake Hills for almost thirty years, Nell's spirits still lifted whenever she first came in sight of the lake, choked at this end with hundreds of water lilies, and then began the climb, past four- and five-acre lots, with rambling houses and woods on some, and more formal houses with meticulous landscaping on others—how people expressed themselves, even in the exteriors of their houses!—and up, almost to the very top, to "their" home: she still thought of it as theirs.

I hope Leonard didn't mind it too much when we didn't buy that old yachtsman's house in St. Dunstan's Forest, she thought, feeling her body grow lighter as she rose into sunlight and air; but, honestly, it was so damp and dark and smug. I do believe he came to love this house. And St. Dunstan's Forest would have affected the girls; it was bound to. Lydia could never have kept up with those Forest girls, who had their New York hairdressers flown down for their special parties, and went off to expensive finishing schools in Switzerland. We just didn't have that kind of money, and even if we had, I hate to think what it would have done to her. As for Cate, with her tendency to *react*, why, she would have picked up at once on the anti-Semitism, and by this time she might have become a citizen of Israel.

Nell smiled to herself at the thought of Cate's extremes. But she could not repress her annoyance when she crested the hill and saw Cate's red Volkswagen parked in the driveway.

That was just like Cate. To say she was coming on Sunday and arrive at midday Saturday. Surprise, everybody, the free spirit has flown in. Regardless of what everybody's plans might have been. Lydia had a point.

Nell seriously considered driving on past the house and looping around, back down past the golf course, and perhaps parking beside the lake for a few minutes, to prepare herself. She had been planning to use the rest of this day to prepare herself to welcome her daughter tomorrow. Certain things went smoother when they were prepared for. But now Cate might already have glimpsed the car; she would wonder what was going on if it sped on past and disappeared around the curve.

Oh damn, thought Nell, nevertheless fixing her face in a semblance of surprised welcome as she pulled in behind Cate's car. In case Cate was watching from . . . wherever she was.

Where was she? Her small car was packed to the hilt, but she was not in it. And, Nell remembered, she couldn't be in the house, because Nell had to lock the house, now that the burglar-alarm system had been installed—at Max's insistence.

Nell went around to the back of the house and found Cate asleep in a redwood chaise, in the garden. She was frowning in her sleep, probably because her head was wrenched into an uncomfortable angle by the slant of the chaise. Why hadn't she lowered the chaise to one level *before* she fell asleep? But that was Cate, wasn't it?

She looked unrestful even in sleep. She looked spent. Middle-aged. Nell, gazing down at Cate, in her twisted shirt and jeans, experienced a disturbing surge of pity and shame for her child. This was followed by anger. But the anger was ambivalent, too. It was an anger against whatever in life had robbed her daughter of her attractive vitality; but it was also an anger at Cate for letting herself be spent by life to this degree. She had obviously driven all night; it would not have been the first time. But there had been no *reason* to drive all night, other than for the thrill of being caught up in momentum. How much of Cate's life had been just . . . wasteful momentum? Movement for movement's sake? How much had been conviction; and how much had been action for the sake of action—and reaction?

Then Nell felt a strong but utterly impractical urge to *seize control* of Cate's life. She wished she could pick her up, figuratively, and clean off the spoilage, whether world-caused or Cate-caused; just as she had picked her up, literally, as a baby, to sponge off yard dirt or feces. If only you could sponge off grown people and make them clean and new as a freshly powdered baby's bottom.

Cate woke and caught Nell in the act of thinking these things. As if aware of her mother's less-than-flattering musings about her, she straightened regally and stuck her chin up. "Where were you?" she asked casually, as if they had seen each other as recently as this morning. Her hands went up to her sliding topknot: she refastened a few loose hairpins.

"I went out to the mall to buy a bathing suit," said Nell, stooping to kiss her daughter, who smelled of perspiration and tiredness. "Or rather, I ended up buying two; but if I don't get fat, they ought to last me the rest of my life. Then I went by the hospital to see Theodora. She's had a stroke. How long have you been here? From the looks of it, you drove straight through."

"Oh, I got in about eleven. What happened was, I had planned to leave Iowa very early this morning and spend the night somewhere in eastern Kentucky, just the other side of the Appalachians, and tootle in leisurely sometime tomorrow, but I got the creeps about six o'clock last evening. I had everything all packed up in the car, except for the sheets I was going to sleep on, but when the sun disappeared from that bare apartment, it started filling up with ghosts. I knew I could never last the night, so I left the key in my landlords' box and got in the car and started driving. I just kept on driving. Did Aunt Thea have a bad stroke?"

"She's conscious. They're talking of an operation to seal off the aneurysm in the brain. That's always a good sign, when they can talk about surgery. She's pretty much paralyzed on her left side, but that may get better. I think she's aware of what's going on, though she may not be able to attach names and dates yet."

Nell recalled how Theodora's eyes had slammed shut at the mention of Cate. Had she connected Cate's name with a picture of Cate; or had the sound *Cate* sent a simple message meaning "trouble" to her shaky thought-centers?

"Well, I'm sorry," said Cate defiantly, as though she expected to be blamed for Theodora's stroke. "You don't think *I* ought to go and see her, do you?"

"Not just at the *moment*," replied Nell. "She's still in danger of hemorrhage, and—"

Cate cackled, "—and you're afraid I might make her hemorrhage. Well, I might. How did she happen to have a stroke, anyway?"

Nell sat down on the edge of Cate's chaise and related the events leading to Theodora's collapse on Azalea's porch.

"I told you that Wickie Lee was the Third World," said Cate. "Why is it imperialists are never prepared for insurrection, I wonder? I mean, it's the logical next step. When you feed and enlighten people, you give them the tools to free themselves from you. But I am sorry about poor Aunt Thea. She isn't going to like being paralyzed one bit. Why have you got the house locked up so tight? I tried to crawl into Daddy's study, like we sometimes did when we came home late from our dates, but the window wouldn't budge."

"I have to lock those low front windows now. It's this new burglar alarm. Max talked me into having the house wired with that new Safeguard System they have here."

"That sounds like Max. Wire yourself from all the dangers outside. Never mind all the dangers building up *inside*."

Nell stood up from the chaise. "Why don't I go and fix us some lunch. I've got some homemade soup and some of that salt-rising bread from the bakery that you used to like. And then you ought to take a real nap in a proper bed."

"I suppose I should. I suppose I should also start unloading my car. The trouble is, I'm not sure where to put things. And what to take with me to the beach cottage. I wish my mind weren't so muddled today."

"You've just driven seventeen hours." Nell went over to the peony bushes and snapped off three pink peonies and two white ones. She had planned to put a large bowl of peonies in Cate's room before her daughter's arrival. "Why not wait till you've rested, to decide what you're going to do with things." She puffed out her cheeks and blew some ants off one of the peonies.

"I wish I knew what I was going to do, *period*," said Cate from the chaise.

"Well, why not have lunch and a nap before you get into *that*," suggested Nell, trying to keep the rising aggravation out of her voice. "I'll go on up and warm the soup. Why don't you just . . . sit here and enjoy the garden. I'll call you when to come."

"Okay," said Cate, rather morosely. "If you're sure you don't need help."

"To warm up some soup?" Nell had already started up the steep, grassy bank with her bunch of peonies. She planned to have a long nap herself, immediately after lunch. She needed her resources. Cate's needs, Cate's style, demanded one's resources, if one were to remain civilized. Why was it she was never quite prepared for Cate's incorrigible . . . *Cate*-ness? She kept thinking her daughter would mellow, but each time they met again, the impact was the same: Cate's steamroller judgments on everything and everybody; the way she had of just walking in and dumping her ghosts and muddle into your lap. Yet Nell wantd to understand Cate. Why, in a sense, wanting to understand Cate had been the frustrated project of her life. If she could ever understand Cate, perhaps she would be able to give her . . . what?

What, if anything, could she give Cate? What, if anything, did Cate want from her? What kind of person would you have to be, to help Cate?

The trouble was, decided Nell, continuing to pursue the Cate problem after lunch, restfully sealed off from her daughter in the sanctuary of the master bedroom; the trouble was, trying to approach Cate's mind was like walking toward the repellent forces of a magnet.

Do those forces emanate from her, wondered Nell, pulling the silken comforter up to her chin, which somehow helped her to concentrate better; or do they come from me; or do we repel each other, as the like poles of magnets do?

But wouldn't that mean we were natural enemies? How could that be? How could my daughter be my natural enemy? I mean, Cate's head floated inside me for nine months; my blood furnished her brain with the cells to *build* those thoughts of hers.

Stymied by her own questions, Nell picked up a book she kept by her bedside and opened it to today's date, June 2. The book was the nature diary of a New England naturalist. She read in it to calm her mind, as some people read religious meditations. Today's entry was about newts. The naturalist, a modest, unpretentious sort of observer who never tried to see more than was there, or to force what he did see into any earthshaking applications, described the newt in his hollow; then, admitting that his mind was too impatient to try to bridge the span between himself and the small, moist creature who contained the beginnings of his own backbone and brain, the naturalist went on to describe a salamander.

Nell closed the book and sighed.

She recalled a hot August day in 1942. One of those true "dog days" when you sat very still and imagined Heaven as a cool body of water in which you could drench yourself. She was six months pregnant with Lydia, and, in those days, visibly pregnant women did not parade themselves at swimming pools. But Leonard's father, who had a car, was coming to take them out to a lake.

Well, he came. But they never got to the lake. Cate, who was three at the time, bounded out to the car with her bucket and shovel. Her grandfather, smoking one of his strong cigars, reached across and opened the passenger's door. "Come on, missy. Ride up front with the old man."

But Cate had taken one whiff of the inside of the car and said, "*Pe*-yew! I'm not riding in that smelly car."

"How are you going to get to the lake, then?"

By the time Nell and Leonard reached the car, Strickland Senior was visibly angry, but there was still a chance of reconciliation.

"She says she won't ride in this 'smelly car,'" Leonard's father reported to his son. "Can't you all bring up your little gal better than that?"

"Cate," said Leonard, "apologize at once to Grandpop. Say 'I'm sorry, Grandpop.'"

"No," said three-year-old Cate.

"You don't apologize, I'm going to drive off without you," said old Strickland menacingly. "Your momma and daddy and I will just drive off and leave you here all by yourself."

"I don't care," said the child. But she looked frightened.

Nell took Cate back toward the house and tried to reason with her in a low voice. "Honey, you've hurt Grandpop's feelings. Nobody likes to be told their car is smelly. Just say you're sorry, like a good girl, and climb in the car and try not to think about the smell, and soon we'll be at a nice cool lake. Won't that be nice?"

"No. He's mean. And the car *smells!*"

"Cate, please. It's so hot and we'd all like to go to the lake."

"Go on, then," said the child, and marched up to the front door and stood with her straight little back to them, holding her pail and shovel. No threats or entreaties could budge that rigid little figure.

Leonard suggested that he stay behind so that Nell, who was heavy and uncomfortable, could go to the lake with his father.

Nell, by this time in tears, insisted Leonard go alone with his father, and she would stay home and discipline Cate.

"Well, dammit, you all two make up your minds," old Strickland had shouted at last, curling up his lip to show his teeth, browned from cigars. He was mad and hurt; he had taken a fancy to Cate—or as near a fancy as a selfish man like himself could take.

The result was, Mr. Strickland had driven away all by himself, Leonard had taken Cate back in the house and pulled down the pants of her little swimsuit and smacked her bottom, she screaming all the while in an unrepentant little chant, "It *smells*, it *smells*!" And the family had spent the remainder of the day prostrate with heat and out of sorts with one another. "What a will that child has," Leonard had remarked after Cate was asleep, and Nell had been furious and disdainful of the admiration in his tone.

Yes, it smelled, thought Nell, thirty-seven summers later. A lot of things smell. But people are more important.

Cate's trouble was that she was always sacrificing people to ideals.

But if that was Cate's trouble, how were she and Leonard to blame? For wasn't it always the "parents' fault"?

Leonard had had lofty ideals, a yearning for fair play; but he had never bypassed people to get to his ideals. The St. Dunstan's Forest anti-Semitism, for instance: Leonard deplored racism. He spoke out against it, in his slow, patient singsong. But he would have been willing to live in The Forest so that his little girls would have the advantage of unrestricted romps in a vast, police-protected park.

Leonard had deplored the suppression of the people in Spain, and, as an idealistic young man, just out of law school, had wanted to go over there and risk his life for the rights of some Spanish people he had never laid eyes on. But, though Leonard had always been mysterious about the details, he had listened to reason—from Osgood—and stayed home.

Was it reason or compromise? *"Compromise!"* Cate would have cried if this man had been described to her as anybody but her father. That was natural: to have a blind spot about your own father. Wasn't it? Yet, Nell thought, I saw through my father pretty thoroughly. But he didn't love me much. Leonard loved Cate. I think that, in some way he didn't even understand completely, Leonard wanted Cate to be the hard idealist he was too soft to be.

He sacrificed "people at a distance" for the real, known, concrete people he loved.

Cate sacrifices real, flesh-and-blood people she knows for . . . people she's never met. "People." She sacrificed her job and her godmother for the Cambodians, for instance. And what good did that do either Theodora or the Cambodians?

What good did it do poor Cate?

Oh, my poor child, thought Nell: the way you have chosen *dooms* you to personal unhappiness.

If Leonard had known this, surely he wouldn't have abetted this streak in her? But how did he abet it? I can't put my finger on anything definite. He never said, in so many words, Now, you go out and defend the oppressed and forget about your personal happiness. Ah, but he admired her "will"; he looked more interested in life whenever he would say, "I wonder what Cate will do *next*?"

And that night, after Theodora's party, that fatal night coming home in the car, when I said, "I wish Cate would hurry up and find . . . happiness," wasn't there something like pride in his voice when he answered, "Maybe she's looking for something else"?

Nell heard her crows, in the white pine Leonard had

planted. There were several little crows now, though she couldn't see them to count how many. Their wistful, high-pitched squawks were so funny and touching.

Wawk! wawk! wawk! came the angry, staccato scoldings of the parent crows: warning, disciplining, constantly pointing out dangers.

Wa-wawk, *wa*-wawk, *wa*-wawk, piped the high-pitched junior imitations, drawling out the plaintiveness of their nest needs, but lacking the dark, sharp urgency of the experienced cries.

I suppose I was to blame, too, thought Nell. Leonard subversively encouraged Cate; I . . . what did I do? It's always easier to figure out what somebody else's fault was, but where did my own lie? Cate was born with a stubborn will. Her father admired it and abetted it on the sly. I preached, begged, wept at times, in trying to correct her. ("Nobody likes to be told their car is smelly. Just say you're sorry, like a good girl, and climb in the car and try not to think about the smell and soon we'll be at a nice cool lake.") That made her, of course, label me a hypocrite.

And I resented her. Oh, how I resented that rigid little figure with her back to us, clutching her pail and shovel so righteously and ruining our day.

But she was only a three-year-old child! How could anyone resent a three-year-old child?

Nevertheless, I did.

Nell started to drop off to sleep just as she heard Cate running water for a bath. Nell dreamed she and Cate were swimming in a curious body of water. It had the horizon of an ocean, but it was muddy and the stems of water lilies kept wrapping themselves around her legs as she swam. Cate swam on ahead, with thrashing, determined strokes. She was more like a plump baby in the dream, though she had Cate's adult face. Why, she's only a baby, thought Nell, she shouldn't be out that far. But she was afraid to enlighten Cate with the fact, because she knew that if Cate were to look down and see that she had the body of a little baby, she would panic and drown.

*   *

When Nell emerged from her room, at half past four, feeling bone-tired, as if she literally had been thrashing through resistant, tangling elements, she found Cate, her hair freshly washed and drying naturally, unpacking her clothes and sorting them in piles; she smelled of some exotic soap she must have brought with her, and had managed, at least for the time being, to wrest back from her turbulent existence her God-given attractiveness.

"You must not have slept much," said Nell, admiring a little enviously, the resilience of the comparatively young: apparently Nature still granted to thirty-nine-year-olds dispensations she withheld from sixty-three-year-olds.

"No," said Cate cheerfully. "My mind was too active. Besides, I don't know how anybody could sleep with the racket those crows were making. We never used to have crows, did we? You ought to borrow a shotgun and dispatch the lot of them."

Though she said this in play, Nell flinched. "I don't know," said Nell. "I'm sorry they disturbed you, but I've gotten rather attached to them. They're very interesting birds, actually. Extremely smart. I've read up on them. They're supposed to be the most intelligent of all birds. They can learn to mimic human sounds, and their instinct for survival is so keen that they can sometimes recognize a person who's been a hunter, even if he isn't carrying a gun."

"I like them better already," said Cate, who was perceptive enough to see that she had overstepped. "Poor Mother. I barge in here a day early and ruin your afternoon just because I got the heebie-jeebies in my empty apartment, and then I criticize your intelligent birds. Why don't you send me back where daughters come from and get a refund?"

"I don't want to send you back," Nell said, touched. "What am I going to do with a refund? I've got way too much money, as it is. Speaking of which, why not let's eat out tonight? There's a new place that's supposed to be very chic: Jamal's, it's called; everybody keeps telling me about it, but I haven't wanted to go there all by myself. Would you like to go with your old mother?"

"I'd love it," said Cate. "Let's get all dolled up to the nines

356 ~ GAIL GODWIN

and go to Jamal's. I need to iron something, though. Do you still keep the iron in the same place?"

"Same old place," said Nell. "I'll make a reservation."

The two women, looking their best, drove through the early-summer dusk. Nell was wearing the gray linen dress that she had worn for her Book Club, and Cate, coincidentally, had chosen to put on a soft gray shirt of Indian cotton, with white embroidery. Each was aware that she did credit to the other, and this further enhanced the atmosphere of hopeful solidarity between them.

"By the way," said Cate, "thanks for those peonies in my room. I can't remember the last time somebody put flowers in a bedroom for me. When I came up, after lunch, and saw them floating in that silver bowl, I wanted to thank you then, but you had already closed your door."

"You're very welcome. I like your hair in that French twist. It looks very chic."

"Thank you. After all, you're taking me to a chic restaurant."

It was exactly as if they had set out to court each other.

Jamal's had taken over the old building of the furniture store that had moved out to the mall. Many of the abandoned buildings in the old business section of town were being appropriated and renovated by young entrepreneurs and craftsmen—or what Theodora still called "hippies." The stationer's store was now a stained-glass and leather shop. The old fabric shop, where you used to be able to buy such lovely silks and tweeds, had been turned into a health-food market, where you could buy "organic" produce and vitamin pills. But the owners of the new stores on this street had chosen, in many instances, to keep the fronts and logos of the old stores in which they lodged. So the stained-glass and leather shop was still called Rolfe's Commercial Stationers, and the owners of the health-food market had gone so far as to keep the old handpainted sign of a thumb and forefinger threading a needle above their market, which was called The Fine Fabrics Natural Foods Store.

As mother and daughter held on to each other to balance themselves in the high heels neither was in the habit of wearing anymore, except for special occasions, Nell expressed aloud her unease at seeing this street where she had formerly done her shopping turned into a sort of "nostalgia lane."

"It's as if they're making fun of us in some way," she said. "Or . . . I don't know . . . embalming us while we're still alive."

Cate laughed, rather loudly, in appreciation of Nell's comparison. Then she said, "*Anything* makes me uneasy when it poses as something else."

They entered Jamal's under the sign of a winking neon sheikh. A tall young man in tight dark trousers and shirt and an Arab headdress sauntered airily toward them.

"Hello," said Nell, "we have reservations for two. Strickland."

"Hello again!" cried the young man, as if Nell were a long-lost friend. "Did you buy that black one, like I told you to?"

It was the young "checker" from Blum's under the white headdress.

"Oh," said Nell. "*You* certainly do get around. I liked it so well, as a matter of fact, that I bought two. But you were gone when I came out again."

"I only work half days on Saturday, because I have to be here until two in the morning. I'm saving up to go to the Big Apple in September." He twirled away from them to consult a reservations schedule in a fake Koran. "Strickland, two. Right here. Will you follow me?" He held aside a clattering curtain of glass beads for them and then led the way past an ornate "mosque," ablaze with colored lights; the mosque was a revolving salad bar.

The only Western note was a series of framed glossies of Hollywood stars (circa 1940), one of which hung over each of the small tables next to the wall.

"We've put you all under Joan Crawford," he said. "Unless

you'd rather have Hedy Lamarr. If you'd rather have Hedy, I can switch the reservation cards. The other couple will never have to know."

"Well," mused Nell, as she and Cate exchanged smiles. A notorious exposé of Joan Crawford's cruelty had recently been published by the late movie star's daughter. "What do you think, Cate?" To the young man, she said, "This is my daughter."

"Oh my *God*," he cried, loving it, "then of *course* you can't sit there. You can't possibly sit under Mommie Dearest. I won't permit it."

"I think we might be happier under Hedy," agreed Cate, playing along.

They all laughed, and he seated each woman with exaggerated gallantry and presented them with shiny brown menus on which the winking sheikh was embossed in gold. "Your waiter will be along in a minute, but I recommend that you order different dishes and share. For instance, for an appetizer one of you could have the Saudi Sampler, which is a mixture of little dishes like hommus and tahina and baba ghanoush, and the other could have, say, the Baghdad Prawns, which is a sort of Easternized shrimp cocktail. Then for a main course, one of you could order the Cairo Special, which comes with either chicken or lamb on a skewer, and the other could order the Tehran Treat, which is a delicious vegetarian quiche made with okra and cherry tomatoes and mushrooms and three kinds of cheese. Mmm. I had that myself tonight. Meanwhile, you all go and help yourself at our mosque salad bar."

"Is there a wine list?" asked Cate. "Or are we supposed to drink orangeade or something, like true Arabs?"

"Heavens forbid! The wines are on the back of the menu. I personally think you ladies would enjoy the Pouilly-Fumé the best."

When he had gone, Cate said, "Twenty-four dollars for a bottle of Pouilly-Fumé. An Arab restaurant in Mr. Madison's furniture store. And our prancing young sheikh. Mountain City will never be the same."

"That's for sure," agreed Nell. "But please don't worry about the prices. I was warned ahead of time about them. You have to consider the prices as part of the experience."

"The man I was seeing in Iowa had a son like our sheikh," said Cate, still frowning down at the wine list, "only Jody was much more handsome than the sheikh. Oh, they have Piesporter Goldtröpfchen. Remember, Aunt Thea served that at the linen shower she gave me before I married Pringle? It's only eighteen dollars. 'Only'! Maybe we should order it and drink to her recovery, for good luck. I wonder why so many good-looking young men nowadays turn out to be gay?"

"I don't know," said Nell. "It does seem a shame. Let's do order the Piesporter. Whatever happened with your man in Iowa?"

Cate shrugged. "Oh, nothing. Everything." A guilty smile flitted across her features. "What I mean is, everything led to nothing. He actually proposed, you know." She tipped up her chin defiantly. "He invited me up to his castle on the river and introduced me to his other son, a sweet retarded man—but he looks okay, not like some. I was very properly proposed to on a picnic. If I had accepted, I would have been packing my bags right now to accompany my husband to an Integrated Pest Management Conference in Switzerland." Cate dropped her head suddenly and became extremely busy with the unfolding of her napkin.

"I don't suppose you were even tempted?" asked Nell wistfully.

"Oh sure, I was tempted. Ah, here's our waiter."

They ordered the Piesporter and the selection of dishes their "sheikh" had recommended. "He's good on bathing suits," Nell had said, "we might as well try him on food." Nell was dying to hear more about the proposal, but wanted to tread carefully.

They made a pilgrimage to the revolving salad bar and returned with croutons and chick-peas and bacon bits sprinkled over their iceberg lettuce and cucumbers. "Some mosque," commented Cate. "A mosque harboring bacon bits. And that fake

Koran where they write the reservations. Some Arab would have a heart attack if he came in here."

"Did he really live in a castle?" asked Nell, pushing bacon bits around in her dressing with her fork, trying not to seem desperately interested.

"Oh yes. It had all the requisite crenellations and towers. And an absent housekeeper who prepared enough food for an army and labeled every little container so they'd know which meal it went with." Plunged in thought, Cate began to eat her salad.

"He would probably have wanted you to stay home a lot," ventured Nell, "and look after the retarded son?"

"Oh no. He said I could come and go as I liked. Roger Jernigan admired my independence. I think it was the thing that attracted him to me initially."

"You probably weren't sufficiently attracted to *him*," suggested Nell. "It's probably not a good idea to marry someone if there isn't attraction. I know I never could. Though women do it every day."

"Oh, I was attracted to him, all right. He was no beauty, but he was an extremely warm and vital man," Cate rejoined with fervor, confounding her mother.

Nell raised her eyebrows and smiled inquiringly, but she was damned if she was going to be trapped into asking, *"Well, then . . . ?"* as she had so many times before.

The mood cooled between them. Each picked intently at her salad. Then Cate said offhandedly, "No, I couldn't have married Jernigan. I would have made him into a father figure just as sure as Jake made me into a mother figure. People aren't really marrying when they just shelter under a parent figure."

"I didn't realize Jake tried to make you into a mother figure. I thought you two seemed like . . . well, passionate young rebels in league against the world." Nell remembered Leonard's baffled politeness and her own embarrassed welcome when Cate brought home, as her new husband, a rather rude, though good-looking, young man with his hair plaited in two braids.

"We *were* passionate, but remember: he was younger than I was."

"Only four years," Nell said.

"Four years was enough," retorted Cate, who formerly had been precipitate to point out that four years was "nothing." "It was enough to give him the leeway he needed to pervert marriage into a mother-son relation; he reverted into childishness and then madness. The whole thing was predictable, only I didn't see it at the time. Not that I regret marrying Jake. It was the right thing to do at the time; I'll never go back on *that*."

"Of course not," murmured Nell. "And if you think Mr. Jernigan would have been . . . a *father* . . . it's right that you didn't marry him. Maybe one does learn from"—she had been on the verge of saying "one's mistakes," but no, that would be wrong: hadn't Cate just said it was the right thing to do at the time?—"from one's experiences."

"Yes," replied Cate glumly. "I made the right decision about Roger Jernigan. I would have regressed into dependency. He was just too good a father; it was the thing he did best, I think. He would have been perfectly willing to be father to one more child."

Then a queer, startled expression came on her face. She blushed. "I meant that figuratively, of course," she said, rather aggressively.

"Well, of course," said Nell. "I knew you did. Poor man. One son retarded, the other . . . uh—" She couldn't yet use the word "gay": it still had resonances from her own generation, when it had simply meant being in a good mood. "I'm sure the poor man had his hands full as it was."

In that way that she had, Cate made it clear that the Jernigan topic was closed for the evening. Nell felt, almost like a sudden wind blowing in her face, the repellent forces from Cate's mind.

After they had toasted to Theodora's recovery with the Piesporter, Nell—by way of trying to reestablish rapport with Cate by abusing someone they both disliked—related her conversation with Latrobe Bell in the hospital parking lot. "It's amazing," concluded Nell, "when you think that Latrobe actually represented this state in the U.S. Congress."

"It's not amazing," said Cate. "Politicians are reflections of the people they represent." Then she added, ungraciously, "You and Daddy voted for him, didn't you?"

After all these years, thought Nell, stung; and I still haven't learned to see the trap before I walk into it. "We did," she replied calmly. "He was someone we knew ... and ... quite frankly, he was better than the old fogey he was running against."

"The lesser of two evils," sneered Cate. Then, looking up, she saw that she had wounded her mother and tried to make amends. "I'm sorry, but lately this country has really begun to depress me," she said. "This past month and a half I've been a news addict. I don't know why. Something ghoulish in my nature, I guess. I would sit there *mesmerized* in front of the little color TV my landlords gave me—he repaired TV sets, you know—and the gorge would just rise in my throat at practically every item on the news. I really do think we've blown it, Mother. Rich, promising, adventuresome, imaginative America has blown it. We started off with more than anybody else as a nation—more land, more dreams, more freedom—and just look what we've made of our abundance: we poison and blow one another up with our science and technology; we've bought pretty packaged lies for so long that if the truth walked into this restaurant right now we wouldn't recognize it; we've gotten lazy and smug and greedy and inept; no wonder our planes fall out of the sky and kill hundreds of people—some goddamned lazy mechanic was probably reading *Playboy* instead of checking a screw—that is, if he could read—he was probably getting off on the centerfold, is what I mean. And the makers of nuclear reactors and sporty little cars don't give a damn how many people they poison or turn into human torches, as long as they can collect their sneaky profits. And we've got a bunch of assholes like Latrobe Bell who sit up there in Washington and play at "running the country" like it was some kind of *Monopoly* game, or something. Only nobody's told them that if they make a mistake, Mother's not going to comfort them with milk and brownies and tell them to get a good night's rest and they can start all fresh again tomorrow on a clean board. And then we've got whitewashed delinquents like Buddy Bell making missiles, for God's sake . . . *missiles*: this civilization's latest toy. Mother, do *you* actually think we can go on much longer? Truthfully? There have been times this spring when I'd be in my apartment and I'd hear a military plane scream over-head—you know, they make that awful sound when they break the sound barrier—and my head would almost burst with rage. For all I know, some moron has started the next . . . the *last* . . . World War, I'd think, and there's not a goddamned thing I can do about it. I have no power. For as long as I can remember, I've had the feeling that my life was being controlled by people less intelligent that I am—" She flushed, checked Nell's face guiltily, and hastened to add, "You and Daddy, of course, are exceptions to that statement."

"Well, thank you," said Nell dryly.

"Don't *you* get depressed?" asked Cate. "I mean, how can any intelligent person who has kept up with what's going on in the world for the last six months *not* get depressed?"

"I did have a sort of . . . thought today," said Nell. "About how . . . well, sometimes wisdom comes too late. To nations as well as individuals. I was thinking that, with this oil crisis, the last thing we need to do is drive thirty or forty miles just to do our shopping. But if you'd told the city fathers that a decade ago when they were getting all fired up about their shopping-mall plans, would they have listened? People don't listen . . . I decided . . . they *can't* listen until they're ready. Then you have to hope it's not too late."

"What we need is a few more city *mothers*," said Cate. "Honestly, Mother, don't you believe . . . just between us . . . you could do a better job running this town . . . or this state . . . or this country than the goons we've chosen to represent us?"

Nell pondered this question. The waiter arrived with enough little dishes to make up an entire meal; and this was only the appetizer. "I don't know," she said at last. "Of course, it's al-ways easy to be a backseat driver. If you mean me personally, I don't think I would be qualified. I just don't know enough. I don't know enough about science or government or ... why, there are countries on the map I couldn't point out to you. I'm not sure I could locate all the continental states on the map anymore, though we had to do that in school. What I'm saying is, I don't have the groundwork. Besides, I'm too old."

"Oh nonsense," snapped Cate, eating an "Easternized" shrimp with her fingers. "You can't use age as an excuse. The majority of the leaders of Europe and Asia are older than you. Some are doddering old men. As for *groundwork*, it's foresight we need more than facts. You can always look up the facts."

"I'm not sure I have any more foresight than anybody else," said Nell. "I'm getting pretty good at hindsight, but that isn't the same thing."

"So you're copping out on me," said Cate, tearing a piece of pita bread violently in half. "Just like Daddy did."

"What do you mean?" asked Nell.

"Oh, once he was pointing out to me the discrepancies in some law Congress had made, and I said, 'Why don't *you* run for Congress, Daddy?' And he said he didn't think he could be a politician, they have to tell too many lies and make too many compromises before they get anyplace. Then I said, 'Well, why don't you become the first honest, uncompromised congressman?' and he said he doubted he could raise the money or get the votes, and besides, he was too old. And that was years ago."

Yes, thought Nell, that sounded like Leonard, all right; but she didn't want to be disloyal. "Well, you're still young," she said, "and you seem to be developing *your* foresight—"

"Oh no," Cate said quickly. "I've already got my profession. If my colleges would quit closing on me. I can't believe I've had two colleges close down on me in less than three years. First the one in New Hampshire and now Melanchthon. And it was bad planning in both cases. Bad planning I had nothing to do with. No, as long as I can teach, I feel I'm making my contribution. Margaret Mead says there is a certain type of person, a person who has an affection for the culture into which he was born, but is impatient with some of its old habits and rules. She says all he needs is a few disciples, what she calls a *cluster*, who are attached to him . . . or her . . . and excited by his teachings and eager to spread his ideas. She says this person may not be an acknowledged leader in history, but that he and his cluster are the means by which the small changes in a society get made, one by one. Just give me my little cluster and I'm all right. Do you know, about three weeks ago I received a wonderful letter from one of my former students at that girls' school that fired me in New York. It was a kind of *fan* letter—you must have seen it, you forwarded it to me."

"Oh yes. I wondered who you still knew in New York."

"Well, this girl, Mimi Vandermark, had gone back to that school and got my address from their files because she wanted to tell me that she had never forgotten that day when I led her class to the Lincoln Tunnel. She wrote that it was one of the most important days in her life, next to her marriage and the birth of her child. She's only twenty-one, but she's married to some rich man whose family runs a foundation, and she had this little baby who only lived for a year. Isn't that terrible? She wrote that she had been brooding over what his short little life had meant, and that led her to thoughts about the meaning of life, and *that* led her back to that afternoon in 1970 when I bundled them all into taxis and we went down and linked hands right across the mouth of the tunnel. She said"—Cate's face started to work strangely—"she said she considered it a privilege to have known me, and that I was . . . oh God . . . the only real-life heroine she'd ever known. And then you know what she wrote? She wrote that it was my face she thought of whenever she needed to summon up courage—"

Here Cate broke down and started to sob. She snatched up her napkin and hid her face in it. "Sorry," came her muffled voice. "I'm just very tired, I guess."

The waiter, as waiters often do, chose this moment to come and ask them if everything was all right.

"Everything is just lovely," replied Nell firmly. He took one look at Cate behind her napkin and fled.

Cate put down the napkin, chuckling. "God, Mother, it was

wonderful, the way you said that." There were still tears coming out of her eyes. "You're the glue that holds civilization together. Ha, ha, ha." She went off into spasms of laughter. Nell thought she was slightly hysterical.

"I think you probably *are* a very powerful teacher," Nell said. "You're bound to get another job. Have you started making inquiries yet?"

It took Cate a minute to get herself in hand. "I've made some phone calls, that's about all I've had time for. The college didn't let us know till the last minute. That's another thing, Roger Jernigan was supporting the school just long enough for his son to graduate . . . but I don't want to start on *him* again. I phoned several people I knew in grad school. One of them has just been let go himself. I got a few quasi-leads. Mostly rumors of a *perhaps* one-year fill-in at the Gila Monster Community College in the Arizona desert, or a maybe-but-please-don't-say-I-said-so opening in Freshman Composition at the Underground Coal Mine College in Depression, West Virginia. I'm exaggerating, of course, but things are not much better. I plan to write a whole lot of letters this summer while I'm living in the cottage. Who knows, maybe Skylab will fall on me and solve the whole thing. It's going to fall somewhere. Maybe it'll come down right in the middle of Ocracoke and make a great big crater. That would be fitting, in a way. Daddy used to say American history really began about where Ocracoke is now, when Verrazano looked across the Outer Banks from the Atlantic and mistook Pamlico Sound for the Pacific Ocean and went back to Europe and told the mapmakers that America had this teeny-tiny waistline where North Carolina is now; and the Europeans accepted this for a hundred and fifty years. Wouldn't it be *symmetrical* if our hubristic chunk of spacecraft wiped out the beginnings of American history? Miscalculation from beginning to end. The American Dream devouring its own tail."

Nell decided to take the expressway home. She felt bloated from all the rich, spicy food, and her head ached from the wine;

she was not used to drinking wine. Cate, having run through more moods than Nell used up in a week, sat docilely on the passenger's side, looking out at the skyful of early summer stars and humming softly. Her appetite had lasted right up until the end of the meal. She had helped Nell finish off her Cairo Special. Cate seemed to possess amazing regenerative powers of the spirit as well as the body, thought Nell; or was it only a surface resilience masking a dangerous imbalance? Was Cate simply exhibiting the healthy, elastic signs of a soul in progress? Or was she sending distress signals of a personality about to fly out of control?

Worn out as she was, Nell determined to make one more attempt at solving the riddle of her firstborn. Choosing, as near as she could remember, the spot on the expressway where she and Leonard had had their last exchange about Cate—as a sort of way of enlisting his aid—she asked their daughter, trying to strike the right balance between nonthreatening humor and committed affection, "If Skylab *doesn't* fall on you, and if we *don't* manage to blow ourselves up in the next few years, how would you like to live?"

At first she wasn't sure Cate had heard the question. At least a half mile went by and there was no answer. Or maybe Cate had heard the question and resented something in its tone or formulation and was not going to answer.

Another half mile went by. Soon, now, they would pass the spot Nell could never not be conscious of when she drove this route.

"I want to understand," said Cate, just as Nell had abandoned her attempt as ill-timed, or possibly presumptuous. "I want to be free to conduct my own sustained inquiry into this maddening, fascinating, infuriating world I was born into. I don't particularly want to starve or live in ugly places, and I'd like a few friends, and if I can't teach in a college or university, maybe I can find a *cluster*, in the Margaret Mead sense. They don't even have to be disciples, just a few engaged minds, so I won't go crazy with loneliness. But I've done a lot of thinking on the subject, this past month and a half, and I've come to the conclusion I can forgo the luxuries. I think of them as luxuries now, though"—she gave a low, sharp single note of a laugh—"I once thought of them as my simple entitlements."

"Like what?" Nell asked softly.

"Oh, I've decided I can stand being obscure. I can stand being by myself. I can even stand growing old alone, without an 'admiring bog,' or a man to love me, or children to 'invest my unfulfilled dreams in.' " She said this last in a parodying tone.

"That sounds"—there was a congestion of sorrow in Nell's throat—"very brave."

"I don't know about brave," said Cate, slipping into her old ironic singsong (the irony Nell's; the singsong Leonard's); "I only know it's possible . . . just. I think I can forgo the luxuries if I can have the freedom and mobility to investigate things as they are, and maybe call a few truths as I see them, without getting arrested or put away in a madhouse. If I can be allowed to do that for a few more years, I think I will have fulfilled my purpose in life. Oh, and I'd like to keep my health, if possible."

"That's certainly to be desired," agreed Nell.

They were driving past the place where Leonard had gone off the road. *My life could have ended that night, too,* thought Nell. Cate was looking intently out her window, but Nell could not tell whether their thoughts were on the same thing. The stars were very clear and close tonight, just as they had been on the night of December 16. Nell spotted the Big Dipper. Leonard had once shown her how to use it to locate his name star. But now was not the time to try; she didn't want to drive herself and Cate off the road.

They completed the trip in silence, Nell thinking about Cate's words (were they the words of a "real-life heroine" or were they the words of a very disappointed, no-longer-quite-so-young woman whose American Dream had failed to materialize?) and Cate thinking—Nell knew not what.

On Monday afternoon, Nell went to the hospital, in a last-minute burst of compunction, to see Theodora once more, in case things took a turn for the worse while she and the girls were in Ocracoke. Cate, taking advantage of her time alone in the house, was in her father's study. Except for the mail on his desk which had required answering, everything had been left exactly as it had been at his death.

During her last weeks in Iowa, Cate had been in a sensitive, agitated state and had dreamed heavily. One of the sharpest dreams had been about her father. It couldn't have lasted more than a minute, even in dream time, but the image remained as clear-cut as a memorable film sequence: her father, his glasses sitting low on his nose, as they did when he had been reading, stood at the door of his study and beckoned her in. As she entered, he already had his back to her. He was leaning forward across his desk to reach for some book on his personal shelf where he kept all his favorites. The dream was so sharp she could see the wrinkles in the silk of his vest, where his back must have sweated as he sat pressed against a chair. It was the tattersall vest, his old favorite. She knew in the dream he was reaching for something in one of the books that he wanted to point out to her. He reached; she waited for his revelation; and that was the end of the dream.

Now she stood in the afternoon shadows of the real study, trying to force an extension of the dream. There was the row of books, each filled with half a dozen or more white paper markers, sticking up like sails becalmed. Above the shelf were two of his Ocracoke paintings, done from the porch of the cottage where she planned to sit out the summer, reassessing her life and drawing up a plan of action for the future. She was already thinking ahead till next week, after Mother and Lydia would have left the island. She still had great faith in her powers of regeneration. She would plan her post-forty years, celebrating her birthday alone, sipping wine, calling on the gods, summoning up ghosts, making herself hospitable, at the mystical sunset hour of her birth, to whatever came next.

It had occurred to her that, alone in this house—assuming she maintained the proper receptive attitude—she might find her way to the passage her father had been about to point out to her in the dream. She believed in significances that arrived costumed in the garb of the accidental: it was up to her to find the connections; she liked the challenge to her mental powers, the chasing down of clues. If a D. H. Lawrence novel, picked up "by accident" on the wrong bookshelf in Iceland could lead her to a husband and a Ph.D. in New Mexico, wasn't it possible that her father's passage—if she could find it—might indicate to her what she was supposed to do next?

She leaned forward across the desk, trying to imagine herself inside her father, inside the tattersall vest with its sweat-dampened back. She was Leonard Strickland, going for a book which would save his daughter's life. . . .

Her spine went prickly. The house itself was as quiet as a house in a dream. The afternoon light filtering through the slats in the blinds made the room a soft, watery gold. Montaigne? Emerson? Cicero? Orwell? Why did Daddy have three different editions of *Homage to Catalonia*? He couldn't forget he might have been fighting in Spain with Orwell in 1936, she supposed. But if he had, where might she have been? Nowhere? In the "limbo" the nuns used to tell them that unbaptized babies went to?

Unfortunate train of thought. There came, unbidden, into Cate's imagination a future scene that could now never take place: a young man, alone in some room filled with afternoon light, safe in the knowledge that he exists, muses on what the universe would have been like without him if his mother had decided not, after all, to have him.

Grasping at a straw rather than a clue, Cate snatched the Emerson from her father's shelf. For some reason, she connected Emerson with common sense. ("What was it, could you tell?" she had asked, her legs up, on the table in Chicago. "Are you sure you want to know?" The doctor's reply came after an interim of silence, in which Cate had still heard echoes of the horrible sucking sound that had transported the life in her womb to a large, plastic-lined aluminum garbage pail. "I do and I don't," faltered Cate, remorse battling with her need to know. "Well, make up your mind," said the doctor, whose tone was not as reassuring as it had been when he had first instructed her to lie down on the table. Cate had made up her mind. "It was a boy, then," came the doctor's grudging reply, at last. Had it been grudging because the world had lost one of his own sex? Or because her curiosity had obliged him to poke for some time among the bloody debris in the plastic-lined pail before he could answer her?)

Cate turned through the pages of the Emerson, which were marked with paper strips. But her heart was no longer in the game. Faint pencil lines, scored vertically in the margins, attested to her father's approval of many passages. Almost too many. But wait: he had a discriminatory system: some passages had two vertical lines scored beside them. Cate read one of these, in the essay on "Illusions."

> From day to day the capital facts of human life are hidden from our eyes. Suddenly the mist rolls up, and reveals them, and we think how much good time is gone, that might have been saved, had any hint of these things been shown. A sudden rise in the road shows us the system of mountains, and all the summits, which have been just as near us all the year, but quite out of mind. . . .

Her eyes filled at the stately prose rhythms, the pictures that sprang instantly to the mind. Why had she never read Emerson before? Because he was an abolitionist, she supposed, and, most of her teachers having been Southern, they had not assigned him. And in graduate school, her specialty had been *English* literature, so she had avoided him altogether. An "educated" American who had never read Emerson.

Well, if she ever got another teaching job, she would have her class read Emerson, so she would be obliged to read him thoroughly herself.

> But these alternations are not without their order, and we are parties to our various fortune. If life seems a succession of dreams, yet poetic justice is done in dreams also. The visions of good men are good. . . .

Yes, Daddy would have liked that passage. It vindicated the armchair visionaries. What "capital facts of human life" had been revealed to Daddy when *his* mist rolled up? Could she know for certain that it ever had?

Was there ever a moment when Daddy had called himself to account for being an armchair visionary? Or did the evidence of this double-marked passage testify to his self-vindication? ("The visions of good men are good. . . .") Did Daddy believe it was good enough to have good visions?

If so, what made her so certain she wanted him for a teacher?

She was wrestling with the guilt of having had such a mutinous thought in her father's study, when she was rescued from her confusion by the clear, sharp sound of a very efficient engine idling to a stop in the driveway outside.

That was unmistakably Lydia's Volvo. Cate replaced the Emerson and left the trancelike gloom of her dead father's haven. She went out into the bright sunshine, blinking and frowning. She was frankly curious to see what Lydia had been making of herself and her new freedom.

Lydia stood on tiptoe, her back to Cate, sliding shut the sunroof of her car. She was wearing crisply tailored safari shorts and a while halter top and her Dr. Scholl's sandals. Her shoulders and arms were pink from sun. Depend on Lydia to get two things done at once: working on her suntan while driving. She turned at the sound of the screen door's slamming and saw Cate, looking pale and rather drawn around the eyes, ambling toward her with that pelvis-first gait of hers.

"Hi," said Cate, tipping up her chin. As she came closer, a superior little smile sketched itself across the face Lydia had been judging haggard, and reverted things instantly to the way they had always been: Lydia, in the pink of health and success and self-approval, found herself judged and possibly wanting, just as she had all the other times in the past when the sisters had met after an interval of separation.

I'm thirty-six years old, thought Lydia. I am the mother of two almost-grown sons. I have coped admirably with a very complex and trying spring. I got A's in all my courses (despite the B-plus Renee felt she had to give me on that "Eros" paper, which I agree could have been better organized) and I am going to be on television. I left my lover's bed less than four hours ago and was feeling, in every sense, a satisfied woman until I drove into this driveway and saw her car and felt my heart begin to pound. *Why?* It's time I analyzed this. Maybe if I can analyze it, I can outgrow it.

"Hi," said Lydia, clopping the few remaining steps in her exercise sandals and puckering her lips against her sister's. "What's new?"

"Oh, let me see." Cate rolled her eyes upward and looked amused. "I'm out of a job and just about broke, for one thing. Aunt Thea's had a stroke—you probably knew about that, though. And the country's going to hell in a handbasket, though some would say that's nothing new. Here, let me help you unload your car."

"There's just this one overnight bag. Everything else can be left in; it's already packed for the beach."

"My, how *organized*," said Cate, with just a touch too much mirth. With a simple tone of voice, she could turn things around so, making her own joblessness into a sort of achievement while rendering Lydia's careful planning slightly ludicrous. Lydia, burning, hefted her little tote bag by its shoulder strap and started up the walk ahead of Cate, vowing inwardly not to say another word until Cate made a friendly overture.

This came before she had even reached the front door. Cate, who could be uncannily alert to people after she got their backs up, called winningly, "Mother ran over to the hospital to look in on poor Aunt Thea. I'm on bartending duty this time. Remember how you saved my life with that lovely bourbon when I dragged in off the bus last December? How about a mint julep? I'll run down to the garden and pick some mint while you wash up. Though, I must say, you look like you just stepped out of the shower."

Lydia had to admit she'd love a mint julep, though she had resolved to stick to thin white-wine spritzers on this vacation.

She was dieting; Calvin had told her she was just a tad too heavy for television. "Perfect for life, but the camera puts on ten pounds" had been his tactful wording. Lydia, mounting the stairs to her girlhood room, while Cate nipped down to the garden to pick mint, suddenly felt homesick for her reassuring new friends. In some ways, she felt closer to Renee than to her own sister.

Cate had been right about the shower, however. She had taken a shower with Stanley, at his place. What a shower! Then he got in his car and drove back to the office from his "lunch hour," and she got in her car and headed west on I-40 to her mother's. Already she missed Stanley, too, though she still couldn't decide what to do about him.

Motivated, despite herself, by Lydia's elegant management of trivia, Cate decided to go all out on the mint juleps. She gathered a generous bunch of mint; pressing the hairy, aromatic leaves to her face, in a gesture of solitary ecstasy, she headed toward Mother's kitchen, full of purpose. Once there, she stowed the washed-off mint in a glass pitcher filled with water, got two of Daddy's silver julep cups from their velvet-lined mahogany case in the third drawer of the dining-room buffet, and, running water over them lightly so they would frost in a hurry, stowed them for the moment in the freezer of the refrigerator. Now the bourbon, which looked like the same bottle that had been there at Christmas, and two ice trays—that should be enough crushed ice, even when packed tightly, with some to go. Cate crushed the ice. She could hear Lydia clopping around, between the bedroom and bathroom upstairs. Lydia looked good. Of course, Lydia always looked good, but now there was a sort of glow added to her usual svelteness. Mother had said she was going to be a regular on some cooking show with an old lady who went into interesting people's homes; Lydia had got on the show by accident, and then the station had had letters and phone calls from people saying how much they had liked her.

She must be feeling pleased with herself, thought Cate, rummaging through the utensil drawer for Daddy's wooden muddler; where in hell was the muddler? No self-respecting Southerner could make a julep without a muddler. She went into a brief panic, for somehow it had become important for her to have the juleps ready, or at least well in hand, by the time Lydia came down again. I must remember to praise Lydia about the TV show, thought Cate. Damn it, Daddy, where is your muddler? Then, in a burst of reflective inspiration, she remembered having seen it, out of the corner of her eye, in the drawer of the buffet; Mother had probably put it away there to protect herself from having to come across it every time she opened the utensil drawer. For the well-made little tool, carved of walnut, resembling a miniature policeman's billy stick, had been one of Daddy's favorite possessions.

Am I jealous of Lydia's new progress through life? wondered Cate as she got out the sugar and, slipping on a pot-holder mitt so she wouldn't fingerprint the frost on the silver cups, bruised four mint leaves against two teaspoonful of sugar in the bottom of each cup with the muddler. Wouldn't it be something if Lydia, after hibernating all these years, suddenly charged out of her cave and became a huge success? Little Sister coming into her own just as Big Sister edges into the crumbly landslide leading to the abyss of decay. . . .

Lydia, entering the kitchen at that moment, saw Cate smiling mysteriously as she poured generous amounts of bourbon into two frosted silver cups packed to the rim with crushed ice.

"Oh look, Daddy's julep cups," said Lydia, pleased. "What were you smiling at in that strange way just now?"

"Oh," said Cate provocatively, sticking a large, wavy sprig of mint into each cup, "I was having a sort of Hegelian meditation about the contrasting progresses of people's lives."

"Which people?" asked Lydia casually, lowering her lashes as she accepted her julep. Since she had last seen Cate, she had amassed a considerable amount of lore about the worship of Eros; she had learned what Marx thought, and Descartes and William James; but she had not got around to Hegel. Was the disparity between them never going to end?

Then Cate floored her by saying, "You and me. I was thinking how you're blossoming about the same time I'm going to seed."

"Oh nonsense," said Lydia, blushing brightly because in past weeks she had entertained the merest outline of the same thought. But it embarrassed and hurt her to hear it voiced so blatantly by Cate. She felt as if she had to protect some ideal of her sister from this unflatteringly honest denigrator. "I mean, it's not *your* fault that your college went bankrupt and closed." She realized she was taking her mother's side of the argument last week, when she herself had been attacking Cate's lack of planning.

"No, I didn't mean that," said Cate, raising her frosted silver cup. "Cheers. I think we should drink to Daddy. These are probably the first juleps under this roof that he didn't make. Are they all right? Truthfully, now."

"To Daddy." Lydia sipped. "They're divine. I'm drunk already." She sank, with a sensuous roll of her shoulders, into the nearest chair.

Cate sat down on the other side of the kitchen table, the same table into which she and Lydia had once smeared their food when they were learning to eat. She sipped, and licked her lips. "Mmm. Not bad, if I do say so myself. No kidding, baby, you look really fine. What is that extra *shining* something? You look . . . I don't know . . . all buffed up with attention and love. I know. You've got a lover."

Lydia, taken by surprise, felt her lips draw back from her teeth in a guilty smirk.

"Aha! I was right, eh?"

Lydia lowered her head demurely in reply. She marshaled attractive descriptions of Stanley, in case she was asked. But Cate switched back to the previous subject.

"What I meant, actually, was that your star seems to be rising just as mine seems to be fading into the morning light of somebody else's day. God, Cate. That's enough metaphors for a whole week. Stars, blossoms, caves, and abysses. Probably what I'm having is simple middle-aged panic. I'll be forty this month, you know. But we English teachers have to doll things up with fancy language." Cate's voice had acquired a forced heartiness. She drained the remainder of the liquid in her cup and sucked crushed ice.

She didn't say anything about caves and abysses, thought Lydia. Was Cate going to be eccentric in her middle age? Was she, perhaps, just a little mad? But then, Lydia had a sharp sense of déjà vu: how many times before, upon meeting Cate after an interval, had she, Lydia, gone through just this sequence of thought? It had something to do with the fact that Cate's higher intensity threw her into what Daddy used to call a swivet. She became confused, lost control of the situation, and projected her confusion back on Cate in the form of "madness." Was that it? A faint ripple of pleasure swept over Lydia as she realized that she had (a) begun to analyze the problem for the first time, and (b) felt strong enough to blame herself a little in order to protect Cate. On top of this, she suddenly remembered Stanley's last kiss in the shower: it was true, she was all glossy and polished with love. Added to this came the not unpleasant realization that, as she grew stronger in the coming years, she would have to protect her sister more and more.

"What does Hegel have to do with all this?" Lydia felt she had strength enough to admit her ignorance and ask. She was wondering if there was still time to slip out and get something for Cate's birthday.

"Oh, just that things swing one way for a while, then they swing in the opposite direction, and out of this comes a synthesis which is good for the world soul, though I'm not sure where that leaves us individual souls. We're dispensable, I guess, after we've completed our swing. To tell the truth, it's been years since I read Hegel. I was just playing a little fast and loose with him to impress you. But now you've gone back to college and you aren't impressed. I don't blame you. I never really approved of his endorsement of monarchy as the highest form of government. I guess we all have our blind spots."

Though Lydia wore her rapt "classroom" gaze of attention, she was mentally cruising the aisles of stores out at the mall. How late did the mall stay open? What pretense could she use to get away? What would Cate *want* for her fortieth birthday? Lydia had her charge cards with her. Maybe a pretty little clock? No, Cate might attach the wrong metaphor to a clock. What had she given Cate in the old days, when they lived in the same house and still exchanged presents? French soaps; thick vellum note-paper in a perky buff color Cate had liked; and, when they were younger, a paperweight that snowed on a little orphan selling matches. And then it came to Lydia what Cate would love; and she would not even have to go anywhere to get it. It was her new summer shawl, a gorgeous paisley triangle of green and tur-quoise and deep purple. She had seen it last week while shop-ping for a bathing suit. It had been too expensive, but she had imagined herself dropping by to see Stanley on summer eve-nings, the shawl thrown casually around her suntanned shoul-ders, and she had not been able to resist buying it. Now, basking in her own generosity, she imagined Cate, walking alone on the beach at Ocracoke, her blond hair whipped by the sea breeze. It would be about dusk and some nice man, maybe someone who owned a little yacht which he had docked on the island for the night, would see Cate and be attracted to the independent woman with her passionate meditative air, striding along the beach and clutching the pretty, feminine shawl about her shoul-ders. And maybe later, after Cate and this man were married, Lydia would laughingly confide how she had known something like this was going to happen when she first decided to give Cate the shawl. And maybe much later, when she and Cate were an-cient and had outlived the men who had loved them, the two of them would take a long cruise or a trip together and swap the real stories of their lives.

Lydia isn't even listening to me, thought Cate, winding down on Hegel. In some ways she hasn't changed a bit. I remem-ber how she used to ask Daddy some question she thought she ought to know the answer to, and then her eyes would glaze over and she wouldn't hear a thing. The same way with Max: I've seen her ask Max something about the stock market and, as soon as he began to explain, her big lavender-blue eyes would go all fuzzy and distant and she wouldn't take in one word.

Some demon stirred in Cate, one of the same tribe which had been egging her on to dramatize her failures today, and she was dangerously on the verge of announcing in a dry, ironic voice, "*Another* reason I'm kind of down at the moment is, well . . . less than two months ago, I had this abortion." That would snap Lydia out of her reverie. And Cate was even considering telling Lydia about her confrontation, the evening before the abortion, with the Right-to-Life woman who had followed her from the clinic, when both sisters—looking slightly reprieved and trying not to show it—heard the sound of Nell's big car purring down the incline and into the garage, just below this kitchen.

The Oldsmobile door slammed. Cate got up from the table and removed two more ice trays from the refrigerator. "I'm going to make another round of these, for Mother."

Nell's familiar step was heard on the basement stairs leading to the kitchen.

Suddenly Lydia said, "Don't say anything about my having a lover. I haven't told her about it yet."

"Of course not," said Cate, dumping more cubes into the crusher.

Their mother's handsome face, assured of its welcome, appeared around the door. "Well. Both my girls. Just like old times."

Lydia jumped up to kiss her mother and relieved her of the brown paper bag she was carrying. She peeked boldly inside: a daughter's right. "Lord, where did you get such perfect tomatoes this early in the season?"

"I detoured out to the Farmers' Market. Of course, these were probably shipped up from Georgia, it's a little too early here. But after I saw Thea, I decided we should get our savor out of life while we can. I've been thinking of a good, ripe tomato all day."

"I'm making mint juleps," said Cate. "In Daddy's silver

cups. How's that for savoring? Lydia and I had one already. We drank a toast to Daddy, since he always made them."

"How nice," said Nell, though a little shadow of sadness darted across her brow.

"How's Aunt Thea?" asked Lydia.

"If her condition continues to improve, they'll take her down to Duke by ambulance next week. The Harley 'brothers' were visiting when I came, and Al Harley actually made her smile. It's the first time anybody's done that, the nurse said. It pleased both of them no end. Both Harleys, I mean. You know, I was thinking how they complement each other—in the fulfilling sense. They balance each other as people do who really *are* together. Why, they will have been together as long as your father and I were married, by next year. That's what made Thea smile, actually. Al was telling her she had to be up on her feet in time for their fortieth anniversary." Nell blushed. "Why, I guess it really *is* like a marriage, though I don't think I could have said such a thing ten years ago. Maybe not even thought it."

"Onward, toward the fulfillment of the world soul," chanted Cate, a bitter-ironic edge in her voice, as she marched out to get another silver julep cup from the dining room.

Nell raised her eyebrows inquiringly at Lydia. The gesture meant: Is something about to go wrong? Lydia gave a tiny shrug, accompanied by a smile and a shake of her head. Which meant: It's okay; Cate's just being Cate; no immediate cause for alarm.

"You look so . . . I don't know . . . happy and rested," said Nell to Lydia.

From the dining room, Cate chortled.

The three women set off next morning, about an hour later than planned. First Cate had been unable to find her bathing suit she had been sure she had packed, and then, when she unpacked everything and found it, decided to try it on and discovered the time for bikinis was past. She had gone into a tirade of self-hatred, had even cried, and said she thought she'd postpone her departure until tomorrow—after all, they were going in two cars—and do some last-minute shopping where she knew the stores, and get her ego together. Nell had come to the rescue with the offer of her extra new bathing suit, which fit Cate perfectly, though, even while admiring herself in the mirror, she berated herself for "stealing" her mother's brand-new suit. "You're not stealing it, I'm giving it to you," said Nell. "I can't wear them both at once. That would look kind of silly. If it makes you feel better, consider it a loan until the end of the summer." Nell was impatient to be on the road. She had forgotten how emotions could crowd a house; she and her thoughts had rambled so spaciously these past few months.

Then Lydia had neglected to shut her bedroom window, activating the burglar alarm as soon as Nell locked the front door, and they had all had to wait for Nell to go back in and phone Safeguard Systems to say it was the family's mistake.

"That Jerome Ennis is such a nice man," she said, coming out and locking up again. "He is in love with his business, you can tell. He clucks over it like a mother hen. He answered the phone himself. It's just a shame he lost a leg in Vietnam."

"Oh Jesus," said Cate. "Not the same Jerome Ennis I went to high school with. Not the football player."

"I think it must be," said Nell. "He said he grew up here. We had a nice long talk when he came by to show his men how to wire the screened porch."

"Oh *Jesus!*" Cate stamped her foot and glared at the sky, which was a cloudless, hazy blue; it was going to be a hot day. "That goddamn war."

Lydia rolled her eyes: her "here-we-go-again" look.

Nell said, "Yes. But he's pleased to be alive. He has a wife and several children. Poor Sicca's boy was killed. Now, girls, what shall we do about lunch? Shall we try to keep more or less together and stop somewhere in about three hours?"

It had been decided that Nell would go in Lydia's Volvo, which had more room; Cate was taking along a great deal of stuff in her VW for her sojourn on the island.

Lydia checked her watch and said, somewhat petulantly, that, as it was already past nine, they probably couldn't get farther than Winston-Salem by lunchtime. She had just driven *from*

Winston-Salem yesterday, and the idea of going back over old territory irritated her, though she knew she couldn't blame it on anybody.

"I hate driving in tandem," said Cate, "always having to be squinting up ahead or looking in the rearview mirror." She needed to be alone. The news about Jerome Ennis's leg had ruined the morning for her.

And so they had agreed not to meet for lunch but "sometime around sundown," each car driving at its own pace across the length of the long state; Lydia had reserved a room for the three of them at the Buccaneer Motel in Morehead City, in Nell's name.

When they were out on the I-40, going east into the sun, Lydia turned the air conditioner on high. "What do you think she'll *do?*" she asked Nell.

They had exhausted the subject of Dickie and Leo before they even got to the expressway entrance. Dickie would be going to music camp in Brevard as soon as school was out (meaning Lydia would have to drive *west* on I-40 again in less than two weeks), and Leo, all on his own, was writing to schools in England. Renee had been quite a help; even Renee's daughter, Camilla, had been enlisted in the cause. Camilla herself had written Leo a lovely little note, on school stationery, suggesting he might like Tunbridge, a school near her Battle Abbey. And now, since Lydia had to retrace the boring route of exactly the day before, she felt she owed it to herself to talk about something interesting. And Cate, though sometimes exasperating in person, was always interesting in principle. Though Lydia knew Mother would not "betray" Cate; and depended on Lydia not to overstep certain bounds, either.

"Well, right now," said Nell, warming, as Lydia did, to the subject, "I think she needs to *rest.* Her nerves are very much on edge. She needs to swim and get some sun and eat fresh fish and go to bed early. What she'll do after a couple of months of that . . . well! Your guess is as good as mine. I'm fairly certain she'll get another job at a college. Things can't be all *that* bad, can they? I mean, she *is* an attractive, intelligent woman. Anyone will surely see that she'd be an asset." Nell's voice rose rather aggressively, as if arguing with someone who had just disagreed with her. "And, as for the rest . . . I mean the rest of her life . . . well, things have a way of turning up in Cate's life, don't they? Did she tell you she was proposed to by a millionaire this spring?"

They talked about Cate's millionaire all the way to Statesville; and about Cate's reasons for turning him down almost to Winston-Salem. Lydia drove at a steady sixty-five, keeping her eye out for a sneaky Highway Patrolman mean enough to quibble over a mere ten miles; her heart was divided between jealousy at how *animated* Mother had become since the discussion had turned to Cate, and fascination at Cate's latest adventure. A millionaire. A castle. The two sons. *Lord. . . .*

Cate, fiddling with AM radio stations, which were all she could get, thought about Jerome Ennis. Had he married Teenie Wilson? Before or after he lost his leg? Jerome and Teenie had been one of those legendary high-school couples so exalted in their beauty and popularity that you were just grateful to them for bothering to walk past you on the same level of ground. Teenie had been head cheerleader and president of the Boosters, a social club Cate had made it into only by the skin of her teeth. Teenie's father had owned a drive-in barbecue pit, right in the middle of colored town, where, even before integration, whites and blacks parked side by side to partake of Mr. Wilson's barbecued pork slathered in his secret sauce. Jerome was captain of the football team the year Cate and Teenie were juniors and he was a senior. Cate still remembered his number: 22. Jerome's father was a plumber.

One of the things I liked about that school, thought Cate, as Bonnie Raitt's "Sweet Forgiveness" filled the car, was that you had to make it on your own; nobody got a head start because of what his or her father did. If you were good-looking or athletic, or at least (in my case) good-looking enough and very good at something (in my case, the debating team), you became one of the stellar ones. Not that my star was anywhere close to Jerome's and Teenie's.

She smiled to herself then, remembering what a stir she had caused when she debated *"for* our recognition of Red China"; and won, because her argument was better prepared.

She switched away from Bonnie Raitt. The words of the song reminded her of Jernigan. Bonnie Raitt was admitting to some man that she needed him, after all. Jernigan would have liked it if she, Cate, had turned her car around that day and driven back, admitting, "I need you, after all."

The sucking pull downward . . . and backward . . . thought Cate, fiddling restlessly with the dial again. For every giant step forward, there were six baby steps backward. Like that maddening May I? game we played as children. If you forgot to say "May I?" you had to start all over again at the beginning. What a disgusting game. Why had she ever played it? In hopes of beating it, she supposed; yet she, of all people, was the one who most often forgot to say "May I?" and had to go back to square one. What tyrannical son of a bitch ever invented that game? wondered Cate. Some bewhiskered Victorian father, I'll just bet.

The terrifying swing of the pendulum. Diastole/systole. Hegel's thesis/antithesis. Forward, backward. You had to, somehow, keep moving forward, without getting sucked into the abysses or hit by the pendulum.

Now Red China was "recognized" and nobody was shocked anymore. A crafty-eyed old man with the smile of a Cheshire cat had, just this year, been serenaded by America's performing artists in Washington and made Man of the Year by *Time* magazine.

Jerome Ennis had been hit by the pendulum.

She, Cate, kept moving, still miraculously in one piece; time had even proved her right on many unpopular stands. (Mimi Vandermark had called her the only real-life heroine she had ever known.) But what fun is it to be right, thought Cate mournfully, when people like Jerome Ennis are hobbling around on plastic legs? She probably hadn't spoken more than three sentences to Jerome the whole time she had been in high school, but that such splendor had been damaged—needlessly, in her opinion—made her feel old and defeated.

But then she tuned in to a Back-to-the-Bible station and her mood improved. The announcer was offering listeners their choice of three free pamphlets: *Why Every Word of the Bible Is True; What to Do, Based on the Inspired Word of Jesus Christ, When Your Marriage Goes Sour;* and *An Anticursing Chart.* An anticursing chart? What would that be like? Cate waited through the next hymn, "How Great Thou Art," and through his next message (". . . the only thing you can count on in our lost and dying world is the one and only inspired word of Jesus Christ"), hoping to hear more about the anticursing chart. Would it have *synonyms* for the bad words? Or would it have suggested Bible passages to mutter, like imprecations, every time you felt like saying the words? Would the pamphlet actually spell the curse words out, or just write "d——," "f——," "s——," etcetera? Or maybe the curse words of this particular Back-to-the-Bible sect were altogether different from the ones she considered curse words. But no more was said about the anticursing chart, and Cate did not really feel she could last through the sermon, which was beginning now. She listened for several minutes, not to the sermon's *words*, variations of which she had heard a million times in her life, but to the conviction of the preacher. He spoke as if there were only one way to live and he was letting you in on the secret right now.

Just as the Right-to-Life woman, urgently sipping her mai tai (paid for by Cate), had done at Trader Vic's in Chicago. The awful color photographs, which Cate had yet to be shown, lay on the table between them, harmless as yet in the leather portfolio from Gucci's with the woman's own initials stenciled at the bottom in gold.

What a bunch of loonies we are, on this doomed planet, thought Cate, switching back to a country-music station. She smiled to herself, a lopsided, ironic smile, and lifted her chin and stepped on the gas. But one thing for damn sure: we're *interesting.*

*   *

Lydia and Nell were the first to arrive at the Buccaneer Motel, and when Cate arrived they both had showered already and were into their second drink: Lydia had brought along a bar suitable for a small Shriners' convention. Cate saw they were eager to eat, and so, like a good sport, splashed water on her face, reknotted her hair, and put on a clean blouse over her jeans. If she had been alone, she would have taken a leisurely sunset dip in the motel pool, which looked inviting at this hour, with no children in it.

After an unremarkable supper in the restaurant, they took a short constitutional, lifting their faces and trying to sniff the sea air, which was somewhere just the other side of the gasoline fumes of cars and trucks. When they got back to their room, the clearest TV channel was showing *The Ghost and Mrs. Muir*, and they decided to watch it and sip a little brandy on ice till they got sleepy. The sisters lay side by side on one king-sized bed, and Nell stretched out on the other one. Lydia complained of a stiff neck and Cate gave her a sisterly rub, and then Lydia got up and made Cate a refill of her drink. Nell, absently watching this movie she had seen years before, about a widow who rents the house of a dead sea captain who falls in love with her, was actually more affected by her daughters' show of rapport and was glad she had this opportunity to spy on it while ostensibly watching the movie.

But Lydia, catching the wistful expression on Nell's face, asked, "Now Mother, this movie isn't bothering you, is it?"

At the end of the movie, when Rex Harrison vanishes for the last time through the windblown curtains, after giving the sleeping Gene Tierney a farewell speech of all the things they could have done together if only he had still been alive, Cate broke down and sobbed quietly into her pillow. "But Cate," said Lydia, disturbed and fascinated by the intensity of her sister's reaction, "he did it because he wanted her to go on and marry that man in the village. A live lover's better than a dead sea captain, even if he is Rex Harrison. Look at it that way."

"That's not the point," snuffled Cate, casting glances toward

Nell, who had undressed and gone to sleep sometime before. She kept her voice low, so as not to wake her mother.

"Would you like to go out and walk around the pool?" offered Lydia, who was still full of nervous energy from driving all day. Maybe Cate would tell her something about the millionaire that she had not told Mother.

But Cate said she was too tired to move. Lydia, after helping her undress, took some change from her own purse and went to the pay phone she had seen earlier in the motel office and called Stanley, whom she certainly preferred to Rex Harrison, who was at least seventy by now.

Out of habit, Lydia had brought along a loaf of stale commercial bread to feed to the gulls as soon as the Cedar Island Ferry churned out of its moorings for its two-hour voyage across the Sound to Ocracoke; feeding the gulls had always been the high point of the trip for Leo and Dickie. But as soon as the ferry engines started and people began getting out of their cars (other parents with *their* loaves of stale bread), Lydia saw that the bread would be wrong for the family today. For the first half hour, all three Strickland women were subdued. Each was aware, in her own way, that here was the same expanse of water, the same sky, the familiar channel markers and sandbars, the agile gulls hovering and diving and competing against one another for the bread the passengers tossed to them in bits—or held up sadistically in whole pieces to force the braver gulls to eat out of their hands. But the one person who had perhaps enjoyed it more than anybody was not there to enjoy it anymore.

I believe this part of the world was his favorite anywhere, Nell thought, leaning over the rail, her hands clasped in the hot sun. The hands were mottled with the hated brown spots now, but, somehow, she found them comforting. Leonard had never minded them; he had had them himself. Four hands, full of age spots, keeping one another company.

The first time she had visited Ocracoke, just after they were married in the summer of 1938, she and Leonard had come on the mail boat; there was no state-run ferry in those days, and you had to leave your car at Atlantic, on the mainland. The cottage belonged to Leonard's father then, and Leonard, on the trip over, had told Nell about his first trip to the island with his father. It was for the opening of duck-hunting season, in November, and Leonard was twelve that year. His mother had not wanted him to go. ("I reckon she knew Daddy, when he got together with his cronies, two lawyers from Beaufort that he hunted with, liked to drink a lot, and I expect she thought one of them might shoot me by mistake. But I had my heart set on going, and go I did. It took us two whole days to drive across the state, and toward sundown of day two, I was feeling kind of feverish, but I attributed it to excitement. But, lo and behold, no sooner had we embarked on the mail boat and gone too far to turn back than the Captain took one look at me and told my father, 'That boy has the measles; he'll have to go below board with the freight; I can't have him infecting the other passengers.' Well, it just so happened that the 'freight,' that particular trip, included a dead woman. She was in a coffin, down in the hold where I had to spend the night; she was an old resident of Ocracoke and they were taking her back to bury her on the island. The Captain didn't want me to know she was down there, but he told my father and, just before I went below, Daddy told me. I guess he just thought it was too good to keep to himself. Well, I tell you, I didn't get much sleep that night. I made up this little sentence I kept saying to myself, 'She's just a poor old dead woman, can't harm a soul.' I reckon I must have said that sentence a thousand times before we landed in Ocracoke. Daddy got a woman on the island who nursed people to come take care of me in the cottage and he went on to the hunting lodge and stayed with his friends. I had to stay there two weeks and take the mail boat back by myself and then get the bus on home, after I was well. But that was when I got to love the island, I think. Despite the fact that Mother always claimed it ruined my eyes. When the nurse would go out, you see, I'd pull up the shade in my room and watch for ships passing, way out in the Sound. I decided I'd be a sailor when I grew up. Nobody told me you weren't supposed to stare into the light when you had measles, but I guess I found out the hard way.")

That damned selfish old man, thought Nell now. How could anyone be so cruel to a child. Or so careless!

It still broke her heart to think of that poor boy, gazing out to sea with his inflamed eyes. He would have liked to be an officer in the Navy, he had told her, were it not for the fact he had had to wear thick glasses since the age of twelve.

The sins of the fathers. Did any child ever, ever, ever escape? The sins of the mothers, too, of course.

And yet, perhaps it averaged out. One reason Nell was sure Leonard had been such a good father and faithful husband was that he wanted to be different from his own father.

Their first stop on Ocracoke Island was at Mr. Jack's store. Not because they needed anything (Lydia's booze and mixers and the food Nell had brought in the ice chest would last them for the week) but because Mr. Jack would be hurt if they didn't stop, especially when he found out Leonard was dead and he hadn't been the first on the island to know.

Nell and Lydia waited for Cate, who had got stuck behind a trailer coming off the ferry, and together they went into Mr. Jack's and bought a carton of milk, a box of Ritz crackers, and some tonic water they didn't need. Mr. Jack took the news with the stoic equanimity of the born Ocracoker. "Oi'm sorry to hear it," he said. "He was a good-tempered man. Oi disremember him saying a harsh word to anyone." He rang up their purchases on his new electronic cash register and, speaking deep from the back of his throat in the same unhurried voice, told them, "C'am today and tomorrow, but hoigh winds come Froiday." He packaged their three items, adding, "Couple from Wirginia's staying in the Hollowell house, next to yours. He's a Reverend."

"That wasn't so bad," Nell told Lydia when they were back in the Volvo. "One of the hardest things about being a widow is having to *tell* people who don't know. They think they have to say all kinds of unnecessary things that confuse the issue. I like the way Mr. Jack put Leonard's death right in the same category with the weather. You know Mr. Jack believes in the weather; therefore he believes in Leonard's death. The trouble with most sympathizers is, they try to pretend death isn't real. Or natural. And it is. Just as natural as the 'hoigh winds' coming on Friday. I do hope they won't stay long and ruin our week."

"No," said Lydia, watching Cate's red VW following them through her rearview mirror. "Daddy loved the way the older people talked here. He said the accent went all the way back to Elizabethan times when their ancestors first got shipwrecked here."

"Yes, he loved that sort of thing," said Nell, thinking of the boy with measles, struck with the romance of the sea, staring, hour after hour, at the bright horizon for ships.

The cottage sat, isolated between dunes, on the easternmost tip of the island, just to the right of the entrance to Silver Lake Harbor, where their ferry could be seen reloading next to the Coast Guard station for the trip back to the mainland. They had already passed within a hundred yards of the cottage while still on the ferry: high noon was not its best hour; it looked drab and exposed amid the low-lying shrubs. Its best time was just after sunset, when shadows added denseness to the wild-grape vines, and the mildest breeze from the Sound caused the white-backed leaves of the one stunted aspen to flutter and quake, and the steep, pale roof the Navy had put on in 1945 (in lieu of the payment Leonard had refused for the garrisoning of two officers' families there) glowed with an appealing, nacreous forlornness.

Nell, despite having prepared for this moment ahead of time, was moved to a level of grief she had thought she was done with. Not only had this cottage been one of the dearer things of this world to Leonard, but it was so close to his spirit; it was like him, in some way: plain and unfurbished and *lonely*, especially in this bright public midday light which turned a blind eye to the softer, attractive shadings of those simple qualities.

This is *not* the way I want to begin this week, thought Nell, getting out of Lydia's car. I have come here to be with my daughters, to go on where he left off. If I start crying now, I'll set Cate off, and the last thing she needs is to be set off, she's too depressed as it is.

For Nell had heard Cate's muffled sobbing, the evening before, after the movie, but had forced herself to lie still. I'm best out of this, she had thought. Let the sisters tend to each other. And they had. It was sweet, lying there and hearing Lydia's sensible solicitations and Cate's self-mocking gratitude when Lydia helped her undress. It was like . . . having a preview of their rapport when she would not be around to interfere, anyway.

Nell's eyes were misted over, and she didn't want her daughters to see. They would make *her* the center of their solicitations and impede the whole process of getting over what must be gotten over. She squinted toward the Hollowells' driveway across the dune and focused on a serviceable green Chevrolet, about a decade old. "That must be the Reverend's car," she said dryly. "How unusual of old Mary Hollowell, to rent to a Reverend. She's usually out for fatter summer prices."

The daughters flanked their mother protectively as she took the old key, with its cardboard label made out in Leonard's writing, and unlocked the door. Then she had to pull it toward her and kick it several times, as Leonard always had, and it burst open, revealing a room caught in the act of existing without humans. The cane-backed furniture with its water-marked pillows, the bookcase full of left-behind paperbacks and old magazines, the threadbare Oriental rug with its still lovely remnants of blues and oranges, which, in its prime, had been the pride of Leonard's mother's living room—all were bathed in a lively golden dust which streamed through a large crack in the faded draperies. It was as if, thought Nell, entering first and breathing the dampish odor of unused things, the outdoor elements of sun and sea and air were conducting their own sort of exchange with the inanimate inhabitants of this room. (*"You'll be one of us, someday, if they leave you alone for enough summers and winters."*)

So will we all, thought Nell, and the sharp grief she had been feeling the moment before mellowed into a more bearable, elemental resignation. She took a look around her and made up her mind to get rid of the girls for a while.

"Now listen here," she told them. "Let's bring things in from the cars, and then I want you all to do what you have always done in the past. Put on your suits and drive over to the ocean beach and leave me to get things organized."

"We wouldn't think of it!" protested Lydia.

"Don't be silly, Mother," said Cate.

"Well, of course I can't *force* you," said Nell, taking a new tack, "but it would be the nicest thing you could do for me. I want to be alone, in this place, just for a while."

"Oh," said Cate, understanding first. "In that case—"

"Well, if you'll promise not to *clean* or anything," said Lydia. "Promise you'll leave the dirty work till we get back."

Nell promised.

As soon as she heard them drive off in Cate's VW, Nell abandoned herself to sorrow. She walked about in the two downstairs rooms, then the two upstairs rooms, letting memories flow unchecked while she dusted windowsills and tables; she encouraged herself to recall, in as much detail as possible, scenes available to her memory alone now. Then she went down again and opened up the doors to the screened porch: the Sound at midday was a brilliant sheet of light; it seemed to draw her personal grief into its great, warm, impersonal body. Nell uttered a deep, shuddery sigh and carried a few pieces of porch furniture out and arranged them around a giant piece of driftwood somebody had once dragged back from the beach. She dusted the furniture, but left undisturbed an impressive spider who had constructed an intricate web between two prongs of the driftwood.

She transferred the food they had brought with them from the picnic chest to the refrigerator, after she plugged it in; she was just about to fill the ice trays from the tap when she remembered that the water hadn't been turned on yet. You had to open the main valve in the pipe under the sink that led to their well, and then throw the switch on the pump.

She knelt under the sink and twisted the valve with all her strength. It would not budge. This had always been Leonard's job. And sometimes he had found it so tight he had to use a rag to get a better grip. She found a rag and tried some more, until her palms seemed to have sprouted blisters and her face was bathed in sweat.

She stood up, frustrated, and gazed out the window above the sink. No use killing herself. She would wait for the girls. If they couldn't manage it, Mr. Jack would send someone. Nevertheless, how infuriating!

She saw a bare-chested man in shorts come out onto Mary Hollowell's flagstone patio. He sat down and began to do something to a fishing rod. The Reverend? Well, he looked strong enough for her purposes. Knowing that he was a Reverend made it easier to ask.

Nell wiped her face on a dish towel and smoothed her hair and went purposefully across the sand dune between the houses. She prepared her face with a businesslike expression and rehearsed her opening.

His chair scraped back and he was on his feet as soon as he saw that she was headed for the patio. Probably thinks I'm a nosy neighbor, thought Nell.

"How do you do," she called, puffing a little from her trudge through the hot sun. "I'm Nell Strickland. That's our cottage just over there. I'm terribly sorry to disturb you, it won't be for long. The thing is—"

"Not at all," he said at once, with the automatic courtesy of a gentleman. "I'm Marcus Chapin." He offered his hand. He was about her own age, of stocky, athletic build, with white hair cut militarily short and rather distant light blue eyes. "Won't you sit down a minute?" he added, with the air of a man who is used to being disturbed and has acquired an elegant, but not over-friendly, manner of hiding his irritation. "My wife is inside," he said. "We just returned from the beach and she's lying down now. She's been ill this winter." He put aside his fishing rod and was about to pull up one of the chairs for her.

"Thank you, but I really can't. My daughters and I just arrived and I sent them off to the beach, and then I found I couldn't turn on the main water valve by myself. I looked out and saw you, and I wondered—"

"My God!" came a woman's impassioned cry from inside the house.

Marcus Chapin, looking extremely alarmed, was on his way to the door, when it burst open and out rushed a lovely little woman, her arms raised to her head as she hurriedly tied a lavender kerchief around it. There were grayish shadows under her large eyes, and her skin was slightly jaundiced, but she was beaming ecstatically at Nell. "I saw you through the bathroom window, darling," she said to Nell as she knotted the kerchief at the nape of her neck, "I saw you step up on that patio and I said to myself, 'Unless I'm hallucinating, that's Nell Purvis.' And it *is* you, isn't it?"

"Merle! I don't believe this!"

For Nell, in the interim, had discerned, in the ultrafeminine movements of the little woman and in the heart shape of the face, even without the masses of auburn hair that used to fly about it like an electric aureole, the identity of her charming little school friend who used to snuggle up to her and demand, "Nell, why won't you *really* love us?"

"Yes, darling, it's Merle. I know I look hideous, I've been so sick, but you! The years have done you nothing but good."

With an exhausted leap, Merle attached herself to Nell. Nell smelled some elusive scent on Merle's neck as she returned her friend's embrace; the scent brought with it all Nell's old adolescent agonies over her own lack of elusive arts. *My God, I'm still jealous of Merle*, Nell realized, hugging her. But Merle was so weightless, it came as a surprise.

"You're so light, Merle. I don't remember you being so light," she exclaimed, and then could have bitten off her tongue. The reason Merle was light was because, under her loose robe, she no longer had her large breasts. The illness. Of course.

"Oh yes, I'm light," replied Merle at once, with an eagerly offhand manner, meant to distract Nell from her blunder. "And

I'll tell you something else that's changed: somebody's taught *you* how to hug!"

Merle's generosity of spirit, and her perception, made Nell choke up. Then she looked over at Marcus Chapin, who had been watching the women's reunion, and saw a look of pure anguish cross his face.

"But what are you doing here?" demanded Merle. "To think, after all this time! You promised to write and you never did. Marcus, here in the flesh stands one of my dearest old friends from Farragut Pines, Nell Purvis. Though I always loved her more than she did me."

"That's hard to believe," said Marcus Chapin, smiling as he shook Nell's hand for a second time. He had got his anguish in hand enough to make this gallant remark seem a tribute to each woman. "But it's Nell Strickland now, isn't it?"

"How silly of me!" cried Merle. "Of course you would have gotten married."

"Not necessarily," said Nell wryly. "I was lucky enough to find someone willing to put up with me."

"I want to meet him! Is he here?"

"Oh, dear Merle," said Nell helplessly. "There is so much to catch up on. Leonard died six months ago."

"Oh Nell!" wailed Merle. And would have burst into tears if Nell had not gone on quickly, in as cheerful and practical voice as she could manage:

"I've come here with my two daughters, whom I want you to meet. Actually, I was having trouble turning on a valve and I looked out and saw . . . Marcus . . . and I came over to borrow his strength."

"Well, you came to the right place," said Merle. But she leaned against Nell and slipped her arm around Nell's waist in a gesture of sympathy. "Marcus has oodles of strength. Come on, Marcus, let's go help Nell with her valve."

"Of course. But hadn't you better rest?" said her husband.

"No sirree," said Merle, clasping Nell tightly. "I'm not letting her out of my clutches, now that I've caught her again. Besides, I'm not at all tired now."

As the three of them crossed the sand to Nell's house, Merle snuggled against her friend and asked gently, "Was it a long illness, darling, or did he go quickly?"

Nell described the accident. "He had a massive coronary just before our car turned over. I doubt if he suffered more than a few moments of pain."

"Oh God!" cried Merle. "You could have been killed. Oh Nell, how lucky you're alive." She tightened her hold around Nell's waist.

"Yes," murmured Nell. "At first I didn't think of it as lucky, but I'm pretty much over that, now. Life can't ever be the same without him, but I do want to go on living."

"Of course you do! Don't we all!"

Marcus Chapin, who had been completely silent during the short walk, opened the valve in the kitchen with one turn of his wrist.

Merle laughed. "You have just witnessed, Nell, what I call the 'mayonnaise-jar syndrome.' The poor woman struggles and struggles to open the jar and can't. Then, just when she gets it all loosened up to the place it will open, she suddenly gives up and hands it to the man and says, 'Honey, can you open this jar?' and of course he gets it with the next twist." But Merle looked proudly at Marcus, who was running Nell's taps for her until they cleared of rust. "Would you ever have imagined, Nell, that a flibbertigibbet like me would end up marrying an Anglican priest?"

Nell, who had never been good at countering this type of self-denigrating repartee with any flair, replied simply that she had never thought of Merle as a flibbertigibbet. Then, despite a sudden shyness unusual for her, Nell asked them, "Would you two like to come over for drinks after supper and meet my daughters?"

The Chapins exchanged the glance of the truly married.

"If Merle is up to it, we'd be delighted," said Marcus, but only after having read his wife's clear wish on her face.

"Of course I'm up to it!" said Merle, smiling radiantly at her long-lost friend.

Nell, watching them go back across the dune, Merle's arm linked through his, her small figure leaning into him, felt a pang that her own married life was over.

10.
CONFLICT

Lydia stood in the shallows, letting the tamed and broken waves nip at her toes, and watched Cate *battling* the breakers. That was the only word for it. Cate would swim toward the angriest-looking part of a wave, and then, just when she should be diving under it or getting ready to ride it, she would propel herself up and try to confront it, chest to chest. After a messy collision, during which Lydia usually squinched shut her eyes, or looked away, Cate would emerge, triumphantly battered from her defeat, motion Lydia to come and join the fray, and then head out for the next beating.

When Lydia was smaller, this "invitation to the fray" from Cate had put her through torturous indecision: should she try to copy her sister's boldness and get rudely slammed about by the waves, or should she submerge herself gradually in this chancy element, at her own secure style and pace—and be thought a coward?

And she had not resolved this dilemma until, at almost this exact spot on the lovely, wild beach, she had been teaching her children how to go into the ocean, explaining to them how it was different from going into a wading pool. She had chosen her words carefully because she did not want to frighten them into being sissies or coax them into a false confidence that could get them drowned. It was sometime during this beach lecture to the little boys that her own ambivalence about going into the ocean left her for good. "If you respect its moods and learn to anticipate its rhythms, then you can use it to have lots of fun," she had said, or something like that; and after that time, whenever she entered the surf, her own motherly advice drowned out the taunting urge to compete with the Cates of the world: she no longer felt wanting in vitality or daring just because she wouldn't hurl herself at the might of the waves. She could now go into the ocean like a Lydia, and like herself very much in the process.

Which she proceeded to do now, wading in deeper, a level at a time, letting a small wave break over the tops of her thighs, then a larger one over her belly; at this point, she always stopped: she needed an inner goad to surrender her bosom and bare neck to the chilly water. ("If I get completely wet by the count of three, I can have—")

The water was very chilly. It would have to be something very desirable. What did she want, too forcefully to risk losing if she didn't go down by the count of three? She raised her face to the sun and summoned supremely eligible desires to make themselves known. Soon she had one she liked. "I want to be—" She considered, then rejected, the word "famous": it had an adolescent inflation about it.

"I want to be a widely admired and influential woman before I'm forty," she wished aloud.

And plunged wholeheartedly into the water, and swam, with deft, strong strokes toward Cate, who was just being mauled by a new breaker.

"Let's walk up the beach as far as that old shipwreck and get our backs dry," said Cate. "Then we'll walk back and get our fronts dry."

"We shouldn't leave Mother *too* long."

"She wants to be left alone. I don't blame her. She's saying good-bye to Daddy. This place was special to him. If he decides to haunt anywhere, it'll probably be here. I wonder if the spirits of the dead have problems traveling. I mean, if you died in Mountain City, what would be the afterlife mechanics of getting four hundred miles to the coast?"

"I really couldn't say," replied Lydia, feeling it was disrespectful to talk of Daddy as some kind of commuting ghost. "You know, Mother was telling me one of the worst things about being a widow was having to break the news to people. It must be awkward. I don't think I want to be a widow."

"Well, don't be married when your husband dies and you won't."

"What's that supposed to mean?" Lydia frowned, mentally working out the implications of Cate's ambiguous retort.

"Oh, forget it, baby," said Cate with a weary sigh. She kicked a broken shell and sent it skittering ahead of them into the surf. "I was just working up a little homily on appearances versus feeling, but I'm getting kind of sick of my homilies." She put her arm around Lydia's shoulder and playfully bumped Lydia's hip with her own. "Tell me about your lover. That would be much more fun."

"I'll tell you about my lover," said Lydia, won over by Cate's agile shift of mood, "if you'll tell me about the millionaire who proposed to you, first." She bumped Cate's hip back.

"Ha, so you and Mother have been discussing me."

"Not as much as I wanted. I want to know all."

"You want to know all, eh?" said Cate thoughtfully. She took her arm away from Lydia's shoulder and bowed forward, watching her own feet make tracks in the sand. Then, with a sudden decisiveness, she threw back her head. Her nostrils flared once. She sucked in her stomach and made herself taller. "Well, my fling with Roger Jernigan just about destroyed me," she pronounced ominously. "He was my match, in a lot of ways. If only he hadn't been what he was and . . . a lot of other factors . . . I think he might have been just the sort of man I could get along with. But I couldn't see myself being Mrs. Pesticide Queen of Iowa and living his kind of life, for one thing. . . ."

That's exactly the way I feel! Lydia all but blurted out. *I don't want to be Mrs. Podiatrist. I don't want to be Mrs. anybody, really, anymore.* But she wanted Cate to go on talking.

"And then, he was that kind of man who wants to take care of everything. And everybody. I didn't trust myself. It would have been very easy just to lie back and let him slip the ring on my finger and say, You give up now, and I'll take care of everything. I would have been a zombie before the year was out."

"You mean, he wouldn't have let you work?"

"Oh, he would have 'let' me work. Christ, he was paying my salary as it was, he was financing the goddamn school till his son could graduate. But there was something else that had to be done before I could work. You see, I got pregnant."

"You got—" Lydia stared at Cate's stomach. Many things raced through her mind. Cate, at Mother's house yesterday, sobbing because she couldn't fit into a bikini anymore. Was that why Cate wanted to exile herself to the island? But there wasn't even a doctor here. If Cate wants to be unfettered, I could take the child, thought Lydia. Dickie would find it a lark, helping bring up Cate's little baby. I could adopt it, even. And Stanley would help out. He said he wished he had a little baby all his own. We could take turns keeping it.

"No, no," said Cate crossly, following Lydia's stare. "There's nothing in there now. It's quite empty. I had an abortion. Don't ever have one if you can help it. Not that I regret my choice. I think it's every woman's right to have the choice. But just try to be careful so you won't have to make the choice. Though, God knows, I thought I *was* being careful, I—"

"I could *never*—" began Lydia fervently, before she managed to stop herself. "I mean, I don't think I could ever—" She could not bring herself to finish the sentence. She was deeply shocked, and she was shocked at herself for being so shocked. She was a modern woman; she had friends who'd had abortions. But Cate's abortion was too close to home. There had been a little cousin in the offing for Leo and Dickie, the cousin she had promised them for years, to no avail, and now it was gone. Lydia felt the family had been cheated, though she knew it was not modern to feel so. "Did it hurt?" was the only thing she could think of to say next.

"It hurt my soul more than it did my body. And I don't mean that in any religious sense. I mean it just hurt my soul deep down."

"Oh, Cate," said Lydia mournfully. She reached over and touched her sister's arm.

They walked on, toward the agreed-upon marker of the old shipwreck, which was not in sight.

"I know I can trust you not to tell Mother," said Cate.

"You can trust me."

"You know what? I think our old shipwreck has been covered up by new dunes. We should have been able to spot it by now. This whole chain of islands along the Outer Banks is eroding, you know. I read an article about it. The more people try to stop it by building jetties and things, the faster it erodes." There was an uncomfortable edge of satisfaction in her voice.

"I don't think Ocracoke is eroding all that much," said Lydia, scanning the wild curve of shore possessively. Up ahead, several dozen long-legged seabirds had gathered to peck for the fresh load of coquinas washed in by the last wave; you could see hundreds of holes in the wet sand, as the tiny shellfish struggled to bury themselves before they were eaten. Lydia wanted Leo and Dickie to bring their families here one day, to teach their children how to swim, safely but with gusto, in this sea. "Maybe we should start on back," she suggested. It seemed a shame to disturb all those birds. And the hopeful note on which they had begun their walk had turned into the beginnings of tension.

"As you like," said Cate, wheeling around instantly, in midstep, and striding back, toward the sun, with her aggressive gait. She closed her eyes; she stuck up her chin; she shut Lydia out.

She's miffed because I didn't show enough sympathy about her ordeal, thought Lydia.

Matching Cate's stride as they headed back down the beach, Lydia asked, in as loving a voice as she could, "Your soul . . . is it starting to heal a little, do you think?"

"Oh, my soul will be all right. It's a tough old soul," said Cate humorously. "But you know what I still can't get out of my mind is this woman who actually followed me from the clinic, the day before I was to have the abortion."

"She followed you? But why?"

"To talk me out of having my abortion. This woman—" and

Cate launched into her slightly satirical, raconteur's rhythm— "drove all the way in to Chicago, from her six-bedroom home on the western shore of Lake Michigan, twice a week, in order to sit in the waiting room of this clinic and study the clientele who'd come to have their preabortion checkups. She'd pick out a likely candidate, and then follow her out on the street and introduce herself as a sort of liaison lady of the clinic who volunteered to answer any *questions* you might have about . . . what you were going to go through the next day. Well, when she collared me, I smelled a rat, but it was an interesting kind of rat: a very personable, well-spoken, elegantly dressed, *dedicated* kind of rat, and so I invited her to have a drink at Trader Vic's, at the Palmer House, where I had a room.

"We ordered mai tais, and sat there very agreeably, talking about everything but The Subject for the first half hour or so. She was a few years older than me, her husband was a lawyer and traveled a lot, she had four children, all but the youngest in college, and *lots* of time on her hands. First she'd gone back to college and got herself an M.A., and then she'd taught in a high school for a while, but they let her go because they said they had to hire more blacks—or at least that was her story. So then she took a travel agent–training course and worked in a travel agency for a while. But that didn't satisfy her; it lacked a sense of purpose, just helping people plan trips to go off and have fun, she said. Meanwhile, she had persuaded her husband to have another baby, and she duly got pregnant, but then, about the third month into the pregnancy, she was standing in the kitchen on the maid's day off, peeling some vegetables, and she got terrible cramps, and by the time she managed to get to the bathroom she had miscarried.

"At this point in the conversation, she very adroitly changed subjects and asked me about what I did, and we ended up discussing the Romantic poets for a while, whether we preferred Keats or Shelley—she preferred Shelley—and whether Wordsworth and his sister had known they had an incestuous attachment. We ordered another round of mai tais. I was considering asking her to have dinner with me; after all, I had nothing better to do, and wasn't particularly relishing the empty hours until I had to go back to the clinic.

"And then she reached into a Marshall Field's shopping bag and pulled out this smart leather portfolio, and at first I thought she was going to show me this Gucci portfolio she'd just bought; but then she got this earnest look on her face and turned the portfolio around so her initials were facing me, and then, after a quick look to see that no waiters were hovering, she opened it and there were all these . . . *photographs*, in color, of fetuses.

"I was angry. I opened my purse to pay for the drinks. I was just going to walk out on her. Leave her sitting there with her portfolio of those terrible pictures. But then I couldn't resist asking her what motivated a woman like herself to do what she did. She explained to me, in her pleasant, well-modulated voice, that she'd had a religious experience the day of her miscarriage. When she'd gone to the bathroom to stanch the flow of blood, a perfectly formed litle baby about the size of a mouse had dropped into her pants. She washed the blood off and was just cradling it in her hands, marveling at all its fully formed parts, when . . . IT SPOKE TO HER. According to her, it said, '*It's too late to save me, Mother. But save the others.*' "

"Oh *God*!" cried Lydia. She put her arms around herself; she had shivers in the hot sun. "She was mad!"

"Maybe she was and maybe she wasn't," said Cate, matter-of-factly. "She gave me her card. Francine J. Armbruster, Lake Forest, Illinois. I've still got it in my wallet. I can show it to you, if you like."

"You could have reported her to the clinic," said Lydia.

"Yes, I considered that. Then I figured she had an 'in' there, to get away with coming as often as she did. It's a very controversial issue in Illinois at the moment. But then I figured, let her keep her mission in life. She may save some babies and that will make her feel good, and it will maybe make the mothers feel good. To each his own. To each *her* own. I did tell her I thought she had abused my hospitality, though; I couldn't resist that. And you know, it hurt her. Despite her mission, she's still got all her upper-middle-class baggage intact. But it wasn't too pleasant having those photographs in my mind the next day, I can tell you that."

"I wish you'd called me," said Lydia, after they had walked for a few minutes. Lydia saw herself flying to Cate, sitting across the table from Cate, maybe in some nice restaurant, talking to Cate in a low, well-modulated voice, but not a *mad* voice. *I might have been able to change her mind*, thought Lydia.

"Why should I have called you?" asked Cate, surprised.

"Well," began Lydia, "I don't know, because—" But then she gave it up. It was too late. Why cause Cate more pain? "—because I'm your sister," she finished lamely.

"Well, thank you, baby." Cate veered sideways toward Lydia and gave her a little squeeze around the shoulders, then released her. "But there are some things even a sister can't help you with. Now, let's put it out of our minds, and remember: Mother is never to know."

"Of course not," said Lydia, slightly indignant. "I already said I wouldn't tell."

They did not find their mother in the subdued state they had anticipated. Cheeks flushed, damp hairs curling loose from her usually sedate gray-blond knot, she was putting the finishing touches on an arrangement of sea oats and dune grasses in an old cider jug; a rag and a spray can of Lemon Pledge on a table testified that she had not been keeping her promise.

"Mother, you *said* you wouldn't clean," accused Lydia.

"I know, I know." Nell gave them a sheepish grin; her eyes were bright with barely restrained excitement. "But you'll just never *believe* what has happened."

And she related to them the events of her past hour. "I'm sure you've heard me talk about my old school friend Merle Meekins, from Farragut Pines Academy. I know I've mentioned her: she was the school's charmer. We even roomed together for a while. I must have mentioned her many times."

The daughters shook their heads. Neither could remember Mother's ever mentioning the charming Merle Meekins.

"Oh. Well, maybe I didn't. Maybe I just thought about her

to myself," said Nell, with an air of disappointment. "But anyway, I told them we'd expect them around sunset, when the lighthouse goes on. They can see it from their window, too. Lydia, don't you think we should set up a little bar in that corner, where people can help themselves from the porch? I think it will still be warm enough for the porch, after dark. Cate, you looked so lovely in that gray outfit you wore to the restaurant the other night; I hope you brought it with you."

"You'd think the Governor was coming," said Lydia to Cate after the early supper, following which they had been all but "sent upstairs to dress." She was lying, still in her shorts, which Mother had suggested might not be appropriate for an Episcopal priest, on the freshly made double bed with the sagging mattress which the sisters always shared. Cate was having first turn at the dressing-table mirror; she had decided that she might as well go all out, and was applying gray eye shadow to go with the requested gray outfit. In the pinkish light of the setting sun, Cate's reflection, which Lydia could watch from the bed, was that of a woman confident that she could still make herself beautiful if she tried, but whose experience had convinced her that it was no more than a game, which she could play as well as anyone else, in a self-mocking way.

"*I* never heard her mention this person, did you?" inquired Cate, knowing she was being watched, not unadmiringly, by Lydia. It was a gratifying moment, just like old times, when Big Sister sat before her mirror, preparing her face for a date, and Little Sister from behind reverently memorized the rituals for when her time would come.

"Never!" agreed Lydia fervently. "She talked about the school some, and how lonely she had been, and about having to visit her mother in that sanatorium on the hill, but never about any *friends*."

"Oh well, now is the time Mother needs friends, so maybe this Merle is a good thing. When people are married, they close themselves off from friendships. At least, people like Mother and

Daddy did. Mother had her Book Club gang, but she wasn't close to any of them; and Daddy didn't have any friends, really. His books were his friends: when he had free time, he preferred to be alone with them."

"But this Merle still has her husband," said Lydia. She was looking forward to telling Cate about her new friend Renee, who was by far the most superior friend Lydia had ever had, but now, in this soft light, with Cate looking such a poignant mixture of arrogant and haunted, was not the time to introduce a stranger. Cate's harrowing tale of her recent ordeal, while at first repelling and then saddening Lydia, had had the effect, in the intervening hours, of sharpening Lydia's already pronounced protective instincts toward her tribe. She had lost a little niece or nephew: which had it been? All the more reason to hold on to her one and only sister, whatever the shortcomings of their sisterly relations. Or so she felt at this moment, farther from her friend and from her lover than from Cate, whose plight had given her center stage in Lydia's heart for now. (Though, on their way back from the beach, Lydia had asked Cate to stop at the pay phone outside the Island Inn; after hearing of Cate's lost child, Lydia had had a sudden, ferocious urge to check on the well-being of the boys.)

"Oh well," said Cate. "He's a priest, isn't he? Maybe he'd rather be off with God." She dipped into a little glass jar of rouge and, with a dramatic flourish, drew a mauve slash upward on each of her cheeks. "There: I have half a mind to go down just like that!" She gave a wicked wink to Lydia in the mirror. Their solidarity had been increased by their mother's unexpected defection to this unheard-of old school friend.

On a sudden, affectionate impulse, Lydia bounded from the bed and unzipped her suitcase. She drew out the soft, gorgeous shawl with its silky fringe, marched formally up behind Cate, and adorned her sister with it.

"What's this?" Cate had just begun to blend in the rouge slash on her right cheek.

"It's your birthday present. I know it's not till the twenty-fifth, but I won't be here then. I wanted to see you in it."

"But it's lovely! These beautiful colors. This purple would go so well with your eyes. Lydia, this is much too elegant for me."

"No, it isn't. And look how the turquoise brings out the gold lights in your hair."

"Oh baby. You shouldn't have. We haven't exchanged presents in years. . . ." Cate was arranging the folds of the shawl in a more casual, asymmetrical way: it did suit her.

"Well, but this is a special birthday. When I turn forty, I'll expect a present from you. This shawl is going to bring you luck. It's a magic shawl. Any woman who wears this shawl will be irresistible to men." Lydia leaned down and put her head against her sister's. They smiled at each other's reflections. At the moment, each thought herself handsome and each was proud that the other was handsome.

"That's all I need, is another man," said Cate ironically.

"Oh no. That's another thing. This shawl only attracts the *right* man," added Lydia, pursuing her own whimsy.

The last portion of the Chinese-red sun disappeared below the calm, silvery-gray waterline. Suddenly, uncannily, the tip of the lighthouse began to glow. The effect was always spooky, even when you knew that a timed automatic switch had activated a mere 250-watt bulb, magnified by a special lens. In the old days, the lighthouse keeper trudged up the stairs at dusk, lit the oil lamp, then went up several more times during the night to check the wicks; now the Coast Guard checked things out once a week. The sisters had learned these facts from Daddy; Daddy had loved information like this.

"Are you girls about ready?" Nell's voice from below. She had dressed before supper. She must have been watching the lighthouse from the kitchen window.

"Oh Lord, what am I going to wear?" said Lydia. "I don't *feel* like getting dressed up, my first night at the beach, for strangers."

"Why not put on that peasant skirt? The blouse you have on is perfectly fine. I and my shawl ought to be enough grandeur for any visitors. Let's watch through the window and see how prompt they are."

Lydia straggled into the suggested skirt, and the two of them crouched like spies at the upstairs window overlooking the Hollowell house.

"Here they come," whispered Cate, with mock conspiracy. "Out their front door. Ah, she has on high-heeled sandals; they've decided to use the road."

The couple seemed to float toward them out of the gathering blue dusk; they moved in rhythmical step, the woman leaning into the man, as if they had walked through decades together.

"Girls?" called Nell from below. "They're coming!"

Cate raised her eyebrow at Lydia. "Shall we descend in our splendor, *ma petite jolie soeur?*"

"Oh wait!" Lydia laughed. "You forgot to do your other cheek. Here, let me." She rubbed Cate's rouge streak into her left cheek with practiced, circular strokes. "That ought to do."

"Thank you, baby." Cate puckered her lips at Lydia. She drew her new shawl about her regally, and the two of them clopped down the creaky stairs in their high heels to impress their mother's guests.

"This is Cate, my older daughter, and this is Lydia, my younger daughter." Nell presented them with pride to the older couple. Cate had *really* outdone herself, and Lydia, even in her simple, rustic skirt, looked streamlined as always. "Girls, these are my friends the Chapins. Rather"—she laughed nervously—"Merle is my very old friend, and Marcus is new, from just this afternoon."

"I honestly don't believe," said Merle, after kissing and hugging Nell and pressing each daughter's hand warmly, "I have ever seen three such nice-looking women in one family." She wore a dark-green silk turban pinned with a jeweled scarab. Tonight she felt more like the old Merle: there were falsies under the loose-flowing dress; Nell felt them when she hugged her.

"Should we call you Reverend or Father?" Cate asked Merle's husband as she was shaking his hand.

"Please call me Marcus," he replied, in the easygoing slightly abstracted manner of a man accustomed to being made much of at social functions. He wore a rumpled cotton cord suit and spoke his name as "Mah-cus." Cate, on the alert, sniffed out a decadent Tidewater aristocrat.

Plans for sitting on the porch were quickly revised when Marcus Chapin said that Merle had had a cough. The two comfortable cane-backed chairs that had been dragged out onto the porch were brought in again, a corner lamp turned on, and Lydia, appointing herself bartender, took everybody's drink order. Marcus Chapin drank scotch on the rocks; Merle said ginger ale or tonic would suit her fine. ("Ordinarily I'm a bourbon aficionado, but right now I'm taking some medication that just won't mix.")

Merle, seated beside Nell on the sofa, drank in her friend with her eyes. "You bad old thing." She picked up Nell's hand and pretended to slap it. "Promised to write and never did. As a punishment, I'm going to make you tell me *everything* you should have put in all those letters. We'll start in the present and then work backward. I want to know all about these lovely girls of yours." She looked eagerly toward Lydia, then Cate. "Marcus and I wanted children, but the good Lord didn't see fit to send us any. You must be so proud of them."

"Why, yes, I am, of course," said Nell, a little self-conscious to be talking about her daughters like this while they could hear. And she remembered why, in the old days, she had sometimes found Merle hard to take: it was her dogged *enthusiasm* for everything and everybody—some would call it effusiveness—which made Nell, in comparison, seem standoffish. But then she felt churlish for even having had this thought, and, taking a deep swig from her gin and tonic, began to relate her daughters' admirable statistics, even though in their hearing. "Lydia's got two fine boys and has gone back to college at UNC–Greensboro, and Cate has a Ph.D. in English and has been teaching at a private Lutheran college in Iowa."

"So you're a teacher," said Marcus Chapin, seated next to Cate.

"A teacher without a school, actually. My college just went bankrupt."

"Ah. I'm sorry to hear it." He sat forward, clasping his drink between his knees. "That puts us in the same boat. I'm a priest without a church."

"What happened to your church?"

"Oh, the church is still there." He smiled ruefully. "Or rather, the building is still there. I can't say it much resembles the church I knew. I was 'rotated' up the river by the Bishop. To a very small church with a congregation thought to be as regressive as myself. This past year, I took a leave of absence, for personal reasons. They've got themselves a nice young rector for the interim. He's full of schemes and dreams. I go over and say Mass once a month, just to keep the old knee joints from getting stiff. But they're better off with him, so we'll probably leave things the way they are indefinitely. What was the topic of your doctoral thesis?"

"Well, it was called 'Designs for a New World in the Poetry of D. H. Lawrence.' " Cate rearranged her shawl and threw back her shoulders, on the offensive, just in case. On this subject, she had learned to divide educated people into two categories: the Lawrence haters and the Lawrence lovers. There seemed to be no in-between state.

"I regret to admit, I've never read any of his poetry." demurred Chapin, in his Tidewater accent. "I did try one of his novels once. To tell the truth, I found it a little strident. I'm sure his poetry's different. Don't you find he cants too much in his prose?"

"Oh, he does just as much in his poetry. That's because he found himself in a world where people wouldn't listen." Cate sipped bourbon and gazed challengingly over the rim of her glass at the Virginia Gentleman. It would be interesting to test the borders of his politeness.

Lydia had pulled her chair over beside the sofa and was telling Merle about Leo and Dickie.

"I see," said Chapin, smiling down into his drink. "And what was his design for a new world? One where people would listen to him?"

Cate detected—or thought she detected—just the slightest condescension in the Reverend's tone, as he hunched his muscular shoulders forward like some silvery-haired Patton. He looked more like a retired Army officer than he did a priest.

"Not so much listen *to him*, as to just listen," said Cate. "Most people can't listen, so no wonder they can't hear."

Chapin nodded, as if in tentative agreement with this view. "But what was his design for a new world?"

"Designs," corrected Cate, taking another sip of bourbon. "It took me almost three hundred pages to explicate what I thought they were. I doubt if I could satisfy your question in a chat over drinks."

Smiling faintly, Chapin raised his eyebrows.

"I mean," Cate amended, feeling he thought her rude, "it's a rather large topic. Could you sum up the whole meaning of your ministry over a glass of scotch?"

"The meaning, no. It's still working itself out. The message, yes. The message of my ministry has been the urgency of our getting to know the wisdom and love of God and becoming possessed of these attributes ourselves."

Chapin was clearly no boob; he could think logically, and he politely let you know when he thought you were taking shortcuts. Even though that "message" of his ministry had come a little too fluidly off his elegant tongue. Nevertheless, his performance made Cate wish she had some fluent "message" already prepared, with which she could attractively describe her mission in life to strangers.

"Now what was Mr. Lawrence's message?" asked Chapin pleasantly.

Cate, feeling put on the spot, sorted rapidly through her hard-won findings, searching for something striking that would impress Chapin. But why did she want to impress him? She wasn't sure she even liked him very much. He seemed the sort of man who, if asked, could recite his deepest beliefs while doing a minuet and never miss a step.

"Lawrence says our epoch is over. Our activity has lost its meaning, and even our emotions have become mechanical. We're just ghosts, going through the motions of the outmoded old dance steps of our civilization." The dance part was improvised, but since he'd never read the poems, she counted on getting away with it.

"Ah, but where is the hopeful prognosis? What about Mr. Lawrence's designs for us poor ghosts?"

"I'm coming to that," Cate said, rather irritably. She sighed. She bolted the last of her bourbon. She bunched up her face in concentration. If they *had* been dancing, she would have missed a step. "We're ghosts, he says, but we are also *seeds*. What we have to do, though it's very hard, is 'give up the ghost' and let the old world die with us. Then we've got to go underground and start over. . . ."

Everyone else in the room had stopped to listen. Cate felt self-conscious, but Chapin had turned toward her expectantly, waiting for her to go on.

"We have to start over with"—she faltered, thinking it out as she went, not sure if it was Lawrence's idea or hers she was explicating—"with what's true and living and indestructible in us . . . even though it's very tiny and unimpressive at first . . . and—" She stopped cold, unnerved by the cluster of faces turned toward her. Did she detect the slightest shadow of nervousness in Mother's rosy countenance? Had she gone on too long, gotten "too intense" for what was supposed to be a convivial social hour? "Anyway," she concluded with an attempt at self-mocking humor, "while we're waiting for our seeds to sprout, would anybody like a refill?"

"Might as well," said Marcus Chapin, handing up his glass to Cate, who had risen. "Got to keep them watered."

A murmur of relieved laughter, as Cate—and then Lydia, who jumped up to help—collected empty or dwindling glasses.

"You know, Marcus," said Merle Chapin, sitting forward

raptly, "I couldn't help thinking, when Cate was talking about how we had to be brave and go underground and start over . . . why, that's just what you're doing, in a way. Like the early Christians, when they were being persecuted."

"Now darling, I wouldn't say I was persecuted. I wouldn't go that far," her husband corrected her.

"But you are!" cried the little woman passionately. "Do you mind if I tell them about . . . the Norfolk church? And your run-in with the Bishop?"

Marcus Chapin spread his hands helplessly. With a smile, he said, "You can hardly do otherwise, now."

For everyone had perked up with expectation. "Oh, *do* tell about your run-in with the Bishop," urged Nell, who was rather overexcited tonight.

"Why don't you tell it, love?" Chapin suggested to his wife. "Thank you," he said to Cate, who had brought him a fresh scotch. Quietly raising his glass to her, he murmured, "To the indestructible seed."

Merle had already embarked on her breathy, ardent narrative about how it had been "a bolt out of the blue" when the Bishop had sent Marcus a female seminarian to assist him in his Norfolk church.

"At first, he decided he'd just keep real quiet, as it was just for the summer; she had another year in seminary. So poor Marcus just closed his eyes and thought about Higher Things when she marched up to the lectern, with her Hush Puppies showing under her cassock, to read the Epistle. But she liked Marcus's church so well, she asked to come back as assistant rector after she'd taken Orders. What really happened was, she fancied the church's music director, *another* young woman who wears Hush Puppies under *her* robe—"

"Merle honey, we don't know that for certain," put in Chapin; but with a forbearing smile that indicated he believed it to be so.

"Oh, all right, Marcus. Marcus is always so *fair*—too fair for his own good, if you ask me. *Anyway*, being a full-fledged 'priest' now—though it beats me how a woman can be a priest any more than a man can be, say, a mother—it was Jim's right to serve Communion. That's right, her name was Jim: her parents had actually named her James, after the James River; that's where the whole trouble started, if you ask me; how can a woman be named *James*? She was one of those horsey girls, from an old family; I'm sure her family put pressure on the Bishop, because it was always considered a plum for any young priest to get to be assistant rector in Marcus's church—"

"Honey, we don't know that her family put pressure on anyone," corrected Chapin once more, smiling pensively into his drink.

"Well, I know what I know," said Merle, with a toss of her green-silk-turbaned head. "And you know it, too, but you're so doggone fair. Anyway, one Sunday Jim was handing round the wine while Marcus gave out the wafers—it was her first time, helping with Communion; Marcus had tried to put her off as long as possible, but now she had *insisted*—and one of our most devout old parishioners, Mrs. Leeds, whose chauffeur has to bring her to the communion rail in her wheelchair, well! Mrs. Leeds just about fainted when she looked up from swallowing her wafer and saw Jim in her Hush Puppies bearing down with that chalice. She almost had a heart attack right there on the spot, and she motioned frantically to her chauffeur to come wheel her away from that rail! Well, Marcus saw this happen, and he understood, and so, after everyone else had finished taking Communion, Marcus, instead of just drinking the rest of the wine himself, as it calls for in the service, well, Marcus took the chalice and marched down into the congregation to where Mrs. Leeds was, still shaking with shock in her wheelchair, and he finished administering the sacrament. Well, Jim couldn't wait to hop into her little foreign car and dash over to the Bishop's to tattle on Marcus. And then there was a great big fracas. The congregation took sides. Of course, all Marcus's parishioners were fiercely loyal, but this Jim and her friend the music director had brought a certain number of new people into the church—a certain element of people, you might say—and the result was, Marcus was 'rotated' up to Gloucester, which is a very picturesque little place, full of fine old estates, but nobody in the congregation much a day under seventy, and they were much more interested in restoring the eighteenth-century baptismal font or cleaning off the first settlers' gravestones in the churchyard than they were in God. So when I got so sick last year, Marcus decided to take a leave of absence, and now, except for once a month, Marcus says Mass just for the two of us, up in his study. We've made ourselves a little altar of sorts, and that's what we do. We've gone underground, but we've kept the faith."

"Oh dear, how unfortunate," said Nell. "About the Norfolk church, I mean. But what about the other little one? The one in Gloucester. Won't you go back? Couldn't you, I don't know, have a membership drive for members under seventy? We're doing that in my Book Club at home. One needs new blood."

"To tell the truth . . . Nell," said Marcus, using her name for the first time, "the church I've known and loved is pretty much shot to hell. Just when people are galloping off in all directions on their pale horses and need its unchanging stability more than ever, what does it do but clamber aboard its own horse and start galloping in circles." He swirled the melting ice in his glass meditatively. "I probably won't go back, no. I'm due to retire soon, anyway, and the Bishop won't be heartbroken to get me out of the way sooner. If I can keep alive *my* church for a congregation of two—Merle and myself—that will be enough."

"I don't know," said Cate, whose face had gone through a number of expressions during Merle's narration and Marcus's conclusion. "It sounds a little to me like one more example of the Elegant Defeatist attitude we Southerners have become so adept at. It also sounds like desertion of your beliefs."

Marcus Chapin raised his eyebrows. This time he did not smile.

"Oh, nobody *believes* more than Marcus!" protested Merle. She doubled over in a little flurry of coughing.

"You're overtired, honey. We ought to be going," said Marcus.

"No, no, I'm not," insisted Merle. "Please don't drag me away from Nell. I haven't had a woman friend in years." She put a pert smile on her yellowish-pale, heart-shaped little face. "We can stay a little longer."

"I didn't desert the church," said Chapin, turning to face Cate. "The church deserted me. My beliefs remain as firm as ever. But the church no longer allows me to act on them." He seemed to want to impress this point on Cate.

"Wait a minute," said Cate, rather fiercely. "I want to clarify something. Is it that you don't approve of homosexuals or of women being priests?" Cate's eyes glittered boldly at Chapin.

Nell caught Lydia's eye and sent a signal: Head her off if you can. *Please.*

"I think when our institutions let us down, we have to give them a good shake," put in Lydia, speaking up with authority. "What I think is, we have to keep alive the principles they've deserted until we force them to come back to their senses. *Meanwhile,*" she continued, with a lovely lift of her head, "we must take our business elsewhere. I mean, when American cars get shoddy, we have to show Detroit that *we* still value honest workmanship by going to the foreign markets. And, well, I'll give you another example: this spring, my son's school let him down. They care more about a sort of sociable herd mentality than they do about standards. So he's applying for English boarding schools. He's writing the letters himself. We—"

"We're not talking about *products*, Lydia. We're talking about beliefs," interrupted Cate, somewhat menacingly.

"You call *education* a product?"

"Of course it's a product." Cate stuck up her chin and grinned patronizingly across the room at her sister. "What else? You know yourself that you pay so much for so many credit hours and that, in turn, eventually buys you a degree. You said at supper you wanted one in sociology. So you pay your money and this gives you a piece of paper that will allow you to go around snooping in the homes of the underprivileged."

"Would anyone like another refill?" inquired Nell, with a sharp look at Cate, who chose not to acknowledge it.

"That's not fair, Cate. We were talking about Leo's high school, and you don't pay for semester hours in a high school.

What about your Ph.D. in English? I suppose that's not a product. I suppose that's a belief, because you seem to have cornered the market on beliefs."

"Lydia, I need more ice," said Nell, to no avail. She and Merle exchanged a look. Merle smiled encouragingly, as if to say, It's all right, darling, they're still *wonderful* girls.

"Of course it's a product," said Cate, smiling dangerously. "I paid my money and I bought my product, and now no one wants it. I find myself in the same position as Detroit. If you're getting Mother more ice, would you mind getting me a teensy refill of Old Crow while you're up?"

"Why, certainly," replied Lydia, in her sugariest tone, forced into good manners by Cate, who surely didn't need another drink. Thin-lipped, she took Mother's glass and Cate's.

There was a tense silence as Lydia, at the bar, clinked ice loudly into one glass and sloshed bourbon into the other.

Marcus Chapin, who had been patiently biding his time, said, still facing Cate, "The question under consideration here, I believe, is whether a devout parishioner is to be denied the Blood of Christ, shed for her two thousand years ago, because she could not bring herself to accept the highly controversial decision of a convocation of somewhat confused churchmen in 1976."

"But you could have brought her around to it," said Cate, reaching eagerly for the fresh drink Lydia had just handed her with a mock curtsy. "You were her priest and she was your loyal parishioner."

"But I can't accept it, either," he explained gently.

"Aha! Got you!" said Cate excitedly, springing forward as if to pounce on him. "That's exactly what I asked in the first place. Now, is it that she's a lesbian or a woman that you object to?"

Nell felt tiny prickles, all over her face and neck, like bubbles bursting.

"She can be anything she likes and I won't object," said Marcus Chapin cordially. "But nowhere in the Thirty-nine Articles of Religion is there any provision for a woman being a priest."

"Or even in the Bible!" put in Merle.

"Now, wait a minute," said Cate. And she made them all wait while she took a long, thoughtful sip of bourbon. "You said earlier that the message of your ministry was getting people to know the wisdom and love of God and become possessed of these attributes themselves."

"I did," said Chapin, somewhat formally.

"Well, then!" concluded Cate triumphantly. "Couldn't this Jim, or James, or whatever she calls herself, be just as much possessed of them as you are?" Her mind was a little fuzzy with bourbon, and something told her she had left out a step in her argument; but she willed *momentum* to get her through.

"I should hope she is very much possessed of them," replied Chapin, making it clear by his look that he doubted it. "But that can't make her a priest."

"Well, priestess, then. Maybe we're just quibbling over nomenclature. Do you acknowledge this woman's right to be a priestess in your church?"

"I'm afraid I don't," he replied. "She can be a priestess in the Temple of Isis, or a vestal virgin if she likes, or even an Anglican nun if she wants, but she cannot be a priest in the church." He said it as if the subject were closed.

"But she is, isn't she?" insisted Cate.

Marcus Chapin, for the first time, began to look annoyed. Nell closed her eyes.

Merle, seeing her old friend's embarrassment, submitted to another coughing spell, which, though less genuine than the previous ones, brought Marcus Chapin to his feet.

"We're getting you home right now," he said, going over to his wife. "I allowed myself to get so involved in discussion that I've neglected your welfare."

There followed a round of cordial good-byes, in which Marcus Chapin went so far as to *thank* Cate for her stimulating conversation. There were enthusiastic pleadings on Merle's part for them all to get together again: the Chapins would be staying another week. And before the couple finally headed off, arm in arm, into the balmy, salt-smelling darkness, Merle had secured Nell's promise to spend the next afternoon with her, while Marcus was sailing with some young man with a thirty-three-foot yawl who had invited them both, "But I get horribly seasick and Marcus refuses to leave me by myself. So now, Nell, you and I will have our chance for lots of girl talk and reminiscing, without boring everybody else to death!"

"I'll stay downstairs and read for a while," said Lydia, as soon as the three of them were alone. "I can wash up these glasses, Mother, leave it to me."

"Well, thank you," said Nell, looking vaguely in the direction of Lydia, but not meeting her eyes. "I am kind of tired." Lydia could not tell whether Mother was miffed with her or not. But why should she be miffed with *me*? she thought, defensively.

"And I'm a little drunk, I'm afraid," said Cate, with determined heartiness. She gave her mother a peck on the cheek. "Don't worry about your friend's husband. He can take it. It's just that his brand of Old Guard complacency always sets me off."

"So it *seems*," said Nell dryly. But then, with a little half-smile, she returned Cate's peck. "Anyway, you *looked* lovely. Especially in that shawl."

"Isn't it beautiful? Lydia gave it to me. It's an early fortieth-birthday present, to grace my declining years. Lydia honey, I didn't mean to jump on you about the education thing, but you were diverting my attack on Marcus Chapin. Mother, according to Lydia, this is a magic shawl; it attracts men." Winking roguishly at Lydia, Cate wrapped the shawl vampishly about her; she was trying to make up, but Lydia wasn't having any.

"Well, you're going to need it," Nell said, "if you treat them like poor Marcus Chapin."

"Oh, he'll survive. I only wish I'd been the teensiest bit more sober and I could have won that argument. I know exactly where I fell into the trap." She yawned. "God, I'm tired. I'm also a little dizzy. Well, good night all." She swept upstairs, unrepentant.

"Good night," said Nell, turning back toward her younger daughter, whom she hadn't kissed goodnight yet. But Lydia, looking rather grim and unkissable, had begun gathering up the glasses. "Good night," she called gruffly to her mother and disappeared into the kitchen.

Nell, deciding not to force the issue, went up to her own room, glad for bed.

Lydia sudsed each glass liberally in liquid detergent. She rinsed and dried them thoroughly and lined them up on a folded paper towel. She wished there were fifty more of them to wash. She had no intention of climbing into that bed with Cate until Cate was sure to be asleep. Lydia could not trust herself not to start a fight. Especially about Cate's remark concerning that sociology degree. That was below the belt; just the sort of thing Cate had done in the old days: wormed some admission from Lydia about something she, Lydia, desired, and then, at the first opportunity, thrown it back in Lydia's face. Made it seem ludicrous . . . or not worth having.

But Lydia did not want to start a fight, especially not tonight, after she had given Cate the shawl. It would be just like Cate never to wear the shawl again because she and Lydia had had a fight on the same day, and it was too nice a shawl to go to waste. Lydia regretted her impulsive generosity a little, but it was too late, so she determined to make the best of it.

My only chance for respect in this family, thought Lydia, is to be *forbearing*, to be a person everyone else can count on. I was the one Mother turned to for help when Cate started in on that man, and then look who gets kissed goodnight and who doesn't. Well, thank the Lord I have another family, too. Dickie adores kissing me goodnight; so does Leo, in his way. It will be nice, being back in the big house with both of them this summer, while Leo goes to summer school. It was generous of Max to swap places with me. Even though we both know he's at Lizzie's place a good bit of the time. Well, I've got Stanley, though *Lord* knows what I'm going to do with *him.* Stanley wouldn't mind kissing me goodnight, either.

Lydia got her library book and settled down on the sofa facing the empty fireplace, beside which Mother had placed the cider jug full of dune grasses and sea oats. It had seemed really important to Mother to please those people. To think: that haggard little woman with all the eye makeup had been a girl with Mother. Mother said she had been the most charming girl in school, she could win over anyone. Lydia had found her agreeable—especially when she seemed so interested in Leo and Dickie—but a little too determined to see the bright side of everything. Those people always made Lydia tired. (What would Mother have been like as a girl?)

She opened her library book and took out several sheets of folded paper. These were Xerox copies of the letters people had sent to the TV station, praising—or mentioning—Lydia. Calvin had sent her the copies; and rereading them even for the hundredth time or more still caused a feeling of joy and untapped power to surge through her body.

Lydia kicked off her high-heeled sandals and, curling her toes indulgently, reread them once more.

... just a note to congratulate you on last Tuesday's show (Captain LaForgue's crabmeat soufflés) and to say how *delightful* that Mrs. Manning from Mountain City was! I hope Miss Mary Turnbull will have more guests like that. (Maybe she will have Mrs. Manning again!)

> (signed by a lady from a
> rural address in Level Cross, N.C.)

After all the air time you TV people give to those strident women's libbers and the "disaffected generation of the sixties," thank you for letting us see a living refutation to the usual "pop" garbage. I am referring, of course, to the lovely young lady who broke those eggs on the cooking show I happen to watch occasionally with my wife since I retired. That young lady in the green dress reminded me of the real ladies of my generation: she had poise, charm, *respect for her elders*, and a pride in being just what God made her, a woman. In the last year, I have written many letters of complaint to stations and newspapers for harping so unceasingly on despicable topics. It gives me a real pick-me-up to find one opportunity for a letter of praise.

(signed by a doctor from
Archdale, N.C.)

. . . the main reason I am writing is to ask whether it is possible to buy one of those "sunburst" clocks like the one on the brick chimney in Captain LaForge's Beaufort home; or is it an antique? Also, I enjoyed that girl who told the story about "the hill that disappeared" up in Mountain City. She reminded me of when I used to keep my Grandmother company in the kitchen while she made her cakes. We had such wonderful talks, just the way Mary McGregor Turnbull and that girl did.

(signed by a woman in Greensboro)

P.S. Do you think Captain LaForge would be interested in selling that clock?

That Lydia Mansfield you had on the last Mary McGregor Turnbull show really did inspire me. I, too, am a young mother, left at home a lot, and I get depressed occasionally, wondering if it is too late to make anything of my life. But she made me feel better and I hope to see her again.

(signed by a woman in a lower-income-
housing section of Greensboro)

With a gratified sigh, Lydia refolded the Xerox pages. She sniffed the paper's chemical odor and musingly rubbed the corners of the folded pages against her cheek. Her original plan had been to show Mother these letters, on their first night alone in the cottage. Then, when Cate announced she was coming, Lydia had envisioned an occasion on which she might show them *both* the letters. But now she wasn't sure. It might seem as if she were flaunting her "blossoming," as Cate had called it, just when Cate, what with the loss of her job and . . . her other loss . . . was feeling on the way down. And if Cate happened to be in an argumentative mood, or had had one too many bourbons, she might say something about the letters that would render them less gratifying to Lydia. Lydia tucked the letters firmly into the back pages of the book and reopened it to the chapter where she had left off. It was Bob Shanks's *Cool Fire: How to Make It in Television*, highly recommended by Calvin.

There are four people in this world who felt better about life after seeing me, thought Lydia. I mean, I have proof of four. There may be a whole lot of others who didn't write in. Is it wrong that this knowledge gives me pleasure and a sense of my potential for making this world a little better? If so, I'm sorry.

She remembered that she must buy a nice card, something with Ocracoke on it—maybe the wild ponies—to send to Mary McGregor Turnbull. No, maybe more than a card: Miss Mary might feel slighted by a mere card. And Lydia did not want Miss Mary to feel slighted or usurped, in any way. Lydia was willing to play respectful granddaughter until . . . well, until she established herself. Even in subservient roles, you could exercise considerable influence—if you did what you did well, with poise and charm, and did not act pushy.

Nell, though exhausted from the day's spectrum of events, found herself unable to sleep. She lay for the first time in the Ocracoke bed without Leonard, and her thoughts were churning about so, she couldn't even acknowledge the occasion with the proper level of regret. Where was the resigned serenity she had gained these past six months, when she had become able to look down, down, through the layers of her life—as though it were a deep, still pond—and see, beyond her own reflection, both the earthy bottom and the sky overhead?

It had to do with the evening, of course; all the crosscurrents and turbulences between various individuals—she, Nell, wanting to impress Merle with her daughters; Merle, wanting to act properly impressed; then Cate's intenseness about what seemed to be a philosophical subject she and Marcus Chapin were discussing; then Cate's tiff with Lydia; then Cate's rudeness to Marcus, who, after all, was a minister, and old enough to be Cate's father; and then the look Lydia had given Nell when she had agreed to spend the next afternoon with Merle.

But how could I have said no to Merle, thought Nell, turning in the soft bed, which flipped up uncomfortably on the side no longer weighted down by Leonard. How can anyone say no to Merle. And especially now, when she's been so obviously sick. I didn't like that cough. I wonder if they caught that cancer in time. That turban she wears: I'm sure she's had chemotherapy ... how could I have *not* said I'd come over tomorrow. Merle, never having had children, can't know how easily the little resentments and jealousies spring up: poor Lydia—first she thought she was going to have me all to herself; then she had to share me with Cate on this trip; and now, out of the blue, comes this girlhood friend who wants her chunk of my time.

How odd that neither of the girls remembers my mentioning Merle. Come to think of it, I had more or less forgotten those old school days until just recently, when I found myself with the time to look back on things. Maybe I never did mention Merle to them.

But why is it that meeting Merle again, even when we're both old women, has the power to dredge up all that painful adolescent *turbulence* in me again? She connects me with feelings I thought I was rid of for good. Mercifully rid of. I don't even know what to call the feelings. They have to do with a fear of some insufficiency in myself ... just as I thought I was rid of my troublesome old self, too! They have to do with a dread. A dread of what? A dread of losing more than I could survive losing ... oh God, I want to sleep! I wish Leonard were still weighting down his half of the bed. And that's another thing. Seeing Merle with her husband, even though he is rather aloof—to everyone but her, that is—makes me feel the full force of what being a widow means. Socially, you're half of a whole that no longer exists. You have to arrive places by yourself and go home by yourself, and if you get a coughing spell there's nobody to hustle you off to bed. Your hosts probably sit nervously, hoping you won't get sick in their house.

Now I'm getting melodramatic. Besides, back in Mountain City, with my contemporaries there, I won't stick out like a sore thumb. There's Grace Hill, who's been widowed so long most people think she's an old maid; and Sicca, whose husband stays home drunk while she goes out and drinks, when she goes out at all; and I'd rather have been single all my life than have to be married to Latrobe Bell; and poor Theodora never married. I do hope Theodora recovers completely or not at all. Thank God I've still got my health. Perhaps I should get a job, like Grace Hill. But what could I do? I could do private nursing, like Mrs. Talmadge. But somehow that doesn't appeal to me. . . .

The tide lapped continually upon the little beach below her window. The channel markers in the Sound flashed red-green, green-red, and would do so throughout the night. Having resigned herself stoically to wakefulness at about one in the morning, Nell was as surprised as if she had been visited by an unexpected lover when she felt, at her extremities, the first loosenings of sleep.

Cate, her feet trapped in shoes the size of small boats, had been given the task of sorting the sand on the beach. With only the aid of several little shallow baking pans, she was supposed to separate the grains into sizes and colors and remove extraneous matter. She attempted to do this for some time. Her mouth felt dry and nasty and her head ached, but still she went on. She *had* to. And yet, she didn't seem to be making much progress. From close by, a hoarse blast of a horn warned her that time was almost up. Oh no! How was she ever going to—

She looked down at her feet in the big shoes. The shoes were Hush Puppies. Now wait just a minute, she thought; I don't have to put up with this a moment longer. This is just a goddamned dream.

She woke and saw daylight through the corner of the window shade, and checked Lydia's watch, on the bedside table.

That blast must have been the seven a.m. ferry leaving Ocracoke. She had a hangover. She closed her eyes and tried to go back to sleep and *rest* a little, after that exhausting dream, but Lydia was breathing in a particularly irritating way, in affronted, snuffly gasps, as if she were being surprised by something repeatedly in a dream she had no control over.

Cate took her shirt and jeans and went downstairs to dress in the bathroom. She took a dose of vitamin B for the hangover, and washed the capsules down with a glass of soda water and some Ritz crackers. Then she brushed her teeth until the bad taste had subsided, got her car keys and wallet, and drove to the twelve-mile stretch of beach on the ocean side of the island.

Ah, morning at the beach. Surely this was one of the last beautiful beaches left on earth. Clean, empty, wild. Nobody could ever put up a sign here or build little gimcrack houses on stilts. The National Park Service owned it now and would protect and maintain its purity until it sank into the sea. Unless the National Park Service sank first. There was always that chance.

Cate turned left, away from the two dune buggies parked right in the surf, where four or five men were casting their lines. She faced the sun and the empty beach: miles of freshly washed sand, all to herself, except for a few breakfasting birds and ghost crabs, who scuttled sideways from her path, their eyes on stalks, their bodies almost transparent against the sand.

A new day. A new beginning. I'll be all right, thought Cate, setting herself a brisk marching pace up the beach. In a way, I'm starting completely over. It's nice to start over. My future, at this juncture, is as clear of impediments as this beach. I don't know what's coming next, but here I go, striding forward, taking deep breaths, to meet it. I shall walk on the beach every morning, at just this hour, and get myself in shape for the coming year. My fortieth year—no, actually my forty-first. I'll establish a regimen this summer: exercise, meditation, letter writing. I've got my ream of Melanchthon College stationery I nicked from the supply office—well, why not? They won't be needing it anymore—and I intend to send out letters to every friendly contact in my address book. I'll begin the letter in a sportive tone ("I am writing to you because the institution represented by this letterhead has ceased to exist . . .") and go on from there. Something will come up. It always has. In a way, it's nice not knowing exactly what form it will take.

I can't do much of anything till they leave, though. I can't even be myself around them. Mother stifles me; I can just glance at her and see her expecting some kind of excessive behavior from me; it's as if she predicts it, knows what it's going to be before it comes. Now, why is that? Because she's got the same seeds in herself and is piqued with me for not stifling them as well as she has?

No, let's not start on seeds. Unfortunate. I had just a wee bit too much bourbon last night. I'm usually not rude. I lost my cool.

And Lydia! Well, she's my sister. I do feel affection, even a certain *attraction* to her, up to a point. We're the same blood, but we're a different species of soul. It's quixotic of me to keep trying to make her see the world from my viewpoint; and it's naughty of me to bait her the way I do. She brings it out in me, though. I can just be in a room with her and start itching to shock her out of her complacency.

Maybe that's my mission in life: to keep people from being complacent.

Excuse me, Dr. Galitsky, but could you sum up the meaning of your ministry for us?

Why certainly. The meaning of my ministry is to shock people out of their complacency. As for the *message*, I'm still working on that. . . .

A figure, some distance up the beach, was walking toward Cate. Instinctively, Cate veered toward the surf so she would not be required to speak.

Also, it was a mistake telling Lydia about the abortion, thought Cate. I knew it was a mistake as soon as the words were out of my mouth. When Lydia says she wants to know "all" about my life, what she means is she wants to savor, or sample, my experiences vicariously—as she might dip into some book about an adventurous character willing to go further than Lydia would. Then she draws back, with an offended little recoil, as I've seen her do right here on the beach when a wave dares to touch her body at a higher level than she had planned for, and she says, "Oh, I would *never*—!" She wants to hear about the turmoils of my life, but she doesn't want to take responsibility for sharing what I tell her. So I end up feeling plundered and she retains her irreproachability. Maybe I'm not sorry I said that about her being a sociologist; maybe she needed to hear it.

The figure heading Cate's way was a woman, a rather strange-looking woman, and she seemed to have moved toward the surf. Unless one of them changed course quickly, they would be obliged to speak. The woman was about fifty, thin and sunburned, too much so for her coloring. She had short red hair, cut almost like a crew cut, with a streak of dead white down the middle. She wore a transparent plastic jacket over an old-fashioned bathing suit with a skirt. She was already eyeing Cate brightly from behind her glasses—ordinary glasses, not sunglasses. Yes, we're going to have to speak, you and I, her expression clearly read, but we'll think of something to say.

"Good morning," called Cate. "Isn't it beautiful out here?"

"Oh yes," replied the other woman, in an arch, knowing way, as if she herself were somehow responsible for it all. She stopped, facing Cate, still eyeing her brightly. At closer range, Cate saw that beneath the woman's freckles the skin was different colors of red and pink on her face and scrawny neck. The woman was smiling now; she had good teeth, at least.

"Do you happen to know if that old shipwreck is still up the beach?" Cate asked, pointing in the direction from which the woman had come. "I tried to find it yesterday, but I couldn't. Either the sand has covered it up since the last time I was here, or somebody's moved it."

"My mirage is in *that* direction," replied the woman, pointing the opposite way. "I walk to it every day, and then I walk back, regardless of the weather." She stopped, smiled more broadly at Cate, and waited. Just as Cate was about to respond to her remark about the mirage (whatever that meant; did the woman mean she thought Cate's shipwreck was a mirage?), the woman continued, "What I like about the walk is the *planes*."

"The planes?" Cate looked up at the quiet morning sky, dotted only by a few winging gulls.

"Yes, the planes," said the woman, with a little too much fervor. "There are so many planes, so many perspectives," and her hands, also red and freckled, began dividing up the air between them, making choppy, bracketing motions around portions of the landscape. "That's why *I* like the walk," concluded the woman, watching Cate closely, as a lonely (or slightly mad) person watches another to see how her "unusual" statement has been received.

She's probably trying to tell me she's an artist, thought Cate, but felt a strong disinclination to indulge the woman by asking her what kinds of pictures she painted, or whether she lived here all year round, or what she had done with her life before she came here. The woman's eyes looked so eager, so ready to claim her. Cate, usually so curious about strangers, even eccentric ones, felt a powerful physical revulsion. She did not want to meet this woman every morning of the summer, walking the beach.

"Well, I guess I'll go on and see if I can't find my shipwreck," said Cate, remembering to add, "It's been nice talking to you."

The woman, still smiling brightly at Cate, shrugged. Then she refocused her eyes in such a way that she seemed to be looking right *through* Cate, at more of her "planes." "You probably won't find it," she said pleasantly, and turned to go.

Cate walked at least half a mile before she dared to look back. Far, far down the beach, beyond the two dune buggies, a solitary figure walked, but Cate couldn't be absolutely sure it was the woman.

On Cate's return walk, she worried all the way to her car, which she had left in the sandy parking space next to the island's landing strip, that she might meet the woman returning from *her* walk.

She drove to the Island Inn and treated herself to a big breakfast: two eggs, country ham, grits, and fresh biscuits. When she returned to the cottage, Lydia and Mother were just having coffee on the porch. They appeared cheerful enough and even pleased to see her. No criticisms of her behavior the night before seemed to be on the agenda. When Lydia asked her what she had "been up to," Cate said she had walked for quite a while on the beach, and it was very lovely, but she did not mention the woman, who had seemed a bad omen, a projection of what she herself did not want to become.

Merle, sipping iced tea under the shade of an umbrella on the Hollowell patio, looked out across the Sound, where, until recently, they had been able to watch Marcus departing for his sail with the young man on the yawl. "I don't know about you," she said to Nell, "but I'm grateful to have lived when I did. I mean, I'm glad I had my best years when I did, and not now. So much of life these days is just a freak show. Don't you feel that way?"

"On *some* days I do," said Nell. "There are times when I seem to hit a pocket of bad air, and everything is so accelerated and confused and shoddy, and I think, Well, if this is progress they can have it! But then I remember that I'm still included in the 'they,' and I have to admit to myself that I find it pretty interesting. The young don't seem to mind it all that much. Of course they can't remember things being different. I wonder if things *were* all that different. Or will the youth of today be sitting around in the middle of the next century, shaking their heads and recalling the good old eighties, when things were so much more coherent and attractive?"

"Yes!" exclaimed Merle. "Maybe it's just the course of things. People always remember the past as better." (And Nell recalled how Merle always had been eager to revise herself, like this, for the sake of preserving a congenial conversational flow.) "Frankly," Merle went on, "I believe it gets to Marcus worse than it does me. Poor Marcus, his whole world is falling around his feet; the two things he cares most for in this world are just crumbling before his eyes: I mean, first the church, and then me, in that order of importance." She looked at Nell keenly. "You know what my illness was, don't you, Nell? You've guessed, haven't you? Now that I know you were a nurse, I'm sure you have. Am I right? I thought so. Darling, I've been *through* it these past three years. Everything hit us at once. Marcus was banished to Gloucester, then I found a lump in my breast. Well! When I was younger, I was sure I'd rather die than lose a breast. But you get over *that* right quick, when it's a choice between— You gather your pride again, go out and buy your falsie, throw out your low-cut blouses, and start your five-year countdown. I only made it to two and a half. Then I found another lump. After they took the second breast, they detected a little something in the axillary nodes, and so I got these follow-up hormone injections. Male hormones! Oh Nell, it was a trial. My hair started coming out in clumps, and I grew some whiskers, and then I got jaundice, so they took me off that and put me on regular chemotherapy. First my hair, then my femininity, then my energy . . . I think that was the worst: I didn't even have the energy to smile at Marcus. I'm only just now beginning to feel human again. They think they caught it, whatever little *residue* was left. They say so, anyway. It's probably ungrateful of me, but doctors are so . . . well, even when they're kind, you can't help but feel like a guinea pig when you've been through what I have."

"So you've stopped having the chemotherapy?" Nell asked.

"Yes, praise the Lord! And my hair is starting to come back, but there's hardly any color left in it. I tried a wig, but it looked ludicrous. I prefer my Carmen Miranda turbans. But all this is *trivial*, if I can just have the rest of my simple life, watering my houseplants and talking to Marcus and puttering around the house. I value things like just getting up in the morning, feeling *able* to get up, and looking out to see what kind of day it's going to be. I don't care if it's a rainy day or a hot day or an icy, sleety day . . . as long as I can see it!" She became breathless and dissolved into a flurry of coughs.

Nell wanted to ask her how long she had had the cough, but

could not bring herself to, just now, after Merle's determined hymn to life.

Then Merle laughed and said, with the gay petulance of a popular girl used to getting what she wants, "I refuse to die and let Mary Hollowell get Marcus."

"Mary *Hollowell*?"

"Do you know her? The woman who owns this cottage?"

"Not well. She wasn't here very often at the same time we were. She liked to rent this cottage for the whole season if she could. She gave me the impression of being a hardheaded businesswoman. Doesn't she run a realty agency in Norfolk?"

Merle, eyes narrowed, nodded knowingly. "That's right, darling. She was one of our Norfolk parishioners. Since we were transferred up to Gloucester, she drives up to consult Marcus on 'spiritual matters' at least once a month. Does she strike you as the spiritual type? Ha! Of course, she always says she just had to be in the area, anyway, showing a client some old estate, but where is the client? Why, she even took it on herself to find us the house we now live in—we only rent, of course. Nell, I could write a thousand-page exposé about how our church treats its clergy: we have never lived in a house we owned; we never, until a few years ago, when, thank God, we bought a Blue Cross policy, had any health insurance; why, once, in the rectory in Norfolk, it was a boiling hot day, in the upper nineties, and Marcus and I had to go out for about an hour on Sunday afternoon, and when we got home we thought the air conditioner had broken down, because it was running when we left, and you know what had happened? One of the parishioners had walked right in our house and *turned it off*, because he thought we were wasting the church's money! Have you ever heard of anything to beat that? Not only do they keep you poor as the proverbial church mouse, but you have literally no privacy. Nell, do *you* have your own home?"

"Yes, I'm very fortunate there," said Nell. She sat quietly for a moment, thinking of all Merle had told her. "I would love it if you and Marcus would come and visit me in it. There's plenty of room." She laughed. "*Too* much, for just me. October is a beautiful time in our mountains. Why not speak to Marcus, and you all plan to come then?"

"Oh Nell! You know, we just might do it? I mean, why not? It would be something to plan for, and as long as there's something to plan for—" She hestitated, thought better of whatever she had been going to say, and then seized Nell's arm excitedly. "We could go visit old Farragut Pines Academy. Is the building still there? And I remember this enchanting old meadow, with crabapple trees, where we used to have picnics. . . ."

"That's gone, I'm afraid. It's a shopping mall. I'll have to check about Farragut Pines. I know for years it was there, up on its hill; we used to drive by it whenever we were on that side of town. But then they put in a bypass. . . ."

"Ah, everything changes!" lamented Merle. She, too, was silent for a moment. Then she asked, "Nell, if it isn't too painful for you, would you mind telling me what it's like to be . . . well, to be the one who's *left?*"

Nell thought. Merle was the first person to ask her this question. She had lain awake last night, thinking about the ever-new implications of being "the one who's left." But how much of her real feelings could she share with Merle, or anyone? Wasn't it different for each person? Was Merle asking for herself or for Marcus? Nell suspected for Marcus. In that case, it would not do to emphasize the most wrenching emotions. Yet she had to say something, and it had to be true. Merle would know if it weren't true.

"Well," said Nell, purposely dryly, "for one thing, I think I've set the table for two, or got out two glasses at cocktail time, at least a hundred times since Leonard died." To Nell's surprise, and dismay, her eyes filled up, and Merle saw.

"Oh darling, it *is* painful," cried Merle. "I'm so sorry I brought it up." She took Nell's hand and laced her fingers through Nell's. "It was selfish of me to ask. It's just that . . . oh, I feel so much better now, there's probably nothing to worry about, but . . . I can't bear the thought of Marcus alone, saying his poor little underground Mass, with the old prayer book, alone in his study. You know what I'm really afraid of? I might as well say it. I'm afraid if I . . . go first . . . he'll get bitter and lose his faith. I've seen people in the church do that. And Marcus has such a beautiful, stalwart faith. He really believes, Nell, he really does. I've seen him down on his knees sometimes, when he thinks I'm already asleep, and I can't tell you how moving it is to see a virile man like him just . . . offering himself wholeheartedly to God. I'm so afraid he'll get bitter or angry at God for taking me, and then he'll lose his faith, and Mary Hollowell . . . she's giving us this cottage, Nell, free, for ten whole days, and as tight as she is, you know she's doing it for a motive! It's to impress Marcus with how nice she is . . . for *later*! Oh Nell, what if he loses his God and then Mary Hollowell will snap him up and he'll spend his old age sitting around with those types who have old *Horse and Hounds* stacked on their dusty coffee tables and sipping port and talking about restoring old houses . . . I can't bear to think of Marcus being *debased* like that!"

"Merle, it's not going to happen." Nell, still holding Merle's hand, gazed across at her own cottage. Cate had just come out onto the screened porch and was setting herself up with clipboard and paper to write something. "Mary Hollowell isn't his type. I don't know her well, but from what I do know, she's your complete opposite: tough-talking and . . . and—" Nell cast back in her memory for something unpleasant about the woman who owned the patio on which they were sitting. "I don't think she shaves her legs. I remember once I was standing over there talking to her and—"

Merle let out a peal of laughter at this. Cate, across the way, looked up at the sound. She waved. The women waved back. Cate returned to her writing.

"Poor Cate's probably drafting her letter," explained Nell to Merle when they had stopped laughing, and almost crying, at the same time. It was time to get off this level of intensity—for everyone's good. "Her college went bankrupt and she has to write to all her old contacts to see what jobs are available."

"Marcus *said* she had no school, just as he had no church. Marcus liked her."

"He did?" Nell looked closely at her friend to see whether she was joking.

"He did. Really. He said she had an inquiring mind. Anyone can see she's very intelligent. Now, myself, I liked Lydia so much, but then I talked to her more than I did to Cate."

Mr. Jack's weather forecast proved accurate. In the predawn hours of Friday, the usual breeze that eddied casually from the Sound, playing about in the low-lying shrubs around the cottage, suddenly increased its intensity and changed its mood; it whipped rather than caressed the aspen, causing the leaves to set up an incessant, clattering protest; it hissed through the stunted cedars; it nosed its way importunately under the eaves of the cottage, drummed on windowpanes, and sent a small, unidentified object—plastic, from the sound of it—skittering across the cement floor of the Stricklands' screened porch. The shallows sprouted small breakers, which dashed themselves against the stones of the narrow strip of beach, making an urgent, gulping sound, like a thirsty animal drinking.

The noise woke Nell briefly. Those must be Mr. Jack's "hoigh winds," she thought, then drowsed off again, having identified the natural causes of the disturbance.

The winds did not completely wake Cate, but they infiltrated her sleep. She dreamed agitatedly of bashed ships' timbers and sailors' cries, and was just in the process of figuring out what she was doing in this dream—for she was neither on the endangered ship nor safe on land, but hovering insubstantially somewhere in the ether—when the clatter of the little plastic item on the porch below woke her; she recognized it at once: it was the coaster she had put under her glass of soda water when she had been drafting her letter about jobs.

Each time the wind rattled the window of the sisters' room, Lydia emitted a disturbed little moan, sounding like a much younger version of herself, but she slept on.

When daylight came, the Coast Guard station, visible from the Stricklands' living-room window, had its red flag flying.

Nell and Cate met downstairs before seven, and drank their coffee together, sitting on the sofa.

"God," said Cate, still in her nightgown, her long hair hanging in several uncombed portions, "that wind reminds me of when Pringle and I spent our year in Keflavík. The winds in winter were maddening. The trees there were no more than waist-high because the soil was mostly volcanic ash, and we lived in this ultramodern apartment complex with lots of glass, and the wind would come howling around the corner windows until it's a wonder we all didn't go mad. Then, when the long daylight period came, in summer, most Americans would put aluminum foil on their windows because the night light made them crazy. But the light never bothered me. I rather liked having that eerie dawn, all night long." She took a deep, gratifying slurp of coffee from her mug, her eyes gone distant in the remembrance of another time in her life when things were breaking up. Before they shaped themselves into the next pattern.

"It's fortunate that Marcus Chapin got his sail in yesterday," said Nell, gazing through the window at the small-craft-warning flag being whipped about on its pole.

"Mmm," murmured Cate, wanting to skirt controversial topics this morning. The wind set her on edge; she didn't want to create any more disquiet.

"He told Merle he liked you," said Nell, arching her eyebrows at Cate over her coffee cup. "He said you had an inquiring mind."

"Ha!" laughed Cate. "Well, he won't neutralize me with compliments." But she was pleased.

They sipped their coffee. The wind whooped suddenly around their corner of the cottage, as if seeking entry to their conversation. Nell considered telling Cate about her afternoon with Merle, which was very much on her mind. But to share fully the reasons why it *was* on her mind, she would have to tell about Merle's illness. Nell always felt uncomfortable when people traded off someone's illness or disaster for the sake of lively conversation.

What had struck Nell was how a sanguine person like Merle

could make the best of what she had, even when circumstances narrowed her expectations down to being able to get up in the morning and see what the weather was. At the moment, Nell found herself more engaged with Merle's prospects, threatened as they seemed, than with those of herself or her daughters. She was with Merle in imagination, waking up to this day and discovering the weather in store for her. Would Merle love the storm? Probably.

Nell asked Cate, "How did the letter writing go?"

"It didn't go much of anywhere. I mistakenly thought I could draft one letter and then copy it over for everybody. But as soon as I leafed through my address book, I realized my folly. They're all such damned individuals. My former chairman at New Mexico is a traditionalist. My ex-boss at the defunct New Hampshire college is an innovator. What I'll have to do is create myself over for each letter, and that takes time and energy."

"I should think so!" agreed Nell.

Lydia, who had slept through the winds, was wakened by Cate's laugh below. Mother and Cate were down there talking. She tried to make out their words, but the wind interfered. She pulled aside the shade and looked out on a slate-gray sky, tempest-tossed trees and grasses, angry-looking waves in their usually calm Sound. She was glad she had got a good start on her tan yesterday. How long were these winds supposed to last? She needed a couple more days to attain the shade she had hoped to be when she returned to Stanley. And she and Mother were leaving Tuesday.

What to do with the day? Lydia had sent all her cards—and the note to Mary McGregor Turnbull—yesterday. She had bought an Ocracoke tote bag in a gift shop for each of her sons.

We can clean, thought Lydia, with a slight lift of spirit. We can empty the closets and pack up Daddy's stuff and the family belongings that Cate doesn't need, and then it will be ready to rent out, first thing *next* summer.

She got up and put on slacks. It was too chilly for shorts today. And brushed her short, easy-to-keep, curly hair, and went downstairs to the bathroom. Mother and Cate, no longer talking, were sitting side by side on the sofa, their faces pensive and grainy in the austere light. Neither looked as if she would mind being mobilized.

"Hey, everybody," said Lydia. "Why don't I fix one of my Western omelets? And then, I was thinking, we could go through the closets and clean out all our old stuff."

"What's the point of that?" asked Cate. "I mean, if you're doing it for my sake, it's a sweet thought, but I can live with it. As a matter of fact, I like having our old stuff around."

"It will make it easier for you," said Lydia. "Then you won't have to do it when you leave, at the end of the summer . . . or whenever you leave."

"But why should anybody do it? Why can't we leave it like it is?" Cate wanted to know.

"*Because*"—Lydia struggled to keep her patience—"Mother had planned to rent it out."

"Lydia," put in Nell quickly, "there's really no hurry. We've only just got here. There's not all that *much* old stuff. . . ."

"I didn't know you *had planned* to rent the cottage, Mother," said Cate. "Had you planned it for this summer? Is my sojourn interfering with the family economy? You didn't say anything to me about wanting to rent the cottage, Mother, or I would have made other plans."

"It was just an idea," said Nell, "and, as far as I'm concerned, it's an idea that can wait. I've been left more than I know what to do with, and two houses. Many people in this world don't even have *one* house." She stood up and, looking at neither daughter, gave a small sigh of exasperation. "Let's all try to get through the day peaceably. By the looks of this weather, we're going to be trapped inside. Lydia, that omelet sounds like a very good idea. And I'll make more coffee for everybody. . . ." She started for the kitchen.

"Well, I don't intend to be trapped by a little wind," said Cate, setting her mug down with a bang on the nearest table. "And count me out on the omelet. I'm going to take a walk." Off she went, up the stairs, her chin stuck out grimly, to dress.

Oh dear, thought Nell, standing in the kitchen. She looked through the window at the Hollowell cottage, across the dune. The wind, caught in a loose shingle somewhere, set up an unnerving percussion sound. Nell had the discomforting thought that Merle, trapped inside that other house with the attentive Marcus, would probably yearn less for her old school friend than the other way around.

Cate, in a headscarf, head ducked against the wind, walked halfway around Silver Lake and then decided to have breakfast at the Inn before walking on to the North Point, to the old cemetery, which had been her original goal. But it wasn't much fun, this wind keening in your ears, sand flying in your face. Maybe after breakfast the wind would have changed, or would seem less of a deterrent to a full stomach. She wanted to stay out of that cottage as long as possible. This morning with her mother and sister had brought back the bitter taste of revolt that she recalled from her teen years, when she had gone around in a more or less constant state of alienation from family. Why in God's name did people form families? What made them imprison themselves in the separate pressure cookers referred to as "nuclear families"? Of course, children didn't form them; children came to consciousness and found themselves already bubbling away in the pot. But then what made these children grow up and start another pressure cooker all their own? What an unholy process! First the smug exclusion of all others, of the "outside world"; then the grim multiplication of oneself and one's partner behind closed doors; then the nauseating, unclean moiling about of all the family members in their "nuclear" caldron, bumping against one another, everyone knowing all too well everyone else's worst faults—all of them *stewing* themselves in one another's juices.

And, oh God, the polarizations, the trade-offs, the assignment of family "roles." ("Let's see, what have we got here? One calm man, one excitable woman. Put them together as 'husband and wife,' and look how *well* they complement each other. The wife's passionate nature is kept in check by the husband's pru-

dence—or vice versa, depending on which marriage we're discussing—and the husband's passiveness seems more attractive
when given shape by the agitating molecules of his wife's surrounding energies. He may even become known, in that marriage, as 'The Rock,' or 'The Anchor,' or 'The Grounding
Force,'—pick your favorite metaphor.

"And now, to make this mixture complete, let's throw one
or two children into the pressure cooker. That one's a little wild;
well, we'll balance her off with a tame one. That child's too fearful; never mind, we'll even out our mixture by making the other
one too bold.")

Nobody who is, first and foremost, a "family member" has a
hope in hell of becoming a whole person, concluded Cate, entering the Inn's restaurant with such a fierce scowl that the cashier,
an observant, matronly woman, asked her if anything was
wrong.

Cate was not so far gone in her inner diatribe that she
couldn't assume a friendly mask at once and reply with sociable
heartiness, "Oh, it's just this *wind!*"

That was something the woman could understand, and,
picking up a menu, she led Cate the Restaurant Goer to a better
table, in the convivial center of the dining room, than she would
have led Cate the Rebel to. Even Ocracoke, that rustic, pure
haven from the decadent mainland, was beginning to get its
share of kooks, though, as yet, there was no call for a policeman.
The only island "crime" was manifested in the occasional fist-
fight or in rowdy behavior as a result of drunkenness. Once in a
while, someone might make off with a car or a bicycle that didn't
belong to him, but—as Leonard Strickland used to say humorously—"What is the thief going to do with his stolen goods?
Take them down to the Coast Guard station to wait for the next
ferry?" The car or bicycle always found its way back to its owner.

Cate ordered the same breakfast she had eaten here yesterday morning and took a paperback book out of her bag. One of
the basic pleasures of the independent life was being able to

order a huge breakfast in a restaurant and sit there in warm solitude, reading your book, letting snatches of neighboring conversations play around the edges of your attention.

Five men—locals, judging from their speech—sat at the
large round table behind Cate. They were discussing a proposed
new health unit that would serve the island. But there was, it
seemed, a woman on the planning board who "wanted to run
everything." The woman's name was Joyce. "I don't fault her for
effort," said one man, the oldest at the table, "but she's wanting
to do it all by herself, then she mommicks things up." "Best
thing to do is praise her, then work around her," said a younger
man with a shy demeanor. "Work *over* her's more like it," said a
gruff voice. General laughter. Cate tried to guess, from these remarks, how old Joyce was and what she looked like and why
she'd gotten on the board in the first place.

Cate opened her book. She was two thirds through it. The
book had been highly recommended by several women colleagues. It was about a young woman who flees modern technology to rediscover her basic instincts in the honesty of the deep
woods. In the past year, Cate had read at least three novels about
women fleeing into the honesty of the woods. In the first book,
the woman fell in love with a bear; in the second, the woman
discovered latent artistic impulses; in this book, the woman
was, at the moment, down on all fours naked in the forest,
rooting and snuffling around, trying to get back to her basic
instincts and wondering if she could grow hair over her whole
body.

In the past year or two, Cate had read at least three novels
by well-known men writers about men who had gotten themselves in prison, one way or another, and were trying to restruc-
ture their psyches inside their jail cells.

The women were fleeing into the wilderness and the men
were putting themselves in prison. What does that mean,
thought Cate, as the woman in her book leaned against a tree and
tried to imagine the act from the tree's side: we're seeking more
space and they're trying to shrink theirs down to something
manageable? Will we end up retreating to cells after we've had

our share of running through the woods and sitting on town boards?

But at least these writers are trying to stretch the limits of communal imagination and envision new ways to live. At the moment, they seem to be stuck in wilderness or prison—both excellent places for reflection and stoking up one's energies for what comes next: what have we done wrong, and how can we do better next time? I don't knock these writers; how can I? I'm stuck in the same place—between reassessment and what comes next—but I allow myself the right to be impatient with them, all the same. Why can't they come up with something marvelous to solve my life?

And what, about your life, do you want solved? This sensible inner voice spoke in a tone much resembling Mother's.

Well ... *solvency* first, replied Cate, playing on words in a play for time.

And then her breakfast came and she escaped heartily into her basic instincts.

At the cottage, Lydia and Nell were finishing their Western omelet.

"Do you think she'd mind if we just cleared out one or two closets?" asked Lydia. "I brought empty boxes just for the purpose."

"She *shouldn't* mind. ..." Nell hesitated; she saw how Lydia was dying to "accomplish something," to give a form and structure to her day. On the other hand, what if it aggravated Cate, to return from her walk and find them cleaning the place that was supposed to be hers for the summer—as if they couldn't wait to clean *her* out, too. Nell wondered if she should have told Cate earlier about the rental plans. But Cate would only have been set off, just as she had been set off by Max's burglar alarm: one more example of Max's (and Lydia's, by association) decadent Capitalistic impulses. "But why don't we wait until she gets back, before we start anything. Let's see what her mood is."

"Oh, her moods," said Lydia through clenched teeth. She sprang up from her seat and began clearing the dishes.

*   *

But Cate returned in the jolliest of moods. Any resentments she might have had seemed to have blown away like trifles on her windy walk. She recounted her adventures of the past hour, making her expedition sound like an odyssey of significance which the folks who had stayed safely at home should be sorry to have missed.

Cate has this knack, thought Lydia, as her sister told them about hot biscuits and country ham and Joyce, the woman on the board of the proposed new health unit who wanted to run everything; she just walks through a village shut down by bad weather, or climbs aboard a Greyhound bus, and all of a sudden things start popping. The air is filled with tasty bits of overheard conversation, a bizarre couple passes a lunch bag back and forth, but the fat man doesn't eat anything. . . .

"And then I went on to the cemetery," Cate was saying. "The British flag was flapping away over the little 'forever England' plot where those British sailors that got torpedoed by the Nazi submarine are buried, and then I went and paid my respects to all the generations of Williamses and Howards and Wahabs—you know, it just struck me this morning, there are no Jews in the cemetery. They've got all the Wahabs there, descended from that first Arab boy who washed up here on an oar in the seventeen-hundreds, and they've got their one black family, a descendant of which baked my biscuits this morning, but *no Jews.* I wonder why that is?"

"Did you say hello to Love and Pinta?" put in Lydia, hoping to head off an inquiry into racial prejudice on Ocracoke Island. Love was the first name of a man and Pinta of a woman, and, in past years, the sisters, charmed by the names on the old stones, had speculated on how Love and Pinta might have married, had they been born in the same century.

"Oh yes," recalled Cate offhandedly, " 'Love loves Pinta, and Pinta loves Love.' " Quoting their old chant. But even in their young days, Cate had been able to construct a tale of inequality out of that. "Love loves Pinta," she would say, "but you *could* construe it to mean that Pinta only loves *love.*"

"That's very promising news, about the new health unit," said Nell. "When you girls were small, I used to worry what would happen if you got sick or hurt."

"God, I have half a ton of sand in my hair," said Cate, "and I was wearing a scarf. Also my right ear is ringing from walking back along the lake. The wind cut right through the scarf."

"Why don't you take a hot shower and wash the sand out of your hair?" suggested Nell. "And then, would you mind if we went through some of our things in the closets and decided what we want to throw away and what we want to keep?"

"I think I will take a shower," mused Cate, looking absently around her. Then added, maddeningly, "Of course I don't mind. I'll help, if you wait till I have my shower. It'll be fun, going through our old stuff. There's not much *else* we can do today."

A Dutch painter might have captured us, Cate thought, as the three women, equipped with dust mop, rags, spray can of Lemon Pledge, and empty cardboard boxes, climbed the stairs single file to begin on the upstairs closets. *The stark light from windows against the shadows of corners; the complacent harmony of housebound women embarking on a communal task.*

In the sisters' closet, Lydia found the missing shoe of a once-favored doll. She had liked that doll so much that she had kept it, wrapped in tissue, for her own eventual daughter. But she had had sons. She held up the little shoe, a white Mary Jane with a tiny button made of imitation pearl, and a real buttonhole. "Just look at the craftsmanship of this little shoe," she said, forcing the others to stop what they were doing and admire it. If Cate had had a little girl, thought Lydia, I could have presented her with my old doll, with both her shoes. "They don't make dolls or dollclothes like they used to," said Lydia sadly.

In Mother and Daddy's closet, they found Daddy's paint set. "Most of the oils look dried up, to me," said Nell. "He hadn't painted a picture for at least ten years." "No, wait, let's keep the paints," said Cate. "I might try my hand at art this summer." But then a scowl flashed over her face as she remembered the mad artist woman on the beach with her mirages and "planes." "No, throw it away," she said.

In the downstairs closet, off the kitchen, they found Daddy's boots and fishing cap, and Granddaddy Strickland's mildewed waders, the wrong size for Leonard, even if he had hunted ducks, but he couldn't bear to throw them away; and there were fly rods and spinning rods, and Daddy's prized English fly box, with the beautiful, feathery fake insects, their colorful names labeled on pieces of tape over their transparent cubicles.

"There's his Grizzly Wulff," said Lydia fondly, "and his Grasshopper, and his Royal Coachman. Oh, and there's *my* favorite, his Golden Witch, for channel bass. Lord, just look at the way these things are made." She took the Witch out of its cubicle and, holding it cautiously by its hook, flashed it through the air in mimic flight. "Look at those greens and golds!"

"This fly rod is almost brand new," said Nell. "I remember when he ordered it from Bean's." She wondered if it would be appropriate to offer Leonard's fishing rods to Marcus Chapin. At least someone would get use from them.

"We'll save them for the boys," said Lydia. "One of these days, Leo and Dickie will be coming here with their friends to fish."

On second thought, Cate decided, *Norman Rockwell might do us better. The Mother leaning pensively against the fly rod; the Younger Daughter packing things greedily into cardboard boxes; the Older Daughter empty-handed, with a faintly sarcastic look on her face. Titled: "The Breakup of the Nuclear Family."*

By early afternoon, they had finished their project. Nell, worn out emotionally from the memories connected to all these artifacts, shut herself in her room for a long nap. The wind continued its ceaseless howling and pummeling of the cottage. It was the sort of wind which, like the sirocco and the mistral, oppresses its captive audience.

I'm glad I didn't say we should give those rods to Marcus Chapin, thought Nell, really relieved to be by herself. She had completely forgotten that Leo and Dickie might want Leonard's fishing gear. Already, she was looking forward to being back in her own house, weeding her garden, spying on her crow family. In peace. She loved her girls, of course, but she loved them better when she could love them separately, reflectively, in peace. She had forgotten the tension the three of them could generate under one roof. It seemed worse than ever today. Why was that? Had Leonard's restraining presence made that much difference? Had the mere knowledge that he was under the same roof with them—though far away in his study, far away in war-torn Spain or at Cicero's summer villa—kept them from blowing the roof off?

Of course, if we hadn't come here, I wouldn't have seen Merle again, thought Nell. But this is not the place to see too much of Merle. That will cause more tension.

Before she dropped off to sleep, suddenly not minding the wind outside, Nell began to plan how she would entertain Merle and Marcus if they came to see her in Mountain City. October would be the best. The trees all scarlet and yellow. She would take them to the famous château. She would take them through the famous novelist's house. She even knew a church where Marcus could worship comfortably: Theodora's Episcopal church. She recalled Theodora's saying how the rector was a renegade after her own heart who continued to use the 1928 prayer book.

Lydia stood at the living-room window overlooking the Sound and watched the two p.m. ferry bound for Ocracoke approach over the squallish gray waters.

"Here comes the ferry," she said. "Boy, I'll bet there are a few seasick children on that ferry today."

"Mmm," replied Cate, curled up on the sofa with her novel. She had washed her hair earlier, after the cleaning, and she had her new shawl tied around her shoulders, squaw-style. The clean, beige-colored hair, always rather wispy, floated about her shoulders.

Lydia continued to stand post by the window. She knew she could watch the ferry's approach just as well from their bedroom window, but some stubbornness kept her down here, trying to draw Cate out, even though Cate was immersed in her book, which she had almost finished.

Out in the Sound, the ferry began the first part of its devious entrance into the harbor. As if it had suddenly changed its mind and decided to go to some other island, it turned sharply south and crossed directly in front of the cottage; then, just as sharply, it turned north, and, at a slightly different angle, retraced its route toward the harbor again. When the girls were small, the strange behavior of the ferry had delighted them; they thought the whole performance had something to do with *them*: that the ferry was paying its respects to their cottage by zigzagging back and forth like that. Then Daddy had explained how all the ferries, entering and leaving the harbor, had to follow a labyrinth of precise channel markers in order not to be wrecked on the treacherous shoals. The most deceptive shoals on the East Coast, some said. That was why the greatest pirate of all had chosen to anchor his last ship, the *Adventure*, right here on this side of the island, "just a couple of doors down from us, back in those days," as Daddy put it. And then Edward Teach, the great "Blackbeard," would wait gleefully for ships to run aground, practically on his doorstep.

"Do you remember how you and Daddy used to walk down to Teach's Hole after I had been put to bed?" asked Lydia, staring out at the ferry. "I would watch you all from the upstairs window. You walked right down there on the flats when it was low tide."

"So we did," agreed Cate, but not quite looking up from her book.

"And then, when I got old enough to stay up later and go with you," continued Lydia, watching the ferry do its about-face north, "do you know what you did?"

"What did I do?" Still not looking up.

"You told me that anybody who went down to Teach's Hole who was the least little bit scared would see the ghost of his head glowing at them from just below the surface of the water."

Cate laughed. "God, did I say that? What an awful little girl I must have been." This time, she looked up from the book. She cocked her head and seemed to be looking into the past. "Oh yes, now I remember. It scared you so badly, you decided you didn't want to go. We would invite you, but you never would go."

"No," said Lydia. "I never did."

Cate returned to her book. Lydia watched the ferry, rocking from side to side, enter the mouth of the harbor. "There sure must be some seasick people on that ferry," she repeated. She seemed to have an irrepressible urge to talk.

"Oh shit!" cried Cate vehemently. She flung the book across the room, where it hit the side of the fireplace with a *thwack*.

Lydia, shocked, turned around. "What's the matter?" she asked, pretending ignorance, though she was positive Cate's outburst had been brought on by her own constant interruptions.

"Oh, I'd like to smack the woman who wrote that book, that's all," replied Cate more calmly, with a touch of humor.

"Oh, why?" asked Lydia, interested and relieved. She sat down in the nearest chair.

Cate sighed. Lydia could see her sister mounting an invisible platfrom from which to hold forth. "I'm getting tired of novels about women who go off to the woods to find themselves. Then they learn to chop wood or skin a rabbit, or they have a few epiphanies or suddenly produce a volume of poems or a roomful of canvases, and then back they go, right down to the wicked city again. In this case, the woman was just getting somewhere. But she discovers she's pregnant and so, of course, goes back to town. She even resigns herself to the fact that she'll probably marry another second-rate man, because that's all there is. Or so she says. Damn."

"Well, what would you have liked her to do?"

Cate frowned. "I'd have liked her to have a little more confidence in her hard-earned visions. She was just beginning to see what was wrong. If she'd had a little more courage, maybe she could have changed things. But no, back she goes, dragging her tail behind her in fashionable angst. The book ends on a note of almost *gloating* resignation. How I wish there were a roaring fire in that fireplace. That's what that book deserves, a roaring fire."

"Oh damn," said Lydia. "I knew I forgot something. I was going to bring some nice splits of wood so we could have a fire. In just such an eventuality as today's weather. And I forgot."

"You can't prepare for *every* eventuality, Lydia," said Cate, with what Lydia thought sounded very much like the "gloating resignation" she had just been criticizing the other woman for.

"I guess not. Still, a fire would have been nice. It would help. This wind—I don't know—what is it about this wind? It sets you on edge, doesn't it?"

"Yes! You can't concentrate, or read, or reflect, or plan, or anything. It just ... twines itself around you and makes you a sort of prisoner. It makes you *wait* ... that's it! You *wait*, in a wind like this, for something to happen. Some culmination or cessation or *something*." Cate looked pleased with herself for having figured the wind out intellectually, even though it was still keening and thumping the house, hard as ever.

Lydia was thinking about the woman in Cate's book. "Maybe," she ventured, "the *baby* was a symbol of hope." She felt rather proud of this insight; and Cate approved of symbols.

"What baby?"

"Didn't you say the woman in the book found out she was pregnant? Well, maybe that was the author's way of saying the baby was a chance to start over. A sign of new beginnings. Like your seed you and Marcus Chapin were discussing."

"Well, if that was her idea, it's not good enough for me. It's a fallacy, that whole notion of starting over with a baby. It evades the challenge of your own adulthood. Nothing ever evolves that way."

"I only meant as a *symbol*," said Lydia, in a small but determined voice.

"A baby's not a symbol," said Cate. "A flesh-and-blood baby means you have to go back into the fallen world and take what you can get till that baby grows up. The baby keeps you a hostage in that world." Her voice was rising aggressively.

Lydia felt a dangerous lump of gorge collecting in her chest. Her eyes roved the room, looking for some safety valve. "I know what," she said. "I'll drive down to Mr. Jack's and see if he has any fresh crabmeat. I'll treat the family to Captain LaForgue's crabmeat soufflé. That's the recipe we were making on the Mary McGregor Turnbull show, the day I was 'discovered.'" Though she made her voice light, this was the nearest Lydia had come to boasting to Cate about her television breakthrough. She, Lydia Strickland Mansfield, was going to appear weekly on a television show. People she couldn't see would be able to see *her*, and she would be able to express herself to them, perhaps to influence their lives; she would have a platform larger than any teacher's; maybe she could change a few things in the world Cate called "fallen."

"That's going to a lot of trouble, isn't it, making a soufflé?" asked Cate. "Just for your mother and your mean old sister?"

"I don't mind going to a little trouble," said Lydia. "We need something to look forward to, as Dickie puts it."

"Dear old Dickie," mused Cate, remembering their evening together watching that disappointing Dracula documentary. When she'd broken her tooth on the peanut brittle. Cate smiled. "Yes, why not? It'll give you something to accomplish and it will give us something to look forward to. I'll go with you to Mr. Jack's. I want to get a newspaper and see what's been happening."

But Lydia's soufflé supper was not a success. The crabmeat was fresh and succulent, the mixture had been followed to perfection, she had even made complicated calculations to compensate for the slow oven; but when she removed her masterpiece (which hadn't risen as high as it should have) and carried it in pot-holder mitts to the table, and plunged in the big spoon to begin apportioning servings, the deceptively firm crust of the soufflé caved into a soupy morass.

Lydia had had to *fry* the soufflé in a hot skillet, before it was edible. Though Mother and Cate assured her that "looks didn't count," and that it was the most delicious crabmeat *omelet* they had ever eaten, Lydia was inconsolable. She had not had a dish fail on her in *years*. And it seemed a bad omen: to fail at something so closely connected to her future ambitions seemed ominous.

"That oven has always been slow," Nell comforted her. "I can't tell you how many fallen cakes I've pulled out of it. But they tasted fine."

What does it mean? thought Lydia. Does it mean that I am guilty of counting my chickens before they hatch? Or does it mean that, no matter how well I do in the world, I will never be a success to my mother and my sister?

And Cate's dinner conversation hadn't helped matters, either. In the *News and Observer*, Cate had found a news item that reconfirmed her worst fears for the evolution of any new world. A seventeen-year-old girl flutist had been pushed onto the subway tracks, two days before, in New York, by a black man. Though the news item reported the miraculous reattachment of the girl's hand, which had been severed by the train, she probably would not be able to bend her wrist or play the flute again.

"There you have it," Cate kept saying angrily. "The downward forces triumphing over the upward. She'll never play a Bach sonata again. And if they catch him, it won't even be murder, so he'll get off with six months and go and do it again. Just like that other one who pushed the airline stewardess off the subway platform. Did you read about that? It makes you despair. And the thing is, he's a victim, too. He was probably crazed by drugs, which he got hooked on by the goddamned Mafia, and so it's not his fault, either."

Lydia had looked down at the fried remnants of her ruined soufflé. She thought of its collapsed craters swimming in unappetizing yellow fluid. She tried not to think of a metal wheel running over a human wrist.

Nell had endeavored to channel the topic into its most hopeful aspect: the delicate microsurgery that had been performed successfully, reattaching the girl's hand. "When I was in nursing school, such a thing wasn't even a dream yet."

"It just makes you want to give up," said Cate grimly, taking an abandoned gulp of wine.

The three women cleared the dishes and took a long time washing up. They even dried the dishes and pots and put everything away. It was too early to go to bed—it wasn't even dark—and yet each was looking forward to escaping from the others in the only acceptable way possible to them: sleep.

They dragged themselves dutifully into the living room. Outside, in the eerie half-light, several of the long-legged birds stood disconsolately on the marshy flats. It was low tide, about sunset time, but the sun was hidden behind the greeny-gray, impacted sky. Nell, with her "jet pilot's vision," could see the feathers on the birds' sides ruffling in the wind.

Cate paced up and down angrily and then, suddenly, dropped to the sofa with a loud sigh. She picked up the *News and Observer* and leafed impatiently through its pages—looking for more bad news? She glared defiantly at the empty fireplace. "Too bad you aren't perfect, Lydia. You would have planned for every eventuality and we could have had a nice fire. A nice family fire to gather around. And tell a few ghost stories."

"I know what," said Lydia, suddenly inspired. "We can burn that old piece of driftwood on the porch. It's plenty big. It'll make a nice fire, just for long enough till time to go to bed. Is anybody in love with that old piece of driftwood? Mother?"

"Not me," said Nell. "Just be sure to let that red spider who lives on it have a chance to get away."

"Great idea, Lydia," said Cate, springing to her feet.

The sisters carried in the unwieldy driftwood. A fierce gust of wind barged into the house with them.

"Now, be sure the flue is opened right," cautioned Nell. "That damper has to be felt from inside the chimney to make sure it's opened."

Cate stuck her head into the grate and reached into the recesses of the chimney. She grunted. "There. It's open. Now! What are we going to use for kindling? Shit, there's no kindling."

"We can ball up your newspaper in little bits," said Lydia. "Max always does that, anyway, to start a fire going."

"Oh well, if *Max* does it . . ." said Cate sarcastically. She seized her paper and began ripping off pages and balling them up in her fists.

We'll get through the rest of this day, thought Nell, and then tomorrow is Saturday, and then we've got Sunday and Monday, and Lydia and I leave on Tuesday.

The driftwood turned out to be too big to go into the fireplace. "I know," said Cate. "We'll knock off its prongs. That'll be better, anyway. They can serve as more kindling."

The sisters dragged the driftwood back out on the windy porch, and Lydia held down the main body of the log while Cate stamped and tore the prongs off.

They had just got a blazing fire going, and Lydia had opened another bottle of wine, and they were each making an effort to have a semblance of family harmony at the end of this trying day, when someone knocked at the door.

It was Marcus Chapin. He took one look at the fire, the women, and their wine, then said, "I'm sorry to barge in, Nell, but Merle has been having some difficulty breathing. I was wondering if you'd mind coming over." He would not even come in. He stood on the doorstep, the wind whipping through his shirt sleeves; he was breathing hard himself.

"Of course," said Nell. "Let's go right away." She put down her wineglass, feeling guilty for having answered the door with it, and was heading out into the wind with Marcus Chapin, when Cate, snatching up the shawl, which lay in a crumpled heap on the sofa, jumped up and fastened it around her mother. "You can't go out in that wind without some kind of wrap," she said with benevolent authority.

"Quite right," said Chapin, helping Nell adjust the shawl. Though visibly distraught, he was still gallant. He gave Cate a look of approval for her daughterly gesture.

"Thank you, darling," said Nell, also rewarding Cate with a look of affection. "Be good, girls," she called to both of them, closing the door behind her.

*   *

"I wonder what's wrong with her," said Lydia.

"I don't know. Difficulty breathing is lungs, isn't it. Or asthma? Maybe it's psychosomatic. She looked a bit like that sort. 'Frailty, thy name is woman.' You know."

"I don't know. She didn't look well to me when they were here night before last."

"Well, you probably can judge better than I can. I was stuck with *him*," said Cate. Though it was gratifying to know he admired her mind.

The subject of Merle was dropped. Neither sister knew her well enough or cared enough about her to start a fight over her or how ill she was.

When the fire, after its initial burst of glory, began to dwindle, Cate got a stack of the magazines from the shelf and brought them over to the fireplace. She found that by shoving a magazine under the glowing log she could get a little more action.

They drank more wine.

"I can't get that girl out of my mind," said Cate softly. She was sitting on the floor so she could feed the fire another magazine whenever it was hungry.

"That girl in New York? I know. Once it's *in* your mind, you can't get it out. It's awful. But at least they saved her hand."

"But such a waste. Such needless waste."

Lydia stared at the fire. She thought about the black man who had done it. Then she thought about Renee and Calvin. She wanted to tell Cate about her friends, and this seemed a fortuitous time. "You know, I used to be as bad as everybody else," she began. "I blamed the blacks for everything. Whenever I heard about anybody getting robbed or mugged or worse, I'd just automatically think, What color was the criminal? I'll bet he was black. And he *was*, a lot of the time. But since I've met these friends of mind in Greensboro, these really smart, sensitive, *achieving* people—who happen to have been born black—I resent the bad publicity people like that man in New York, who was probably crazed on drugs like you said, give to people like Calvin and Renee, who are really contributing to the world."

"How are they contributing?" asked Cate, sticking in another magazine over the blackened corpse of the previous one.

She seemed really interested. And so Lydia presented her friends to Cate, making them as interesting as possible, trying to build toward her best revelations suspensefully, as Cate did when telling stories, and not give away all the good parts first. So she began with Calvin, her entrée to the world of TV, and how he had grown up right in Greensboro and yet managed to overcome all that *that* implied when people like Calvin were growing up; how he got an M.A. in Theater from Chapel Hill and went up to the RCA Institute in New York, which he found too cynical when there was so much opportunity back home in North Carolina. And about his samovar and his quick, anxious (though Lydia called them quick, *sensitive*) eyes that monitored everybody's thoughts; and how he had a dream of establishing a network of pure culture, to be beamed from North Carolina and financed completely by private subscriptions.

"And then, *Renee* . . ." As Lydia launched into her description of Renee, she realized how often she must have fantasized telling Cate about Renee, because the words poured out in sentences and phrases already long-formed. "She has her doctorate from *Harvard*, and the Harvard University Press is going to publish her thesis . . . she is probably the most articulate person I have ever met in my life, and yet she loves to slip into jive talk, just to shake people up when they're least expecting it . . . she's perfectly beautiful, with these elongated, aristocratic features . . ."

Cate, arching her eyebrows, poked at the embers under the simmering log and added another magazine from the pile. "How did she get those aristocratic features?"

Which led right into the whole Peverell-Watson history. The beautiful great-great-grandmother from the West Indies who was auctioned to the Reverend Peverell with real gold in her pierced ears. Her daguerreotyped alliance with the plantation-owning Reverend, and their descendants. How all the members of Renee's family on her mother's side had kept Peverell in their name.

"I mean, Renee can trace her family back much farther than *our* family can, on either side," said Lydia.

"I don't know," mused Cate. "All this foraging around in family roots makes my heart sink a little. It's enough having to deal with the family in one's living memory."

Daunted slightly, Lydia nevertheless continued her celebratory chronicle of the Peverell-Watsons. "Renee's parents both went to this chic school in Greensboro, a boarding school for upper-class blacks—it was called Palmer, have you ever heard of it?" Cate never had. "And Renee's daughter, Camilla—she's the same age as Leo—is at boarding school in England. When Leo and I were over at Renee's one day—she has this beautiful house—she showed us some photographs of Camilla jumping her horse just like some black Princess Anne."

Cate snickered. "Really, Lydia, the way you put things."

"Well," said Lydia, smiling, "you know what I mean." Though she certainly hadn't meant it as a slur. She decided not to darken her story any more by telling about Camilla's jailbird father.

"Well," said Cate slowly, after meditating into the fire for a few minutes, "they certainly do sound like . . . paragons, your friends. Paragons of *what*, I'm not quite sure, but—" She meditated some more. "What did Renee *Peverell*-Watson do her dissertation on?"

"Oh, that's fascinating, too," said Lydia. "Renee did her dissertation, which is going to be published, on 'Social Class in Black America.' "

" 'Social Class in Black America'?" asked Cate incredulously. "I didn't realize there was one."

"Oh Lord," said Lydia. "Do they ever have one. For instance, just about the best thing you can be if you're black is a *Vaughn*, from the Scipio Vaughn branch in Camden, South Carolina. I mean, they have the same criteria for their best families as we do for ours. Money is never the primary thing, though it helps. What counts is how far you can trace back and how much accomplishment goes with the background."

There was a silence. The magazine pile was exhausted. Cate

looked toward the other magazines, still on the shelf. Then she said, "I hate to use Daddy's *National Geographics*; why don't we burn one of those empty boxes we didn't use this afternoon?"

Lydia got up and fetched a box. Cate tore it savagely into pieces and tucked a big piece under the smoldering log, which didn't seem to want to blaze on its own. Wasn't Cate going to comment anymore on all that Lydia had told her?

Then Cate said, drawling her words out ironically, "I don't know, baby. You sure do pick 'em."

"What do you mean?" At Cate's tone, Lydia's heart had begun to thump.

"Well!" Cate gave a short, sharp laugh. "No, nothing. Forget it."

"Cate, that's not fair. You can't start something and not finish it."

"No, Lydia, I'd rather not; you might not like how I finished, if I did finish."

"Well, I can't promise whether I'll like it or not, but I want to hear, anyway."

"You always want to 'hear,' Lydia, but then, as soon as you hear anything scary, you run away."

"Scary? I don't see how you can make anything scary out of what we've been talking about."

"But it *is* scary, Lydia. Your friends Calvin and Renee strike me as *mighty* scary. They sound like just about the scariest things imaginable. Boy, you did tell a ghost story tonight, Lydia. My pirate's head glowing beneath the water wasn't half as scary as Calvin and Renee."

"What do you *mean*?" demanded Lydia, her voice rising.

"Well, hell, baby. They're walking dead people."

"I don't see how you can say that. They've accomplished a heck of a lot more than—" She reined herself in with every ounce of remaining self-control, to stop herself from adding what she had so much wanted to add: More than you have, or probably ever will. "—more than most people do. And damn it, Cate, they're my friends. I was telling you about my friends, and you—" She stopped, to keep from crying.

"I know. I'm sorry. But—" Cate was fighting to keep herself calm. "God*damnit*, you can't just turn me on, Lydia, and then expect to turn me off again like a . . . faucet. . . ."

"Well, go on!" cried Lydia. "Don't turn off, then. *Finish!*"

Cate took a deep breath and threw back her shoulders. She spun around on her bottom to face Lydia. "All right," she said wearily. "Your friends are living in a world—living *for* a world, I should say—that doesn't even exist anymore. If it ever did exist. I mean it's just goddamned pitiful! Stacking up all the old status symbols—or what you call accomplishments—like people hoarding Confederate dollars or something. Just perpetuating all the old crap that's finished! Gone!"

"It's not finished for them," said Lydia. "Or for me, either."

"I know, baby," Cate said sorrowfully. "That's why it's so damn pitiful. Oh Jesus *Christ.* 'Social Class in Black America.' A network of 'pure culture,' privately subscribed to. The daughter 'taking her fences' in England. It's like some horrible parody. Instead of using their obviously good minds—I'll give them that, they sound very intelligent, especially *her*—to create themselves afresh, out of the ruins of that old oppressive society, they assimilate all its pretensions and start the whole goddamn cycle over again. Can't *you* see how depressing it is?"

"I'll tell you what I see," said Lydia, who had gone suddenly so buoyant with anger that she hardly felt her body as it rose from the chair. "I see a woman, about forty, who happens to be my sister. She was brought up with all the advantages any American girl has the right to expect. And as far as I can see, she has nothing to show for it except an endless capacity to criticize, criticize, *criticize!*"

"If I criticize, criticize, criticize, it is in hopes that people like you will wake up and see farther than your safe, circumscribed, orderly little kingdom, your pretend world. I mean, it's a very pretty, neat, admirable little *table-model* kingdom, but—" She took a deep breath, and as she did so, Lydia could see in the firelight of the almost-dark room that her accusation had just hit Cate midway through her countercharge. Cate was wounded. But binding her wounds in thick sarcasm, she went on, "—nobody in your pretend kingdom would dream of taking a real chance or making a real choice. I mean, let's face it, Lydia, you can't stand safely on the edge of the shore and stick your little toe in the water and say, 'Oh yes, this is the ocean. Now I know what the ocean is all about. I am a citizen of the ocean.' " She made her voice high, mimicking a little girl's voice.

"What do you advise?" challenged Lydia. "Taking a ship into the middle of the Atlantic and jumping overboard naked? What is that going to accomplish?"

"Oh, accomplishment, accomplishment, accomplishment!" chanted Cate. "Go and accomplish your little accomplishments. Get your little M.A. and your little Ph.D. and putter around in people's lives, wearing your little Ivy League outfits and calling yourself a sociologist, and cook little soufflés on your little TV show while you make harmless chitchat with some old harridan who still knows Calvin is her personal slave, and then lie in your cozy little bed with your cozy little lover and congratulate yourself on all the things you managed to 'accomplish' without once climbing down off your little table-model kingdom. You'll die surrounded by your little accomplishments, Lydia, without ever once having left your dollhouse." Cate turned away her head. She savagely fed the fire another slab of cardboard, as if she were relegating Lydia's entire "table-model kingdom" to the flames.

Lydia, standing above, watched this hateful creature crouched below her. She hardened her heart against this creature.

Lydia got her sweater and her purse. When she came back, Cate still sat, hunched and scowling, feeding more cardboard to the flames.

"Well, I may not set the world on fire," said Lydia, feeling her knees begin to tremble in the knowledge of what she was powerless to stop herself from saying, "but at least I've never murdered anybody. If that's 'creating yourself afresh,' I prefer my doll kingdom."

And then she ran out of the cottage, slamming the door, into the wind. Away from that face slowly dawning with wrath. She got in her car and locked the doors before she got her key out.

Her hands felt numb. Even as she backed out onto the sand-swept road, she expected to see the door of the cottage flung open and her older sister, always bigger and stronger and bolder, to come charging out and ... what? The days were over when Cate could frighten her out of a walk, or come racing after her in fury and hurl her to the ground and pummel her to her heart's content.

The door stayed closed as long as Lydia could watch it out of the rearview mirror as she drove away in her Volvo.

"Nell, I'm much better now. You don't need to stay."

"I'll stay a little longer. If it's all right with you, that is. Are you sure you wouldn't like to try to sleep?"

"No, honey. That's when the whole thing started, when I was lying here, kind of dozing, like, and then that *wind* would rattle those panes, and that's when I began to notice I couldn't breathe so well. But then, as soon as I sat up, it got better, and I wanted to talk Marcus out of going and getting you, but he thought you ought to come. He wanted to go down to the Inn to see if there were any doctors staying there, but I talked him out of that."

"I'm glad I came. Do me a favor, Merle, and lie back and tell me if you feel any obstruction anymore."

"It seems to be gone. Isn't that the funniest thing? Do you think maybe it was the position I was lying in? Maybe I was lying in some peculiar position that would make *anyone* short of breath."

"It's possible. But Merle, when you get back home, why not go to see your doctor, to put your mind at rest?"

"I know, I know. I was supposed to go before we came, but I didn't want to find out anything that might spoil our vacation. It's been the first one we've had since all this started. I didn't want to go asking for trouble."

"He might not find anything. And then *you'd* be less troubled. And you should have that cough seen to."

"Oh Nell, you think there's something wrong, don't you? Be honest."

"Merle, I'm not a doctor. I haven't even practiced nursing in . . . oh Lord . . . forty years. But I do believe, when in doubt, *ask*. You've come this far. I'd like to see you watering your plants and looking at the weather for a long time to come."

"Oh Nell, I'm so happy we found each other again. If I *were* to get ill again, would you be willing to come and stay for a while? We have a very nice guest room, with its own half bath. The Bishop slept in it once. I think he felt bad about banishing Marcus, and came up to see how we were. Would you come? I'm so terrified of hospitals. If I *were* to be ill, I'd want to be at home."

"Merle dear, please. It may be nothing. Don't upset yourself imagining—"

"But if it is, will you come?"

"Well . . . goodness. I mean, if you want it, of course I will."

"Thank you, darling. That means a lot. Nell, you've changed so much since our Farragut Pines days. I mean, I always loved you, Nell, you were so funny and clever, but back then you had a shell around you a foot thick. Nobody could get past it. And now you're just as warm and loving and natural as can be. I think you must have had a wonderful marriage. You love yourself more now, Nell, and it's just beautiful on you. You're just a beautiful, beautiful woman. Well, you are! You're light-years away from that poor girl who wouldn't even let me hug her when her mother died. I tried to put my arms around you, to comfort you and share your pain, and you said, 'It's all right. She wanted to die.' It gave me chills for years, darling, every time I remembered the way you said that. But then I finally understood that you were holding on for dear life behind that shell. You were afraid, if you let yourself go, you might just fall to pieces. You needed that shell, and I'm glad you had one. And now I'm so happy you don't need one anymore. Why, hello, Marcus. See, I'm all better. Marcus, what on earth is the matter?"

"Nell," said Marcus Chapin. "I just looked out the window and your house is on fire."

When one is an American given adequate cause for anger—and given a car, of course—one *drives* until the anger wears away or becomes merged with the illusion of going somewhere. Lydia's first impulse, as she barreled off in the Volvo, was to drive. Although the island in its entirety was only sixteen miles long, there was a straight, twelve-mile stretch of road all the way to the Hatteras Inlet, and Lydia envisaged herself hurtling obdurately down this road, then circling around and hurtling obdurately back again. But what would be the point of that, with the gas crisis? She had topped off her tank before they left Morehead City in the event that the gas pumps in Ocracoke ran out, and if she was careful between now and Tuesday, they'd be fine till they got back to Morehead City.

Just thinking about the end of this "vacation" made her feel better—much better than the wasteful twenty-four-mile drive would have made her feel—and she parked her car across from the Island Inn and, using her purse to shield her eyes from the flying sand, ran toward the public phone box and shut herself into the narrow cubicle, away from the wind. Now for a few calls to the "dolls" in her "table-model kingdom." She took out her Southern Bell charge card, which Max had gotten for her, and dialed 0.

The line was busy at Max's house. Who was talking? Max to Lizzie? Max on business? Leo to a new girl friend? Or to one of the diminished Ghouls?

She tried Stanley. But there was no answer. She looked at her watch: nine-thirty. Maybe he had gone to a movie by himself. But she was disappointed in him for not being there when she needed him.

Renee was home. God bless Renee. "Am I calling at a bad time?" demanded Lydia, and burst promptly into sobs.

"Child, what's *wrong*?" Renee's voice was so truly concerned that, if Lydia had been with her, she would have laid her head on her friend's breast and cried her heart out.

Lydia spent forty-five minutes telling Renee what was wrong. Or a version of it. She left out Renee and Calvin's part in the fight. It was the underside of the fight she tried to describe to Renee: how she and Cate had been locked in mortal combat since . . . since Lydia's *birth*, it seemed, and "tonight she said the unforgivable to me, she found words to undermine my whole life, and then I said something unforgivable back." Lydia also did not tell Renee about Cate's abortion, which she felt was generous of herself: hating Cate, she could still be loyal. "The thing is, she despises the things I live for and I can't *stand* the way she blames everybody else in the world for the mess she's in," said Lydia. "Oh Renee, you're closer to me than my own sister." Overcome, Lydia began to cry once more into the receiver; the high winds rattled the panes of the phone box.

"Hush, girl," soothed Renee. "Nobody, but *nobody*, is closer than your own kin, but I appreciate what you're trying to tell me. You *like* me better than Cate, for now, and I'm happy you like me. Listen, I know what these fights are. I almost killed my brother, Warren, one time. It was the same kind of thing. He was trying to put me down, the way big brothers and big sisters do. I broke a Coke bottle over his head and knocked him clean out. They said I could have killed him, no joke. And he and I still have our tiffs. He's very conservative, and he thinks I ought to marry some nice conservative man like himself and give Camilla a 'proper home.' Well, now, I tell him, that's some more of his business. Hey, when am I going to see you again? I got a letter from the Harvard Press yesterday. They say I'll have the proofs of the book by the end of the summer. Isn't that exciting? And Camilla's bringing a houseguest for the summer. Her little Persian roommate. The poor little girl has nowhere to go. Her father's stuck in Tehran, trying to keep a low profile, and her mother is holed up in this little apartment in Paris, but what the poor child's really sick about is, she's afraid she'll never see her two Corgi dogs again. I told Camilla it might cheer her up some to have our Judge around."

People like Renee and Calvin, thought Lydia, emerging from the phone booth in a much better state of mind than she had entered it, *and people like Stanley* (whom she had succeeded in reaching the second time around—he had been out with a real-estate agent looking at a farm), *and people like ME,* want to claim their share of what Cate calls the "dying world" because they haven't *had* their share yet. So they need to protect what's left of it until they can get what they never had out of it. So let Renee publish her book, and let Calvin have his cultural network, and let Stanley have his farm with horses, and let me have a little spotlight and influence in this world. If it's a "pretend world" to some people, well, "that's some more of their business," as Renee would say.

Lydia's own line—or rather, the line of Max and the boys—was still busy.

Well, she could try again in a few minutes. Go and sit in the lobby of the Inn and wait for whoever was on the phone in Winston-Salem to get off. The island had no bar, even if she had been the kind of woman who sits in a bar alone. Just so Mother would have returned to the cottage by the time Lydia got back, that's what was important. She didn't want to face Cate alone. She would get a blanket and sleep downstairs; she was not getting into the same bed with Cate. How they were going to get by in the same house till Tuesday, Lydia hadn't figured out yet.

As she was heading for the Inn, she heard the siren go off. There was a fire somewhere on the island. She decided to wait in her car until the fire trucks came out of the road where the firehouse was—she could see the road from her car—and follow the trucks to the fire. A harmless and perfectly human pastime. She waited. Presently they came. Two fire trucks, followed by a convoy of private cars and pickups: the overflow of the volunteer fire department, which everyone on this island took seriously. Then she had to wait some more, because other fire chasers, including guests from the Inn, who had been shut up in their rooms all day by the wind, were backing out into the road to follow the trucks.

It did not occur to Lydia, until she had joined the excited stream of traffic pressing eagerly around the road beside the lake, that she might be following the trucks to her own house.

Cate found herself out in the dark, on the marshy flats of low tide, walking south toward Teach's Hole. She was barefoot, but did not recall removing her shoes. She had put on a sweater, but had forgotten to defend her face and head against the wind with a scarf.

She had heard Lydia's car driving off, and had continued to sit for some time on the floor, feeding the remaining pieces of cardboard to the fire that didn't seem to want to burn by itself. The cardboard would appear to pass its flame to the driftwood; then the fire would lose its force as soon as the cardboard had burned.

So she had abandoned the room and its intolerable echoes.

She considered returning to get her scarf; but no, she chose to have her head mauled by the wind, her windward cheek like ice. Rather than go back to the room that had overheard such a vicious, disgusting exchange.

She was more disgusted with herself than with Lydia. If that were possible. Though she could gladly go without seeing Lydia for years to come, Cate's revulsion against her sister in no way lessened the shame she felt at her own proclivity toward belittling others. The acknowledgment of this in herself hurt her more than Lydia's worst remark. (Yet even there they differed: Lydia obviously thought her final accusation had been the worst, that's why she had saved it for last; but for Cate, who had no thoughts of herself as a "murderer," though she did feel remorse for lost possibilities, it was the "nothing to show for it" remark, coming as it did from her baby sister, that really hurt. Those words, though spoken in anger and self-defense, had been like the light push of a finger against a structure about to collapse.)

But, though it was chastening to be told you had done nothing with your life, it was surely worse to be a destroyer. And Cate had been out to destroy Lydia. Once Cate and a Catholic friend had been speculating on what the sin against the Holy Ghost—the worst sin, according to Catholics—consisted of. And the friend said he thought it had something to do with making a human being despise his own nature, the nature God had given him and that he had to live with. Tonight, Cate had exerted her entire intellectual force toward making Lydia acknowledge that she was trivial, insignificant, banal—no matter what she could or would do with her life.

I was contemptible, thought Cate, trudging on through the muck. At this extreme low tide, she was able to walk to within a few feet of the blinking channel markers and thus to avoid having to clamber over the jetties that stuck out from the private cottages along her way. Her right cheek, by this time, had gone completely numb from the sharp wind.

She waded in and sat down in the familiar sheltered spot. Here, at one time, the water had been deep enough to anchor a pirate ship. This was Teach's Hole, the destination of Daddy's and her old walk.

From here, the hairy, fearless brigand, who wore red ribbons in the plaits of his thick, black, waist-length beard, and often set his hat on fire, while it was on his head, to frighten people, had conducted his business. The ships that did not wreck on his doorstep at night, he went out and plundered in daylight. He built himself a castle on Ocracoke. He shot his first mate under the table, on a dare, crippling the man for life. He was said to have had four wives in towns along the Carolina coast; the youngest, sixteen, he made mistress of his castle. The Governor of North Carolina was reputedly in his pay, and it was the Governor of Virginia who finally got fed up and sent the raiding party of British sailors who did him in.

The National Park Visitors Center presented a "Blackbeard skit" for children, several times a day in summer. Local actors, dressed like pirates or sailors in the Royal Navy, went through the whole thing, again and again. Again and again the ambushed pirate was dealt the final killing blow by Lieutenant Maynard (a name most children immediately forgot), but the last part of the saga was never, of course, acted out. The "narrator," a young National Parks man or woman, would simply step forward, and, with a reassuring smile for the children, tell how the *legend* said Blackbeard's beheaded body had so much energy left that it had swum seven times around his ship before sinking.

But, thought Cate, smiling mournfully down into the lapping waters where, to frighten Lydia, she had said the head floated and glowed (it was too dark tonight even to see an outline of her own head), I'll bet I am the only child—*the only child*—whose parent saw fit to complicate its mind by telling Teach's side of the story.

As an impressionable young sailor, Teach had served aboard a British privateer during Queen Anne's War, when it had been his *patriotic duty* to loot cargo from French ships. He got so good at it that he didn't want to stop, said Daddy, but then the War came to an end and he was told to stop; what had been patriotism now had its name changed to piracy. "The way Teach felt," explained Daddy in his patient singsong, sitting beside Cate in this very cove, "was that he had been trained to do something, and then, just when he got to where he could do it well, they made it a crime. So, even though he later did commit some deplorable deeds, and really overstepped himself in the end— why, he was actually making plans to turn Ocracoke into a refuge for all pirate ships, from which he would collect a 'protection fee,' and that's when the Governor of Virginia stepped in—he felt he'd been dealt with unfairly. And, in a sense, he had."

And then they had walked, hand in hand, back through the shallows, the impressionable daughter sunk deep in the boldness and the contradictions of her father's tale.

Were you aware, Father, that you sometimes sent very contradictory messages? Cate thought. She had endured enough windy assault on her body for the day. She stood up and headed back, ducking her head and shielding her newly windward cheek with her upraised arm.

But, be that as it may, I loved you and still do. You have made me part of what I am.

She walked fast, eager for the shelter of the cottage, even if it must contain the presence of Lydia. They would just have to coexist, somehow, until Tuesday. I'll sleep downstairs, thought Cate, keeping her head down and her eyes narrowed to slits as sand flew at her across the dunes.

From far across the island came the sound of a siren, fading in and out, in competition with the wind. But then a spreading glow arrested her shuttered vision, and she looked up to see giant, unruly tongues of flame rushing at the black sky, crimsoning the tip of the island toward which she was bound.

11.
FORTY

Given the prevailing twenty-to-thirty-knot winds, and the fact that the roof was a sheet of flame by the time the island's fire trucks arrived, it was a testimony to the efficiency and pride of the firefighters that the cottage was not allowed to burn to the ground. But what was left, when the flames had been extinguished and the weary volunteers had gone to their homes for a much-deserved rest, offered very little basis for rebuilding. Max would fly in sometime tomorrow, or as soon as the winds subsided; he would bring the claims adjuster, and see what could—or could not—be done. Meanwhile, he instructed Lydia over the phone, the women were not to say anything to anyone about hard-to-open dampers, and certainly nothing about anyone's burning cardboard.

"I thought I'd taught you better than that," said Max. "I bet sparks were just raining down on that roof."

"I wasn't thinking properly," Lydia told him. "Cate and I were having this terrible argument, and I watched her stick in those pieces of cardboard, but I guess I didn't really register it. . . ."

"Cate *would* do something so careless."

"It was partly my fault for not stopping her." But to herself Lydia thought, It was Cate's fault. If she hadn't gone out and left it, maybe it could have been saved. Of course I left, too. "Well, at least everybody's safe," she told Max.

Lydia did not mention to Max the awful fear she had suffered when she first saw the cottage in flames; she had been sure that Cate, undone with remorse over what Lydia had said about being a murderer, had decided to make the cottage into her own funeral pyre. And then she, Lydia, would have had to live the rest of her life knowing she had as good as murdered her own sister.

But when Cate had come running up from the flats, and Mother, with the strangest cry, had rushed to Cate and embraced her and then started laughing hysterically, shouting over the wind and the cries of the firemen, "The cottage doesn't matter! It doesn't matter!" Lydia's heart, cleansed so briefly by repentance, had begun to fill up with new resentment. She knew she should go over and say something to Cate: now would be the time, before their conflict hardened. But why? What had altered, really, since she had fled from the cottage? Only that Cate, somehow, had let it burn down.

And then there had been a second emergency. Mrs. Chapin, who had come out in her raincoat with her nightgown showing underneath, had succumbed to an awful coughing attack, and the next thing everybody knew, there she was, lying flat on her back on the road, one of the firemen breathing into her mouth. A Coast Guard helicopter had been radioed for, and by now the Chapins were at the Norfolk Hospital. Although the poor woman had seemed restored by the oxygen from the paramedics' van, Mother had said that with her medical history they'd decided it would be dangerous for her to spend another night on the island.

Cate and Mother were now installed in the Chapins' cottage, but Lydia had taken a room for herself at the Island Inn. By setting herself up as phone liaison with Max, who might need to relay further advice via the Inn's telephone—available only to guests—she had managed to justify her separateness and thus avoid any possible confrontation with Cate. Thank God she still had her credit cards, to pay for the hotel room. All Cate's and Mother's cash and cards had been burned up. Cate was lucky still to have her car. And that, ironically, was due to her carelessness: she had left the keys in the ignition, and quick-thinking

Mother had driven it away from the flames while Mr. Chapin rushed off in his car to summon the fire squad. (Which, it turned out, had already been summoned by a Coast Guardsman, who, for some time, had been keeping watch from the teletype room over sparks shooting wildly from the chimney of the cottage.)

Now Lydia lay in the dark, in the room she had bought for herself, wearing her underclothes, as her nightgown and everything else had been destroyed by the fire. To think they had worked so hard, packing everything up in boxes and labeling each box, and now all was ashes. Pulling the hotel blanket up to her chin, Lydia ticked off in her mind the things she would have to replace. That done, she turned one cheek to the pillow, drew up her knees, and went on to enumerate, for her own comfort, the important people and things in her life untouched by tonight's events. As she made this vital list, she felt the hard knot in the upper region of her chest begin to dissolve. Nothing irreplaceable had been lost. The cottage was most likely beyond repair, but the person who had loved it most for what it was in itself was dead. Objectively, everybody admitted it was poorly designed and a little ramshackle. And only that one little bathroom. Before Lydia slept, she had already left the island. In her mind she was getting Dickie ready for music camp, moving her belongings back to the old house, helping Max move his things into her apartment, temporarily. And Leo's summer school . . . And, oh Lord, what about Dickie's cat? Would Gregory get along with Leo's old dog, Fritz? Would Leo really stick to his guns about going to school in England? If she knew Leo, he would.

It was past midnight, but Nell and Cate were still sitting in the living room of the Chapins' cottage—or rather, Mary Hollowell's cottage. They had been going over the events of the past few hours in a stunned, desultory manner, sometimes repeating themselves or asking the same questions in different ways, and often letting long silences elapse, during which one or the other, or both, stared out of the window at the darkness on the other side of the dune where formerly they could have seen the roof and upper story of their cottage.

"Marcus will call Mary Hollowell," said Nell, "but I'm sure I'll be out of here by Monday. As soon as Max flies in and we've settled everything. I'll drive the Chapins' car to Norfolk, or Gloucester, depending on what they decide about Merle. Then I'll get a flight back to Mountain City."

"I'd like to get out of here tomorrow," said Cate. It had been decided that she would drive back to Mountain City, staying at Mother's until she got herself reorganized. "I can start phoning the credit card people. I can make myself useful for *something*."

"There's no great rush," said Nell. "They were burned up. It's not as if they'd been stolen." But she had caught Cate's subserviently remorseful tone. Already Cate was blaming herself for the fire, repeating that if she hadn't left the cottage it would still be there. Nell hoped she wouldn't make a crusade of the remorse. They had all been absent when it caught fire; in that sense, wasn't it the fault of all? And why waste time apportioning blame? The cottage was gone.

Nell knew her daughters had had a fight. That was clear from their behavior to each other at the fire and afterward. They had been spoiling for a clash all day. As to what had finally brought it to a head, well . . . either one of them might tell her, or again, they might not. Tonight she was just as content not to know. Right now, she needed to sort the basics out. Her daughters were alive. For one awful moment, when Lydia had driven up to the burning house and Nell had seen no Cate in the Volvo—for Nell had assumed that both sisters had rushed out of the cottage when it had caught fire; she had assumed they had gone for the firemen; though Marcus had said he'd better go, too, just to make certain—and then, when Lydia had jumped out of the Volvo, shouting, "Cate can't be in there! She can't be in the cottage!" (meaning Cate could; meaning Lydia had reason to believe she might be), well, Nell had glimpsed a new horror that could still lie in wait for a widow who had survived the loss of her husband, and for a woman who, when she was still a girl, had survived the loss of her mother when she most needed one.

So Merle had puzzled over it all these years and figured out why an old friend, whom she had not laid eyes on in almost fifty years, had needed her shell. Imagine Merle thinking about Nell all these years, when Nell had given Merle—let's face it—scarcely a thought at all.

And yet, scarcely four hours ago, Nell had promised Merle that she would come and stay if Merle got ill again. Merle was ill; that was clear. And in several days, Nell would be driving the Chapins' car to Virginia. In the space of a few hours, everything had shifted. A cottage had burned down, a sick woman had been lifted away, accompanied by her anxious huband, into the sky— and everybody's plans had changed. Nature is a humbling force, thought Nell, whose mind was still ablaze with how *fast* the house had gone. And then, there lay poor Merle on the road. She had insisted on coming out in all that smoke: if your friend's house is burning down, the least you can do is stand by her and watch it burn.

Would they operate on Merle? What would they find? Nell was pretty certain they would find something. Would Merle still want her to stay? When faced with the real and immediate prospect rather than some distant, sentimental possibility, Nell was filled with uncertainty . . . and some embarrassment. Yet she felt sure that if they were in reversed places, Merle would drop everything and fly to Nell's bedside and devote herself to her friend completely.

And after all, what other duties do I have? thought Nell, who had been trained to put duty before pleasure, or peace, or "self-realization."

". . . and when you come home," Cate was saying, "I'll vacate the house the minute I get on your nerves."

"Don't be silly." Nell shelved her own dilemma for the moment. "Where would you go?"

"I'll take a room somewhere. I'll get a job as a waitress or a short-order cook. Don't worry. I won't do it *right in* Mountain City. That would embarrass you. It will do me good to get down to the realities. I've done too much sitting up in my ivory tower, complaining."

The last part was true, thought Nell, but why did Cate always have to go to extremes? "Look, if you want to cook or wait table, it's fine with me, and wherever you do it, it's not going to embarrass me." (Which was not wholly true.) "But why not use your time looking for another teaching job, and let me tide you over until—"

"Mother, I am not going to be another Taggart McCord, sponging off Mother every time she—"

"You are *not* Taggart McCord!" Nell's vehemence shocked them both. "You're alive; Taggart McCord's dead! When you're alive, you do what you *can* do. That's the duty, that's the privilege of the living. I'm not sure the rest matters very much. If you love me, if you honor me at all, you will accept what I offer out of love—and because I *have* it to offer. Otherwise"—Nell spread her arms in an exasperated gesture—"what has it all been *for?*"

Cate left the island the next day, on the early-afternoon ferry. Max had not arrived yet, but Cate's departure money had been provided indirectly by Lydia, who had cashed a check at the Inn and then "lent" the money to her mother, who then "lent" it to Cate. Cate knew all this, but her desire to leave was stronger than her desire to save face. But when Nell tried to give Cate back her shawl, Cate refused, saying she would never wear it again and that Nell should keep it for herself. Shortly before ferry time, Lydia drove up to the Hollowell house, and the sisters, in the presence of their mother, managed a decent, if guarded, farewell. Neither made any attempt to look the other in the eye.

And then Cate, sticking up her chin, drove off to the ferry, and, a few minutes later, underwent the chastening, somewhat haunting ordeal of having to pass, and then repass, the desolate view of the blackened remains of the cottage, as the ferry performed its circuitous route around the hazardous shoals. The wind of the day before had died down. The experience had the flavor of the last act of a Greek play, in which everything portended in the first act is fulfilled. Four days ago, at exactly this hour, the three of them had approached by this same route, passing and repassing their house. Had they been shown a vision of it as it was now, what would they have made of it? Would they have been able to predict the ways in which they would bring this vision to pass? Would they, even armed with their fore-knowledge, have been able to prevent it from happening? What one thing, had it been different, could have kept it from happening? Cate had some ideas on this last question, but none of them lightened her heart.

She had planned to drive straight through, in her usual style—the urgency and the exhaustion would have a purgative effect—but because of a warning twinge in her right jaw, decided to stop for the night in Goldsboro. In her Holiday Inn, she had dinner and washed it down with a bottle of wine, willing the incipient toothache to be a false alarm. Then, just to be on the safe side, she asked the waitress to bring her a double brandy in a paper cup to take to her room, where, with the additional aids of aspirin and sleep, she hoped to nip the toothache in the bud. Sometimes before, when she had been tired, the nerve of a tooth had jangled threateningly, but usually she had been able to pacify it again.

When she woke, the twinge, or whatever it was, hadn't gone away. Actually, it was more like an uncomfortably acute consciousness of the right side of her face: an unnatural sensitivity, that's what it felt like. She was on the road by seven, and crossed the state at a steady speed, with relatively little reflection. There was nothing like an awareness of something gone even slightly wrong in the body to diminish the urge to rehash or philosophize. Every hour that passed without the sudden, dreaded explosion of pain in the offended tooth (whichever one it should eventually reveal itself to be), she counted a victory. When she reached Old Fort, she placed a call to the dentist in Mountain City, that same Dr. Musgrove of the sporty plaid smock and the gold neck chain who had made her gold crown back in December, when she had bit down wrong on Dickie's peanut brittle. Although he was clearly less than pleased about the Sunday emergency, he agreed to meet her down at his office at the medical center in about an hour; she would go straight there. After all, the trouble was on the right side of the face, and might—Cate reminded him—be something to do with that same tooth, gone bad under its gold crown. The whole right side of her face was numb by now, and she was beginning to have trouble closing her right eye.

Within the hour, Cate sat humbly in the dentist's chair, allowing him to take as many "pictures" as he liked. Not a word did she utter concerning the dangers of unnecessary X rays. She was becoming a little scared, as she had never experienced such a lack of sensation in her life. It was as if, she told him, attempting to cheer herself up by an apt figure of speech, someone had taken an eraser and simply rubbed out the right half of her face—she traced the line of the eraser with her fingertip—from the middle of her forehead down to her neck.

"Well, it's not any *tooth* that I can see," he told her when he came back from developing the X rays. "It could be an insect bite ... although, in that case, there'd be facial swelling." He wrapped a black cloth tightly around the crook of her arm and began to take her blood pressure. "Now, if it were on the left side of your face, I'd say you'd be a good candidate for Bell's palsy."

"What's that?"

"Paralysis of the facial nerves. Wind can bring it on. Driving a car with the wind blowing on one side of the face is a frequent cause. But this isn't your driver's side. Hmm. Your pressure's a little high. Tell you what, I'm going to arrange for you to see a neurologist."

"Tomorrow?"

"No, today. I'm going to see if I can reach Dick Brant at home."

"I'm not really in *pain*," said Cate. "Don't you think it could wait until tomorrow?" She half hoped he would say yes; that would mean it wasn't serious.

"Frankly no. Whatever it is, the sooner we catch it, the more chance there is of full recovery."

Full recovery?

"Am I having a stroke?" asked Cate.

"Seems unlikely, but ... you sit right here in the chair," said the dentist. "I'm going to see if I can reach Dick Brant. And try to relax."

"Oh sure," said Cate, managing weak sarcasm.

The neurologist's office was in the same wing of this particular medical center. There was *something* to be said for these ugly, sprawling complexes where doctors bunched together.

Cate sat humbly in *his* chair while he poked needles around in the right side of her face and asked her to say when it hurt. He was still wearing his tennis clothes; he was tanned an almost brutal shade of brown, which rendered his immobile features even more expressionless. Cate wished he would talk more. She also wished the needles hurt more. Some of them she couldn't feel at all, even though she saw him stick them in.

"Sure looks like Bell's palsy," he said at last. "Have you been sleeping near a fan on that side, or an air conditioner?"

"I was walking in a lot of wind, day before yesterday. Could that have done it?"

"Might have. If it was localized on this side more than the other. Whatever did it, it's done. I'm going to put you on cortisone for three days. The sooner you get started, the better. And I'd advise complete rest for one week. Two, if you can manage it." He sat down on a high stool and began to scribble off a prescription. "And I want you to call me when you finish these. Or before, of course, if there are any complications."

"Wait a minute," Cate interrupted him. "I'm not sure I want to take cortisone. It's a very strong drug."

He looked up. The browned face registered surprise only by an infinitesimal enlargement of the whites of his eyes as he lifted his eyebrows. "That's why I'm giving it to you," he said. "The sooner we get started on those nerves, the less likely you'll be to have a facial disfigurement for the rest of your life."

"Is there . . . some chance of that?" She added one more charge against doctors to her thickening file of complaints: the way they always managed to win by scaring you if you questioned their authority.

"There is. Some cases recover completely, some partially;

some never get over it. Once, during my residency, I treated a woman whose family owned practically the whole town. But she never recovered. And you can be sure she had the best medical treatment."

"I'll take the cortisone," said Cate.

"It would be the wise thing." He went back to his scribbling. His tennis socks had a red stripe around each top. "Though even then, there's no complete guarantee. But we'll do the best we can. A lot depends on the body's natural healing capacities."

Cate kept looking at herself in the rearview mirror as she drove to the drugstore to get her prescription filled. Even when she kept her face perfectly still, the right side sagged a little. It was like one of those unkind photo simulations you sometimes saw in magazines, showing how beautiful or famous people would look in twenty years. And when she moved her mouth, the effect was grotesque. She almost drove off the road once, she alarmed herself so badly. How could she ever stand in front of a class and teach, with such a face? The worst part was the eye. It wouldn't close at all. The neurologist had advised her to buy a large pair of sunglasses and wear them whenever she had to go out, to prevent eye infections. How did a person sleep with one eye staring open?

She bought the largest pair of glasses she could find, and put them on while waiting for her prescription. Then she drove to Lake Hills, stopping at a bare-looking new ranch-style house to pick up Mother's extra set of keys (the originals had been in Nell's burned-up purse) from some neighbors. They were a young couple trying desperately to hold on to this house, which they had waited so long to build. Just after they had moved in, the husband had been laid off at his textile plant, and, though the wife still had her good job as a legal secretary, the man mowed lawns and did light landscaping work and even watered houseplants when his client-neighbors went away. He was watering a young birch in his own front yard when Cate drove in, and did not seem to notice her face when she asked for the set of keys.

Either he was being polite or he had his own problems, she decided.

The first thing she did, out of weariness and preoccupation with her illness, was activate the burglar alarm by accident. She forgot to turn the little key which switched the red light to green, before unlocking the main door. She phoned Safeguard Systems to report her mistake. "Code number?" asked a woman. "Look, I don't know the goddamned code number. Our house at the beach burned down and we had other things on our mind." "Could I have your name?" And then Cate had to spell "Galitsky" twice for the woman, who couldn't seem to get it through her head that Cate could have a different name from Mrs. Strickland's and still be her daughter. Perhaps she should just have kept things simple and given her name as Cate Strickland, to start with.

She took her first cortisone pill in the kitchen, and stood at the row of windows above the sink, looking out at the familiar mountain ranges turning their late-afternoon purples. She gazed at their peaks, which had always reminded her of great slumbering beasts, in a kind of hypnotic despair. Here she was, in the same place she had started from: her parents' house. In fifteen days she would be forty years old. And—in Lydia's hateful words—nothing to show for it. How had this happened? What ought she to do about it? What could she do about it? Mother's impassioned words, as the two of them had sat, gazing out at where their cottage had been, came back to her: "You do what you *can* do. That's the duty, that's the privilege of the living."

"What can I do?" Cate asked her old friends, the mountains. She felt her mouth pull to one side and realized she had spoken aloud. What *may* I do, was more like it, given the progressive diminishment of all that was hers. If she had still believed in God, she would have asked Him, "What are You going to *let* me do? Is there some kind of message You're trying to send me by divesting me of everything I have?"

As she slowly climbed the stairs, the ghosts of her arrogant young dreams clustered around her like frightened children seeking protection from the lengthening shadows. The light in the house was at that dreaded melancholy-orange stage that had always set off her claustrophobia. All her life, even before she had anything to run from, she had been fleeing this thickening, dusty half-light, as if it possessed some spiritual chemical that could destroy her. Now she knew what the chemical was composed of: it was made up of all the ingredients of her own history—those she could control and those she could not. She had been fleeing from the premonition of just such a moment as this, when that history would have had enough time to assume a shape.

Her room looked as if it had been freshly painted in the melancholy color: everything was bathed in the reproachful orange. Her room! Was this where all her running had landed her? Right back, face-to-face with the young Cate who had lain on that bed and stared out that window and made bold and sweeping plans for the romance of her future? How infinite the possibilities had seemed; how limitless the frontiers! But now, many of the possibilities had been exhausted, or tried and found wanting, or rejected beforehand in favor of a better possibility that might never be forthcoming. And the frontiers were shrinking. Deterioration had set in. When even an angry walk on a windy beach exacts such a price, one comes to the end of one's romance about oneself, and one's entitlement to limitless fresh starts. There were no more physical frontiers—this side of the grave—where she could seek refuge from her history or her ghosts.

And so she lay down with them, in her girlhood bed, under the crumbling Klee poster, *Saint at a Window*. She was wearing one of her mother's nightgowns, as hers had been burned up in the cottage. For the first time in her life that she could recall, she went to bed without looking in the mirror first.

Propped on pillows, she watched the sun descend in the western sky until, at last, it hid itself partially behind great Pisgah and its ratlike junior peaks; and then, as if eager to be done with that day, it plunged out of sight.

As light ebbed from the room, she felt, with relief and a certain interest, her own resistance merging into the growing obscurity: its hard center seemed to break slowly into fragments and disperse. Resistance to what? It had been her stance for so long that it had become a way of life. She felt her actions, to date, had been paid for. The problems ahead, while they did not solve themselves, seemed to be dissolving, like the light, into the rich, gathering dark. Could this be the effect of the cortisone? She could not say she felt hopeful, but neither did she miss the hope. Her characteristically tensed, charged readiness—a kind of athletic readiness—for Whatever Came Next relaxed into a different kind of readiness: a bemused, restful offering of herself to whatever out there in the growing darkness would have her . . . or would know what to do with her. As she lay there, not sleeping, but with her breathing growing calmer and deeper, she felt both sentenced and redeemed. And accepted both.

At about nine o'clock, she took another cortisone pill and went downstairs to open a can of soup, which she was doing when the door chimes rang. Grabbing her father's old raincoat from the hall closet, she slipped it over her nightgown. She caught a weird glimpse of herself in the oval mirror. With the unfamiliar clothes and the twisted face, she looked like some degenerate interloper.

The man at the door must have thought so, too, because he instinctively reached inside his windbreaker, the way men in detective movies reach for hidden guns.

It was Jerome Ennis, ex–football star from her high school. She recognized him at once, despite the added flesh and unfriendly look. He was still quite attractive. He had come over to check on her call to Safeguard Systems. "It was the second time in one week you all had called in, and I thought I'd check to see if something in the system wasn't working right. I just came back from driving my wife down to Gastonia, and when I saw the strange name in the log, and no code number, I decided I'd better hit your place before I turned in."

"Did you marry Teenie?" asked Cate.

"Hell, she wouldn't of let me marry anybody else." He

smiled his old cocky smile for the first time. Her question must have removed any doubts in his mind that she was a twisted-faced burglar in disguise, trying to pose as the daughter of the house.

"Won't you come in? I was just making myself some soup. I've come down with Bell's palsy, from being out in the wind, but it's not catching. The doctor tells me if I'm lucky my face won't stay like this."

"I thought you looked a little peculiar when you answered the door," said Jerome. "I knew a guy in basic training got that, from driving around with the window opened. He got over it pretty quick, as I remember."

"That's the best news I've heard all day." Cate smiled up at him, then instinctively put her hand to her cheek when she felt how grotesque she must look.

"Maybe I will come in, just for a minute," said Jerome. "Did your mother tell you what I got over in Nam?" He stuck out a stiff trouser leg. He was wearing cowboy boots.

"She did. I was sorry to hear it. But you're looking great, Jerome."

"I feel great. He followed her into the kitchen with a swinging, slightly off-balance walk. "I'm getting along just fine. Lots worse happened to guys I knew. Did you know you were in here without your alarm system on? The light was on green. Somebody could of broke right in."

"I would have scared him off with this face," said Cate, emptying a can of Campbell's chicken noodle into a saucepan.

"Mountain City's changed," he said, looking around the kitchen with interest, as if he might be comparing its amenities with his own. "People keep their doors locked now; it's not like when we were growing up. I'm expanding my business to include a Patrol Service. You know, the thieves check the papers for weddings, and then they go to the bride's home while everybody's at church and make off with all the presents. My son Johnny's in business with me now; the Patrol's going to be his baby."

"God, Jerome, you have a son that old?"

"Hell, I'll be forty-two in August. Teenie's going on forty, though she don't look it. You must be getting up there yourself."

"I'll be there in two weeks. Would you like a drink?"

"You wouldn't have a beer, would you?"

There was no beer. Jerome settled for a scotch. "Chivas Regal! Fancy stuff."

"My father liked it. It's left over from before he died."

"Yeah, we saw about that, in the paper. Teenie's father passed away, too. No more secret-formula barbecue sauce. He left Teenie and her sister a right nice inheritance each. Sissy spent hers on a damn Porsche. Teenie used hers to invest in this nursery school she and some friends started in town."

"Teenie sounds like a sensible woman," said Cate, who had not really known Teenie that well. She had seated herself to Jerome's right, so he would be spared her worst contortions as she slurped her soup.

"I'll send her over to see you when she gets back. She's due back Friday. Sissy's gone and had herself another baby, so Teenie and our girls went down to help out."

"How old are your girls?"

"Six and sixteen. The little 'un's a kind of celebration for my coming back. I was flown home in 'seventy-two and old Melody came along about nine months later. You have any children?"

"No."

"Didn't you marry some Air Force guy? But not the name I saw in the log tonight. I'm sure of that."

"Pringle was my first husband, the one in the Air Force."

"He didn't leave you a *widow,* did he?" Jerome looked at her with growing respect.

"No, we got divorced. Later he went to Vietnam. Now he lives in Texas."

"So what about this other name in the log?"

"Jake Galitsky was my second husband. We're divorced." She saw no reason to complicate Jerome's view of her post–high-school life further by adding that Jake had been in a mental institution for the past six years.

"You've had a tough time," said Jerome, rattling the ice in

his scotch. He studied her from under his light eyebrows. "Teenie and I almost got divorced once. That's when I enlisted. I figured I'd be better off fighting gooks than fighting my wife. And my first business venture flopped. I had me a little camera and record store. But the kids would come in and steal me blind. The same ones who made all those *protests* so they wouldn't have to go over there and risk their skins. Well, the hell with them. All that's over. Since I've been back, it seems everything I touch turns to gold. Got all the business I can handle, and Teenie and I don't fight anymore. Guess I paid the price, eh?" He tapped his false leg with a fingernail. It made a resonant *pok-pok* sound. Then he pondered something for a moment and looked up at her and laughed. "You know what Teenie used to call you, back when you were all in Boosters together?"

"No, what?"

He laughed some more. "No, I probably shouldn't tell you."

"You have to, now. You can't start and not finish." (The echo of Lydia's words came back to her.) "Come on, what did Teenie call me?"

"You won't be mad?"

"I promise."

He slugged back the last of his fancy scotch. "Joan of Arc." He laughed. "Because you were always crusading for causes."

He was relieved when Cate laughed, too. But she kept her palm over the right side of her face to hide the distortion. Would she have the bad luck to turn out like that rich woman the doctor mentioned rather than the good luck of Jerome's friend in basic training?

Jerome refused a second scotch. "You look like you could use some rest. How long you going to be in town?"

She explained about her mother and the burned cottage and how she herself was between jobs.

"What kind of job are you looking for?"

"Teaching. If my face improves. I can't very well stand in front of a class with a face like one of those old drama masks, smiling on one side and crying on the other. Meanwhile, I'll take anything where I can be useful."

"Maybe Teenie could use you in her nursery school. She needs someone to stay there all the time. This woman they have is getting too old. The girls run it on a rotation system, see, each of them takes a turn, but this one woman stays there all the time. She has a nice apartment on the premises and all. Would you be interested in that?"

"No, thank you," Cate said, laughing a bit sharply. "I don't think I want to be quite *that* useful."

Jerome looked offended. But then he shrugged and said good-naturedly, "It wouldn't be for you, I guess. Well, I've got to go. Old Johnny'll be wondering what's kept me." He reached underneath the table, and Cate could see him adjusting the position of his false leg, which had been stretched out straight. Tensing his powerful arms against the seat of his chair, he hauled himself up.

"I'm sorry you have to go," Cate said. "I was enjoying your company." She hadn't meant to hurt his feelings about Teenie's nursery school.

"Maybe I'll drop by tomorrow evening," he surprised her by replying. "See how you're getting on."

She accompanied him to the front door. "Now I want you to lock that door after me," he said, "and turn that system on. I want to see that little button turn red."

"Oh, all right," said Cate, giving him an amused look. Then there was a funny moment when she could swear he was going to kiss her. She quickly made up her mind to let him—after all he'd been through. But he only touched her face, on the stiff side.

"Don't worry, it'll get better," he said.

He waited outside until she turned on the system. Cate switched on the porch light and watched him down the walk. He had developed for himself a sort of swinging, giant-step gait, which, though it emphasized his fake leg, made it clear that he intended to use it, that special piece of equipment, to get there as quickly, maybe quicker, than someone with ordinary legs.

By the time Nell phoned, late Monday afternoon, Cate could almost close her right eye again, though the rest of her face hadn't shown much progress. She had debated whether or not to tell Mother she had Bell's palsy. On the one hand, it was nice to have sympathy, and also her illness might redeem her a little for letting the cottage burn down. But on the other hand, Mother might feel obligated to rush home, when, Cate suspected strongly, she'd really rather nurse her long-lost old school friend. That would certainly be more satisfying that knocking about in the old nuclear-family pressure cooker with an aging prodigal daughter. Besides, thought Cate, I'm nursing myself perfectly well and—to be frank—I like having the house to myself.

Nell was getting ready to lock up the Hollowell cottage and drive to Virginia in the Chapins' car. She was uncertain of her plans after that. She seemed to be working them out as she talked to Cate. Merle was set on her staying at their house for a few weeks, at least. "I want to finish our reunion!" was how Merle had put it. In Norfolk, they had done an open lung biopsy and decided to treat the tumor they had found in the interstices of the lungs with a combination of chemotherapy and cortisone. The treatments could be administered in Gloucester, where Merle could have them from her own doctor.

"But why didn't they cut the tumor out?" Cate asked.

Nell sighed. "The chemotherapy will shrink it enough to keep her comfortable. Oh Cate, I'm afraid it's what they call 'palliation' treatment, though nobody's said so. Merle is so determined to be brave and see the hopeful side of things."

"Do you think there *is* a hopeful side?"

"As long as there's life, there's hope. And so much depends on the individual. They know for a fact that tumors shrink more in optimistic people than in pessimistic ones. She's a very optimistic person. What worries me is ... well ... where do I fit into this? Marcus says she has her heart set on my staying with her, and I promised I would go, but ... it's awkward! I mean, shouldn't they have this time to themselves? If you want to know the truth, I don't know what to do."

"What do you want to do?"

"Oh, want!" Nell scoffed. "I was getting along just fine puttering in the garden and watching my crows. But my garden will be there, and there will be next summer's crows. How are they, by the way?"

"They're keeping fit. They woke me at five this morning."

After a pause, Nell said, "I *can* make her comfortable. And we're old friends. And they have so little money for hired nurses. Perhaps ... if you wouldn't mind packing my summer things and sending them on ... oh, and Max has already called Mr. Bowers at our bank. Go on up there and sign your name, and our joint account is officially open. I've put three thousand in; I can always put more."

"Old Max flew in, then, and settled everything?"

"Very handsomely. He wants to buy the land and build a duplex cottage in the boys' names. Until they're old enough to use it, the rental income will be theirs."

"That's handsome, all right."

"He feels guilty, I think."

"Why should *he* feel guilty?"

"He's thinking of marrying again, when the divorce comes through. After all his protestations of undying love for Lydia. He and Lydia discussed it when he came, that's how I know. She didn't seem particularly upset. She told me she has a boyfriend, though she's not thinking of marrying."

"Who on earth is Max thinking of marrying?" Cate did not feel like discussing her sister just yet.

"Lizzie Broadbelt. The granddaughter. She works in the bank now."

"That's convenient, isn't it?"

"Isn't it!" Nell permitted herself a short laugh. "But I like Max. He will do right by everybody. It gives him pleasure to do it." A pause. "Cate, am *I* doing right to go on up there and stay in their guest room? If only ... this sounds terrible, but I don't mean it that way ... if only I had some idea of *how long.* I know she wouldn't expect me to stay on and on...." Her voice trailed away on a distraught note.

Cate decided not to mention the Bell's palsy. "You do what you *can* do, Mother. It's the duty and privilege of the living. Remember?"

Nell laughed. "Well, fancy your remembering my advice."

"Miracles do happen," replied Cate.

"Oh," said Nell, more somberly. "If only one would happen for poor Merle!"

Awhile later, Jerome Ennis phoned. "How's the face?"

"It's actually better. My eye almost closes."

"What'd I tell you?" He sounded as if he had worked the magic himself. "Look, I'm planning to knock off here soon. If I brought you some Chinese food, would you eat it? There's a pretty good takeout place here."

"Well ... sure," said Cate, her mind quickly processing possible permutations if Jerome Ennis, already speaking in that protective tone, brought Chinese food to the house. "That's very kind of you, to want to do that," she added. Maybe I can keep things on a simple, friendly level, she thought: two high-school acquaintances, the former president of the debating team and the former captain of the football team, one chastened, one harrowed by life, get together for a little Chinese food. I mean, we were worlds apart then; we still are now.

Who do you think you're kidding? the voice of experience laughed, as she sat in front of her mirror and tried various ways of pinning her hair to offset the lopsided face.

Nevertheless, she would look back on the week with a special, tender amusement. She would come to think of it as The Healing Week, though she kept its contents discreetly to herself. In her fortune cookie, included with the Chinese meal, had been the message LEARN FROM THE MISTAKES OF OTHERS. YOU CAN'T MAKE THEM ALL YOURSELF. It set the tone, somehow; that and the touchingly dainty expertise with which Jerome handled his chopsticks. They had both been over these mountains and back, and here they still were, survivors of mishaps caused by themselves and others, but able to laugh and enjoy a good meal despite it all. They could enjoy each other: the crusading debater who could, at the moment, talk out of only one side of her mouth, and the football hero who'd left part of his leg in a rice field. One person couldn't do it all, but two persons might do a lot for each other, even in a week.

It was a surprisingly sweet week—or rather, five days—for Cate. Once more, The Unexpected had proved itself her ally. She woke with the crows, watched the room fill with light, then went to the mirror to check her face. Each morning of the first week brought dramatic improvement, though it would be a year before she regained full use of the muscles. (And she would always look slightly asymmetrical to herself in mirrors.)

After breakfast, she sat propped in a little nest of pillows in Mother's bed (where, on Monday night, she had moved to accommodate her lover) and wrote letters, in varying styles and tones, alerting those who might be interested and able to do something about it to her availability in the job market. Luckily most of the addresses were care of some English department, as her address book had been lost in the fire. She ended up writing Mimi Vandermark, her former student and admirer (c/o Astra Foundation, 2 Park Avenue: she remembered that address), a wry-witty, four-page account of her adventures and journeys since 1970, when she had been fired from the girls' school for her Cambodian protest. There: Mimi would enjoy the letter, would perhaps laugh aloud at parts. Cate did not mention her Chicago ordeal, but she could not resist a short paragraph about her weekend at the castle and her proposal from the Pesticide Baron.

Another reason it was a healing week was that, after Jernigan, Cate wondered if she would ever want to make love with another man. She did. Though, in many ways, Jerome was like Jernigan. He loved the "taking-care" part. He mailed off the box of her mother's clothes; he took charge (or rather, he had his secretary take charge) of replacing all Nell's and Cate's burned-up credit cards; he even said things that reminded her of Jernigan. When, for instance, lying next to her, Jerome had summed up his feelings about Vietnam by concluding, "Well, I didn't save the Vietnamese from Communism, but I guess I can save my hometown from a bunch of thieves," Cate had heard echoes of Jernigan's gruffer, Midwestern voice: "I believe in taking care of what is mine."

I guess, thought Cate, I'm one of those women who don't want to be taken care of by a man, but want him to offer—and to be able to back his offer, if the need arises. Marrying Jernigan was one thing. Whereas Teenie would be back on Friday.

In closing her letter to Mimi Vandermark, Cate wrote: "I was so terribly sorry to hear of the loss of your baby. To have a little *person*, to have time enough to discover all the ways in which he is uniquely lovable, uniquely himself, and then to lose him, is a sorrow beyond my imagination. I wouldn't dare try to console you, but please know I feel it with you, as much as anyone can without having suffered it herself."

Teenie Ennis "called on" Cate during the middle of Cate's second week in her mother's house. It was a slightly stiff visit, Teenie having obviously been told by Jerome . . . what would he have told Teenie? "Listen, hon, go on over to Lake Hills and see old Joan of Arc. Remember, from the Boosters? I know you two weren't best friends, or anything like that, but she's had a hard time. Lost her job, their beach house burned down, then on top of everything she came down with that palsy. I tried to help her out a little last week."

Teenie sat on the edge of Daddy's favorite blue chair and sipped a glass of iced orange juice. She had wanted a Coke, but Cate didn't have any. She looked very much as she had in high school: her pert-featured prettiness had simply hardened into a sharper version of itself. She inquired tentatively into Cate's life after high school, expressing the praise that was expected of her for Cate's higher degrees and travel experiences. She skirted indelicate subjects, such as divorces, joblessness, and childlessness: Jerome must have filled her in there. But when Cate, pretending interest in Teenie's nursery school, tried to inject some life into the dreary visit, Teenie warmed up. She spoke animatedly of the problems and successes of her venture with the relish of the obsessed businesswoman. She lamented how Mrs. Murphy, their mainstay, was getting too old, and they were looking for another live-in woman to help her, but did not make the mistake of thinking Cate might be interested in the job. Accepting a second glass of orange juice so she could complete the tale of her successes, Teenie told how her school had a waiting list, how it had such a good reputation that some people—"some of the best people in town"—were now enrolling their children before birth. Teenie and her partners were thinking seriously of expanding to include an infant center.

"Well," said Cate, "it's an idea whose time has certainly come."

But something in the lazy, ironic tone of Cate's voice froze Teenie again. She looked carefully at Cate to see if some sort of slight had been intended; apparently decided it hadn't; then, thanking Cate for the delicious juice, rose to go.

As they walked together to the front door, Teenie, who was about five inches shorter than Cate—thus the high-school nickname that had stuck—looked Cate up and down. "Your face isn't bad at all," she said. "It doesn't even show when you aren't talking. I expected much worse."

"Well, thank you," said Cate dryly.

"Now you must come and see me while you're still in Mountain City," said Teenie, flashing Cate a sociable, dimpled smile.

"When I get organized, I certainly will," said Cate.

"I'll look forward to that," said Teenie. They were at the door. With just an edge of warning in her voice, she added, "Jerome said you'd been having trouble with the alarm system. Have you learned how to work it now?"

"I've got everything under control now," replied Cate. "Jerome shouldn't have any more alarms from this address. That is, unless a *real* thief gets in."

"Well," said Teenie, her point having been made, "don't forget to come and see me, hear?"

"I won't!" said Cate sweetly.

The women parted, each happy in the knowledge that she would probably not be seeing the other again.

Teenie missed my thief innuendo, thought Cate later, but

that's okay; on the whole, we conducted ourselves pretty well, exactly like the Southern Ladies we were raised to be.

On her fortieth birthday, Cate received a card from Mother and one from Lydia's son Dickie. "Merle is putting up a splendid fight," wrote Mother. "Meanwhile, it makes me feel better that someone's in the house. You may have to hold the fort for the whole summer. I am doing what I can here, and, I must say, it is appreciated. Please buy yourself a bottle of good wine or champagne and drink to your own happiness. I have faith in you."

"I'm at Brevard Music Camp again," wrote Dickie. "We are playing lots of good music, but they starve us at meals. Happy Birthday, Aunt Cate. Please come out and see me when you can. Bring some more peanut brittle, ha, ha."

Cate detected Lydia behind Dickie's card, as this was the first one he'd ever sent her on his own. She could hear Lydia driving Dickie to camp: "Oh, and be sure and send your aunt Cate a birthday card. Don't forget. Do it for me." That would be Lydia's style: delegating to Dickie the upkeep of "family solidarity" so she could hold her grudge with impunity.

The Unexpected also had two surprises for Cate on her fortieth birthday. They were in order of appearance, a small family revelation and an interesting reconciliation.

The first occurred when she went out to Big Sandy to visit Uncle Osgood. She had not seen the old man since Daddy's funeral, when he had asked about her "purty black-haired" Jake, and told her to come and see him again.

How shamefully we neglect the old, thought Cate; for it had been twelve years since she and Jake had gone to Osgood's. That day, she had purposely taken the long, circuitous route, going miles out of her way, because she had wanted Jake to have the pure, dramatic approach to Big Sandy, that high and isolated kingdom of peaks and hollows out of which she, through her father, partially derived.

But today she drove the direct route, which had been "built up" since her childhood and led through an uninspiring clutter of Discount Citys, shoe factory outlets, car washes, and fast-food chains—all the eyesores of twentieth-century progress on display. Yet she was a product of her century and its consequences and corruptions. More so, really, than she was a product of Osgood's uncorrupted mountain. So there was a certain justice in her driving this route, as if the God of Progress were saying, You can't expect to drive your modern car up into the unadulterated mountain cove of your ancestors in less than one hour without paying some price.

Jake had not been willing to pay *any* price, to tolerate any amount of adulteration of his dreams. Which was why her practicalities (such as going out to work every day, into the corrupted bourgeois world he despised, in order to feed them) had made him cease loving her. Which was also probably why he eventually found the whole outside world intolerable and opted out through madness.

I might have done better to have taken him this route twelve years ago, thought Cate. To have led him safely through the detestable realities while we were still connected by passion. I might have saved him if I had tried to protect him less. But I wanted it to be perfect for him, a flawless, memorable day. As it was. For as long as we stayed together, he never stopped raving about the day we went to see Uncle Osgood. That day was one of the few that lived up to his standards of purity: the breathtaking approach, up from the river into the first of the alpine valleys with their fresh-plowed, rich, dark, clayey fields; and the steep, grassy pastures with their strange, terracelike indentations. Jake had looked out of the car window and pronounced the strange grassy stairsteps the mysterious handiwork of the old gods, before man came and spoiled everything.

But Cate had explained, as her father had explained to her, that the indentations on the slopes came from generations of cows, ridging the hills as they grazed.

She could still see Jake's dark, nervous eyes glowing at her with a mixture of hostility and respect as she explained about the cows. He would have preferred the story of the gods, but was impressed by her knowledge. They were not yet into the bad times, when he would regard any intelligence from her as an outright attack on his precarious, illusion-structured world.

Now Roger Jernigan would not have minded this "impure" route to Osgood's. He would have got a kick out of the contrasts. Cate smiled to herself as she saw the road she was driving through Jernigan's sharp and curious eyes. He would take in the spectacle of the ugly chain stores, wondering aloud which suppliers were local, which out-of-state; he would want to know, as the road grew narrower and snaked upward into the hilly farmlands, where the people who lived in those trailers worked, the ones who didn't farm; what did the factories around here make? He would have something to say about those two turkeys racing around that trailer that sat by itself on a lonely hill: were they pets, or were they destined to be a little extra income around Thanksgiving? He would appreciate, as she did, the incongruous sight of a cow grazing next to an overturned pink bathtub set in the middle of the treeless lawn of a brand-new, rather pretentious brick house. They would perhaps discuss how progress itself was a sum of incongruities which you either accepted, as best you could, or else (as he had put it, that first night he had walked into her office, sat down, and plucked off his cap, exposing a headful of electrically charged hair) "it plows you under. I'm not ready to become fertilizer yet."

She missed Jernigan; missed his bright curiosity, the way he saw things; his sturdy style of enduring his fate; his pragmatic, uncringing attitude toward his mistakes.

One nice thing about not running from your history anymore (as she had given up trying to do) was that you could incorporate into yourself the people who had meant something, even if the experience itself had hurt. Jerome Ennis had helped her incorporate Jernigan. Having satisfied herself that Jernigan had not ruined men for her forever, she could allow herself to remember him fondly. She could even *become* Jernigan a little bit; could absorb into herself the strengths and qualities she admired in and needed from Jernigan.

And she did need them. Though she could never, never,

never have married him and gone to live in that castle in order to get them.

She drove as far as she could up into Osgood's cove, then parked her car next to a pasture gate and completed the climb by foot up Osgood's terrible road. She had to stop several times to get her breath. The air was thinner up here, but it felt good. The road seemed different, somehow; neatened up. The angle was as steep as ever, but someone had graded out the potholes and removed the large rocks.

Alarmed, Cate wondered if—? But surely, if anything had happened to Osgood, the family would have been informed.

She crested the hill, one hand on her heart, which was beating rapidly from the climb. There was nobody on the porch, but Osgood's chair was there. Maybe history would repeat itself and her voice would summon his old legs out of one of the apple trees, as it had twelve years ago.

"Osgood?" she called, heading for the orchard. She walked through the rows of low, curling trees, scanning the leafy branches for a sign of dangling legs.

Then she collided with a bare-chested creature in jeans, wearing the face of a bug. She screamed before she could stop herself, even after her mind had registered that the apparition was a young man wearing a gas mask. He had put down his spray pump against the side of a tree, and was already unfastening the mask.

"Scared you, huh?" He was very young, no more than fifteen or sixteen. But his childish features were alight with his power, as Cate embraced the bark of a tree, panting furiously.

"I just didn't . . . expect you," she said when she got herself in hand. "I was looking for my cousin Osgood." The boy was watching her face as she talked. Probably fascinated by the asymmetry caused by the Bell's palsy. A whole scenario flashed across her mind: Osgood dead, the house and land sold, the son of the new owner spraying the orchard; or, Osgood gone to a retirement home, having sold his place to finance his last days. Dexter Everby, who was always prowling around here, could have arranged it all, without the family's knowing—it would be in his interest if the family didn't know.

One more lost opportunity to add to the pile. Why hadn't she come sooner, kept in touch, cultivated this last living scion of the Strickland line?

"Last I saw, he was up at the chicken house, playing with his silkies," said the boy.

"Then who are you?"

"I'm his summer aide."

"His what?"

"It's a project at our school. We live with an Appalachian family for the summer, help out and all, take down their stories and learn their crafts. You get credit for it, just like a real course."

"You're living here with Osgood?"

"Been here for two weeks. Boy, there sure was a lot to do around here. Berry and I couldn't even get our Jeep up his road till we cleared it. Did you notice how much better the road was?"

"I did. Who is Berry?"

"He's the other aide. Usually there's only one aide to a house, but old Grandpop said he'd take two of us, being as how he was all alone. He's a real old-timer, isn't he? None of the other aides got anyone near as interesting. Berry's gone to town to pick up some more spray."

"And what's your name?"

"Oh, I'm Rick." He swelled out his chest, which was still more boyish than mannish. He looked quite pleased with himself as he offered her a firm, sweaty handshake.

"I'm Cate."

"Please to meet you, ma'am."

Cate gave a surprised laugh. That's right, to this boy she was "ma'am." This was her fortieth birthday, after all. "Well, same here," she said. "I'm sure you're going to get an A in your summer course, Rick. See you later." She started up a further hill, to Osgood's chicken house.

The old man stood with his back to her, surrounded by a semicircle of Chinese silkies, their soft white floating feathers covering them all over except for their black beaks and black toes. The sun, starting its afternoon descent, lit up Osgood's thin hair as if it were gossamer; his shoulders looked painfully frail without a coat. He appeared to be in rapt communication with the fluffy white chickens before they saw her and scattered with clucks of annoyance.

Osgood turned to see what had startled them. The absence of a normal nose was always a shock, no matter how you prepared yourself. If my crooked face lasts, thought Cate, I will have to learn to prepare myself for other people's curiosity, or their careful preparations to keep from showing anything.

"Well, hello, young lady," said Osgood, ambling forward on his cane. "You've come out to see me, have you?"

They sat on Osgood's porch, sipping Dr Peppers. Their view encompassed a widening V-shape of valley and a ridge above that was changing by the minute as the sun made its afternoon passage. The wind was soft and visible. A rooster crowed repeatedly. The other summer aide, Berry, had bumped up the hill in an old camouflaged Army Jeep, and from time to time the boys' voices could be heard, calling out to each other as they finished spraying the orchard.

"Them boys is good, but they talk me to death," said Osgood. "Sometimes I go to bed early, just to stop talking." He put down his Dr Pepper can and rummaged in a cardboard box until he found the piece of wood and the tool he wanted. He sat back in his chair, with a little snort, and began nudging the wood with the tool until it lost its edge.

"What do they talk about?" asked Cate, who suddenly felt perfectly happy sitting here, talking or not, watching the changes in the blue valley, being part of the landscape.

"They make me talk, that's what. Everything from what I recall about my folks to how I make my corn bread. They get me wound up. I have to go to bed to *stop* talking. You ever hear me talk so much?"

Cate hadn't, but she didn't want to discourage him. "You're fascinating to them, Uncle Osgood. The things you know and take for granted are very exciting and pioneering to them. They're having the time of their lives. I'm sure they wouldn't work this hard at home, for their own parents."

"Oh, they're good boys. Their cooking don't always turn out. They tried to make some brownies in the Dutch oven, the way I taught 'em to do the corn bread, over the coals. Them brownies tasted awful funny. Dusty or something. I et one and it give me so bad a headache I had to go for a walk. But them boys was just crowing with pleasure over those brownies. They called 'em their Alice-be-something brownies. They got all silly and began dancin' around and I didn't have the heart to complain about the dust."

"Alice B. *Toklas*?"

"That's it! You ever had any?"

"Yes," said Cate. "I wouldn't eat too many, Uncle Osgood, if they make them again."

"Don't you worry," said Osgood.

They sat on quietly for a while, Osgood patiently shaping his piece of wood, Cate drinking in the enchantment of this lovely cove. What if her grandfather Strickland had decided this cove was all he wanted out of life? And had his family out here. And some other version of her father had married and had some version of her. A country Cate. Would she have been very different from the self that sat on this porch? She might have been a grandmother by now. On the other hand, if the country Cate had been anything like the city Cate, she would have fled these mountains as soon as she could, to see what was on the other side.

"How long you stayin' this time?" asked Osgood.

Cate told Osgood all her recent history, beginning with the closing of Melanchthon and ending with the fire. "So Mother's letting me stay in her house while she's nursing this old school friend in Virginia. I've been writing letters for another job. And then I came down with this nerve paralysis from walking in the wind. Haven't you noticed anything strange about my face, Uncle Osgood?"

She turned her face to him. "Tell me, honestly."

The old man stopped his work and looked up. Then Cate felt appalled at her tactlessness: drawing attention to her facial abnormality when his was so much worse. But he didn't seem to make any connection or comparison. He studied her face like a problem. She noticed for the first time how beautiful his eyes were. Even set in their droopy sockets, the clear green of the irises changed into a startling brown around the rims of the pupils.

"Now you speak of it," said Osgood, "it looks like you might have yourself a little toothache. But you're still purty enough. Won't it get better?"

"The doctor says I'm showing good progress. Which is true. You should have seen me two weeks ago. God! Well, I brought it on myself, storming around in that wind."

"Well," said Osgood, dipping his head down to his carving again, "I brought my ugly nib on myself, too."

This was the first time Cate had ever heard Osgood refer to his War injury. "It's hardly the same thing, Uncle Osgood. You got your . . . injury . . . in the line of duty. Mine was pure carelessness. You got yours in the *War*."

Osgood went on shaving the wood, almost as if he had not heard Cate's reply. But then, without missing a beat with his knife, he said, "I never got to no War. Didn't yore daddy ever tell you that?"

He's getting senile, thought Cate sadly. "On the contrary, Uncle Osgood. Daddy often said he admired your bravery."

"Hnn." The old man snorted through the ragged cartilage of his nose. "If he said that, he must of meant something else."

Scrape, scrape, went Osgood's knife. Cate did not know what to say. Perhaps it would be kinder not to try to argue him out of his delusion. Most old soldiers exaggerated their former prowess, but if Osgood had chosen to deny his altogether, wasn't that his business? Maybe each old person had to construct his own mythical tapestry to the specifications of a pall he would feel comfortable lying under. She supposed she ought to be getting back to town.

"When yore daddy was a young man, he come out here one

day all het up to go fight in Spain," said Osgood, just as she was preparing to offer some practical excuse for leaving. "I could see he was divided in his mind, so I told him what I had never told another living soul. God bless that boy. He sure could keep a secret. But you're his child, so I'll tell you what I told him. Me and this boy got in a fight down at Camp Greene, Charlotte, just before we was to get shipped off to France. We'd been drinking likker, and he called me a name and I called him one, and afore either one of us knew it, there we was on the ground. I got one of his eyes, he bit off my nose. Chewed it plumb off. They almost saved the eye. I watched them changing bandages on it in the hospital. We was in the same ward. The day we heard that eye of his had to come out, we both cried like babies. We was both so sick and ashamed of ourselves. Neither one of us had the nerve to go home, we was too ashamed to face our people. So the Army let us finish out the Great War not ten miles away from where you and me sit right now. Our folks never found out. They thought we was overseas fighting the Huns, and all the time we was guards up at this prison camp they had at Hot Springs for some Germans that was seized off civilian ships when the War broke out. Harmless fellers, not even soldiers, but they had to keep 'em someplace. We'd get them cabbage from the local farms and they showed us how to make sauerkraut. That feller who bit off my nose is dead now. But we used to exchange Christmas cards every year, after we got out of the Army. He married a girl, but it didn't last. I got to where I used to look out for that Christmas card. In some ways, me and him was close. Seems strange, don't it? When we ruined one another like that. The only way I can figure yore daddy meant my bravery was that I've lived quiet with my foolishness without inflicting any more of it on any living soul. I told him that day because it seemed right. Him wanting to fly off over there and fight because he thought he ought to. 'Make sure things is right at home first,' I told him"—and the old man took the blade of his knife and tapped the handle against his chest—" 'if things ain't right at home, you won't make them right anywhere else. You're like to do more harm than good.' Just between you and me, I think he was plain relieved to be talked out of going. Leonard was a gentle boy. Now I was an ornery critter. If I hadn't of gotten into that fight with Percy Clamp, I'd of killed somebody sure as anything before too long. And I don't just mean Huns. Percy Montraville Clamp, from Rock Hill. You ever hear such a fancy name in your life? I told him what I thought of it after he called me an ignorant hillbilly. For that, we ruined our lives. Animals have better sense. At least they fight for something they *need*."

Cate sat back in her chair. She gazed through, rather than at, the soft, pastoral rises and hollows before her.

Scrape, scrape, went Osgood's knife again. Had it ever ceased during the telling of his story? What ought she to say, in return for such a story? *Ruined our lives.* The sacred calm of this high-up hollow dispersed such a human statement, seemed to smooth it out, making it one more echo in a vast valley with a long history of echoes: the place was large and lonely enough to absorb many such sweeping statements about lives gone by. And still have room left over. Perhaps Osgood derived comfort from such a milieu, forgiving by its very impersonality. But she felt more akin than ever to her old cousin and wanted to give him something personal as acknowledgment.

Then she remembered her father's words, that night after he hit Lydia, when she, Cate, had been lurking outside in the hall.

"Once I heard Daddy say that if it weren't for you, our lives might have turned out very differently. I assumed he meant that you, in a general way, by going to fight in the War, had kept the world free. But now I see that he meant it specifically: if he hadn't come to see you that day, Lydia and I might never have existed. Today's my birthday, Uncle Osgood, so it's a very appropriate time for me to thank you for my life."

The scraping stopped. The old man bowed his head. The piece of wood and the knife rested in his curled hands. A strange noise came from the abbreviated nose. "I'm glad you come," he said in a frail voice. "Them boys has loosened my tongue to the place I was telling closer and closer to that time. And that story don't belong to strangers. It's for one family member, and let it rest there. You wait here."

He reached for his cane and, rising slowly, went into the white frame house that Cate could still remember as a log cabin with a tin roof. Daddy had helped Osgood modernize it, about twenty years ago. "Those chickens live drier than he does," she remembered Daddy saying.

She was beginning to worry about him, when he came back with a carton of eggs. He placed the carton formally in her hands, as if it were a much larger gift. "My silkies lay small eggs, but they're the best in the world for cakes. You make yourself a birthday cake with these, you hear? And don't give them away to nobody, these eggs. They're for you."

On the way back to Lake Hills, Cate stopped off at the supermarket, where you could now buy wine from the shelves—except before noon on Sunday. Following her mother's request, she bought herself a bottle of Moët et Chandon.

At six o'clock, she was standing in the kitchen, trying to make up her mind whether to chill the champagne quickly in the freezer so she could drink it before the sun went down, thus commemorating the actual moment of her birth (seven-fifteen p.m.), or to let it get good and cold while she baked herself a cake with Osgood's eggs, and have cake and champagne, at about nine o'clock, in the garden under the stars. People had certainly had less agreeable decisions to make on their fortieth birthdays. Even though she was alone and, in Lydia's phrase, had "nothing to show" for her four-decade sojourn on the earth, she couldn't help feeling positive about life. Maybe it was the rarefied mountain air up at Osgood's: an infusion of good oxygen masquerading as a resurgence of her old arrogance. Well, if so, at least she knew where to go to get some more.

She was just thinking how people's lives—even when they proclaimed them "ruined"—continued to bounce off one another, adding new evidence, opening up more and more secret hollows in the complex human soul, thus changing the perspectives and possibilities for everyone, when the phone on the kitchen wall rang. She thought it might possibly be Lydia, unable to hold out against her own inveterate habit of phoning on family birthdays.

Squaring her shoulders, Cate let the phone ring twice more. Then she answered in a breezy, caught-in-the-middle-of-life voice so no one would think she was sitting around feeling sorry for herself on her birthday.

"Nell?" Not Lydia. A weary, deep drawl that Cate at first took for a man's.

"Mother's up in Virginia. This is Cate."

An offended "Oh." Then silence.

"Can I take a message?" Then, realizing who it was, "Aunt Thea?"

Another silence. Cate wondered if her godmother would hang up. Then, neither denying nor affirming the identity, "When will she be back?"

"That's hard to say. She's nursing an old friend. The friend's pretty ill."

"I see."

Cate could feel Theodora's stubbornness emanating into this kitchen. Theodora wanted to extract the needed information from her without having to acknowledge her existence. How long could they keep up the game: Cate providing one stingy reply at a time to Theodora's haughty questions and coercive "I see"s?

But why on earth should they keep it up? Their estrangement seemed quaintly outdated, like some tired old war kept going on principle, long after both enemies had turned their real attentions toward fresher, graver concerns. So much had happened since Theodora had predicted Cate's eventual residence in prison or bedlam, and Cate, in retaliation, had declared Theodora's brain atrophied by its refusal to admit new ideas. Since that day, both of them had found (and lost) new people; had had new fights; had known humbling defenselessness in the face of illness: perhaps the ultimate opponent this side of death. It really did seem superfluous to carry on this old animosity. Cate and Lydia had said worse things to each other less than three weeks ago, and Cate had been ready to talk when the phone had rung. Even Osgood and Percy Clamp had gone on to exchange Christmas cards.

Cate took a deep breath. "Is there anything I can tell her for you, Aunt Thea?"

A throat was cleared. "Thank you, no. There was a little errand I wanted her to run for me. I've been sick and they won't let me go anywhere."

"I was very sorry to hear about it, Aunt Thea. But you must be better now. You sound very lucid—"

"Well, of course I'm lucid," snapped Theodora. "I was down at Duke, you know. My neurosurgeon said I have an excellent prognosis. My *mind* was never affected, I was always lucid—even when some people thought I wasn't. But I haven't quite regained use of my fool leg, and that's why I can't get out myself. That's why I wanted Nell."

"Is there anything *I* could do?"

A brief, miffed pause, during which pride was obviously battling it out with need. "I wouldn't dream of troubling you." Another pause. "*What* friend did Nell go to nurse in Virginia? I don't recall her ever mentioning any friend in Virginia."

"Merle Chapin. They were at Farragut Pines as girls. Her maiden name was something else. Mother told me, but it's slipped my mind."

"Hmpff," said Theodora. "I don't ever recall Nell's mentioning any Merle." Then, with a touch of reproach, "I considered asking Nell to come stay with me when I got back from Duke, but I got the idea she was doing fine all by herself. If I'd known she was looking out for somebody to *nurse*, I could have suggested an old friend closer to home."

"It was all very spur-of-the-moment," Cate explained. "Merle and her husband were staying in the cottage next door on the island—we'd gone to Ocracoke, you know—oh, of course you haven't heard: Aunt Thea, we lost our cottage. It burned down while we were there."

"Poor Leonard's cottage burned *down*? How could it have, while you all were there? Why didn't you stop it?"

"We were all three out at the time," Cate abbreviated.

"Well. For pity's sake. Faulty wiring?"

"No, a chimney fire that spread up and down at the same time. It was windy. Lydia and I had made a fire—"

"You don't mean you went out and *left* a fire? Why, I won't even go to bed until I've doused the embers in my fireplace with my watering can. I'm surprised at Nell. She's usually so sensible."

"Mother had gone next door to be with her friend. She had every reason to believe we were taking care of things. But Lydia had to go out suddenly, and ... um ... I went out for a short walk, which I'll always regret. It was really all my fault."

"Oh pshaw. Nothing is ever *all* anybody's fault. You overestimate your importance. Some new aberration in the modern character, in my opinion. Like all these terrorists phoning in at the same time to claim responsibility for every little bomb blast. Everyone wants all the guilt for himself. Or *herself.*"

Cate burst out laughing. "Aunt Thea, you're in fine form. Nobody would know you'd been so ill."

"They'd know if they could see my dern leg. However, I don't intend to let it"—significant pause—"*atrophy.* Azalea gives me a workout every morning—she sleeps over at my house now; the physical therapist showed her how to do the exercises." But Theodora sounded pleased by Cate's remark.

"This errand you wanted Mother for. Could I do it?"

Theodora hesitated. "Oh dear. It's so complicated. Perhaps we'd better leave it. It's just that I believe a little girl who stayed with me for a while is trying to get in touch with me. But Azalea answered the phone both times, and she said all she heard was someone breathing and some babies crying and then the party hung up. Lucy Bell and Latrobe told me the child had gone back to her home, which is one big fib. She has no home to go back to, but they don't know I know that. I was going to ask Nell if she wouldn't mind going over to that old green tenement house on Depot Street to see if Wickie was still there or not. Without any *fuss.* I'm disappointed with the girl, she acted very ugly, but if she's in trouble I want to know. I have a duty toward her. *When* did you say Nell was coming back?"

"I didn't. She doesn't know herself."

"What sort of illness has this Merle *got*?"

"Lung cancer, I'm afraid."

Theodora gave an affronted intake of breath. "That's not so good. Better count my blessings, I reckon. And you? In town between adventures, I suppose?"

"That's one way of putting it," said Cate dryly. "I'm here for the summer. May I come over and see you sometime?"

"If you want," said the other, after a pause. Then, with a sigh, as if realizing she had been ungracious, she added wearily, "Well, it's been nice talking to you, but I won't keep you any longer. I hear Azalea bringing my tray."

"Call me, Aunt Thea, if you need anything?"

"Mmpf," mumbled Theodora noncommittally. She hung up without ever once having spoken Cate's name.

"Headstrong old devil," said Cate. She put the champagne, and Osgood's egg carton, in the refrigerator and took a stroll around the downstairs rooms, which were filling with the mellow light of the impending sunset. She stuck her finger in the soil of a couple of Mother's flowerpots, and returned with a glass pitcher filled with water, pouring in a dollop at a time until she heard the little sucking, hissing sounds of the water loosening the soil as it made its way down to the roots. On the way back to the kitchen, she stopped in front of the hall mirror and tried some new expressions she had worked out to minimize the lopsidedness of her face. In this gentle light, she was able to reassure herself that, even if this were to be the total extent of her recovery, she could get by on good days, in the right light, with a look of permanent wryness, a sort of chronic "looking askance" at whatever was in front of her. Some people earned such a look naturally; perhaps she also would have, in time.

It would be at least an hour before the champagne was even drinkable. Not only that, but Theodora's call had had the effect of making the prospect of a solitary champagne party seem blandly solipsistic; moreover, Cate could feel the inner radar of her curiosity swinging irresistibly toward Depot Street, refuge of the mysterious girl whom Theodora had taken in—or been taken in by: if the latter, it would be interesting to meet such a girl. Cate even felt she knew her, in a vague, symbolic way. All last spring, the girl's life had moved—based on Mother's reports— like a counterpoint shadow behind Cate's own crises. Alternately she had resented her, then cheered her on: resented her for being able, so effortlessly, to dazzle a bunch of privileged, middle-class ladies with her stark, womanly drama; cheered her on as the shy, but perhaps cunning, underdog intent on wresting some comfort and protection from their overabundant privilege. And the fact that she had been able to walk out on the easy life at Theodora's and move down to Depot Street testified to something, though whether to the girl's spirit of independence or simply the impossibility of living with Theodora, Cate was not sure.

Perhaps the girl *is* in trouble, thought Cate, fetching her car keys with the unmistakable lift of heart she always felt whenever she escaped the dead spots in life by following her instincts toward conflict and drama. As she drove from Lake Hills to the expressway which would take her to the opposite end of town, she recalled how, as a child and as a young girl, she had spent a large portion of her waking hours having rescue fantasies in which she saved people from danger or oppression, often risking her own life, and usually meting out delicious punishments to the oppressors afterward: the punishments were often the best part.

Depot Street, and its surrounding environs, was a rather sad little area, but by no means a slum. In the heyday of the railroads, it had been a bustling enclave of shops, restaurants, a few commercial hotels, serving the needs of the passengers who arrived and departed on the thirty or forty trains a day. Now, as in several other formerly prosperous areas in town—the downtown area where she and her mother had dined at Jamal's, for instance—the landlords were engaged in a sort of holding action between past and future, willing to accept low rents on their properties, just enough to cover taxes, until the longed-for giant corporation or powerful combination of "interests" should sweep magnanimously into town, bearing cash, demolition squads, and blueprints for climate-controlled shopping malls or factories for the assemblage of foreign cars, and reward them for their patience. The Depot Street area did not have the hippie chic of the downtown area with its crafts shops and restaurants and self-conscious nostalgia, but, shabby as it was, Cate warmed to it. In tone, it reminded her of where she had lived in Iowa, down by the river, above the TV repair shop: it had that same humble, wistful quality of *waiting* to see what the future would make of it; but until that day of transformation, it did not try to cover up its past.

It occurred to Cate as she parked in front of the building described by Theodora as a "green tenement" (it was not; it was one of the old commercial hotels, renovated into an apartment building, though it was painted an unpleasant shade of yellowish-green) that, if she had come to Mountain City to work, she might have chosen this honest little between-worlds neighborhood as her first home. (What, for that matter, would Theodora have called Cate's residence in Iowa, if she had seen it?)

Cate studied the names on the wall of metal mailboxes in a dim hallway in which a few too many cooking smells conflicted. What had she been expecting: a clear, handlettered sign that said "Wickie Lee"? But if she eliminated married couples (R. and J. Dobbs, etcetera) and old calling cards (which she did not think Wickie Lee would have), that left just six mailboxes. She was feeling perfectly capable of knocking on six doors when she heard, somewhere on the floor above, the opening chords of two babies crying at once. Hadn't Mother said Wickie Lee was living with another woman who'd also just had a baby?

She headed upstairs and soon located the door from behind which the cries came. She could hear a woman's voice cajoling and chiding the babies in a rhythmic, repetitious way. Cate knocked loudly enough to be heard above the din.

All noise inside stopped instantly. Light footsteps approached. "Who is it?" the woman inside called out.

"I'm looking for Wickie Lee," Cate called back.

One of the babies began to whimper again and the other

joined in. "Who is that out there?" demanded the voice, more suspiciously.

"It's Cate. On behalf of Theodora Blount. Have I got the right place?"

Silence. More whimpering, in duet, from the babies. Then a slow unbolting of a lock and unfastening of a chain. The door opened. A small, pale girl in tight jeans, a baby slung over each shoulder, looked defiantly out at Cate.

"So you're the crazy one," she said, in a flat, twangy voice.

"If you've been told *that*, then you must be Wickie Lee," Cate countered dryly. "May I come in? I promise my craziness is neither dangerous nor catching."

The other did not reply, but she stepped aside.

The room was cluttered and depressing: a "suite" of sofa and chairs in a garish, furry material of brown-and-orange swirl design; the ubiquitous neutral wall-to-wall shag carpeting, which hid spillage and wore well; a chrome-and-Formica dinette set on whose tabletop were several unopened boxes of disposable diapers, a dish with one forlorn taco on it, and a half-drunk glass of milk.

"I've interrupted your supper," said Cate. In the far corner of the room, she now noticed another child, of about a year, strapped into a sort of indoor swing; neither asleep nor awake, he nodded hypnotically at a TV program with the sound turned-off, as the swing, which seemed to be self-propelling, rocked him back and forth.

"No, they did," said the girl, indicating the babies she joggled in her arms. "The minute I put them down so I could eat, they started. They're so spoiled. They like to be *walked* to sleep, and if you stop for even a minute, they start crying."

"Which one is yours?"

The girl turned sideways to show the face of the baby on the left. "This one. This is Tiffany." Then, as though reminding herself she must be fair, she turned to the other side and showed the other baby. "And this is Scott, Rita's baby. That over there in the swing is Sam. He's Rita's, too. He's the best-tempered."

"And where is Rita?"

The girl's face darkened. "She's over at her boyfriend's."

"And you're baby-sitting?"

"Looks like it, doesn't it?" said Wickie Lee, with a flat, rude tone that dismissed Cate's question as imbecilic.

"Look, I'll get right to the point," said Cate. "Theodora just called our house—actually, she wanted Mother, but she got me, which was awkward for her because she has made a point of not speaking to me for years—"

"She *called*?" The girl's eyes widened as she stood holding the babies. "You mean she's conscious?"

"She sounded very conscious to me. Just like her old self. Judging everyone right and left. Apparently, it's only her leg that's been affected. Didn't you know she was conscious?"

Wickie Lee had sat down on the arm of a chair. Immediately the babies started squalling in duet. It was as if their reflexes were linked together. She stood up again and dutifully joggled them, pacing up and down. She had extremely small, bare feet. The toenails were polished a bright, careful pink. Her beigy-brown hair hung to her shoulders, except for two chunks that had been chopped off on either side of her face just above the ears: in an attempt at "style"? Cate wondered.

"I don't know who to believe," she said in her twangy voice.

"You mean someone's told you differently?" asked Cate, deciding to sit down on the sofa without being asked. In the process of clearing herself a space, between baby garments and soft toys, she found a very interesting doll: its face had been made out of a mesh stocking pulled over cotton, and the expression, even the wrinkles, of the lady doll had been stitched in; it was an uncannily human, but also parodic, little creature. Was this one of Wickie Lee's famous dolls? Cate had expected something more innocent and folksy.

"Do you know Mr. Bell?" asked the girl.

"Latrobe Bell? I'm afraid so. He's not one of my favorite people."

Wickie Lee gave Cate an almost-friendly look. "He came by again last week. He said they'd taken her down to Duke for some operation that didn't work. And they didn't ever expect her to regain consciousness."

"Why, that perfidious old sot!"

"He tried to give me some money, but I wouldn't take it. Rita said I was a fool, but I didn't want his old money. Besides, it was for me to go home on, and I can't do that."

"Yes. That's what Theodora said."

"What did she tell you about me?" asked Wickie Lee suspiciously.

"Just that. That you had no home to go back to. And that she thought you'd been trying to phone her but hung up when Azalea answered. She wanted to know if you were in trouble. *Are* you in trouble?"

Wickie Lee gave a short, mirthless laugh. "Not any more than usual, I don't guess. At least I've got a roof over my head. Sometimes Rita takes advantage, that's all."

"How does she do that?"

Wickie Lee paced back and forth a few times with the babies. Cate thought she had decided not to answer. *Squeak, squeak,* went the self-propelled little swing which lulled Rita's other baby. "All the time leaving me with the kids," Wickie Lee finally admitted. "Not that I mind kids. I raised my baby brother, and my sister's first two babies when I went to live with her after Momma died, but Rita promised we'd take equal turns."

"How about this sister? Could you go back there? Or—"

"Look," said the girl, narrowing her eyes, "I don't want to be rude, but it isn't any of your business. I mean, I still don't understand why you're here."

"To check on you for Aunt Thea. Actually, it was my mother she wanted to come, but Mother's out of town. The Bells told Theodora that you had gone back home, but she didn't believe them. She thought it was you, calling the house and then hanging up. Also, I admit, I was just plain curious to see you. Mother's spoken of you in a couple of our phone conversations. *Was* that you, who called Theodora's and then hung up?"

"I didn't do anything wrong. I was only trying to find out

how she was. That Mrs. Bell spread it around that I hit her and caused her to have that stroke. That was a lie. I may have said some pretty harsh things, but she did, too. That day she followed me here, she said things nobody has a right to say to anybody."

"Aunt Thea can do that only too well," agreed Cate. "She and I had quite an exchange a few years back. We both said things."

"Then why are you over here running her errands? Have you all made up?"

"Not really. I mean, she hasn't made up with me. I'm willing to be friendly. I've got bigger problems on my mind than keeping up old animosities. Look, I told you, I was curious about you. Also, driving over here, I wondered if I could be of any help."

"I know why you've come!" said the girl with sudden passion. "You want to offer me money, too. To go and get lost. You've all found out about me, and you want to get me out of the way. Especially now that she's *conscious!* Ouch!" One of the babies, roused by her voice, had grabbed a fistful of hair. "I swear, I'm going to have to cut it *all* off just to keep you meanies from pulling it to death."

"You can be at rest in your mind about my offering you any money," said Cate, understanding now why the girl had lopped off those two chunks of hair. "I don't have any to offer. And what could I, or anyone else, find out about you that would make us want you out of the way?"

Wickie Lee looked hard at Cate. "Are you playing dumb, or you really don't know?"

"Know what?"

"She didn't tell you? Then why else are you all over here in *shifts,* trying to drive me out of town? You're all scared to death of me. Well, I can't change what I *am,* but I don't want her old money. I'd rather let Rita take advantage of me than have to knuckle under to your lot. I could *never* have pleased her, never, without giving up my soul."

She spun away on her heel and gave the babies another turn. A tear had started down one cheek, but her fierce little face was as defiant as ever.

"Wickie Lee," said Cate quietly. "I'm sorry I've upset you, and I'll leave if you like. I honestly don't know anything about you. I don't know what you're talking about. Whatever secrets you two had over there on Edgerton Road, she's certainly kept. At least, from me. All she said when she called was that though you had 'talked ugly' to her, she felt it was her duty to help you if you were in trouble."

Cate stood up to go, feeling in her shirt pocket for her keys. "Shall I tell her I came by and you're fine, or would you rather I didn't say anything at all?"

"You do what you please," said the girl. "You probably will, anyway." She bit down hard on her lower lip; she was trying hard not to sob. "She said you never listened to anybody."

"I listen quite a lot, actually," said Cate. "What she meant was that I don't knuckle under. Like you, I may end up in tatters, but I'll still have my soul. Poor Theodora. She's unlucky in her protégées, isn't she? She picks people as hardheaded as herself. I could tell her that, but *she* wouldn't listen. What she's looking for is a docile young thing who would let Theodora run her life for her; only, if she found such a person, Aunt Thea would end up despising her."

"That's what she tried to do with me, run my life," said Wickie Lee, nuzzling her face against one of the babies' little T-shirts; then Cate realized the girl was merely wiping her eyes in this manner, as she had no hand free. "Some of it was all right, like her teaching me how to read better and giving me that pretty room—I miss that room—but then it turned out she wanted me to read better so I could go back to school, and I wanted to stay home with my baby. Tiffany will never have any father, so I don't intend to cheat her out of her full-time mother. And then, that was another thing. She wanted to name Tiffany *Fletcher*. Can you imagine anyone wanting to name a girl Fletcher?"

"Fletcher? Why Fletcher?" asked Cate, jingling her keys. "Though I roomed with a girl in college whose name was Cecil. It was her mother's maiden name—"

"You really *don't* know, do you?" Wickie Lee was peering earnestly up at Cate. She was even smaller than Teenie Ennis.

"Well, maybe if I tell you, you can keep those Bells away. I trust you more than them, I think. You don't seem as crazy as she said, either."

"Why, thank you," said Cate, but her irony was lost on Wickie Lee, who, perversely, was now pursuing Cate with her secret, just when Cate had convinced herself it would be better to forfeit her curiosity and leave this girl in peace.

"I mean, she was going to have this great big christening and announce it to everybody," said Wickie Lee, "so I'm not giving away anything she wasn't intending to. Come to think of it, I'm not giving away anything that's not mine to give away. I'm who I am." The defiance shone brightly.

Cate waited.

"She wouldn't let me tell it, all those months, though it was her that wanted me to go and live at her house." The girl gave a sharp, bitter laugh. "I was sure jumping from the frying pan into the fire, only I didn't know it. She was so nice on the desk that day I showed up at New Hope, where I'd heard once from a girl you could go and get private help without having to report yourself to the government. She starts asking me these questions about where I come from, which I wasn't about to tell, on account of I was afraid my brother-in-law'd come and drag me back, and that would have been worse than any frying pan *or* fire. And I couldn't tell my age, or they would of sent me back with him if he *had* come. But then she said I talked like I was from Sharpe County and said her people had come from there, and she asked me if I ever knew any Blounts. That's when I made my mistake. But I couldn't help it. Hearing the name made me so homesick for Momma, even though she's dead. I told her Momma's name was that, but Momma's family spelled theirs without the *o*. That was when she told me to shut up in front of the other women, because they were busybodies. And before I could say 'boo,' I was living on Edgerton Road. She felt bad about lying to just one person, and that was your daddy. She wanted to keep things secret for a while—for my own good, was what she said, but I think because she wanted to test me out and see if I was worth claiming. And also"—another sharp laugh—

"see that my baby turned out not to have two heads, or be the wrong color. She didn't have to worry about neither, but she didn't know that."

"So—you really are related to Theodora."

"She's my second cousin, twice removed," said the girl, somewhat proudly. "We figured it out. She and my momma's daddy were second cousins. See, Momma's great-grandfather was named Fletcher Blount, and he was the brother of . . . of Theodora's grandfather." The girl's cheeks flushed up as she forced herself to use Theodora's name as Cate did. "It was my granddaddy who dropped the *o* out of the name; we figured that out, too."

"So that's what the Fletcher was all about." A smile twitched at the corners of Cate's mouth. "Won't the Bells just die when they find out you're a Blount . . . unless they already have."

"They haven't unless *she's* told them," said the girl. "On account of, my name is something else. My daddy's name wasn't Blunt. But nobody is going to find out what it was if I can help it. I'm not going back there, ever. Tiffany has 'baby girl Blount' on her birth certificate, and I guess that's the best thing for her to have. It's me that's trapped because I can't show proof of myself existing."

"How are you trapped?"

"How? How would you like it if you couldn't get a job, couldn't even get money from the state like Rita does, because you couldn't own up to your name? I don't have any proof of my age, neither. I've turned sixteen now, but I can't prove it, so Rita says I can't even get a social security card. I guess I am lucky to have found her. I mean, she lets me and Tiffany stay here, and we can't pay nothing for our room and board—not that Tiffany takes up much space. John—that's Rita's boyfriend—has sold a few of my dolls, and that's brought some pin money in. He takes 'em to some place up on the parkway where they sell mountain crafts, and tells 'em I'm an old woman lives up in the hills and makes these dolls. People like that better, he says. But I got more for my dolls at that Republican women's bazaar than I do from that fancy parkway place, and it's for tourists. I think they ought to pay more than five dollars for a doll that's got its own expression and every stitch of clothing hemmed, and no two alike. And it's so hard, with these babies, and Rita gone so much, to find time to sit down and make a doll. When I was living over on Edgerton Road, I had all day to sit around and make 'em. And she had such nice scraps. . . ." The girl's voice rose plaintively: "I don't have any control over my own life. It's like I just keep jumping from one frying pan into the next!"

Cate's nostrils dilated. She sniffed the unmistakable odor of exploitation. This Rita, whatever *her* hard-luck story, had her welfare check, her boyfriend, and her built-in baby-sitter: built-in *slave* was more like it. The babies' heads drooped on either side of Wickie Lee's slight, rounded shoulders as she gave them another weary turn up and down the depressing room; the single, unappealing cold taco awaited her on the table, next to the boxes of disposable diapers; and she had just "turned sixteen." Cate at sixteen had also felt "trapped": after school, she had shut herself in her room, while Mother began supper in the kitchen below, and read *The Prophet* aloud, sometimes watching herself in the mirror, other times gazing with determination at the mountains over which she intended to fly as soon as possible, to escape the shackles of family, region, and all less-than-noble concerns. What would she be like today if, at sixteen, she had had Wickie Lee's shackles?

The plight of the girl—Theodora's little cousin, or not (Cate would almost have preferred *not*, as Theodora would surely reassert her claims, was already preparing the way)—aroused in Cate a sudden, new maternal desire to protect and defend Wickie Lee from her exploiters as well as from her benefactors; and she saw a way to do it without becoming either, herself: the girl certainly didn't need another frying pan to hop into. She needed a guide, perhaps: someone to abet and cheer her on to her goal—which was, from the looks of it, freedom in its simplest and most fundamental aspects.

"Listen!" exclaimed Cate, with the excitement from her idea, "I think I—"

"Shh!" hissed Wickie Lee. "These two're about out. I'm

going to walk 'em a few more minutes and then see if I can't put them down. I'm not saying for you to leave or anything, but could you keep your voice down?"

"I have an idea," said Cate, with exaggerated softness. Her pride was hurt, but it would be foolish to let the girl's abruptness dampen her inspiration. "While you get all your babies settled, why don't I go out and pick up a couple of hamburgers. I saw a McDonald's on the way here. I haven't eaten, and I don't imagine you're exactly looking forward to that taco."

"It wasn't a very good taco," admitted Wickie Lee. "It set in the refrigerator too long."

"French fries?" Cate twirled her keys. She narrowed her eyes wickedly.

She read the hesitation in the girl's face and didn't like her less for her pride.

"I think I know a job that's just tailor-made for you, Wickie Lee. We can talk about it while we eat. And you can pay me back later."

When Cate returned home, around nine, the phone was ringing. It was Mother, calling to say happy birthday.

"Where have you been? I've been trying to reach you all day."

"Oh," said Cate, "I've been keeping myself amused."

"You . . . have?" Nell sounded surprised and slightly wary.

"I went out to see Uncle Osgood this afternoon. God, it's so beautiful. It's another world. Those runic rocks sticking up in the fields, those straight-up green pastures. I'm going to go out there often while I'm here."

"How *is* Osgood?"

"Talkative. He's got two roommates."

"*What?*"

Cate enjoyed her mother's bewilderment. She was well aware that she was the member of the family who could always bring back an element of surprise, some startling new fact, from the simplest journey, even into old familiar territory. She explained about Osgood's two summer aides, and even about the

Alice B. Toklas brownies. Nell laughed and laughed. But Cate did not tell about Percy Clamp; "It's for one family member, and let it rest there," Osgood had said.

"Did you just get back from Big Sandy, then?" asked Nell.

"Oh no, I came back around six. I bought a bottle of champagne, like you told me to, but I haven't even had a chance to open it yet. Aunt Thea called—"

"Aunt *Thea*? Have you been mending your fences, then?"

"Not exactly. She really wanted you, but she had to make do with me."

"How is she?"

"She's going to recover, apparently. One of her legs doesn't work, but she's got Azalea exercising it."

"Did you go over there? Was that where you were when I called about an hour go?"

"No, we're not that chummy yet. I expect I will go over and see her. Maybe tomorrow. I need to discuss something with her. No, actually I've just come back from a very nice visit with Wickie Lee."

"Well!" Nell said, laughing. "Now you really have got my curiosity aroused."

"Mine was aroused, too. That's why I went over there myself. That's what Aunt Thea wanted you to do. She thought her ex-protégée might be in distress. Wickie Lee had been phoning, then hanging up when Azalea answered."

"*Is* she in distress?"

"She is, but if things work out like I want them to, she won't be much longer. That Rita she's living with has been intimidating her about the intricacies of the system in order to exploit her."

"Did you meet Rita?"

"No, she was out with her boyfriend. They sound like pros, I must say. He's the father of both children, and apparently visits a lot and loves them and all that, but—get this: they're saving their money for a house. And if he lived with Rita, then she couldn't get her welfare check. And he sells Wickie Lee's dolls somewhere up on the parkway, at a fancy crafts shop, for five dollars. You know he's pocketing most of it. Even those tacky little apple dolls you always see too many of at the Mountain Crafts Fair cost that much. By the way, would you mind if Wickie Lee had some of your scraps? Don't you have a lot of old scraps from when you made our dresses when we were young?"

"She's welcome to whatever she wants," said Nell. "But how are things going to work out for her?"

"Well, Jerome Ennis's wife came over to see me—we were in high school together—and she just happens to be looking for a woman to live in at her nursery school. It would be perfect for Wickie Lee. She wants to stay home all day with her baby, anyway. So she can stay home with a dozen or so others as well, and get paid for it. I've got to call Teenie Ennis. But I want to consult Aunt Thea first. If she's willing to claim Wickie Lee as her relative, that would be an excellent reference. Teenie is a bit of a snob. Oh, wait! I haven't told you! Wickie Lee is Theodora's cousin."

"You *are* full of surprises. But how—who—" Nell laughed at her own eagerness.

Cate explained about Theodora's great-uncle Fletcher. ". . . and Aunt Thea knew it from the beginning. She was on the desk that day. The other women weren't even involved. When she found out Wickie Lee was a Blount, she whisked her right off to Edgerton Road. She felt bad about lying to Daddy, though. But she wanted to see how things worked out first. Wickie Lee thinks she wanted to be sure the baby didn't come out too dark—or with some telltale sign of incest."

"Did you find out who the father was?"

"Now, Mother. Don't expect too much in one day. No, she's very closemouthed about that. But I have my ideas. She was living with her married sister, taking care of her sister's children—and she seemed scared to death her brother-in-law would find out where she was and come and drag her back."

"Oh, poor child. Wouldn't it be nice if you could help her." A pause. "You certainly have been busy today."

"What about you? How are things there? How is she?"

Nell sighed. "I'll have to speak low. Though I don't think they can hear. I'm downstairs and they're in her room watching a

movie on television. After she went to the doctor for her first in-
jection, she was euphoric for several days. But ... well, she's
sinking a little. And something else bothers me, I can see it in her
face. I think she's giving up. I don't think"—and Nell lowered
her voice almost to a whisper—"I'll be here too much longer."

"Oh, Mother. I'm sorry."

"So am I. But don't be sorry for me. I had the strangest
thoughts this evening. After Marcus and I washed the dishes, I
went out for a walk. There were such unusual clouds in the sky,
and I was thinking how I was happy being right where I was at
the moment, all by myself on some strange street in Virginia.
And I was remembering how uncomfortable I was, the first few
days here. I didn't tell you, but I really felt cramped and resentful
about giving up my self-contained life in Lake Hills. I mean, I
had said I would come, and she's been so affectionate and
they've both been so appreciative and careful of my privacy, but
I had gotten used to my self-contained existence. And then I had
the strangest thought. It was almost as if I heard my own voice
coming out of the clouds, saying 'You can be self-contained in the coffin.' And I thought, I'm not ready for the coffin. I've felt almost ...
immortal these past few weeks. That's partly a feeling you do get
from being around people whose mortality is ... all too evident;
I remember it from nursing. But I do feel so very alive and fortunate. When I get back to Mountain City, I'm going to look for a
job. I'd like to work in a hospital again, or maybe a clinic. I'd
probably have to take lots of refresher courses, there are so many
new things since my day ... I would have liked to have been up
on the needle techniques that would have qualified me for giving
Merle her injections. I could have made that seven minutes pass
faster for her, talking about old times. Oh Cate, I have so much
time. I feel as if I ought to *pay* something for my own good fortune."

Then she gave the dry laugh which Cate knew well. It was a
laugh that meant Nell felt she had been on the verge of being
embarrassingly "intense." Who would have been embarrassed?
Certainly not Cate.

"You'd be a wonderful nurse," said Cate.

"I wasn't such a bad one before you were born." Then, as if to remove any unintentional accusation her words might have conveyed, she added in a gentle, rather shy voice, "I thought of you at seven-fifteen tonight. I usually do, on this day. I remember the way I felt, not at seven-fifteen so much—those were the days before natural childbirth was widely practiced, and I was so groggy—but later, when they brought you to me. You were screaming and beating your little fists against the air; your eyes were swollen shut with that silver nitrate they put in. You were a seven-pound bundle of aching, miserable *questions*, and there was no way I could explain to you what was going on. It was so terrifying to me that you were so new and little and didn't understand whether what had happened to you was the end of your world or the beginning. I was your *mother* and there was no language, no way I could get the message across. You broke my heart. I felt so inadequate because all I could do was just hold you. And you did stop crying eventually and took your bottle. It wasn't the end of anybody's world. But I'll never forget that awesome helplessness. You were . . . completely beyond me. With Lydia, it was so easy. They brought her in, she was crying; I held her and I knew that was all I was expected to do. And she seemed to accept it, and stopped crying at once. It was as if I had conveyed my certainty to her, the certainty I didn't have with you. You missed the certainty, but in a way, Lydia got shortchanged, too. I was so busy doing what I knew to do that I skipped over the awe."

"I'd rather have had the awe," said Cate. "Too much certainty, right there at the beginning, might have cramped my style."

"Well, that's convenient, isn't it?" said Nell after a moment. She laughed. But it was a thankful, reprieved laugh.

"Isn't it!" agreed her daughter, laughing also.

EPILOGUE

1984

We are not strong by our power to penetrate, but by our relatedness.
The world is enlarged for us, not by new objects, but by finding
more affinities and potencies in those we have.
—Emerson, "Success"

Lydia turned off the main highway into the county road leading up to Big Sandy. "They've paved it," she said. "When Daddy brought us out here as children, it was just an old dirt road." The new car handled well: it took the turn with a graceful, pivoting motion and slipped smoothly into its climbing gear. But she missed her sturdy old Volvo, in which she had got to do the shifting. She was furious with Dickie for smashing it up but, of course, thankful he had not been hurt. And as her life was not her own anymore, she had felt obligated to buy a new American car and set a good example.

"It's beautiful out here," said Stanley. "Just imagine what powerful upheavals in the earth must have caused this landscape. Hey, Liza Bee"—he turned to the child buckled into her little traveling throne behind them—"look out there at that red tree. You ever see such a red tree?"

"You ever *see* such a red tree?" repeated the child, in a precise, comical imitation of the man's tone.

Liza Bee, just turned four in September, was going through a mimicking phase. They all found it disconcerting, because she had an uncanny knack for picking up certain idiosyncrasies in speech and emphasis that revealed the intention behind the voice. Just now she had captured exactly the fond falsetto he slipped into only with her, and the emphasis which made it quite plain that he cared more about her reaction than the existence of any red tree.

Stanley, charmed, exchanged a "did-you-hear-that?" look with Lydia, above the child's head. Lydia was not as charmed, although she was pleased that Liza was such a bright child. It was right that Max's daughter should be bright. And pretty, too, in a fairy-delicate way that had aspects of Leo's baby beauty; in absentminded moments, Lydia sometimes completely forgot that this was Lizzie's child and not her own. But they were spoiling her rotten, all of them: herself, Stanley, Dickie, Leo, Mother; Renee and Camilla; and Lizzie, when she was home. Already, Liza Bee (Eliza Broadbelt Mansfield) at four had been to more places with more people than Lydia had been in the first eighteen years of her life. But somebody in this indulgent bunch of family and near-family had to make clear to this bold sprite that there were boundaries, and Lydia suspected she was going to be that person. She owed it to Max, who had missed seeing his only daughter born by three months.

"This place seems neater than it used to," said Lydia, as the car continued to climb and circle into the hills. "It doesn't look more built up, or spoiled, of anything, just . . . neater. It's probably all the hidden money. The Sufis have a place in here somewhere and the Buddhists have a monastery, and I was reading in the paper that some citizens' corporation has bought a thousand acres, right up at the top of Big Sandy: they're going to have one of those 'metaindustrial villages' and make little computers. Or maybe that's the Sufis I read about who are going to make the computers." She looked out her window at a field of dried cornstalks and sighed deeply. "I just wish I knew what to expect today. Oh *Lord.*"

"Oh *Lord!*" echoed Liza Bee, her little voice a microversion of Lydia's tone.

Stanley burst out laughing. Then, glancing at Lydia, sobered at once. "It can't be too bad, can it?" he asked. "She's giving the party in Leo and Camilla's honor. That shows her good intentions to you as well as them, I would think."

"Leo and Camilla," sang the child. "We going to see Leo and Camilla?" Her voice rose in a little squeak.

"Yes, Liza," Lydia said. "They're driving up specially, from Chapel Hill." Lydia made a mental note to eliminate "Oh Lord" from her vocabulary; did she really sound so put-upon, at times? If so, it wasn't very attractive.

"Specially to see me?" inquired the child.

"Specially to see you," crowed Stanley adoringly.

"Specially to see all of us," Lydia corrected.

Stanley saw Lydia's hands, in her driving gloves, tighten on the wheel. She looked different from the woman who had come sauntering toward him, outside the Health Club, five years ago: that young woman had been softer, rounder-checked; just as proud in demeanor, but her feelings had been nearer the surface. But when you had so much practice at monitoring your smallest reactions, seeing yourself as thousands of others saw you at a given moment, he supposed you learned to anticipate yourself— to show however much or little of the reaction you wanted to be seen. And, just as he had learned to accept (somewhat reluctantly) the paring down of her body from its curvy size twelve to its present boyish eight, he had also learned to anticipate and interpret her pared-down signals for help. The clenched gloved fingers she had meant for him to see; she wanted reassurance. Though she could call up the Governor and be put through at once for an interview, or raise a quarter of a million in donations for a youth center in one hour, or cause a thousand women to return a certain brand of chutney to their supermarkets because the makers had cheated on the mangoes, she still needed as much reassurance as the old "soft" Lydia, whose feelings had crowded into her face with such touching visibility.

"Hey, pull over in that wide spot and let's get out and look at the view," he said. "Come on, let's stretch our legs down in that meadow. We've got time."

"That's true," said Lydia, pulling over. "I certainly don't want to be the first one there."

They unbuckled Liza Bee and, walking her in the air between them, descended the steep, grassy slope into the meadow. Below them were farms and fields of dark clay, nestled in the curves of the valley; on the far side rose the jagged, towering peaks of neighboring ranges.

Lydia filled her lungs deeply with the good air and gave a profound sigh. "Thanks. I needed this. How clean and isolated it is up here. You could almost pretend the twentieth century never happened."

"It happened, all right. The thing that surprises me is, it continues to happen."

Laughing softly, she leaned her head against him. "When I first met you, you said we were all going to have to run for our lives. You were trying to get everybody's feet in shape."

"Well, I still am. Feet are getting better. But I'm not so sure we won't still have to make a dash for it. Just because it hasn't happened yet doesn't mean we shouldn't be prepared." He put his arm around her, and watched Liza Bee run toward a clump of blue flowers she had just spotted under a scarlet-leafed dogwood. "I know you and Dickie think my bomb shelter is a lark," he teased with mock reproach. "I hope we never have to use it, but, all the same, I'm glad we have it."

"So am I. Have I ever said I didn't enjoy spending the night down there?" She nudged her hip suggestively against his. Then she looked serious, signaling, as he had seen her do on TV, that she was about to present some new idea she thought well of: "You know, it seems to me there are people who worry about catastrophe in a *general* way—like you do; and then there are people who worry about it in a more personal way—I guess I'm one of those. When you picture catastrophe, you picture a cast of thousands, whereas I worry about Leo and Dickie and Mother— and you, of course. I'm not saying my way is better, it's just the difference in the way we worry about things. Maybe it has something to do with being masculine or feminine. But, the point is—I was just thinking about this as we drove up here today—neither of us can ever predict, or ever thoroughly prepare for, the *specific* way the things we dread are going to happen. I mean, God forbid, if there is a nuclear attack on North Carolina, we may be among the lucky ones because of your dried food and thick concrete walls under your farmhouse, but, on the other hand, God forbid, we could be driving along this road today and some hillbilly might not like our looks and use us for target practice. You just *never know.* If anybody had told me five years ago that there would be a personal catastrophe in our family, well, I would have prepared myself for something to do with Cate; the last thing I would have predicted would be Max just . . . crumpling like that. Just sitting quietly in his office, figuring up something on his calculator." Lydia's eyes filled; even after four years, she could not speak of Max without tears. "I mean, there he was with everything going for him . . . Lizzie . . . the baby on the way . . . he'd even lost all the weight he wanted to lose. You never can *prepare.* Just when you think you've covered all the possibilities, something totally unexpected sneaks up from behind."

She bit down hard on her lower lip to get herself under control. "Liza Bee," she called, "if you're going to pick those flowers, pick them nice and long. That's right. Pick a nice long-stemmed bunch for Cate." She slipped her arm around Stanley's waist and said for the second time, "If I just knew what to expect today. . ."

"You're complicating things," said Stanley, who knew of the rift between the sisters. Before he'd met Cate, at Max's funeral, *he* hadn't known what to expect. He had been pleasantly surprised at the normal-seeming woman who had flown down from her job in New York, wearing appropriate clothes, showing concern for everybody, and being a great comfort to Dickie, who had taken his father's death hard. "Why not look at the simple side of things? She's giving a party because it's a nice time of year, and because she was out west at that summer school and couldn't make it to Leo's wedding, and because she has a place of her own now. Remember the shindig *I* gave when I bought my farm? Why not take her at her word? This is a family get-together in honor of the newlyweds."

"You're right," sighed Lydia. "It's just that, with Cate, there's always some extra you can't prepare for."

"That's life, honey. You just said so yourself. That's not just Cate." He nuzzled the top of her head. The fragrance of her hair still gave him erotic pleasure. She was the woman of his life, he had accepted that. He had also accepted—the way you accepted nearsightedness or a limp in your beloved—that Lydia could never completely enjoy life. Her temperament did not seem to be able to accommodate those bouts of rapport with the world that people call happiness. Lydia would never be completely happy. Having her own television show, making money, even his continued adoration, had not dispersed the little cloud of unease she carried with her everywhere. However safe or famous or beloved she was, she would never quite believe in her security: she would be anticipating something up ahead that she would be unable to prepare for. She didn't want to get married, she said, because it would be tempting the gods: look at what had happened to Max and Lizzie.

However, every few months or so, or when Lydia's self-esteem dropped, she would ask him, "Stanley, are you still willing to marry me?" And his unvarying answer would raise her spirits again and get her through another few months. Until she'd feel guilty. ("If I weren't in the way, you could marry a younger woman and have children." "I don't want another woman, and I've got Liza. I'm practically her father; she spends weekends with me, keeps her pony at my place. I might not like another child as well as I like her. Liza Bee's just what I would have ordered.")

"I don't know why you keep putting up with me," said Lydia now, as they stood in the meadow. In her present agitation, brought on by the imminent meeting with Cate, she was likely to ask if he was still willing to marry her. He didn't trust himself in this heady air. Surrounded by these great blue protecting ranges, he was dangerously parted from his old consoler and rationalizer, Impending Catastrophe. Up here, it was all too possible to believe they would live well into the new century. *Why not marry?* He saw himself shaking her shoulders. *You can still be independent and mine, at the same time. You are those two things now. What's really holding us back?*

But what would she answer if backed into a corner? After all this time, he was not sure. He preferred to hold on to what he had; so he gave Lydia the reassuring squeeze she required and called to Liza Bee. The child came running to them on her sweet, stick-shaped legs, her hands filled with blue flowers and weeds, pulled up by the roots. Stanley herded his strange little makeshift family back to the car.

"If only Renee had come with Leo and Camilla," said Lydia. "I could have faced Cate better with Renee along. But all she does is live in that law library. It's as if she's sworn off ever having fun again, since that awful mess happened in Greensboro. Now who could have predicted *that*!"

"Leo, isn't that your momma's new car parked over there?"
"Yes, it's her license plate."
"Shouldn't we stop?"
"No. Liza Bee probably had to go to the bathroom."
"That poor child." Camilla craned her long, graceful neck to look back as their car continued up and around the curve. "Yes, I see your mother and Stanley hugging down there."

Leo frowned. "Liza Bee's hardly poor. She's got people standing in line to entertain her, and she'll be very rich someday."

"Ah, but her momma's always off on some business trip, and she never knew that nice daddy of hers," said Camilla in her low, English voice that made all other women's voices seem grating or crude to Leo. "All the people and money in the world can't make up for that."

"Come over here. Why are you hugging that window?" He remembered that Camilla had not had her mother, either, when she was growing up; like Lizzie Broadbelt, Renee had been off tending her career. And as for Camilla's father—well, Leo supposed it was better never to have known a dead father, who everybody agreed had been wonderful, than to have been worried all the time, as Camilla had been, that your jailbird father would come leering over the school fence at you every time he got paroled. He was back "in" now, which had saved them from wondering whether they ought to invite him to the wedding and then having to worry that he would show up. They had sent him some Polaroid pictures of the reception and a piece of wedding cake.

Camilla slid over, touching her hip to his. "But don't put your arm around me. You need both hands on this road."

"I learned to drive in these mountains. My grandfather took me out on a road like this when I was fourteen and taught me how to drive."

"I wish I could have known him. I'm jealous of your past. I wish there were one long movie I could sit and watch, of you going through your life from the day you were born in that London clinic all the way up to the time you came over to visit me, your first week at Tunbridge—to 'call on me' at Battle Abbey."

"Silly, if there were such a movie, it would take you sixteen years to watch it. And while you were watching it, what would I do, the present me you've got now?"

"Hmm. I hadn't considered that. Well, I could watch it in little swatches, like a TV series . . . a little every night."

"No. You have to be with the real me. I've got you booked for every night. Why would you want to watch an ordinary little boy grow up into a teenage blur? My life didn't focus until I walked into that parlor at Battle Abbey."

"I . . . was just . . . a teenage blur," she sang in her silky voice, making a little rhythm-and-blues song out of it. But she put her left hand, the one with the wide gold band, on his knee, and squeezed it. He felt their union flow between them like a current; he actually counted the number of hours they had to get through before he could be alone with her. Grandmother would want them to spend the night at her house in Lake Hills. He had already planned to tell her they had to get back to Chapel Hill— Camilla had tests, he had tests; and they could be by themselves in a motel by seven. Since this party was for them, they would be expected to stay most of the afternoon.

"Anyway," he said, his lungs expanding with happiness at the thought of seven o'clock, "you'll get to meet one new character in the old family serial. My crazy aunt Cate."

"Tell me something crazy she's done."

He cast back in his memory. There was that children's protest march his aunt had led, years ago. Taking all those little girls to block traffic at the Lincoln Tunnel. He had been a little boy then, but he could remember how shocked and exasperated his parents had been. Now, suddenly, it didn't seem very shocking. Camilla's uncle, who was a prominent Atlanta lawyer, was always taking part in those silent protest marches; every time the Klan or some new offshoot of the White Coalition perpetrated some new ugliness, Warren Peverell-Watson would put on his suit and tie, just as if he were going off to church, and meet his friends downtown for a march. And hadn't Aunt Cate gone back to New York, a few years ago, and worked for the husband of one of those little girls, in some foundation? So the march probably hadn't shocked others as much as it had shocked his family.

"It's not anything she does," he said, "so much as it is . . . well, you never quite know what she's going to do next. I mean, with most people, after you know them, you can think about them when you're not with them and more or less know where they are. With her you can't. Just when you've got her imagined in one place, she shows up somewhere else."

"*El camino es mejor que la posada,*" said Camilla. "Or is it *está mejor que?*" Spanish was one of the two languages she was taking. They both planned to enter the Foreign Service if they passed the big exam next spring. The officer from Washington who had interviewed them on campus had come right out and said that couples like themselves were just what the Service was looking for now—"global couples" had been his phrase. "Maybe your aunt Cate's kind of a Don Quixote," said Camilla, "and prefers the road to the inn."

"Yes. I remember Mother's address book had two pages filled up completely with my aunt's addresses, each one crossed out when she moved to the next. Moving around all the time is okay when you're young, but Aunt Cate's getting up there. Mother says it's probably a good thing Granddaddy's crazy old cousin left her his place. Though it rightfully should have gone to both sisters. But Mother's been pretty fair about it. She says she never did get to know the old man too well, whereas he and Aunt Cate got close at the end. And it's not as if Mother needs the house. Aunt Cate needs it more. If only she won't go and do something foolish with the land."

"Like what, for instance?"

"There's a lot of foolish things you can do with a hundred acres. Set up a trailer park for paroled prisoners . . . or establish a refuge for abandoned cats and dogs . . . her head is probably teeming with ideas."

"Well, I can't wait to meet her. Every family needs one Aunt Cate. And it wasn't at all crazy of her to send me this beautiful poncho from New Mexico. It suits my coloring perfectly."

"Everything suits your coloring perfectly." It was a simple fact. Camilla was the most beautiful color on earth. She *was* the color of earth. Leo felt sure that if a creature from another planet, arriving here without prejudices, only with a love of beauty, were to see Camilla placed next to beautiful women of all the earth's races, he would just *assume* she was the healthiest member, the superlative flower, of the species.

And yet, he had overheard a woman, in the supermarket where they shopped in Chapel Hill, say to her friend as Leo and Camilla passed with their cart, "A striking couple, *in themselves*, but"—lowering her voice, but not quite low enough—"who I feel sorry for are the *children*." Leo had glanced quickly at Camilla, who skimmed right on behind the cart, her head with its single thick braid lifted like a proud young queen's, smiling faintly at a top shelf of canned fruit juices; then he had looked angrily back at the woman: narrowed eyes in a face like a dried prune confronted him belligerently, but the thin, red-painted mouth, though clamped firm, wobbled slightly at the corners. *She wanted us to hear,* Leo had realized, appalled; now she's scared I'm going to say something back—or maybe even go over and assault her; but she'd like that, too; what she'd *really* like is if I were Camilla's color and went over there and assaulted her. He had turned away, sickened by this ugly knowledge; Camilla had been right not to turn around, though he was sure she had overhead; but Camilla had had years more practice.

"Why do you young folks want to give yourselves so much trouble?" Camilla's uncle Warren, Renee's brother, had asked when Leo, traditional chap that he was, had gone to Atlanta to ask the current patriarch of the Peverell-Watson family for Camilla's hand in marriage. "We love each other," Leo had replied, as if he were the first in history to utter the magic words. "You all have been over in England," Warren had said; "it's not quite reality. You might even say it's reality twice-removed. They could accept you just fine because, in the first place, neither of you is English, and, in the second place, they knew you'd be going home." "But we've been home three years," Leo had reminded him. "We've been going out almost every night in Chapel Hill, and nobody's stoned us yet." "Chapel Hill is an oasis of sophistication in a surrounding desert of bigotry," Warren had reminded him. Then the older man had asked, "What does your mother say?" "My mother is your sister's best friend," Leo had protested. "Best friend isn't being married; just like going out every night in Chapel Hill isn't being married. What did your mother say?" Warren had looked him hard in the eye; it was as if Warren somehow had had access to a closed-circuit performance of Lydia's first reaction to Leo's news; had seen her turn white, then pink, then make a lot of nervous movements with her eyes, as if she were trying to escape, before she finally said what Leo could repeat honestly that she had said: "Camilla is a perfect lady, and I guess I always knew you would never be satisfied with less." "Besides," Leo had added, after repeating his mother's words to Warren, "this is 1984." "So it is," said Warren, his voice a little softer, "and Big Brother's done his best to warn you. You all just be sure you two have got more love than all those people out there have got hate." "We have," Leo had replied, undaunted. Then he couldn't resist his last argument, which he had prepared for the eventuality of real resistance on Camilla's uncle's part: "I feel this way. Camilla and I and people like us *are* the future, if we're going to *have* a future. The way races have always stopped killing each other is to marry instead. Look at the Ostrogoths and the Italians. Look at the Egyptians. Look at the Brazilians." Leo was double-majoring in history and political science. And then his final coup, or so he thought: "Look at the Peverell-Watsons." "Ah," countered Camilla's lawyer uncle, resting his warm, sad-wise eyes on his future nephew, "but the Reverend Peverell never *married* our great-grand-mother."

Cate stood, with arms folded, on the sloping lawn of her domain, doing a last-minute surveillance of the preparations. Two tables had been set up at the edge of the orchard, where the terrain was as level as it was going to get around here. One table for food, to be brought out after the guests had arrived, and one for drinks, on which two kegs of cider were already fixed in place: alcoholic cider for the adults, and unfermented for the children and teetotalers, such as Wickie Lee and her husband, and Mother's widowed friend Sicca Dowling. After Sicca's husband died, not leaving her very well provided for, Mother had taken her into her own home and helped her dry out. Now Sicca lived in Mother's basement, which had been made over into a sunny apartment overlooking the back garden.

"Thank God the weather held," she said to her two helpers, one of whom was laying out individual place settings of silver-ware wrapped in napkins on the food table, the other of whom was taking considerable trouble, but obviously enjoying it, over a complicated geometrical arrangement of the glasses on the other table. "This time of year can be tricky. But look at it. Not an ominous cloud in the sky. Trees decked out in their fall fin-ery. All *nature* conspires to make our party a success; it remains to be seen what the *people* will do with it."

At her words, the man doing the complicated arrangement with the party glasses (plastic, in deference to the expected con-tingent of children) smiled to himself; he was apparently familiar with her views on life.

"Which part of a party do you like best?" asked the young woman who was setting out the bundles of silverware. "Just be-fore people come, when everything is all set up but nothing's happened yet; or while the party's actually going on; or after-ward, when you can look back and know how everything's turned out—assuming there's been no fiasco?" The young woman blushed as she spoke; she was still a little afraid of Cate,

of the older woman's sarcastic bent and her sharp pronounce-
ments on people and things, even though they had been living
together for almost two months, and she knew Cate was the most
decent and entertaining of women.

"If it's somebody else's party, that's easy: I enjoy the party
in progress. If it's my party, well, sometimes I enjoy the beforehand part, when anything is possible, and probably *less* often I
enjoy the aftermath; but that's because I'm a die-hard idealist
and will always expect more than I can get. However, there have
been one or two worthy aftermaths in my history of party giving.
But"—Cate tipped up her chin and appeared to consult the Octo-
ber-blue sky as oracle—"it's hard to say, about this party. It's a
sort of hybrid party. Anything's possible, of course, but, in another sense, this party started happening a long time ago."

"Oh," said the young woman. Then, after she had counted
the bundles of silverware already laid out, she added, "I think I
know what you mean."

"Of course you do, Heather," replied Cate. She smiled
fondly at her housemate and at her houseguest, who was completing his geometric design of plastic glasses. Cate was in a very
good mood today.

"I hear a motor," said the man.

They all three straightened up and cocked their heads.
"Please, Lord, don't let the first one be Lydia," muttered Cate.
Heather burst out laughing. "We'll protect you," she said.

The motor sound got louder. "Whoever it is is coming up
the hill," said Cate. "That means it can't be Lydia. Only intrepid
souls, or people with trucks or Jeeps, try the hill."

"It's an intrepid soul with a truck," said the houseguest as
the vehicle bounced into sight, making a great clatter.

"It's Tom," said Cate. "Oh good, he's brought the chairs."
She went over to greet the man climbing out of the truck that had
his name and GENERAL CONTRACTOR written on the door. "But
where's Wickie Lee?" she asked him.

"Down at the bottom of the hill. She brought the Royal
Family in our car," said the man. Two towheaded boys jumped
down from the back of the truck and began unloading brightly

colored canvas chairs from the nursery school. "You all set the chairs up wherever Miss Cate wants, you hear?" he said to the boys. To Cate, "I've got to go back down and carry up the Queen Mother." Off he went, a heavily built figure with a bald spot the size of a half-dollar at the crown of his head: a rather serious man, who allowed himself this one joke.

Through the high, clear air came the sound of car doors slamming below. "The party's begun," announced Cate.

"What a sweet place!" exclaimed Theodora, a bit breathlessly because of her semireclining position in Tom's hefty arms. "But somehow I imagined it would be more *rustic*. Old Osgood was so rustic. I expected . . . I don't know . . . logs. And"—she chortled gruffly—"one or two skinny old hound dogs."

"You sound like me," said Heather, who had met Theodora on a previous occasion, "when I arrive here fresh from medical school to help the picturesque Appalachians."

"There are logs," said Cate, "but they're under the siding. Daddy helped Osgood remodel back in the fifties. There are plenty of picturesque Appalachians, too. You just have to catch them when they come out of their coves."

"Well, aren't you lucky to have such a sweet place. You're lucky with your weather, too." She sounded as if Cate didn't quite deserve all her luck. "Tom, put me down. I could have made that hill. Azalea did. Barely. Azalea, you're puffing like an old steam engine. You're the one ought to have been carried."

Azalea, carrying a pair of matching tartan lap rugs, and leaning heavily on Wickie Lee, did not answer. Wickie Lee was pregnant. She and Tom, whose boys had been under her care at Teenie Ennis's nursery school, had married after the boys' mother had left Tom to join a folk-dancing team.

Tiffany, a prim five-year-old, formally presented Cate with a small box. "There's the bride and groom inside," she announced importantly.

"Poor Wickie liked to worry herself sick over that bride doll," Tom informed them, helping Theodora gently to a standing position.

"Tom, I'll kill you!" Wickie Lee shook her fist at him. To Cate she explained, "I made you a little bride and groom to go on top of your cake."

"Want to see?" asked Tiffany, whose fingers were already scrabbling at the box top. Two little cornshuck dolls lay on a bed of tissue paper. "Oh, what exquisite clothes!" said Cate. "His little morning coat . . . those tiny pearls on her veil."

Tom and Heather walked ahead with the two old ladies, to get them settled in their big armchairs brought out from the house. All of them matched their pace to Theodora's slow gait; since her stroke she dragged a leg, but had managed to turn her performance into a sort of ceremonious wedding-march step.

"I wanted to do real faces on the dolls," said Wickie Lee confidentially to Cate. "But then I got all worried about what *color*." She flushed. "Tom said just make them both a kind of dark pinky color, but I said no, that might seem a slight. And to make them different colors might seem worse of one. I didn't know *what* to do, so I just went on ahead and played it safe with cornshucks, though they're not half as nice."

"These have their simple charm," Cate assured her. "And they'll be honored you did it for them. We won't tell them about your masterpieces."

"You wouldn't believe the orders I've got for Christmas for my portrait dolls," said Wickie Lee complacently. "The only trouble is, when am I going to find time to do them all? If this baby decides to come early, like Tiffany here did, I'm *sunk*." Wickie Lee's latest creations were custom-made dolls that looked like particular people; all she needed was a color photo of the person and she would do the rest. She charged fifty dollars for a small doll and one hundred for a big one, and got it. She was now a partner in the expanded infant center, started several years back by Teenie Ennis and her friends. Prosperity and self-satisfaction had filled out her cheeks and put color in her wan face; she was probably going to be overweight before long.

"You'll be fine," Cate told her. And, of course, Wickie Lee would, barring some misfortune. Wickie Lee *had* sunk, thought Cate, into the system—as easily as someone sinking with a sigh of relief into a warm bath. Or maybe Cate was being unfair. Maybe Wickie Lee was simply one of the lucky ones, whose needs for themselves corresponded exactly with the needs of others for them. Yet Cate couldn't help preferring the lean defiance of the Wickie Lee she had first known. Well, she had done her share in changing her. She wondered if the twenty-one-year-old matron ever had nightmares about her previous life, no member of which had ever shown up to claim her—to anybody's knowledge.

The houseguest, also officiating as bartender, was serving the first glasses of hard cider to Theodora and Azalea, tucked into their special chairs. They were dressed outrageously alike, especially since Azalea had taken to wearing a brooch Theodora had given her exactly as Theodora wore *her* brooch: pinned dead center in the décolletage. "I don't believe we've met," Theodora said rather flirtatiously to the man handing each old lady a glass with a paper napkin, and Cate was about to approach and introduce them when more guests arrived. It was the newlyweds, followed almost immediately by Lydia and Stanley and little Liza Bee, who stalked forward as though she were the guest of honor and presented Cate with the bouquet of uprooted flowers. (Lydia had picked out the weeds.)

"But these are bottle gentians!" exclaimed Cate. "And some of them still have their roots. I wonder, if we stuck them right into the ground . . . Heather, do you think they might revive and grow?"

"We could try," said Heather, touching the roots gently. "I ought to get them in the ground right away, though." She went off to plant them, calling back that she would "meet everybody" later.

"Heather's shy. She hates formalities," explained Cate. "But she can make anything grow. You should have seen her summer garden. And she's a wonderful doctor."

"Does she live around here?" asked Lydia, looking around Osgood's old homestead and convincing herself it was much too isolated to have been of use to her; she waved at Theodora.

"Heather lives right here," said Cate. "With me."

Lydia swallowed. "Oh." She willed her face not to register anything. "How nice." Cate was watching her with a strange little smile. Just after Daddy's death in 1978, Cate had given Lydia just such a smile after announcing that, if she got lonely enough, she might try women. Cate's face was much better; it had still been a little lopsided at Max's funeral. On the other hand, Cate had looked much slimmer then; that was when she had been living in New York. People in New York lived on their nerves; that's what Calvin wrote Renee. Poor Calvin, after his disenchantment with his home state, had given up his dream of an arts channel and gone back to New York to work for a national network.

"It suits us both, for the time being," replied Cate, aware of what Lydia was thinking and willing to let her stew in her own suspicions for a while. *Yet, here we are, starting the whole routine over again,* she realized, turning to greet Stanley, whom she liked, and then to devote her attention to the newlyweds, especially Camilla. *It's as if we've learned nothing.* Yet she was helpless to stop herself from baiting Lydia.

Well, at least she could take the arm of her new niece-in-law and walk her off for a gracious little aside. God, the girl was lovely. "I was so sorry I couldn't make your wedding," Cate told Camilla, "I really wanted to be there. But since I've been creating these temporary jobs for myself, I have to be where I've contracted to go. I sell a course, you see; it's a package deal: for three weeks, six weeks, a semester—whatever my market will bear. And I sign a contract and go and teach it. This Lawrence course that conflicted with your wedding is the nearest thing I have to a steady job; I've been going to Taos for three years now."

"Oh, we understood," said Camilla in her caressing low voice with its British intonations. "That's so enterprising, to sell a *course.*"

Cate threw back her head and laughed. "Enterprise born of necessity. No, that's not quite true. I had a perfectly good, steady job at this plush foundation in New York—my own office; God, I even had a pension plan—but it was boring me to death after the first year. I missed teaching. But there didn't seem to be any jobs. Then, while I was reading all these piles of grant applications for the most outlandish projects, I suddenly got this idea. Some of those applications were presented so intriguingly—they were packaged so attractively! Even though, if you had half a brain, you could see they were pure bunkum. So I decided to package my job applications in an irresistible way. I wrote up some proposals for courses I would really be interested in teaching—'Prophets of Apocalypse,' one was called, because apocalypse was very much on my mind at the time—and I sent them out in spiffy folders, typed up impeccably by one of the foundation secretaries, and what do you know, I got three offers for that 'Apocalypse' course. So I quit my job and did those, and then I got interested in doing a course on 'Fantasy'; and guess where I was first hired to do that one? At a hostel for elders in Hawaii, of all places. They flew me out. I was charmed by my elderly students. In some ways, older people aren't as afraid to use their imagination, which was the whole point of the course."

"It sounds fascinating," agreed Camilla, who had been sizing up her new aunt: she was not at all like Leo's poised and pretty mother. Except for a similarity around the mouth, you'd never know they were sisters. But this aunt had a certain elusive, lively attraction; and, aside from the extravagant way she stuck out her chin, and a bold glitter in the amber eyes, she didn't seem too dangerous.

"Yes," conceded Cate, "it was. Now a police academy in Texas wants to me to it. A retired police officer in my Hawaii course recommended me. I haven't decided yet whether I'm going. To tell the truth, I'm a little tired. It would be fun to hole up here for the winter and let Heather bring the groceries in her Jeep. Also, I suspect their motives. I think they're hoping I'll provide them with some easy insights into the criminal mind."

"But the course isn't about criminals, is it?"

"In a sense it is. I make them read Blake and Jung and Kafka . . . and Doris Lessing." She squeezed Camilla's arm and narrowed her eyes challengingly: "There's a thin line between the artistic and the criminal mind. Both create fresh difficulties for everybody."

Perhaps a *little* crazy, decided Camilla, but I don't mind. "I want to thank you again for this beautiful poncho," she told her new aunt, getting back on safe ground.

"I'm glad you like it. I liked your note. But you're the first bride I ever heard of who sent her thank-you notes out the same week as her wedding. At least mine was, I noticed the postmark."

"I wrote most of them on our honeymoon," confessed Camilla. "We went to Leo and Dickie's house on Ocracoke, and it rained the first three days, and I thought I ought to use the time for something."

"*That* was enterprising of you," commented Cate. Heavens, she thought, Camilla reminds me a little of Lydia. "Now I've hogged you long enough." She steered her lovely niece back toward the group. "You'd better come be presented to Theodora. She's the nearest thing we have to a reigning queen."

Theodora looked Camilla up and down and seemed gratified. But Azalea, to everybody's surprise, was rather formal and oblique. Theodora made the girl bend down and kiss her, while Azalea only offered a dubious handshake.

This introduction performed, Cate swaggered, smiling, over to the bar, where Lydia and Stanley were in conversation with her houseguest. "Have you all met my old friend from Iowa?" she asked Lydia and Stanley. "Roger, this is my sister, Lydia, and her friend, Stanley Edelman."

"We've just introduced ourselves," said Roger Jernigan. "Are you ready for some cider, Cate?"

"I certainly am. The alcoholic, please."

Lydia was looking slightly disoriented.

Heather returned to join them.

"Will the patients live?" asked Cate.

"They're pretty droopy. But I've watered them. We'll just have to keep our fingers crossed."

Cate introduced the young doctor to Lydia and Stanley. Liza Bee had already begun to boss around her little contemporary, Tiffany, and Stanley was keeping one eye on her as she organized a tree-climbing contest in the orchard.

"Heather took care of Uncle Osgood two winters ago when he fell and broke his hip," Cate told Lydia. "She was out here one night when it snowed, and she couldn't get down the road, and he asked her to stay over. And she's been here ever since, which was a stroke of good luck for him, as it now is for me."

"It worked out well for everybody," explained Heather, blushing. "I had just come here and I was trying to commute from Mountain City to our clinic out here. That first snowy night, he said, 'Young lady, why not just stay here?' And the next day, when I got ready to leave, he said, 'Young lady, why not just stay *on* here?' I got really fond of him. He'd be here today if he hadn't got that pneumonia."

"Now Heather keeps threatening to move out," said Cate. "Afraid she'll cramp my style. But I keep explaining I only drop down to recuperate. What better person to have in the house than a doctor?"

"And so you—?" Lydia's question to Heather was interrupted by the arrival of Nell and Marcus and Sicca.

"It's all my fault we're late!" cried Sicca. "My hairdresser had lead in her fingers today." She wore a trailing chiffon scarf around her coiffure, which was much too elaborate for a party outdoors in the country. But Siccca took great care over her hairdos, especially now that she had her new face; after she had been on the wagon one full year, Nell and Theodora had treated her to a facelift.

"Well, here we all are, anyway," called Nell. Her arm through Marcus's, she paused with him at the top of the hill, smiling at everyone while, ostensibly, they both caught their breath from the climb: Marcus suffered from emphysema. Leaning against Marcus, Nell counted faces. "I see everyone but Dickie. Lydia, isn't Dickie coming?"

"I'm afraid not," said Lydia. "He and his group had an engagement. He was getting ready to leave right after me, this morning." Dickie still lived with his mother; he was at the School of the Arts in Winston-Salem, and, with three friends, had formed a musical group; they called themselves The Wandering Winds and went around the state playing at weddings and parties.

"What a pity," sighed Nell. "But an engagement is an engagement."

"It is these days, isn't it," agreed Roger Jernigan, "with a bunch of free lancers like us. Nell, Marcus, which will you have? Cider with or without a kick?"

"Oh with, please. For both of us," said Nell. "Sicca Dowling, this is Roger Jernigan. You didn't get a chance to meet him when Cate stopped by yesterday on the way from the airport."

"I live in Nell and Marcus's basement," explained Sicca coyly, batting her eyelashes at Mr. Jernigan. Had Nell said he was "a friend" of Cate's, or just a friend? He was younger than herself, of course, but not all *that* young. Sicca was not averse to marrying again. It had been one thing to keep Nell company when they were both widows, but since Nell had finally given in and married Marcus, Sicca worried about being a third wheel. Not that she didn't adore her little apartment; and Nell and Marcus were always including her in things. But being sober gave you so many more hours in the day. And especially now, with her new face, Sicca enjoyed meeting men again. *She* would certainly not go on and on about "just being good friends" with any man who paid court to her the way poor Marcus had to Nell, practically *commuting* from Virginia until, as Sicca enjoyed telling people, she almost proposed to Marcus herself. Finally, Marcus had brought Nell to her senses by making plans to enter the Episcopal Retirement Home, just outside Mountain City. To be near Nell. He had even put down a nonreturnable deposit. But Sicca still enjoyed telling her little story about threatening to marry him herself if Nell couldn't see what she had right in front of her nose. "I'll have a glass of the nonalcoholic, please," Sicca told Mr. Jernigan, who had very sexy green eyes.

"And so, how did you and Mr. Lawrence get on out in Taos this summer?" Marcus Chapin asked his stepdaughter pleasantly.

"We got along as we always have. Other people continue to misunderstand him, but that's nothing new. During this year's festival, which winds up the summer, I almost knocked down a so-called famous critic who maintained Lawrence would have been forgotten by now if it hadn't been for the feminists reviving him in order to prove what a sexist he was."

"I would have liked to see that." Marcus smiled—remembering, perhaps, another exchange over the controversial Lawrence. But Marcus had read *Women in Love*, at Cate's recommendation; he had read it diligently, as if it had been an assignment, on the nights Nell taught Emergency Techniques at the new Rescue Center. Although Nell had urged Marcus to take Leonard's study, Marcus preferred reading in bed. For his own books, he had a nice office out at the Episcopal Retirement Home, where he had almost incarcerated himself in order to be closer to Nell. Theodora had arranged for him to be chaplain at the Home.

"You wouldn't have seen anything," Cate told him. "I controlled myself. The Lawrence course is my only standing gig, as Dickie would say, and I want to be invited back next summer."

"Just so long as you didn't sacrifice any principles." The Virginia gentleman raised an eyebrow. The two of them laughed. Sparring had remained a formality with them, like an opening dance. On occasion they had discussions about the collapse of the society they knew. Marcus would say, shaking his head gently, that it was imminent; Cate would laugh and tell him it had happened already.

"Cate?" It was Heather. "Should we start bringing out the food?"

"Good idea."

Lydia suddenly materialized. "May I help?" she asked rather wistfully.

"Why, thank you, baby." Whether from the sun and the potent cider, or from the general goodwill Cate was feeling toward all, she found it surprisingly easy to slip her arm around her sister's thin shoulders (Lydia had dieted herself to the bone!). "That would be nice."

As the sisters followed Heather toward Osgood's house, they overheard Sicca asking Roger Jernigan, "What did you say you did?"

"I declare, Azalea," said Theodora, when the two of them were briefly alone in their armchairs, Theodora's stiff leg and

Azalea's swollen ones tucked under their tartan lap-robes, "you'd think you were prejudiced or something. The girl's from a *very* old family. Why, the Peverells of Halifax County go back even further, on this side of the water, than Blount of Beaufort."

"I don't care if they go back to the Queen of Sheba. Ain't no good ever come out of mixing."

"Indiscriminate mixing, yes. Like everything else, Azalea, there's a right way and a wrong way to do things. But in this case they're both good-looking, educated, well-bred young people, and they're going to represent our country abroad; think what a marvelous advertisement they'll be."

"I don't care," repeated Azalea, shaking her head adamantly.

Somewhere, in rather recent memory, Theodora could recall having argued the other side of this subject—the side Azalea was now arguing. She understood that Azalea had every right to be miffed, having the rules switched on her like that, but really, how were *their* existences threatened or altered by Leo's marrying this girl? Just to see how far she could venture into this "new" side of an old argument, Theodora forged briefly into the thickets (in her own mind, of course). Now what if Leo had been *her* child? Still all right, pretty much. As long as the girl looked and behaved like this one. She was a little lady. Her features weren't— Taking a deep breath, Theodora took a step nearer the heart of the real forest; she imagined herself a girl of nineteen again, engaged to a young man she loved: good-looking, intelligent, well-bred. Only—he was a Negro. Well, not a dark one. And his features weren't— Could she have? Not in 1930, of course—but in 1984?

Theodora sighed. The trouble was, she told herself, backing off from the shadows, she was beyond imagining being in love with *any* man. She could not even remember being in love with Latrobe. (Last year, they had buried him; watching his coffin being lowered into the earth, Theodora had admitted to herself that he had never had a good character.)

And though, until recently, she had flirted with the idea of adopting some grateful young person who would bless her name

after she was gone, she knew that was not the same thing as actually raising a child, which she couldn't imagine, either.

What she *could* imagine, increasingly well, was the rest of
her own life, which she intended to have as much control over as
possible. Her stroke had taught her a lesson. Never again would
she lie helpless on her back while fools lied to her and plotted
her future to suit themselves. She already had places reserved for
herself and Azalea at the Episcopal Retirement Home, for when
they got too feeble to do for themselves on Edgerton Road. And
she had already donated a sizable chunk of her fortune to that
institution: right now, the Theodora Blount Medical Wing was
going up. She would live to see it completed (*Deo volente*); she
hoped she would not, in her last days, have to use any of its
awful machines, but best to have them there in the Wing, where
they knew who Theodora Blount was, than at some vast, impersonal hospital. And if they treated her right to the *very* end, there
would be another handsome bequest.

So let the young marry whomever they liked, and let them
take care of themselves, she thought. (There would, of course, be
a little legacy for her country cousin, Wickie Lee, who had made
herself useful to society and found herself a good man to take
care of her—Tom had fixed Theodora's rotting back porch and
charged only for materials; and a little something for her godson,
Buddy Bell—Theodora guessed she knew her obligations—if he
didn't invent some weapon that blew them all up first—he and
his team were working on railguns now: you could shoot at one
another in outer space; and a little something for Cate, as well.
Theodora had been so relieved when Osgood left her his place;
now Cate could always have a truck garden or keep bees or sell
off some timber when she got too old for this itinerant teaching;
at least Cate had a *base*. As long as a woman had a base, she could
afford to be a little eccentric.)

But, just to have the last word about Leo's marriage, she said
to Azalea, "The old order changes, Azalea. Why, look at us. Who
would ever have thought you and I'd be coughing each other to
sleep on the opposite sides of our wall?"

Azalea gave Theodora a level look. "You perfectly capable

of winning any argument all by yourself, Miss Thea, but you know and I know there's still that wall." She settled back in her chair with a dark smile, looking for all the world as if *she* had won.

"I'm in integrated pest management," Roger Jernigan told Sicca.

"Oh! What exactly is that? It sounds—" And Sicca had to suppress the laughter burbling up her windpipe as she pictured roaches being forced to mix with ants, and termites with cutworms, as the world became more democratic. But she didn't know Mr. Jernigan well enough to entertain him with this little scene. One had to be so careful now. And especially *today*, of all days. Sicca's hairdresser had told her the cutest joke about a Negro, a Jew, and a Pole traveling together on a space shuttle. But here in plain sight was Nell's grandson with his dark bride, and Nell's daughter Lydia with her nice Jewish boyfriend, and Wickie Lee's husband with his last name she had never been able to pronounce, which might be either Russian or Polish—so there went Sicca's joke. Well, she could live without it, as she could live without her booze. "—it sounds fascinating," Sicca told the stocky, green-eyed man with those adorable little sun wrinkles fanning out to his hairline and down into his cheeks.

"It is to me. I doubt if it would be to you."

But Sicca assured him she wanted to know all about it. (Always ask a man about his work.) She kept her gaze trained assiduously on his face as he explained about releasing armies of wasps into gardens to devour the eggs of the cabbage worm, and about infecting some bugs with a virus and then grinding them up into powder to spray on other bugs.

"But isn't that dangerous? Couldn't you get stung? Or catch some virus?"

He was smiling, but whether at her or just because he felt good (he had been drinking the twelve-proof cider), Sicca couldn't tell. "Sure. There are still lots of risks. You got to take risks if you want to plow new ground." His mind seemed to be wandering off his subject. He watched Cate emerge from the house. She and Lydia and that shy doctor-girl were carrying out the food.

"Have you known Cate long?" Might as well find out what was what, thought Sicca.

"She taught my son some years ago. At a college in Iowa that no longer exists. And she and I kept each other company some. Then, you might say, we went our separate ways."

"Ah," sighed Sicca. Then, more brightly, as though she *hoped* it were the case, "And now you've found each other again?"

"No, she found me." He laughed to himself. "I was right where I always was. But this past summer, she was driving through Iowa, and she missed my signs and got worried about me." He chuckled. "She thought I'd died."

"Your signs?"

"My billboards. Advertising my chemical company. The past two years, see, she'd driven through Iowa on her way to summer school, and she'd seen my signs and told herself I was still okay, so she could forget about me. But this year, the signs were gone, on account of I dissolved my company. Got to be more trouble than it was worth, and it wasn't keeping me interested anymore. Keeping interested in life is one of my priorities. *The* priority, you might say. I decided to chuck the production end and go back and see what my old buddies the scientists were doing. I'm a consultant now. Free-lance, like Cate. I keep my own hours and go where I want, when I want. My sons live in California. I go back and forth a lot to visit with them."

He took out his wallet and handed Sicca a folded page from one of those newspaper color supplements. "My sons."

She unfolded it and screamed, "But I know him! He's that famous model. I have him on the cover of one of my magazines at home. . . ." She scanned the newsprint beneath the full-page photograph, then read it aloud: 'Jody and his bodyguard set off in the fashion star's vintage Bentley for a typical day's work.' That's right, Jody. He doesn't use a last name, or I would have connected . . . and he's your son?"

"That one, too." Jernigan's sun-browned finger pointed to a

man with short, graying blond hair and sunglasses and those muscles body-builders get. He was identified only as a body-guard, though.

"Oh," said Sicca, taken aback. "You mean he's your son, too?"

"That's right. That's Sunny. The boys have different mothers."

"But—is he *really* his brother's bodyguard? Or is it some kind of joke?"

"It's no joke at all," said Jernigan. "It's his job. He's very happy at it. Being happy at your job is no small thing." He took the page back and placed it, refolded, in his wallet.

Sicca had the feeling she had said something wrong. "And how do you like it here in our mountains?" she asked, changing the subject.

"The farmlands are wonderful. It's a treat to see more than an inch of good topsoil these days. I wish I could stay longer. I've just come up from Raleigh-Durham. We had an international conference on microscopic insect killers at the Research Triangle there. I thought I'd drop in and pay a visit to Cate, since I was so near. You know what we saw when she was driving me up here yesterday? An old man, at least eighty, standing on a handmade wooden sled, letting his horse pull him down the dirt road."

"You ought to retire here," encouraged Sicca magnani-mously, for she was beginning to see how the terrain lay; she had just seen the way Jernigan looked at Cate as she carried out a platter of fried chicken. It was obvious *Cate* was "keeping him interested." Sicca consoled herself by creating her story for some future occasion ("I had to practically propose to him myself, to make Cate see what she had right under her nose!").

"Thanks for the suggestion," said Jernigan, smiling. "I'll re-member it. When I get ready to retire."

Cate, returning to the kitchen to see if everything had been carried out, found Lydia there, ostensibly examining Heather's wall map of all the coves in the county where her patients lived.

But something in the way she stood, stiff-shouldered but tentative, made Cate think that Lydia had been waiting to catch her alone.

Well, it has to come sometime, thought Cate; we can't go on contriving never to be alone in the same room—as we did at Max's funeral and Mother's wedding. If the world stays in one piece, Lydia and I may have to coexist in it for decades more. That's one reason—the main reason, if I'm honest—I had this party. To make sure if we were alone it would be on my territory. And now, obviously, she's picked the time, so it won't be all my show. Now let's see how we finally manage to do this thing.

And though she was nervous, fearful of wounding and fearful of being wounded, Cate felt a part of her consciousness detach itself and stand to one side, *its* only desire being to observe. She was becoming increasingly aware of this "separate self" as an ally: it had stood beside her when she had almost punched that critic at the Lawrence festival; had it not been for its cool, clinical eye, that critic would have landed in a muddy meadow—and she, Cate, would not be teaching her favorite writer next year. Old age has some compensations, Cate thought wryly.

Lydia was saying what a likable person Heather was: so shy and so *feminine* and yet, obviously, so competent. "How lucky you are to have her as a tenant," said Lydia. "What a load off your mind, when you travel around so much, to have her here looking after the place."

While Cate sent her emotions toward Lydia, in experimental, short forays, to determine how much jealousy she was feeling toward her glamorous younger sister, who had become so necessary and popular to more people than all Cate's students, past and future, would ever add up to, Cate's trusty "detached observer" kept track of what Lydia was saying, and even provided a subtext: *I compliment you on your housemate as a form of complimenting you, which I can't quite manage yet. It's also my way of saying I'm glad you have a place of your own, even if Osgood was my cousin, too. And also that I know you were just teasing outside, trying to make me think you'd turned lesbian.*

When Cate's turn came, she said, "I was really sorry your

friend Renee couldn't make it today. I sent her a note specially. But Camilla says she's studying hard to pass the bar."

"She loved your note," said Lydia. "I spoke to her on the phone. I was hoping right up to the last that she'd drive up with them from Chapel Hill. But, well, honestly, I think Renee's sworn off pleasure of any kind until she can get out there as a lawyer and avenge herself on all the hate and injustice in this country."

"She may have to wait a long time to have any pleasure, in that case." But Cate spoke softly, with no irony. She regretted, in the light of later events, what she had said about Lydia's friends Calvin and Renee on the night of the fight. The bourgeois castles she had mocked them for trying to build on the rubble of their dying society had collapsed in a series of bizarre happenings. It was as if, suddenly, a dragon had wakened and crawled out from beneath the foundations . . . when everybody had started to believe dragons were dead, or had never really existed. In 1980, Renee had given a student a D. The student's father, angered, paid a visit to Renee and said he never thought he'd see the day when "a person like Renee" could give his daughter a D. Renee replied that she gave students the grades they earned, regardless of whose children they happened to be. When she got home that night, she found her beautiful Japanese maple in a heap on the ground. Some men in a truck had come by, the neighbors told her, who said Renee wanted the tree cut down. The next day, Renee received a telephone call from the student's father, who hoped, in silky, courteous tones, that she would change that D to a C before noon, when final grades were due in; at noon, he called her once more, to see if she'd changed her mind. "Your daughter's D has been turned in," she told him coldly. But she was scared, and left school immediately. She wanted to be safe inside her house, with her dog, The Judge . . . neither of which she ever saw again. The house, on which she had lavished so much taste and care, was firebombed within minutes of her last words to the man on the phone; The Judge had been waiting for her inside.

It was for the dog she couldn't forgive them; it was the dog. Imagining it and reimagining it almost drove Renee wild. It was as if she deflected all her disbelief that such a thing could be done to *her*, by dwelling, until her friends worried that her mind would snap, on the senseless killing of the dog.

And no evidence could be found that the man, a prominent churchgoing citizen, had been connected in any way with the tough bunch of men in the truck who had come to cut down the tree; and nobody had seen the firebomb thrown. "Law officials" concluded that it was one more in a series of regrettable incidents that had dotted the country like a sudden rash.

That was when Renee resolved to become a "law official" herself. She took the entrance exam and was enrolled in the law school over at Chapel Hill (where the Reverend Peverell's papers were housed); she had begun studying before an all-white jury—which tried (and later acquitted) some Klan members involved in an earlier shooting of some Communists—was sworn in over in Greensboro.

Several months later, Calvin took Miss Mary to a secluded marsh for some bird-watching, and they had the ill luck to stumble right into a paramilitary training camp of the Klan. The fact that Miss Mary was with him probably saved Calvin's life. He got the old lady home and gave her a brandy and then rode back to the site with a cameraman from the TV station. Not a trace of anybody. Just a few smoking fires any picnickers could have left; and some holes where tent stakes had been pulled from the marshy ground. Calvin felt like a fool, but he had Miss Mary as a witness. Though she didn't seem to want to talk about it anymore. Even the station didn't seem too hot on his exploring it further. A few days later, he found a smoking cross in his mailbox. Then he received a letter composed of words cut out of magazines announcing his imminent death. When he let himself into his carefully locked apartment the next night and found a .38-caliber bullet lying in the center of his pillow, Calvin decided that his home state did not love him as much as he had been trying to convince himself he loved it. He was safe in New York before the date prophesied for his death.

"Renee is going to be a formidable lawyer," Lydia said. "She's so dedicated ... and intense. She has a real *cause*. She makes me feel almost trivial sometimes. What good am I doing, really, showing people how they can be healthy and furnish their houses with taste on a budget and be powerful if they organize as consumers and parents? Compared with Renee, I'm so—" She went red in the face. Both sisters realized that Lydia had caught herself in the middle of accusing herself of the thing Cate, on that night five years ago, had accused her of.

"Don't underestimate what you do," said Cate. "People need to feel they can manage their lives. Where would we be if everybody despaired even of putting their own house in order?"

"I suppose so." Lydia gave Cate a wary look. Here they were, cautiously trying out each other's viewpoints; replaying the fight, but each from the other's side.

It was Lydia's turn again. "Isn't that the man ... Jernigan? The one with the castle?" Cate said he was. And heard in her mind what Lydia probably still thought was her worst accusation to Cate of five years ago ("*I may not set the world on fire. But at least I've never murdered anybody!*"). And she guessed, from Lydia's face, that she, too, was hearing it in her own mind.

"How did you two happen to get together again?"

"We're not exactly 'together.' We're just on good visiting terms. I told him, 'Next time you're in North Carolina ...' And here he came." Cate told how, driving west through Iowa this past summer, she had missed his signs and mourned him all the way to New Mexico, where, unable to stand not knowing, one way or the other, she had telephoned the castle. "I didn't know whether to hang up or cry when he answered the phone himself."

"What *did* you do?"

"Both. I hung up, then called back. And cried. At first he thought it was a wrong number ... a crazy woman. Then, when he found out who it was, he was a little distant. But after we'd talked for a while and filled each other in on our lives, he got friendlier. The son I taught is quite famous as a model, and the other one lives with his brother most of the time. He's his body-guard out in California. Anyway, Roger said be sure and call him on my way back east, and if he wasn't off on one of his consulting trips, he'd take me to lunch or dinner. I arranged it very carefully so I'd get there for lunch, so I could always say I had to drive on afterward."

"And did you? Drive on?" It was the old, wide-eyed Lydia, demanding the denouements of her sister's adventures.

"Ah," stalled Cate, looking mysterious, while she debated whether or not to reestablish the old intimate routine with Lydia, whose *real* worst accusation still rankled.

(If I have "nothing to show" for my life, Lydia, then what is it about me you're always so intent on seeing?)

But she was spared having to make a precipitate decision either to accept or to deny the old terms with Lydia by the arrival of a deus ex machina, which chose that very moment to come bouncing up Cate's last hill—the one for Jeeps, trucks, or intrepid souls. Delighted cries rang out among the guests as the purple hearse, with its logo, THE WANDERING WINDS, shuddered to a stop on its efficient old springs.

"My Lord!" exclaimed Lydia, looking out the window. "It's Dickie and his group. That devil. He told me he had an engagement."

"He has." Cate smiled. "It was supposed to be a surprise for Leo and Camilla." She relented a little. "And for you."

While his group set up music stands and unpacked their instruments, Dickie balanced his little half sister, Liza Bee, on one hip and ate a piece of fried chicken. "This is just to keep me going," he explained to his mother and aunt. "We always wait to eat till afterward so we won't be short of wind." But the women saw him take a quick, worried survey of the guests depleting the table as they heaped their plates with the chicken and slices of country ham and chunky mounds of potato salad and little slippery ovals of deviled egg.

"We've got a whole separate batch of everything put away just for you hungry musicians," said Cate, reading his look. She and her nephew had become good friends since that time he had stayed with her in New York, when she had that godsend of a job through Mimi at the Astra Foundation (though it had very soon got boring); Dickie had poured out his young soul to Cate—how he had never been able to please Max, his father, and then just when Leo went away to school and Dickie and Max were getting close, Max had died.

"I was so *surprised* when you all drove up," Lydia said, beaming at her younger son with irrepressible delight. He was still too fat—and would probably be a lot fatter before his life was over—but his zest for living and his sweet temper and his musical talent would, she hoped, distract notice from his rotundity. She and Stanley had given up nagging him. He teased Stanley that there would be plenty of opportunity for dieting when they all had to live on dried food in Stanley's bomb shelter.

"That's the general idea of a surprise," Dickie told his mother.

"I'm just going to enjoy this to pieces," Theodora told her neighbor, Mr. Jernigan, Cate's friend from somewhere out west. "When I was a child, we *always* had live musicians for our picnics."

"Those must have been some picnics," commented Jernigan.

"Ladies and Gentlemen," announced Dickie. "More to the point, Brides and Grooms . . . what, Mother?" (Lydia, seated low in one of the nursery-school chairs, her knees clamped together to balance her plate of food, had called something discreetly behind her hand.) "Oh. Mother says I have a crumb on my mouth. Good-bye, crumb." He scrubbed his mouth with the back of his sleeve. Liza Bee, standing between the legs of Stanley, who was reclining against a warm, friendly-looking rock, gave a shriek of laughter and called back, "Good-bye, crumb!"

Chuckles rose indulgently from the well-disposed group, and floated away through the blue air, into the valleys below.

"Let's see, where was I?" said Dickie, obviously relishing it all. "Brides and Grooms, Old Family, New Family, Old Friends, New Friends . . . have I left anybody out?"

"Children!" shouted Liza Bee.

"Ah, how could I leave out children!" Dickie smote his well-padded breast with a fist. "Anyway, the first thing we're going to play for you is a cassation, for Oboe (that's Potter there, taking a debonair bow), Clarinet (Yours Truly), Horn (that's Jim), and Bassoon (Neal). Now, a cassation, for those of you who don't know, is an instrumental composition to be played outdoors. They were very popular in the seventeenth and eighteenth centuries, to celebrate the birthdays of wealthy patrons, the marriages of the nobility—that sort of thing; Mozart liked to write them, and some people believe he wrote the one we're going to play for you now—I myself think he probably did—but, you see, the manuscript of this work was found in somebody's old trunk in Austria in 1910, and then all the music scholars swooped in, and one said, 'No, no, Mozart would never end his divertimento with a coda,' and another said, 'I'm *sure* this was written by the young Beethoven,' and . . . you know how it goes. Anyway, whoever wrote it, I think you'll enjoy it. It's in E-flat major, and Liza Bee says the allegro sounds exactly like mice having a party. Later on in the program, there will be another divertimento written expressly for this occasion by a promising young North Carolina composer still in his teens, whose name you may recognize."

Dickie bowed modestly, sat down in his chair, arranged the voluminous flowing robe he wore on these occasions (so his waistline would not be constricted), and, after blowing fussily into the mouthpiece of his instrument, as if clearing out dust, caught the eye of the other musicians. There followed a significant hush—almost an opening note in itself—during which The Wandering Winds relinquished their separate identities so they could sound, as one body, the opening chord.

It may turn out, thought Lydia, as Dickie's clarinet, having stated the theme with the other instruments, detached itself and went wandering, light as gossamer, up the scale, that we will all be a footnote in his biography. And under the influence of the blithe and graceful music, she allowed herself to bask, for the duration of her son's brief solo, in the sunshine of her accomplishments: she had finished her education; she had raised her sons, both of whom were interesting, likable young men; she had a good job, a sort of continuing education in itself, which brought her the bonuses of fan mail, influence, and money; she was still a good-looking woman (though she had to work at it harder now); and she had a lover who pleased her and who was also a good and gentle man.

Why, then, did she feel—as the darker, reedier oboe intertwined its melancholy voice with that of the brighter instrument—this sudden yearning, profound and unfulfillable, up here in Cate's kingdom? She had known she was going to feel it, had prepared herself ahead of time, and here it was. But what *was* it? What was missing? For what or for whom did she yearn? What else was there to aspire to? What was it in Cate's atmosphere that had the power to do this to her? It surely wasn't jealousy; she surely wasn't petty enough to be *jealous* of Cate because she had a plain little house and a hundred acres and an insecure series of self-created "courses" which meant she had to fly who knew where at very little notice, wearing herself out; surely Lydia was glad for Cate that the man from Iowa was here today: he must care for her, or he wouldn't have come. (If Cate had gone on and had that baby, it would be halfway between Tiffany's age and Liza Bee's; it would be running around playing with them today. Lydia wondered if Mr. Jernigan, sitting over there beside Aunt Thea, apparently enjoying himself, had had that thought.) But what was it, here, that made it seem as if all the windows and doors of her own carefully appointed house had blown open, and a capricious wind had come whooshing through, and then, just as she had got over her fear that it might break or upset something, had gone blowing out again, bound for somewhere else, leaving her wistfully behind to watch it disappear into the unexplored distance?

"That's the mouse party, isn't it?" Stanley whispered into Liza Bee's neck, damp with sweet-tasting perspiration. "I'd recognize it anywhere." The child rewarded him with an exuberant nod, then could contain herself no longer; she wriggled free and joined her friend Tiffany and the older boys. With a little coaxing on her part, she soon had the other children running in circles to the music and tilting their arms like butterflies, or airplanes.

Lydia, seeing Stanley's lips brush the child's neck, felt a corresponding quiver of desire, as if he had kissed her own neck. What if Cate surprises everyone and ends up marrying Mr. Jernigan? she thought; then I'll be the only old maid in the family. Earlier, Lydia had noticed Stanley in earnest conversation with Heather; they were probably discussing medicine. Her face had dropped so woefully as she conjured up the thought of Mother with Marcus, Cate with Jernigan, Stanley with Heather, and herself with no one, that Stanley would ask her later that night, when they were curled together in bed, "Who walked over your grave this afternoon, honey, when Dickie and his friends were playing that mouse part?" And she would say, "Stanley, I think I'm serious this time. Do you still want to marry me?" And burst into tears whose meaning she herself didn't understand.

Mother's face, thought Leo, sitting next to Camilla on the ground, as the elfin music went chattering and chasing up and down the scale; my mother's face as she ran out of that house when Dickie arrived. It was ecstatic, that's the only word for it. She admires me and approves of my character, she knows she can depend on me to do what I say I will, but it's Dickie, secretly, who makes her happiest. Leo's fingers went wandering until they found his wife's, and they played sensuous finger-and-palm games under a corner of the poncho.

Marcus Chapin was always glad for an occasion to see his "new daughters," as he gallantly called them. At first, his clear preference had been for Cate. If he could have a stimulating exchange with Cate at least twice a year, he told her, his mind wouldn't go senile. When he was at the theological seminary way back when, one of his more radical teachers had put forth the theory that God, in order to become more conscious of Himself, experimented with certain people. These people felt a greater need than others to fling themselves against the world, to let it pierce them and knock them about; they absorbed the world's good or evil, or both, and went on to transmute it into something else. Depending on what the something else was, they became saints or sinners. This view had been a little too Manichaean for Marcus's idealistic sensibility, but he never quite forgot it; and when Cate came into his life, he tended to remember it more often. Not that she was one of the extreme ones; and she had mellowed a lot, Nell said. She certainly didn't look extreme now, leaning back on her elbows in the grass, her head thrown back, her eyes shuttered like a contented cat's in the sun; but there *was* an extra intensity there; she gave herself up to the moment more than most; this moment just happened to be a sunny, contented one. (Here Marcus saw that he was not the only one observing Cate keenly; he nodded politely to Mr. Jernigan, whom Cate had brought by the house to meet them yesterday, and shifted his attention to the musicians.)

Lydia, for him, had been an acquired taste, but now that he had acquired it, he liked her more and more. She was not the hard, calculating person he had first mistaken her for; on the contrary, she was softer than even she suspected, and as for her relentless drive, it seemed to be bound up with a formidable sense of responsibility. If Cate was God experimenting with His consciousness, then Lydia was, as Mr. Wordsworth had so aptly put it in his "Ode to Duty," His stern daughter. For whatever reason, Marcus felt more fatherly toward Lydia than toward Cate; and it was a feeling he treasured, never having had children of his own.

The stately march of the adagio came, like a change of light in the sky. The red-cheeked oboist named Potter bent forward from the waist, swaying and frowning with the poignancy of his own solo. A young maple on the ridge behind Osgood's old chicken house suddenly changed color before everyone's eyes. Up and down the register the pungent notes went, probing gently but insistently at the hearts of the listeners: *Do you remem-*

ber? . . . Does it still hurt here? . . . Oh, it all passes, but that's the beauty of it, too.

Some of the listeners, sitting in the colorful chairs brought by Tom from the nursery school, found themselves looking through the landscape as if it were a veil; behind the veil, each saw other landscapes, other faces, certain ghosts.

Oof, thought Dickie, Potter hit a wrong note; he looked around at everybody quickly: nobody seemed to have noticed.

What a mysterious thing music is, thought Nell, especially like this, played by these fresh-cheeked young men, under the open sky. The way it draws people together—yet, at the same time, you can see each person having his own reveries.

And what a mysterious thing *we* are, all of us gathered here on old Osgood's mountaintop aerie. I'll bet he never saw this many people up here at one time in his whole life, though he did get almost sociable at the end. Perhaps he was never a real hermit, but was simply waiting for somebody to come to see him.

And another mysterious thing—I just thought of it—if it weren't for me . . . and Leonard . . . most of these people wouldn't be here. There wouldn't be Lydia, or Leo and his bride, or Dickie playing, or Cate to have this party. And not Cate's friend Heather, or Mr. Jernigan, either; and not Stanley, who's so sweet to poor Max's child. And not poor Max's child, either. So, good heavens, who would be here? Theodora, of course: a Party of One; her own law. And her Azalea. And Sicca, who was Theodora's school friend long before I knew her. How about Wickie Lee and her brood? That's a toss-up: Theodora found her first, but Cate brought her back.

That leaves Marcus. He's here because Merle was my old school friend. And Merle was my old school friend because my mother got sick and had to come to Mountain City. But I might never have seen Merle again if Leonard hadn't died and the girls and I hadn't gone to Ocracoke to clear out the cottage. So I owe Marcus's presence here, in my life, to them: to my mother and Merle and Leonard.

Driving home the other night, after teaching Emergency Techniques to a new class down at the Rescue Center, Nell, passing the spot where she and Leonard had gone off the road six years ago this December 16, had started to cry. She had cried because how could it be that she could still miss him and yet be happy? The tears seemed a bond between the two states, and she did not mind them.

When she got home, she found Marcus waiting up for her in bed. He was the first man she had ever known who read in bed; she had always assumed that was something only women did. But she liked it. She liked him waiting for her in that way, the evidences of his mental life stacked right there on the bedside table for her to inspect. Leonard had always shut himself away in his study and communed privately with his philosophers and historians; and then he would come up to bed with an enlightened look, or a worried look, on his face, and she was never sure who had given him cause for hope or reason to fret. Marcus even wrote in his notebook in bed, working out his sermons for the Retirement Home, copying down memorable sentences from books he was reading, continually striving—with a touching faith in his scholarship—to form a philosophy that could reconcile all the disturbing new developments in the world with his deeply felt traditions. Sometimes he would write things about Merle in the notebook; and sometimes he wrote about Nell herself, and about aspects of their new life together. He would, on occasion, read passages aloud to her, with an affecting, shy formality.

The night she had come home after crying on the expressway, she had asked Marcus if he also felt at times this sense of a double existence: one part of him in the present with her, and one part in the past with Merle. Of course he did, he had replied. And then they had lain in bed, holding each other, and remembering things about Merle and Leonard. It was almost as if the four of them were there, together.

And then . . . well, that was another mysterious thing: how, at her age, at Marcus's age . . . how they could enjoy a side of life she had thought was over forever. A warmth spread over her whole body and into her face,, and she felt the corners of her mouth turn up as she dwelt with amazement on some recent nights. She closed her eyes, as if such a seemly gesture could render her strange flush invisible.

Oh my, look, thought Dickie, who happened to glance at his grandmother as he launched into his duet with the horn, we've made her rapturous with our playing.